THE PORTABLE GRAHAM GREENE

The Portable

GRAHAM GREENE

Edited by Philip Stratford

The Viking Press | *New York*

First published in 1973 by The Viking Press, Inc.
625 Madison Avenue, New York, N.Y. 10022

SBN 670-56566-0 (hardbound)
    670-01075-8 (paperbound)

Library of Congress catalog card number: 72-78990

Printed in U.S.A.

Contents

III.   CRITICISM

IV.   COMMITMENTS

Editor's Introduction

After more than forty years in the métier and over thirty books, Graham Greene is drawing into perspective. Such a mobile writer has never been easy to fix. In the thirties, after a false start as poet and historical novelist, he broke out as a writer of contemporary thrillers, and on the side became known as one of London's cleverest cinema critics and book reviewers. That was his English period. In the decade of the war he made his reputation as a major Catholic novelist, added Mexico and West Africa to his fictional territory, and began to work in film. In the early fifties he forsook Catholic themes, extended the range of his travels to the Far East, took to journalism, and tried his hand at drama. Having passed the grand climacteric of *A Burnt-Out Case*, by the sixties he had relaxed into comedy and political fiction and, stepping outside the novel, became an effective *franc-tireur* on international issues. Now, at the beginning of the seventies (at sixty-eight Greene is not quite as old as the century), he is writing prefaces to the Collected Edition of his novels and has published a volume of autobiography, *A Sort of Life*, which closes the circle on the unknown early years.

There have been many other complete men of letters but few have resisted definition better. Edward Sackville-West once called Greene "the electric hare whom the greyhound critics are not meant to catch." His pursuit fiction was criminal-centered; his Catholic novels skirted heresy; his journalism espoused unpopular causes; his comedies were sad and his politics paradoxical.

At the root of these contradictions lies a carefully nurtured ambiguity. From his earliest memories, when he used to play a game in the family garden called "England and France," Greene has been irresistibly drawn to frontiers. Where they didn't exist, he invented them; where they did, he assiduously sought out some of the remoter of them; once across, he hearkened back to the place he had left; when caught in some no-man's-land, he suffered from it, exquisitely. In *Another Mexico* (*The Lawless Roads*) Greene describes how, at thirteen, he lived a divided life between the bleak school where he was a boarder and his father was headmaster and—across an almost invisible boundary line—the weekend world of home and family, where his father was just his father. This passage is related to another further on in the book where, twenty years later, we find him hovering restlessly on the American side of the Mexican border, waiting "on the dangerous edge of things." The situation inspires this reflection:

> The world is all of a piece, of course; it is engaged everywhere in the same subterranean struggle, lying like a tiny neutral state, with whom no one ever observes his treaties, between two eternities of pain and—God knows the opposite of pain, not we. It is a Belgium fought over by friend and enemy alike. There is no peace anywhere where there is human life, but there are, I told myself, quiet and active sectors of the line. Russia, Spain, Mexico—there's no fraternization on Christmas morning in those parts. . . .

This is typical of the way that Greene broadens the significance of his own border experiences.

A physical frontier occurs in many Greene novels: Dr. Czinner, the exiled revolutionary in *Orient Express* (*Stamboul Train*), crosses home to his death in Subotica; Pinkie disputes territorial claims with a rival gang in the wasteland of Brighton; the Mexican priest in *The Power and the Glory* tastes momentary peace on one side of the border before being drawn back to capture and a firing squad; Scobie, in a key scene in *The Heart of the Matter*, stands peering into Vichy France and sees his destiny carried toward him on a stretcher across a boundary river; Harry Lime is betrayed and shot on an underground frontier in the sewers of occupied Vienna. . . . Even a buoyant character like Aunt Augusta in *Travels with My Aunt*, who can hardly be said to suffer from frontier-phobia, depends absolutely on international boundaries for her brisk contraband trade.

But more important than the mere presence of a border is the sense of conflicting allegiances that it breeds. With a headmaster-father, Greene likens his fate to that of being "Quisling's son." Betrayal has always been the capital sin in Greene's book, and the classical dilemma of his hero is to find himself unwillingly but inevitably forced to betray someone or something he holds dear. The problem was set in his first novel, *The Man Within*, which took its title from Sir Thomas Browne's phrase: "There's another man within me that's angry with me." The crux of nearly every subsequent novel was to be some variation on the Judas theme: Pinkie's betrayal of Rose; the whisky priest's presumed betrayal of his office and the mestizo's betrayal of the priest; Scobie's triple betrayal of his wife, his mistress, and his God, which leads him to the self-betrayal of suicide. . . . Even Greene's predilection for espionage and counterespionage, for agents and double agents, points to the obsessive nature of the theme.

Of course his treatment of the border psychosis is never simplistic nor exclusive. No one escapes it. Just as he describes the world as "a tiny neutral state . . . warred over by friend and enemy alike," so Greene considers it the general human condition to be a victim of divided loyalties. When he deals with this universal predicament in a comic and not a tragic way, he becomes an exponent of "the virtue of disloyalty," as in *Our Man in Havana*, or in that anarchic little tale "The Destructors." In yet another light he has described as the only distinguishing mark of a Christian civilization "the divided mind, the uneasy conscience, and the sense of personal failure."

The possibility of living under a double standard is also for Greene fundamental to the art of the novel. One must be able to write, he says, recalling Bishop Blougram's chessboard, "from the point of view of the black square as well as of the white." An expert in creative duplicity himself, he has drawn his characters from both sides of the board (or the border), presenting them always with their full share of inner contradictions. If he has shown a preference at all, it has been for the black, for the doubters and dissenters, because they offer more of a challenge to the imagination. "Disloyalty," he writes, "encourages you to roam through any human mind: it gives the novelist an extra dimension of understanding." This was one of the main lines he developed in his literary criticism, finding the extra dimension in James, Ford, Mauriac, Waugh, and a few others. He sometimes called it "a religious sense" but meant nothing more parochial by that than: "The creative act seems to remain a function of the religious mind."

In theory and practice Greene applied the liberating principle of disloyalty. But, turning the coin, one must admit that disloyalty has a dark face too. If, as Greene seems to suggest, it is the human lot to be led into the temptation of betrayal—"In the lost boyhood of Judas / Christ was betrayed"—is there no way to ward off the temptation, or to transcend betrayal? The answer is, of course, that while there is plenty of despair in Green's fiction, there is also an unbroken thread of hope, and even his most illusive characters do aspire to virtues less unconventional than the virtue of disloyalty.

The prerequisite to virtue of any kind in Greene's catechism is an act of humility, performed by a conditional admission of failure. Heroes as different as Wormold in *Our Man in Havana*, Fowler, the jaded British war correspondent in *The Quiet American*, Father Clay in *The Heart of the Matter* (their very names smack of mortality), are obsessed with a sense of personal failure, as is Greene himself. The pious, the powerful, and the self-righteous in Greene's fiction—the Captain Seguras, the Pyles, the Wilsons—exist as foils to the unsuccessful characters; and even in the proud, Greene tries to trip the trigger of humility by subjecting them to minor humiliations.

From this base, the next quality that Greene's uncertain

heroes share is not an overwhelming faith but a small tough core of faithfulness. "If you have abandoned one faith, do not abandon all faith," Doctor Magiot writes to his friend Brown in *The Comedians*, and agnostic Doctor Colin in *A Burnt-Out Case* tells the sceptic Querry that a man needs, if not a faith, at least "a superstition to live by." This irreducible grain of faith is the weight that sways the balance in many Greene stories. The split-second of doubt that flashes through the World Dictator's mind as he personally executes the last Pope is an extreme illustration of Greene's faith in the dogged persistence of faith.

But faith in what? What is it that is so bitter to betray?

Faith in individuals, not creeds, in the first instance. "Would the world be in the mess it is now if we were loyal to love and not to countries?" exclaims Beatrice in *Our Man in Havana*. The Mexican priest's virtue resides in the fact that in the prison cell he is ready to trust murderers—and they respond to that trust. The saddest admission that Scobie makes, just before the murder of Ali, is that he has "lost the trick of trust." The element that lifts *The Third Man* above the level of fast-paced thriller is Rollo Martins' fidelity to the memory of his shifty schoolboy friend Harry Lime. This personal involvement puts him on the track of the mystery quicker than the police. (Colonel Calloway attributes it to the fact that he is "an amateur" and, in the most literal sense, his analysis is quite correct.) It also gives to the capture of the criminal an extra dimension—the significance of betrayal—for betrayal isn't worthy of the name if one doesn't love what one betrays.

Faithfulness to others as persons then, and, as far as oneself is concerned, faithfulness to a kind of residual innocence. A characteristic of Greene's fiction is that childhood plays such a large part in it—either a child's actual experience, like Francis Morton's mortal terror of the dark in one of Greene's earliest stories, "The End of the Party," or the childlike reflexes that mark the old man's fear of loneliness in one of his latest stories, "Cheap in August." Many of

Greene's characters are situated in relation to a childhood or schooltime image of themselves: Harris, Wilson, and Helen Rolt are examples of this in *The Heart of the Matter*, and the short story "The Innocent" is a perverse little paradigm of Greene's belief in innocence.

Critics have delighted in underscoring the atmosphere of tawdry, monotonous degeneracy which prevails in Greene's fiction and which they call Greeneland, as we find it, for example, in Minty's character, room, and habits in *The Shipwrecked (England Made Me)*. What they have failed to see is that other quality—now heroic, now merely pathetic—which throws the "seediness" into relief: a remembered idealism, a latent purity, the residual innocence. Even in Minty's case, his threadbare fantasies of family and school provide another standard, make room for that other voice, however wavering, that speaks from the past in criticism of the inadequate present. "To render the highest justice to corruption, you must retain your innocence," Greene writes. "You have to be conscious all the time within yourself of treachery to something valuable."

Chekhov may seem a strange writer to invoke here, but Greene has frequently referred to his views on the role of the writer. "The best artists are realistic and paint life as it is," Chekhov had written and Greene quoted approvingly, "but because every line is permeated as with a juice by awareness of a purpose, you feel, besides life as it is, also life as it ought to be." Chekhov's double standard is the heritage of most of Greene's characters. Minty, the whisky priest, Scobie, Pinkie, bound though they may seem to be by life as it is, never completely lose sight of life as it ought to be; the possibility of change endures like an indissoluble sediment of hope at the bottom of the brain.

To discover the presence of such characteristics in Greene's fiction shows him for what, essentially, he has always been: a subversive romantic. His trek through the hinterlands of Liberia at the beginning of his novelist's career was an attempt to cut back through the crust of civilization to an age of innocence, to "the finer taste, the finer pleasure, the finer terror on which we might have built." Thirty-five years later, in his recent introduction to *Brighton Rock*, he confesses that the kind of book he had always wanted to write was "the high romantic tale, capturing us in youth with hopes that prove illusions, to which we return in age in order to escape the sad reality." The ambivalent play between the light and dark faces of faithfulness and failure, innocence and seediness, hope and despair, realism and romance, has always characterized Greene's creative outlook. Is it any wonder that his restless, disloyal heroes inhabit a twilight borderland?

But here I must abandon my pretence to deliver "the heart of the matter" and ask the reader to be content with "the hint of an explanation" only. Despite the misleading title of the novel, hints are all we ever do get in Scobie's story—or in any other of Greene's inventions. It is tempting to say that all the hints add up to a cryptic message of love. But that, perhaps, is too unqualified a statement to make about a writer who, after so many journeys in fact and imagination, and after so many different fictional incarnations, has never consented to reveal himself directly. Nevertheless, one *can* say that for more than forty years he has, with courage and tenderness, explored the unmapped region that lies between the risk of betrayal and the risk of love. And that, I think, is the extra dimension that Graham Greene has added to the twentieth-century novel.

I am extremely grateful to him for having freely discussed the contents of this book with me, for providing material, approving the choice of texts, and checking my translations, and for permitting a very few minor amendments to make certain excerpts read more smoothly.

And now, having led the reader up to the frontier of Greene's world, I must leave him the excitement of making his own discoveries in "the outlands of danger."

PHILIP STRATFORD

Principal Dates, Travels, Books

October 2, 1904
Born at Berkhamsted, Hertfordshire, son of Charles Henry Greene, history and classics master and later headmaster at Berkhamsted School

1912–1922
Berkhamsted School

1922–1925
Balliol College, Oxford   *Babbling April* (verse), 1925

February 1926
Nottingham; received into Roman Catholic Church

1926–1930
Sub-editor on *The Times*

October 1927
Marries Vivien Dayrell-Browning   *The Man Within*, 1929

1932–
Begins regular book reviewing for *The Spectator*; continues until the early 1940s   *Stamboul Train (Orient Express)*, 1932
                                              It's a Battlefield, 1934

Winter 1934–35
Journey to Liberia   *England Made Me (The Shipwrecked)*, 1935

July 1935–March 1940
Regular film critic for *The Spectator*   *Journey Without Maps* (travel), 1936
                                              A Gun for Sale (This Gun for Hire), 1936

July–December 1937
Co-editor and film critic of *Night and Day*

Winter 1937–38
Journey to Mexico   *Brighton Rock*, 1938

1939
First of many film scenarios   *The Lawless Roads (Another Mexico)*, 1939
                                              The Confidential Agent, 1939

1940–1941
Literary editor and drama critic for *The Spectator*; Ministry of Information, London   *The Power and the Glory*, 1940

1941
Hawthornden Prize for *The Power and the Glory*

1941–1943
Department of Foreign Office, Sierra Leone

The Ministry of Fear, 1943

1943–1944
Department of Foreign Office, London

1944–1948
Director, Eyre & Spottiswoode

June–October 1945
Book reviewer for *The Evening Standard*

Nineteen Stories, 1947

January 1948
Speaker, with François Mauriac, at Les Grandes Conférences Catholiques, Brussels; visits Czechoslovakia; Vienna

The Heart of the Matter, 1948

The Third Man, 1950

1951
Malaya for *Life;* Indochina

The Lost Childhood (essays), 1951
The End of the Affair, 1951

1952
Indochina for *Paris-Match*

1953
Kenya for *The Sunday Times*

The Living Room (drama), 1953
Essais catholiques, 1953

1954
Indochina for *The Sunday Times* and *Le Figaro;* Cuba; Haiti

Twenty-One Stories, 1954

1955
Indochina and Poland for *The Sunday Times* and *Le Figaro*

Loser Takes All, 1955
The Quiet American, 1955

1956
Haiti

1957
Cuba; China; Russia (twice)

The Potting Shed (drama), 1957

1958
Cuba

Our Man in Havana, 1958

1958–1968
Director, The Bodley Head

1959
Cuba; Congo

The Complaisant Lover (drama), 1959

1960
Russia; Brazil for PEN

1961
Honorary Associate, American Institute of Arts and Letters (resigned May 1970); Tunis

In Search of a Character (travel), 1961
A Burnt-Out Case, 1961

1962
Hon.Litt.D., Cambridge; Rumania

1963
Honorary Fellow, Balliol College; Cuba, Haiti for *The Sunday Telegraph*; Goa for *The Sunday Times*; Berlin and East Germany

A Sense of Reality (stories), 1963

Carving a Statue (drama), 1964

1965
Santo Domingo

1966
Named Companion of Honour; Cuba for *The Sunday Telegraph*; settles in France

The Comedians, 1966

1967
Hon.D.Litt., Edinburgh; Israel for *The Sunday Times*; Sierra Leone for *The Observer*; Dahomey

May We Borrow Your Husband? (stories), 1967

1968
Shakespeare Prize, Hamburg; Istanbul for the BBC

1969
Chevalier de la Légion d'Honneur; Paraguay for *The Sunday Telegraph*; Argentina; Czechoslovakia

Collected Essays, 1969
Travels with My Aunt, 1969

1970
Argentina

1971
Chile for *The Observer*; Argentina

A Sort of Life (autobiography), 1971

Bibliographical Notes

Greene's novels have appeared in England in several editions: Heinemann's Uniform Edition, Heinemann's Library Edition, Penguin Books paperback edition. A new definitive edition, revised and with introductions by Greene, is being published jointly by Heinemann and The Bodley Head; nine titles have now appeared and others will be forthcoming at the rate of one or two a year. In the United States most of Greene's works, with the exception of some of his very earliest novels and *A Sort of Life*, are available from The Viking Press. In the following selected bibliography only first English and American editions are listed, except in the case of books originally published by Doubleday and later reissued by Viking. Four of Greene's books were issued under different titles in the States; in this bibliography the English title is given first, as it usually appeared first; in my editorial notes, the order is reversed.

Books by Greene

Babbling April. Oxford: Basil Blackwell, 1925; New York: Doubleday, 1925.

The Man Within. London: Heinemann, 1929; New York: Doubleday, 1929; Viking, 1947.

The Name of Action. London: Heinemann, 1930; New York: Doubleday, 1931.

Rumour at Nightfall. London: Heinemann, 1931; New York: Doubleday, 1932.

Stamboul Train. London: Heinemann, 1932; New York: Doubleday, 1933 (under the title *Orient Express*).

It's a Battlefield. London: Heinemann, 1934; New York: Doubleday, 1934; Viking, 1948.

England Made Me. London: Heinemann, 1935; New York:

Doubleday, 1935 (under the title *The Shipwrecked*); Viking, 1953.

Journey Without Maps. London: Heinemann, 1936; New York: Doubleday, 1936; Viking, 1961.

A Gun for Sale. London: Heinemann, 1936; New York: Doubleday, 1936 (under the title *This Gun for Hire*); Viking, 1952 (in *Three by Graham Greene*) and 1971 (in *Triple Pursuit*).

Brighton Rock. London: Heinemann, 1938; New York: Viking, 1938.

The Lawless Roads: A Mexican Journey. London: Longmans, Green, 1939; New York: Viking, 1939 (under the title *Another Mexico*).

The Confidential Agent. London: Heinemann, 1939; New York: Viking, 1939.

The Power and the Glory. London: Heinemann, 1940; New York: Viking, 1940 (under the title *The Labyrinthine Ways*; reissued 1946 under the original title).

The Ministry of Fear. London: Heinemann, 1943; New York: Viking, 1943.

Nineteen Stories. London: Heinemann, 1947; New York: Viking, 1949 (one story changed). Reissued as *Twenty-One Stories* (with three stories added and one omitted). London: Heinemann, 1954; New York: Viking, 1962.

The Heart of the Matter. London: Heinemann, 1948; New York: Viking, 1948.

Why Do I Write? An exchange of views between Elizabeth Bowen, Graham Greene, and V. S. Pritchett. London: Marshall, 1948.

The Third Man. London: Heinemann, 1950; New York: Viking, 1950.

The Lost Childhood and Other Essays. London: Eyre & Spottiswoode, 1951; New York: Viking, 1952.

The End of the Affair. London: Heinemann, 1951; New York: Viking, 1951.

The Living Room. London: Heinemann, 1953; New York: Viking, 1954.

Essais catholiques. Paris: Editions du Seuil, 1953.

Loser Takes All. London: Heinemann, 1955; New York: Viking, 1957.

The Quiet American. London: Heinemann, 1955; New York: Viking, 1956.

The Potting Shed. New York: Viking, 1957; London: Heinemann, 1958.

Our Man in Havana. London: Heinemann, 1958; New York: Viking, 1958.

The Complaisant Lover. London: Heinemann, 1959; New York: Viking, 1961.

A Burnt-Out Case. London: Heinemann, 1961; New York: Viking, 1961.

In Search of a Character: Two African Journals. London: Bodley Head, 1961; New York: Viking, 1962.

A Sense of Reality. London: Bodley Head, 1963; New York: Viking, 1963.

Carving a Statue. London: Bodley Head, 1964.

The Comedians. London: Bodley Head, 1966; New York: Viking, 1966.

May We Borrow Your Husband? London: Bodley Head, 1967; New York: Viking, 1967.

Collected Essays. London: Bodley Head, 1969; New York: Viking, 1969.

Travels with My Aunt. London: Bodley Head, 1969; New York: Viking, 1970.

A Sort of Life. London: Bodley Head, 1971; New York: Simon & Schuster, 1971.

Nearly all Greene's novels have been filmed. Besides several original scenarios and adaptations, he has written film plays for five of his own stories: *Brighton Rock*, 1948; *The Fallen Idol*, 1948; *The Third Man*, 1949; *Our Man in Havana*, 1960; and *The Comedians*, 1967. Of these, only one has been published, *The Third Man* (London: Lorrimer, 1968). A collection of Greene's film criticism, edited by John Russell

Taylor, is being published under the title *The Pleasure Dome* by Secker & Warburg, London, and under the title *The Collected Film Criticism of Graham Greene* by Simon & Schuster, New York, in 1972.

Books about Greene

BIBLIOGRAPHIES

A complete bibliography of Greene's work by Neil Brennan, Frank Redway, and Cecil Woolf is in preparation. In the meantime, the most up-to-date bibliography is Neil Brennan's in R. O. Evans' *Graham Greene: Some Critical Considerations* (Lexington: University of Kentucky Press, 1963). As for criticism of Greene's work, J. Don Vann has recently published *Graham Greene: A Checklist of Criticism* (Kent, Ohio: Kent State University Press, 1970). A good short bibliography is included in The Viking Critical Library edition of *The Power and the Glory*, edited by R. W. B. Lewis and Peter J. Conn (New York: Viking, 1970).

CRITICISM

Allott, Kenneth, and Miriam Farris. *The Art of Graham Greene.* London: Hamish Hamilton, 1951; New York: Russell & Russell, 1963.

Atkins, John. *Graham Greene.* London: Calder, 1957; New York: Roy Publishers, 1957.

DeVitis, A. A. *Graham Greene.* New York: Twayne Publishers, 1964.

Kunkel, F. L. *The Labyrinthine Ways of Graham Greene.* New York: Sheed & Ward, 1959.

Lodge, David. *Graham Greene.* New York: Columbia University Press, 1966.

Mesnet, Marie-Béatrice. *Graham Greene and the Heart of the Matter.* London: Cresset Press, 1954.

Pryce-Jones, David. *Graham Greene*. Edinburgh: Oliver & Boyd, 1963.

Stratford, Philip. *Faith and Fiction: Creative Process in Greene and Mauriac*. Notre Dame, Ind.: University of Notre Dame Press, 1964.

Turnell, Martin. *Graham Greene: A Critical Essay*. Grand Rapids, Mich.: Eerdmans, 1967.

Wyndham, Francis. *Graham Greene*. London: Longmans, Green, 1955.

I. REMINISCENCES

The creative writer perceives his world once
and for all in childhood and adolescence, and
his whole career is an effort to illustrate his
private world in terms of the great public
world we all share.

—"The Young Dickens," *Collected Essays*

EDITOR'S PREFACE

Greene's autobiography of his first twenty-seven years, *A Sort of Life*, was not available when *The Portable Graham Greene* was being prepared. That might seem like a major handicap, for any book on Greene must begin with those all-important years when his creative sensibilities were forming and his obsessions were being struck. Fortunately, in several essays and in two travel books, he had already described the most significant events in his lost childhood, so it was possible to make a montage of impressions which parallels the autobiography and goes a little beyond it.

A parallel implies a difference as well as similarity, and it should be interesting for those who have read the graceful, meditative *A Sort of Life* to try the sharper, more nervous style of the earlier reminiscences. I have relied heavily on *Journey Without Maps*, a neglected book, but one which Greene recently called "a watershed" in his writing, ". . . a book which gave one a kind of switch and rivers ran a different way afterwards." Using this source gives an African slant to these memories. But that is not out of keeping, for, apart from Mexico, which he visited in the winter of 1937–1938, West Africa was the only part of the world outside England that Greene knew at all well until his early fifties.

The African emphasis also sets up the choice of *The Heart of the Matter* as the one complete novel to be included in this anthology. With this book in mind, I close the section of reminiscences with Greene's account of a Christmas spent in Freetown, Sierra Leone, in 1968—twenty-five years after the experiences which formed the background to Scobie's story.

Primary Symbols

The first thing I can remember at all was a dead dog at the bottom of my pram; it had been run over at a country cross-roads, where later I saw a Jack-in-the-Green, and the nurse put it at the bottom of the pram and pushed me home. There was no emotion attached to the sight. It was just a fact. At that period in life one has an admirable objectivity. Another fact was the man who rushed out of a cottage near the canal bridge and into the next house; he had a knife in his hand; people ran after him shouting; he wanted to kill himself. . . .

The earliest dream that I can remember, earlier than the witch at the corner of the nursery passage, is the dream of something outside that has got to come in. The witch, like the masked dancers, has form, but this is simply power, a force exerted upon a door, an influence that drifted after me upstairs and pressed against the windows.

Later the presence took many odd forms: a troop of black-skinned girls who carried poison flowers which it was death to touch; an old Arab; a half-caste; armed men with shaven heads and narrow eyes and the appearance of Tibetans out of a travel book; a Chinese detective.

You couldn't call these things evil, as Peter Quint in *The Turn of the Screw* was evil, with his carroty hair and his white face of damnation. That story of James's belongs to the Christian, the orthodox imagination. Mine were devils only in the African sense of beings who controlled power. They were not even always terrifying. I remember that at the age of sixteen it was a being with the absurdly symbolic title of the Princess of Time who haunted my sleep. The poisoned flowers, the Tibetan guards, the old Arab . . . were all in her service. I can still recall the dull pain in my palms and my insteps when I deliberately touched the flowers, for I was always trying to escape her, her kindliness as well as her destructiveness. Once I was incited to kill her: I was given a book of ritual, bound in limp leather like an Omar Khayyám at Christmas-time, and a dagger. But she survived into many later dreams. Any dream which opened with terror, with flight, with falling, with unseen presences and opening doors, might end with her cruel and reassuring presence.

It was only many years later that Evil came into my dreams: the man with gold teeth and rubber surgical gloves; the old woman with ringworm; the man with his throat cut dragging himself across the carpet to the bed. . . .

1936   from *Journey Without Maps*

The Future Strikes

I remember distinctly the suddenness with which a key turned in a lock and I found I could read—not just the sentences in a reading book with the syllables coupled like railway carriages, but a real book. It was paper-covered, with the picture of a boy, bound and gagged, dangling at the end of a rope inside a well with the water rising above his waist —an adventure of Dixon Brett, detective. All a long summer holiday I kept my secret, as I believed: I did not want anybody to know that I could read. I suppose I half consciously realized even then that this was the dangerous moment. I was safe so long as I could not read—the wheels had not begun to turn, but now the future stood around on bookshelves everywhere waiting for the child to choose—the life of a chartered accountant perhaps, a colonial civil servant, a planter in China, a steady job in a bank, happiness and misery, eventually one particular form of death, for surely we choose our death much as we choose our job. It grows out of our acts and our evasions, out of our fears and out of our moments of courage. I suppose my mother must have discovered my secret, for on the journey home I was presented for the train with another book, a copy of Ballantyne's *Coral Island* with only a single picture to look at, a coloured frontispiece. But I would admit nothing. All the long journey I stared at the one picture and never opened the book.

But there on the shelves at home (so many shelves for we were a large family) the books waited. Each was a crystal in which the child dreamed that he saw life moving. Here in a cover stamped dramatically in several colours was Captain Gilson's *The Pirate Aeroplane.* I must have read that book six times at least—the story of a lost civilization in the Sahara and of a villainous Yankee pirate with an aeroplane like a box kite and bombs the size of tennis balls who held the golden city to ransom. It was saved by the hero, a young subaltern who crept up to the pirate camp to put the aeroplane out of action. He was captured and watched his enemies dig his grave. He was to be shot at dawn, and to pass the time and keep his mind from uncomfortable thoughts the amiable Yankee pirate played cards with him—the mild nursery game of Kuhn Kan. The memory of that nocturnal game on the edge of life haunted me for years, until I set it to rest at last in one of my own novels with a game of poker played in remotely similar circumstances.

And here is *Sophy of Kravonia* by Anthony Hope—the story of a kitchen-maid who became a queen. One of the first films I ever saw, about 1911, was made from that book, and I can hear still the rumble of the Queen's guns crossing the high Kravonian pass beaten hollowly out on a single piano. Then there was Stanley Weyman's *The Story of Francis Cludde*, and above all other books at that time of my life, *King Solomon's Mines.*

This book did not perhaps provide the crisis, but it certainly influenced the future. If it had not been for that romantic tale of Allan Quatermain, Sir Henry Curtis, Captain Good, and, above all, the ancient witch Gagool, would I at nineteen have studied the appointments list of the Colonial

Office and very nearly picked on the Nigerian Navy for a career? And later, when surely I ought to have known better, the odd African fixation remained. In 1935 I found myself sick with fever on a camp bed in a Liberian native's hut with a candle going out in an empty whisky bottle and a rat moving in the shadows. Wasn't it the incurable fascination of Gagool with her bare yellow skull, the wrinkled scalp that moved and contracted like the hood of a cobra, that led me to work all through 1942 in a little stuffy office in Freetown, Sierra Leone? There is not much in common between the land of the Kukuanas, behind the desert and the mountain range of Sheba's Breast, and a tin-roofed house on a bit of swamp where the vultures moved like domestic turkeys and the pye-dogs kept me awake on moonlit nights with their wailing, and the white women yellowed by atebrin drove by to the club; but the two belonged at any rate to the same continent, and, however distantly, to the same region of the imagination—the region of uncertainty, of not knowing the way about. . . .

1947   from "The Lost Childhood," *Collected Essays*

Life on the Border

I was, I suppose, thirteen years old. Otherwise why should I have been there—in secret—on the dark croquet lawn? I could hear the rabbit moving behind me, munching the grass in his hutch; an immense building with small windows, rather like Keble College, bounded the lawn. It was the school; from somewhere behind it, from across the quad, came a faint sound of music: Saturday night, the school orchestra was playing Mendelssohn. I was alone in mournful happiness in the dark.

Two countries just here lay side by side. From the croquet

lawn, from the raspberry canes, from the greenhouse and the tennis lawn you could always see—dominatingly—the great square Victorian buildings of garish brick: they looked down like skyscrapers on a small green countryside where the fruit trees grew and the rabbits munched. You had to step carefully: the border was close beside your gravel path. From my mother's bedroom window—where she had borne the youngest of us to the sound of school chatter and the disciplinary bell—you looked straight down into the quad, where the hall and the chapel and the classrooms stood. If you pushed open a green baize door in a passage by my father's study, you entered another passage deceptively similar, but none the less you were on alien ground. There would be a slight smell of iodine from the matron's room, of damp towels from the changing rooms, of ink everywhere. Shut the door behind you again, and the world smelt differently: books and fruit and eau-de-Cologne.

One was an inhabitant of both countries: on Saturday and Sunday afternoons of one side of the baize door, the rest of the week of the other. How can life on a border be other than restless? You are pulled by different ties of hate and love. For hate is quite as powerful a tie: it demands allegiance. In the land of the skyscrapers, of stone stairs and cracked bells ringing early, one was aware of fear and hate, a kind of lawlessness—appalling cruelties could be practised without a second thought; one met for the first time characters, adult and adolescent, who bore about them the genuine quality of evil. There was Collifax, who practised torments with dividers; Mr. Cranden with three grim chins, a dusty gown, a kind of demoniac sensuality; from these heights evil declined towards Parlow, whose desk was filled with minute photographs—advertisements of art photos. Hell lay about them in their infancy.

There lay the horror and the fascination. One escaped surreptitiously for an hour at a time: unknown to frontier guards, one stood on the wrong side of the border looking back—one should have been listening to Mendelssohn, but instead one heard the rabbit restlessly cropping near the croquet hoops. It was an hour of release—and also an hour of prayer. One became aware of God with an intensity—time hung suspended—music lay on the air; anything might happen before it became necessary to join the crowd across the border. There was no inevitability anywhere . . . faith was almost great enough to move mountains . . . the great buildings rocked in the darkness.

And so faith came to one—shapelessly, without dogma, a presence above a croquet lawn, something associated with violence, cruelty, evil across the way. One began to believe in heaven because one believed in hell, but for a long while it was only hell one could picture with a certain intimacy—the pitch-pine partitions in dormitories where everybody was never quiet at the same time; lavatories without locks: "There, by reason of the great number of the damned, the prisoners are heaped together in their awful prison . . ."; walks in pairs up the suburban roads; no solitude anywhere, at any time. The Anglican Church could not supply the same intimate symbols for heaven; only a big brass eagle, an organ voluntary, "Lord, Dismiss Us with Thy Blessing," the quiet croquet lawn where one had no business, the rabbit, and the distant music.

Those were primary symbols; life later altered them; one began slowly, painfully, reluctantly, to populate heaven. The Mother of God took the place of the brass eagle: one began to have a dim conception of the appalling mysteries of love moving through a ravaged world—the Curé d'Ars admitting to his mind all the impurity of a province, Péguy challenging God in the cause of the damned. It remained something one associated with misery, violence, evil, "all the torments and agonies," Rilke wrote, "wrought on scaffolds, in torture chambers, madhouses, operating theatres, underneath vaults of bridges in late autumn. . . ."

1939   from *Another Mexico* (*The Lawless Roads*)

Russian Roulette

The wilderness of gorse, old trenches, abandoned butts was the unchanging backcloth of most of the adventures of childhood. It was to the Berkhamsted Common I had decamped for my act of rebellion some years before, with the intention, expressed in a letter left after breakfast on the heavy black sideboard, that there I would stay, day and night, until either I had starved or my parents had given in; when I pictured war it was always in terms of this Common, and myself leading a guerrilla campaign in the ragged waste, for no one, I was persuaded, knew its paths so intimately (how humiliating that in my own domestic campaign I was ambushed by my elder sister after a few hours).

Beyond the Common lay a wide grass ride known for some reason as Cold Harbour to which I would occasionally with some fear take a horse, and beyond this again stretched Ashridge Park, the smooth olive skin of beech trees and the thick last year's quagmire of leaves, dark like old pennies. Deliberately I chose my ground, I believe without any real fear—perhaps because I was uncertain myself whether I was play-acting; perhaps because so many acts which my elders would have regarded as neurotic, but which I still consider to have been under the circumstances highly reasonable, lay in the background of this more dangerous venture.

There had been, for example, perhaps five or six years before, the disappointing morning in the dark-room by the linen cupboard on the eve of term when I had patiently drunk a quantity of hypo under the impression that it was poisonous; on another occasion the blue glass bottle of hay-fever lotion which, as it contained a small quantity of cocaine, had probably been good for my mood; the bunch of deadly nightshade that I had eaten with only a slight narcotic effect; the twenty aspirins I had taken before swimming in the empty out-of-term school baths (I can still remember the curious sensation of swimming through wool): these acts may have removed all sense of strangeness as I slipped a bullet into a chamber and, holding the revolver behind my back, spun the chambers round.

Had I, at seventeen, romantic thoughts about my sister's governess? Undoubtedly I must have had, but I think that at the most they simply eased the medicine down. Boredom, aridity, those were the main emotions. Unhappy love has, I suppose, sometimes driven boys to suicide, but this was not suicide, whatever a coroner's jury might have said of it: it was a gamble with five chances to one against an inquest. The romantic flavour—the autumn scene, the small heavy compact shape lying in the fingers—that perhaps was a tribute to adolescent love, but the discovery that it was possible to enjoy again the visible world by risking its total loss was one I was bound to make sooner or later.

I put the muzzle of the revolver in my right ear and pulled the trigger. There was a minute click, and looking down at the chamber I could see that the charge had moved into place. I was out by one. I remember an extraordinary sense of jubilation. It was as if a light had been turned on. My heart was knocking in its cage, and I felt that life contained an infinite number of possibilities. It was like a young man's first successful experience of sex—as if in that Ashridge glade one had passed a test of manhood. I went home and put the revolver back in the corner cupboard.

The odd thing about this experience was that it was repeated several times. At fairly long intervals I found myself craving for the drug. I took the revolver with me when I went up to Oxford, and I would walk out from Headington towards Elsfield down what is now a wide arterial road, smooth and shiny like the walls of a public lavatory. Then it was a sodden unfrequented country lane. The revolver would be whipped behind my back, the chambers twisted, the muzzle quickly and surreptitiously inserted beneath the black and ugly winter tree, the trigger pulled.

Slowly the effect of the drug wore off—I lost the sense of

jubilation, I began to gain from the experience only the crude kick of excitement. It was like the difference between love and lust. And as the quality of the experience deteriorated, so my sense of responsibility grew and worried me. I wrote a very bad piece of free verse (free because it was easier in that way to express my meaning without literary equivocation) describing how, in order to give a fictitious sense of danger, I would "press the trigger of a revolver I already know to be empty." This piece of verse I would leave permanently on my desk, so that if I lost my gamble, there would be incontrovertible evidence of an accident, and my parents, I thought, would be less troubled than by an apparent suicide—or than by the rather bizarre truth.

But it was back at Berkhamsted that I paid a permanent farewell to the drug. As I took my fifth dose it occurred to me that I wasn't even excited: I was beginning to pull the trigger about as casually as I might take an aspirin tablet. I decided to give the revolver—which was six-chambered—a sixth and last chance. Twirling the chambers round, I put the muzzle to my ear for the last time and heard the familiar empty click as the chambers revolved. I was through with the drug, and walking back over the Common, down the new road by the ruined castle, past the private entrance to the gritty old railway station—reserved for the use of Lord Brownlow—my mind was already busy on other plans. One campaign was over, but the war against boredom had got to go on.

I put the revolver back in the corner cupboard, and going downstairs I lied gently and convincingly to my parents that a friend had invited me to join him in Paris.

1946   from "The Revolver in the Corner Cupboard,"
The Lost Childhood

First Travels

Arrived about nine o'clock at the Gare St.-Lazare, Easter 1924, went to an hotel, then on to the Casino to see Mistinguette, the thin insured distinguished legs, the sharp "catchy" features like the paper faces of the Ugly-Wuglies in *The Enchanted Castle* (" 'Walk on your toes, dear,' the bonneted Ugly-Wugly whispered to the one with the wreath; and even at that thrilling crisis Gerald wondered how she could, since the toes of one foot were but the end of a golf club and of the other the end of a hockey stick"). The next night the Communists met in the slums at the end of a cul-de-sac. They kept on reading out telegrams from the platform and everyone sang the *Internationale*; then they'd speak a little and then another telegram arrived. They were poor and pinched and noisy; one wondered why it was that they had so much good news coming to them which didn't make any difference at all. All the good news and the singing were at the end of an alley in a wide cold hall; they couldn't get out; in the little square the soldiers stood in tin helmets beside their stacked rifles. That night from the window of an hotel I saw a man and woman copulating; they stood against each other under a street lamp, like two people who are supporting and comforting each other in the pain of some sickness. The next day I read in the paper how the Reds had tried to get out, but the soldiers had stopped them; a few people were hurt, a few went to prison. . . .

The aeroplane rocked over Hanover, the last of the storm scattering behind it, dipped suddenly down five hundred feet towards the small air station, and soared again eastwards. Behind the plane the sun set along the clouds; we were above the sunset; looking back it lay below, long pale ridges of stained clouds. The air was grey above the lakes; they were sunk in the ground, like pieces of lead; the lights of villages in between. It was quite dark long before Berlin, and the city came to meet the plane through the darkness as a gorse fire does, links of flame through the heavy green night. A sky-sign was the size of a postage stamp; one could see the whole plan of the city, like a lit map in the Underground when you press a button to find the route. The great rectangle of the Tempelhof was marked in scarlet and yellow lights; the plane swerved away over the breadth of Berlin, turned back and down; the lights in the cabin went out and one could see the headlamps sweeping the asphalt drive, the sparks streaming out behind the grey Lufthansa wing, as the wheels touched and rebounded and took the ground and held. That was happiness, the quick impression; but on the ground, among the swastikas, one saw pain at every yard. . . .

Coming into Riga, I had deceived myself into thinking I was on the verge of a relationship with something new and lovely and happy as the train came out from the Lithuanian flats, where the peasants were ploughing in bathing-slips, pushing the wooden plough through the stiff dry earth, into the shining evening light beside the Latvian river. I had left Berlin in the hard wooden carriage at midnight; I hadn't slept and I'd eaten nothing all day. There was a Polish Jew in the carriage who had been turned out of Germany; he couldn't speak any English and I could speak no German, but a little stout Estonian girl who had been a servant in London could speak both. She was an Estonian patriot, she hadn't a good word for Riga, she regarded the grey spires beyond the river with firm peasant contempt.

And there *was* something decayed, "Parisian," rather shocking in an old-fashioned way about the place. One could see why someone so fresh and unspoiled was disgusted. The old bearded droshky drivers and their bony haggard horses at the station were like the illustrations to a very early translation of *Anna Karenina*; they were like crude and foxed wood engravings. They must have dated back to the days when Riga was a pleasure resort for Grand Dukes, a kind of aristocratic Brighton to which one slipped away from a duchess's bed with someone from the theatre, someone to be described in terms of flowers and pink ribbons, chocolates and champagne in the slipper, of black silk stockings and corsets. All the lights in Riga were dimmed by ten: the public gardens were quite dark and full of whispers, giggles from hidden seats, excited rustles in the bushes. One had the sensation of a whole town on the tiles. It was fascinating, it appealed immensely to the historical imagination, but it certainly wasn't something new, lovely and happy.

1936   from *Journey Without Maps*

A Salmon Tea

It was a late winter evening when I drove through into the Nottingham suburb from the station, round streets quite as dark as Riga's, down and down below the castle rock and the municipal art gallery with the rain breaking on the windows. I had a job; it excited and scared me; I was twenty-one, and you couldn't talk of darkest Africa with any conviction when you had known Nottingham well: the dog sick on the mat, the tinned salmon for tea and the hot potato chips for supper carried into the sub-editor's room ready-salted in strips of newspaper (if you had won the football sweep you paid for the lot). The fog came down in the morning and stayed till night. It wasn't a disagreeable fog; it lay heavy and black between the sun and the earth; there was no light but the air was clear. The municipal "tart" paced up and down by the largest cinema, old and haggard and unused. Her trade was spoilt; there were too many girls about who hadn't a proper sense of values, who would give you a good time in return for a fish tea. The trams creaked round the goose market, and day after day the one bookshop displayed a card in the window printed with Mr. Sassoon's poem:

> Have you forgotten yet? . . .
> Look up, and swear by the green of the
> Spring that you'll never forget.

Somebody must have put it in the window for Armistice Day, and there it stayed, like the Poppy Day posters in Freetown, through the winter months, black sooty dripping months.

In Nottingham I was instructed in Catholicism, travelling here and there by tram into new country with the fat priest who had once been an actor. (It was one of his greatest sacrifices to be unable to see a play.) The tram clattered by the Post Office: "Now we come to the Immaculate Conception"; past the cinema: "Our Lady"; the theatre: a sad slanting look towards *The Private Secretary* (it was Christmastime). The cathedral was a dark place full of inferior statues. I was baptized one foggy afternoon about four o'clock. I couldn't think of any names I particularly wanted, so I kept my old name. I was alone with the fat priest; it was all very quickly and formally done, while someone at a children's service muttered in another chapel. Then we shook hands and I went off to a salmon tea, the dog which had been sick again on the mat. Before that I had made a general confession to another priest: it was like a life photographed as it came to mind, without any order, full of gaps, giving at best a general impression. I couldn't help feeling all the way to the newspaper office, past the Post Office, the Moroccan café, the ancient whore, that I had got somewhere new by way of memories I hadn't known I possessed. I had taken up the thread of life from very far back, from so far back as innocence.

1936   from *Journey Without Maps*

Journey Back

The motive of a journey deserves a little attention. It is not the fully conscious mind which chooses West Africa in preference to Switzerland. The psychoanalyst, who takes the images of a dream one by one—"You dreamed you were asleep in a forest. What is your first association to forest?"—finds that some images have immediate associations; to others the patient can bring out nothing at all; his brain is like a cinema in which the warning "Fire" has been cried; the exits are jammed with too many people trying to escape, and when I say that to me Africa has always seemed an important image, I suppose that is what I mean, that it has represented more than I could say. "You dreamed you were in Africa. Of what do you think when I say the word Africa, Africa?" and a crowd of words and images, witches and death, unhappiness and the Gare St.-Lazare, the huge smoky viaduct over a Paris slum, crowd together and block the way to full consciousness. . . .

It is not *any* part of Africa which acts so strongly on this unconscious mind; certainly no part where the white settler has been most successful in reproducing the conditions of his country, its morals and its popular art. A quality of darkness is needed, of the inexplicable. This Africa may take the form of an unexplained brutality, as when Conrad noted in his Congo diary: "Thursday, 3rd July. . . . Met an officer of the State inspecting. A few minutes afterwards saw at a camp place the dead body of a Backongo. Shot? Horrid smell"; or a sense of despair, as when M. Céline writes: "Hidden away in all this flowering forest of twisted vegetation, a few decimated tribes of natives squatted among fleas and flies, crushed by taboos and eating nothing all the time but rotten tapioca." The old man whom I saw beaten with a club outside the poky little prison at Tapee-Ta, the naked widows at Tailahun covered with yellow clay squatting in a

hole, the wooden-toothed devil swaying his raffia skirts between the huts seem like images in a dream to stand for
something of importance to myself.

Today our world seems particularly susceptible to brutality. There is a touch of nostalgia in the pleasure we take in
gangster novels, in characters who have so agreeably simplified their emotions that they have begun living again at a
level below the cerebral. We, like Wordsworth, are living
after a war and after a revolution, and these half-castes
fighting with bombs between the cliffs of skyscrapers seem
more likely than we to be aware of Proteus rising from the
sea. It is not, of course, that one wishes to stay for ever at
that level, but when one sees to what unhappiness, to what
peril of extinction centuries of cerebration have brought us,
one sometimes has a curiosity to discover if one can from
what we have come, to recall at which point we went astray.

1936   from *Journey Without Maps*

A Discovery

The fever would not let me sleep at all, but by the early
morning it was sweated out of me. My temperature was a
long way below normal, but the worst boredom of the trek
for the time being was over. I had made a discovery during
the night which interested me. I had discovered in myself a
passionate interest in living. I had always assumed before, as
a matter of course, that death was desirable.

It seemed that night an important discovery. It was like a
conversion, and I had never experienced a conversion before. (I had not been converted to a religious faith. I had
been convinced by specific arguments in the probability of
its creed.) If the experience had not been so new to me, it
would have seemed less important, I should have known

that conversions don't last, or if they last at all it is only as a little sediment at the bottom of the brain. Perhaps the sediment has value, the memory of a conversion may have some force in an emergency; I may be able to strengthen myself with the intellectual idea that once in Zigi's Town I had been completely convinced of the beauty and desirability of the mere act of living.

1936   from *Journey Without Maps*

Return

One was back, or, if you will, one had advanced again, to the seedy level. This journey, if it had done nothing else, had reinforced a sense of disappointment with what man had made out of the primitive, what he had made out of childhood. Oh, one wanted to protest, one doesn't believe, of course, in "the visionary gleam," in the trailing glory, but there was something in that early terror and the bareness of one's needs, a harp strumming behind a hut, a witch on the nursery landing, a handful of kola nuts, a masked dancer, the poisoned flowers. The sense of taste was finer, the sense of pleasure keener, the sense of terror deeper and purer. It isn't a gain to have turned the witch or the masked secret dancer, the sense of supernatural evil, into the small human viciousness of the thin distinguished military grey head in Kensington Gardens with the soft lips and the eye which dwelt with dull lustre on girls and boys of a certain age.

He was an Old Etonian. He had an estate in the Highlands. He said, "Do they cane at your school?" looking out over the wide flat grass, the nursemaids and the children, with furtive alertness. He said, "You must come up and stay with me in Scotland. Do you know of any girls' school where they still—you know——" He began to make confidences, and then, suddenly taking a grip of the poor sliding brain, he rose and moved away with stiff military back, the Old Etonian tie, the iron-grey hair, a bachelor belonging to the right clubs, over the green plain among the nursemaids and the babies wetting their napkins.

I could hear a policeman talking to Vande under the wall, and suddenly I remembered (though I told myself still that I was dead sick of Africa) the devil's servant at Zigita waving away the lightning and the rain with an elephant-hair fan, the empty silent town after the drums had beaten the devil's warning. There was cruelty enough in the interior, but had we done wisely exchanging the supernatural cruelty for our own?

I was looking out of the window of the day nursery when the aeroplane fell. I could see it crash out of sight on to the playing fields at the top of the hill. The airman had dived, playing the fool before his younger brother and the other boys, he had miscalculated the height and struck the ground and was dead before he reached hospital. His small brother never looked, never waited to hear if he were alive, but walked steadily away down the hill to the school and shut himself tearlessly in a lavatory. Someone went and found him there, there were no locks on any lavatory doors, nowhere where you could be alone.

Major Grant said, "And in a cupboard they keep birches. . . ."

The lorries drove up and down the day of the General Strike loaded with armed men. The café had been turned into a dressing station and a squad of Garde Mobile moved down the wide boulevard that runs from Combat to Ménilmontant searching everyone on the pavement for arms. The whole of Paris was packed with troops; every corner, every high building sheltered a troop, they clustered along the walls in their blue steel helmets like wood-lice. The road of the Revolution from Vincennes to the Place de la Concorde was lined with guns and cavalry. No breaking out here, no return to something earlier, something communal, something primitive.

More police were coming up to get their pickings beneath

the wall. Vande and Amah were being persuaded towards the wooden station. I thought of Vande in the dark urging the carriers over the long gaping swaying bridge at Duogobmai; I remembered they had never had the goat to guard them from the elephants. It wouldn't have been any use now. We were all of us back in the hands of adolescence, and I thought rebelliously: I am glad, for here is iced beer and a wireless set which will pick up the Empire programme from Daventry, and after all it is home, in the sense that we have been taught to know home, where we will soon forget the finer taste, the finer pleasure, the finer terror on which we might have built. . . .

But what had astonished me about Africa was that it had never been really strange. Gibraltar and Tangier—those extended just parted hands—seemed more than ever to represent an unnatural breach. The "heart of darkness" was common to us both. Freud has made us conscious as we have never been before of those ancestral threads which still exist in our unconscious minds to lead us back. The need, of course, has always been felt, to go back and begin again. Mungo Park, Livingstone, Stanley, Rimbaud, Conrad represented only another method to Freud's, a more costly, less easy method, calling for physical as well as mental strength. The writers, Rimbaud and Conrad, were conscious of this purpose, but one is not certain how far the explorers knew the nature of the fascination which worked on them in the dirt, the disease, the barbarity and the familiarity of Africa.

The captain leant over the rail, old and dissatisfied, complaining of his men: "Boil the whole bloody lot of the men in the ship together and you wouldn't make an ordinary seaman"; he was looking back—to the age of sail. At Freetown guests came on board and we drank ourselves free from Africa. An officer came and eyed me like an enemy across the table in the smoking-room. "I'd send my ticket to the Board of Trade, my dear friend, and tell them to—— I tell you, my dear friend. . . ." The captain stuck his fingers down his throat, brought up his drink and was dead sober again, and the ship went out of harbour, out of Africa. But their dissatisfaction was like a navel-string that tied them to its coast.

For there are times when the nearest the European has ever got to the interior, to the communal life with its terror and its gentleness, seems to be the Coast; Major Grant ringing up the brothel in Savile Row, the Old Etonian in Kensington Gardens, the Nottingham "tart" and the droshky-drivers of Riga dwell on that rim of land which is known all the world over as the Coast, the one and only coast. They are not, after all, so far from the central darkness: Miss Kilvane listening to the ghost of Joanna just as the circle of blacks in Tailahun listened to the enigmatic speech of Landow; the Catholic priest saying, "And now the Immaculate Conception," as the tram drove through the market, the tangle of stalls and overhead wires, the neo-Gothic hotels under the black overhead Midland fog. This may explain the deep appeal of the seedy. It *is* nearer the beginning; like Monrovia its building has begun wrong, but at least it has only begun; it hasn't reached so far away as the smart, the new, the chic, the cerebral.

It isn't that one wants to stay in Africa: I have no yearning for a mindless sensuality, even if it were to be found there: it is only that when one has appreciated such a beginning, its terrors as well as its placidity, the power as well as the gentleness, the pity for what we have done with ourselves is driven more forcibly home.

> While I was fishing in the dull canal
> On a winter evening round behind the gashouse
> Musing upon the king my brother's wreck
> And on the king my father's death before him.

After the blinding sunlight on the sand beyond the bar, after the long push of the Atlantic sea, the lights of Dover burning at four in the morning, a cold April mist coming out from shore with the tender. A child was crying in a tenement not far from the Lord Warden, the wail of a child too young to speak, too young to have learnt what the dark may conceal in the way of lust and murder, crying for no intelligible reason but because it still possessed the ancestral fear, the devil was dancing in its sleep. There, I thought, standing in the cold empty customs shed with a couple of suitcases, a few pieces of silver jewellery, a piece of script found in a Bassa hut, an old sword or two, the only loot I had brought with me, was as far back as one needed to go, was Africa: the innocence, the virginity, the graves not opened yet for gold, the mine not broken with sledges.

1936   from *Journey Without Maps*

Africa Revisited

A ghost—a *revenant*—does not expect to be recognized when he returns to the scenes of his past; if he communicates to you a sense of fear, perhaps it is really his own fear, not yours. Places have so changed since he was alive that he has to find his way through a jungle of new houses and altered rooms (concrete and steel can proliferate like vegetation). Because *he* hasn't changed, because his memories are unaltered, the *revenant* believes that he is invisible. Coming back to Freetown and Sierra Leone last Christmas, I thought I belonged to a bizarre past which no one else shared. It was a shock to be addressed by my first name on my first night, to feel a hand squeeze my arm and a voice say, "Scobie, eh, who's Scobie?" and "Pujehun, don't you remember we met in Pujehun? I was in P.W.D. Let's have a drink at the City."

I came to Sierra Leone to work more than a quarter of a century ago, landing in Freetown from a slow convoy four weeks out of Liverpool. I felt a strong sense of unreality: how had this happened? A kitchen orchestra of forks and frying-pans played me off the Elder Dempster cargo ship into a motor launch where my temporary host, the Secretary of Agriculture, awaited me, expecting something less flippant. The red Anglican cathedral looked down on my landing as it had done in 1935 when I first visited Freetown. Nothing in the exhausted shabby enchanted town of bougainvillaea and balconies, tin roofs and funeral parlours, had changed, but I never imagined on my first visit that one day I would arrive like this to work, to be one of those tired men drinking pink gin at the City bar as the sun set on the laterite.

The sense of unreality grew stronger every hour. A passage by air had been arranged to Lagos where I was to work for three months before returning, and I thought it best to warn my host that he would be seeing me again. "What exactly are you going to do here?" he asked, and I was studiously vague, for no one had yet told me what my "cover" in this far-from-James-Bond world was to be. I knew my number, and that was all (it was not 007). I was glad when a major with a large moustache looked in, with an air of stern premeditation, for drinks, and the subject could be changed. "Come for a walk?" he suddenly asked. It seemed an odd thing to do at that hour of the day, but I agreed. We set out down the road in the haze of the harmattan.

"Find it hot, I suppose?" he said.

"Yes."

"Humidity is ninety-five per cent."

"Really?"

He swerved sideways into a garden. "This house is empty," he said. "Fellow's gone on leave." I followed him obediently. He sat down on a large rock and said, "Got a message for you." I sat gingerly down beside him, remembering the childhood warning that sitting on a stone in the heat gives you piles.

"Signal came in last Friday. You're an inspector of the D.O.T. Got it?"

"What's D.O.T.?"

"Department of Overseas Trade," he said sharply. Ignorance in this new intelligence world was like incompetence.

All the same I felt relieved to know and at lunch gently led the conversation back to my future in Freetown. "As a matter of fact," I said to my host, "I can tell *you*, though it's not been officially announced yet, that I am to be an inspector of the D.O.T."

"D.O.T.?"

"Department of Overseas Trade."

He looked a little sceptical. He had every right to be, for by the time I returned I had become something quite different. The D.O.T., I learnt too late in Lagos, had refused to give cover to a phoney inspector, and an equally unsuccessful attempt had been made on the virginity of the British Council. After that I was threatened in turn with a naval rank and an air force rank, until it was found that unless I was given the rank of commander or group-captain I could not have a private office and a safe for my code-books. When I flew up to Freetown again it was with a vague attachment to the police force which was a little difficult to explain to those who awaited an inspector of Overseas Trade.

The whole of my life in Freetown had the same unreality; for the secretariat I did not exist, for I was not on the Colonial Office list where everyone's salary and position were set down, and for the Sierra Leonians I was another unapproachable Government servant. I lived alone in a small house on the edge of what in the rains became a marsh, with a Nigerian transport camp opposite me which helped to collect the vultures and behind the scrub which collected flies, for it was used as a public lavatory. Over this I had one successful brush with the administration. When I wrote to the Colonial Secretary demanding a lavatory for the Africans, he replied that my request should go through the proper channels by way of the Commissioner of Police; I quoted in reply what Churchill had said of "proper channels" in wartime, and the shed was built. I wrote back that in the annals of Freetown my name like Keats's would be writ in water. My isolation for a while was increased when I quarrelled with my boss 1200 miles away in Lagos and he ceased to send me any money to live on (or to pay my almost non-existent agents).

During that long silence I had plenty of time to wonder again why I was here. Our lives are formed in the years of childhood, and when a while ago I began writing an account of my first twenty-seven years, I was curious to discover any hints of what had led a middle-aged man to sit there in a humid solitude, far from his family and his friends and his real profession. Out of my experience was to come my first popular success, *The Heart of the Matter*, but I did not begin to write that book for another four years, after the absurdities had already faded from my mind. I had been instructed not to keep a diary for security reasons, just as I was taught the use of secret inks that I never employed and of bird-droppings if these were exhausted. (Vultures were the most common bird—there were usually three or four on my tin roof—but I doubt whether their droppings had been contemplated.)

The start of my life as 59200 was not propitious. I announced my safe arrival by means of a book code (I had chosen a novel of T. F. Powys from which I could detach sufficiently lubricious phrases for my own amusement), and a large safe came in the next convoy with a leaflet of instructions and my codes. The code-books were a constant source of interest, for the most unexpected words occurred in their necessarily limited vocabulary. I wondered how often use had been made of the symbol for "eunuch," and I was not content until I had found an opportunity to use it myself in a message to my colleague in Gambia: "As the chief eunuch said I cannot repeat cannot come." (Strange the amusements one finds in solitude. I can remember standing for half an hour on the staircase to my bedroom watching two flies make love.)

The safe was another matter. I am utterly incapable of reading instructions of a technical nature. I chose my combination and set it as I believed correctly, put away my newly acquired code-books, shut the safe and tried in vain to reopen it. Very soon I realized the fault I had made: my eye had passed over one line in the instructions and the combination was set now to some completely unknown figure. Telegrams were waiting to be decoded and telegrams to be sent. Laboriously with the help of T. F. Powys I lied to London that the safe had been damaged in transit; they must send another by the next convoy. The code-books were rescued with a blow flame and lodged temporarily in Government House.

I used to look forward to the evenings, when I would take a walk along the abandoned railway track on the slopes below Hill Station, returning at sunset to get my bath before the rats came in (at night they would swing on my bedroom curtains). Then—free from telegrams—I would sit down to write *The Ministry of Fear*. Whisky, gin and beer were severely rationed, but some friendly naval officers supplied me with demijohns of wine which had come from Portuguese Guinea without passing the customs. On nights of full moon the starving pye-dogs kept me awake with their howling, and I would rise, pull boots over my pyjamas, and get rid of my rage by cursing and throwing stones in the lane behind my house where the very poor lived. My boy told me I was known there as "the bad man," so before I went away from Freetown as I believed for ever, I sent some bottles of wine to a wedding in one of the hovels, hoping to leave a better memory behind.

It was not very often I went to the City Hotel, where *The Heart of the Matter* began. There one escaped the protocol-conscious members of the secretariat. It was a home from home for men who had not encountered success at any turn of the long road and who no longer expected it. They were not beachcombers, for they had jobs, but their jobs had no prestige value. They were failures, but they knew more of Africa than the successes who were waiting to get transferred to a smarter colony and were careful to take no risks with their personal file. In the City bar were the men who had stayed put into the beginnings of old age, and yet they were immeasurably younger than the new assistant secretaries. The dream which had brought them to Africa was still alive: it didn't depend on carefully mounting the ladder of a career. I suppose I felt at home at the City because, after six months or more, I was beginning to feel a failure too.

All my brighter schemes had been firmly turned down: the rescue by bogus Communist agents of a left-wing agitator who was under house-arrest (I intended to have him planted in Vichy-held Conakry believing himself to be an informant for Russia); a brothel to be opened in Bissau for visitors from Senegal. The Portuguese liners came in and out carrying their smuggled industrial diamonds, and not one search—from the rice in the holds to the cosmetics in the cabins—had ever turned up a single stone. In the City bar I could occasionally forget the insistent question what am I doing here? because the answer was probably much the same as my companions might have given: an escape from schools? a recurring dream of adolescence? a book read in childhood?

The City Hotel I found on my return last Christmas had not altered at all. A white man looked down from the balcony where my character Wilson sat watching Scobie pass in the street below, and he waved to me as if it was but yesterday that I looked in last for a coaster. Only the turbaned Sikh was absent who used to tell fortunes—in the communal bathroom for the sake of privacy. A Sierra Leonian played sad Christmas calypsos in a corner of the balcony and a tart in a scarlet dress danced to attract attention (tarts were not allowed inside). Even the kindly sad Swiss landlord was still the same; he hadn't left Freetown in more than thirty years. He had survived, and to that extent he was successful, but perhaps it was the very meagreness of the success which made his shabby bar the "home from home."

Next day I went to look for my old house. A quarter of a century ago it had been condemned by the health authorities, so it might well have disappeared, and I thought at first it had. A brand-new Italian garage stood on the site of the

Nigerian transport camp, the bush where the lavatory had been built had disappeared under a housing-estate, and there were very superior houses now in the lane where the pye-dogs had howled (one was occupied by the Secretary General of the National Reform Council which at that moment was governing Sierra Leone). It took me quite a while to recognize my old home, brightly painted, with a garden where the mud had been. The little office had become a kitchen, the sitting-room which had been bleak with P.W.D. furniture was gay with the abstract paintings of a Sierra Leone young woman. I went upstairs and looked into the bedroom where the rats had swung—there were still rats, the owner said—and I stopped on the stairs where I had watched for so long a fly's copulation. The image brought back the boredom of my adolescence, a youth playing at Russian roulette . . . perhaps that had been a stage towards this barren hermitage on the Brookfield flats.

The Brookfield church was unchanged, where my friend Father Mackie used to preach in Creole: the same bad statue of St. Anthony over the altar, the same Virgin in the butterfly blue robe. At Midnight Mass I could have believed myself back in 1942 if in that year I had not missed the Mass. A fellow Catholic, the representative of the rival secret service, S.O.E., had come to dine with me tête-à-tête and we were soon too drunk on Portuguese wine to stagger to the church. Now the girl in front of me wore one of the surrealist Manchester cotton dresses which are rarely seen since Japanese trade moved in. The word "soupsweet" was printed over her shoulder, but I had to wait until she stood up before I could confirm another phrase: "Fenella lak' good poke." Father Mackie would have been amused, I thought, and what better description could there be of this poor lazy lovely coloured country than "soupsweet"?

It was with some shame that my companion, Mario Soldati, and I moved out of the old City Hotel for the conventional comfort of the new luxury Paramount built up the hill behind the former police station where I used to come every day to collect my cables from the Commissioner. The old man would not have approved this change in Freetown, and I remembered the morning in the rains when he went out of his mind under the pressure of overwork, the strain of controlling corrupt officers, the badgering of M.I.5 bureaucrats from home. He was not a drinking man, but in his knowledge and humanity he was more akin to the inhabitants of the City Hotel than I was now. I had been spoilt for the communal bathroom and the bare bedroom. They treated me with great charity when I left, they gave me a warm welcome whenever I returned for a drink, but I felt the guilt of a beachcomber *manqué:* I had failed at failure. How could they tell that for a writer as much as for a priest there is no such thing as success?

1968   "The Soupsweet Land," *Collected Essays*

II. FICTION

If I were to choose an epigraph for all the
novels I have written, it would be from *Bishop
Blougram's Apology*:

> Our interest's on the dangerous edge
>   of things.
> The honest thief, the tender murderer,
> The superstitious atheist, demi-rep
> That loves and saves her soul in new
>   French books—
> We watch while these in equilibrium keep
> The giddy line midway.

—*A Sort of Life*

In the introduction to a three-volume French edition of his novels, Greene wistfully looks back over a long line of books and writes: "I sometimes see myself as a ragged troop commander driving his exhausted column on towards the last frontier. I have no wish to march at the pace of the stragglers; they must be left to the mercies, however harsh, that a hostile population may perhaps accord them." And on the strength of this assessment he drops *The Man Within* and *Orient Express* (*Stamboul Train*) from this edition of his *Oeuvres choisies.*

The editor of a book like *The Portable Graham Greene* must be even more ruthless: the squad is reduced to a few picked men; forces must be deployed to mask the many inevitable gaps. My strategy has been to balance excerpts from six of the novels with six short stories—including two of the longer ones and an uncollected story, "The Blessing." These elements flank two of Greene's most characteristic works which are reprinted complete in their definitive versions: *The Heart of the Matter* and *The Third Man.* The order of march is chronological, and individual units have been chosen to show not only the consistency of Greene's vision but also his versatility as a storyteller.

Still it was painful to omit so much. Two of his best entertainments, *This Gun for Hire* (*A Gun for Sale*) and *The Ministry of Fear*, had to be jettisoned; his most beautifully articulated novel, *The End of the Affair*, is not represented; *A Burnt-Out Case* and *The Comedians* are given only a token role in a later section; and for reasons of space none of his plays is included. When one is in charge of an austere operation of this kind, one is well aware that another choice might have had other virtues. But it is some consolation to think that, whatever the choice, there would still have been untapped resources and quality to spare.

The End of the Party

Peter Morton woke with a start to face the first light. Rain tapped against the glass. It was January the fifth.

He looked across a table, on which a night-light had guttered into a pool of water, at the other bed. Francis Morton was still asleep, and Peter lay down again with his eyes on his brother. It amused him to imagine it was himself whom he watched, the same hair, the same eyes, the same lips and line of cheek. But the thought palled, and the mind went back to the fact which lent the day importance. It was the fifth of January. He could hardly believe a year had passed since Mrs. Henne-Falcon had given her last children's party.

Francis turned suddenly upon his back and threw an arm across his face, blocking his mouth. Peter's heart began to beat fast, not with pleasure now but with uneasiness. He sat up and called across the table, "Wake up." Francis's shoulders shook and he waved a clenched fist in the air, but his eyes remained closed. To Peter Morton the whole room seemed to darken, and he had the impression of a great bird swooping. He cried again, "Wake up," and once more there was silver light and the touch of rain on the windows. Francis rubbed his eyes. "Did you call out?" he asked.

"You are having a bad dream," Peter said. Already experience had taught him how far their minds reflected each other. But he was the elder, by a matter of minutes, and that brief extra interval of light, while his brother still struggled in pain and darkness, had given him self-reliance and an instinct of protection towards the other who was afraid of so many things.

"I dreamed that I was dead," Francis said.

"What was it like?" Peter asked.

"I can't remember," Francis said.

"You dreamed of a big bird."

"Did I?" The two lay silent in bed facing each other, the

same green eyes, the same nose tilting at the tip, the same firm lips, and the same premature modelling of the chin. The fifth of January, Peter thought again, his mind drifting idly from the image of cakes to the prizes which might be won. Egg-and-spoon races, spearing apples in basins of water, blind-man's-buff.

"I don't want to go," Francis said suddenly. "I suppose Joyce will be there . . . Mabel Warren." Hateful to him, the thought of a party shared with those two. They were older than he. Joyce was eleven and Mabel Warren thirteen. Their long pigtails swung superciliously to a masculine stride. Their sex humiliated him, as they watched him fumble with his egg, from under lowered scornful lids. And last year . . . he turned his face away from Peter, his cheeks scarlet.

"What's the matter?" Peter asked.

"Oh, nothing. I don't think I'm well. I've got a cold. I oughtn't to go to the party."

Peter was puzzled. "But, Francis, is it a bad cold?"

"It will be a bad cold if I go to the party. Perhaps I shall die."

"Then you mustn't go," Peter said, prepared to solve all difficulties with one plain sentence, and Francis let his nerves relax, ready to leave everything to Peter. But though he was grateful he did not turn his face towards his brother. His cheeks still bore the badge of a shameful memory, of the game of hide-and-seek last year in the darkened house, and of how he had screamed when Mabel Warren put her hand suddenly upon his arm. He had not heard her coming. Girls were like that. Their shoes never squeaked. No boards whined under their tread. They slunk like cats on padded claws. When the nurse came in with hot water Francis lay tranquil, leaving everything to Peter. Peter said, "Nurse, Francis has got a cold."

The tall starched woman laid the towels across the cans and said, without turning, "The washing won't be back till tomorrow. You must lend him some of your handkerchiefs."

"But, Nurse," Peter asked, "hadn't he better stay in bed?"

"We'll take him for a good walk this morning," the nurse said. "Wind'll blow away the germs. Get up now, both of you," and she closed the door behind her.

"I'm sorry," Peter said. "Why don't you just stay in bed? I'll tell mother you felt too ill to get up." But rebellion against destiny was not in Francis's power. If he stayed in bed they would come up and tap his chest and put a thermometer in his mouth and look at his tongue, and they would discover he was malingering. It was true he felt ill, a sick empty sensation in his stomach and a rapidly beating heart, but he knew the cause was only fear, fear of the party, fear of being made to hide by himself in the dark, uncompanioned by Peter and with no night-light to make a blessed breach.

"No, I'll get up," he said, and then with sudden desperation, "But I won't go to Mrs. Henne-Falcon's party. I swear on the Bible I won't." Now surely all would be well, he thought. God would not allow him to break so solemn an oath. He would show him a way. There was all the morning before him and all the afternoon until four o'clock. No need to worry when the grass was still crisp with the early frost. Anything might happen. He might cut himself or break his leg or really catch a bad cold. God would manage somehow.

He had such confidence in God that when at breakfast his mother said, "I hear you have a cold, Francis," he made light of it. "We should have heard more about it," his mother said with irony, "if there was not a party this evening," and Francis smiled, amazed and daunted by her ignorance of him. His happiness would have lasted longer if, out for a walk that morning, he had not met Joyce. He was alone with his nurse, for Peter had leave to finish a rabbit-hutch in the woodshed. If Peter had been there he would have cared less; the nurse was Peter's nurse also, but now it was as though she were employed only for his sake, because he could not be trusted to go for a walk alone. Joyce was only two years older and she was by herself.

She came striding towards them, pigtails flapping. She glanced scornfully at Francis and spoke with ostentation to the nurse. "Hello, Nurse. Are you bringing Francis to the party this evening? Mabel and I are coming." And she was off again down the street in the direction of Mabel Warren's home, consciously alone and self-sufficient in the long empty road. "Such a nice girl," the nurse said. But Francis was silent, feeling again the jump-jump of his heart, realizing how soon the hour of the party would arrive. God had done nothing for him, and the minutes flew.

They flew too quickly to plan any evasion, or even to prepare his heart for the coming ordeal. Panic nearly overcame him when, all unready, he found himself standing on the door-step, with coat collar turned up against a cold wind, and the nurse's electric torch making a short trail through the darkness. Behind him were the lights of the hall and the sound of a servant laying the table for dinner, which his mother and father would eat alone. He was nearly overcome by the desire to run back into the house and call out to his mother that he would not go to the party, that he dared not go. They could not make him go. He could almost hear himself saying those final words, breaking down for ever the barrier of ignorance which saved his mind from his parents' knowledge. "I'm afraid of going. I won't go. I daren't go. They'll make me hide in the dark, and I'm afraid of the dark. I'll scream and scream and scream." He could see the expression of amazement on his mother's face, and then the cold confidence of a grown-up's retort. "Don't be silly. You must go. We've accepted Mrs. Henne-Falcon's invitation."

But they couldn't make him go; hesitating on the door-step while the nurse's feet crunched across the frost-covered grass to the gate, he knew that. He would answer, "You can say I'm ill. I won't go. I'm afraid of the dark." And his mother, "Don't be silly. You know there's nothing to be afraid of in the dark." But he knew the falsity of that reasoning; he knew how they taught also that there was nothing to fear in death, and how fearfully they avoided the idea of it. But they couldn't make him go to the party. "I'll scream. I'll scream."

"Francis, come along." He heard the nurse's voice across the dimly phosphorescent lawn and saw the yellow circle of her torch wheel from tree to shrub. "I'm coming," he called with despair; he couldn't bring himself to lay bare his last secrets and end reserve between his mother and himself, for there was still in the last resort a further appeal possible to Mrs. Henne-Falcon. He comforted himself with that, as he advanced steadily across the hall, very small, towards her enormous bulk. His heart beat unevenly, but he had control now over his voice, as he said with meticulous accent, "Good evening, Mrs. Henne-Falcon. It was very good of you to ask me to your party." With his strained face lifted towards the curve of her breasts, and his polite set speech, he was like an old withered man. As a twin he was in many ways an only child. To address Peter was to speak to his own image in a mirror, an image a little altered by a flaw in the glass, so as to throw back less a likeness of what he was than of what he wished to be, what he would be without his unreasoning fear of darkness, footsteps of strangers, the flight of bats in dusk-filled gardens.

"Sweet child," said Mrs. Henne-Falcon absent-mindedly, before, with a wave of her arms, as though the children were a flock of chickens, she whirled them into her set programme of entertainments: egg-and-spoon races, three-legged races, the spearing of apples, games which held for Francis nothing worse than humiliation. And in the frequent intervals when nothing was required of him and he could stand alone in corners as far removed as possible from Mabel Warren's scornful gaze, he was able to plan how he might avoid the approaching terror of the dark. He knew there was nothing to fear until after tea, and not until he was sitting down in a pool of yellow radiance cast by the ten candles on Colin Henne-Falcon's birthday cake did he become fully conscious of the imminence of what he feared. He heard Joyce's high voice down the table, "After tea we are going to play hide-and-seek in the dark."

"Oh, no," Peter said, watching Francis's troubled face, "don't let's. We play that every year."

"But it's in the programme," cried Mabel Warren. "I saw it myself. I looked over Mrs. Henne-Falcon's shoulder. Five o'clock, tea. A quarter to six to half-past, hide-and-seek in the dark. It's all written down in the programme."

Peter did not argue, for if hide-and-seek had been inserted in Mrs. Henne-Falcon's programme, nothing that he could say could avert it. He asked for another piece of birthday cake and sipped his tea slowly. Perhaps it might be possible to delay the game for a quarter of an hour, allow Francis at least a few extra minutes to form a plan, but even in that Peter failed, for children were already leaving the table in twos and threes. It was his third failure, and again he saw a great bird darken his brother's face with its wings. But he upbraided himself silently for his folly, and finished his cake encouraged by the memory of that adult refrain, "There's nothing to fear in the dark." The last to leave the table, the brothers came together to the hall to meet the mustering and impatient eyes of Mrs. Henne-Falcon.

"And now," she said, "we will play hide-and-seek in the dark."

Peter watched his brother and saw the lips tighten. Francis, he knew, had feared this moment from the beginning of the party, had tried to meet it with courage and had abandoned the attempt. He must have prayed for cunning to evade the game, which was now welcomed with cries of excitement by all the other children. "Oh, do let's." "We must pick sides." "Is any of the house out of bounds?" "Where shall home be?"

"I think," said Francis Morton, approaching Mrs. Henne-Falcon, his eyes focused unwaveringly on her exuberant breasts, "it will be no use my playing. My nurse will be calling for me very soon."

"Oh, but your nurse can wait, Francis," said Mrs. Henne-Falcon, while she clapped her hands together to summon to her side a few children who were already straying up the wide staircase to upper floors. "Your mother will never mind."

That had been the limit of Francis's cunning. He had refused to believe that so well prepared an excuse could fail. All that he could say now, still in the precise tone which other children hated, thinking it a symbol of conceit, was, "I think I had better not play." He stood motionless, retaining, though afraid, unmoved features. But the knowledge of his terror, or the reflection of the terror itself, reached his brother's brain. For the moment, Peter Morton could have cried aloud with the fear of bright lights going out, leaving him alone in an island of dark surrounded by the gentle lapping of strange footsteps. Then he remembered that the fear was not his own, but his brother's. He said impulsively to Mrs. Henne-Falcon, "Please. I don't think Francis should play. The dark makes him jump so." They were the wrong words. Six children began to sing, "Cowardy, cowardy custard," turning torturing faces with the vacancy of wide sunflowers towards Francis Morton.

Without looking at his brother, Francis said, "Of course I will play. I am not afraid. I only thought . . ." But he was already forgotten by his human tormentors. The children scrambled round Mrs. Henne-Falcon, their shrill voices pecking at her with questions and suggestions. "Yes, anywhere in the house. We will turn out all the lights. Yes, you can hide in the cupboards. You must stay hidden as long as you can. There will be no home."

Peter stood apart, ashamed of the clumsy manner in which he had tried to help his brother. Now he could feel, creeping in at the corners of his brain, all Francis's resentment of his championing. Several children ran upstairs, and the lights on the top floor went out. Darkness came down like the wings of a bat and settled on the landing. Others began to put out the lights at the edge of the hall, till the children were all gathered in the central radiance of the chandelier, while the bats squatted round on hooded wings and waited for that, too, to be extinguished.

"You and Francis are on the hiding side," a tall girl said, and then the light was gone, and the carpet wavered under his feet with the sibilance of footfalls, like small cold draughts, creeping away into corners.

"Where's Francis?" he wondered. "If I join him he'll be less frightened of all these sounds." "These sounds" were the casing of silence: the squeak of a loose board, the cautious closing of a cupboard door, the whine of a finger drawn along polished wood.

Peter stood in the centre of the dark deserted floor, not listening but waiting for the idea of his brother's whereabouts to enter his brain. But Francis crouched with fingers on his ears, eyes uselessly closed, mind numbed against impressions, and only a sense of strain could cross the gap of dark. Then a voice called "Coming," and as though his brother's self-possession had been shattered by the sudden cry, Peter Morton jumped with his fear. But it was not his own fear. What in his brother was a burning panic was in him an altruistic emotion that left the reason unimpaired. "Where, if I were Francis, should I hide?" And because he was, if not Francis himself, at least a mirror to him, the answer was immediate. "Between the oak bookcase on the left of the study door and the leather settee." Between the twins there could be no jargon of telepathy. They had been together in the womb, and they could not be parted.

Peter Morton tiptoed towards Francis's hiding place. Occasionally a board rattled, and because he feared to be caught by one of the soft questers through the dark, he bent and untied his laces. A tag struck the floor and the metallic sound set a host of cautious feet moving in his direction. But by that time he was in his stockings and would have laughed inwardly at the pursuit had not the noise of someone stumbling on his abandoned shoes made his heart trip. No more boards revealed Peter Morton's progress. On stockinged feet he moved silently and unerringly towards his object. Instinct told him he was near the wall, and, extending a hand, he laid the fingers across his brother's face.

Francis did not cry out, but the leap of his own heart revealed to Peter a proportion of Francis's terror. "It's all right," he whispered, feeling down the squatting figure until he captured a clenched hand. "It's only me. I'll stay with you." And grasping the other tightly, he listened to the cascade of whispers his utterance had caused to fall. A hand touched the bookcase close to Peter's head and he was aware of how Francis's fear continued in spite of his presence. It was less intense, more bearable, he hoped, but it remained. He knew that it was his brother's fear and not his own that he experienced. The dark to him was only an absence of light; the groping hand that of a familar child. Patiently he waited to be found.

He did not speak again, for between Francis and himself touch was the most intimate communion. By way of joined hands thought could flow more swiftly than lips could shape themselves round words. He could experience the whole progress of his brother's emotion, from the leap of panic at the unexpected contact to the steady pulse of fear, which now went on and on with the regularity of a heart-beat. Peter Morton thought with intensity, "I am here. You needn't be afraid. The lights will go on again soon. That rustle, that movement is nothing to fear. Only Joyce, only Mabel Warren." He bombarded the drooping form with thoughts of safety, but he was conscious that the fear continued. "They are beginning to whisper together. They are tired of looking for us. The lights will go on soon. We shall have won. Don't be afraid. That was only someone on the stairs. I believe it's Mrs. Henne-Falcon. Listen. They are feeling for the lights." Feet moving on a carpet, hands brushing a wall, a curtain pulled apart, a clicking handle, the opening of a cupboard door. In the case above their heads a loose book shifted under a touch. "Only Joyce, only Mabel Warren, only Mrs. Henne-Falcon," a crescendo of reassuring thought before the chandelier burst, like a fruit tree, into bloom.

The voices of the children rose shrilly into the radiance. "Where's Peter?" "Have you looked upstairs?" "Where's Francis?" but they were silenced again by Mrs. Henne-Falcon's scream. But she was not the first to notice Francis Morton's stillness, where he had collapsed against the wall at the touch of his brother's hand. Peter continued to hold the clenched fingers in an arid and puzzled grief. It was not merely that his brother was dead. His brain, too young to realize the full paradox, wondered with an obscure self-pity why it was that the pulse of his brother's fear went on and on, when Francis was now where he had always been told there was no more terror and no more darkness.

1929   *Twenty-One Stories*

Minty's Day

EDITOR'S NOTE

Ferdinand Minty, shabby remittance man, high Anglican and old Harrovian, is employed by a Stockholm newspaper to shadow the industrial giant Erik Krogh and report on his movements. Minty is one of Greene's first comic characters. Greene has often singled him out as an example, in his creative experience, of a secondary character who unexpectedly "comes alive" and commandeers more than his share of the action. We see him here, in an early chapter of The Shipwrecked (England Made Me), *as he first stirs into life.*

Minty knew the moment that he got up in the morning that this was one of his days. He sang gently to himself as he shaved, "This is the way that Minty goes, Minty goes,

Minty goes." Although he had a new blade he did not cut himself once; he shaved cautiously rather than closely, while the pot of coffee, which his landlady had brought him, grew cold on the washstand. Minty liked his coffee cold; his stomach would bear nothing hot. A spider watched him under his tooth glass; it had been there five days; he had expected his landlady to clear it away, but it had remained a second day, a third day. He cleaned his teeth under the tap. Now she must believe that he kept it there for study. He wondered how long it would live. He watched it and it watched him back with shaggy patience. It had lost a leg when he put the glass over it.

Above his bed was a house group, rows of boys blinking against the sun above and below the seated figures of the prefects, the central figure of the housemaster and his wife. It was curious to observe how a moustache by being waxed at the tips could date a man as accurately as a woman's dress, the white blouse, the whalebone collar, the puffed sleeves. Occasionally Minty was called on to identify himself; practice had made him perfect; there had been a time of hesitation when he could not decide whether Patterson seated on the housemaster's left or Tester standing rather more obscurely behind, his jaw hidden by a puffed sleeve, best acted as his proxy. For Minty himself did not appear; he had seen the photograph taken from the sick-room window, a blaze of light, the blinking, blackened faces, the photographer diving beneath his shade.

"This is the way that Minty goes." He picked up a stump of cigarette from the soap tray and lit it. Then he studied his hair in the mirror of the wardrobe door; this was one of his days; he must be prepared for anything, even society. The scurf worried him; he rubbed what was left of the pomade upon his scalp, brushed his hair, studied it again. Minty was satisfied. He drank his tepid coffee without taking the cigarette from his mouth; the smoke blew up and burned his eyes. He swore so gently that no one but himself would have known that he swore. "Holy Cnut." The phrase was his own; always, instinctively, like a good Anglo-Catholic, he had disliked "smut"; it was as satisfying to say "Holy Cnut" as words that sullied, Minty believed.

Minty put on his black overcoat and went downstairs. It was Tuesday, the twenty-third. A letter from home was due. For nearly twenty years Minty had fetched his monthly letters from the General Post Office; it prevented embarrassment. On occasion it was necessary to change a lodging without the usual notice. He found the sun quite hot in the square by the station, but he always wore a coat when he went to fetch his letters. He parked his cigarette outside in a spot where a beggar was unlikely to find it. Presenting a dog-eared card at the Poste Restante counter, he believed that, as an Englishman and an old Harrovian, he honoured Stockholm by choosing it as his home. For no one could deny that he was a gentleman of leisure who might have lived in any place with a post office and scope for personality.

To his surprise there were two letters; this was something which had to be celebrated with another cup of tepid coffee. He chose a leather armchair facing the street in the lounge opposite the station and sat there waiting for his coffee to cool. He was so certain that this was one of his days that he ground out the stump of his cigarette and bought a packet. Then he tried a little coffee in a spoon, but it was still too hot.

On the point of opening one of the letters he paused, his eye caught by an unusual activity at the station. Several men were running across the road with movie cameras. He saw Nils darting by outside and waved to him. He remembered what it was all about. "The film star's return home." He had earned sixty crowns a few days ago translating into Swedish all the dope he could discover in the movie magazines. "The screen's greatest lover." "The mystery woman of Hollywood." A number of people (were they hired by the hour? Minty wondered) began to cheer, and several businessmen, with portfolios under their arms, stopped on the pavement and scowled at the station. They obscured Minty's view. Minty stood on his chair. It was just as well to keep an eye open even if it was not his own pigeon. The actress was not very popular in Sweden; something disgraceful might happen; something which someone would want hushed up. If, for example, she was hissed . . .

But nothing happened. A woman came out of the station in a camel-hair coat with a big collar; it was just possible to see that she was wearing grey flannel trousers; Minty had one glimpse of a pale haggard humourless face, a long upper lip, the unreal loveliness and the unreal tragedy of a mask like Dante's known too well. The movie cameras whirred and the woman put her hands in front of her face and stepped into a car. Somebody threw an expensive bouquet of flowers (who paid for that? Minty wondered) which missed the car and fell in the road. Nobody took any notice. A little woman in heavy black weeds and a black veil scuttled into the car and it drove away. The newspapermen came together in front of the station and Minty could hear their laughter.

He opened the first letter. Scott and James, solicitors. "Enclosed find money order for £15, being your allowance for the month ending next September 20th. Please sign and return the enclosed receipt. Reference GL/RS." GL, Minty pondered. I haven't had those initials before. New blood in the old firm. After twenty years it amused him to find the smallest variation in the letter's form. Before he opened the second letter he drank his coffee for luck

Holy Cnut, it's Aunt Ella. I'd quite forgotten the old—the old woman (be careful, Minty) was alive.

"Dearest Ferdinand." The name checked Minty. He had not seen that particular arrangement of letters for a very long while. One signed one's Christian name on cheques, of course, but somehow Minty carried off the burden of the name. "Dearest Ferdinand." He laughed and stirred his coffee; that's me.

"It seems a long while since I heard from you." A long

while, Minty thought. I should think it is a long while: the best part of twenty years. "I happened to come across an old letter of yours the other day when I was clearing out my drawers preparatory to my latest move. It had got pushed to the back of a drawer where I keep my old sketching blocks. The thought came to me that we are the last of the immediate Mintys. Your cousin Delia's family, of course, still go on, and there are the Hertfordshire Mintys, but we have never had much to do with them, and there is your mother of course, but she is only a Minty by marriage. I suppose—an odd thought, isn't it?—that we are all only Mintys by marriage. Anyway, there was your letter, and it was such a pleasure to read it over again. Characteristically it is undated, so I cannot tell you how long it is since I received it. It must be some years now, I expect. I see that you say that you enjoy Stockholm and hope that is still true. I can't quite remember now why you went to Stockholm, I must remember to ask your mother when I next see her, her memory, poor dear, is not what it was, and it would not surprise me at all to hear that she had forgotten what position it is that you occupy. It must, at any rate, be satisfactory financially or you would not have stayed away from England all these years. I notice that my brokers have just bought me some Norwegian State Bonds; rather a coincidence, isn't it? Curious—I am reading your old letter as I write—I see that you ask me for the loan of five pounds; it must indeed have been written many years ago when you were first starting whatever work it is you do. Doubtless I sent you the money, but I wonder whether you ever repaid me. However, we'll be charitable and take it for granted that you did. It's an old story now, anyway. You'll be wondering what news there is of home, but you will have heard about Uncle Laurie's death and the affair of Delia's twins from your mother. She'll have told you everything important. I saw a Harrow boy on Fakenhurst platform the other day; another coincidence. Your loving Aunt, Ella"

Well, Minty thought, this is indeed a proud day. To have

heard from the family. How long this coffee takes to cool. I've a good mind to write to mother on the strength of it. "Aunt Ella when she last wrote mentioned . . ." What a start it would give the dear woman to see my handwriting on an envelope. Not sweet enough. Another lump. But I don't know her address, and if I sent it to the solicitors they would return it. Reference GL/RS. Cool enough now. I could send it under cover to Aunt Ella and ask her to stamp and forward it. My handwriting under an English stamp. What a surprise for mother, but cautious, Minty, cautious. Your imagination runs away with you, Minty. Nothing must endanger the fifteen pounds a month so regularly and gracefully paid. Reference GL/RS.

"I see you, Nils," Minty said, wagging his finger roguishly at the young man on the pavement. "You knew it was pay-day and you want a cup of coffee. And you shall have one. This is a special day. I have had a letter from the Family."

Nils came up the steps from the street, shy and graceful as a young fawn pressing its nose against a fence and seeing life go by behind the rails. Minty was life. Minty sipping his cold coffee, Minty yellow about the lips, "Have a cigarette," Minty munificent.

"Thank you, Mr. Minty."

"Quite a commotion at the station."

"Yes, Mr. Minty. She is a fine actress."

"Did she pay for the bouquet?"

"No, I do not think that she did, Mr. Minty. The card fell off. I have it here."

Minty said, "Give it to me."

"I thought it might be useful to you, Mr. Minty."

"You're a good lad, Nils," Minty said. "Take another cigarette. Put it in your pocket." He looked at the card. "Take the whole packet."

"No, really, Mr. Minty."

"Well," Minty said, "if you won't—" He put the cigarettes quickly into his pocket and got up. "Business calls. Bread and butter. The squalid necessity of earning money."

"The editor," Nils said, "wants to see you."

"Trouble?"

"Yes, I think so."

"I can face him," Minty said. "I have fifteen pounds in my pocket; I have heard from the Family." He walked boldly out and round the corner; his shortness, his long black coat, made him ridiculous; people smiled at him and he knew why they smiled. It had been poison to him once, but that was many years ago. He had taken the poison so often in small doses, dodging between side street and side street, that now like Mithridates he was immune. He could come out into the main streets, he could stand and talk to himself and plume his dusty image in the windows of haberdashers, minding the smiles hardly at all; only a little malice stirred in his veins, moved with the bloodstream.

It stirred, after the long stairs, the machine room, the opening and closing of glass doors, at sight of the editor. He resented the red military moustache, the curtness, the efficiency; one might as well work in a factory and have done with it. "Well, Herr Minty?"

"I was told you wanted to see me."

"Where was Herr Krogh yesterday evening?"

"I just went to snatch a cup of tea. There was no reason why he should leave the Legation like that."

The editor said, "We are not receiving very much from you, Herr Minty. There are plenty of men we can employ for outside work. I think we may have to try someone else. You haven't a trained eye for news." He blew out his chest and said suddenly, "Your health is not good enough, Herr Minty. That cup of tea. A Swede would not have needed a cup of tea. Poison. You probably take it strong."

"Very weak, Herr Redaktör, cold, with lemon."

"You should exercise yourself, Herr Minty. Have you a wireless set?"

Minty shook his head. Patience, he thought with venom, patience.

"If you had a wireless set you could exercise as I do every

morning under a first-class instructor. Do you take a cold bath?"

"A tepid bath, Herr Redaktör."

"All my reporters take cold baths. You cannot be efficient, Herr Minty, with a bent back, an undeveloped chest, poor muscles."

But this was the familiar poison. He had been slowly broken in by parents, by schoolmasters, by strangers in the street. Crooked and yellow and pigeon-chested, he had his deep refuge, the inexhaustible ingenuity of his mind. He blinked his scorched eyes and said with brave perkiness, "So I'm discharged?"

"The next time you slip an opportunity—"

"I would rather leave now," Minty said, "when I have something to sell."

"What have you to sell?"

"A friend of mine, Miss Farrant's brother, has joined the firm. A confidential position."

"You know very well that you get the best price from us."

"For that," Minty said, "but for this?" and he snapped a visiting card on to the desk. It was stained with mud. "She never got the flowers," Minty said. "They just fell in the road. That's what comes of employing athletic reporters. They can't throw straight. You ought to have come to Minty." He wagged his finger and left the room; he was quite drunk on two cups of coffee, his monthly cheque, on Aunt Ella's letter. In the reporters' room he saw Nils. "I put him in his place," he said. "He won't trouble me again for a while. Has Krogh left the flat yet?"

"No. I've just rung up the porter."

"He's late," Minty said. "Reunion, eh, Nils? A Night of Love. We're all human," he said, sucking in his cheeks, shivering in the draught from the wide window, seeking malevolently for a stray cigarette packet on an empty desk and finding none. "It's turning cold. It's going to rain again," and while he searched the rain came; a great blown cloud from over the lake drifted like a derelict airship above the

roofs, bringing shadow, bringing the first slow deliberate
drops which stung the window sill, broke and ran down the
wall.

1935   from *The Shipwrecked* (*England Made Me*)

The Innocent

It was a mistake to take Lola there, I knew it the moment
we alighted from the train at the small country station. On
an autumn evening one remembers more of childhood than
at any other time of year, and her bright veneered face, the
small bag which hardly pretended to contain our "things"
for the night, simply didn't go with the old grain warehouse
across the small canal, the few lights up the hill, the posters
of an ancient film. But she said, "Let's go into the country,"
and Bishop's Hendron was, of course, the first name which
came into my head. Nobody would know me there now, and
it hadn't occurred to me that it would be I who remembered.

Even the old porter touched a chord. I said, "There'll be a
four-wheeler at the entrance," and there was, though at first
I didn't notice it, seeing the two taxis and thinking, "The
old place is coming on." It was very dark, and the thin autumn mist, the smell of wet leaves and canal water were
deeply familiar.

Lola said, "But why did you choose this place? It's grim."
It was no use explaining to her why it wasn't grim to me,
that that sand heap by the canal had always been there
(when I was three I remember thinking it was what other
people meant by the seaside). I took the bag (I've said it was
light; it was simply a forged passport of respectability) and
said we'd walk. We came up over the little humpbacked

bridge and passed the almshouses. When I was five I saw a middle-aged man run into one to commit suicide; he carried a knife, and all the neighbours pursued him up the stairs. She said, "I never thought the country was like *this*." They were ugly almshouses, little grey stone boxes, but I knew them as I knew nothing else. It was like listening to music, all that walk.

But I had to say something to Lola. It wasn't her fault that she didn't belong here. We passed the school, the church, and came round into the old wide High Street and the sense of the first twelve years of life. If I hadn't come, I shouldn't have known that sense would be so strong, because those years hadn't been particularly happy or particularly miserable: they had been ordinary years, but now with the smell of wood fires, of the cold striking up from the dark damp paving stones, I thought I knew what it was that held me. It was the smell of innocence.

I said to Lola, "It's a good inn, and there'll be nothing here, you'll see, to keep us up. We'll have dinner and drinks and go to bed." But the worst of it was that I couldn't help wishing that I were alone. I hadn't been back all these years; I hadn't realized how well I remembered the place. Things I'd quite forgotten, like that sand heap, were coming back with an effect of pathos and nostalgia. I could have been very happy that night in a melancholy, autumnal way wandering about the little town, picking up clues to that time of life when, however miserable we are, we have expectations. It wouldn't be the same if I came back again, for then there would be the memories of Lola, and Lola meant just nothing at all. We had happened to pick each other up at a bar the day before and liked each other. Lola was all right, there was no one I would rather spend the night with, but she didn't fit in with *these* memories. We ought to have gone to Maidenhead. That's country too.

The inn was not quite where I remembered it. There was the Town Hall, but they had built a new cinema with a

Moorish dome and a café, and there was a garage which hadn't existed in my time. I had forgotten too the turning to the left up a steep, villaed hill.

"I don't believe that road was there in my day," I said.

"Your day?" Lola asked.

"Didn't I tell you? I was born here."

"You must get a kick out of bringing me here," Lola said. "I suppose you used to think of nights like this when you were a boy."

"Yes," I said, because it wasn't her fault. She was all right. I liked her scent. She used a good shade of lipstick. It was costing me a lot, a fiver for Lola and then all the bills and fares and drinks, but I'd have thought it money well spent anywhere else in the world.

I lingered at the bottom of that road. Something was stirring in the mind, but I don't think I should have remembered what, if a crowd of children hadn't come down the hill at that moment into the frosty lamplight, their voices sharp and shrill, their breath fuming as they passed under the lamps. They all carried linen bags, and some of the bags were embroidered with initials. They were in their best clothes and a little self-conscious. The small girls kept to themselves in a kind of compact, beleaguered group, and one thought of hair ribbons and shining shoes and the sedate tinkle of a piano. It all came back to me: they had been to a dancing lesson, just as I used to go, to a small square house with a drive of rhododendrons half-way up the hill. More than ever I wished that Lola were not with me, less than ever did she fit, as I thought "Something's missing from the picture," and a sense of pain glowed dully at the bottom of my brain.

We had several drinks at the bar, but there was half an hour before they would agree to serve dinner. I said to Lola, "You don't want to drag round this town. If you don't mind, I'll just slip out for ten minutes and look at a place I used to know." She didn't mind. There was a local man, perhaps a schoolmaster, at the bar simply longing to stand her a drink:

I could see how he envied me, coming down with her like this from town just for a night.

I walked up the hill. The first houses were all new. I resented them. They hid things like fields and gates I might have remembered. It was like a map which had got wet in the pocket and pieces had stuck together; when you opened it there were whole patches hidden. But half-way up, there the house really was, the drive; perhaps the same old lady was giving lessons. Children exaggerate age. She may not in those days have been more than thirty-five. I could hear the piano. She was following the same routine. Children under eight, 6–7 p.m. Children eight to thirteen, 7–8. I opened the gate and went in a little way. I was trying to remember.

I don't know what brought it back. I think it was simply the autumn, the cold, the wet frosting leaves, rather than the piano, which had played different tunes in those days. I remembered the small girl as well as one remembers anyone without a photograph to refer to. She was a year older than I was: she must have been just on the point of eight. I loved her with an intensity I have never felt since, I believe, for anyone. At least I have never made the mistake of laughing at children's love. It has a terrible inevitability of separation because there *can* be no satisfaction. Of course one invents tales of houses on fire, of war and forlorn charges which prove one's courage in her eyes, but never of marriage. One knows without being told that that can't happen, but the knowledge doesn't mean that one suffers less. I remembered all the games of blind-man's-buff at birthday parties when I vainly hoped to catch her, so that I might have the excuse to touch and hold her, but I never caught her; she always kept out of my way.

But once a week for two winters I had my chance: I danced with her. That made it worse (it was cutting off our only contact) when she told me during one of the last lessons of the winter that next year she would join the older class. She liked me too, I knew it, but we had no way of expressing it. I used to go to her birthday parties and she would come to mine, but we never even ran home together after the dancing class. It would have seemed odd; I don't think it occurred to us. I had to join my own boisterous teasing male companions, and she the besieged, the hustled, the shrilly indignant sex on the way down the hill.

I shivered there in the mist and turned my coat collar up. The piano was playing a dance from an old C. B. Cochran revue. It seemed a long journey to have taken to find only Lola at the end of it. There *is* something about innocence one is never quite resigned to lose. Now when I am unhappy about a girl, I can simply go and buy another one. Then the best I could think of was to write some passionate message and slip it into a hole (it was extraordinary how I began to remember everything) in the woodwork of the gate. I had once told her about the hole, and sooner or later I was sure she would put in her fingers and find the message. I wondered what the message could have been. One wasn't able to express much, I thought, in those days; but because the expression was inadequate, it didn't mean that the pain was shallower than what one sometimes suffered now. I remembered how for days I had felt in the hole and always found the message there. Then the dancing lessons stopped. Probably by the next winter I had forgotten.

As I went out of the gate I looked to see if the hole existed. It was there. I put in my finger, and, in its safe shelter from the seasons and the years, the scrap of paper rested yet. I pulled it out and opened it. Then I struck a match, a tiny glow of heat in the mist and dark. It was a shock to see by its diminutive flame a picture of crude obscenity. There could be no mistake; there were my initials below the childish, inaccurate sketch of a man and woman. But it woke fewer memories than the fume of breath, the linen bags, a damp leaf, or the pile of sand. I didn't recognize it; it might have been drawn by a dirty-minded stranger on a lavatory wall. All I could remember was the purity, the intensity, the pain of that passion.

I felt at first as if I had been betrayed. "After all," I told myself, "Lola's not so much out of place here." But later that night, when Lola turned away from me and fell asleep, I began to realize the deep innocence of that drawing. I had believed I was drawing something with a meaning unique and beautiful; it was only now after thirty years of life that the picture seemed obscene.

1937   *Twenty-One Stories*

A Marriage Proposal

EDITOR'S NOTE
Brighton Rock *began as a detective story describing the take-over of Kite's race-track gang by the adolescent hero, Pinkie. But as the novel developed, a moral and religious dimension asserted itself and the retributive murders of Hale and Spicer became less important than Pinkie's own Catholic sense of the appalling certainty of his self-damnation.*

This is highlighted in the excerpts that follow, in which Pinkie decides to marry Rose, the waitress from Snow's Restaurant who knows too much of the gang's crimes and must be silenced, not by murder but by marriage, for a wife cannot give evidence against her husband. The horror of his sacrilegious union with Rose weighs more heavily on the Boy's conscience than his carvings and killings, and she, through her love for him, represents a last chance, "between the stirrup and the ground," for the saving intervention of the mercy of God.

The Boy looked down at the body, spread-eagled like Prometheus, at the bottom of Frank's stairs. "Good God," Mr. Prewitt said, "how did it happen?"

The Boy said, "These stairs have needed mending a long while. I've told Frank about it, but you can't make the bastard spend money." He put his bound hand on the rail and pushed until it gave. The rotten wood lay across Spicer's body, a walnut-stained eagle couched over the kidneys.

"But that happened *after* he fell," Mr. Prewitt protested; his legal voice was tremulous.

"You've got it wrong," the Boy said. "You were here in the passage and you saw him lean his suitcase against the rail. He shouldn't have done that. The case was too heavy."

"My God, you can't mix me up in this," Mr. Prewitt said. "I saw nothing. I was looking in the soap dish, I was with Dallow."

"You both saw it," the Boy said. "That's fine. It's a good thing we have a respectable lawyer like you on the spot. Your word will do the trick."

"I'll deny it," Mr. Prewitt said. "I'm getting out of here. I'll swear I was never in the house."

"Stay where you are," the Boy said. "We don't want another accident. Dallow, go and telephone for the police—and a doctor, it looks well."

"You can keep me here," Mr. Prewitt said, "but you can't make me say——"

"I only want you to say what you want to say. But it wouldn't look good, would it, if I was taken up for killing Spicer, and you were here—looking in the soap dish. It would be enough to ruin some lawyers."

Mr. Prewitt stared over the broken gap at the turn of the stairs where the body lay. He said slowly, "You'd better lift that body and put the wood under it. The police would have a lot to ask if they found it that way." He went back into the bedroom and sat down on the bed and put his head in his hands. "I've got a headache," he said, "I ought to be at home." Nobody paid him any attention. Spicer's door rattled in the draught. "I've got a splitting headache," Mr. Prewitt said.

Dallow came lugging the suitcase down the passage: the

cord of Spicer's pyjamas squeezed out of it like toothpaste. "Where was he going?" Dallow said.

"The Blue Anchor, Union Street, Nottingham," the Boy said. "We'd better wire them. They might want to send flowers."

"Be careful about finger prints," Mr. Prewitt implored them from the washstand without raising his aching head, but the Boy's steps on the stairs made him look up. "Where are you going?" he asked sharply. The Boy stared up at him from the turn in the stairs. "Out," he said.

"You can't go now," Mr. Prewitt said.

"I wasn't here," the Boy said. "It was just you and Dallow. You were waiting for me to come in."

"You'll be seen."

"That's your risk," the Boy said. "I've got things to do."

"Don't tell me," Mr. Prewitt cried hastily and checked himself. "Don't tell me," he repeated in a low voice, "what things . . ."

"We'll have to fix that marriage," the Boy said, sombrely. He gazed at Mr. Prewitt for a moment—the spouse, twenty-five years at the game—with the air of someone who wanted to ask a question, almost as if he were prepared to accept advice from a man so much older, as if he expected a little human wisdom from the old shady legal mind.

"It had better be soon," the Boy went softly and sadly on. He still watched Mr. Prewitt's face for some reflection of the wisdom twenty-five years at the game must have given him, but saw only a frightened face, boarded up like a store when a riot is on. He went on down the stairs, dropping into the dark well where Spicer's body had fallen. He had made his decision; he had only to move towards his aim; he could feel his blood pumped from the heart and moving indifferently back along the arteries like trains on the inner circle. Every station was one nearer safety, and then one farther away, until the bend was turned and safety again approached, like Notting Hill, and afterwards receded. The middle-aged whore on Hove front never troubled to look round as he came up behind her: like electric trains moving on the same track there was no collision. They both had the same end in view, if you could talk of an end in connexion with that circle. Outside the Norfolk bar two smart scarlet racing models lay along the kerb like twin beds. The Boy was not conscious of them, but their image passed automatically into his brain, released his secretion of envy.

Snow's was nearly empty. He sat down at the table where once Spicer had sat, but he was not served by Rose. A strange girl came to take his order. He said awkwardly, "Isn't Rose here?"

"She's busy."

"Could I see her?"

"She's talking to someone up in her room. You can't go there. You'll have to wait."

The Boy put half a crown on the table. "Where is it?"

The girl hesitated. "The manageress would bawl hell."

"Where's the manageress?"

"She's out."

The Boy put another half-crown on the table.

"Through the service door," the girl said, "and straight up the stairs. There's a woman with her though——"

He heard the woman's voice before he reached the top of the stairs. She was saying, "I only want to speak to you for your own good," but he had to strain to catch Rose's reply.

"Let me be, why won't you let me be?"

"It's the business of anyone who thinks right."

The Boy could see into the room now from the head of the stairs, though the broad back, the large loose dress, the square hips of the woman nearly blocked his view of Rose, who stood back against the wall in an attitude of sullen defiance. Small and bony in the black cotton dress and the white apron, her eyes stained but tearless, startled and determined, she carried her courage with a kind of comic inadequacy, like the little man in the bowler put up by the management to challenge the strong man at a fair. She said, "You'd better let me be."

It was Nelson Place and Manor Street which stood there in the servant's bedroom, and for a moment he felt no antagonism but a faint nostalgia. He was aware that she belonged to his life, like a room or a chair: she was something which completed him. He thought, "She's got more guts than Spicer." What was most evil in him needed her: it couldn't get along without goodness. He said softly, "What are you worrying my girl about?" and the claim he made was curiously sweet to his ears, like a refinement of cruelty. After all, though he had aimed higher than Rose, he had this comfort: she couldn't have gone lower than himself. He stood there, with a smirk on his face, when the woman turned. "Between the stirrup and the ground"—he had learned the fallacy of that comfort: if he had attached to himself some bright brassy skirt, like the ones he'd seen at the Cosmopolitan, his triumph after all wouldn't have been so great. He smirked at the pair of them, nostalgia driven out by a surge of sad sensuality. She was good, he'd discovered that, and he was damned: they were made for each other.

"You leave her alone," the woman said. "I know all about you." It was as if she were in a strange country: the typical Englishwoman abroad. She hadn't even got a phrase book. She was as far from either of them as she was from hell—or heaven. Good and evil lived in the same country, spoke the same language, came together like old friends, feeling the same completion, touching hands beside the iron bedstead. "You want to do what's Right, Rose?" she implored.

Rose whispered again, "You let us be."

"You're a Good Girl, Rose. You don't want anything to do with *him*."

"You don't know a thing."

There was nothing she could do at the moment but threaten from the door. "I haven't finished with you yet. I've got friends."

The Boy watched her go with amazement. He said, "Who the hell is she?"

"I don't know," Rose said.

"I've never seen her before." A memory pricked him and passed: it would return. "What did she want?"

"I don't know."

"You're a good girl, Rose," the Boy said, pressing his fingers round the sharp wrist.

She shook her head. "I'm bad." She implored him, "I want to be bad if she's good and you——"

"You'll never be anything but good," the Boy said. "There's some wouldn't like you for that, but I don't care."

"I'll do anything for you. Tell me what to do. I don't want to be like her."

"It's not what you do," the Boy said, "it's what you think." He boasted. "It's in the blood. Perhaps when they christened me, the holy water didn't take. I never howled the devil out."

"Is *she* good?"

"She?" The Boy laughed. "She's just nothing."

"We can't stay here," Rose said. "I wish we could." She looked round her at a badly foxed steel engraving of Van Tromp's victory, the three black bedsteads, the two mirrors, the single chest of drawers, the pale mauve knots of flowers on the wallpaper, as if she were safer here than she could ever be in the squally summer night outside. "It's a nice room." She wanted to share it with him until it became a home for both of them.

"How'd you like to leave this place?"

"Snow's? Oh no, it's a good place. I wouldn't want to be anywhere else than Snow's."

"I mean marry me."

"We aren't old enough."

"It could be managed. There are ways." He dropped her wrist and put on a careless air. "If you wanted. I don't mind."

"Oh," she said. "I want it. But they'll never let us."

He explained airily. "It couldn't be in church, not at first. There'd be difficulties. Are you afraid?"

"I'm not afraid," she said. "But will they let us?"

"My lawyer'll manage somehow."

"Have you got a lawyer?"

"Of course I have."

"It sounds somehow—grand—and old."

"A man can't get along without a lawyer."

She said, "It's not where I always thought it would be."

"Where what would be?"

"Someone asking me to marry him. I thought—in the pictures or maybe at night on the front. But this is best," she said, looking from Van Tromp's victory to the two looking glasses. She came away from the wall and lifted her face to him. He knew what was expected of him; he regarded her unmade-up mouth with faint nausea. Saturday night, eleven o'clock, the primeval exercise. He pressed his hard puritanical mouth on hers and tasted again the sweetish smell of the human skin. He would have preferred the taste of Coty powder or Kissproof lipstick or any chemical compound. He shut his eyes and when he opened them again it was to see her waiting like a blind girl, for further alms. It shocked him that she had been unable to detect his repulsion. She said, "You know what that means?"

"What means?"

"It means I'll never let you down, never, never, never."

She belonged to him like a room or a chair: the Boy fetched up a smile for the blind lost face, uneasily, with obscure shame.

§

He had sent Rose back home the night before and now draggingly he rejoined her. It was no good rebelling any more; he had to marry her: he had to be safe. The children were scouting among the rubble with pistols from Woolworth's; a group of girls surlily watched. A child with its leg in an iron brace limped blindly into him; he pushed it off; someone said in a high treble, "Stick 'em up." They took his mind back and he hated them for it; it was like the dreadful appeal of innocence, but *there* was not innocence; you had to go back a long way further before you got innocence; innocence was a slobbering mouth, a toothless gum pulling at the teats; perhaps not even that; innocence was the ugly cry of birth.

He found the house in Nelson Place, but before he had time to knock the door opened. Rose had spied him through the broken glass. She said, "Oh, how glad I am . . . I thought perhaps . . ." In the awful little passage which stank like a lavatory she ran quickly and passionately on. "It was awful last night . . . you see, I've been sending them money . . . they don't understand everyone loses a job some time or another."

"I'll settle them," the Boy said. "Where are they?"

"You got to be careful," Rose said. "They get moods."

"Where are they?"

But there wasn't really much choice of direction: there was only one door and a staircase matted with old newspapers. On the bottom steps between the mud marks stared up the tawny child face of Violet Crow violated and buried under the West Pier in 1936. He opened the door and there beside the black kitchen stove with cold dead charcoal on the floor sat the parents. They had a mood on: they watched him with silent and haughty indifference: a small thin elderly man, his face marked deeply with the hieroglyphics of pain and patience and suspicion: the woman middle-aged, stupid, vindictive. The dishes hadn't been washed and the stove hadn't been lit.

"They got a mood," Rose said aloud to him. "They wouldn't let me do a thing. Not even light the fire. I like a clean house, honest I do. Ours wouldn't be like this."

"Look here, Mr.—" the Boy said.

"Wilson," Rose said.

"Wilson. I want to marry Rose. It seems as she's so young I got to get your permission."

They wouldn't answer him. They treasured their mood as

if it were a bright piece of china only they possessed: something they could show to neighbours as "mine."

"It's no use," Rose said, "when they got a mood."

A cat watched them from a wooden box.

"Yes or no?" the Boy said.

"It's no good," Rose said; "not when they've got a mood."

"Answer a plain question," the Boy said. "Do I marry Rose or don't I?"

"Come back tomorrow," Rose said. "They won't have a mood then."

"I'm not going to wait on them," he said. "They oughter be proud——"

The man suddenly got up and kicked the dead coke furiously across the floor. "You get out of here," he said. "We don't want any truck with you," he went on, "never, never, never," and for a moment in the sunk lost eyes there was a kind of fidelity which reminded the Boy dreadfully of Rose.

"Quiet, father," the woman said, "don't talk to them," treasuring her mood.

"I've come to do business," the Boy said. "If you don't want to do business——" He looked round the battered and hopeless room. "I thought maybe ten pounds would be of use to you," and he saw swimming up through the blind vindictive silence incredulity, avarice, suspicion. "We don't want——" the man began again and then gave out like a gramophone. He began to think: you could see the thoughts bob up one after another.

"We don't want your money," the woman said. They each had their own kind of fidelity.

Rose said, "Never mind what they say. I won't stay here."

"Stop a moment. Stop a moment," the man said. "You be quiet, mother." He said to the Boy, "We couldn't let Rose go, not for ten nicker, not to a stranger. How do we know you'd treat her right?"

"I'll give you twelve," the Boy said.

"It's not a question of money," the man said. "I like the

look of you. We wouldn't want to stand in the way of Rose bettering herself—but you're too young."

"Fifteen's my limit," the Boy said. "Take it or leave it."

"You can't do anything without we say yes," the man said.

The Boy moved a little away from Rose. "I'm not all that keen."

"Make it guineas."

"You've had my offer." He looked with horror round the room: nobody could say he hadn't done right to get away from this, to commit any crime. . . . When the man opened his mouth he heard his father speaking, that figure in the corner was his mother: he bargained for his sister and felt no desire. . . . He turned to Rose, "I'm off," and felt the faintest twinge of pity for goodness which couldn't murder to escape. They said that saints had got—what was the phrase?—"heroic virtues," heroic patience, heroic endurance, but there was nothing he could see that was heroic in the bony face, protuberant eyes, pallid anxiety, while they bluffed each other and her life was confused in the financial game. "Well," he said, "I'll be seeing you," and made for the door. At the door he looked back: they were like a family party. Impatiently and contemptuously he gave in to them. "All right. Guineas. I'll be sending my lawyer," and as he passed into the evil passage Rose was behind him panting her gratitude.

He played the game to the last card, fetching up a grin and a compliment: "I'd do more for you."

"You were wonderful," she said, loving him among the lavatory smells, but her praise was poison: it marked her possession of him: it led straight to what she expected from him, the horrifying act of a desire he didn't feel. She followed him out into the fresh air of Nelson Place. The children played among the ruins of Paradise Piece, and a wind blew from the sea across the site of his home. A dim desire for annihilation stretched in him: the vast superiority of vacancy.

She said, as she had said once before, "I always wondered how it'd be." Her mind moved obscurely among the events of the afternoon, brought out the unexpected discovery. "I've never known a mood go so quick. They must have liked you."

§

At the bottom of the steps the Boy waited. The big municipal building lay over him like a shadow—departments for births and deaths, for motor licences, for rates and taxes, somewhere in some long corridor the room for marriages. He looked at his watch and said to Mr. Prewitt, "God damn her. She's late."

Mr. Prewitt said, "It's the privilege of a bride."

Bride and groom: the mare and the stallion which served her: like a file on metal or the touch of velvet to a sore hand. The Boy said, "Me and Dallow—we'll walk and meet her."

Mr. Prewitt called after him, "Suppose she comes another way. Suppose you miss her. . . . I'll wait here."

They turned to the left out of the official street. "This ain't the way," Dallow said.

"There's no call on us to wait on her," the Boy said.

"You can't get out of it now."

"Who wants to? I can take a bit of exercise, can't I?" He stopped and stared into a small news-agent's window—two-valve receiving sets, the grossness everywhere.

"Seen Cubitt?" he asked, staring in.

"No," Dallow said. "None of the boys either."

The daily and the local papers, a poster packed with news: Scene at Council Meeting. Woman Found Drowned at Black Rock. Collision in Clarence Street: a Wild West magazine, a copy of *Film Fun*; behind the inkpots and the fountain pens and the paper plates for picnics and the little gross toys, the works of well-known sexologists. The Boy stared in.

"I know how you feel," Dallow said. "I was married once

myself. It kind of gets you in the stomach. Nerves. Why," Dallow said, "I even went and got one of those books, but it didn't tell me anything I didn't know. Except about flowers. The pistils of flowers. You wouldn't believe the funny things that go on among flowers."

The Boy turned and opened his mouth to speak, but the teeth snapped to again. He watched Dallow with pleading and horror. If Kite had been there, he thought, he could have spoken—but if Kite had been there, he would have had no need to speak . . . he would never have got mixed up.

"These bees . . ." Dallow began to explain and stopped. "What is it, Pinkie? You don't look too good."

"I know the rules all right," the Boy said.

"What rules?"

"You can't teach me the rules," the Boy went on with gusty anger. "I watched 'em every Saturday night, didn't I? Bouncing and ploughing." His eyes flinched as if he were watching some horror. He said in a low voice, "When I was a kid, I swore I'd be a priest."

"A priest? You a priest? That's good," Dallow said. He laughed without conviction, uneasily shifted his foot so that it trod in a dog's ordure.

"What's wrong with being a priest?" the Boy asked. "They know what's what. They keep away—" his whole mouth and jaw loosened: he might have been going to weep: he beat out wildly with his hands towards the window: Woman Found Drowned, two-valve, *Married Passion*, the horror—"from this."

"What's wrong with a bit of fun?" Dallow took him up, scraping his shoe against the pavement edge. The word "fun" shook the boy like malaria. He said, "You wouldn't have known Annie Collins, would you?"

"Never heard of her."

"She went to the same school I did," the Boy said. He took a look down the grey street and then the glass before *Married Passion* reflected his young and hopeless face. "She put her head on the line," he said, "up towards Hassocks. She had to wait ten minutes for the seven-five. Fog made it late from Victoria. Cut off her head. She was fifteen. She was going to have a baby and she knew what it was like. She'd had one two years before, and they could've pinned it on twelve boys."

"It does happen," Dallow said. "It's the luck of the game."

"I've read love stories," the Boy said. He had never been so vocal before, staring in at the paper plates with frilly edges and the two-valve receiving set: the daintiness and the grossness. "Frank's wife reads them. You know the sort. Lady Angeline turned her starry eyes towards Sir Mark. They make me sick. Sicker than the other kind"—Dallow watched with astonishment this sudden horrified gift of tongues—"the kind you buy under the counter. Spicer used to get them. About girls being beaten. Full of shame to expose herself thus before the boys she stooped. . . . It's all the same thing," he said, turning his poisoned eyes away from the window, from point to point of the long shabby street: a smell of fish, the sawdusted pavement below the carcasses. "It's fun. It's the game."

"The world's got to go on," Dallow said uneasily.

"Why?"

"You don't need to ask me," Dallow said. "You know best. You're a Roman, aren't you? You believe . . ."

"Credo in unum Satanum," the Boy said.

"I don't know Latin. I only know . . ."

"Come on," the Boy said. "Let's have it. Dallow's creed."

"The world's all right if you don't go too far."

"Is that all?"

"It's time for you to be at the registrar's. Hear the clock? It's striking two now." A peal of bells stopped their cracked chime and struck—one, two——

The Boy's whole face loosened again: he put his hand on Dallow's arm. "You're a good sort, Dallow. You know a lot. Tell me—" his hand fell away. He looked beyond Dallow down the street. He said hopelessly, "Here she is. What's she doing in *this* street?"

"She's not hurrying either," Dallow commented, watching the thin figure slowly approach. At that distance she didn't even look her age. He said, "It was clever of Prewitt to get the licence at all, considering."

"Parents' consent," the Boy said dully. "Best for morality." He watched the girl as if she were a stranger he had got to meet. "And then, you see, there was a stroke of luck. I wasn't registered. Not anywhere they could find. They added on a year or two. No parents. No guardian. It was a touching story old Prewitt spun."

She had tricked herself up for the wedding, discarded the hat he hadn't liked: a new mackintosh, a touch of powder and cheap lipstick. She looked like one of the small gaudy statues in an ugly church: a paper crown wouldn't have looked odd on her or a painted heart: you could pray to her but you couldn't expect an answer.

"Where've you been?" the Boy said. "Don't you know you're late?"

They didn't even touch hands. An awful formality fell between them.

"I'm sorry, Pinkie. You see"—she brought the fact out with shame, as if she were admitting conversation with his enemy—"I went into the church."

"What for?" he said.

"I don't know, Pinkie. I got confused. I thought I'd go to confession."

He grinned at her. "Confession? That's rich."

"You see, I wanted—I thought——"

"For Christ's sake, what?"

"I wanted to be in a state of grace when I married you." She took no notice at all of Dallow. The theological term lay oddly and pedantically on her tongue. They were two Romans together in the grey street. They understood each other. She used terms common to heaven and hell.

"And did you?" the Boy said.

"No. I went and rang the bell and asked for Father James. But then I remembered. It wasn't any good confessing. I went away." She said with a mixture of fear and pride, "We're going to do a mortal sin."

The Boy said, with bitter and unhappy relish, "It'll be no good going to confession ever again—as long as we're both alive." He had graduated in pain: first the school dividers had been left behind, next the razor. He had a sense now that the murders of Hale and Spicer were trivial acts, a boy's game, and he had put away childish things. Murder had only led to this—this corruption. He was filled with awe at his own powers. "We'd better be moving," he said and touched her arm with next to tenderness. As once before he had a sense of needing her.

Mr. Prewitt greeted them with official mirth. All his jokes seemed to be spoken in court, with an ulterior motive, to catch a magistrate's ear. In the great institutional hall from which the corridors led off to deaths and births there was a smell of disinfectant. The walls were tiled like a public lavatory. Somebody had dropped a rose. Mr. Prewitt quoted promptly, inaccurately: "Roses, roses all the way, and never a sprig of yew." A soft hollow hand guided the Boy by the elbow. "No, no, not that way. That's taxes. That comes later." He led them up great stone stairs. A clerk passed them carrying printed forms. "And what is the little lady thinking?" Mr. Prewitt said. She didn't answer him.

Only the bride and groom were allowed to mount the sanctuary steps, to kneel down within the sanctuary rails with the priest and the Host.

"Parents coming?" Mr. Prewitt said. She shook her head. "The great thing is," Mr. Prewitt said, "it's over quickly. Just sign the names along the dotted line. Sit down here. We've got to wait our turn, you know."

They sat down. A mop leant in a corner against the tiled wall. The footsteps of a clerk squealed on the icy paving down another passage. Presently a big brown door opened: they saw a row of clerks inside who didn't look up: a man and wife came out into the corridor. A woman followed them and took the mop. The man—he was middle-aged—said "thank you," gave her sixpence. He said, "We'll catch the three-fifteen after all." On the woman's face there was a look of faint astonishment, bewilderment, nothing so definite as disappointment. She wore a brown straw and carried an attaché case. She was middle-aged too. She might have been thinking, "Is that all there is to it—after all these years?" They went down the big stairs walking a little apart, like strangers in a store.

"Our turn," Mr. Prewitt said, rising briskly. He led the way through the room where the clerks worked. Nobody bothered to look up. Nibs wrote smooth numerals and ran on. In a small inner room with green washed walls like a clinic's the registrar waited: a table, three or four chairs against the wall. It wasn't what she thought a marriage would be like—for a moment she was daunted by the cold poverty of a state-made ceremony.

"Good morning," the registrar said. "If the witnesses will just sit down—would you two—" he beckoned them to the table and stared at them with gold-rimmed and glassy importance: it was as if he considered himself on the fringe of the priestly office. The Boy's heart beat: he was sickened by the reality of the moment. He wore a look of sullenness and of stupidity.

"You're both very young," the registrar said.

"It's fixed," the Boy said. "You don't have to talk about it. It's fixed."

The registrar gave him a glance of intense dislike; he said, "Repeat after me," and then ran too quickly on: "I do solemnly declare that I know not of any lawful impediment," so that the Boy couldn't follow him. The registrar said sharply, "It's quite simple. You've only to repeat after me . . ."

"Go slower," the Boy said. He wanted to lay his hand on speed and brake it down, but it ran on: it was no time at all, a matter of seconds, before he was repeating the formula "my lawful wedded wife." He tried to make it careless, he kept his eyes off Rose, but the words were weighted with shame.

"No ring?" the registrar asked sharply.

"We don't need any ring," the Boy said. "This isn't a church," feeling he could never now rid his memory of the cold green room and the glassy face. He heard Rose repeating by his side: "I call upon these persons here present to witness . . ." and then the word "husband," and he looked sharply up at her. If there had been any complacency in her face then he would have struck it. But there was only surprise as if she were reading a book and had come to the last page too soon.

The registrar said, "You sign here. The charge is seven and sixpence." He wore an air of official unconcern while Mr. Prewitt fumbled.

"These persons," the Boy said and laughed brokenly. "That's you, Prewitt and Dallow." He took the pen and the Government nib scratched into the page, gathering fur; in the old days, it occurred to him, you signed covenants like this in your blood. He stood back and watched Rose awkwardly sign—his temporal safety in return for two immortalities of pain. He had no doubt whatever that this was mortal sin, and he was filled with a kind of gloomy hilarity and pride. He saw himself now as a full-grown man for whom the angels wept. . . .

1938   from *Brighton Rock*

The Prison Cell

EDITOR'S NOTE

This is a key scene from The Power and the Glory, *the novel that Greene considers to be his best, or at least the one that*

*gives him the most satisfaction. The scene stands very well
alone, but as background one should know that religion has
been banned in this socialist state, churches are destroyed or
closed, the clergy are outlawed. The hero is one of the last
priests to remain. He lingers on, dogged by the sense of his
own uselessness and unworthiness, for he is a drunkard, has
a bastard child, and endangers all those he helps or those
who help him, because he has been denounced as a criminal
and there is a price on his head. Travelling incognito, he has
been picked up on a charge of illegal possession of alcohol
and has been thrown into the common cell.*

*The setting is Tabasco in the middle thirties, a few years
before Greene visited the state to report on religious
persecution there. The travel book that resulted from that
trip and appeared a year before* The Power and the Glory
was Another Mexico (The Lawless Roads).

A voice near his foot said, "Got a cigarette?"

He drew quickly back and trod on an arm. A voice said
imperatively, "Water, quick," as if whoever it was thought
he could take a stranger unawares, and make him fork out.

"Got a cigarette?"

"No." He said weakly, "I have nothing at all," and imagined he could feel enmity fuming up all round him. He
moved again. Somebody said, "Look out for the bucket."
That was where the stench came from. He stood perfectly
still and waited for his sight to return. Outside the rain
began to stop: it dropped haphazardly and the thunder
moved away. You could count forty now between the lightning flash and the roll. Half-way to the sea, or half-way to
the mountains. He felt around with his foot, trying to find
enough space to sit down, but there seemed to be no room at
all. When the lightning went on he could see the hammocks
at the edge of the courtyard.

"Got something to eat?" a voice said, and when he didn't
answer, "Got something to eat?"

"No."

"Got any money?" another voice said.

"No."

Suddenly, from about five feet away, there came a tiny scream—a woman's. A tired voice said, "Can't you be quiet?" Among the furtive movements came again the muffled cries. He realized that pleasure was going on even in this crowded darkness. Again he put out his foot and began to edge his way inch by inch away from the grill. Behind the human voices another noise went permanently on: it was like a small machine, an electric belt set at a certain tempo. It filled any silences that there were louder than human breath. It was the mosquitoes.

He had moved perhaps six feet from the grill, and his eyes began to distinguish heads—perhaps the sky was clearing: they hung around him like gourds. A voice said, "Who are you?" He made no reply, feeling panic edging in. Suddenly he found himself against the back wall: the stone was wet against his hand—the cell could not have been more than twelve feet deep. He found he could just sit down if he kept his feet drawn up under him. An old man lay slumped against his shoulder; he told his age from the feather-weight lightness of the bones, the feeble uneven flutter of the breath. He was either somebody close to birth or death—and he could hardly be a child in this place. The old man said suddenly, "Is that you, Catarina?" and his breath went out in a long patient sigh, as if he had been waiting for a long while and could afford to wait a lot longer.

The priest said, "No. Not Catarina." When he spoke everybody became suddenly silent, listening, as if what he said had importance: then the voices and movements began again. But the sound of his own voice, the sense of communication with a neighbour, calmed him.

"You wouldn't be," the old man said. "I didn't really think you were. She'll never come."

"Is she your wife?"

"What's that you're saying? I haven't got a wife."

"Catarina?"

"She's my daughter." Everybody was listening except the two invisible people who were concerned only in their cramped pleasure.

"Perhaps they won't allow her here."

"She'll never try," the old hopeless voice pronounced with absolute conviction. The priest's feet began to ache, drawn up under his haunches. He said, "If she loves you . . ." Somewhere across the huddle of dark shapes the woman cried again—that finished cry of protest and abandonment and pleasure.

"It's the priests who've done it," the old man said.

"The priests?"

"The priests."

"Why the priests?"

"The priests."

A low voice near his knees said, "The old man's crazy. What's the use of asking him questions?"

"Is that you, Catarina?" He added, "I don't really believe it, you know. It's just a question."

"Now *I've* got something to complain about," the voice went on. "A man's got to defend his honour. You'll admit that, won't you?"

"I don't know anything about honour."

"I was in the cantina and the man I'm telling you about came up to me and said, 'Your mother's a whore.' Well, I couldn't do anything about it: he'd got his gun on him. All I could do was wait. He drank too much beer—I knew he would—and when he was staggering I followed him out. I had a bottle and I smashed it against a wall. You see, I hadn't got my gun. His family's got influence with the jefe or I'd never be here."

"It's a terrible thing to kill a man."

"You talk like a priest."

"It was the priests who did it," the old man said. "You're right, there."

"What does he mean?"

"What does it matter what an old man like that means? I'd like to tell you about something else. . . ."

A woman's voice said, "They took the child away from him."

"Why?"

"It was a bastard. They acted quite correctly."

At the word "bastard" his heart moved painfully, as when a man in love hears a stranger name a flower which is also the name of his woman. "Bastard!" the word filled him with miserable happiness. It brought his own child nearer: he could see her under the tree by the rubbish-dump, unguarded. He repeated "Bastard?" as he might have repeated her name—with tenderness disguised as indifference.

"They said he was no fit father. But, of course, when the priests fled, she had to go with him. Where else could she go?" It was like a happy ending until she said, "Of course she hated him. They'd taught her about things." He could imagine the small set mouth of an educated woman. What was she doing here?

"Why is he in prison?"

"He had a crucifix."

The stench from the pail got worse all the time; the night stood round them like a wall, without ventilation, and he could hear somebody making water, drumming on the tin sides. He said, "They had no business . . ."

"They were doing what was right, of course. It was a mortal sin."

"No right to make her hate him."

"They knew what's right."

He said, "They were bad priests to do a thing like that. The sin was over. It was their duty to teach—well, love."

"You don't know what's right. The priests know."

He said after a moment's hesitation, very distinctly, "I am a priest."

It was like the end: there was no need to hope any longer. The ten years' hunt was over at last. There was silence all round him. This place was very like the world: overcrowded with lust and crime and unhappy love, it stank to heaven; but he realized that after all it was possible to find peace there, when you knew for certain that the time was short.

"A priest?" the woman said at last.

"Yes."

"Do *they* know?"

"Not yet."

He could feel a hand fumbling at his sleeve. A voice said, "You shouldn't have told us. Father, there are all sorts here. Murderers . . ."

The voice which had described the crime to him said, "You've no cause to abuse me. Because I kill a man it doesn't mean . . ." Whispering started everywhere. The voice said bitterly, "I'm not an informer just because when a man says, 'Your mother's a whore . . .'"

The priest said, "There's no need for anyone to inform on me. That would be a sin. When it's daylight they'll discover for themselves."

"They'll shoot you, father," the woman's voice said.

"Yes."

"Are you afraid?"

"Yes. Of course."

A new voice spoke, in the corner from which the sounds of pleasure had come. It said roughly and obstinately, "A man isn't afraid of a thing like that."

"No?" the priest said.

"A bit of pain. What do you expect? It has to come."

"All the same," the priest said, "I *am* afraid."

"Toothache is worse."

"We can't all be brave men."

The voice said with contempt, "You believers are all the same. Christianity makes you cowards."

"Yes. Perhaps you are right. You see I am a bad priest and a bad man. To die in a state of mortal sin"—he gave an uneasy chuckle—"it makes you think."

"There. It's as I say. Believing in God makes cowards."

The voice was triumphant, as if it had proved something.

"So then?" the priest said.

"Better not to believe—and be a brave man."

"I see—yes. And, of course, if one believed the Governor did not exist or the jefe, if we could pretend that this prison was not a prison at all but a garden, how brave we could be then."

"That's just foolishness."

"But when we found that the prison was a prison, and the Governor up there in the square undoubtedly existed, well, it wouldn't much matter if we'd been brave for an hour or two."

"Nobody could say that this prison was not a prison."

"No? You don't think so? I can see you don't listen to the politicians." His feet were giving him great pain: he had cramp in the soles, but he could bring no pressure on the muscles to relieve them. It was not yet midnight; the hours of darkness stretched ahead interminably.

The woman said suddenly, "Think. We have a martyr here . . ."

The priest giggled: he couldn't stop himself. He said, "I don't think martyrs are like this." He became suddenly serious, remembering Maria's words—it wouldn't be a good thing to bring mockery on the Church. He said, "Martyrs are holy men. It is wrong to think that just because one dies . . . no. I tell you I am in a state of mortal sin. I have done things I couldn't talk to you about. I could only whisper them in the confessional." Everybody, when he spoke, listened attentively to him as if he were addressing them in church. He wondered where the inevitable Judas was sitting now, but he wasn't aware of Judas as he had been in the forest hut. He was moved by an irrational affection for the inhabitants of this prison. A phrase came to him: "God so loved the world . . ." He said, "My children, you must never think the holy martyrs are like me. You have a name for me. Oh, I've heard you use it before now. I am a whisky priest. I am in here now because they found a bottle of brandy in my pocket." He tried to move his feet from under him: the cramp had passed: now they were lifeless: all feeling gone. Oh, well, let them stay. He wouldn't have to use them often again.

The old man was muttering, and the priest's thoughts went back to Brigitta. The knowledge of the world lay in her like the dark explicable spot in an X-ray photograph; he longed—with a breathless feeling in the breast—to save her, but he knew the surgeon's decision—the ill was incurable.

The woman's voice said pleadingly, "A little drink, father . . . it's not so important." He wondered why she was here —probably for having a holy picture in her house. She had the tiresome intense note of a pious woman. They were extraordinarily foolish over pictures. Why not burn them? One didn't need a picture. . . . He said sternly, "Oh, I am not only a drunkard." He had always been worried by the fate of pious women. As much as politicians, they fed on illusion. He was frightened for them: they came to death so often in a state of invincible complacency, full of uncharity. It was one's duty, if one could, to rob them of their sentimental notions of what was good. . . . He said in hard accents, "I have a child."

What a worthy woman she was! her voice pleaded in the darkness; he couldn't catch what she said, but it was something about the Good Thief. He said, "My child, the thief repented. I haven't repented." He remembered her coming into the hut, the dark malicious knowing look with the sunlight at her back. He said, "I don't know how to repent." That was true: he had lost the faculty. He couldn't say to himself that he wished his sin had never existed, because the sin seemed to him now so unimportant and he loved the fruit of it. He needed a confessor to draw his mind slowly down the drab passages which led to grief and repentance.

The woman was silent now: he wondered whether after all he had been too harsh with her. If it helped her faith to believe that he was a martyr . . . but he rejected the idea:

one was pledged to truth. He shifted an inch or two on his hams and said, "What time does it get light?"

"Four . . . five . . ." a man replied. "How can we tell, father? We haven't clocks."

"Have you been here long?"

"Three weeks."

"Are you kept here all day?"

"Oh no. They let us out to clean the yard."

He thought: that is when I shall be discovered—unless it's earlier, for surely one of these people will betray me first. A long train of thought began, which led him to announce after a while, "They are offering a reward for me. Five hundred, six hundred pesos, I'm not sure." Then he was silent again. He couldn't urge any man to inform against him— that would be tempting him to sin—but at the same time if there was an informer here, there was no reason why the wretched creature should be bilked of his reward. To commit so ugly a sin—it must count as murder—and to have no compensation in this world. . . . He thought: it wouldn't be fair.

"Nobody here," a voice said, "wants their blood money."

Again he was touched by an extraordinary affection. He was just one criminal among a herd of criminals. . . . He had a sense of companionship which he had never experienced in the old days when pious people came kissing his black cotton glove.

The pious woman's voice leapt hysterically out at him: "It is so stupid to tell them that. You don't know the sort of wretches who are here, father. Thieves, murderers . . ."

"Well," an angry voice said, "why are you here?"

"I had good books in my house," she announced, with unbearable pride. He had done nothing to shake her complacency. He said, "They are everywhere. It's no different here."

"Good books?"

He giggled. "No, no. Thieves, murderers . . . Oh, well,

my child, if you had more experience you would know there are worse things to be." The old man seemed to be uneasily asleep; his head lay sideways against the priest's shoulder, and he muttered angrily. God knows, it had never been easy to move in this place, but the difficulty seemed to increase as the night wore on and limbs stiffened. He couldn't twitch his shoulder now without waking the old man to another night of suffering. Well, he thought, it was my kind who robbed him: it's only fair to be made a little uncomfortable. . . . He sat silent and rigid against the damp wall, with his dead feet under his haunches. The mosquitoes droned on; it was no good defending yourself by striking at the air: they pervaded the whole place like an element. Somebody as well as the old man had somewhere fallen asleep and was snoring, a curious note of satisfaction, as though he had eaten and drunk well at a good dinner and was now taking a snooze. . . . The priest tried to calculate the hour: how much time had passed since he had met the beggar in the plaza? It was probably not long after midnight: there would be hours more of this.

It was, of course, the end, but at the same time you had to be prepared for everything, even escape. If God intended him to escape he could snatch him away from in front of a firing squad. But God was merciful. There was only one reason, surely, which would make Him refuse His peace—if there was any peace—that he could still be of use in saving a soul, his own or another's. But what good could he do now? They had him on the run; he dared not enter a village in case somebody else should pay with his life—perhaps a man who was in mortal sin and unrepentant. It was impossible to say what souls might not be lost simply because he was obstinate and proud and wouldn't admit defeat. He couldn't even say Mass any longer—he had no wine. It had all gone down the dry gullet of the Chief of Police. It was appallingly complicated. He was still afraid of death, he would be more afraid of death yet when the morning came, but it was beginning to attract him by its simplicity.

The pious woman was whispering to him. She must have somehow edged her way nearer. She was saying, "Father, will you hear my confession?"

"My dear child, here! It's quite impossible. Where would be the secrecy?"

"It's been so long . . ."

"Say an Act of Contrition for your sins. You must trust God, my dear, to make allowances . . ."

"I wouldn't mind suffering . . ."

"Well, you are here."

"That's nothing. In the morning my sister will have raised the money for my fine."

Somewhere against the far wall pleasure began again; it was unmistakable: the movements, the breathlessness, and then the cry. The pious woman said aloud with fury, "Why won't they stop it? The brutes, the animals!"

"What's the good of your saying an Act of Contrition now in this state of mind?"

"But the ugliness . . ."

"Don't believe that. It's dangerous. Because suddenly we discover that our sins have so much beauty."

"Beauty," she said with disgust. "Here. In this cell. With strangers all round."

"Such a lot of beauty. Saints talk about the beauty of suffering. Well, we are not saints, you and I. Suffering to us is just ugly. Stench and crowding and pain. *That* is beautiful in that corner—to them. It needs a lot of learning to see things with a saint's eye: a saint gets a subtle taste for beauty and can look down on poor ignorant palates like theirs. But we can't afford to."

"It's mortal sin."

"We don't know. It may be. But I'm a bad priest, you see. I know—from experience—how much beauty Satan carried down with him when he fell. Nobody ever said the fallen angels were the ugly ones. Oh no, they were just as quick and light and . . ."

Again the cry came, an expression of intolerable pleasure.

The woman said, "Stop them. It's a scandal." He felt fingers on his knee, grasping, digging. He said, "We're all fellow prisoners. I want drink at this moment more than anything, more than God. That's a sin too."

"Now," the woman said, "I can see you're a bad priest. I wouldn't believe it before. I do now. You sympathize with these animals. If your bishop heard you . . ."

"Ah, he's a very long way off." He thought of the old man now—in Mexico City, living in one of those ugly comfortable pious houses, full of images and holy pictures, saying Mass on Sundays at one of the cathedral altars.

"When I get out of here, I shall write . . ."

He couldn't help laughing: she had no sense of how life had changed. He said, "If he gets the letter he'll be interested to hear I'm alive." But again he became serious. It was more difficult to feel pity for her than for the half-caste who a week ago had tagged him through the forest, but her case might be worse. The other had so much excuse—poverty and fever and innumerable humiliations. He said, "Try not to be angry. Pray for me instead."

"The sooner you are dead the better."

He couldn't see her in the darkness, but there were plenty of faces he could remember from the old days which fitted the voice. When you visualized a man or woman carefully, you could always begin to feel pity—that was a quality God's image carried with it. When you saw the lines at the corners of the eyes, the shape of the mouth, how the hair grew, it was impossible to hate. Hate was just a failure of imagination. He began again to feel an overwhelming responsibility for this pious woman. "You and Father José," she said. "It's people like you who make people mock—at real religion." She had, after all, as many excuses as the half-caste. He saw the kind of salon in which she spent her days, with the rocking-chair and the family photographs, meeting no one. He said gently, "You are not married, are you?"

"Why do you want to know?"

"And you never had a vocation?"

"They wouldn't believe it," she said bitterly.

He thought: poor woman, she's had nothing, nothing at all. If only one could find the right word . . . He leant hopelessly back, moving carefully so as not to wake the old man. But the right words never came to him. He was more out of touch with her kind than he had ever been; he would have known what to say to her in the old days, feeling no pity at all, speaking with half a mind a platitude or two. Now he felt useless: he was a criminal and ought only to talk to criminals. He had done wrong again, trying to break down her complacency. He might just as well have let her go on thinking him a martyr.

His eyes closed and immediately he began to dream. He was being pursued; he stood outside a door banging on it, begging for admission, but nobody answered—there was a word, a password, which would save him, but he had forgotten it. He tried desperately at random—cheese and child, California, excellency, milk, Vera Cruz. His feet had gone to sleep and he knelt outside the door. Then he knew why he wanted to get in: he wasn't being pursued after all: that was a mistake. His child lay beside him bleeding to death and this was a doctor's house. He banged on the door and shouted, "Even if I can't think of the right word, haven't you a heart?" The child was dying and looked up at him with middle-aged complacent wisdom. She said, "You animal," and he woke again crying. He couldn't have slept for more than a few seconds because the woman was still talking about the vocation the nuns had refused to recognize. He said, "That made you suffer, didn't it? To suffer like that—perhaps it was better than being a nun and happy," and immediately after he had spoken he thought: a silly remark, what does it mean? Why can't I find something to say to her which she could remember?

He didn't sleep again: he was striking yet another bargain with God. This time, if he escaped from the prison, he would escape altogether. He would go north, over the border. His escape was so improbable that, if it happened, it couldn't be anything else but a sign—an indication that he was doing more harm by his example than good by his occasional confessions. The old man moved against his shoulder and the night just stayed around them. The darkness was always the same and there were no clocks—there was nothing to indicate time passing. The only punctuation of the night was the sound of urination.

Suddenly, he realized that he could see a face, and then another; he had begun to forget that it would ever be another day, just as one forgets that one will ever die. It comes suddenly on one in a screeching brake or a whistle in the air, the knowledge that time moves and comes to an end. All the voices slowly became faces—there were no surprises. The confessional teaches you to recognize the shape of a voice—the loose lip or the weak chin and the false candour of the too straightforward eyes. He saw the pious woman a few feet away, uneasily dreaming with her prim mouth open, showing strong teeth like tombs: the old man: the boaster in the corner, and his woman asleep untidily across his knees. Now that the day was at last here, he was the only one awake, except for a small Indian boy who squatted cross-legged near the door with an expression of interested happiness, as if he had never known such friendly company. Over the courtyard the whitewash became visible upon the opposite wall. He began formally to pay his farewell to the world: he couldn't put any heart into it. His corruption was less evident to his sense than his death. One bullet, he thought, is almost certain to go directly through the heart—a squad must contain one accurate marksman. Life would go out in a "fraction of a second" (that was the phrase), but all night he had been realizing that time depends on clocks and the passage of light. There were no clocks and the light wouldn't change. Nobody really knew how long a second of pain could be. It might last a whole purgatory—or for ever. For some reason he thought of a man he had once shrived who was on the point of death with cancer—his relatives had had to bandage their faces, the smell of the rotting interior was so appalling. He wasn't a saint. Nothing in life was as ugly as death.

A voice in the yard called, "Montez." He sat on upon his dead feet; he thought automatically: This suit isn't good for much more. It was smeared and fouled by the cell floor and his fellow prisoners. He had obtained it at great risk in a store down by the river, pretending to be a small farmer with ideas above his station. Then he remembered he wouldn't need it much longer—it came with an odd shock, like locking the door of one's house for the last time. The voice repeated impatiently, "Montez."

He remembered that that, for the moment, was his name. He looked up from his ruined suit and saw the sergeant unlocking the cell door. "Here, Montez." He let the old man's head fall gently back against the sweating wall and tried to stand up, but his feet crumpled like pastry. "Do you want to sleep all day?" the sergeant complained testily: something had irritated him: he wasn't as friendly as he had been the night before. He let out a kick at a sleeping man and beat on the cell door. "Come on. Wake up, all of you. Out into the yard." Only the Indian boy obeyed, sliding unobtrusively out with his look of alien happiness. The sergeant complained, "The dirty hounds. Do they want us to wash them? You, Montez." Life began to return painfully to his feet. He managed to reach the door.

The yard had come sluggishly to life. A queue of men were bathing their faces at a single tap; a man in a vest and pants sat on the ground hugging a rifle. "Get out into the yard and wash," the sergeant yelled at them, but when the priest stepped out he snapped at him, "Not you, Montez."

"Not me?"

"We've got other plans for you," the sergeant said.

The priest stood waiting while his fellow prisoners filed out into the yard. One by one they went past him; he looked at their feet and not their faces, standing like a temptation at the door. Nobody said a word: a woman's feet went drag- gingly by in black worn low-heeled shoes. He whispered without looking up, "Pray for me."

"What's that you said, Montez?"

He couldn't think of a lie; he felt as if ten years had ex- hausted his whole stock of deceit.

"What's that you said?"

The shoes had stopped moving. The woman's voice said, "He was begging." She added mercilessly, "He ought to have more sense. I've nothing for him." Then she went on, flat-footed, into the yard.

"Did you sleep well, Montez?" the sergeant badgered him.

"Not very well."

"What do you expect?" the sergeant said. "It'll teach you to like brandy too well, won't it?"

"Yes." He wondered how much longer all these prelimi- naries would take.

"Well, if you spend all your money on brandy, you've got to do a bit of work in return for a night's lodging. Fetch the pails out of the cells and mind you don't spill them—this place stinks enough as it is."

"Where do I take them to?"

The sergeant pointed to the door of the excusados beyond the tap. "Report to me when you've finished that," he said, and went bellowing orders back into the yard.

The priest bent down and took the pail. It was full and very heavy: he went bowed with the weight across the yard. Sweat got into his eyes. He wiped them free and saw one be- hind another in the washing queue faces he knew—the hos- tages. There was Miguel, whom he had seen taken away; he remembered the mother screaming out and the lieutenant's tired anger and the sun coming up. They saw him at the same time; he put down the heavy pail and looked at them. Not to recognize them would have been like a hint, a claim, a demand to them to go on suffering and let him escape. Mi- guel had been beaten up: there was a sore under his eye—

flies buzzed round it as they buzz round a mule's raw flank. Then the queue moved on; they looked at the ground and passed him; strangers took their place. He prayed silently: O God, send them someone more worthwhile to suffer for. It seemed to him a damnable mockery that they should sacrifice themselves for a whisky priest with a bastard child. The soldier sat in his pants with his gun between his knees paring his nails and biting off the loose skin. In an odd way he felt abandoned because they had shown no sign of recognition.

The excusados was a cesspool with two planks across it on which a man could stand. He emptied the pail and went back across the yard to the row of cells. There were six: one by one he took the pails: once he had to stop and retch: splash, splash, to and fro across the yard. He came to the last cell. It wasn't empty; a man lay back against the wall; the early sun just reached his feet. Flies buzzed around a mound of vomit on the floor. The eyes opened and watched the priest stooping over the pail: two fangs protruded. . . .

The priest moved quickly and splashed the floor. The half-caste said in that too-familiar nagging tone, "Wait a moment. You can't do that in here." He explained proudly, "I'm not a prisoner. I'm a guest." The priest made a motion of apology (he was afraid to speak) and moved again. "Wait a moment," the half-caste commanded him again. "Come here."

The priest stood stubbornly, half-turned away, near the door.

"Come here," the half-caste said. "You're a prisoner, aren't you?—and I'm a guest—of the Governor. Do you want me to shout for a policeman? Then do as you're told: come here."

It seemed as if God were deciding . . . finally. He came, pail in hand, and stood beside the large flat naked foot, and the half-caste looked up at him from the shadow of the wall, asking him sharply and anxiously, "What are you doing here?"

"Cleaning up."

"You know what I mean."

"I was caught with a bottle of brandy," the priest said, trying to roughen his voice.

"I know you," the half-caste said; "I couldn't believe my eyes, but when you speak . . ."

"I don't think . . ."

"That priest's voice," the half-caste said with disgust. He was like a dog of a different breed: he couldn't help his hackles rising. The big toe moved plumply and inimically. The priest put down the pail. He argued hopelessly, "You're drunk."

"Beer, beer," the half-caste said, "nothing but beer. They promised me the best of everything, but you can't trust them. Don't I know the jefe's got his own brandy locked away?"

"I must empty the pail."

"If you move, I'll shout. I've got so many things to think about," the half-caste complained bitterly. The priest waited: there was nothing else to do; he was at the man's mercy—a silly phrase, for those malarial eyes had never known what mercy was. He was saved at any rate from the indignity of pleading.

"You see," the mestizo carefully explained, "I'm comfortable here." His yellow toes curled luxuriously beside the vomit. "Good food, beer, company, and this roof doesn't leak. You don't have to tell me what'll happen after—they'll kick me out like a dog, like a dog." He became shrill and indignant. "What have they got you here for? That's what I want to know. It looks crooked to me. It's my job, isn't it, to find you? Who's going to have the reward if they've got you already? The jefe, I shouldn't wonder, or that bastard sergeant." He brooded unhappily. "You can't trust a soul these days."

"And there's a Red Shirt," the priest said.

"A Red Shirt?"

"He really caught me."

"Mother of God," the mestizo said, "and they all have the ear of the Governor." He looked up beseechingly. He said, "You're an educated man. Advise me."

"It would be murder," the priest said, "a mortal sin."

"I don't mean that. I mean about the reward. You see, as long as they don't *know*, well, I'm comfortable here. A man deserves a few weeks' holiday. And you can't escape far, can you? It would be better, wouldn't it, to catch you out of here. In the town somewhere. I mean nobody else could claim . . ." He said furiously, "A poor man has so much to think about."

"I dare say," the priest said, "they'd give you *something* even here."

"Something," the mestizo said, levering himself up against the wall. "Why shouldn't I have it all?"

"What's going on in here?" the sergeant said. He stood in the doorway, in the sunlight, looking in.

The priest said slowly, "He wanted me to clear up his vomit. I said you hadn't told me . . ."

"Oh, he's a guest," the sergeant said. "He's got to be treated right. You do as he says."

The mestizo smirked. He said, "And another bottle of beer, sergeant?"

"Not yet," the sergeant said. "You've got to look round the town first."

The priest picked up the pail and went back across the yard, leaving them arguing. He felt as if a gun were levelled at his back. He went into the excusados and emptied the pail, then came out again into the sun—the gun was levelled at his breast. The two men stood in the cell door talking. He walked across the yard: they watched him come. The sergeant said to the mestizo, "You say you're bilious and can't see properly this morning. You clean up your own vomit then. If you don't do *your* job . . ." Behind the sergeant's back the mestizo gave him a cunning and unreassuring wink. Now that the immediate fear was over, he felt only regret. God had decided. He had to go on with life, go on making decisions, acting on his own advice, making plans. . . .

It took him another half-hour to finish cleaning the cells, throwing a bucket of water over each floor; he watched the pious woman go off through the archway to where her sister waited with the fine; they were both tied up in black shawls like something bought in the market, things hard and dry and second-hand. Then he reported again to the sergeant, who inspected the cells and criticized his work and ordered him to throw more water down, and then suddenly got tired of the whole business and told him he could go to the jefe for permission to leave. So he waited another hour on the bench outside the jefe's door, watching the sentry move lackadaisically to and fro in the hot sun.

And when at last a policeman led him in, it wasn't the jefe who sat at the desk, but the lieutenant. The priest stood not far from his own portrait on the wall and waited. Once he glanced quickly and nervously up at the old crumpled newspaper cutting and thought, It's not very like me now. What an unbearable creature he must have been in those days—and yet in those days he had been comparatively innocent. That was another mystery: it sometimes seemed to him that venial sins—impatience, an unimportant lie, pride, a neglected opportunity—cut you off from grace more completely than the worst sins of all. Then, in his innocence, he had felt no love for anyone; now in his corruption he had learnt . . .

"Well," the lieutenant asked, "has he cleaned up the cells?" He didn't take his eyes from his papers. He went on, "Tell the sergeant I want two dozen men with properly cleaned rifles—within two minutes." He looked abstractedly up at the priest and said, "Well, what are you waiting for?"

"For permission, Excellency, to go away."

"I am not an excellency. Learn to call things by their right names." He said sharply, "Have you been here before?"

"Never."

"Your name is Montez. I seem to come across too many people of that name in these days. Relations of yours?" He sat watching him closely, as if memory were beginning to work.

The priest said hurriedly, "My cousin was shot at Concepción."

"That was not my fault."

"I only meant—we were much alike. Our fathers were twins. Not half an hour between them. I thought your Excellency seemed to think . . ."

"As I remember him, he was quite different. A tall thin man . . . narrow shoulders . . ."

The priest said hurriedly, "Perhaps only to the family eye . . ."

"But then I only saw him once." It was almost as if the lieutenant had something on his conscience, as he sat with his dark Indian-blooded hands restless on the pages, brooding. . . . He asked, "Where are you going?"

"God knows."

"You are all alike, you people. You never learn the truth —that God knows nothing." Some tiny scrap of life like a grain of smut went racing across the page in front of him; he pressed his finger down on it and said, "You had no money for your fine?" and watched another smut edge out between the leaves, scurrying for refuge: in this heat there was no end to life.

"No."

"How will you live?"

"Some work perhaps . . ."

"You are getting too old for work." He put his hand suddenly in his pocket and pulled out a five-peso piece. "There," he said. "Get out of here, and don't let me see your face again. Mind that."

The priest held the coin in his fist—the price of a Mass. He said with astonishment, "You're a good man."

1940   from *The Power and the Glory*

The Heart of the Matter

EDITOR'S NOTE

It should be said immediately that despite public and critical acclaim The Heart of the Matter *is not Greene's favorite novel. He thinks that* The Power and the Glory *is his best book "by quite a long head," and currently running second in his esteem is* Travels with My Aunt. *In the new prefaces he has been writing for the Collected Edition he sees some of his best work in earlier novels—in the last sixty pages of* It's a Battlefield *and in* Brighton Rock—*and he has always had a soft spot for the entertainment* The Ministry of Fear.

Obviously these preferences, while not to be discounted, are just too ample to be covered in a volume like this which could physically accommodate only one major novel. The Power and the Glory was seriously considered as first choice but was discarded because Viking had already published a critical edition of the novel. Travels with My Aunt was too recent and too long. Brighton Rock, a strong contender, was felt to be "period" Greene, and its length, too, would have meant sacrificing variety of selection. Finally, with some reluctance on Greene's part, The Heart of the Matter was chosen. I do not share his hesitation and feel not only that this novel is central and representative but also that it is the most beautiful and provocative of all his books.

But a word should be said about Greene's reservations. The Heart of the Matter was his first popular success, and this was enough, with his fixation on failure, to make him dislike it. Second, it pinned the tag of "Catholic novelist" on him, and he prefers to think of himself as a novelist who happens to be a Catholic. Third, there was the usual amount, perhaps in this case an unusual amount, of faulty

*identification between the author and his hero. Greene
thought of Scobie as a man in error, as a just man corrupted
by pity. But many readers felt that he was condoning
Scobie's flaw. This has led Greene, in retrospect, to treat
him somewhat harshly, to say that his scruples were
grotesquely exaggerated and to describe him categorically as
"a weak man with good intentions and doomed by pride."
In fact, in his personal life at about this time, Greene shared,
if not Scobie's attitudes, at least some of his difficulties.*

*A combination of these effects led to his disenchantment
with* The Heart of the Matter. *He found himself in the
public eye, the center of a sometimes passionate, often silly
public debate. He was pursued, as he tells us in his new
preface to* A Burnt-Out Case, *by all manner of cranks and
unhappy people, mostly women and priests, who hoped he
could solve their problems, theological and other: "A young
woman wrote a rather drunken letter of invitation from a
Dutch fishing boat; another wrote from Switzerland
suggesting I join her 'where the snow can be our
coverlet'—a fate worse than martyrdom." Elsewhere,
referring to his Catholic pursuers, "I began to resent it," he
writes. "I began to feel as though I were being made into a
father confessor for people who should have been confessing
me."*

*Out of this persecution came the hunted character of
Querry in* A Burnt-Out Case. *In that sense we should be
thankful for the bad taste* The Heart of the Matter *left in
Greene's memory. But I have no wish to reopen old wounds
or to reanimate the Scobie debate. It is easier for us now to
read the book not as a problem but as a story. And that is
the way it should be read, for it is a deeply touching story,
beautifully textured and complete in itself, and one that has
more in common with classical tragedy than with Catholic
melodrama.*

*The present version is the definitive one. It includes
Greene's introduction to the novel, numerous emendations
which tone down the pathos, and an added scene—*

eliminated from the original manuscript and from all editions until 1971, when Greene restored it to the British Collected Edition.

To V.G., L.C.G. and F.C.G.

Le pécheur est au coeur même de
chrétienté. . . . Nul n'est aussi compétent
que le pécheur en matière de chrétienté.
Nul, si ce n'est le saint.

—Péguy

Introduction

Evelyn Waugh once wrote to me that the only excuse he could offer for *Brideshead Revisited* was "Spam, black-outs and Nissen huts." I feel much the same towards *The Heart of the Matter*, though my excuse might be different—"swamps, rain and a mad cook"—for our two wars were very different.

In the six years that separated the end of *The Power and the Glory* from the start of *The Heart of the Matter* my writing had become rusty with disuse and misuse (the misuse included innumerable telegrams and reports from Freetown in Sierra Leone to my headquarters in London). I began the book soon after the war was over in 1946, three years after I had closed my small office and burnt my files and code-books. For reasons of security I had been unable to keep a proper diary, but looking at the few random notes which survive I seem to have been already, between telegrams and reports, playing with the idea of a novel—though not the novel I eventually wrote.

There had been a chance encounter during one of my journeys up-country with a Father B. whom I have now completely forgotten, though I must have been remembering him when I wrote of Father Clay whom Scobie met when he went to Bamba to inquire into young Pemberton's suicide. "Poor little red-headed north country boy neglected by his fellows," I read in my notebook. "His account of the blackwater fever. 'I walk up and down here.' [These were Father Clay's very words.] £38 in cash at the Mission when he arrived, but a £28 bill. Apparently no interests. 6 year tour—3½ done. The old raincoat over a dirty white shirt."

I had no idea of Major Scobie in those days. It was the young north country priest who grew in my imagination, so that I find a few lines in faded pencil beginning his story.

If I were a writer, I would be tempted to turn this into a novel. I imagine this is what writers feel—the haunting presence of an individual whom they wish to understand. But I haven't the time or the skill for such work and all I have been able to do is to gather the impressions that this man made on others who knew him, the documents as it were in the case of Father ——. I am afraid a character can hardly emerge from such a collection as this. In the reviews I have read novelists are praised or blamed for their success or failure in creating a character, but such characters usually seem to bear about the same relation to life as the pictures in the country that you see painted on the mud walls of the native huts. A train is represented by a row of rectangles, each rectangle balanced on two circles. So a "character" is simplified by the novelist: the contradictions you find in human beings are pared or explained away. The result is Art—which is arrangement and simplification for the purpose of conveying a mental condition. This book cannot pretend to be art because the compiler has left in all the contradictions: its only purpose is to present as truthfully as possible an enigma, though I daresay it is an enigma common to most of us if every man had his own case-book.

My name is . . . I am a line agent for . . .

The name and the firm were never filled in and the novel went no further. It was just another object abandoned on the coast like the old guns on Bunce Island in Sierra Leone river. I am glad to put up this small memorial to what might well have been a better book than *The Heart of the Matter.*

Looking through my old notebook I find stray incidents and characters which could have been included in my novel; they formed part of the routine life of an S.I.S. representative in Freetown, and some of them may have found a hole or corner in the book which came to be written—but I don't want to search for them now.

The German agent's letters. The list of ships which have called. Tell so-and-so he's too optimistic when he says no ships can call here. The touch of pacifism: "What would Livingstone have said?" [Who was that agent? Forgotten as deeply as Father B.]

The small brown kid dead in the middle of the road between the shops, and the vulture hopping round, looking back towards the gutter when cars came by.

The suitcase of the suspect—the squalor and intimacy of a man's suitcase.

The funeral party going home outside—I had thought it was a wedding. The crowd of women in bright native dress wearing a kind of black apron and overshirt. The trombone players going Dum, dum, dum, and the women making little dancing steps and posturing and shouting to the soldiers in the camp as they went by. All a little tipsy. At the house young men were kicking a football. The last mourners seem sedate and sombre, carrying handkerchiefs. One woman in white European dress walking alone.

My boy's brother dying. Of gonorrhoea. He too has had g. "Cured now." "Injections?" "No." He makes an expressive gesture with his hands. "Doctor throw it out." His stilted walk with buttocks projecting and the smell of drink. "You drink if you see your brother—own father, own mother—lying on bed, not seeing you. You drink to keep water out of eyes." He cannot yet tell his brother's wife. If people know he's dying they'll all come in and steal his things. All night he's going to have a party at his brother's, drinking so that water doesn't come out of eyes, and quietly checking on his brother's belongings and getting his small brother to write them down. Next morning he tells me with interest that there are two sewing machines—but his brother isn't dead yet.

This must have been my first unsatisfactory boy, a Mende, whom my mad cook tried to kill with a hatchet because he had borrowed a cooking utensil—an empty sardine tin. I thankfully lost the boy when he went to prison for perjury, an offence beyond his comprehension. My cook was later accused of taking money for witchcraft and not fulfilling his promise. I found my house deserted one night when I returned from a long trek with no one to cook me an evening meal. The cook, I learnt from a neighbour, was in prison. When I visited him there I couldn't bear to see him in his grim cell. I got in touch, but it wasn't easy, with a Vichy district commissioner across the border in French Guinea and had him returned to his native village, where he would end his days well looked after, at liberty except for an iron ring round his ankle to show that he had been afflicted by God.

The letter to the African agitator in his internment who has married again and who in England seems to have had relations with an ardent humanitarian Englishwoman who financed him. It is from an African in the Gower Street–Gray's Inn district. First about letting him have collars left at the laundry. Reference to the agitator's new romance. "Oh, she will be jealous when she hears the news. You are a real heart-breaker." The photo of the heart-breaker on the files. The respectable humanitarian names chiming in the right places—Victor Gollancz, Ethel Mannin. . . .

The Court Messenger at Yengema [the headquarters of

the diamond mines] with his senseless face and his bandy legs suffering from ju-ju. [He had to be sent back to his native village to be treated by a witch doctor.]

The mammas in the market wrapping up their fruit and vegetables in confidential telegrams from the secretariat files.

The Commissioner back subdued from a hanging. "I can't eat meat for a week after a hanging."

There was another event which I couldn't put down in the notebook and which sickened me—the interrogation of a young Scandinavian seaman from Buenos Aires who was suspected of being a German agent. I knew from a report about the girl he had loved in Buenos Aires—a prostitute probably, but he was really in love in his romantic way. If he came clean he could go back to her, I told him; if he wouldn't speak he would be interned for the duration of the war. "And how long do you think she'll stay faithful to you?" It was a police job, an M.I.5 job. I was angry that I had been landed with it. It was a form of dirty work for which I had not been engaged. I gave up the interrogation prematurely, without result, hating myself. He may even have been innocent. To hell, I thought then, with M.I.5.

There was another occasion when I was going through an address book of a man on a Portuguese liner who was believed to be a spy, and I found the name and address of the best friend I had in France (she died later in a concentration camp). I asked London what it all meant, but they never replied. I had no right to be curious about even a friend's fate.

The experience was rich enough, but I have never been satisfied with what I made of it. My critics have complained, perhaps with justice, that "I laid it on too thick," but the material *was* thick. The real fault, as I have written, lay in the rustiness of my long inaction. What I was engaged on in those war years was not genuine action—it was an escape from reality and responsibility. To a novelist his novel is the only reality and his only responsibility. Like the man suffering from ju-ju I had to go back to my proper region to be cured.

In 1946 I felt myself at a loss. How had I in the past found the progressions from one scene to another? How confine the narrative to one point of view, or at most two? A dozen such technical questions tormented me as they had never done before the war when the solution had always come easily. Work was not made easier because the booby-traps I had heedlessly planted in my private life were blowing up in turn. I had always thought that war would bring death as a solution in one form or another, in the blitz, in a subma-rined ship, in Africa with a dose of blackwater, but here I was alive, the carrier of unhappiness to people I loved, tak-ing up the old profession of brothel-child. So perhaps what I really dislike in the book is the memory of a personal an-guish. As Scott Fitzgerald wrote, "A writer's temperament is continually making him do things he can never repair." I was even contemplating one night the first move to suicide when I was interrupted in that game by the arrival at ten in the evening of a telegram (I had never known they delivered telegrams so late) from someone whom I had made suffer and who now felt anxious about my safety.

But long before that point of despair was reached I had found myself so out of practice and out of confidence that I couldn't for months get the character Wilson off his balcony in the hotel from which he was watching Scobie, the Com-missioner of Police, pass down the wide unpaved street. To get him off the balcony meant making a decision. Two very different novels began on the same balcony with the same character, and I had to choose which to write.

One was the novel I wrote; the other was to have been an "entertainment." I had long been haunted by the possibility of a crime story in which the criminal was known to the reader, but the detective was carefully hidden, disguised by false clues which would lead the reader astray until the cli-max. The story was to be told from the point of view of the criminal, and the detective would necessarily be some kind of undercover agent. M.I.5 was the obvious organization to use, and the character Wilson is the unsatisfactory relic of the entertainment, for when I left Wilson on the balcony and joined Scobie I plumped for the novel.

It was to prove a book more popular with the public, even with the critics, than with the author. The scales to me seem too heavily weighted, the plot overloaded, the religious scruples of Scobie too extreme. I had meant the story of Scobie to enlarge a theme which I had touched on in *The Ministry of Fear*, the disastrous effect on human beings of pity as distinct from compassion. I had written in *The Ministry of Fear*: "Pity is cruel. Pity destroys. Love isn't safe when pity's prowling round." The character of Scobie was intended to show that pity can be the expression of an almost monstrous pride. But I found the effect on the reader was quite different. To them Scobie was exonerated, Scobie was "a good man," he was hunted to his doom by the harshness of his wife.

Here was a technical fault rather than a psychological one. Louise Scobie is mainly seen through the eyes of Scobie, and we have no chance of revising our opinion of her. Helen, the girl whom Scobie loves, gains an unfair advantage. In the original draft of the novel a scene was played between Mrs. Scobie and Wilson on their evening walk along the abandoned railway track below Hill Station. It occurred in Book One, Part II, between the end of Chapter 1 and the beginning of Chapter 2. This put Mrs. Scobie's character in a more favourable light, but the scene had to be represented through the eyes of Wilson. This scene—so I thought when I was preparing the novel for publication— broke Scobie's point of view prematurely; the drive of the narrative appeared to slacken. By eliminating it I thought I had gained intensity and impetus, but I had sacrificed tone. Now I have reinserted the passage,* so that this edition for the first time presents the novel as I first wrote it, apart from minor revisions, perhaps more numerous than in any other novel in this edition.

* Pp. 169–174.

Maybe I am too harsh to the book, wearied as I have been by reiterated arguments in Catholic journals on Scobie's salvation or damnation. I was not so stupid as to believe that this could ever be an issue in a novel. Besides I have small belief in the doctrine of eternal punishment (it was Scobie's belief not mine). Suicide was Scobie's inevitable end; the particular motive of his suicide, to save even God from himself, was the final twist of the screw of his inordinate pride. Perhaps Scobie should have been a subject for cruel comedy rather than for tragedy. . . .

All this said, there are pages in the book (and one character, Yusef) for which I care, descriptions of Freetown and the interior of Sierra Leone which bring back many happy months and some unhappy ones. The Portuguese liners with their smuggled letters and smuggled diamonds were very much a part of the odd life I led there in 1942–43. Scobie was based on nothing but my own unconscious. He had nothing to do with my Commissioner of Police, whose friendship was the human thing I valued most during fifteen rather lonely months. Nor was Wilson—who obstinately refused to come alive—based on any of the M.I.5 agents who trailed—in two cases disastrously—down the West African coast in those days.

"Those days"—I am glad to have had them; a love of Africa deepened there, in particular a love for what is called the world over, "the Coast." I have often been accused of inventing a country called Greeneland, but this world of tin roofs, of vultures clanging down, of laterite paths turning rose in the evening light does exist. My cook who went to prison for witchcraft, my steward who was sentenced unjustly for perjury, the boy from the bush who arrived with no recommendation from anyone and took charge of me as faithfully as Ali did of Scobie, refusing the bribes offered by the representative of another secret service, S.O.E., to leave my employ—were they just inhabitants of Greeneland? As well tell a man in love with a woman that she is only a figment of his romantic imagination.

BOOK ONE

Part I

[1]

i

Wilson sat on the balcony of the Bedford Hotel with his bald pink knees thrust against the ironwork. It was Sunday and the Cathedral bell clanged for matins. On the other side of Bond Street, in the windows of the High School, sat the young negresses in dark-blue gym smocks engaged on the interminable task of trying to wave their wirespring hair. Wilson stroked his very young moustache and dreamed, waiting for his gin-and-bitters.

Sitting there, facing Bond Street, he had his face turned to the sea. His pallor showed how recently he had emerged from it into the port: so did his lack of interest in the schoolgirls opposite. He was like the lagging finger of the barometer, still pointing to Fair long after its companion has moved to Stormy. Below him the black clerks moved churchward, but their wives in brilliant afternoon dresses of blue and cerise aroused no interest in Wilson. He was alone on the balcony except for one bearded Indian in a turban who had already tried to tell his fortune: this was not the hour or the day for white men—they would be at the beach five miles away, but Wilson had no car. He felt almost intolerably lonely. On either side of the school the tin roofs sloped towards the sea, and the corrugated iron above his head clanged and clattered as a vulture alighted.

Three merchant officers from the convoy in the harbour came into view, walking up from the quay. They were surrounded immediately by small boys wearing school caps. The boys' refrain came faintly up to Wilson like a nursery rhyme: "Captain want jig jig, my sister pretty girl schoolteacher, captain want jig jig." The bearded Indian frowned over intricate calculations on the back of an envelope—a horoscope, the cost of living? When Wilson looked down into the street again the officers had fought their way free, and the schoolboys had swarmed again round a single ableseaman: they led him triumphantly away towards the brothel near the police station, as though to the nursery.

A black boy brought Wilson's gin and he sipped it very slowly because he had nothing else to do except to return to his hot and squalid room and read a novel—or a poem. Wilson liked poetry, but he absorbed it secretly, like a drug. *The Golden Treasury* accompanied him wherever he went, but it was taken at night in small doses—a finger of Longfellow, Macaulay, Mangan: "Go on to tell how, with genius wasted, Betrayed in friendship, befooled in love. . . ." His taste was romantic. For public exhibition he had his Wallace. He wanted passionately to be indistinguishable on the surface from other men: he wore his moustache like a club tie—it was his highest common factor, but his eyes betrayed him—brown dog's eyes, a setter's eyes, pointing mournfully towards Bond Street.

"Excuse me," a voice said, "aren't you Wilson?"

He looked up at a middle-aged man in the inevitable khaki shorts with a drawn face the colour of hay.

"Yes, that's me."

"May I join you? My name's Harris."

"Delighted, Mr. Harris."

"You're the new accountant at the U.A.C.?"

"That's me. Have a drink?"

"I'll have a lemon squash if you don't mind. Can't drink in the middle of the day."

The Indian rose from his table and approached with deference. "You remember me, Mr. Harris. Perhaps you would tell your friend, Mr. Harris, of my talents. Perhaps he would like to read my letters of recommendation. . . ." The grubby sheaf of envelopes was always in his hand. "The leaders of society."

"Be off. Beat it, you old scoundrel," Harris said.

"How did you know my name?" Wilson asked.

"Saw it on a cable. I'm a cable censor," Harris said. "What a job! What a place!"

"I can see from here, Mr. Harris, that your fortune has changed considerably. If you would step with me for a moment into the bathroom . . ."

"Beat it, Gunga Din."

"Why the bathroom?" Wilson asked.

"He always tells fortunes there. I suppose it's the only private room available. I never thought of asking why."

"Been here long?"

"Eighteen bloody months."

"Going home soon?"

Harris stared over the tin roofs towards the harbour. He said, "The ships all go the wrong way. But when I do get home you'll never see me here again." He lowered his voice and said with venom over his lemon squash, "I hate the place. I hate the people. I hate the bloody niggers. Mustn't call 'em that you know."

"My boy seems all right."

"A man's boy's always all right. He's a real nigger—but these, look at 'em, look at that one with a feather boa down there. They aren't even real niggers. Just West Indians and they rule the coast. Clerks in the stores, city council, magistrates, lawyers—my God. It's all right up in the Protectorate. I haven't anything to say against a real nigger. God made our colours. But these—my God! The Government's afraid of them. The police are afraid of them. Look down there," Harris said, "look at Scobie."

A vulture flapped and shifted on the iron roof and Wilson looked at Scobie. He looked without interest in obedience to a stranger's direction, and it seemed to him that no particular interest attached to the squat grey-haired man walking alone up Bond Street. He couldn't tell that this was one of those occasions a man never forgets: a small cicatrice had been made on the memory, a wound that would ache whenever certain things combined—the taste of gin at mid-day, the smell of flowers under a balcony, the clang of corrugated iron, an ugly bird flopping from perch to perch.

"He loves 'em so much," Harris said, "he sleeps with 'em."

"Is that the police uniform?"

"It is. Our great police force. A lost thing will they never find—you know the poem."

"I don't read poetry," Wilson said. His eyes followed Scobie up the sun-drowned street. Scobie stopped and had a word with a black man in a white panama: a black policeman passed by, saluting smartly. Scobie went on.

"Probably in the pay of the Syrians too if the truth were known."

"The Syrians?"

"This is the original Tower of Babel," Harris said. "West Indians, Africans, real Indians, Syrians, Englishmen, Scotsmen in the Office of Works, Irish priests, French priests, Alsatian priests."

"What do the Syrians do?"

"Make money. They run all the stores up-country and most of the stores here. Run diamonds too."

"I suppose there's a lot of that."

"The Germans pay a high price."

"Hasn't he got a wife here?"

"Who? Oh, Scobie. Rather. He's got a wife. Perhaps if I had a wife like that, I'd sleep with niggers too. You'll meet her soon. She's the city intellectual. She likes art, poetry. Got up an exhibition of arts for the shipwrecked seamen. You know the kind of thing—poems on exile by aircraftsmen, water-colours by stokers, pokerwork from the mission schools. Poor old Scobie. Have another gin?"

"I think I will," said Wilson.

ii

Scobie turned up James Street past the Secretariat. With its long balconies it had always reminded him of a hospital. For fifteen years he had watched the arrival of a succession of patients; periodically at the end of eighteen months certain patients were sent home, yellow and nervy, and others took their place—Colonial Secretaries, Secretaries of Agriculture, Treasurers and Directors of Public Works. He watched their temperature charts every one—the first outbreak of unreasonable temper, the drink too many, the sudden stand for principle after a year of acquiescence. The black clerks carried their bedside manner like doctors down the corridors; cheerful and respectful they put up with any insult. The patient was always right.

Round the corner, in front of the old cotton tree, where the earliest settlers had gathered their first day on the unfriendly shore, stood the law courts and police station, a great stone building like the grandiloquent boast of weak men. Inside that massive frame the human being rattled in the corridors like a dry kernel. No one could have been adequate to so rhetorical a conception. But the idea in any case was only one room deep. In the dark narrow passage behind, in the charge-room and the cells, Scobie could always detect the odour of human meanness and injustice—it was the smell of a zoo, of sawdust, excrement, ammonia, and lack of liberty. The place was scrubbed daily, but you could never eliminate the smell. Prisoners and policemen carried it in their clothing like cigarette smoke.

Scobie climbed the great steps and turned to his right along the shaded outside corridor to his room: a table, two kitchen chairs, a cupboard, some rusty handcuffs hanging on a nail like an old hat, a filing cabinet: to a stranger it would have appeared a bare uncomfortable room but to Scobie it was home. Other men slowly build up the sense of home by accumulation—a new picture, more and more books, an odd-shaped paper-weight, the ash-tray bought for a forgotten reason on a forgotten holiday; Scobie built his home by a process of reduction. He had started out fifteen years ago with far more than this. There had been a photograph of his wife, bright leather cushions from the market, an easy-chair, a large coloured map of the port on the wall. The map had been borrowed by younger men: it was of no more use to him; he carried the whole coastline of the colony in his mind's eye: from Kufa Bay to Medley was his beat. As for the cushions and the easy-chair, he had soon discovered how comfort of that kind down in the airless town meant heat. Where the body was touched or enclosed it sweated. Last of all his wife's photograph had been made unnecessary by her presence. She had joined him the first year of the phoney war and now she couldn't get away: the danger of submarines had made her as much a fixture as the handcuffs on the nail. Besides, it had been a very early photograph, and he no longer cared to be reminded of the unformed face, the expression calm and gentle with lack of knowledge, the lips parted obediently in the smile the photographer had demanded. Fifteen years form a face, gentleness ebbs with experience, and he was always aware of his own responsibility. He had led the way: the experience that had come to her was the experience selected by himself. He had formed her face.

He sat down at his bare table and almost immediately his Mende sergeant clicked his heels in the doorway. "Sah?"

"Anything to report?"

"The Commissioner want to see you, sah."

"Anything on the charge sheet?"

"Two black men fight in the market, sah."

"Mammy trouble?"

"Yes, sah."

"Anything else?"

"Miss Wilberforce want to see you, sah. I tell her you was at church and she got to come back by-and-by, but she stick. She say she no budge."

"Which Miss Wilberforce is that, sergeant?"

"I don't know, sah. She come from Sharp Town, sah."

"Well, I'll see her after the Commissioner. But no one else, mind."

"Very good, sah."

Scobie, passing down the passage to the Commissioner's room, saw the girl sitting alone on a bench against the wall: he didn't look twice: he caught only the vague impression of a young black African face, a bright cotton frock, and then she was already out of his mind, and he was wondering what he should say to the Commissioner. It had been on his mind all that week.

"Sit down, Scobie." The Commissioner was an old man of fifty-three—one counted age by the years a man had served in the colony. The Commissioner with twenty-two years' service was the oldest man there, just as the Governor was a stripling of sixty compared with any district officer who had five years' knowledge behind him.

"I'm retiring, Scobie," the Commissioner said, "after this tour."

"I know."

"I suppose everyone knows."

"I've heard the men talking about it."

"And yet you are the second man I've told. Do they say who's taking my place?"

Scobie said, "They know who isn't."

"It's damned unfair," the Commissioner said. "I can do nothing more than I have done, Scobie. You are a wonderful man for picking up enemies. Like Aristides the Just."

"I don't think I'm as just as all that."

"The question is what do you want to do? They are sending a man called Baker from Gambia. He's younger than you are. Do you want to resign, retire, transfer, Scobie?"

"I want to stay," Scobie said.

"Your wife won't like it."

"I've been here too long to go." He thought to himself, poor Louise, if I had left it to her, where should we be now? and he admitted straight away that they wouldn't be here— somewhere far better, better climate, better pay, better position. She would have taken every opening for improvement: she would have steered agilely up the ladders and left the snakes alone. I've landed her here, he thought, with the odd premonitory sense of guilt he always felt as though he were responsible for something in the future he couldn't even foresee. He said aloud, "You know I like the place."

"I believe you do. I wonder why."

"It's pretty in the evening," Scobie said vaguely.

"Do you know the latest story they are using against you at the Secretariat?"

"I suppose I'm in the Syrians' pay?"

"They haven't got that far yet. That's the next stage. No, you sleep with black girls. You know what it is, Scobie, you ought to have flirted with one of their wives. They feel insulted."

"Perhaps I ought to sleep with a black girl. Then they won't have to think up anything else."

"The man before you slept with dozens," the Commissioner said, "but it never bothered anyone. They thought up something different for him. They said he drank secretly. It made them feel better drinking publicly. What a lot of swine they are, Scobie."

"The Chief Assistant Colonial Secretary's not a bad chap."

"No, the Chief Assistant Colonial Secretary's all right." The Commissioner laughed. "You're a terrible fellow, Scobie. Scobie the Just."

Scobie returned down the passage; the girl sat in the dusk. Her feet were bare: they stood side by side like casts in a museum: they didn't belong to the bright smart cotton frock. "Are you Miss Wilberforce?" Scobie asked.

"Yes, sir."

"You don't live here, do you?"

"No! I live in Sharp Town, sir."

"Well, come in." He led the way into his office and sat down at his desk. There was no pencil laid out and he opened his drawer. Here and here only had objects accumu-

lated: letters, india-rubbers, a broken rosary—no pencil.
"What's the trouble, Miss Wilberforce?" His eye caught a
snapshot of a bathing party at Medley Beach: his wife, the
Colonial Secretary's wife, the Director of Education holding
up what looked like a dead fish, the Colonial Treasurer's
wife. The expanse of white flesh made them look like a gathering of albinos, and all the mouths gaped with laughter.

The girl said, "My landlady—she broke up my home last
night. She come in when it was dark, and she pull down all
the partition, an' she thieve my chest with all my belongings."

"You got plenty lodgers?"

"Only three, sir."

He knew exactly how it all was: a lodger would take a
one-roomed shack for five shillings a week, stick up a few
thin partitions and let the so-called rooms for half a crown
apiece—a horizontal tenement. Each room would be furnished with a box containing a little china and glass
"dashed" by an employer or stolen from an employer, a bed
made out of old packing-cases, and a hurricane-lamp. The
glass of these lamps did not long survive, and the little open
flames were always ready to catch some spilt paraffin; they
licked at the plywood partitions and caused innumerable
fires. Sometimes a landlady would thrust her way into her
house and pull down the dangerous partitions, sometimes
she would steal the lamps of her tenants, and the ripple of
her theft would go out in widening rings of lamp thefts until
they touched the European quarter and became a subject of
gossip at the club. "Can't keep a lamp for love or money."

"Your landlady," Scobie told the girl sharply, "she say
you make plenty trouble: too many lodgers: too many
lamps."

"No, sir. No lamp palaver."

"Mammy palaver, eh? You bad girl?"

"No, sir."

"Why you come here? Why you not call Corporal Laminah in Sharp Town?"

"He my landlady's brother, sir."

"He is, is he? Same father same mother?"

"No, sir. Same father."

The interview was like a ritual between priest and server. He knew exactly what would happen when one of his men investigated the affair. The landlady would say that she had told her tenant to pull down the partitions and when that failed she had taken action herself. She would deny that there had ever been a chest of china. The corporal would confirm this. He would turn out not to be the landlady's brother, but some other unspecified relation—probably disreputable. Bribes—which were known respectably as dashes—would pass to and fro, the storm of indignation and anger that had sounded so genuine would subside, the partitions would go up again, nobody would hear any more about the chest, and several policemen would be a shilling or two the richer. At the beginning of his service Scobie had flung himself into these investigations; he had found himself over and over again in the position of a partisan, supporting as he believed the poor and innocent tenant against the wealthy and guilty house-owner. But he soon discovered that the guilt and innocence were as relative as the wealth. The wronged tenant turned out to be also the wealthy capitalist, making a profit of five shillings a week on a single room, living rent free herself. After that he had tried to kill these cases at birth: he would reason with the complainant and point out that the investigation would do no good and undoubtedly cost her time and money; he would sometimes even refuse to investigate. The result of that inaction had been stones flung at his car window, slashed tyres, the nickname of the Bad Man that had stuck to him through all one long sad tour—it worried him unreasonably in the heat and damp; he couldn't take it lightly. Already he had begun to desire these people's trust and affection. That year he had blackwater fever and was nearly invalided from the service altogether.

The girl waited patiently for his decision. They had an in-

finite capacity for patience when patience was required—
just as their impatience knew no bounds of propriety when
they had anything to gain by it. They would sit quietly all
day in a white man's backyard in order to beg for something
he hadn't the power to grant, or they would shriek and fight
and abuse to get served in a store before their neighbour. He
thought: how beautiful she is. It was strange to think that
fifteen years ago he would not have noticed her beauty—the
small high breasts, the tiny wrists, the thrust of the young
buttocks; she would have been indistinguishable from her
fellows—a black. In those days he had thought his wife
beautiful. A white skin had not then reminded him of an al-
bino. Poor Louise. He said, "Give this chit to the sergeant at
the desk."

"Thank you, sir."

"That's all right." He smiled. "Try to tell him the truth."

He watched her go out of the dark office like fifteen
wasted years.

iii

Scobie had been out-manoeuvred in the interminable war
over housing. During his last leave he had lost his bungalow
in Cape Station, the main European quarter, to a senior
sanitary inspector called Fellowes, and had found himself
relegated to a square two-storeyed house built originally for
a Syrian trader on the flats below—a piece of reclaimed
swamp which would return to swamp as soon as the rains set
in. From the windows he looked directly out to sea over a
line of Creole houses; on the other side of the road lorries
backed and churned in a military transport camp and vultures strolled like domestic turkeys in the regimental refuse.
On the low ridge of hills behind him the bungalows of the
station lay among the low clouds; lamps burned all day in
the cupboards, mould gathered on the boots—nevertheless
these were the houses for men of his rank. Women depended
so much on pride, pride in themselves, their husbands, their

surroundings. They were seldom proud, it seemed to him, of the invisible.

"Louise," he called, "Louise." There was no reason to call: if she wasn't in the living-room there was nowhere else for her to be but the bedroom (the kitchen was simply a shed in the yard opposite the back door), yet it was his habit to cry her name, a habit he had formed in the days of anxiety and love. The less he needed Louise the more conscious he became of his responsibility for her happiness. When he called her name he was crying like Canute against a tide— the tide of her melancholy and disappointment.

In the old days she had replied, but she was not such a creature of habit as he was—nor so false, he sometimes told himself. Kindness and pity had no power with her; she would never have pretended an emotion she didn't feel, and like an animal she gave way completely to the momentary sickness and recovered as suddenly. When he found her in the bedroom under the mosquito-net she reminded him of a dog or a cat, she was so completely "out." Her hair was matted, her eyes closed. He stood very still like a spy in foreign territory, and indeed he was in foreign territory now. If home for him meant the reduction of things to a friendly unchanging minimum, home to her was accumulation. The dressing-table was crammed with pots and photographs— himself as a young man in the curiously dated officer's uniform of the last war: the Chief Justice's wife, whom for the moment she counted as her friend: their only child, who had died at school in England three years ago—a little pious nine-year-old girl's face in the white muslin of first communion: innumerable photographs of Louise herself, in groups with nursing sisters, with the Admiral's party at Medley Beach, on a Yorkshire moor with Teddy Bromley and his wife. It was as if she were accumulating evidence that she had friends like other people. He watched her through the muslin net. Her face had the ivory tinge of atebrin: her hair which had once been the colour of bottled honey was dark and stringy with sweat. These were the times of ugliness when he loved her, when pity and responsibility reached the intensity of a passion. It was pity that told him to go: he wouldn't have woken his worst enemy from sleep, leave alone Louise. He tiptoed out and down the stairs. (The inside stairs could be found nowhere else in this bungalow city except in Government House, and she had tried to make them an object of pride with stair-carpets and pictures on the wall.) In the living-room there was a bookcase full of her books, rugs on the floor, a native mask from Nigeria, more photographs. The books had to be wiped daily to remove the damp, and she had not succeeded very well in disguising with flowery curtains the food safe which stood with each foot in a little enamel basin of water to keep the ants out. The boy was laying a single place for lunch.

The boy was short and squat with the broad ugly pleasant face of a Temne. His bare feet flapped like empty gloves across the floor.

"What's wrong with Missus?" Scobie asked.

"Belly humbug," Ali said.

Scobie took a Mende grammar from the bookcase: it was tucked away in the bottom shelf where its old untidy cover was least conspicuous. In the upper shelves were the flimsy rows of Louise's authors—not so young modern poets and the novels of Virginia Woolf. He couldn't concentrate: it was too hot and his wife's absence was like a garrulous companion in the room reminding him of his responsibility. A fork fell on the floor and he watched Ali surreptitiously wipe it on his sleeve, watched him with affection. They had been together fifteen years—a year longer than his marriage—a long time to keep a servant. He had been "small boy" first, then assistant steward in the days when one kept four servants, now he was plain steward. After each leave Ali would be on the landing-stage waiting to organize his luggage with three or four ragged carriers. In the intervals of leave many people tried to steal Ali's services, but he had never yet failed to be waiting—except once when he had been in prison. There was no disgrace about prison; it was an obstacle that no one could avoid for ever.

"Ticki," a voice wailed, and Scobie rose at once. "Ticki." He went upstairs.

His wife was sitting up under the mosquito-net, and for a moment he had the impression of a joint under a meat-cover. But pity trod on the heels of the cruel image and hustled it away. "Are you feeling better, darling?"

Louise said, "Mrs. Castle's been in."

"Enough to make anyone ill," Scobie said.

"She's been telling me about you."

"What about me?" He gave her a bright fake smile; so much of life was a putting off of unhappiness for another time. Nothing was ever lost by delay. He had a dim idea that perhaps if one delayed long enough, things were taken out of one's hands altogether by death.

"She says the Commissioner's retiring, and they've passed you over."

"Her husband talks too much in his sleep."

"Is it true?"

"Yes. I've known it for weeks. It doesn't matter, dear, really."

Louise said, "I'll never be able to show my face at the club again."

"It's not as bad as that. These things happen, you know."

"You'll resign, won't you, Ticki?"

"I don't think I can do that, dear."

"Mrs. Castle's on our side. She's furious. She says everyone's talking about it and saying things. Darling, you aren't in the pay of the Syrians, are you?"

"No, dear."

"I was so upset I came out of Mass before the end. It's so mean of them, Ticki. You can't take it lying down. You've got to think of me."

"Yes, I do. All the time." He sat down on the bed and put his hand under the net and touched hers. Little beads of sweat started where their skins touched. He said, "I do think of you, dear. But I've been fifteen years in this place. I'd be lost anywhere else, even if they gave me another job. It isn't much of a recommendation, you know, being passed over."

"We could retire."

"The pension isn't much to live on."

"I'm sure I could make a little money writing. Mrs. Castle says I ought to be a professional. With all this experience," Louise said, gazing through the white muslin tent as far as her dressing-table: there another face in white muslin stared back and she looked away. She said, "If only we could go to South Africa. I can't bear the people here."

"Perhaps I could arrange a passage for you. There haven't been many sinkings that way lately. You ought to have a holiday."

"There was a time when you wanted to retire too. You used to count the years. You made plans—for all of us."

"Oh well, one changes," he said.

She said mercilessly, "You didn't think you'd be alone with me then."

He pressed his sweating hand against hers. "What nonsense you talk, dear. You must get up and have some food. . . ."

"Do you love anyone, Ticki, except yourself?"

"No, I just love myself, that's all. And Ali. I forgot Ali. Of course I love him too. But not you," he ran on with worn mechanical raillery, stroking her hand, smiling, soothing. . . .

"And Ali's sister?"

"Has he got a sister?"

"They've all got sisters, haven't they? Why didn't you go to Mass today?"

"It was my morning on duty, dear. You know that."

"You could have changed it. You haven't got much faith, have you, Ticki?"

"You've got enough for both of us, dear. Come and have some food."

"Ticki, I sometimes think you just became a Catholic to

marry me. It doesn't mean a thing to you, does it?"

"Listen, darling, you want to come down and eat a bit. Then you want to take the car along to the beach and have some fresh air."

"How different the whole day would have been," she said, staring out of her net, "if you'd come home and said, 'Darling, I'm going to be the Commissioner.'"

Scobie said slowly, "You know, dear, in a place like this in war-time—an important harbour—the Vichy French just across the border—all this diamond smuggling from the Protectorate, they need a younger man." He didn't believe a word he was saying.

"I hadn't thought of that."

"That's the only reason. You can't blame anyone. It's the war."

"The war does spoil everything, doesn't it?"

"It gives the younger men a chance."

"Darling, perhaps I'll come down and just pick at a little cold meat."

"That's right, dear." He withdrew his hand: it was dripping with sweat. "I'll tell Ali."

Downstairs he shouted "Ali" out of the back door.

"Massa?"

"Lay two places. Missus better."

The first faint breeze of the day came off the sea, blowing up over the bushes and between the Creole huts. A vulture flapped heavily upwards from the iron roof and down again in the yard next door. Scobie drew a deep breath; he felt exhausted and victorious: he had persuaded Louise to pick a little meat. It had always been his responsibility to maintain happiness in those he loved. One was safe now, for ever, and the other was going to eat her lunch.

iv

In the evening the port became beautiful for perhaps five minutes. The laterite roads that were so ugly and clay-heavy by day became a delicate flower-like pink. It was the hour of

content. Men who had left the port for ever would sometimes remember on a grey wet London evening the bloom
and glow that faded as soon as it was seen: they would wonder why they had hated the Coast and for a space of a drink
they would long to return.

Scobie stopped his Morris at one of the great loops of the
climbing road and looked back. He was just too late. The
flower had withered upwards from the town; the white
stones that marked the edge of the precipitous hill shone like
candles in the new dusk.

"I wonder if anybody will be there, Ticki."

"Sure to be. It's library night."

"Do hurry up, dear. It's so hot in the car. I'll be glad
when the rains come."

"Will you?"

"If only they just went on for a month or two and then
stopped."

Scobie made the right reply. He never listened while his
wife talked. He worked steadily to the even current of sound,
but if a note of distress were struck he was aware of it at
once. Like a wireless operator with a novel open in front of
him, he could disregard every signal except the ship's symbol and the SOS. He could even work better while she
talked than when he was silent, for so long as his ear-drum
registered those tranquil sounds—the gossip of the club,
comments on the sermons preached by Father Rank, the
plot of a new novel, even complaints about the weather—he
knew that all was well. It was silence that stopped him
working—silence in which he might look up and see tears
waiting in the eyes for his attention.

"There's a rumour going round that the refrigerators were
all sunk last week."

He considered, while she talked, his line of action with the
Portuguese ship that was due in as soon as the boom opened
in the morning. The fortnightly arrival of a neutral ship
provided an outing for the junior officers: a change of food,

a few glasses of real wine, even the opportunity of buying some small decorative object in the ship's store for a girl. In return they had only to help the Field Security Police in the examination of passports, the searching of the suspects' cabins: all the hard and disagreeable work was done by the F.S.P., in the hold, sifting sacks of rice for commercial diamonds, or in the heat of the kitchen, plunging the hand into tins of lard, disembowelling the stuffed turkeys. To try to find a few diamonds in a liner of fifteen thousand tons was absurd: no malign tyrant in a fairy-story had ever set a goose girl a more impossible task, and yet as regularly as the ships called, the cypher telegrams came in—"So and so travelling first class suspected of carrying diamonds. The following members of the ship's crew suspected. . . ." Nobody ever found anything. He thought: it's Harris's turn to go on board, and Fraser can go with him. I'm too old for these excursions. Let the boys have a little fun.

"Last time half the books arrived damaged."

"Did they?"

Judging from the number of cars, he thought, there were not many people at the club yet. He switched off his lights and waited for Louise to move, but she just sat there with a clenched fist showing in the switchboard light. "Well, dear, here we are," he said in the hearty voice that strangers took as a mark of stupidity. Louise said, "Do you think they all know by this time?"

"Know what?"

"That you've been passed over."

"My dear, I thought we'd finished with all that. Look at all the generals who've been passed over since 1940. They won't bother about a deputy-commissioner."

She said, "But they don't like me."

Poor Louise, he thought, it is terrible not to be liked, and his mind went back to his own experience in that early tour when the blacks had slashed his tyres and written insults on his car. "Dear, how absurd you are. I've never known anyone with so many friends." He ran unconvincingly on. "Mrs. Halifax, Mrs. Castle . . ." and then decided it was better after all not to list them.

"They'll all be waiting there," she said, "just waiting for me to walk in. . . . I never wanted to come to the club to-night. Let's go home."

"We can't. Here's Mrs. Castle's car arriving." He tried to laugh. "We're trapped, Louise." He saw the fist open and close, the damp inefficient powder lying like snow in the ridges of the knuckles. "Oh, Ticki, Ticki," she said, "you won't leave me ever, will you? I haven't got any friends— not since the Tom Barlows went away." He lifted the moist hand and kissed the palm: he was bound by the pathos of her unattractiveness.

They walked side by side like a couple of policemen on duty into the lounge where Mrs. Halifax was dealing out the library books. It is seldom that anything is quite so bad as one fears: there was no reason to believe that they had been the subject of conversation. "Goody, goody," Mrs. Halifax called to them, "the new Clemence Dane's arrived." She was the most inoffensive woman in the station; she had long untidy hair, and one found hairpins inside the library books where she had marked her place. Scobie felt it quite safe to leave his wife in her company, for Mrs. Halifax had no malice and no capacity for gossip; her memory was too bad for anything to lodge there for long: she read the same novels over and over again without knowing it.

Scobie joined a group on the verandah. Fellowes, the sanitary inspector, was talking fiercely to Reith, the Chief Assistant Colonial Secretary, and a naval officer called Brigstock. "After all this is a club," he was saying, "not a railway refreshment-room." Ever since Fellowes had snatched his house, Scobie had done his best to like the man—it was one of the rules by which he set his life, to be a good loser. But sometimes he found it very hard to like Fellowes. The hot evening had not been good to him: the thin damp ginger hair, the small prickly moustache, the goosegog eyes, the scarlet cheeks, and the old Lancing tie. "Quite," said Brigstock, swaying slightly.

"What's the trouble?" Scobie asked.

Reith said, "He thinks we are not exclusive enough." He spoke with the comfortable irony of a man who had in his time been completely exclusive, who had in fact excluded from his solitary table in the Protectorate everyone but himself. Fellowes said hotly, "There are limits," fingering for confidence the Lancing tie.

"Tha's so," said Brigstock.

"I knew it would happen," Fellowes said, "as soon as we made every officer in the place an honorary member. Sooner or later they would begin to bring in undesirables. I'm not a snob, but in a place like this you've got to draw lines—for the sake of the women. It's not like it is at home."

"But what's the trouble?" Scobie asked.

"Honorary members," Fellowes said, "should not be allowed to introduce guests. Only the other day we had a private brought in. The army can be democratic if it likes, but not at our expense. That's another thing, there's not enough drink to go round as it is without these fellows."

"Tha's a point," Brigstock said, swaying more violently.

"I wish I knew what it was all about," Scobie said.

"The dentist from the 49th has brought in a civilian called Wilson, and this man Wilson wants to join the club. It puts everybody in a very embarrassing position."

"What's wrong with him?"

"He's one of the U.A.C. clerks. He can join the club in Sharp Town. What does he want to come up here for?"

"That club's not functioning," Reith said.

"Well, that's their fault, isn't it?" Over the sanitary inspector's shoulder Scobie could see the enormous range of the night. The fireflies signalled to and fro along the edge of the hill and the lamp of a patrol-boat moving on the bay could be distinguished only by its steadiness. "Black-out time," Reith said. "We'd better go in."

"Which is Wilson?" Scobie asked him.

"That's him over there. The poor devil looks lonely. He's only been out a few days."

Wilson stood uncomfortably alone in a wilderness of arm-chairs, pretending to look at a map on the wall. His pale face shone and trickled like plaster. He had obviously bought his tropical suit from a shipper who had worked off on him an unwanted line: it was oddly striped and liverish in colour. "You're Wilson, aren't you?" Reith said. "I saw your name in Col. Sec.'s book today."

"Yes, that's me," Wilson said.

"My name's Reith. I'm Chief Assistant Col. Sec. This is Scobie, the deputy-commissioner."

"I saw you this morning outside the Bedford Hotel, sir," Wilson said. There was something defenceless, it seemed to Scobie, in his whole attitude: he stood there waiting for people to be friendly or unfriendly—he didn't seem to expect one reaction more than another. He was like a dog. Nobody had yet drawn on his face the lines that make a human being.

"Have a drink, Wilson."

"I don't mind if I do, sir."

"Here's my wife," Scobie said. "Louise, this is Mr. Wilson."

"I've heard a lot about Mr. Wilson already," Louise said stiffly.

"You see, you're famous, Wilson," Scobie said. "You're a man from the town and you've gate-crashed Cape Station Club."

"I didn't know I was doing anything wrong. Major Cooper invited me."

"That reminds me," Reith said, "I must make an appointment with Cooper. I think I've got an abscess." He slid away.

"Cooper was telling me about the library," Wilson said, "and I thought perhaps . . ."

"Do you like reading?" Louise asked, and Scobie realized with relief that she was going to be kind to the poor devil. It was always a bit of a toss-up with Louise. Sometimes she could be the worst snob in the station, and it occurred to him with pity that perhaps now she believed she couldn't afford to be snobbish. Any new face that didn't "know" was welcome.

"Well," Wilson said, and fingered desperately at his thin moustache, "well . . ." It was as if he were gathering strength for a great confession or a great evasion.

"Detective stories?" Louise asked.

"I don't mind detective stories," Wilson said uneasily. "Some detective stories."

"Personally," Louise said, "I like poetry."

"Poetry," Wilson said, "yes." He took his fingers reluctantly away from his moustache, and something in his dog-like look of gratitude and hope made Scobie think with happiness: have I really found her a friend?

"I like poetry myself," Wilson said.

Scobie moved away towards the bar: once again a load was lifted from his mind. The evening was not spoilt: she would come home happy, go to bed happy. During one night a mood did not change, and happiness would survive until he left to go on duty. He could sleep. . . .

He saw a gathering of his junior officers in the bar. Fraser was there and Tod and a new man from Palestine with the extraordinary name of Thimblerigg. Scobie hesitated to go in. They were enjoying themselves, and they would not want a senior officer with them. "Infernal cheek," Tod was saying. They were probably talking about poor Wilson. Then before he could move away he heard Fraser's voice. "He's punished for it. Literary Louise has got him." Thimblerigg gave a small gurgling laugh, a bubble of gin forming on a plump lip.

Scobie walked rapidly back into the lounge. He went full tilt into an arm-chair and came to a halt. His vision moved jerkily back into focus, but sweat dripped into his right eye. The fingers that wiped it free shook like a drunkard's. He told himself: Be careful. This isn't a climate for emotion. It's a climate for meanness, malice, snobbery, but anything like hate or love drives a man off his head. He remembered Bowers sent home for punching the Governor's A.D.C. at a party, Makin the missionary who ended in an asylum at Chislehurst.

"It's damned hot," he said to someone who loomed vaguely beside him.

"You look bad, Scobie. Have a drink."

"No, thank you. Got to drive round on inspection."

Beside the bookshelves Louise was talking happily to Wilson, but he could feel the malice and snobbery of the world padding up like wolves around her. They wouldn't even let her enjoy her books, he thought, and his hand began to shake again. Approaching, he heard her say in her kindly Lady Bountiful manner, "You must come and have dinner with us one day. I've got a lot of books that might interest you."

"I'd love to," Wilson said.

"Just ring us up and take pot luck."

Scobie thought: what are those others worth that they have the nerve to sneer at any human being? He knew every one of her faults. How often he had winced at her patronage of strangers. He knew each phrase, each intonation that alienated others. Sometimes he longed to warn her—don't wear that dress, don't say that again, as a mother might teach a daughter, but he had to remain silent, aching with the foreknowledge of *her* loss of friends. The worst was when he detected in his colleagues an extra warmth of friendliness towards himself, as though they pitied him. What right have you, he longed to exclaim, to criticize her? This is my doing. This is what I've made of her. She wasn't always like this.

He came abruptly up to them and said, "My dear, I've got to go round the beats."

"Already?"

"I'm sorry."

"I'll stay, dear. Mrs. Halifax will run me home."

"I wish you'd come with me."

"What? Round the beats? It's ages since I've been."

"That's why I'd like you to come." He lifted her hand and kissed it: it was a challenge. He proclaimed to the whole club that he was not to be pitied, that he loved his wife, that they were happy. But nobody that mattered saw—Mrs. Halifax was busy with the books, Reith had gone long ago, Brigstock was in the bar, Fellowes talked too busily to Mrs. Castle to notice anything—nobody saw except Wilson.

Louise said, "I'll come another time, dear. But Mrs. Halifax has just promised to run Mr. Wilson home by our house. There's a book I want to lend him."

Scobie felt an immense gratitude to Wilson. "That's fine," he said, "fine. But stay and have a drink till I get back. I'll run you home to the Bedford. I shan't be late." He put a hand on Wilson's shoulder and prayed silently: Don't let her patronize him too far: don't let her be absurd: let her keep this friend at least. "I won't say good night," he said; "I'll expect to see you when I get back."

"It's very kind of you, sir."

"You mustn't sir me. You're not a policeman, Wilson. Thank your stars for that."

v

Scobie was later than he expected. It was the encounter with Yusef that delayed him. Half-way down the hill he found Yusef's car stuck by the roadside, with Yusef sleeping quietly in the back: the light from Scobie's car lit up the large pasty face, the lick of his white hair falling over the forehead, and just touched the beginning of the huge thighs in their tight white drill. Yusef's shirt was open at the neck and tendrils of black breast-hair coiled around the buttons.

"Can I help you?" Scobie unwillingly asked, and Yusef opened his eyes: the gold teeth fitted by his brother, the dentist, flashed instantaneously like a torch. If Fellowes drives by now, what a story, Scobie thought. The deputy-commissioner meeting Yusef, the storekeeper, clandestinely at night. To give help to a Syrian was only a degree less dangerous than to receive help.

"Ah, Major Scobie," Yusef said, "a friend in need is a friend indeed."

"Can I do anything for you?"

"We have been stranded a half-hour," Yusef said. "The cars have gone by, and I have thought—when will a Good Samaritan appear?"

"I haven't any spare oil to pour into your wounds, Yusef."

"Ha, ha, Major Scobie. That is very good. But if you would just give me a lift into town . . ."

Yusef settled himself into the Morris, easing a large thigh against the brakes.

"Your boy had better come in at the back."

"Let him stay here," Yusef said. "He will mend the car if he knows it is the only way he can get to bed." He folded his large fat hands over his knee and said, "You have a very fine car, Major Scobie. You must have paid four hundred pounds for it."

"One hundred and fifty," Scobie said.

"I would pay you four hundred."

"It isn't for sale, Yusef. Where would I get another?"

"Not now, but maybe when you leave."

"I'm not leaving."

"Oh, I had heard that you were resigning, Major Scobie."

"No."

"We shopkeepers hear so much—but all of it is unreliable gossip."

"How's business?"

"Oh, not bad. Not good."

"What I hear is that you've made several fortunes since the war. Unreliable gossip, of course."

"Well, Major Scobie, you know how it is. My store in Sharp Town, that does fine because I am there to keep an eye on it. My store in Macaulay Street—that does not bad because my sister is there. But my stores in Durban Street and Bond Street they do badly. I am cheated all the time. Like all my countrymen, I cannot read or write, and everyone cheats me."

"Gossip says you can keep all your stocks in all your stores in your head."

Yusef chuckled and beamed. "My memory is not bad. But it keeps me awake at night, Major Scobie. Unless I take a lot of whisky I keep thinking about Durban Street and Bond Street and Macaulay Street."

"Which shall I drop you at now?"

"Oh, now I go home to bed, Major Scobie. My house in Sharp Town, if you please. Won't you come in and have a little whisky?"

"Sorry. I'm on duty, Yusef."

"It is very kind of you, Major Scobie, to give me this lift. Would you let me show my gratitude by sending Mrs. Scobie a roll of silk?"

"Just what I wouldn't like, Yusef."

"Yes, yes, I know. It's very hard, all this gossip. Just because there are some Syrians like Tallit."

"You would like Tallit out of your way, wouldn't you, Yusef?"

"Yes, Major Scobie. It would be for my good, but it would also be for your good."

"You sold him some of those fake diamonds last year, didn't you?"

"Oh, Major Scobie, you don't really believe I'd get the better of anyone like that. Some of the poor Syrians suffered a great deal over those diamonds, Major Scobie. It would be a shame to deceive your own people like that."

"They shouldn't have broken the law by buying diamonds. Some of them even had the nerve to complain to the police."

"They are very ignorant, poor fellows."

"You weren't as ignorant as all that, were you, Yusef?"

"If you ask me, Major Scobie, it was Tallit. Otherwise, why does he pretend I sold him the diamonds?"

Scobie drove slowly. The rough street was crowded. Thin black bodies weaved like daddy-long-legs in the dimmed headlights. "How long will the rice shortage go on, Yusef?"

"You know as much about that as I do, Major Scobie."

"I know these poor devils can't get rice at the controlled price."

"I've heard, Major Scobie, that they can't get their share of the free distribution unless they tip the policeman at the gate."

It was quite true. There was a retort in this colony to every accusation. There was always a blacker corruption elsewhere to be pointed at. The scandalmongers of the secretariat fulfilled a useful purpose—they kept alive the idea that no one was to be trusted. That was better than complacence. Why, he wondered, swerving the car to avoid a dead pye-dog, do I love this place so much? Is it because here human nature hasn't had time to disguise itself? Nobody here could ever talk about a heaven on earth. Heaven remained rigidly in its proper place on the other side of death, and on this side flourished the injustices, the cruelties, the meanness that elsewhere people so cleverly hushed up. Here you could love human beings nearly as God loved them, knowing the worst: you didn't love a pose, a pretty dress, a sentiment artfully assumed. He felt a sudden affection for Yusef. He said, "Two wrongs don't make a right. One day, Yusef, you'll find my foot under your fat arse."

"Maybe, Major Scobie, or maybe we'll be friends together. That is what I should like more than anything in the world."

They drew up outside the Sharp Town house and Yusef's steward ran out with a torch to light him in. "Major Scobie," Yusef said, "it would give me such pleasure to give you a glass of whisky. I think I could help you a lot. I am very patriotic, Major Scobie."

"That's why you are hoarding your cottons against a Vichy invasion, isn't it? They will be worth more than English pounds."

"The *Esperança* is in tomorrow, isn't she?"

"Probably."

"What a waste of time it is searching a big ship like that for diamonds. Unless you know beforehand exactly where they are. You know that when the ship returns to Angola a seaman reports where you looked. You will sift all the sugar in the hold. You will search the lard in the kitchens because someone once told Captain Druce that a diamond can be heated and dropped in the middle of a tin of lard. Of course the cabins and the ventilators and the lockers. Tubes of toothpaste. Do you think one day you will find one little diamond?"

"No."

"I don't either."

vi

A hurricane-lamp burned at each corner of the wooden pyramids of crates. Across the black slow water he could just make out the naval depot ship, a disused liner, where she lay, so it was believed, on a reef of empty whisky bottles. He stood quietly for a while breathing in the heavy smell of the sea. Within half a mile of him a whole convoy lay at anchor, but all he could detect were the long shadow of the depot ship and a scatter of small red lights as though a street were up: he could hear nothing from the water but the water itself, slapping against the jetties. The magic of this place never failed him: here he kept his foothold on the very edge of a strange continent.

Somewhere in the darkness two rats scuffled. These waterside rats were the size of rabbits. The natives called them pigs and ate them roasted; the name helped to distinguish them from the wharf rats, who were a human breed. Walking along a light railway Scobie made in the direction of the markets. At the corner of a warehouse he came on two policemen.

"Anything to report?"

"No, sah."

"Been along this way?"

"Oh yes, sah, we just come from there."

He knew that they were lying: they would never go alone to that end of the wharf, the playground of the human rats, unless they had a white officer to guard them. The rats were cowards but dangerous—boys of sixteen or so, armed with razors or bits of broken bottle, they swarmed in groups around the warehouses, pilfering if they found an easily opened case, settling like flies around any drunken sailor who stumbled their way, occasionally slashing a policeman who had made himself unpopular with one of their innumerable relatives. Gates couldn't keep them off the wharf: they swam round from Kru Town or the fishing beaches.

"Come on," Scobie said, "we'll have another look."

With weary patience the policemen trailed behind him, half a mile one way, half a mile the other. Only the pigs moved on the wharf, and the water slapped. One of the policemen said self-righteously, "Quiet night, sah." They shone their torches with self-conscious assiduity from one side to another, lighting the abandoned chassis of a car, an empty truck, the corner of a tarpaulin, a bottle standing at the corner of a warehouse with palm leaves stuffed in for a cork. Scobie said, "What's that?" One of his official nightmares was an incendiary bomb: it was so easy to prepare: every day men from Vichy territory came into town with smuggled cattle—they were encouraged to come in for the sake of the meat supply. On this side of the border native saboteurs were being trained in case of invasion: why not on the other side?

"Let me see it," he said, but neither of the policemen moved to touch it.

"Only native medicine, sah," one of them said with a skin-deep sneer.

Scobie picked the bottle up. It was a dimpled Haig, and when he drew out the palm leaves the stench of dog's pizzle and nameless decay blew out like a gas escape. A nerve in his head beat with sudden irritation. For no reason at all he remembered Fraser's flushed face and Thimblerigg's giggle. The stench from the bottle moved him with nausea, and he felt his fingers polluted by the palm leaves. He threw the bottle over the wharf, and the hungry mouth of the water received it with a single belch, but the contents were scattered on the air, and the whole windless place smelt sour and ammoniac. The policemen were silent: Scobie was aware of their mute disapproval. He should have left the bottle where it stood: it had been placed there for one purpose, directed at one person, but now that its contents had been released, it was as if the evil thought were left to wander blindly through the air, to settle maybe on the innocent.

"Good night," Scobie said and turned abruptly on his heel. He had not gone twenty yards before he heard their boots scuffling rapidly away from the dangerous area.

Scobie drove up to the police station by way of Pitt Street. Outside the brothel on the left-hand side the girls were sitting along the pavement taking a bit of air. Within the police station behind the black-out blinds the scent of a monkey house thickened for the night. The sergeant on duty took his legs off the table in the charge-room and stood to attention.

"Anything to report?"

"Five drunk and disorderly, sah. I lock them in the big cell."

"Anything else?"

"Two Frenchmen, sah, with no passes."

"Black?"

"Yes, sah."

"Where were they found?"

"In Pitt Street, sah."

"I'll see them in the morning. What about the launch? Is it running all right? I shall want to go out to the *Esperança.*"

"It's broken, sah. Mr. Fraser he try to mend it, sah, but it humbug all the time."

"What time does Mr. Fraser come on duty?"

"Seven, sah."

"Tell him I shan't want him to go out to the *Esperança.*
I'm going out myself. If the launch isn't ready, I'll go with
the F.S.P."

"Yes, sah."

Climbing again into his car, pushing at the sluggish
starter, Scobie thought that a man was surely entitled to
that much revenge. Revenge was good for the character: out
of revenge grew forgiveness. He began to whistle, driving
back through Kru Town. He was almost happy: he only
needed to be quite certain that nothing had happened at the
club after he left, that at this moment, 10:55 p.m., Louise
was at ease, content. He could face the next hour when the
next hour arrived.

vii

Before he went indoors he walked round to the seaward side
of the house to check the black-out. He could hear the murmur of Louise's voice inside: she was probably reading poetry. He thought: by God, what right has that young fool
Fraser to despise her for that? and then his anger moved
away again, like a shabby man, when he thought of Fraser's
disappointment in the morning—no Portuguese visit, no
present for his best girl, only the hot humdrum office day.
Feeling for the handle of the back door to avoid flashing his
torch, he tore his right hand on a splinter.

He came into the lighted room and saw that his hand was
dripping with blood. "Oh, darling," Louise said, "what have
you done?" and covered her face. She couldn't bear the sight
of blood. "Can I help you, sir?" Wilson asked. He tried to
rise, but he was sitting in a low chair at Louise's feet and his
knees were piled with books.

"It's all right," Scobie said. "It's only a scratch. I can see
to it myself. Just tell Ali to bring a bottle of water." Half-
way upstairs he heard the voice resume. Louise said, "A
lovely poem about a pylon." Scobie walked into the bathroom, disturbing a rat that had been couched on the cool
rim of the bath, like a cat on a gravestone.

Scobie sat down on the edge of the bath and let his hand drip into the lavatory pail among the wood shavings. Just as in his own office the sense of home surrounded him. Louise's ingenuity had been able to do little with this room: the bath of scratched enamel with a single tap which always ceased to work before the end of the dry season: the tin bucket under the lavatory seat emptied once a day: the fixed basin with another useless tap: bare floorboards: drab green black-out curtains. The only improvements Louise had been able to impose were the cork mat by the bath, the bright white medicine cabinet.

The rest of the room was all his own. It was like a relic of his youth carried from house to house. It had been like this years ago in his first house before he married. This was the room in which he had always been alone.

Ali came in, his pink soles flapping on the floorboards, carrying a bottle of water from the filter. "The back door humbug me," Scobie explained. He held his hand out over the washbasin, while Ali poured the water over the wound. The boy made gentle clucking sounds of commiseration: his hands were as gentle as a girl's. When Scobie said impatiently, "That's enough," Ali paid him no attention. "Too much dirt," he said.

"Now iodine." The smallest scratch in this country turned green if it were neglected for an hour. "Again," he said, "pour it over," wincing at the sting. Down below out of the swing of voices the word "beauty" detached itself and sank back into the trough. "Now the Elastoplast."

"No," Ali said, "no. Bandage better."

"All right. Bandage then." Years ago he had taught Ali to bandage: now he could tie one as expertly as a doctor.

"Good night, Ali. Go to bed. I shan't want you again."

"Missus want drinks."

"No. I'll attend to the drinks. You can go to bed." Alone he sat down again on the edge of the bath. The wound had jarred him a little and anyway he was unwilling to join the two downstairs, for his presence would embarrass Wilson. A man couldn't listen to a woman reading poetry in the presence of an outsider. "I had rather be a kitten and cry mew . . ." but that wasn't really his attitude. He did not despise: he just couldn't understand such bare relations of intimate feeling. And besides he was happy here, sitting where the rat had sat, in his own world. He began to think of the *Esperança* and of the next day's work.

"Darling," Louise called up the stairs, "are you all right? Can you drive Mr. Wilson home?"

"I can walk, Mrs. Scobie."

"Nonsense."

"Yes, really."

"Coming," Scobie called. "Of course I'll drive you back." When he joined them Louise took the bandaged hand tenderly in hers. "Oh the poor hand," she said. "Does it hurt?" She was not afraid of the clean white bandage: it was like a patient in a hospital with the sheets drawn tidily up to the chin. One could bring grapes and never know the details of the scalpel wound out of sight. She put her lips to the bandage and left a little smear of orange lipstick.

"It's quite all right," Scobie said.

"Really, sir. I can walk."

"Of course you won't walk. Come along, get in."

The light from the dashboard lit up a patch of Wilson's extraordinary suit. He leant out of the car and cried, "Good night, Mrs. Scobie. It's been lovely. I can't thank you enough." The words vibrated with sincerity: it gave them the sound of a foreign language—the sound of English spoken in England. Here intonations changed in the course of a few months, became high-pitched and insincere, or flat and guarded. You could tell that Wilson was fresh from home.

"You must come again soon," Scobie said, as they drove down the Burnside road towards the Bedford Hotel, remembering Louise's happy face.

viii

The smart of his wounded hand woke Scobie at two in the

morning. He lay coiled like a watch-spring on the outside of the bed, trying to keep his body away from Louise's: wherever they touched—if it were only a finger lying against a finger—sweat started. Even when they were separated the heat trembled between them. The moonlight lay on the dressing-table like coolness and lit the bottles of lotion, the little pots of cream, the edge of a photograph frame. At once he began to listen for Louise's breathing.

It came irregularly in jerks. She was awake. He put his hand up and touched the hot moist hair: she lay stiffly, as though she were guarding a secret. Sick at heart, knowing what he would find, he moved his fingers down until they touched her lids. She was crying. He felt an enormous tiredness, bracing himself to comfort her. "Darling," he said, "I love you." It was how he always began. Comfort, like the act of sex, developed a routine.

"I know," she said, "I know." It was how she always answered. He blamed himself for being heartless because the idea occurred to him that it was two o'clock: this might go on for hours, and at six the day's work began. He moved the hair away from her forehead and said, "The rains will soon be here. You'll feel better then."

"I feel all right," she said and began to sob.

"What is it, darling? Tell me." He swallowed. "Tell Ticki." He hated the name she had given him, but it always worked. She said, "Oh Ticki, Ticki. I can't go on."

"I thought you were happy tonight."

"I was—but think of being happy because a U.A.C. clerk was nice to me. Ticki, why won't they like me?"

"Don't be silly, darling. It's just the heat: it makes you fancy things. They all like you."

"Only Wilson," she repeated with despair and shame and began to sob again.

"Wilson's all right."

"They won't have him at the club. He gate-crashed with the dentist. They'll be laughing about him and me. Oh Ticki, Ticki, please let me go away and begin again."

"Of course, darling," he said; "of course," staring out through the net and through the window to the quiet flat infested sea. "Where to?"

"I could go to South Africa and wait until you have leave. Ticki, you'll be retiring soon. I'll get a home ready for you, Ticki."

He flinched a little away from her, and then hurriedly in case she had noticed, lifted her damp hand and kissed the palm. "It will cost a lot, darling." The thought of retirement set his nerves twitching and straining: he always prayed that death would come first. He had prepared his life insurance in that hope: it was payable only on death. He thought of a home, a permanent home: the gay artistic curtains, the bookshelves full of Louise's books, a pretty tiled bathroom, no office anywhere—a home for two until death, no change any more before eternity settled in.

"Ticki, I can't bear it any longer here."

"I'll have to figure it out, darling."

"Ethel Maybury's in South Africa, and the Collinses. We've got friends in South Africa."

"Prices are high."

"You could drop some of your silly old life insurances, Ticki. And, Ticki, you could economize here without me. You could have your meals at the mess and do without the cook."

"He doesn't cost much."

"Every little helps, Ticki."

"I'd miss you," he said.

"No, Ticki, you wouldn't," she said, and surprised him by the range of her sad spasmodic understanding. "After all," she said, "there's nobody to save for."

He said gently, "I'll try and work something out. You know if it's possible I'd do anything for you—anything."

"This isn't just two-in-the-morning comfort, Ticki, is it? You will do something?"

"Yes, dear. I'll manage somehow." He was surprised how quickly she went to sleep: she was like a tired carrier who has slipped his load. She was asleep before he had finished his sentence, clutching one of his fingers like a child, breathing as easily. The load lay beside him now, and he prepared to lift it.

[2]

i

At eight in the morning on his way to the jetty Scobie called at the bank. The manager's office was shaded and cool: a glass of iced water stood on top of a safe. "Good morning, Robinson."

Robinson was tall and hollow-chested and bitter because he hadn't been posted to Nigeria. He said, "When will this filthy weather break? The rains are late."

"They've started in the Protectorate."

"In Nigeria," Robinson said, "one always knew where one was. What can I do for you, Scobie?"

"Do you mind if I sit down?"

"Of course. I never sit down before ten myself. Standing up keeps the digestion in order." He rambled restlessly across his office on legs like stilts: he took a sip of the iced water with distaste as though it were medicine. On his desk Scobie saw a book called *Diseases of the Urinary Tract* open at a coloured illustration. "What can I do for you?" Robinson repeated.

"Give me two hundred and fifty pounds," Scobie said with a nervous attempt at jocularity.

"You people always think a bank's made of money," Robinson mechanically jested. "How much do you really want?"

"Three fifty."

"What's your balance at the moment?"

"I think about thirty pounds. It's the end of the month."

"We'd better check up on that." He called a clerk and while they waited Robinson paced the little room—six paces to the wall and round again. "There and back a hundred and seventy-six times," he said, "makes a mile. I try and put in three miles before lunch. It keeps one healthy. In Nigeria I used to walk a mile and a half to breakfast at the club, and then a mile and a half back to the office. Nowhere fit to walk here," he said, pivoting on the carpet. A clerk laid a slip of paper on the desk. Robinson held it close to his eyes, as though he wanted to smell it. "Twenty-eight pounds fifteen and sevenpence," he said.

"I want to send my wife to South Africa."

"Oh yes. Yes."

"I daresay," Scobie said, "I might do it on a bit less. I shan't be able to allow her very much on my salary though."

"I really don't see how . . ."

"I thought perhaps I could get an overdraft," he said vaguely. "Lots of people have them, don't they? Do you know I believe I only had one once—for a few weeks—for about fifteen pounds. I didn't like it. It scared me. I always felt I owed the bank manager the money."

"The trouble is, Scobie," Robinson said, "we've had orders to be very strict about overdrafts. It's the war, you know. There's one valuable security nobody can offer now, his life."

"Yes, I see that of course. But my life's pretty good and I'm not stirring from here. No submarines for me. And the job's secure, Robinson," he went on with the same ineffectual attempt at flippancy.

"The Commissioner's retiring, isn't he?" Robinson said, reaching the safe at the end of the room and turning.

"Yes, but I'm not."

"I'm glad to hear that, Scobie. There've been rumours. . . ."

"I suppose I'll have to retire one day, but that's a long way off. I'd much rather die in my boots. There's always my life insurance policy, Robinson. What about that for security?"

"You know you dropped one insurance three years ago."

"That was the year Louise went home for an operation."

"I don't think the paid-up value of the other two amounts to much, Scobie."

"Still they protect you in case of death, don't they?"

"If you go on paying the premiums. We haven't any guarantee, you know."

"Of course not," Scobie said, "I see that."

"I'm very sorry, Scobie. This isn't personal. It's the policy of the bank. If you'd wanted fifty pounds, I'd have lent it you myself."

"Forget it, Robinson," Scobie said. "It's not important." He gave his embarrassed laugh. "The boys at the Secretariat would say I can always pick it up in bribes. How's Molly?"

"She's very well, thank you. Wish I were the same."

"You read too many of those medical books, Robinson."

"A man's got to know what's wrong with him. Going to be at the club tonight?"

"I don't think so. Louise is tired. You know how it is before the rains. Sorry to have kept you, Robinson. I must be getting along to the wharf."

He walked rapidly down-hill from the bank with his head bent. He felt as though he had been detected in a mean action—he had asked for money and had been refused. Louise had deserved better of him. It seemed to him that he must have failed in some way in manhood.

ii

Druce had come out himself to the *Esperança* with his squad of F.S.P. men. At the gangway a steward awaited them with an invitation to join the captain for drinks in his cabin. The officer in charge of the naval guard was already there before them. This was a regular part of the fortnightly routine—the establishment of friendly relations. By accepting his hospitality they tried to ease down for the neutral the bitter pill of search; below the bridge the search party would proceed smoothly without them. While the first-class passengers had their passports examined, their cabins would be ransacked by a squad of the F.S.P. Already others were going through the hold—the dreary hopeless business of sifting rice. What had Yusef said, "Have you ever found one little diamond? Do you think you ever will?" In a few minutes when relations had become sufficiently smooth after the drinks Scobie would have the unpleasant task of searching the captain's own cabin. The stiff disjointed conversation was carried on mainly by the naval lieutenant.

The captain wiped his fat yellow face and said, "Of course for the English I feel in the heart an enormous admiration."

"We don't like doing it, you know," the lieutenant said. "Hard luck being a neutral."

"My heart," the Portuguese captain said, "is full of admiration for your great struggle. There is no room for resentment. Some of my people feel resentment. Me none." The face streamed with sweat, and the eyeballs were contused. The man kept on speaking of his heart, but it seemed to Scobie that a long deep surgical operation would have been required to find it.

"Very good of you," the lieutenant said. "Appreciate your attitude."

"Another glass of port, gentlemen?"

"Don't mind if I do. Nothing like this on shore you know. You, Scobie?"

"No, thanks."

"I hope you won't find it necessary to keep us here to-night, major?"

Scobie said, "I don't think there's any possibility of your getting away before midday tomorrow."

"Will do our best, of course," the lieutenant said.

"On my honour, gentlemen, my hand upon my heart, you will find no bad hats among my passengers. And the crew—I know them all."

Druce said, "It's a formality, captain, which we have to go through."

"Have a cigar," the captain said. "Throw away that cigarette. Here is a very special box."

Druce lit the cigar, which began to spark and crackle. The captain giggled. "Only my joke, gentlemen. Quite harmless. I keep the box for my friends. The English have a wonderful sense of humour. I know you will not be angry. A German yes, an Englishman no. It is quite cricket, eh?"

"Very funny," Druce said sourly, laying the cigar down on the ash-tray the captain held out to him. The ash-tray, presumably set off by the captain's finger, began to play a little tinkly tune. Druce jerked again: he was overdue for leave and his nerves were unsteady. The captain smiled and sweated. "Swiss," he said. "A wonderful people. Neutral too."

One of the Field Security men came in and gave Druce a note. He passed it to Scobie to read. *Steward, who is under notice of dismissal, says the captain has letters concealed in his bathroom.*

Druce said, "I think I'd better go and make them hustle down below. Coming, Evans? Many thanks for the port, captain."

Scobie was left alone with the captain. This was the part of the job he always hated. These men were not criminals: they were merely breaking regulations enforced on the shipping companies by the navicert system. You never knew in a search what you would find. A man's bedroom was his private life. Prying in drawers you came on humiliations; little petty vices were tucked out of sight like a soiled handkerchief. Under a pile of linen you might come on a grief he was trying to forget. Scobie said gently, "I'm afraid, captain, I'll have to look around. You know it's a formality."

"You must do your duty, major," the Portuguese said.

Scobie went quickly and neatly through the cabin: he never moved a thing without replacing it exactly: he was like a careful housewife. The captain stood with his back to Scobie looking out on to the bridge; it was as if he preferred not to embarrass his guest in the odious task. Scobie came to an end, closing the box of French letters and putting them carefully back in the top drawer of the locker with the handkerchiefs, the gaudy ties and the little bundle of dirty handkerchiefs. "All finished?" the captain asked politely, turning his head.

"That door," Scobie said, "what would be through there?"

"That is only the bathroom, the w.c."

"I think I'd better take a look."

"Of course, major, but there is not much cover there to conceal anything."

"If you don't mind. . . ."

"Of course not. It is your duty."

The bathroom was bare and extraordinarily dirty. The bath was rimmed with dry grey soap, and the tiles slopped under his feet. The problem was to find the right place quickly. He couldn't linger here without disclosing the fact that he had special information. The search had got to have all the appearances of formality—neither too lax nor too thorough. "This won't take long," he said cheerily and caught sight of the fat calm face in the shaving-mirror. The information, of course, might be false, given by the steward simply in order to cause trouble.

Scobie opened the medicine-cabinet and went rapidly through the contents: unscrewing the toothpaste, opening the razor box, dipping his finger into the shaving-cream. He did not expect to find anything there. But the search gave him time to think. He went next to the taps, turned the water on, felt up each funnel with his finger. The floor engaged his attention: there were no possibilities of concealment there. The porthole: he examined the big screws and swung the inner mask to and fro. Every time he turned he caught sight of the captain's face in the mirror, calm, patient, complacent. It said "cold, cold" to him all the while, as in a children's game.

Finally, the lavatory: he lifted up the wooden seat: nothing had been laid between the porcelain and the wood. He put his hand on the lavatory chain, and in the mirror became aware for the first time of a tension: the brown eyes were no longer on his face, they were fixed on something else, and following that gaze home, he saw his own hand tighten on the chain.

Is the cistern empty of water? he wondered, and pulled. Gurgling and pounding in the pipes, the water flushed down. He turned away and the Portuguese said with a smugness he was unable to conceal, "You see, major." And at that moment Scobie did see. I'm becoming careless, he thought. He lifted the cap of the cistern. Fixed in the cap with adhesive tape and clear of the water lay a letter.

He looked at the address—a Frau Groener in Friedrich-strasse, Leipzig. He repeated, "I'm sorry, captain," and because the man didn't answer, he looked up and saw the tears beginning to pursue the sweat down the hot fat cheeks. "I'll have to take it away," Scobie said, "and report. . . ."

"Oh, this war," the captain burst out, "how I hate this war."

"We've got cause to hate it too, you know," Scobie said.

"A man is ruined because he writes to his daughter."

"Daughter?"

"Yes. She is Frau Groener. Open it and read. You will see."

"I can't do that. I must leave it to the censorship. Why didn't you wait to write till you got to Lisbon, captain?"

The man had lowered his bulk on to the edge of the bath as though it were a heavy sack his shoulders could no longer bear. He kept on wiping his eyes with the back of his hand like a child—an unattractive child, the fat boy of the school. Against the beautiful and the clever and the successful, one can wage a pitiless war, but not against the unattractive: then the millstone weighs on the breast. Scobie knew he should have taken the letter and gone; he could do no good with his sympathy.

The captain moaned, "If you had a daughter you'd understand. You haven't got one," he accused, as though there were a crime in sterility.

"No."

"She is anxious about me. She loves me," he said, raising his tear-drenched face as though he must drive the unlikely statement home. "She loves *me,*" he repeated mournfully.

"But why not write from Lisbon?" Scobie asked again. "Why run this risk?"

"I am alone. I have no wife," the captain said. "One cannot always wait to speak. And in Lisbon—you know how things go—friends, wine. I have a little woman there too who is jealous even of my daughter. There are rows, the time passes. In a week I must be off again. It was always so easy before this voyage."

Scobie believed him. The story was sufficiently irrational to be true. Even in war-time one must sometimes exercise the faculty of belief if it is not to atrophy. He said, "I'm sorry. There's nothing I can do about it. Perhaps nothing will happen."

"Your authorities," the captain said, "will blacklist me. You know what that means. The consul will not give a navicert to any ship with me as captain. I shall starve on shore."

"There are so many slips," Scobie said, "in these matters. Files get mislaid. You may hear no more about it."

"I shall pray," the man said without hope.

"Why not?" Scobie said.

"You are an Englishman. You wouldn't believe in prayer."

"I'm a Catholic, too," Scobie said.

The fat face looked quickly up at him. "A Catholic?" he exclaimed with hope. For the first time he began to plead. He was like a man who meets a fellow countryman in a strange continent. He began to talk rapidly of his daughter in Leipzig; he produced a battered pocket-book and a yellowing snap-shot of a stout young Portuguese woman as graceless as himself. The little bathroom was stiflingly hot and the captain repeated again and again, "You will understand." He had discovered suddenly how much they had in common: the plaster statues with the swords in the bleeding heart: the whisper behind the confessional curtains: the holy coats and the liquefaction of blood: the dark side chapels and the intricate movements, and somewhere behind it all the love of God. "And in Lisbon," he said, "she will be waiting, she will take me home, she will take away my trousers so that I cannot go out alone: every day it will be drink and quarrels until we go to bed. You will understand. I cannot write to my daughter from Lisbon. She loves me so much and she waits." He shifted his fat thigh and said, "The pureness of that love," and wept. They had in common all the wide region of repentance and longing.

Their kinship gave the captain courage to try another angle. He said, "I am a poor man, but I have enough money to spare. . . ." He would never have attempted to bribe an Englishman: it was the most sincere compliment he could pay to their common religion.

"I'm sorry," Scobie said.

"I have English pounds. I will give you twenty English pounds . . . fifty." He implored. "A hundred . . . that is all I have saved."

"It can't be done," Scobie said. He put the letter quickly in his pocket and turned away. The last time he saw the captain as he looked back from the door of the cabin, he was beating his head against the cistern, the tears catching in the folds of his cheeks. As he went down to join Druce in the saloon he could feel the millstone weighing on his breast. How I hate this war, he thought, in the very words the captain had used.

iii

The letter to the daughter in Leipzig, and a small bundle of correspondence found in the kitchens, was the sole result of eight hours' search by fifteen men. It could be counted an average day. When Scobie reached the police station he looked in to see the Commissioner, but his office was empty, so he sat down in his own room under the handcuffs and began to write his report. *A special search was made of the cabins and effects of the passengers named in your telegrams . . . with no result.* The letter to the daughter in Leipzig lay on the desk beside him. Outside it was dark. The smell of the cells seeped in under the door, and in the next office Fraser was singing to himself the same tune he had sung every evening since his last leave:

> "What will we care for
> The why and the wherefore,
> When you and I
> Are pushing up the daisies?"

It seemed to Scobie that life was immeasurably long. Couldn't the test of man have been carried out in fewer years? Couldn't we have committed our first major sin at seven, have ruined ourselves for love or hate at ten, have clutched at redemption on a fifteen-year-old death-bed? He wrote: *A steward who had been dismissed for incompetence reported that the captain had correspondence concealed in his bathroom. I made a search and found the enclosed letter addressed to Frau Groener in Leipzig concealed in the lid of the lavatory cistern. An instruction on this hiding-place might well be circulated, as it has not been encountered before at this station. The letter was fixed by tape above the water-line. . . .*

He sat there staring at the paper, his brain confused with the conflict that had really been decided hours ago when Druce said to him in the saloon, "Anything?" and he had shrugged his shoulders in a gesture he left Druce to interpret. Had he ever intended it to mean: "The usual private correspondence we are always finding." Druce had taken it for "No." Scobie put his hand against his forehead and shivered: the sweat seeped between his fingers, and he thought, Am I in for a touch of fever? Perhaps it was because his temperature had risen that it seemed to him he was on the verge of a new life. One felt this way before a proposal of marriage or a first crime.

Scobie took the letter and opened it. The act was irrevocable, for no one in this city had the right to open clandestine mail. A microphotograph might be concealed in the gum of an envelope. Even a simple word code would be beyond him; his knowledge of Portuguese would take him no farther than the most surface meaning. Every letter found—however obviously innocent—must be sent to the London censors unopened. Scobie against the strictest orders was exercising his own imperfect judgment. He thought to himself: If the letter is suspicious, I will send my report. I can explain the torn envelope. The captain insisted on opening the letter to show me the contents. But if he wrote that, he would be unjustly blackening the case against the captain, for what better way could he have found for destroying a microphotograph? There must be some lie to be told, Scobie thought, but he was unaccustomed to lies. With the letter in his hand, held carefully over the white blotting-pad, so that he could detect anything that might fall from between the leaves, he decided that he would write a full report on all the circumstances, including his own act.

Dear little money spider, the letter began, *your father who loves you more than anything upon earth will try to send you a little more money this time. I know how hard things are for you, and my heart bleeds. Little money spider, if only I could feel your fingers running across my cheek. How is it that a great fat father like I am should have so tiny and beautiful a daughter? Now, little money spider, I will tell you everything that has happened to me. We left Lobito a week ago after only four days in port. I stayed one night with Señor Aranjuez and I drank more wine than was good for me, but all my talk was of you. I was good all the time I was in port because I had promised my little money spider, and I went to Confession and Communion, so that if anything should happen to me on the way to Lisbon—for who knows in these terrible days?—I should not have to live my eternity away from my little spider. Since we left Lobito we have had good weather. Even the passengers are not sea-sick. Tomorrow night, because Africa will be at last behind us, we shall have a ship's concert, and I shall perform on my whistle. All the time I perform I shall remember the days when my little money spider sat on my knee and listened. My dear, I am growing old, and after every voyage I am fatter: I am not a good man, and sometimes I fear that my soul in all this hulk of flesh is no larger than a pea. You do not know how easy it is for a man like me to commit the unforgivable despair. Then I think of my daughter. There was just enough good in me once for you to be fashioned. A wife shares too much of a man's sin for perfect love. But a daughter may save him at the last. Pray for me, little spider. Your father who loves you more than life.*

Mais que a vida. Scobie felt no doubt at all of the sincerity of this letter. This was not written to conceal a photograph of the Cape Town defences or a microphotograph report on troop movements at Durban. It should, he knew, be tested for secret ink, examined under a microscope, and the inner lining of the envelope exposed. Nothing should be left to chance with a clandestine letter. But he had committed himself to a belief. He tore the letter up, and his own report with it, and carried the scraps out to the incinerator in the yard—a petrol-tin standing upon two bricks with its sides punctured to make a draught. As he struck a match to light the papers, Fraser joined him in the yard. *"What will we care for the why and the wherefore?"* On the top of the scraps lay unmistakably half a foreign envelope: one could even read part of the address—Friedrichstrasse. He quickly held the match to the uppermost scrap as Fraser crossed the yard, striding with unbearable youth. The scrap went up in flame, and in the heat of the fire another scrap uncurled the name of Groener. Fraser said cheerfully, "Burning the evidence?" and looked down into the tin. The name had blackened: there was nothing there surely that Fraser could see—except a brown triangle of envelope that seemed to Scobie obviously foreign. He ground it out of existence with a stick and looked up at Fraser to see whether he could detect any surprise or suspicion. There was nothing to be read in the vacuous face, blank as a school notice-board out of term. Only his own heart-beats told him he was guilty—that he had joined the ranks of the corrupt police officers—Bailey who had kept a safe deposit in another city, Crayshaw who had been found with diamonds, Boyston against whom nothing had been definitely proved and who had been invalided out. They had been corrupted by money, and he had been corrupted by sentiment. Sentiment was the more dangerous, because you couldn't name its price. A man open to bribes was to be relied upon below a certain figure, but sentiment might uncoil in the heart at a name, a photograph, even a smell remembered.

"What sort of day, sir?" Fraser asked, staring at the small pile of ash. Perhaps he was thinking that it should have been his day.

"The usual kind of a day," Scobie said.

"How about the captain?" Fraser asked, looking down into the petrol-tin, beginning to hum again his languid tune.

"The captain?" Scobie said.

"Oh, Druce told me some fellow informed on him."

"Just the usual thing," Scobie said. "A dismissed steward with a grudge. Didn't Druce tell you we found nothing?"

"No," Fraser said, "he didn't seem to be sure. Goodnight, sir. I must be pushing off to the mess."

"Thimblerigg on duty?"

"Yes, sir."

Scobie watched him go. The back was as vacuous as the face: one could read nothing there. Scobie thought, what a fool I have been. What a fool. He owed his duty to Louise, not to a fat sentimental Portuguese skipper who had broken the rules of his own company for the sake of a daughter equally unattractive. That had been the turning point, the daughter. And now, Scobie thought, I must return home: I shall put the car away in the garage, and Ali will come forward with his torch to light me to the door. She will be sitting there between two draughts for coolness, and I shall read on her face the story of what she has been thinking all day. She will have been hoping that everything is fixed, that

I shall say, "I've put your name down at the agent's for South Africa," but she'll be afraid that nothing so good as that will ever happen to us. She'll wait for me to speak, and I shall try to talk about anything under the sun to postpone seeing her misery (it would be waiting at the corners of her mouth to take possession of her whole face). He knew exactly how things would go: it had happened so often before. He rehearsed every word, going back into his office, locking his desk, going down to his car. People talk about the courage of condemned men walking to the place of execution: sometimes it needs as much courage to walk with any kind of bearing towards another person's habitual misery. He forgot Fraser: he forgot everything but the scene ahead: I shall go in and say, "Good evening, sweetheart," and she'll say, "Good evening, darling. What kind of a day?" and I'll talk and talk, but all the time I shall know I'm coming nearer to the moment when I shall say, "What about you, darling?" and let the misery in.

iv

"What about you, darling?" He turned quickly away from her and began to fix two more pink gins. There was a tacit understanding between them that "liquor helped"; growing more miserable with every glass one hoped for the moment of relief.

"You don't really want to know about *me*."

"Of course I do, darling. What sort of a day have you had?"

"Ticki, why are you such a coward? Why don't you tell me it's all off?"

"All off?"

"You know what I mean—the passage. You've been talking and talking since you came in about the *Esperança*. There's a Portuguese ship in once a fortnight. You don't talk that way every time. I'm not a child, Ticki. Why don't you say straight out—'you can't go'?"

He grinned miserably at his glass, twisting it round and

round to let the angostura cling along the curve. He said, "That wouldn't be true. I'll find some way." Reluctantly he had recourse to the hated nickname. If that failed, the misery would deepen and go right on through the short night he needed for sleep. "Trust Ticki," he said. It was as if a ligament tightened in his brain with the suspense. If only I could postpone the misery, he thought, until daylight. Misery is worse in the darkness: there's nothing to look at except the green black-out curtains, the Government furniture, the flying ants scattering their wings over the table: a hundred yards away the Creoles' pye-dogs yapped and wailed. "Look at that little beggar," he said, pointing at the house lizard that always came out upon the wall about this time to hunt for moths and cockroaches. He said, "We only got the idea last night. These things take time to fix. Ways and means, ways and means," he said with strained humour.

"Have you been to the bank?"

"Yes," he admitted.

"And you couldn't get the money?"

"No. They couldn't manage it. Have another gin-and-bitters, darling?"

She held her glass out to him, crying dumbly; her face reddened when she cried—she looked ten years older, a middle-aged and abandoned woman—it was like the terrible breath of the future on his cheek. He went down on one knee beside her and held the pink gin to her lips as though it were medicine. "My dear," he said, "I'll find a way. Have a drink."

"Ticki, I can't bear this place any longer. I know I've said it before, but I mean it this time. I shall go mad. Ticki, I'm so lonely. I haven't a friend, Ticki."

"Let's have Wilson up tomorrow."

"Ticki, for God's sake, don't always mention Wilson. Please, please do something."

"Of course I will. Just be patient a while, dear. These things take time."

"What will you do, Ticki?"

"I'm full of ideas, darling," he said wearily. (What a day it had been.) "Just let them simmer for a little while."

"Tell me one idea. Just one."

His eyes followed the lizard as it pounced; then he picked an ant wing out of his gin and drank again. He thought to himself: what a fool I really was not to take the hundred pounds. I destroyed the letter for nothing. I took the risk. I might just as well . . .

Louise said, "I've known it for years. You don't love me." She spoke with calm. He knew that calm—it meant they had reached the quiet centre of the storm: always in this region at about this time they began to speak the truth at each other. The truth, he thought, has never been of any real value to any human being—it is a symbol for mathematicians and philosophers to pursue. In human relations kindness and lies are worth a thousand truths. He involved himself in what he always knew was a vain struggle to retain the lies. "Don't be absurd, darling. Who do you think I love if I don't love you?"

"You don't love anybody."

"Is that why I treat you so badly?" He tried to hit a light note, and it sounded hollowly back at him.

"That's your conscience," she said, "your sense of duty. You've never loved anyone since Catherine died."

"Except myself, of course. You always say I love myself."

"No, I don't think you do."

He defended himself by evasions. In this cyclonic centre he was powerless to give the comforting lie. "I try all the time to keep you happy. I work hard for that."

"Ticki, you won't even say you love me. Go on. Say it once."

He eyed her bitterly over the pink gin, the visible sign of his failure: the skin a little yellow with atebrin, the eyes bloodshot with tears. No man could guarantee love for ever, but he had sworn fourteen years ago, at Ealing, silently, during the horrible little elegant ceremony among the lace and candles, that he would at least always see to it that she was happy. "Ticki, I've got nothing except you, and you've got —nearly everything." The lizard flicked across the wall and came to rest again, the wings of a moth in his small crocodile jaws. The ants struck tiny muffled blows at the electric globe.

"And yet you want to go away from me," he said.

"Yes," she said. "I know you aren't happy either. Without me you'll have peace."

This was what he always left out of account—the accuracy of her observation. He had nearly everything, and all he needed was peace. Everything meant work, the daily regular routine in the little bare office, the change of seasons in a place he loved. How often he had been pitied for the austerity of the work, the bareness of the rewards. But Louise knew him better than that. If he had become young again this was the life he would have chosen to live; only this time he would not have expected any other person to share it with him, the rat upon the bath, the lizard on the wall, the tornado blowing open the windows at one in the morning, and the last pink light upon the laterite roads at sundown.

"You are talking nonsense, dear," he said, and went through the doomed motions of mixing another gin-and-bitters. Again the nerve in his head tightened; unhappiness had uncoiled with its inevitable routine—first her misery and his strained attempts to leave everything unsaid: then her own calm statement of truths much better lied about, and finally the snapping of his own control—truths flung back at her as though she were his enemy. As he embarked on this last stage, crying suddenly and truthfully out at her while the angostura trembled in his hand, "*You* can't give me peace," he already knew what would succeed it, the reconciliation and the easy lies again until the next scene.

"That's what I say," she said; "if I go away, you'll have your peace."

"You haven't any conception," he accused her, "of what

peace means." It was as if she had spoken slightingly of a woman he loved. For he dreamed of peace by day and night. Once in sleep it had appeared to him as the great glowing shoulder of the moon heaving across his window like an iceberg, arctic and destructive in the moment before the world was struck: by day he tried to win a few moments of its company, crouched under the rusting handcuffs in the locked office, reading the reports from the sub-stations. Peace seemed to him the most beautiful word in the language: My peace I give you, my peace I leave with you: O Lamb of God, who takest away the sins of the world, grant us thy peace. In the Mass he pressed his fingers against his eyes to keep the tears of longing in.

Louise said with the old tenderness, "Poor dear, you wish I were dead like Catherine. You want to be alone."

He replied obstinately, "I want you to be happy."

She said wearily, "Just tell me you love me. That helps a little." They were through again, on the other side of the scene: he thought coolly and collectedly, this one wasn't so bad: we shall be able to sleep tonight. He said, "Of course I love you, darling. And I'll fix that passage. You'll see."

He would still have made the promise even if he could have foreseen all that would come of it. He had always been prepared to accept the responsibility for his actions, and he had always been half aware too, from the time he made his terrible private vow that she should be happy, how far *this* action might carry him. Despair is the price one pays for setting oneself an impossible aim. It is, one is told, the unforgivable sin, but it is a sin the corrupt or evil man never practices. He always has hope. He never reaches the freezing-point of knowing absolute failure. Only the man of good will carries always in his heart this capacity for damnation.

Part II

[1]

i

Wilson stood gloomily by his bed in the Bedford Hotel and contemplated his cummerbund, which lay ruffled like an angry snake; the small room was hot with the conflict between them. Through the wall he could hear Harris cleaning his teeth for the fifth time that day. Harris believed in dental hygiene. "It's cleaning my teeth before and after every meal that's kept me so well in this bloody climate," he would say, raising his pale exhausted face over an orange squash. Now he was gargling: it sounded like a noise in the pipes.

Wilson sat down on the edge of his bed and rested. He had left his door open for coolness, and across the passage he could see into the bathroom. The Indian with the turban was sitting on the side of the bath fully dressed. He stared inscrutably back at Wilson and bowed. "Just a moment, sir," he called. "If you would care to step in here . . ." Wilson angrily shut the door. Then he had another try with the cummerbund.

He had once seen a film—was it *Bengal Lancer?*—in which the cummerbund was superbly disciplined. A native held the coil and an immaculate officer spun like a top, so that the cummerbund encircled him smoothly, tightly. Another servant stood by with iced drinks, and a punkah swayed in the background. Apparently these things were better managed in India. However, with one more effort, Wilson did get the wretched thing wrapped around him. It was too tight and it was badly creased, and the tuck-in came too near the front, so that it was not hidden by the jacket. He contemplated his image with melancholy in what was left of the mirror. Somebody tapped on the door.

"Who is it?" Wilson shouted, imagining for a moment that the Indian had had the cool impertinence to pursue . . . but when the door opened, it was only Harris: the Indian was still sitting on the bath across the passage shuffling his testimonials.

"Going out, old man?" Harris asked, with disappointment.

"Yes."

"Everybody seems to be going out this evening. I shall have the table all to myself." He added with gloom, "Its the curry evening too."

"So it is. I'm sorry to miss it."

"You haven't been having it for two years, old man, every Thursday night." He looked at the cummerbund. "That's not right, old man."

"I know it isn't. It's the best I can do."

"I never wear one. It stands to reason that it's bad for the stomach. They tell you it absorbs sweat, but that's not where I sweat, old man. I'd rather wear braces, only the elastic perishes, so a leather belt's good enough for me. I'm no snob. Where are you dining, old man?"

"At Tallit's."

"How did you meet him?"

"He came into the office yesterday to pay his account and asked me to dinner."

"You don't have to dress for a Syrian, old man. Take it all off again."

"Are you sure?"

"Of course I am. It wouldn't do at all. Quite wrong." He added, "You'll get a good dinner, but be careful of the sweets. The price of life is eternal vigilance. I wonder what he wants out of you." Wilson began to undress again while Harris talked. He was a good listener. His brain was like a sieve through which the rubbish fell all day long. Sitting on the bed in his pants he heard Harris—"You have to be careful of the fish: I never touch it"—but the words left no impression. Drawing up his white drill trousers over his hairless knees he said to himself:

> the poor sprite is
> Imprisoned for some fault of his
> In a body like a grave.

His belly rumbled and tumbled as it always did a little before the hour of dinner.

> From you he only dares to crave,
> For his service and his sorrow,
> A smile today, a song tomorrow.

Wilson stared into the mirror and passed his fingers over the smooth, too smooth skin. The face looked back at him, pink and healthy, plump and hopeless. Harris went happily on, "I said once to Scobie," and immediately the clot of words lodged in Wilson's sieve. He pondered aloud, "I wonder how he ever came to marry her."

"It's what we all wonder, old man. Scobie's not a bad sort."

"She's too good for him."

"Louise?" Harris exclaimed.

"Of course. Who else?"

"There's no accounting for tastes. Go in and win, old man."

"I must be off."

"Be careful of the sweets." Harris went on with a small spurt of energy, "God knows I wouldn't mind something to be careful of instead of Thursday's curry. It is Thursday, isn't it?"

"Yes."

They came out into the passage and into the focus of the Indian eyes. "You'll have to be done sooner or later, old man," Harris said. "He does everybody once. You'll never have peace till he does you."

"I don't believe in fortune-telling," Wilson lied.

"Nor do I, but he's pretty good. He did me the first week I was here. Told me I'd stay here for more than two and a half years. I thought then I was going to have leave after eighteen months. I know better now." The Indian watched triumphantly from the bath. He said, "I have a letter from the Director of Agriculture. And one from D.C. Parkes."

"All right," Wilson said. "Do me, but be quick about it."

"I'd better push off, old man, before the revelations begin."

"I'm not afraid," Wilson said.

"Will you sit on the bath, sir?" the Indian invited him courteously. He took Wilson's hand in his. "It is a very interesting hand, sir," he said unconvincingly, weighing it up and down.

"What are your charges?"

"According to rank, sir. One like yourself, sir, I should charge ten shillings."

"That's a bit steep."

"Junior officers are five shillings."

"I'm in the five-shilling class," Wilson said.

"Oh no, sir. The Director of Agriculture gave me a pound."

"I'm only an accountant."

"That's as you say, sir. A.D.C. and Major Scobie gave me ten shillings."

"Oh well," Wilson said. "Here's ten bob. Go ahead."

"You have been here one, two weeks," the Indian said. "You are sometimes at night an impatient man. You think you do not make enough progress."

"Who with?" Harris asked, lolling in the doorway.

"You are very ambitious. You are a dreamer. You read much poetry."

Harris giggled and Wilson, raising his eyes from the finger which traced the lines upon his palm, watched the fortune-teller with apprehension.

The Indian went inflexibly on. His turban was bowed under Wilson's nose and bore the smell of stale food—he probably secreted stray pieces from the larder in its folds. He said, "You are a secret man. You do not tell your friends about your poetry—except one. One," he repeated. "You are very shy. You should take courage. You have a great line of success."

"Go in and win, old man," Harris repeated.

Of course the whole thing was Couéism: if one believed in it enough, it would come true. Diffidence would be conquered. The mistake in a reading would be covered up.

"You haven't told me ten bob's worth," Wilson said. "This is a five-bob fortune. Tell me something definite, something that's going to happen." He shifted his seat uncomfortably on the sharp edge of the bath and watched a cockroach like a large blood blister flattened on the wall. The Indian bent forward over the two hands. He said, "I see great success. The Government will be very pleased with you."

Harris said, "*Il pense* that you are *un bureaucrat*."

"Why will the Government be pleased with me?" Wilson asked.

"You will capture your man."

"Why," Harris said, "I believe he thinks you are a new policeman."

"It looks like it," Wilson said. "Not much use wasting more time."

"And your private life, that will be a great success too. You will win the lady of your heart. You will sail away. Everything is going to be fine. For you," he added.

"A real ten-bob fortune."

"Good night," Wilson said. "I won't write you a recommendation on that." He got up from the bath, and the cockroach flashed into hiding. "I can't bear those things," Wilson said, sidling through the door. He turned in the passage and repeated, "Good night."

"I couldn't when I first came, old man. But I evolved a system. Just step into my room and I'll show you."

"I ought to be off."

"Nobody will be punctual at Tallit's." Harris opened his door and Wilson turned his eyes with a kind of shame from the first sight of its disorder. In his own room he would never have exposed himself quite like this—the dirty tooth-glass, the towel on the bed.

"Look here, old man."

With relief he fixed his eyes on some symbols pencilled on the wall inside: the letter H, and under it a row of figures lined against dates as in a cash-book. Then the letters D.D., and under them more figures. "It's my score in cockroaches, old man. Yesterday was an average day—four. My record's nine. It makes you welcome the little brutes."

"What does D.D. stand for?"

"Down the drain, old man. That's when I knock them into the wash-basin and they go down the waste-pipe. It wouldn't be fair to count them as dead, would it?"

"No."

"And it wouldn't do to cheat yourself either. You'd lose interest at once. The only thing is, it gets dull sometimes, playing against yourself. Why shouldn't we make a match of it, old man? It needs skill, you know. They positively hear you coming, and they move like greased lightning. I do a stalk every evening with a torch."

"I wouldn't mind having a try, but I've got to be off now."

"I tell you what—I won't start hunting till you come back from Tallit's. We'll have five minutes before bed. Just five minutes."

"If you like."

"I'll come down with you, old man. I can smell the curry. You know I could have laughed when the old fool mixed you up with the new police officer."

"He got most of it wrong, didn't he?" Wilson said. "I mean the poetry."

ii

Tallit's living-room to Wilson, who saw it for the first time, had the appearance of a country dance hall. The furniture all lined the walls: hard chairs with tall uncomfortable backs, and in the corners the chaperons sitting out: old women in black silk dresses, yards and yards of silk, and a very old man in a smoking-cap. They watched him intently in complete silence, and evading their gaze he saw only bare walls except that at each corner sentimental French post-cards were nailed up in a *montage* of ribbons and bows: young men smelling mauve flowers, a glossy cherry shoulder, an impassioned kiss.

Wilson found there was only one other guest besides himself, Father Rank, a Catholic priest, wearing his long soutane. They sat in opposite corners of the room among the chaperons whom Father Rank explained were Tallit's grandparents and parents, two uncles, what might have been a great-great-aunt, a cousin. Somewhere out of sight Tallit's wife was preparing little dishes which were handed to the two guests by his younger brother and his sister. None of them spoke English except Tallit, and Wilson was embarrassed by the way Father Rank discussed his host and his host's family resoundingly across the room. "Thank you, no," Father Rank would say, declining a sweet by shaking his grey tousled head. "I'd advise you to be careful of those, Mr. Wilson. Tallit's a good fellow, but he won't learn what a western stomach will take. These old people have stomachs like ostriches."

"This is very interesting to me," Wilson said, catching the eye of a grandmother across the room and nodding and smiling at her. The grandmother obviously thought he wanted more sweets, and called angrily out for her granddaughter. "No, no," Wilson said vainly, shaking his head and smiling at the centenarian. The centenarian lifted his lip from a toothless gum and signalled with ferocity to Tallit's younger brother, who hurried forward with yet another dish. "That's quite safe," Father Rank shouted. "Just sugar and glycerine and a little flour." All the time their glasses were charged and recharged with whisky.

"Wish you'd confess to me where you get this whisky

from, Tallit," Father Rank called out, and Tallit beamed
and slid agilely from end to end of the room, a word to Wilson, a word to Father Rank. He reminded Wilson of a
young ballet dancer in his white trousers, his plaster of black
hair and his grey polished alien face, and one glass eye like a
puppet's.

"So the *Esperança*'s gone out," Father Rank shouted across
the room. "Did they find anything, do you think?"

"There was a rumour in the office," Wilson said, "about
some diamonds."

"Diamonds, my eye," Father Rank said. "They'll never
find any diamonds. They don't know where to look, do they,
Tallit?" He explained to Wilson, "Diamonds are a sore subject with Tallit. He was taken in by the false ones last year.
Yusef humbugged you, eh, Tallit, you young rogue? Not so
smart, eh? You a Catholic humbugged by a Mahomedan. I
could have wrung your neck."

"It was a bad thing to do," Tallit said, standing midway
between Wilson and the priest.

"I've only been here a few weeks," Wilson said, "and everyone talks to me about Yusef. They say he passes false diamonds, smuggles real ones, sells bad liquor, hoards cottons
against a French invasion, seduces the nursing sisters from
the military hospital."

"He's a dirty dog," Father Rank said with a kind of relish. "Not that you can believe a single thing you hear in this
place. Otherwise everybody would be living with someone
else's wife, every police officer who wasn't in Yusef's pay
would be bribed by Tallit here."

Tallit said, "Yusef is a very bad man."

"Why don't the authorities run him in?"

"I've been here for twenty-two years," Father Rank said,
"and I've never known anything proved against a Syrian
yet. Oh, often I've seen the police as pleased as Punch
carrying their happy morning faces around, just going to
pounce—and I think to myself, why bother to ask them
what it's about? they'll just pounce on air."

"You ought to have been a policeman, father."

"Ah," Father Rank said, "who knows? There are more policemen in this town than meet the eye—or so they say."

"Who say?"

"Careful of those sweets," Father Rank said, "they are harmless in moderation, but you've taken four already. Look here, Tallit, Mr. Wilson looks hungry. Can't you bring on the bakemeats?"

"Bakemeats?"

"The feast," Father Rank said. His joviality filled the room with hollow sound. For twenty-two years that voice had been laughing, joking, urging people humorously on through the rainy and the dry months. Could its cheeriness ever have comforted a single soul? Wilson wondered: had it even comforted itself? It was like the noise one heard rebounding from the tiles in a public baths: the laughs and the splashes of strangers in the steam-heating.

"Of course, Father Rank. Immediately, Father Rank." Father Rank, without being invited, rose from his chair and sat himself down at a table which like the chairs hugged the wall. There were only a few places laid and Wilson hesitated. "Come on. Sit down, Mr. Wilson. Only the old folks will be eating with us—and Tallit of course."

"You were saying something about a rumour?" Wilson asked.

"My head is a hive of rumours," Father Rank said, making a humorous hopeless gesture. "If a man tells me anything I assume he wants me to pass it on. It's a useful function, you know, at a time like this, when everything is an official secret, to remind people that their tongues were made to talk with and that the truth is meant to be spoken about. Look at Tallit now," Father Rank went on. Tallit was raising the corner of his black-out curtain and gazing into the dark street. "How's Yusef, you young rogue?" he asked. "Yusef's got a big house across the street and Tallit wants it, don't you, Tallit? What about dinner, Tallit, we're hungry?"

"It is here, father, it is here," he said, coming away from the window. He sat down silently beside the centenarian, and his sister served the dishes. "You always get a good meal in Tallit's house," Father Rank said.

"Yusef too is entertaining tonight."

"It doesn't do for a priest to be choosy," Father Rank said, "but I find your dinner more digestible." His hollow laugh swung through the room.

"Is it as bad as all that being seen at Yusef's?"

"It is, Mr. Wilson. If I saw you there, I'd say to myself, 'Yusef wants some information badly about cottons—what the imports are going to be next month, say—what's on the way by sea, and he'll pay for his information.' If I saw a girl go in, I'd think it was a pity, a great pity." He took a stab at his plate and laughed again. "But if Tallit went in I'd wait to hear the screams for help."

"If you saw a police officer?" Tallit asked.

"I wouldn't believe my eyes," the priest said. "None of them are such fools after what happened to Bailey."

"The other night a police car brought Yusef home," Tallit said. "I saw it from here plainly."

"One of the drivers earning a bit on the side," Father Rank said.

"I thought I saw Major Scobie. He was careful not to get out. Of course I am not perfectly sure. It *looked* like Major Scobie."

"My tongue runs away with me," the priest said. "What a garrulous fool I am. Why, if it was Scobie, I wouldn't think twice about it." His eyes roamed the room. "Not twice," he said. "I'd lay next Sunday's collection that everything was all right, absolutely all right," and he swung his great empty-sounding bell to and fro, Ho, ho, ho, like a leper proclaiming his misery.

iii

The light was still on in Harris's room when Wilson returned to the hotel. He was tired and worried and he tried to tiptoe by, but Harris heard him. "I've been listening for you, old man," he said, waving an electric torch. He wore his mosquito-boots outside his pyjamas and looked like a harassed air-raid warden.

"It's late. I thought you'd be asleep."

"I couldn't sleep until we'd had our hunt. The idea's grown on me, old man. We might have a monthly prize. I can see the time coming when other people will want to join in."

Wilson said with irony, "There might be a silver cup."

"Stranger things have happened, old man. The Cockroach Championship."

He led the way, walking softly on the boards to the middle of his room: the iron bed stood under its greying net, the arm-chair with collapsible back, the dressing-table littered with old *Picture Posts*. It shocked Wilson once again to realize that a room could be a degree more cheerless than his own.

"We'll draw our rooms alternate nights, old man."

"What weapon shall I use?"

"You can borrow one of my slippers." A board squeaked under Wilson's feet and Harris turned warningly. "They have ears like rats," he said.

"I'm a bit tired. Don't you think that tonight . . . ?"

"Just five minutes, old man. I couldn't sleep without a hunt. Look, there's one—over the dressing-table. You can have first shot," but as the shadow of the slipper fell upon the plaster wall, the insect shot away.

"No use doing it like that, old man. Watch *me*." Harris stalked his prey. The cockroach was half-way up the wall, and Harris, as he moved on tiptoe across the creaking floor, began to weave the light of his torch backwards and forwards over the cockroach. Then suddenly he struck and left a smear of blood. "One up," he said. "You have to mesmerize them."

To and fro across the room they padded, weaving their lights, smashing down their shoes, occasionally losing their heads and pursuing wildly into corners: the lust of the hunt touched Wilson's imagination. At first their manner to each other was "sporting"; they would call out, "Good shot" or

"Hard luck," but once they met together against the wainscot over the same cockroach when the score was even, and their tempers became frayed.

"No point in going after the same bird, old man," Harris said.

"I started him."

"You lost your one, old man. This was mine."

"It was the same. He did a double turn."

"Oh no."

"Anyway, there's no reason why I shouldn't go for the same one. You drove it towards me. Bad play on your part."

"Not allowed in the rules," Harris said shortly.

"Perhaps not in your rules."

"Damn it all," Harris said, "I invented the game."

A cockroach sat upon the brown cake of soap in the washbasin. Wilson spied it and took a long shot with the shoe from six feet away. The shoe landed smartly on the soap and the cockroach span into the basin: Harris turned on the tap and washed it down. "Good shot, old man," he said placatingly. "One D.D."

"D.D. be damned," Wilson said. "It was dead when you turned on the tap."

"You couldn't be sure of that. It might have been just unconscious—concussion. It's D.D. according to the rules."

"Your rules again."

"My rules are the Queensberry rules in this town."

"They won't be for long," Wilson threatened. He slammed the door hard behind him and the walls of his own room vibrated round him from the shock. His heart beat with rage and the hot night: the sweat drained from his armpits. But as he stood there beside his own bed, seeing the replica of Harris's room around him, the washbasin, the table, the grey mosquito-net, even the cockroach fastened on the wall, anger trickled out of him and loneliness took its place. It was like quarrelling with one's own image in the glass. I was crazy, he thought. What made me fly out like that? I've lost a friend.

That night it took him a long while to sleep, and when he slept at last he dreamed that he had committed a crime, so that he woke with the sense of guilt still heavy upon him. On his way down to breakfast he paused outside Harris's door. There was no sound. He knocked, but there was no answer. He opened the door a little way and saw obscurely through the grey net Harris's damp bed. He asked softly, "Are you awake?"

"What is it?"

"I'm sorry, Harris, about last night."

"My fault, old man. I've got a touch of fever. I was sickening for it. Touchy."

"No, it's my fault. You are quite right. It *was* D.D."

"We'll toss up for it, old man."

"I'll come in tonight."

"That's fine."

But after breakfast something took his mind right away from Harris. He had been in to the Commissioner's office on his way down town and coming out he ran into Scobie.

"Hallo," Scobie said, "what are you doing here?"

"Been in to see the Commissioner about a pass. There are so many passes one has to have in this town, sir. I wanted one for the wharf."

"When are you going to call on us again, Wilson?"

"You don't want to be bothered with strangers, sir."

"Nonsense. Louise would like another chat about books. I don't read them myself, you know, Wilson."

"I don't suppose you have much time."

"Oh, there's an awful lot of time around," Scobie said, "in a country like this. I just don't have a taste for reading, that's all. Come into my office a moment while I ring up Louise. She'll be glad to see you. Wish you'd call in and take her for a walk. She doesn't get enough exercise."

"I'd love to," Wilson said, and blushed hurriedly in the shadows. He looked around him: this was Scobie's office. He examined it as a general might examine a battle-ground, and yet it was difficult to regard Scobie as an enemy. The rusty handcuffs jangled on the wall as Scobie leant back from his desk and dialled.

"Free this evening?"

He brought his mind sharply back, aware that Scobie was watching him: the slightly protruding, slightly reddened eyes dwelt on him with a kind of speculation. "I wonder why you came out here," Scobie said. "You aren't the type."

"One drifts into things," Wilson lied.

"I don't," Scobie said, "I've always been a planner. You see, I even plan for other people." He began to talk into the telephone. His intonation changed: it was as if he were reading a part—a part which called for tenderness and patience, a part which had been read so often that the eyes were blank above the mouth. Putting down the receiver, he said, "That's fine. That's settled then."

"It seems a very good plan to me," Wilson said.

"My plans always start out well," Scobie said. "You two go for a walk, and when you get back I'll have a drink ready for you. Stay to dinner," he went on with a hint of anxiety. "We'll be glad of your company."

When Wilson had gone, Scobie went in to the Commissioner. He said, "I was just coming along to see you, sir, when I ran into Wilson."

"Oh yes, Wilson," the Commissioner said. "He came in to have a word with me about one of their lightermen."

"I see." The shutters were down in the office to cut out the morning sun. A sergeant passed through carrying with him, as well as his file, a breath of the zoo behind. The day was heavy with unshed rain: already at 8:30 in the morning the body ran with sweat. Scobie said, "He told me he'd come about a pass."

"Oh yes," the Commissioner said, "that too." He put a piece of blotting-paper under his wrist to absorb the sweat as he wrote. "Yes, there was something about a pass too, Scobie."

[2]

i

Mrs. Scobie led the way, scrambling down towards the bridge over the river that still carried the sleepers of an abandoned railway.

"I'd never have found this path by myself," Wilson said, panting a little with the burden of his plumpness.

Louise Scobie said, "It's my favourite walk."

On the dry dusty slope above the path an old man sat in the doorway of a hut doing nothing. A girl with small crescent breasts climbed down towards them balancing a pail of water on her head; a child naked except for a red bead necklace round the waist played in a little dust-paved yard among the chickens; labourers carrying hatchets came across the bridge at the end of their day. It was the hour of comparative coolness, the hour of peace.

"You wouldn't guess, would you, that the city's just behind us?" Mrs. Scobie said. "And a few hundred yards up there over the hill the boys are bringing in the drinks."

The path wound along the slope of the hill. Down below him Wilson could see the huge harbour spread out. A convoy was gathering inside the boom; tiny boats moved like flies between the ships; above them the ashy trees and the burnt scrubs hid the summit of the ridge. Wilson stumbled once or twice as his toes caught in the ledges left by the sleepers.

Louise Scobie said, "This is what I thought it was all going to be like."

"Your husband loves the place, doesn't he?"

"Oh, I think sometimes he's got a kind of selective eyesight. He sees what he likes to see. He doesn't seem to see the snobbery, and he doesn't hear the gossip."

"He sees you," Wilson said.

"Thank God he doesn't, because I've caught the disease."

"You aren't a snob."

"Oh yes, I am."

"You took *me* up," Wilson said, blushing and contorting his face into a careful careless whistle. But he couldn't whistle. The plump lips blew empty air, like a fish.

"For God's sake," Louise said, "don't be humble."

"I'm not really humble," Wilson said. He stood aside to let a labourer go by. He explained, "I've got inordinate ambitions."

"In two minutes," Louise said, "we get to the best point of all—where you can't see a single house."

"It's good of you to show me . . ." Wilson muttered, stumbling on again along the ridge track. He had no small talk: with a woman he could be romantic, but nothing else.

"There," Louise said, but he had hardly time to take the view in—the harsh green slopes falling down towards the great flat glaring bay—when she wanted to be off again, back the way they had come. "Henry will be in soon," she said.

"Who's Henry?"

"My husband."

"I didn't know his name. I'd heard you call him something else—something like Ticki."

"Poor Henry," she said. "How he hates it. I try not to when other people are there, but I forget. Let's go."

"Can't we go just a little further—to the railway station?"

"I'd like to change," Louise said, "before dark. The rats begin to come in after dark."

"Going back will be downhill all the way."

"Let's hurry then," Louise said. He followed her. Thin and ungainly, she seemed to him to possess a sort of Undine beauty. She had been kind to him, she bore his company, and automatically at any first kindness from a woman love stirred. He had no capacity for friendship or for equality. In his romantic, humble, ambitious mind he could conceive only a relationship with a waitress, a cinema usherette, a landlady's daughter in Battersea or with a queen—this was a queen. He began to mutter again at her heels—"so good" —between pants, his plump knees knocking together on the stony path. Quite suddenly the light changed: the laterite soil turned a translucent pink sloping down the hill to the wide flat water of the bay. There was something happily accidental in the evening light as though it hadn't been planned.

"This is it," Louise said, and they leant and got their breath again against the wooden wall of the small abandoned station, watching the light fade out as quickly as it came.

Through an open door—had it been the waiting room or the stationmaster's office?—the hens passed in and out. The dust on the windows was like the steam left only a moment ago by a passing train. On the forever-closed guichet somebody had chalked a crude phallic figure. Wilson could see it over her left shoulder as she leant back to get her breath. "I used to come here every day," Louise said, "until they spoilt it for me."

"They?"

She said, "Thank God, I shall be out of here soon."

"Why? You are not going away?"

"Henry's sending me to South Africa."

"Oh God," Wilson exclaimed. The news was so unexpected that it was like a twinge of pain. His face twisted with it.

He tried to cover up the absurd exposure. No one knew better than he did that his face was not made to express agony or passion. He said, "What will he do without you?"

"He'll manage."

"He'll be terribly lonely," Wilson said—he, he, he chiming back in his inner ear like a misleading echo I, I, I.

"He'll be happier without me."

"He couldn't be."

"Henry doesn't love me," she said gently, as though she were teaching a child, using the simplest words to explain a difficult subject, simplifying. . . . She leant her head back against the guichet and smiled at him as much as to say, it's quite easy really when you get the hang of it. "He'll be happier without me," she repeated. An ant moved from the woodwork on to her neck and he leant close to flick it away. He had no other motive. When he took his mouth away from hers the ant was still there. He let it run on to his finger. The taste of the lipstick was like something he'd never tasted before and that he would always remember. It seemed to him that an act had been committed which altered the whole world.

"I hate him," she said, carrying on the conversation exactly where it had been left.

"You mustn't go," he implored her. A bead of sweat ran down into his right eye and he brushed it away; on the guichet by her shoulder his eyes took in again the phallic scrawl.

"I'd have gone before this if it hadn't been for the money, poor dear. He has to find it."

"Where?"

"That's man's business," she said like a provocation, and he kissed her again; their mouths clung like bivalves, and then she pulled away and he heard the sad to-and-fro of Father Rank's laugh coming up along the path. "Good evening, good evening," Father Rank called. His stride lengthened and he caught a foot in his soutane and stumbled as he went by. "A storm's coming up," he said. "Got to hurry," and his "ho, ho, ho" diminished mournfully along the railway track, bringing no comfort to anyone.

"He didn't see who we were," Wilson said.

"Of course he did. What does it matter?"

"He's the biggest gossip in the town."

"Only about things that matter," she said.

"This doesn't matter?"

"Of course it doesn't," she said. "Why should it?"

"I'm in love with you, Louise," Wilson said sadly.

"This is the second time we've met."

"I don't see that that makes any difference. Do you like me, Louise?"

"Of course I like you, Wilson."

"I wish you wouldn't call me Wilson."

"Have you got another name?"

"Edward."

"Do you want me to call you Teddy? Or Bear? These things creep on you before you know where you are. Suddenly you are calling someone Bear or Ticki, and the real name seems bald and formal, and the next you know they hate you for it. I'll stick to Wilson."

"Why don't you leave him?"

"I am leaving him. I told you. I'm going to South Africa."

"I love you, Louise," he said again.

"How old are you, Wilson?"

"Thirty-two."

"A very young thirty-two, and I am an old thirty-eight."

"It doesn't matter."

"The poetry you read, Wilson, is too romantic. It does matter. It matters much more than love. Love isn't a fact like age and religion. . . ."

Across the bay the clouds came up: they massed blackly over Bullom and then tore up the sky, climbing vertically: the wind pressed the two of them back against the station. "Too late," Louise said, "we're caught."

"How long will this last?"

"Half an hour."

A handful of rain was flung in their faces, and then the water came down. They stood inside the station and heard the water hurled upon the roof. They were in darkness, and the chickens moved at their feet.

"This is grim," Louise said.

He made a motion towards her hand and touched her shoulder. "Oh, for God's sake, Wilson," she said, "don't let's have a petting party." She had to speak loud for her voice to carry above the thunder on the iron roof.

"I'm sorry . . . I didn't mean . . ."

He could hear her shifting further away, and he was glad of the darkness which hid his humiliation. "I like you, Wilson," she said, "but I'm not a nursing sister who expects to be taken whenever she finds herself in the dark with a man. You have no responsibilities towards me, Wilson. I don't want you."

"I love you, Louise."

"Yes, yes, Wilson. You've told me. Do you think there are snakes in here—or rats?"

"I've no idea. When are you going to South Africa, Louise?"

"When Ticki can raise the money."

"It will cost a lot. Perhaps you won't be able to go."

"He'll manage somehow. He said he would."

"Life insurance?"

"No, he's tried that."

"I wish I could lend it to you myself. But I'm poor as a church-mouse."

"Don't talk about mice in here. Ticki will manage somehow."

He began to see her face through the darkness, thin, grey, attenuated—it was like trying to remember the features of someone he had once known who had gone away. One would build them up in just this way—the nose and then if one concentrated enough the brow; the eyes would escape him.

"He'll do anything for me."

He said bitterly, "A moment ago you said he didn't love you."

"Oh," she said, "but he has a terrible sense of responsibility."

He made a movement and she cried furiously out, "Keep still. I don't love you. I love Ticki."

"I was only shifting my weight," he said. She began to laugh. "How funny this is," she said. "It's a long time since anything funny happened to me. I'll remember this for months, for months." But it seemed to Wilson that he would remember her laughter all his life. His shorts flapped in the draught of the storm and he thought, "In a body like a grave."

ii

When Louise and Wilson crossed the river and came into Burnside it was quite dark. The headlamps of a police van lit an open door, and figures moved to and fro carrying packages. "What's up now?" Louise exclaimed, and began to run down the road. Wilson panted after her. Ali came from the house carrying on his head a tin bath, a folding chair, and a bundle tied up in an old towel. "What on earth's happened, Ali?"

"Massa go on trek," he said, and grinned happily in the headlamps.

In the sitting-room Scobie sat with a drink in his hand. "I'm glad you are back," he said. "I thought I'd have to write a note," and Wilson saw that in fact he had already begun one. He had torn a leaf out of his notebook, and his large awkward writing covered a couple of lines.

"What on earth's happening, Henry?"

"I've got to get off to Bamba."

"Can't you wait for the train on Thursday?"

"No."

"Can I come with you?"

"Not this time. I'm sorry, dear. I'll have to take Ali and leave you the small boy."

"What's happened?"

"There's trouble over young Pemberton."

"Serious?"

"Yes."

"He's such a fool. It was madness to leave him there as D.C."

Scobie drank his whisky and said, "I'm sorry, Wilson. Help yourself. Get a bottle of soda out of the ice-box. The boys are busy packing."

"How long will you be, darling?"

"Oh, I'll be back the day after tomorrow, with any luck. Why don't you go and stay with Mrs. Halifax?"

"I shall be all right here, darling."

"I'd take the small boy and leave you Ali, but the small boy can't cook."

"You'll be happier with Ali, dear. It will be like the old days before I came out."

"I think I'll be off, sir," Wilson said. "I'm sorry I kept Mrs. Scobie out so late."

"Oh, I didn't worry, Wilson. Father Rank came by and told me you were sheltering in the old station. Very sensible of you. He got a drenching. He should have stayed too—he doesn't want a dose of fever at his age."

"Can I fill your glass, sir? Then I'll be off."

"Henry never takes more than one."

"All the same, I think I will. But don't go, Wilson. Stay and keep Louise company for a bit. I've got to be off after this glass. I shan't get any sleep tonight."

"Why can't one of the young men go? You're too old, Ticki, for this. Driving all night. Why don't you send Fraser?"

"The Commissioner asked me to go. It's just one of those cases—carefulness, tact, you can't let a young man handle it." He took another drink of whisky and his eyes moved gloomily away as Wilson watched him. "I must be off."

"I'll never forgive Pemberton for this."

Scobie said sharply, "Don't talk nonsense, dear. We'd forgive most things if we knew the facts." He smiled unwillingly at Wilson. "A policeman should be the most forgiving person in the world if he gets the facts right."

"I wish I could be of help, sir."

"You can. Stay and have a few more drinks with Louise and cheer her up. She doesn't often get a chance to talk about books." At the word books Wilson saw her mouth tighten just as a moment ago he had seen Scobie flinch at the name of Ticki, and for the first time he realized the pain inevitable in any human relationship—pain suffered and pain inflicted. How foolish one was to be afraid of loneliness.

"Good-bye, darling."

"Good-bye, Ticki."

"Look after Wilson. See he has enough to drink. Don't mope."

When she kissed Scobie, Wilson stood near the door with a glass in his hand and remembered the disused station on the hill above and the taste of lipstick. For exactly an hour and a half the mark of his mouth had been the last on hers. He felt no jealousy, only the dreariness of a man who tries to write an important letter on a damp sheet and finds the characters blur.

Side by side they watched Scobie cross the road to the police van. He had taken more whisky than he was accustomed to, and perhaps that was what made him stumble. "They should have sent a younger man," Wilson said.

"They never do. He's the only one the Commissioner trusts." They watched him climb laboriously in, and she went sadly on, "Isn't he the typical second man? The man who always does the work."

The black policeman at the wheel started his engine and began to grind into gear before releasing the clutch. "They don't even give him a good driver," she said. "The good driver will have taken Fraser and the rest to the dance at the Club." The van bumped and heaved out of the yard. Louise said, "Well, that's that, Wilson."

She picked up the note Scobie had intended to leave for her and read it aloud. *"My dear, I have had to leave for Bamba. Keep this to yourself. A terrible thing has happened. Poor Pemberton . . ."*

"Poor Pemberton," she repeated furiously.

"Who's Pemberton?"

"A little puppy of twenty-five. All spots and bounce. He was assistant D.C. at Bamba, but when Butterworth went sick, they left him in charge. Anybody could have told them there'd be trouble. And when trouble comes it's Henry, of course, who has to drive all night. . . ."

"I'd better leave now, hadn't I?" Wilson said. "You'll want to change."

"Oh yes, you'd better go—before everybody knows he's gone and that we've been alone five minutes in a house with a bed in it. Alone, of course, except for the small boy and the cook and their relations and friends."

"I wish I could be of some use."

"You could be," she said. "Would you go upstairs and see whether there's a rat in the bedroom? I don't want the small boy to know I'm nervous. And shut the window. They come in that way."

"It will be very hot for you."

"I don't mind."

He stood just inside the door and clapped his hands softly, but no rat moved. Then quickly, surreptitiously, as though he had no right to be there, he crossed to the window and closed it. There was a faint smell of face-powder in the room—it seemed to him the most memorable scent he had ever known. He stood again by the door taking the whole room in—the child's photograph, the pots of cream, the dress laid out by Ali for the evening. He had been instructed at home how to memorize, pick out the important detail, collect the right evidence, but his employers had never taught him that he would find himself in a country so strange to him as this.

Part III

---

[1]

i

The police van took its place in the long line of army lorries waiting for the ferry. Their headlamps were like a little village in the night. The trees came down on either side smelling of heat and rain, and somewhere at the end of the column a driver sang—the wailing, toneless voice rose and fell like a wind through a keyhole. Scobie slept and woke, slept and woke. When he woke he thought of Pemberton and wondered how he would feel if he were his father—that elderly, retired bank manager whose wife had died in giving birth to Pemberton—but when he slept he went smoothly back into a dream of perfect happiness and freedom. He was walking through a wide cool meadow with Ali at his heels: there was nobody else anywhere in his dream, and Ali never spoke. Birds went by far overhead, and once when he sat down the grass was parted by a small green snake which passed on to his hand and up his arm without fear, and before it slid down into the grass again touched his cheek with a cold, friendly, remote tongue.

Once when he opened his eyes Ali was standing beside him waiting for him to awake. "Massa like bed," he stated gently, firmly, pointing to the camp-bed he had made up at the edge of the path with the mosquito-net tied from the branches overhead. "Two three hours," Ali said. "Plenty lorries." Scobie obeyed and lay down and was immediately back in that peaceful meadow where nothing ever happened. The next time he woke Ali was still there, this time with a cup of tea and a plate of biscuits. "One hour," Ali said.

Then at last it was the turn of the police van. They moved down the red laterite slope on to the raft, and then edged foot by foot across the dark styx-like stream towards the woods on the other side. The two ferrymen pulling on the rope wore nothing but girdles, as though they had left their clothes behind on the bank where life ended, and a third man beat time to them, making do for instrument in this between-world with an empty sardine-tin. The wailing tireless voice of the living singer shifted backwards.

This was only the first of three ferries that had to be crossed, with the same queue forming each time. Scobie never succeeded in sleeping properly again; his head began to ache from the heave of the van: he ate some aspirin and hoped for the best. He didn't want a dose of fever when he was away from home. It was not Pemberton that worried him now—let the dead bury their dead—it was the promise he had made to Louise. Two hundred pounds was so small a sum: the figures rang their changes in his aching head like a peal of bells: 200 002 020: it worried him that he could not find a fourth combination: 002 200 020.

They had come beyond the range of the tin-roofed shacks and the decayed wooden settlers' huts; the villages they passed through were bush villages of mud and thatch: no light showed anywhere: doors were closed and shutters were up, and only a few goats' eyes watched the headlamps of the convoy. 020 002 200 200 002 020. Ali squatting in the body of the van put an arm around his shoulder holding a mug of hot tea—somehow he had boiled another kettle in the lurching chassis. Louise was right—it was like the old days. If he had felt younger, if there had been no problem of 200 020 002, he would have been happy. Poor Pemberton's death would not have disturbed him—that was merely in the way of duty, and he had never liked Pemberton.

"My head humbug me, Ali."

"Massa take plenty aspirin."

"Do you remember, Ali, that two hundred 002 trek we did twelve years ago in ten days, along the border; two of the carriers went sick. . . ."

He could see in the driver's mirror Ali nodding and beaming. It seemed to him that this was all he needed of love or friendship. He could be happy with no more in the world than this—the grinding van, the hot tea against his lips, the heavy damp weight of the forest, even the aching head, the loneliness. If I could just arrange for her happiness first, he thought, and in the confusing night he forgot for the while what experience had taught him—that no human being can really understand another, and no one can arrange another's happiness.

"One hour more," Ali said, and he noticed that the darkness was thinning. "Another mug of tea, Ali, and put some whisky in it." The convoy had separated from them a quarter of an hour ago, when the police van had turned away from the main road and bumped along a by-road farther into the bush. He shut his eyes and tried to draw his mind away from the broken peal of figures to the distasteful job. There was only a native police sergeant at Bamba, and he would like to be clear in his own mind as to what had happened before he received the sergeant's illiterate report. It would be better, he considered reluctantly, to go first to the Mission and see Father Clay.

Father Clay was up and waiting for him in the dismal little European house which had been built among the mud huts in laterite bricks to look like a Victorian presbytery. A hurricane-lamp shone on the priest's short red hair and his young freckled Liverpool face. He couldn't sit still for more than a few minutes at a time, and then he would be up, pacing his tiny room from hideous oleograph to plaster statue and back to oleograph again. "I saw so little of him," he wailed, motioning with his hands as though he were at the altar. "He cared for nothing but cards and drinking. I don't drink and I've never played cards—except demon, you know, except demon, and that's a patience. It's terrible, terrible."

"He hanged himself?"

"Yes. His boy came over to me yesterday. He hadn't seen him since the night before, but that was quite usual after a bout, you know, a bout. I told him to go to the police. That was right, wasn't it? There was nothing I could do. Nothing. He was quite dead."

"Quite right. Would you mind giving me a glass of water and some aspirin?"

"Let me mix the aspirin for you. You know, Major Scobie, for weeks and months nothing happens here at all. I just walk up and down here, up and down, and then suddenly out of the blue . . . it's terrible." His eyes were red and sleepless: he seemed to Scobie one of those who are quite unsuited to loneliness. There were no books to be seen except a little shelf with his breviary and a few religious tracts. He was a man without resources. He began to pace up and down again and suddenly, turning on Scobie, he shot out an excited question. "Mightn't there be a hope that it's murder?"

"Hope?"

"Suicide," Father Clay said. "It's too terrible. It puts a man outside mercy. I've been thinking about it all night."

"He wasn't a Catholic. Perhaps that makes a difference. Invincible ignorance, eh?"

"That's what I try to think." Half-way between oleograph and statuette he suddenly started and stepped aside as though he had encountered another on his tiny parade. Then he looked quickly and slyly at Scobie to see whether his act had been noticed.

"How often do you get down to the port?" Scobie asked.

"I was there for a night nine months ago. Why?"

"Everybody needs a change. Have you many converts here?"

"Fifteen. I try to persuade myself that young Pemberton had time—time, you know, while he died, to realize . . ."

"Difficult to think clearly when you are strangling, father." He took a swig at the aspirin and the sour grains stuck in his throat. "If it was murder you'd simply change your mortal sinner, father," he said with an attempt at humour which wilted between the holy picture and the holy statue.

"A murderer has time . . ." Father Clay said. He added wistfully, with nostalgia, "I used to do duty sometimes at Liverpool Gaol."

"Have you any idea why he did it?"

"I didn't know him well enough. We didn't get on together."

"The only white men here. It seems a pity."

"He offered to lend me some books, but they weren't at all the kind of books I care to read—love stories, novels. . . ."

"What do you read, father?"

"Anything on the saints, Major Scobie. My great devotion is to the Little Flower."

"He drank a lot, didn't he? Where did he get it from?"

"Yusef's store, I suppose."

"Yes. He may have been in debt?"

"I don't know. It's terrible, terrible."

Scobie finished his aspirin. "I suppose I'd better go along." It was day now outside, and there was a peculiar innocence about the light, gentle and clear and fresh before the sun climbed.

"I'll come with you, Major Scobie."

The police sergeant sat in a deck-chair outside the D.C.'s bungalow. He rose and raggedly saluted, then immediately in his hollow unformed voice began to read his report. "At three-thirty p.m. yesterday, sah, I was woken by D.C.'s boy, who reported that D.C. Pemberton, sah . . ."

"That's all right, sergeant, I'll go inside and have a look round." The chief clerk waited for him just inside the door.

The living-room of the bungalow had obviously once been the D.C.'s pride—that must have been in Butterworth's day. There was an air of elegance and personal pride in the furniture; it hadn't been supplied by the Government. There were eighteenth-century engravings of the old colony on the wall and in one bookcase were the volumes that Butterworth had left behind him—Scobie noted some titles and authors, Maitland's *Constitutional History*, Sir Henry Maine, Bryce's *Holy Roman Empire*, Hardy's poems, and the *Doomsday Records of Little Withington*, privately printed. But imposed on all this were the traces of Pemberton—a gaudy leather pouf of so-called native work, the marks of cigarette-ends on the chairs, a stack of the books Father Clay had disliked—Somerset Maugham, an Edgar Wallace, two Horlers, and spread-eagled on the settee, *Death Laughs at Locksmiths*. The room was not properly dusted and Butterworth's books were stained with damp.

"The body is in the bedroom, sah," the sergeant said.

Scobie opened the door and went in—Father Clay followed him. The body had been laid on the bed with a sheet over the face. When Scobie turned the sheet down to the shoulder he had the impression that he was looking at a child in a nightshirt quietly asleep: the pimples were the pimples of puberty and the dead face seemed to bear the trace of no experience beyond the class-room or the football field. "Poor child," he said aloud. The pious ejaculations of Father Clay irritated him. It seemed to him that unquestionably there must be mercy for someone so unformed. He asked abruptly, "How did he do it?"

The police sergeant pointed to the picture-rail that Butterworth had meticulously fitted—no Government contractor would have thought of it. A picture—an early native king receiving missionaries under a State umbrella—leant against the wall and a cord remained twisted over the brass picture-hanger. Who would have expected the flimsy contrivance not to collapse? He can weigh very little, he thought, and he remembered a child's bones, light and brittle as a bird's. His feet when he hung must have been only fifteen inches from the ground.

"Did he leave any papers?" Scobie asked the clerk. "They usually do." Men who are going to die are apt to become garrulous with self-revelations.

"Yes, sah, in the office."

It needed only a casual inspection to realize how badly the office had been kept. The filing cabinet was unlocked: the trays on the desk were filled by papers dusty with inattention. The native clerk had obviously followed the same ways as his chief. "There, sah, on the pad."

Scobie read, in a handwriting unformed as the face, a script-writing which hundreds of his school contemporaries must have been turning out all over the world: *Dear Dad, Forgive all this trouble. There doesn't seem anything else to do. It's a pity I'm not in the army because then I might be killed. Don't go and pay the money I owe—the fellow doesn't deserve it. They may try and get it out of you. Otherwise I wouldn't mention it. It's a rotten business for you, but it can't be helped. Your loving son.* The signature was "Dicky." It was like a letter from school excusing a bad report.

He handed the letter to Father Clay. "You are not going to tell me there's anything unforgivable there, father. If you or I did it, it would be despair—I grant you anything with us. We'd be damned because we know, but *he* doesn't know a thing."

"The Church's teaching . . ."

"Even the Church can't teach me that God doesn't pity the young. . . ." Scobie broke abruptly off. "Sergeant, see that a grave's dug quickly before the sun gets too hot. And look out for any bills he owed. I want to have a word with someone about this." When he turned towards the window the light dazzled him. He put his hand over his eyes and said, "I wish to God my head . . ." and shivered. "I'm in for a dose if I can't stop it. If you don't mind Ali putting up my bed at your place, father, I'll try and sweat it out."

He took a heavy dose of quinine and lay naked between the blankets. As the sun climbed it sometimes seemed to him that the stone walls of the small cell-like room sweated with cold and sometimes were baked with heat. The door was open and Ali squatted on the step just outside whittling a piece of wood. Occasionally he chased away villagers who raised their voices within the area of sick-room silence. The *peine forte et dure* weighed on Scobie's forehead: occasionally it pressed him into sleep.

But in this sleep there were no pleasant dreams. Pemberton and Louise were obscurely linked. Over and over again he was reading a letter which consisted only of variations on the figure 200 and the signature at the bottom was sometimes "Dicky" and sometimes "Ticki"; he had the sense of time passing and his own immobility between the blankets —there was something he had to do, someone he had to save, Louise or Dicky or Ticki, but he was tied to the bed and they laid weights on his forehead as you lay weights on loose papers. Once the sergeant came to the door and Ali chased him away, once Father Clay tiptoed in and took a tract off a shelf, and once, but that might have been a dream, Yusef came to the door.

About five in the evening he woke feeling dry and cool and weak and called Ali in. "I dreamed I saw Yusef."

"Yusef come for to see you, sah."

"Tell him I'll see him now." He felt tired and beaten about the body: he turned to face the stone wall and was immediately asleep. In his sleep Louise wept silently beside him; he put out his hand and touched the stone wall again —"Everything shall be arranged. Everything. Ticki promises." When he awoke Yusef was beside him.

"A touch of fever, Major Scobie. I am very sorry to see you poorly."

"I'm sorry to see you at all, Yusef."

"Ah, you always make fun of me."

"Sit down, Yusef. What did you have to do with Pemberton?"

Yusef eased his great haunches on the hard chair and noticing that his flies were open put down a large and hairy hand to deal with them. "Nothing, Major Scobie."

"It's an odd coincidence that you are here just at the moment when he commits suicide."

"I think myself it is providence."

"He owed you money, I suppose?"

"He owed my store-manager money."

"What sort of pressure were you putting on him, Yusef?"

"Major, you give an evil name to a dog and the dog is finished. If the D.C. wants to buy at my store, how can my manager stop selling to him? If he does that, what will happen? Sooner or later there will be a first-class row. The Provincial Commissioner will find out. The D.C. will be sent home. If he does not stop selling, what happens then? The D.C. runs up more and more bills. My manager becomes afraid of me, he asks the D.C. to pay—there is a row that way. When you have a D.C. like poor young Pemberton, there will be a row one day whatever you do. And the Syrian is always wrong."

"There's quite a lot in what you say, Yusef." The pain

was beginning again. "Give me that whisky and quinine, Yusef."

"You are not taking too much quinine, Major Scobie? Remember blackwater."

"I don't want to be stuck up here for days. I want to kill this at birth. I've too many things to do."

"Sit up a moment, Major, and let me beat your pillows."

"You aren't a bad chap, Yusef."

Yusef said, "Your sergeant has been looking for bills, but he could not find any. Here are IOU's though. From my manager's safe." He flapped his thigh with a little sheaf of papers.

"I see. What are you going to do with them?"

"Burn them," Yusef said. He took out a cigarette-lighter and lit the corners. "There," Yusef said. "He has paid, poor boy. There is no reason to trouble his father."

"Why did you come up here?"

"My manager was worried. I was going to propose an arrangement."

"One needs a long spoon to sup with you, Yusef."

"My enemies do. Not my friends. I would do a lot for you, Major Scobie."

"Why do you always call me a friend, Yusef?"

"Major Scobie," Yusef said, leaning his great white head forward, reeking of hair-oil, "friendship is something in the soul. It is a thing one feels. It is not a return for something. You remember when you put me into court ten years ago?"

"Yes, yes." Scobie turned his head away from the light of the door.

"You nearly caught me, Major Scobie, that time. It was a matter of import duties, you remember. You could have caught me if you had told your policeman to say something a little different. I was quite overcome with astonishment, Major Scobie, to sit in a police court and hear true facts from the mouths of policemen. You must have taken a lot of trouble to find out what was true, and to make them say it. I said to myself, Yusef, a Daniel has come to the Colonial Police."

"I wish you wouldn't talk so much, Yusef. I'm not interested in your friendship."

"Your words are harder than your heart, Major Scobie. I want to explain why in my soul I have always felt your friend. You have made me feel secure. You will not frame me. You need facts, and I am sure the facts will always be in my favour." He dusted the ashes from his white trousers, leaving one more grey smear. "These are facts. I have burned all the IOU's."

"I may yet find traces, Yusef, of what kind of agreement you were intending to make with Pemberton. This station controls one of the main routes across the border from— damnation, I can't think of names with this head."

"Cattle smugglers. I'm not interested in cattle."

"Other things are apt to go back the other way."

"You are still dreaming of diamonds, Major Scobie. Everybody has gone crazy about diamonds since the war."

"Don't feel too certain, Yusef, that I won't find something when I go through Pemberton's office."

"I feel quite certain, Major Scobie. You know I cannot read or write. Nothing is ever on paper. Everything is always in my head." Even while Yusef talked, Scobie dropped asleep—into one of those shallow sleeps that last a few seconds and have only time to reflect a preoccupation. Louise was coming towards him with both hands held out and a smile that he hadn't seen upon her face for years. She said, "I am so happy, so happy," and he woke again to Yusef's voice going soothingly on. "It is only your friends who do not trust you, Major Scobie. I trust you. Even that scoundrel Tallit trusts you."

It took him a moment to get this other face into focus. His brain adjusted itself achingly from the phrase "so happy" to the phrase "do not trust." He said, "What are you talking about, Yusef?" He could feel the mechanism of his brain creaking, grinding, scraping, cogs failing to connect, all with pain.

"First, there is the Commissionership."

"They need a young man," he said mechanically, and thought, if I hadn't fever I would never discuss a matter like this with Yusef.

"Then the special man they have sent from London . . ."

"You must come back when I'm clearer, Yusef. I don't know what the hell you are talking about."

"They have sent a special man from London to investigate the diamonds—they are crazy about diamonds—only the Commissioner must know about him—none of the other officers, not even you."

"What rubbish you talk, Yusef. There's no such man."

"Everybody guesses but you."

"Too absurd. You shouldn't listen to rumour, Yusef."

"And a third thing. Tallit says everywhere you visit me."

"Tallit! Who believes what Tallit says?"

"Everybody everywhere believes what is bad."

"Go away, Yusef. Why do you want to worry me now?"

"I just want you to understand, Major Scobie, that you can depend on me. I have friendship for you in my soul. That is true, Major Scobie, it is true." The reek of hair-oil came closer as he bent towards the bed: the deep brown eyes were damp with what seemed to be emotion. "Let me pat your pillow, Major Scobie."

"Oh, for goodness' sake, keep away," Scobie said.

"I know how things are, Major Scobie, and if I can help . . . I am a well-off man."

"I'm not looking for bribes, Yusef," he said wearily and turned his head away to escape the scent.

"I am not offering you a bribe, Major Scobie. A loan at any time on a reasonable rate of interest—four per cent per annum. No conditions. You can arrest me next day if you have facts. I want to be your friend, Major Scobie. You need not be my friend. There is a Syrian poet who wrote, 'Of two hearts one is always warm and one is always cold: the cold heart is more precious than diamonds: the warm heart has no value and is thrown away.' "

"It sounds a very bad poem to me. But I'm no judge."

"It is a happy chance for me that we should be here together. In the town there are so many people watching. But here, Major Scobie, I can be of real help to you. May I fetch you more blankets?"

"No, no, just leave me alone."

"I hate to see a man of your characteristics, Major Scobie, treated badly."

"I don't think the time's ever likely to come, Yusef, when I shall need *your* pity. If you want to do something for me, though, go away and let me sleep."

But when he slept the unhappy dreams returned. Upstairs Louise was crying, and he sat at a table writing his last letter. "It's a rotten business for you, but it can't be helped. Your loving husband, Dicky," and then as he turned to look for a weapon or a rope, it suddenly occurred to him that this was an act he could never do. Suicide was for ever out of his power—he couldn't condemn himself for eternity—no cause was important enough. He tore up his letter and ran upstairs to tell Louise that after all everything was all right, but she had stopped crying and the silence welling out from inside the bedroom terrified him. He tried the door and the door was locked. He called out, "Louise, everything's all right. I've booked your passage," but there was no answer. He cried again, "Louise," and then a key turned and the door slowly opened with a sense of irrecoverable disaster, and he saw standing just inside Father Clay, who said to him, "The teaching of the Church . . ." Then he woke again to the small stone room like a tomb.

ii

He was away for a week, for it took three days for the fever to run its course and another two days before he was fit to travel. He did not see Yusef again.

It was past midnight when he drove into town. The houses were white as bones in the moonlight; the quiet streets stretched out on either side like the arms of a skeleton, and the faint sweet smell of flowers lay on the air. If he had been returning to an empty house he knew that he would have been contented. He was tired and he didn't want to break the silence—it was too much to hope that Louise would be asleep, too much to hope that things would somehow have become easier in his absence and that he would see her free and happy as she had been in one of his dreams.

The small boy waved his torch from the door: the frogs croaked from the bushes, and the pye-dogs wailed at the moon. He was home. Louise put her arms round him: the table was laid for a late supper, the boys ran to and fro with his boxes: he smiled and talked and kept the bustle going. He talked of Pemberton and Father Clay and mentioned Yusef, but he knew that sooner or later he would have to ask how things had been with her. He tried to eat, but he was too tired to taste the food.

"Yesterday I cleared up his office and wrote my report—and that was that." He hesitated, "That's all my news," and went reluctantly on, "How have things been here?" He looked quickly up at her face and away again. There had been one chance in a thousand that she would have smiled and said vaguely, "Not so bad," and then passed on to other things, but he knew from her mouth that he wasn't so lucky as that. Something fresh had happened.

But the outbreak—whatever it was to be—was delayed. She said, "Oh, Wilson's been attentive."

"He's a nice boy."

"He's too intelligent for his job. I can't think why he's out here as just a clerk."

"He told me he drifted."

"I don't think I've spoken to anybody else since you've been away, except the small boy and the cook. Oh, and Mrs. Halifax." Something in her voice told him that the danger point was reached. Always, hopelessly, he tried to evade it. He stretched and said, "My God, I'm tired. The fever's left me limp as a rag. I think I'll go to bed. It's nearly half-past one, and I've got to be at the station at eight."

She said, "Ticki, have you done anything at all?"

"How do you mean, dear?"

"About the passage."

"Don't worry. I'll find a way, dear."

"You haven't found one yet?"

"No. I've got several ideas I'm working on. It's just a question of borrowing." 200 020 002 rang in his brain.

"Poor dear," she said, "don't worry," and put her hand against his cheek. "You're tired. You've had fever. I'm not going to bait you now." Her hand, her words broke through every defence: he had expected tears, but he found them now in his own eyes. "Go up to bed, Henry," she said.

"Aren't you coming up?"

"There are just one or two things I want to do."

He lay on his back under the net and waited for her. It occurred to him, as it hadn't occurred to him for years, that she loved him. Poor dear, she loved him: she was someone of human stature with her own sense of responsibility, not simply the object of his care and kindness. The sense of failure deepened round him. All the way back from Bamba he had faced one fact—that there was only one man in the city capable of lending him, and willing to lend him, the two hundred pounds, and that was a man he must not borrow from. It would have been safer to accept the Portuguese captain's bribe. Slowly and drearily he had reached the decision to tell her that the money simply could not be found, that for the next six months at any rate, until his leave, she must stay. If he had not felt so tired he would have told her when she asked him and it would have been over now, but he had flinched away and she had been kind, and it would be harder now than it had ever been to disappoint her. There was silence all through the little house, but outside the half-starved pye-dogs yapped and whined. He listened, leaning on his elbow; he felt oddly unmanned, lying in bed alone waiting for Louise to join him. She had always been the one to go first to bed. He felt uneasy, apprehensive, and suddenly his dream came to mind, how he had listened outside the door and knocked, and there was no reply. He struggled out from under the net and ran downstairs barefooted.

Louise was sitting at the table with a pad of notepaper in front of her, but she had written nothing but a name. The winged ants beat against the light and dropped their wings over the table. Where the light touched her head he saw the grey hairs.

"What is it, dear?"

"Everything was so quiet," he said, "I wondered whether something had happened. I had a bad dream about you the other night. Pemberton's suicide upset me."

"How silly, dear. Nothing like that could ever happen with us."

"Yes, of course. I just wanted to see you," he said, putting his hand on her hair. Over her shoulder he read the only words she had written, "Dear Mrs. Halifax" . . .

"You haven't got your shoes on," she said. "You'll be catching jiggers."

"I just wanted to see you," he repeated and wondered whether the stains on the paper were sweat or tears.

"Listen, dear," she said. "You are not to worry any more. I've baited you and baited you. It's like fever, you know. It comes and goes. Well, now it's gone—for a while. I know you can't raise the money. It's not your fault. If it hadn't been for that stupid operation . . . It's just the way things are, Henry."

"What's it all got to do with Mrs. Halifax?"

"She and another woman have a two-berth cabin in the next ship and the other woman's fallen out. She thought perhaps I could slip in—if her husband spoke to the agent."

"That's in about a fortnight," he said.

"Darling, give up trying. It's better just to give up. Anyway, I had to let Mrs. Halifax know tomorrow. And I'm letting her know that I shan't be going."

He spoke rapidly—he wanted the words out beyond recall. "Write and tell her that you can go."

"Ticki," she said, "what do you mean?" Her face hardened. "Ticki, please don't promise something which can't happen. I know you're tired and afraid of a scene. But there isn't going to be a scene. I mustn't let Mrs. Halifax down."

"You won't. I know where I can borrow the money."

"Why didn't you tell me when you came back?"

"I wanted to give you your ticket. A surprise."

She was not so happy as he would have expected: she always saw a little farther than he hoped. "And you are not worrying any more?" she asked.

"I'm not worrying any more. Are you happy?"

"Oh yes," she said in a puzzled voice. "I'm happy, dear."

iii

The liner came in on a Saturday evening; from the bedroom window they could see its long grey form steal past the boom, beyond the palms. They watched it with a sinking of the heart—happiness is never really so welcome as changelessness—hand in hand they watched their separation anchor in the bay. "Well," Scobie said, "that means tomorrow afternoon."

"Darling," she said, "when this time is over, I'll be good to you again. I just couldn't stand this life any more."

They could hear a clatter below stairs as Ali, who had also been watching the sea, brought out the trunks and boxes. It was as if the house were tumbling down around them, and the vultures took off from the roof, rattling the corrugated-iron as though they felt the tremor in the walls. Scobie said, "While you are sorting your things upstairs, I'll pack your books." It was as if they had been playing these last two weeks at infidelity, and now the process of divorce had them in its grasp: the division of one life into two: the sharing out of the sad spoils.

"Shall I leave you this photograph, Ticki?" He took a quick sideways glance at the first-communion face and said, "No. You have it."

"I'll leave you this one of us with the Ted Bromleys."

"Yes, leave that." He watched her for a moment laying out her clothes and then he went downstairs. One by one he took out the books and wiped them with a cloth: the Oxford Verse, the Woolfs, the younger poets. Afterwards the shelves were almost empty: his own books took up so little room.

Next day they went to Mass together early. Kneeling together at the communion rail they seemed to claim that this was not separation. He thought: I've prayed for peace and now I'm getting it. It's terrible the way that prayer is answered. It had better be good, I've paid a high enough price for it. As they walked back he said anxiously, "You are happy?"

"Yes, Ticki, and you?"

"I'm happy as long as you are happy."

"It will be all right when I've got on board and settled down. I expect I shall drink a bit tonight. Why don't you have someone in, Ticki?"

"Oh, I prefer being alone."

"Write to me every week."

"Of course."

"And Ticki, you won't be lazy about Mass? You'll go when I'm not there?"

"Of course."

Wilson came up the road. His face shone with sweat and anxiety. He said, "Are you really off? Ali told me at the house that you are going on board this afternoon."

"She's off," Scobie said.

"You never told me it was close like this."

"I forgot," Louise said, "there was so much to do."

"I never thought you'd really go. I wouldn't have known if I hadn't run into Halifax at the agent's."

"Oh well," Louise said, "you and Henry will have to keep an eye on each other."

"It's incredible," Wilson said, kicking the dusty road. He hung there, between them and the house, not stirring to let them by. He said, "I don't know a soul but you—and Harris of course."

"You'll have to start making acquaintances," Louise said. "You'll have to excuse us now. There's so much to do."

They walked round him because he didn't move, and Scobie, looking back, gave him a kindly wave—he looked so lost and unprotected and out of place on the blistered road. "Poor Wilson," he said, "I think he's in love with you."

"He thinks he is."

"It's a good thing for him you are going. People like that become a nuisance in this climate. I'll be kind to him while you are away."

"Ticki," she said, "I shouldn't see too much of him. I wouldn't trust him. There's something phoney about him."

"He's young and romantic."

"He's too romantic. He tells lies. Why does he say he doesn't know a soul?"

"I don't think he does."

"He knows the Commissioner. I saw him going up there the other night at dinner-time."

"It's just a way of talking."

Neither of them had any appetite for lunch, but the cook, who wanted to rise to the occasion, produced an enormous curry which filled a washing-basin in the middle of the table: round it were ranged the many small dishes that went with it—the fried bananas, red peppers, ground nuts, paw paw, orange slices, chutney. They seemed to be sitting miles apart separated by a waste of dishes. The food chilled on their plates and there seemed nothing to talk about except, "I'm not hungry," "Try and eat a little," "I can't touch a thing," "You ought to start off with a good meal," an endless friendly bicker about food. Ali came in and out to watch them: he was like a figure on a clock that records the striking of the hours. It seemed horrible to both of them that now they would be glad when the separation was complete; they could settle down, when once this ragged leave-taking was over, to a different life which again would exclude change.

"Are you sure you've got everything?" This was another variant which enabled them to sit there not eating but occasionally picking at something easily swallowed, going through all the things that might have been forgotten.

"It's lucky there's only one bedroom. They'll have to let you keep the house to yourself."

"They may turn me out for a married couple."

"You'll write every week?"

"Of course."

Sufficient time had elapsed: they could persuade themselves that they had lunched. "If you can't eat any more I may as well drive you down. The sergeant's organized carriers at the wharf." They could say nothing now which wasn't formal; unreality cloaked their movements. Although they could touch each other it was as if the whole coastline of a continent was already between them; their words were like the stilted sentences of a bad letter-writer.

It was a relief to be on board and no longer alone together. Halifax, of the Public Works Department, bubbled over with false bonhomie. He cracked risky jokes and told the two women to drink plenty of gin. "It's good for the bow-wows," he said. "First thing to go wrong on board ship are the bow-wows. Plenty of gin at night and what will cover a sixpence in the morning." The two women took stock of their cabin. They stood there in the shadow like cave-dwellers; they spoke in undertones that the men couldn't catch: they were no longer wives—they were sisters belonging to a different race. "You and I are not wanted, old man," Halifax said. "They'll be all right now. Me for the shore."

"I'll come with you." Everything had been unreal, but this suddenly was real pain, the moment of death. Like a prisoner he had not believed in the trial: it had been a dream: the condemnation had been a dream and the truck ride, and then suddenly here he was with his back to the blank wall and everything was true. One steeled oneself to end courageously. They went to the end of the passage, leaving the Halifaxes the cabin.

"Good-bye, dear."

"Good-bye. Ticki, you'll write every . . ."

"Yes, dear."

"I'm an awful deserter."

"No, no. This isn't the place for you."

"It would have been different if they'd made you Commissioner."

"I'll come down for my leave. Let me know if you run short of money before then. I can fix things."

"You've always fixed things for me. Ticki, you'll be glad to have no more scenes."

"Nonsense."

"Do you love me, Ticki?"

"What do you think?"

"Say it. One likes to hear it—even if it isn't true."

"I love you, Louise. Of course it's true."

"If I can't bear it down there alone, Ticki, I'll come back."

They kissed and went up on deck. From here the port was always beautiful; the thin layer of houses sparkled in the sun like quartz or lay in the shadow of the great green swollen hills. "You are well escorted," Scobie said. The destroyers and the corvettes sat around like dogs: signal flags rippled and a helio flashed. The fishing boats rested on the broad bay under their brown butterfly sails. "Look after yourself, Ticki."

Halifax came booming up behind them. "Who's for shore? Got the police launch, Scobie? Mary's down in the cabin, Mrs. Scobie, wiping off the tears and putting on the powder for the passengers."

"Good-bye, dear."

"Good-bye." That was the real good-bye, the hand-shake with Halifax watching and the passengers from England

looking curiously on. As the launch moved away she was almost at once indistinguishable; perhaps she had gone down
to the cabin to join Mrs. Halifax. The dream had finished:
change was over: life had begun again.

"I hate these good-byes," Halifax said. "Glad when it's all
over. Think I'll go up to the Bedford and have a glass of
beer. Join me?"

"Sorry. I have to go on duty."

"I wouldn't mind a nice little black girl to look after me
now I'm alone," Halifax said. "However, faithful and true,
old fidelity, that's me," and as Scobie knew, it was.

In the shade of a tarpaulined dump Wilson stood, looking
out across the bay. Scobie paused. He was touched by the
plump sad boyish face. "Sorry we didn't see you," he said
and lied harmlessly, "Louise sent her love."

iv

It was nearly one in the morning before he returned. The
light was out in the kitchen quarters and Ali was dozing on
the steps of the house until the headlamps woke him, passing
across his sleeping face. He jumped up and lit the way from
the garage with his torch.

"All right, Ali. Go to bed."

He let himself into the empty house—he had forgotten
the deep tones of silence. Many a time he had come in late,
after Louise was asleep, but there had never then been quite
this quality of security and impregnability in the silence: his
ears had listened for, even though they could not catch, the
faint rustle of another person's breath, the tiny movement.
Now there was nothing to listen for. He went upstairs and
looked into the bedroom. Everything had been tidied away;
there was no sign of Louise's departure or presence: Ali had
even removed the photograph and put it in a drawer. He
was indeed alone. In the bathroom a rat moved, and once
the iron roof crumpled as a late vulture settled for the night.

Scobie sat down in the living-room and put his feet upon
another chair. He felt unwilling yet to go to bed, but he was

sleepy—it had been a long day. Now that he was alone he could indulge in the most irrational act and sleep in a chair instead of a bed. The sadness was peeling off his mind, leaving contentment. He had done his duty: Louise was happy. He closed his eyes.

The sound of a car driving in off the road, headlamps moving across the window, woke him. He imagined it was a police car—that night he was the responsible officer and he thought that some urgent and probably unnecessary telegram had come in. He opened the door and found Yusef on the step. "Forgive me, Major Scobie, I saw your light as I was passing, and I thought . . ."

"Come in," he said. "I have whisky or would you prefer a little beer . . . ?"

Yusef said with surprise, "This is very hospitable of you, Major Scobie."

"If I know a man well enough to borrow money from him, surely I ought to be hospitable."

"A little beer then, Major Scobie."

"The Prophet doesn't forbid it?"

"The Prophet had no experience of bottled beer or whisky, Major Scobie. We have to interpret his words in a modern light." He watched Scobie take the bottles from the ice chest. "Have you no refrigerator, Major Scobie?"

"No. Mine's waiting for a spare part—it will go on waiting till the end of the war, I imagine."

"I must not allow that. I have several spare refrigerators. Let me send one up to you."

"Oh, I can manage all right, Yusef. I've managed for two years. So you were passing by."

"Well, not exactly, Major Scobie. That was a way of speaking. As a matter of fact I waited until I knew your boys were asleep, and I borrowed a car from a garage. My own car is so well known. And I did not bring a chauffeur. I didn't want to embarrass you, Major Scobie."

"I repeat, Yusef, that I shall never deny knowing a man from whom I have borrowed money."

"You do keep harping on that so, Major Scobie. That was just a business transaction. Four per cent is a fair interest. I ask for more only when I have doubt of the security. I wish you would let me send you a refrigerator."

"What did you want to see me about?"

"First, Major Scobie, I wanted to ask after Mrs. Scobie. Has she got a comfortable cabin? Is there anything she requires? The ship calls at Lagos, and I could have anything she needs sent on board there. I would telegraph my agent."

"I think she's quite comfortable."

"Next, Major Scobie, I wanted to have a few words with you about diamonds."

Scobie put two more bottles of beer on the ice. He said slowly and gently, "Yusef, I don't want you to think I am the kind of man who borrows money one day and insults his creditor the next to reassure his ego."

"Ego?"

"Never mind. Self-esteem. What you like. I'm not going to pretend that we haven't in a way become colleagues in a business, but my duties are strictly confined to paying you four per cent."

"I agree, Major Scobie. You have said all this before and I agree. I say again that I am never dreaming to ask you to do one thing for me. I would rather do things for you."

"What a queer chap you are, Yusef. I believe you do like me."

"Yes, I do like you, Major Scobie." Yusef sat on the edge of his chair which cut a sharp edge in his great expanding thighs: he was ill at ease in any house but his own. "And now may I talk to you about diamonds, Major Scobie?"

"Fire away then."

"You know I think the Government is crazy about diamonds. They waste your time, the time of the Security Police: they send special agents down the coast: we even have one here—you know who, though nobody is supposed to know but the Commissioner: he spends money on every black or poor Syrian who tells him stories. Then he telegraphs it to England and all down the coast. And after all this, do they catch a single diamond?"

"This has got nothing to do with us, Yusef."

"I want to talk to you as a friend, Major Scobie. There are diamonds and diamonds and Syrians and Syrians. You people hunt the wrong men. You want to stop industrial diamonds going to Portugal and then to Germany, or across the border to the Vichy French. But all the time you are chasing people who are not interested in industrial diamonds, people who just want to get a few gem stones in a safe place for when peace comes again."

"In other words you?"

"Six times this month police have been into my stores making everything untidy. They will never find any industrial diamonds that way. Only small men are interested in industrial diamonds. Why, for a whole match-box full of them, you would only get two hundred pounds. I call them gravel collectors," he said with contempt.

Scobie said slowly, "Sooner or later, Yusef, I felt sure that you'd want something out of me. But you are going to get nothing but four per cent. Tomorrow I am giving a full confidential report of our business arrangement to the Commissioner. Of course he may ask for my resignation, but I don't think so. He trusts me." A memory pricked him. "I think he trusts me."

"Is that a wise thing to do, Major Scobie?"

"I think it's very wise. Any kind of secret between us two would go bad in time."

"Just as you like, Major Scobie. But I don't want anything from you, I promise. I would like to give you things always. You will not take a refrigerator, but I thought you would perhaps take advice, information."

"I'm listening, Yusef."

"Tallit's a small man. He is a Christian. Father Rank and other people go to his house. They say, 'If there's such a thing as an honest Syrian, then Tallit's the man.' Tallit's not very successful, and that looks just the same as honesty."

"Go on."

"Tallit's cousin is sailing in the next Portuguese boat. His luggage will be searched, of course, and nothing will be found. He will have a parrot with him in a cage. My advice, Major Scobie, is to let Tallit's cousin go and keep his parrot."

"Why let the cousin go?"

"You do not want to show your hand to Tallit. You can easily say the parrot is suffering from a disease and must stay. He will not dare to make a fuss."

"You mean the diamonds are in its crop?"

"Yes."

"Has that trick been used before on the Portuguese boats?"

"Yes."

"It looks to me as if we'll have to buy an aviary."

"Will you act on that information, Major Scobie?"

"You give me information, Yusef. I don't give you information."

Yusef nodded and smiled. Raising his bulk with some care he touched Scobie's sleeve quickly and shyly. "You are quite right, Major Scobie. Believe me, I never want to do you any harm at all. I shall be careful and you be careful too, and everything will be all right." It was as if they were in a conspiracy together to do no harm: even innocence in Yusef's hands took on a dubious colour. He said, "If you were to say a good word to Tallit sometimes it would be safer. The agent visits him."

"I don't know of any agent."

"You are quite right, Major Scobie." Yusef hovered like a fat moth on the edge of the light. He said, "Perhaps if you were writing one day to Mrs. Scobie you would give her my best wishes. Oh no, letters are censored. You cannot do that. You could say, perhaps—no, better not. As long as *you* know, Major Scobie, that you have my best wishes——" Stumbling on the narrow path, he made for his car. When he had turned on his lights he pressed his face against the glass: it showed up in the illumination of the dashboard, wide, pasty, untrustworthy, sincere. He made a tentative shy sketch of a wave towards Scobie, where he stood alone in the doorway of the quiet and empty house.

BOOK TWO

Part I

[1]

i

They stood on the verandah of the D.C.'s bungalow at Pende and watched the torches move on the other side of the wide passive river. "So that's France," Druce said, using the native term for it.

Mrs. Perrot said, "Before the war we used to picnic in France."

Perrot joined them from the bungalow, a drink in either hand: bandy-legged, he wore his mosquito-boots outside his trousers like riding-boots, and gave the impression of having only just got off a horse. "Here's yours, Scobie." He said, "Of course ye know I find it hard to think of the French as enemies. My family came over with the Huguenots. It makes a difference, ye know." His lean long yellow face cut in two by a nose like a wound was all the time arrogantly on the defensive: the importance of Perrot was an article of faith with Perrot—doubters would be repelled, persecuted if he had the chance . . . the faith would never cease to be proclaimed.

Scobie said, "If they ever joined the Germans, I suppose this is one of the points where they'd attack."

"Don't I know it," Perrot said; "I was moved here in 1939. The Government had a shrewd idea of what was coming. Everything's prepared, ye know. Where's the doctor?"

"I think he's taking a last look at the beds," Mrs. Perrot said. "You must be thankful your wife's arrived safely, Major Scobie. Those poor people over there. Forty days in the boats. It shakes one up to think of it."

"It's the damned narrow channel between Dakar and Brazil that does it every time," Perrot said.

The doctor came gloomily out on to the verandah.

Everything over the river was still and blank again: the torches were all out. The light burning on the small jetty below the bungalow showed a few feet of dark water sliding by. A piece of wood came out of the dark and floated so slowly through the patch of light that Scobie counted twenty before it went into darkness again.

"The Froggies haven't behaved too badly this time," Druce said gloomily, picking a mosquito out of his glass.

"They've only brought the women, the old men and the dying," the doctor said, pulling at his beard. "They could hardly have done less."

Suddenly like an invasion of insects the voices whined and burred upon the farther bank. Groups of torches moved like fireflies here and there: Scobie, lifting his binoculars, caught a black face momentarily illuminated: a hammock pole: a white arm: an officer's back. "I think they've arrived," he said. A long line of lights was dancing along the water's edge. "Well," Mrs. Perrot said, "we may as well go in now." The mosquitoes whirred steadily around them like sewing machines. Druce exclaimed and struck his hand.

"Come in," Mrs. Perrot said. "The mosquitoes here are all malarial." The windows of the living-room were netted to keep them out; the stale air was heavy with the coming rains.

"The stretchers will be across at six a.m.," the doctor said.

"I think we are all set, Perrot. There's one case of black-water and a few cases of fever, but most are just exhaustion —the worst disease of all. It's what most of us die of in the end."

"Scobie and I will see the walking cases," Druce said. "You'll have to tell us how much interrogation they can stand, doctor. Your police will look after the carriers, Perrot, I suppose—see that they all go back the way they came."

"Of course," Perrot said. "We're stripped for action here. Have another drink?" Mrs. Perrot turned the knob of the radio and the organ of the Orpheum Cinema, Clapham, sailed to them over three thousand miles. From across the river the excited voices of the carriers rose and fell. Somebody knocked on the verandah door. Scobie shifted uncomfortably in his chair: the music of the Würlitzer organ moaned and boomed. It seemed to him outrageously immodest. The verandah door opened and Wilson came in.

"Hello, Wilson," Druce said. "I didn't know you were here."

"Mr. Wilson's up to inspect the U.A.C. store," Mrs. Perrot explained. "I hope the rest-house at the store is all right. It's not often used."

"Oh yes, it's very comfortable," Wilson said. "Why, Major Scobie, I didn't expect to see you."

"I don't know why you didn't," Perrot said. "I told you he'd be here. Sit down and have a drink." Scobie remembered what Louise had once said to him about Wilson— phoney, she had called him. He looked across at Wilson and saw the blush at Perrot's betrayal fading from the boyish face, and the little wrinkles that gathered round the eyes and gave the lie to his youth.

"Have you heard from Mrs. Scobie, sir?"

"She arrived safely last week."

"I'm glad. I'm so glad."

"Well," Perrot said, "what are the scandals from the big city?" The words "big city" came out with a sneer—Perrot couldn't bear the thought that there was a place where people considered themselves important and where he was not regarded. Like a Huguenot imagining Rome, he built up a picture of frivolity, viciousness and corruption. "We bush-folk," Perrot went heavily on, "live very quietly." Scobie felt sorry for Mrs. Perrot; she had heard these phrases so often: she must have forgotten long ago the time of courtship when she had believed in them. Now she sat close up against the radio with the music turned low listening or pretending to listen to the old Viennese melodies, while her mouth stiffened in the effort to ignore her husband in his familiar part. "Well, Scobie, what are our superiors doing in the city?"

"Oh," said Scobie vaguely, watching Mrs. Perrot, "nothing very much has been happening. People are too busy with the war . . ."

"Oh, yes," Perrot said, "so many files to turn over in the Secretariat. I'd like to see them growing rice down here. They'd know what work was."

"I suppose the greatest excitement recently," Wilson said, "would be the parrot, sir, wouldn't it?"

"Tallit's parrot?" Scobie asked.

"Or Yusef's according to Tallit," Wilson said. "Isn't that right, sir, or have I got the story wrong?"

"I don't think we'll ever know what's right," Scobie said.

"But what *is* the story? We're out of touch with the great world of affairs here. We have only the French to think about."

"Well, about three weeks ago Tallit's cousin was leaving for Lisbon on one of the Portuguese ships. We searched his baggage and found nothing, but I'd heard rumours that sometimes diamonds had been smuggled in a bird's crop, so I kept the parrot back, and sure enough there were about a hundred pounds' worth of industrial diamonds inside. The ship hadn't sailed, so we fetched Tallit's cousin back on shore. It seemed a perfect case."

"But it wasn't?"

"You can't beat a Syrian," the doctor said.

"Tallit's cousin's boy swore that it wasn't Tallit's cousin's parrot—and so of course did Tallit's cousin. Their story was that the small boy had substituted another bird to frame Tallit."

"On behalf of Yusef, I suppose," the doctor said.

"Of course. The trouble was the small boy disappeared. Of course there are two explanations of that—perhaps Yusef had given him his money and he'd cleared off, or just as possibly Tallit had given him money to throw the blame on Yusef."

"Down here," Perrot said, "I'd have had 'em both in jail."

"Up in town," Scobie said, "we have to think about the law."

Mrs. Perrot turned the knob of the radio and a voice shouted with unexpected vigour, "Kick him in the pants."

"I'm for bed," the doctor said. "Tomorrow's going to be a hard day."

Sitting up in bed under his mosquito-net Scobie opened his diary. Night after night for more years than he could remember he had kept a record—the barest possible record—of his days. If anyone argued a date with him he could check up; if he wanted to know which day the rains had begun in any particular year, when the last but one Director of Public Works had been transferred to East Africa, the facts were all there, in one of the volumes stored in the tin box under his bed at home. Otherwise he never opened a volume—particularly that volume where the barest fact of all was contained—*C. died.* He couldn't have told himself why he stored up this record—it was certainly not for posterity. Even if posterity were to be interested in the life of an obscure policeman in an unfashionable colony, it would have learned nothing from these cryptic entries. Perhaps the reason was that forty years ago at a preparatory school he had been given a prize—a copy of *Allan Quatermain*—for keeping a diary throughout one summer holiday, and the habit had simply stayed. Even the form the diary took had altered very little. *Had sausages for breakfast. Fine day. Walk in morning. Riding lesson in afternoon. Chicken for lunch. Treacle roll.* Almost imperceptibly this record had changed into *Louise left. Y. called in the evening. First typhoon 2 a.m.* His pen was powerless to convey the importance of any entry: only he himself, if he had cared to read back, could have seen in the last phrase but one the enormous breach pity had blasted through his integrity. Y., not Yusef.

Scobie wrote: *May 5. Arrived Pende to meet survivors of s.s. 43* (he used the code number for security). *Druce with me.* He hesitated for a moment and then added, *Wilson here.* He closed the diary, and lying flat on his back under the net he began to pray. This also was a habit. He said the Our Father, the Hail Mary, and then, as sleep began to clog his lids, he added an act of contrition. It was a formality, not because he felt himself free from serious sin but because it had never occurred to him that his life was important enough one way or another. He didn't drink, he didn't fornicate, he didn't even lie, but he never regarded this absence of sin as virtue. When he thought about it at all, he regarded himself as a man in the ranks, the member of an awkward squad, who had no opportunity to break the more serious military rules. "I missed Mass yesterday for insufficient reason. I neglected my evening prayers." This was no more than admitting what every soldier did—that he had avoided a fatigue when the occasion offered. "O God, bless——" but before he could mention names he was asleep.

ii

They stood on the jetty next morning: the first light lay in cold strips along the eastern sky. The huts in the village were still shuttered with silver. At two that morning there had been a typhoon—a wheeling pillar of black cloud driving up from the coast, and the air was cold yet with the rain. They stood with coat-collars turned up watching the French shore, and the carriers squatted on the ground behind them. Mrs. Perrot came down the path from the bungalow wiping the white sleep from her eyes, and from across the water very faintly came the bleating of a goat. "Are they late?" Mrs. Perrot asked.

"No, we are early." Scobie kept his glasses focused on the opposite shore. He said, "They are stirring."

"Those poor souls," Mrs. Perrot said, and shivered with the morning chill.

"They are alive," the doctor said.

"Yes."

"In my profession we have to consider that important."

"Does one ever get over a shock like that? Forty days in open boats."

"If you survive at all," the doctor said, "you get over it. It's failure people don't get over, and this you see is a kind of success."

"They are fetching them out of the huts," Scobie said. "I think I can count six stretchers. The boats are being brought in."

"We were told to prepare for nine stretcher cases and four walking ones," the doctor said. "I suppose there've been some more deaths."

"I may have counted wrong. They are carrying them down now. I think there are seven stretchers. I can't distinguish the walking cases."

The flat cold light, too feeble to clear the morning haze, made the distance across the river longer than it would seem at noon. A native dugout canoe bearing, one supposed, the walking cases came blackly out of the haze: it was suddenly very close to them. On the other shore they were having trouble with the motor of a launch; they could hear the irregular putter, like an animal out of breath.

First of the walking cases to come on shore was an elderly man with an arm in a sling. He wore a dirty white topee and a native cloth was draped over his shoulders; his free hand tugged and scratched at the white stubble on his face. He said in an unmistakably Scottish accent, "Ah'm Loder, chief engineer."

"Welcome home, Mr. Loder," Scobie said. "Will you step up to the bungalow and the doctor will be with you in a few minutes?"

"Ah have no need of doctors."

"Sit down and rest. I'll be with you soon."

"Ah want to make ma report to a proper official."

"Would you take him up to the house, Perrot?"

"I'm the District Commissioner," Perrot said. "You can make your report to me."

"What are we waitin' for then?" the engineer said. "It's nearly two months since the sinkin'. There's an awful lot of responsibility on me, for the captain's dead." As they moved up the hill to the bungalow, the persistent Scottish voice, as regular as the pulse of a dynamo, came back to them. "Ah'm responsible to the owners."

The other three had come on shore, and across the river the tinkering in the launch went on: the sharp crack of a chisel, the clank of metal, and then again the spasmodic putter. Two of the new arrivals were the cannon fodder of all such occasions: elderly men with the appearance of plumbers who might have been brothers if they had not been called Forbes and Newall, uncomplaining men without authority, to whom things simply happened. One had a crushed foot and walked with a crutch; the other had his hand bound up with shabby strips of tropical shirt. They stood on the jetty with as natural a lack of interest as they would have stood at a Liverpool street corner waiting for the local to open. A stalwart grey-headed woman in mosquito-boots followed them out of the canoe.

"Your name, madam?" Druce asked, consulting a list. "Are you Mrs. Rolt?"

"I am not Mrs. Rolt. I am Miss Malcott."

"Will you go up to the house? The doctor . . ."

"The doctor has far more serious cases than me to attend to."

Mrs. Perrot said, "You'd like to lie down."

"It's the last thing I want to do," Miss Malcott said. "I

am not in the least tired." She shut her mouth between every sentence. "I am not hungry. I am not nervous. I want to get on."

"Where to?"

"To Lagos. To the Educational Department."

"I'm afraid there will be a good many delays."

"I've been delayed two months. I can't stand delay. Work won't wait." Suddenly she lifted her face towards the sky and howled like a dog.

The doctor took her gently by the arm and said, "We'll do what we can to get you there right away. Come up to the house and do some telephoning."

"Certainly," Miss Malcott said, "there's nothing that can't be straightened on a telephone."

The doctor said to Scobie, "Send those other two chaps up after us. They are all right. If you want to do some questioning, question them."

Druce said, "I'll take them along. You stay here, Scobie, in case the launch arrives. French isn't my language."

Scobie sat down on the rail of the jetty and looked across the water. Now that the haze was lifting the other bank came closer; he could make out now with the naked eye the details of the scene: the white warehouse, the mud huts, the brasswork of the launch glittering in the sun: he could see the red fezzes of the native troops. He thought: Just such a scene as this and I might have been waiting for Louise to appear on a stretcher—or perhaps not waiting. Somebody settled himself on the rail beside him, but Scobie didn't turn his head.

"A penny for your thoughts, sir."

"I was just thinking that Louise is safe, Wilson."

"I was thinking that too, sir."

"Why do you always call me sir, Wilson? You are not in the police force. It makes me feel very old."

"I'm sorry, Major Scobie."

"What did Louise call you?"

"Wilson. I don't think she liked my Christian name."

"I believe they've got that launch to start at last, Wilson. Be a good chap and warn the doctor."

A French officer in a stained white uniform stood in the bow: a soldier flung a rope and Scobie caught and fixed it. *"Bonjour,"* he said, and saluted.

The French officer returned his salute—a drained-out figure with a twitch in the left eyelid. He said in English, "Good morning. I have seven stretcher cases for you here."

"My signal says nine."

"One died on the way and one last night. One from blackwater and one from—from, my English is bad, do you say fatigue?"

"Exhaustion."

"That is it."

"If you will let my labourers come on board they will get the stretchers off." Scobie said to the carriers, "Very softly. Go very softly." It was an unnecessary command: no white hospital attendants could lift and carry more gently. "Won't you stretch your legs on shore?" Scobie asked, "or come up to the house and have some coffee?"

"No. No coffee, thank you. I will just see that all is right here." He was courteous and unapproachable, but all the time his left eyelid flickered a message of doubt and distress.

"I have some English papers if you would like to see them."

"No, no, thank you. I read English with difficulty."

"You speak it very well."

"That is a different thing."

"Have a cigarette?"

"Thank you, no. I do not like American tobacco."

The first stretcher came on shore—the sheets were drawn up to the man's chin and it was impossible to tell from the stiff vacant face what his age might be. The doctor came down the hill to meet the stretcher and led the carriers away to the Government rest-house where the beds had been prepared.

"I used to come over to your side," Scobie said, "to shoot

with your police chief. A nice fellow called Durand—a Nor-
man."

"He is not here any longer," the officer said.

"Gone home?"

"He's in prison at Dakar," the French officer replied,
standing like a figure-head in the bows, but the eye twitching and twitching. The stretchers slowly passed Scobie and
turned up the hill: a boy who couldn't have been more than
ten with a feverish face and a twig-like arm thrown out from
his blanket: an old lady with grey hair falling every way
who twisted and turned and whispered: a man with a bottle
nose—a knob of scarlet and blue on a yellow face. One by
one they turned up the hill—the carriers' feet moving with
the certainty of mules. "And Père Brûle?" Scobie asked.
"He was a good man."

"He died last year of blackwater."

"He was out here twenty years without leave, wasn't he?
He'll be hard to replace."

"He has not been replaced," the officer said. He turned
and gave a short savage order to one of his men. Scobie
looked at the next stretcher load and looked away again. A
small girl—she couldn't have been more than six—lay on it.
She was deeply and unhealthily asleep; her fair hair was
tangled and wet with sweat; her open mouth was dry and
cracked, and she shuddered regularly and spasmodically.
"It's terrible," Scobie said.

"What is terrible?"

"A child like that."

"Yes. Both parents were lost. But it is all right. She will
die."

Scobie watched the bearers go slowly up the hill, their
bare feet very gently flapping the ground. He thought: It
would need all Father Brûle's ingenuity to explain that. Not
that the child would die—that needed no explanation. Even
the pagans realized that the love of God might mean an
early death, though the reason they ascribed was different;
but that the child should have been allowed to survive the

forty days and nights in the open boat—that was the mystery, to reconcile that with the love of God.

And yet he could believe in no God who was not human enough to love what he had created. "How on earth did she survive till now?" he wondered aloud.

The officer said gloomily, "Of course they looked after her on the boat. They gave up their own share of the water often. It was foolish, of course, but one cannot always be logical. And it gave them something to think about." It was like the hint of an explanation—too faint to be grasped. He said, "Here is another who makes one angry."

The face was ugly with exhaustion: the skin looked as though it were about to crack over the cheek-bones: only the absence of lines showed that it was a young face. The French officer said, "She was just married—before she sailed. Her husband was lost. Her passport says she is nineteen. She may live. You see, she still has some strength." Her arms as thin as a child's lay outside the blanket, and her fingers clasped a book firmly. Scobie could see the wedding-ring loose on her dried-up finger.

"What is it?"

"*Timbres,*" the French officer said. He added bitterly, "When this damned war started, she must have been still at school."

Scobie always remembered how she was carried into his life on a stretcher grasping a stamp-album with her eyes fast shut.

iii

In the evening they gathered together again for drinks, but they were subdued. Even Perrot was no longer trying to impress them. Druce said, "Well, tomorrow I'm off. You coming, Scobie?"

"I suppose so."

Mrs. Perrot said, "You got all you wanted?"

"All I needed. That chief engineer was a good fellow. He had it ready in his head. I could hardly write fast enough.

When he stopped he went flat out. That was what was keeping him together—'ma responsibility.' You know they'd walked—the ones that could walk—five days to get here."

Wilson said, "Were they sailing without an escort?"

"They started out in convoy, but they had some engine trouble—and you know the rule of the road nowadays: no waiting for lame ducks. They were twelve hours behind the convoy and were trying to pick up when they were sniped. The submarine commander surfaced and gave them direction. He said he would have given them a tow, but there was a naval patrol out looking for him. You see, you can really blame nobody for this sort of thing," and this sort of thing came at once to Scobie's mind's eye—the child with the open mouth, the thin hands holding the stamp-album. He said, "I suppose the doctor will look in when he gets a chance?"

He went restlessly out on to the verandah, closing the netted door carefully behind him, and a mosquito immediately droned towards his ear. The skirring went on all the time, but when they drove to the attack they had the deeper tone of dive-bombers. The lights were showing in the temporary hospital, and the weight of that misery lay on his shoulders. It was as if he had shed one responsibility only to take on another. This was a responsibility he shared with all human beings, but that was no comfort, for it sometimes seemed to him that he was the only one who recognized his responsibility. In the Cities of the Plain a single soul might have changed the mind of God.

The doctor came up the steps on to the verandah. "Hallo, Scobie," he said in a voice as bowed as his shoulders, "taking the night air? It's not healthy in this place."

"How are they?" Scobie asked.

"There'll be only two more deaths, I think. Perhaps only one."

"The child?"

"She'll be dead by morning," the doctor said abruptly.

"Is she conscious?"

"Never completely. She asks for her father sometimes: she probably thinks she's in the boat still. They'd kept it from her there—said her parents were in one of the other boats. But of course they'd signalled to check up."

"Won't she take you for her father?"

"No, she won't accept the beard."

Scobie said, "How's the school-teacher?"

"Miss Malcott? She'll be all right. I've given her enough bromide to put her out of action till morning. That's all she needs—and the sense of getting somewhere. You haven't got room for her in your police van, have you? She'd be better out of here."

"There's only just room for Druce and me with our boys and kit. We'll be sending proper transport as soon as we get back. The walking cases all right?"

"Yes, they'll manage."

"The boy and the old lady?"

"They'll pull through."

"Who is the boy?"

"He was at a prep school in England. His parents in South Africa thought he'd be safer with them."

Scobie said reluctantly, "That young woman—with the stamp-album?" It was the stamp-album and not the face that haunted his memory for no reason that he could understand, and the wedding-ring loose on the finger, as though a child had dressed up.

"I don't know," the doctor said. "If she gets through to-night—perhaps——"

"You're dead tired, aren't you? Go in and have a drink."

"Yes. I don't want to be eaten by mosquitoes." The doctor opened the verandah door, and a mosquito struck at Scobie's neck. He didn't bother to guard himself. Slowly, hesitatingly, he retraced the route the doctor had taken, down the steps on to the tough rocky ground. The loose stones turned under his boots. He thought of Pemberton. What an absurd thing it was to expect happiness in a world so full of misery. He had cut down his own needs to a minimum, photographs were put away in drawers, the dead were put out of mind: a razor-strop, a pair of rusty handcuffs for decoration. But one still has one's eyes, he thought, one's ears. Point me out the happy man and I will point you out either extreme egotism, evil—or else an absolute ignorance.

Outside the rest-house he stopped again. The lights inside would have given an extraordinary impression of peace if one hadn't known, just as the stars on this clear night gave also an impression of remoteness, security, freedom. If one knew, he wondered, the facts, would one have to feel pity even for the planets? if one reached what they called the heart of the matter?

"Well, Major Scobie?" It was the wife of the local missionary speaking to him. She was dressed in white like a nurse, and her flint-grey hair lay back from her forehead in ridges like wind erosion. "Have you come to look on?" she asked forbiddingly.

"Yes," he said. He had no other idea of what to say: he couldn't describe to Mrs. Bowles the restlessness, the haunting images, the terrible impotent feeling of responsibility and pity.

"Come inside," Mrs. Bowles said, and he followed her obediently like a boy. There were three rooms in the rest-house. In the first the walking cases had been put: heavily dosed they slept peacefully, as though they had been taking healthy exercise. In the second room were the stretcher cases for whom there was reasonable hope. The third room was a small one and contained only two beds divided by a screen: the six-year-old girl with the dry mouth, the young woman lying unconscious on her back, still grasping the stamp-album. A night-light burned in a saucer and cast thin shadows between the beds. "If you want to be useful," Mrs. Bowles said, "stay here a moment. I want to go to the dispensary."

"The dispensary?"

"The cook-house. One has to make the best of things."

Scobie felt cold and strange. A shiver moved his shoulders. He said, "Can't I go for you?"

Mrs. Bowles said, "Don't be absurd. Are you qualified to dispense? I'll only be away a few minutes. If the child shows signs of going call me." If she had given him time, he would have thought of some excuse, but she was already out of the room and he sat heavily down in the only chair. When he looked at the child, he saw a white communion veil over her head: it was a trick of the light on the mosquito net and a trick of his own mind. He put his head in his hands and wouldn't look. He had been in Africa when his own child died. He had always thanked God that he had missed that. It seemed after all that one never really missed a thing. To be a human being one had to drink the cup. If one were lucky on one day, or cowardly on another, it was presented on a third occasion. He prayed silently into his hands, "O God, don't let anything happen before Mrs. Bowles comes back." He could hear the heavy uneven breathing of the child. It was as if she were carrying a weight with great effort up a long hill: it was an inhuman situation not to be able to carry it for her. He thought: this is what parents feel year in and year out, and I am shrinking from a few minutes of it. They see their children dying slowly every hour they live. He prayed again, "Father, look after her. Give her peace." The breathing broke, choked, began again with terrible effort. Looking between his fingers he could see the six-year-old face convulsed like a navvy's with labour. "Father," he prayed, "give her peace. Take away my peace for ever, but give her peace." The sweat broke out on his hands. "Father . . ."

He heard a small scraping voice repeat, "Father," and looking up he saw the blue and bloodshot eyes watching him. He thought with horror: this is what I thought I'd missed. He would have called Mrs. Bowles, only he hadn't the voice to call with. He could see the breast of the child struggling for breath to repeat the heavy word; he came

over to the bed and said, "Yes, dear. Don't speak, I'm here."
The night-light cast the shadow of his clenched fist on the
sheet and it caught the child's eye. An effort to laugh convulsed her, and he moved his hand away. "Sleep, dear," he
said, "you are sleepy. Sleep." A memory that he had carefully buried returned and taking out his handkerchief he
made the shadow of a rabbit's head fall on the pillow beside
her. "There's your rabbit," he said, "to go to sleep with. It
will stay until you sleep. Sleep." The sweat poured down his
face and tasted in his mouth as salt as tears. "Sleep." He
moved the rabbit's ears up and down, up and down. Then
he heard Mrs. Bowles's voice, speaking low just behind him.
"Stop that," she said harshly, "the child's dead."

iv

In the morning he told the doctor that he would stay till
proper transport arrived: Miss Malcott could have his place
in the police van. It was better to get her moving, for the
child's death had upset her again, and it was by no means
certain that there would not be other deaths. They buried
the child next day, using the only coffin they could get: it
had been designed for a tall man. In this climate delay was
unwise. Scobie did not attend the funeral service, which was
read by Mr. Bowles, but the Perrots were present, Wilson
and some of the court messengers: the doctor was busy in the
rest-house. Instead, Scobie walked rapidly through the rice-
fields, talked to the agricultural officer about irrigation, kept
away. Later, when he had exhausted the possibilities of irrigation, he went into the store and sat in the dark among all
the tins, the tinned jams and the tinned soups, the tinned
butter, the tinned biscuits, the tinned milk, the tinned pota-
toes, the tinned chocolates, and waited for Wilson. But Wilson didn't come: perhaps the funeral had been too much for
all of them, and they had returned to the D.C.'s bungalow
for drinks. Scobie went down to the jetty and watched the
sailing boats move down towards the sea. Once he found
himself saying aloud as though to a man at his elbow, "Why

didn't you let her drown?" A court messenger looked at him askance and he moved on, up the hill.

Mrs. Bowles was taking the air outside the rest-house: taking it literally, in doses like medicine. She stood there with her mouth opening and closing, inhaling and expelling. She said, "Good afternoon," stiffly, and took another dose. "You weren't at the funeral, major?"

"No."

"Mr. Bowles and I can seldom attend a funeral together. Except when we're on leave."

"Are there going to be any more funerals?"

"One more, I think. The rest will be all right in time."

"Which of them is dying?"

"The old lady. She took a turn for the worse last night. She had been getting on well."

He felt a merciless relief. He said, "The boy's all right?"

"Yes."

"And Mrs. Rolt?"

"She's not out of danger, but I think she'll do. She's conscious now."

"Does she know her husband's dead?"

"Yes." Mrs. Bowles began to swing her arms, up and down, from the shoulder. Then she stood on tip-toe six times. He said, "I wish there was something I could do to help."

"Can you read aloud?" Mrs. Bowles asked, rising on her toes.

"I suppose so. Yes."

"You can read to the boy. He's getting bored and boredom's bad for him."

"Where shall I find a book?"

"There are plenty at the Mission. Shelves of them."

Anything was better than doing nothing. He walked up to the Mission and found, as Mrs. Bowles said, plenty of books. He wasn't much used to books, but even to his eye these hardly seemed a bright collection for reading to a sick boy. Damp-stained and late Victorian, the bindings bore titles like *Twenty Years in the Mission Field, Lost and Found, The Narrow Way, The Missionary's Warning*. Obviously at some time there had been an appeal for books for the Mission library, and here were the scrapings of many pious shelves at home. *The Poems of John Oxenham, Fishers of Men*. He took a book at random out of the shelf and returned to the rest-house. Mrs. Bowles was in her dispensary mixing medicines.

"Found something?"

"Yes."

"You are safe with any of those books," Mrs. Bowles said. "They are censored by the committee before they come out. Sometimes people try to send the most unsuitable books. We are not teaching the children here to read in order that they shall read—well, novels."

"No, I suppose not."

"Let me see what you've chosen."

He looked at the title himself for the first time: *A Bishop Among the Bantus*.

"That should be interesting," Mrs. Bowles said. He agreed doubtfully.

"You know where to find him. You can read to him for a quarter of an hour—not more."

The old lady had been moved into the innermost room where the child had died, the man with the bottle nose had been shifted into what Mrs. Bowles now called the convalescence ward, so that the middle room could be given up to the boy and Mrs. Rolt. Mrs. Rolt lay facing the wall with her eyes closed. They had apparently succeeded in removing the album from her clutch and it lay on a chair beside the bed. The boy watched Scobie with the bright intelligent gaze of fever.

"My name's Scobie. What's yours?"

"Fisher."

Scobie said nervously, "Mrs. Bowles asked me to read to you."

"What are you? A soldier?"

"No, a policeman."

"Is it a murder story?"

"No. I don't think it is." He opened the book at random and came on a photograph of the bishop sitting in his robes on a hard drawing-room chair outside a little tin-roofed church: he was surrounded by Bantus, who grinned at the camera.

"I'd like a murder story. Have you ever been in a murder?"

"Not what you'd call a real murder with clues and a chase."

"What sort of a murder then?"

"Well, people get stabbed sometimes fighting." He spoke in a low voice so as not to disturb Mrs. Rolt. She lay with her fist clenched on the sheet—a fist not much bigger than a tennis ball.

"What's the name of the book you've brought? Perhaps I've read it. I read *Treasure Island* on the boat. I wouldn't mind a pirate story. What's it called?"

Scobie said dubiously, *"A Bishop Among the Bantus."*

"What does that mean?"

Scobie drew a long breath. "Well, you see, Bishop is the name of the hero."

"But you said *a* Bishop."

"Yes. His name was Arthur."

"It's a soppy name."

"Yes, but he's a soppy hero." Suddenly, avoiding the boy's eyes, he noticed that Mrs. Rolt was not asleep: she was staring at the wall, listening. He went wildly on, "The real heroes are the Bantus."

"What are Bantus?"

"They were a peculiarly ferocious lot of pirates who haunted the West Indies and preyed on all the shipping in that part of the Atlantic."

"Does Arthur Bishop pursue them?"

"Yes. It's a kind of detective story too because he's a secret agent of the British Government. He dresses up as an ordinary seaman and sails on a merchantman so that he can be captured by the Bantus. You know they always give the ordinary seamen a chance to join them. If he'd been an officer they would have made him walk the plank. Then he discovers all their secret passwords and hiding-places and their plans of raids, of course, so that he can betray them when the time is ripe."

"He sounds a bit of a swine," the boy said.

"Yes, and he falls in love with the daughter of the captain of the Bantus and that's when he turns soppy. But that comes near the end and we won't get as far as that. There are a lot of fights and murders before then."

"It sounds all right. Let's begin."

"Well, you see, Mrs. Bowles told me I was only to stay a short time today, so I've just told you *about* the book and we can start it tomorrow."

"You may not be here tomorrow. There may be a murder or something."

"But the book will be here. I'll leave it with Mrs. Bowles. It's her book. Of course it may sound a bit different when *she* reads it."

"Just begin it," the boy pleaded.

"Yes, begin it," said a low voice from the other bed, so low that he would have discounted it as an illusion if he hadn't looked up and seen her watching him, the eyes large as a child's in the starved face.

Scobie said, "I'm a very bad reader."

"Go on," the boy said impatiently. "Anyone can read aloud."

Scobie found his eyes fixed on an opening paragraph which stated, *I shall never forget my first glimpse of the continent where I was to labour for thirty of the best years of my life.* He said slowly, "From the moment that they left Bermuda the low lean rakehelly craft had followed in their wake. The captain was evidently worried, for he watched the strange ship continually through his spy-glass. When night fell it was still on their trail, and at dawn it was the first sight that met their eyes. Can it be, Arthur Bishop wondered, that I am about to meet the object of my quest, Blackbeard, the leader of the Bantus himself, or his blood-thirsty lieutenant. . . ." He turned a page and was temporarily put out by a portrait of the bishop in whites with a clerical collar and a topee, standing before a wicket and blocking a ball a Baɲtu had just bowled him.

"Go on," the boy said.

". . . Batty Davis, so called because of his insane rages when he would send a whole ship's crew to the plank? It was evident that Captain Buller feared the worst, for he crowded on all canvas and it seemed for a time that he would show the strange ship a clean pair of heels. Suddenly over the water came the boom of a gun, and a cannon-ball struck the water twenty yards ahead of them. Captain Buller had his glass to his eye and called down from the bridge to Arthur Bishop, 'The jolly Roger, by God.' He was the only one of the ship's company who knew the secret of Arthur's strange quest."

Mrs. Bowles came briskly in. "There, that will do. Quite enough for the day. And what's he been reading you, Jimmy?"

"Bishop Among the Bantus."

"I hope you enjoyed it."

"It's wizard."

"You're a very sensible boy," Mrs. Bowles said approvingly.

"Thank you," a voice said from the other bed and Scobie turned again reluctantly to take in the young devastated face. "Will you read again tomorrow?"

"Don't worry Major Scobie, Helen," Mrs. Bowles rebuked her. "He's got to get back to the port. They'll all be murdering each other without him."

"You a policeman?"

"Yes."

"I knew a policeman once—in our town——" the voice trailed off into sleep. He stood a minute looking down at her face. Like a fortune-teller's cards it showed unmistakably the past—a voyage, a loss, a sickness. In the next deal perhaps it would be possible to see the future. He took up the stamp-album and opened it at the fly-leaf: it was inscribed, "Helen, from her loving father on her fourteenth birthday." Then it fell open at Paraguay, full of the decorative images of parakeets—the kind of picture stamps a child collects. "We'll have to find her some new stamps," he said sadly.

v

Wilson was waiting for him outside. He said, "I've been looking for you, Major Scobie, ever since the funeral."

"I've been doing good works," Scobie said.

"How's Mrs. Rolt?"

"They think she'll pull through—and the boy too."

"Oh yes, the boy." Wilson kicked a loose stone in the path and said, "I want your advice, Major Scobie. I'm a bit worried."

"Yes?"

"You know I've been down here checking up on our store. Well, I find that our manager has been buying military stuff. There's a lot of tinned food that never came from our exporters."

"Isn't the answer fairly simple—sack him?"

"It seems a pity to sack the small thief if he could lead one to the big thief, but of course that's your job. That's why I wanted to talk to you." Wilson paused and that extraordinary tell-tale blush spread over his face. He said, "You see, he got the stuff from Yusef's man."

"I could have guessed that."

"You could?"

"Yes, but you see, Yusef's man is not the same as Yusef. It's easy for him to disown a country storekeeper. In fact, for all we know, Yusef may be innocent. It's unlikely, but not impossible. Your own evidence would point to it. After all you've only just learned yourself what your storekeeper was doing."

"If there were clear evidence," Wilson said, "would the police prosecute?"

Scobie came to a standstill. "What's that?"

Wilson blushed and mumbled. Then, with a venom that took Scobie completely by surprise, he said, "There are rumours going about that Yusef is protected."

"You've been here long enough to know what rumours are worth."

"They are all round the town."

"Spread by Tallit—or Yusef himself."

"Don't misunderstand me," Wilson said. "You've been very kind to me—and Mrs. Scobie has too. I thought you ought to know what's been said."

"I've been here fifteen years, Wilson."

"Oh, I know," Wilson said, "this is impertinent. But people are worried about Tallit's parrot. They say he was framed because Yusef wants him run out of town."

"Yes, I've heard that."

"They say that you and Yusef are on visiting terms. It's a lie, of course, but . . ."

"It's perfectly true. I'm also on visiting terms with the sanitary inspector, but it wouldn't prevent my prosecuting him. . . ." He stopped abruptly. He said, "I have no intention of defending myself to you, Wilson."

Wilson repeated, "I just thought you ought to know."

"You are too young for your job, Wilson."

"My job?"

"Whatever it is."

For the second time Wilson took him by surprise, breaking out with a crack in his voice, "Oh, you are unbearable. You are too damned honest to live." His face was aflame, even his knees seemed to blush with rage, shame, self-depreciation.

"You ought to wear a hat, Wilson," was all Scobie said.

They stood facing each other on the stony path between the D.C.'s bungalow and the rest-house; the light lay flat across the rice-fields below them, and Scobie was conscious of how prominently they were silhouetted to the eyes of any watcher. "You sent Louise away," Wilson said, "because you were afraid of me."

Scobie laughed gently. "This is sun, Wilson, just sun. We'll forget about it in the morning."

"She couldn't stand your stupid, unintelligent . . . you don't know what a woman like Louise thinks."

"I don't suppose I do. Nobody wants another person to know that, Wilson."

Wilson said, "I kissed her that evening. . . ."

"It's the colonial sport, Wilson." He hadn't meant to madden the young man: he was only anxious to let the occasion pass lightly, so that in the morning they could behave naturally to each other. It was just a touch of sun, he told himself; he had seen this happen times out of mind during fifteen years.

Wilson said, "She's too good for you."

"For both of us."

"How did you get the money to send her away? That's what I'd like to know. You don't earn all that. I know. It's printed in the Colonial Office List." If the young man had been less absurd, Scobie might have been angered and they might have ended friends. It was his serenity that stoked the flames. He said now, "Let's talk about it tomorrow. We've all been upset by that child's death. Come up to the bungalow and have a drink." He made to pass Wilson, but Wilson barred the way: a Wilson scarlet in the face with tears in the eyes. It was as if he had gone so far that he realized the only thing to do was to go farther—there was no return the way he had come. He said, "Don't think I haven't got my eye on you."

The absurdity of the phrase took Scobie off his guard.

"You watch your step," Wilson said, "and Mrs. Rolt . . ."

"What on earth has Mrs. Rolt got to do with it?"

"Don't think I don't know why you've stayed behind, haunted the hospital. . . . While we were all at the funeral, you slunk down here. . . ."

"You really are crazy, Wilson," Scobie said.

Suddenly Wilson sat down; it was as if he had been folded up by some large invisible hand. He put his head in his hands and wept.

"It's the sun," Scobie said. "Just the sun. Go and lie down," and taking off his hat he put it on Wilson's head. Wilson looked up at him between his fingers—at the man who had seen his tears—with hatred.

[2]

i

The sirens were wailing for a total black-out, wailing through the rain which fell interminably; the boys scrambled into the kitchen quarters, and bolted the door as though to protect themselves from some devil of the bush. Without pause the hundred and forty-four inches of water continued their steady and ponderous descent upon the roofs of the port. It was incredible to imagine that any human beings, let alone the dispirited fever-soaked defeated of Vichy territory, would open an assault at this time of the year, and yet of course one remembered the Heights of Abraham. . . . A single feat of daring can alter the whole conception of what is possible.

Scobie went out into the dripping darkness holding his big striped umbrella: a mackintosh was too hot to wear. He walked all round his quarters; not a light showed, the shutters of the kitchen were closed, and the Creole houses were invisible behind the rain. A torch gleamed momentarily in the transport park across the road, but, when he shouted, it went out: a coincidence: no one there could have heard his voice above the hammering of the water on the roof. Up in Cape Station the officers' mess was shining wetly towards the sea, but that was not his responsibility. The headlamps of the military lorries ran like a chain of beads along the edge of the hills, but that too was someone else's affair.

Up the road behind the transport park a light went suddenly on in one of the Nissen huts where the minor officials lived; it was a hut that had been unoccupied the day before and presumably some visitor had just moved in. Scobie considered getting his car from the garage, but the hut was only a couple of hundred yards away, and he walked. Except for the sound of the rain, on the road, on the roofs, on the umbrella, there was absolute silence: only the dying moan of the sirens continued for a moment or two to vibrate within the ear. It seemed to Scobie later that this was the ultimate border he had reached in happiness: being in darkness, alone, with the rain falling, without love or pity.

He knocked on the door of the Nissen hut, loudly because of the blows of the rain on the black roof like a tunnel. He had to knock twice before the door opened. The light for a moment blinded him. He said, "I'm sorry to bother you. One of your lights is showing."

A woman's voice said, "Oh, I'm sorry. It was careless . . ."

His eyes cleared, but for a moment he couldn't put a name to the intensely remembered features. He knew everyone in the colony. This was something that had come from outside . . . a river . . . early morning . . . a dying child. "Why," he said, "it's Mrs. Rolt, isn't it? I thought you were in hospital?"

"Yes. Who are you? Do I know you?"

"I'm Major Scobie of the police. I saw you at Pende."

"I'm sorry," she said. "I don't remember a thing that happened there."

"Can I fix your light?"

"Of course. Please." He came in and drew the curtains close and shifted a table lamp. The hut was divided in two by a curtain: on one side a bed, a makeshift dressing-table: on the other a table, a couple of chairs—the few sticks of furniture of the pattern allowed to junior officials with salaries under £500 a year. He said, "They haven't done you very proud, have they? I wish I'd known. I could have helped." He took her in closely now: the young worn-out face, with the hair gone dead. . . . The pyjamas she was wearing were too large for her: the body was lost in them: they fell in ugly folds. He looked to see whether the ring was still loose upon her finger, but it had gone altogether.

"Everybody's been very kind," she said. "Mrs. Carter gave me a lovely pouf."

His eyes wandered: there was nothing personal anywhere: no photographs, no books, no trinkets of any kind, but then he rememberered that she had brought nothing out of the sea except herself and a stamp-album.

"Is there any danger?" she asked anxiously.

"Danger?"

"The sirens."

"Oh, none at all. These are just alarms. We get about one a month. Nothing ever happens." He took another long look at her. "They oughtn't to have let you out of hospital so soon. It's not six weeks . . ."

"I wanted to go. I wanted to be alone. People kept on coming to see me."

"Well, I'll be going now myself. Remember if you ever want anything I'm just down the road. The two-storeyed white house beyond the transport park sitting in a swamp."

"Won't you stay till the rain stops?" she asked.

"I don't think I'd better," he said. "You see, it goes on until September," and won out of her a stiff unused smile.

"The noise is awful."

"You get used to it in a few weeks. Like living beside a railway. But you won't have to. They'll be sending you home very soon. There's a boat in a fortnight."

"Would you like a drink? Mrs. Carter gave me a bottle of gin as well as the pouf."

"I'd better help you to drink it then." He noticed when

she produced the bottle that nearly half had gone. "Have you any limes?"

"No."

"They've given you a boy, I suppose?"

"Yes, but I don't know what to ask him for. And he never seems to be around."

"You've been drinking it neat?"

"Oh no, I haven't touched it. The boy upset it—that was his story."

"I'll talk to your boy in the morning," Scobie said. "Got an ice-box?"

"Yes, but the boy can't get me any ice." She sat weakly down in a chair. "Don't think me a fool. I just don't know where I am. I've never been anywhere like this."

"Where do you come from?"

"Bury St. Edmunds. In Suffolk. I was there eight weeks ago."

"Oh no, you weren't. You were in that boat."

"Yes. I forgot the boat."

"They oughtn't to have pushed you out of the hospital all alone like this."

"I'm all right. They had to have my bed. Mrs. Carter said she'd find room for me, but I wanted to be alone. The doctor told them to do what I wanted."

Scobie said, "I can understand you wouldn't want to be with Mrs. Carter, and you've only got to say the word and I'll be off too."

"I'd rather you waited till the All Clear. I'm a bit rattled, you know." The stamina of women had always amazed Scobie. This one had survived forty days in an open boat and she talked about being rattled. He remembered the casualties in the report the chief engineer had made: the third officer and two seamen who had died, and the stoker who had gone off his head as a result of drinking sea water and drowned himself. When it came to strain it was always a man who broke. Now she lay back on her weakness as on a pillow.

He said, "Have you thought out things? Shall you go back to Bury?"

"I don't know. Perhaps I'll get a job."

"Have you had any experience?"

"No," she confessed, looking away from him. "You see, I only left school a year ago."

"Did they teach you anything?" It seemed to him that what she needed more than anything else was just talk, silly aimless talk. She thought that she wanted to be alone, but what she was afraid of was the awful responsibility of receiving sympathy. How could a child like that act the part of a woman whose husband had been drowned more or less before her eyes? As well expect her to act Lady Macbeth. Mrs. Carter would have had no sympathy with her inadequacy. Mrs. Carter, of course, would have known how to behave, having buried one husband and three children.

She said, "I was best at netball," breaking in on his thoughts.

"Well," he said, "you haven't quite the figure for a gym instructor. Or have you, when you are well?"

Suddenly and without warning she began to talk. It was as if by the inadvertent use of a password he had induced a door to open: he couldn't tell now which word he had used. Perhaps it was "gym instructor," for she began rapidly to tell him about the netball (Mrs. Carter, he thought, had probably talked about forty days in an open boat and a three-weeks'-old husband). She said, "I was in the school team for two years," leaning forward excitedly with her chin on her hand and one bony elbow upon a bony knee. With her white skin—unyellowed yet by atebrin or sunlight—he was reminded of a bone the sea has washed and cast up. "A year before that I was in the second team. I would have been captain if I'd stayed another year. In 1940 we beat Roedean and tied with Cheltenham."

He listened with the intense interest one feels in a stranger's life, the interest the young mistake for love. He felt the security of his age sitting there listening with a glass of gin in his hand and the rain coming down. She told him her school was on the downs just behind Seaport: they had a French mistress called Mlle. Dupont who had a vile temper. The headmistress could read Greek just like English—Virgil. . . .

"I always thought Virgil was Latin."

"Oh yes. I meant Homer. I wasn't any good at Classics."

"Were you good at anything besides netball?"

"I think I was next best at maths, but I was never any good at trigonometry." In summer they went into Seaport and bathed, and every Saturday they had a picnic on the downs—sometimes a paper-chase on ponies, and once a disastrous affair on bicycles which spread out over the whole country, and two girls didn't return till one in the morning. He listened fascinated, revolving the heavy gin in his glass without drinking. The sirens squealed the All Clear through the rain, but neither of them paid any attention. He said, "And then in the holidays you went back to Bury?"

Apparently her mother had died ten years ago, and her father was a clergyman attached in some way to the Cathedral. They had a very small house on Angel Hill. Perhaps she had not been as happy at Bury as at school, for she tacked back at the first opportunity to discuss the games mistress whose name was the same as her own—Helen, and for whom the whole of her year had an enormous *schwärmerei*. She laughed now at this passion in a superior way: it was the only indication she gave him that she was grown-up, that she was—or rather had been—a married woman.

She broke suddenly off and said, "What nonsense it is telling you all this."

"I like it."

"You haven't once asked me about—you know——"

He did know, for he had read the report. He knew exactly the water ration for each person in the boat—a cupful twice a day, which had been reduced after twenty-one days to half a cupful. That had been maintained until within twenty-four hours of the rescue mainly because the deaths had left a small surplus. Behind the school buildings of Seaport, the totem-pole of the netball game, he was aware of the intolerable surge, lifting the boat and dropping it again, lifting it and dropping it. "I was miserable when I left—it was the end of July. I cried in the taxi all the way to the station." Scobie counted the months—July to April: nine months: the period of gestation, and what had been born was a husband's death and the Atlantic pushing them like wreckage towards the long flat African beach and the sailor throwing himself over the side. He said, "This is more interesting. I can guess the other."

"What a lot I've talked. Do you know, I think I shall sleep tonight."

"Haven't you been sleeping?"

"It was the breathing all round me at the hospital. People turning and breathing and muttering. When the light was out, it was just like—you know."

"You'll sleep quietly here. No need to be afraid of anything. There's a watchman always on duty. I'll have a word with him."

"You've been so kind," she said. "Mrs. Carter and the others—they've all been kind." She lifted her worn, frank, childish face and said, "I like you so much."

"I like you too," he said gravely. They both had an immense sense of security: they were friends who could never be anything else than friends—they were safely divided by a dead husband, a living wife, a father who was a clergyman, a games mistress called Helen, and years and years of experience. They hadn't got to worry about what they should say to each other.

He said, "Good night. Tomorrow I'm going to bring you some stamps for your album."

"How did you know about my album?"

"That's my job. I'm a policeman."

"Good night."

He walked away, feeling an extraordinary happiness, but this he would not remember as happiness, as he would remember setting out in the darkness, in the rain, alone.

ii

From eight-thirty in the morning until eleven he dealt with a case of petty larceny; there were six witnesses to examine, and he didn't believe a word that any of them said. In European cases there are words one believes and words one distrusts: it is possible to draw a speculative line between the truth and the lies; at least the *cui bono* principle to some extent operates, and it is usually safe to assume, if the accusation is theft and there is no question of insurance, that something has at least been stolen. But here one could make no such assumption: one could draw no lines. He had known police officers whose nerves broke down in the effort to separate a single grain of incontestable truth; they ended, some of them, by striking a witness, they were pilloried in the local Creole papers and were invalided home or transferred. It woke in some men a virulent hatred of a black skin, but Scobie had long ago, during his fifteen years, passed through the dangerous stages; now lost in the tangle of lies he felt an extraordinary affection for these people who paralysed an alien form of justice by so simple a method.

At last the office was clear again. There was nothing further on the charge-sheet, and taking out a pad and placing some blotting-paper under his wrist to catch the sweat, he prepared to write to Louise. Letter-writing never came easily to him. Perhaps because of his police training, he could never put even a comforting lie upon paper over his signature. He had to be accurate: he could comfort only by omission. So now, writing the two words *My dear* upon the paper, he prepared to omit. He wouldn't write that he missed her, but he would leave out any phrase that told unmistakably that he was content. *My dear, you must forgive a short letter again. You know I'm not much of a hand at letter-writing. I got your third letter yesterday, the one telling me that you were staying with Mrs.*

Halifax's friend for a week outside Durban. Here everything is quiet. We had an alarm last night, but it turned out that an American pilot had mistaken a school of porpoises for submarines. The rains have started, of course. The Mrs. Rolt I told you about in my last letter is out of hospital and they've put her to wait for a boat in one of the Nissen huts behind the transport park. I'll do what I can to make her comfortable. The boy is still in hospital, but all right. I really think that's about all the news. The Tallit affair drags on—I don't think anything will come of it in the end. Ali had to go and have a couple of teeth out the other day. What a fuss he made! I had to drive him to the hospital or he'd never have gone. He paused: he hated the idea of the censors—who happened to be Mrs. Carter and Calloway— reading these last phrases of affection. *Look after yourself, my dear, and don't worry about me. As long as you are happy, I'm happy. In another nine months I can take my leave and we'll be together.* He was going to write, "You are in my mind always," but that was not a statement he could sign. He wrote instead, *You are in my mind so often during the day,* and then pondered the signature. Reluctantly, because he believed it would please her, he wrote *Your Ticki.* For a moment he was reminded of that other letter signed "Dicky" which had come back to him two or three times in dreams.

The sergeant entered, marched to the middle of the floor, turned smartly to face him, saluted. He had time to address the envelope while all this was going on. "Yes, sergeant?"

"The Commissioner, sah, he ask you to see him."

"Right."

The Commissioner was not alone. The Colonial Secretary's face shone gently with sweat in the dusky room, and beside him sat a tall bony man Scobie had not seen before— he must have arrived by air, for there had been no ship in during the last ten days. He wore a colonel's badges as though they didn't belong to him on his loose untidy uniform.

"This is Major Scobie, Colonel Wright." He could tell the Commissioner was worried and irritated. He said, "Sit down, Scobie. It's about this Tallit business." The rain darkened the room and kept out the air. "Colonel Wright has come up from Cape Town to hear about it."

"From Cape Town, sir?"

The Commissioner moved his legs, playing with a pen-knife. He said, "Colonel Wright is the M.I.5 representative."

The Colonial Secretary said softly, so that everybody had to bend their heads to hear him, "The whole thing's been unfortunate." The Commissioner began to whittle the corner of his desk, ostentatiously not listening. "I don't think the police should have acted—quite in the way they did—not without consultation."

Scobie said, "I've always understood it was our duty to stop diamond smuggling."

In his soft obscure voice the Colonial Secretary said, "There weren't a hundred pounds' worth of diamonds found."

"They are the only diamonds that have ever been found."

"The evidence against Tallit, Scobie, was too slender for an arrest."

"He wasn't arrested. He was interrogated."

"His lawyers say he was brought forcibly to the police station."

"His lawyers are lying. You surely realize that much."

The Colonial Secretary said to Colonel Wright, "You see the kind of difficulty we are up against. The Roman Catholic Syrians are claiming they are a persecuted minority and that the police are in the pay of the Moslem Syrians."

Scobie said, "The same thing would have happened the other way round—only it would have been worse. Parliament has more affection for Moslems than Catholics." He had a sense that no one had mentioned the real purpose of this meeting. The Commissioner flaked chip after chip off his desk, disowning everything, and Colonel Wright sat back on his shoulder-blades saying nothing at all.

"Personally," the Colonial Secretary said, "I would always . . ." and the soft voice faded off into inscrutable murmurs which Wright, stuffing his fingers into one ear, leaning his head sideways as though he were trying to hear something through a defective telephone, might possibly have caught.

Scobie said, "I couldn't hear what you said."

"I said personally I'd always take Tallit's word against Yusef's."

"That," Scobie said, "is because you have only been in this colony five years."

Colonel Wright suddenly interjected, "How many years have you been here, Major Scobie?"

"Fifteen."

Colonel Wright grunted non-committally.

The Commissioner stopped whittling the corner of his desk and drove his knife viciously into the top. He said, "Colonel Wright wants to know the source of your information, Scobie."

"You know that, sir. Yusef." Wright and the Colonial Secretary sat side by side watching him. He stood back with lowered head, waiting for the next move, but no move came. He knew they were waiting for him to amplify his bald reply, and he knew too that they would take it for a confession of weakness if he did. The silence became more and more intolerable: it was like an accusation. Weeks ago he had told Yusef that he intended to let the Commissioner know the details of his loan; perhaps he had really had that intention, perhaps he had been bluffing; he couldn't remember now. He only knew that now it was too late. That information should have been given before taking action against Tallit: it could not be an afterthought. In the corridor behind the office Fraser passed whistling his favorite tune; he opened the door of the office, said, "Sorry, sir," and retreated again, leaving a whiff of warm zoo smell behind him. The murmur of the rain went on and on. The Commissioner took the knife out of the table and began to whittle again; it was as if, for a second time, he were deliberately disowning the whole business. The Colonial Secretary cleared his throat. "Yusef," he repeated.

Scobie nodded.

Colonel Wright said, "Do you consider Yusef trustworthy?"

"Of course not, sir. But one has to act on what information is available—and this information proved correct up to a point."

"Up to what point?"

"The diamonds were there."

The Colonial Secretary said, "Do you get much information from Yusef?"

"This is the first time I've had any at all."

He couldn't catch what the Colonial Secretary said beyond the word "Yusef."

"I can't hear what you say, sir."

"I said are you in touch with Yusef?"

"I don't know what you mean by that."

"Do you see him often?"

"I think in the last three months I have seen him three—no, four times."

"On business?"

"Not necessarily. Once I gave him a lift home when his car had broken down. Once he came to see me when I had fever at Bamba. Once . . ."

"We are not cross-examining you, Scobie," the Commissioner said.

"I had an idea, sir, that these gentlemen were."

Colonel Wright uncrossed his long legs and said, "Let's boil it down to one question. Tallit, Major Scobie, has made counter-accusations—against the police, against you. He says in effect that Yusef has given you money. Has he?"

"No, sir. Yusef has given me nothing." He felt an odd relief that he had not yet been called upon to lie.

The Colonial Secretary said, "Naturally sending your wife to South Africa was well within your private means."

Scobie sat back in his chair, saying nothing. Again he was aware of the hungry silence waiting for his words.

"You don't answer?" the Colonial Secretary said impatiently.

"I didn't know you had asked a question. I repeat—Yusef has given me nothing."

"He's a man to beware of, Scobie."

"Perhaps when you have been here as long as I have you'll realize the police are meant to deal with people who are not received at the Secretariat."

"We don't want our tempers to get warm, do we?"

Scobie stood up. "Can I go, sir? If these gentlemen have finished with me. . . . I have an appointment." The sweat stood on his forehead; his heart jumped with fury. This should be the moment of caution, when the blood runs down the flanks and the red cloth waves.

"That's all right, Scobie," the Commissioner said.

Colonel Wright said, "You must forgive me for bothering you. I received a report. I had to take the matter up officially. I'm quite satisfied."

"Thank you, sir." But the soothing words came too late: the damp face of the Colonial Secretary filled his field of vision. The Colonial Secretary said softly, "It's just a matter of discretion, that's all."

"If I'm wanted for the next half an hour, sir," Scobie said to the Commissioner, "I shall be at Yusef's."

iii

After all they had forced him to tell a kind of lie: he had no appointment with Yusef. All the same he wanted a few words with Yusef; it was just possible that he might yet clear up, for his own satisfaction, if not legally, the Tallit affair. Driving slowly through the rain—his windscreen wiper had long ceased to function—he saw Harris struggling with his umbrella outside the Bedford Hotel.

"Can I give you a lift? I'm going your way."

"The most exciting things have been happening," Harris

said. His hollow face shone with rain and enthusiasm. "I've got a house at last."

"Congratulations."

"At least it's not a house: it's one of the huts up your way. But it's a home," Harris said. "I'll have to share it, but it's a home."

"Who's sharing it with you?"

"I'm asking Wilson, but he's gone away—to Lagos for a week or two. The damned elusive Pimpernel. Just when I wanted him. And that brings me to the second exciting thing. Do you know I've discovered we were both at Downham?"

"Downham?"

"The school, of course. I went into his room to borrow his ink while he was away, and there on his table I saw a copy of the *Old Downhamian*."

"What a coincidence," Scobie said.

"And do you know—it's really been a day of extraordinary happenings—I was looking through the magazine and there at the end was a page which said, 'The Secretary of the Old Downhamian Association would like to get in touch with the following old boys with whom we have lost touch' —and there half-way down was my own name, in print, large as life. What do you think of that?"

"What did you do?"

"Directly I got to the office I sat down and wrote—before I touched a cable, except of course the 'most immediates,' but then I found I'd forgotten to put down the secretary's address, so back I had to go for the paper. You wouldn't care to come in, would you, and see what I've written?"

"I can't stay long." Harris had been given an office in a small unwanted room in the Elder Dempster Company's premises. It was the size of an old-fashioned servant's bedroom and this appearance was enhanced by a primitive washbasin with one cold tap and a gas-ring. A table littered with cable forms was squashed between the washbasin and a window no larger than a port-hole which looked straight out on to the water-front and the grey creased bay. An abridged version of *Ivanhoe* for the use of schools, and half a loaf of bread stood in an out-tray. "Excuse the muddle," Harris said. "Take a chair," but there was no spare chair.

"Where've I put it?" Harris wondered aloud, turning over the cables on his desk. "Ah, I remember." He opened *Ivanhoe* and fished out a folded sheet. "It's only a rough draft," he said with anxiety. "Of course I've got to pull it together. I think I'd better keep it back till Wilson comes. You see I've mentioned him."

Scobie read, *Dear Secretary, It was just by chance I came on a copy of the "Old Downhamian" which another old Downhamian, E. Wilson (1923–1928), had in his room. I'm afraid I've been out of touch with the old place for a great many years and I was very pleased and a bit guilty to see that you have been trying to get into touch with me. Perhaps you'd like to know a bit about what I'm doing in "the white man's grave," but as I'm a cable censor you will understand that I can't tell you much about my work. That will have to wait till we've won the war. We are in the middle of the rains now—and how it does rain. There's a lot of fever about, but I've only had one dose and E. Wilson has so far escaped altogether. We are sharing a little house together, so that you can feel that old Downhamians even in this wild and distant part stick together. We've got an old Downhamian team of two and go out hunting together but only cockroaches (Ha! Ha!). Well, I must stop now and get on with winning the war. Cheerio to all old Downhamians from quite an old Coaster.*

Scobie looking up met Harris's anxious and embarrassed gaze. "Do you think it's on the right lines?" he asked. "I was a bit doubtful about 'Dear Secretary.' "

"I think you've caught the tone admirably."

"Of course you know it wasn't a very good school, and I wasn't very happy there. In fact I ran away once."

"And now they've caught up with you."

"It makes you think, doesn't it?" said Harris. He stared out over the grey water with tears in his bloodshot eyes. "I've always envied people who were happy there," he said.

Scobie said consolingly, "I didn't much care for school myself."

"To start off happy," Harris said. "It must make an awful difference afterwards. Why, it might become a habit, mightn't it?" He took the piece of bread out of the out-tray and dropped it into the wastepaper-basket. "I always mean to get this place tidied up," he said.

"Well, I must be going, Harris. I'm glad about the house —and the old Downhamian."

"I wonder if Wilson was happy there," Harris brooded. He took *Ivanhoe* out of the out-tray and looked around for somewhere to put it, but there wasn't any place. He put it back again. "I don't suppose he was," he said, "or why should he have turned up here?"

iv

Scobie left his car immediately outside Yusef's door: it was like a gesture of contempt in the face of the Colonial Secretary. He said to the steward, "I want to see your master. I know the way."

"Massa out."

"Then I'll wait for him." He pushed the steward to one side and walked in. The bungalow was divided into a succession of small rooms identically furnished with sofas and cushions and low tables for drinks like the rooms in a brothel. He passed from one to another, pulling the curtains aside, till he reached the little room where nearly two months ago now he had lost his integrity. On the sofa Yusef lay asleep.

He lay on his back in his white duck trousers with his mouth open, breathing heavily. A glass was on a table at his side, and Scobie noticed the small white grains at the bottom. Yusef had taken a bromide. Scobie sat down at his side and waited. The window was open, but the rain shut out the air as effectively as a curtain. Perhaps it was merely the want of air that caused the depression which now fell on his spirits, perhaps it was because he had returned to the scene of a crime. Useless to tell himself that he had committed no offence. Like a woman who has made a loveless marriage he recognized in the room as anonymous as an hotel bedroom the memory of an adultery.

Just over the window there was a defective gutter which emptied itself like a tap, so that all the time you could hear the two sounds of the rain—the murmur and the gush. Scobie lit a cigarette, watching Yusef. He couldn't feel any hatred of the man. He had trapped Yusef as consciously and as effectively as Yusef had trapped him. The marriage had been made by both of them. Perhaps the intensity of the watch he kept broke through the fog of bromide: the fat thighs shifted on the sofa. Yusef grunted, murmured, "dear chap" in his deep sleep, and turned on his side, facing Scobie. Scobie stared again round the room, but he had examined it already thoroughly enough when he came here to arrange his loan: there was no change—the same hideous mauve silk cushions, the threads showing where the damp was rotting the covers, the tangerine curtains. Even the blue syphon of soda was in the same place: they had an eternal air like the furnishings of hell. There were no bookshelves, for Yusef couldn't read: no desk because he couldn't write. It would have been useless to search for papers—papers were useless to Yusef. Everything was inside that large Roman head.

"Why . . . Major Scobie. . . ." The eyes were open and sought his; blurred with bromide they found it difficult to focus.

"Good morning, Yusef." For once Scobie had him at a disadvantage. For a moment Yusef seemed about to sink again into drugged sleep; then with an effort he got on an elbow.

"I wanted to have a word about Tallit, Yusef."

"Tallit . . . forgive me, Major Scobie. . . ."

"And the diamonds."

"Crazy about diamonds," Yusef brought out with difficulty in a voice half-way to sleep. He shook his head, so that the white lick of hair flapped; then putting out a vague hand he stretched for the syphon.

"Did you frame Tallit, Yusef?"

Yusef dragged the syphon towards him across the table, knocking over the bromide glass; he turned the nozzle towards his face and pulled the trigger. The soda water broke on his face and splashed all round him on the mauve silk. He gave a sigh of relief and satisfaction, like a man under a shower on a hot day. "What is it, Major Scobie, is anything wrong?"

"Tallit is not going to be prosecuted."

He was like a tired man dragging himself out of the sea: the tide followed him. He said, "You must forgive me, Major Scobie. I have not been sleeping well." He shook his head up and down thoughtfully, as a man might shake a box to see whether anything rattles. "You were saying something about Tallit, Major Scobie," and he explained again, "It is the stock-taking. All the figures. Three four stores. They try to cheat me because it's all in my head."

"Tallit," Scobie repeated, "won't be prosecuted."

"Never mind. One day he will go too far."

"Were they your diamonds, Yusef?"

"My diamonds? They have made you suspicious of me, Major Scobie."

"Was the small boy in your pay?"

Yusef mopped the soda water off his face with the back of his hand. "Of course he was, Major Scobie. That was where I got my information."

The moment of inferiority had passed; the great head had shaken itself free of the bromide, even though the limbs still lay sluggishly spread over the sofa. "Yusef, I'm not your enemy. I have a liking for you."

"When you say that, Major Scobie, how my heart beats." He pulled his shirt wider, as though to show the actual movement of the heart and little streams of soda water irrigated the black bush on his chest. "I am too fat," he said.

"I would like to trust you, Yusef. Tell me the truth. Were the diamonds yours or Tallit's?"

"I always want to speak the truth to you, Major Scobie. I never told you the diamonds were Tallit's."

"They were yours?"

"Yes, Major Scobie."

"What a fool you have made of me, Yusef. If only I had a witness here, I'd run you in."

"I didn't mean to make a fool of you, Major Scobie. I wanted Tallit sent away. It would be for the good of everybody if he was sent away. It is no good the Syrians being in two parties. If they were in one party you would be able to come to me and say, 'Yusef, the Government wants the Syrians to do this or that,' and I should be able to answer, 'It shall be so.' "

"And the diamond smuggling would be in one pair of hands."

"Oh, the diamonds, diamonds, diamonds," Yusef wearily complained. "I tell you, Major Scobie, that I make more money in one year from my smallest store than I would make in three years from diamonds. You cannot understand how many bribes are necessary."

"Well, Yusef, I'm taking no more information from you. This ends our relationship. Every month, of course, I shall send you the interest." He felt a strange unreality in his own words: the tangerine curtains hung there immovably. There are certain places one never leaves behind; the curtains and cushions of this room joined an attic bedroom, an ink-stained desk, a lacy altar in Ealing—they would be there so long as consciousness lasted.

Yusef put his feet on the floor and sat bolt upright. He said, "Major Scobie, you have taken my little joke too much to heart."

"Good-bye, Yusef, you aren't a bad chap, but good-bye."

"You are wrong, Major Scobie. I am a bad chap." He said earnestly, "My friendship for you is the only good thing in this black heart. I cannot give it up. We must stay friends always."

"I'm afraid not, Yusef."

"Listen, Major Scobie. I am not asking you to do anything for me except sometimes—after dark perhaps when nobody can see—to visit me and talk to me. Nothing else. Just that. I will tell you no more tales about Tallit. I will tell you nothing. We will sit here with the syphon and the whisky bottle. . . ."

"I'm not a fool, Yusef. I know it would be of great use to you if people believed we were friends. I'm not giving you that help."

Yusef put a finger in his ear and cleared it of soda water. He looked bleakly and brazenly across at Scobie. This must be how he looks, Scobie thought, at the store manager who has tried to deceive him about the figures he carries in his head. "Major Scobie, did you ever tell the Commissioner about our little business arrangement or was that all bluff?"

"Ask him yourself."

"I think I will. My heart feels rejected and bitter. It urges me to go to the Commissioner and tell him everything."

"Always obey your heart, Yusef."

"I will tell him you took my money and together we planned the arrest of Tallit. But you did not fulfil your bargain, so I have come to him in revenge. In revenge," Yusef repeated gloomily, his Roman head sunk on his fat chest.

"Go ahead. Do what you like, Yusef." But he couldn't believe in any of this scene however hard he played it. It was like a lovers' quarrel. He couldn't believe in Yusef's threats and he had no belief in his own calmness: he did not even believe in this good-bye. What had happened in the mauve and orange room had been too important to become part of the enormous equal past. He was not surprised when Yusef, lifting his head, said, "Of course I shall not go. One day you will come back and want my friendship. And I shall welcome you."

Shall I really be so desperate? Scobie wondered, as

though in the Syrian's voice he had heard the genuine accent of prophecy.

v

On his way home Scobie stopped his car outside the Catholic church and went in. It was the first Saturday of the month and he always went to confession on that day. Half a dozen old women, their hair bound like charwomen's in dusters, waited their turn: a nursing sister: a private soldier with a Royal Ordnance insignia. Father Rank's voice whispered montonously from the box.

Scobie, with his eyes fixed on the cross, prayed—the Our Father, the Hail Mary, the Act of Contrition. The awful languor of routine fell on his spirits. He felt like a spectator —one of those many people round the cross over whom the gaze of Christ must have passed, seeking the face of a friend or an enemy. It sometimes seemed to him that his profession and his uniform classed him inexorably with all those anonymous Romans keeping order in the streets a long way off. One by one the old Kru women passed into the box and out again, and Scobie prayed—vaguely and ramblingly—for Louise, that she might be happy now at this moment and so remain, that no evil should ever come to her through him. The soldier came out of the box and he rose.

"In the name of the Father, the Son and the Holy Ghost." He said, "Since my last confession a month ago I have missed one Sunday Mass and one holy day of obligation."

"Were you prevented from going?"

"Yes, but with a little effort I could have arranged my duties better."

"Yes?"

"All through this month I have done the minimum. I've been unnecessarily harsh to one of my men. . . ." He paused a long time.

"Is that everything?"

"I don't know how to put it, father, but I feel—tired of my religion. It seems to mean nothing to me. I've tried to love

God, but——" he made a gesture which the priest could not see, turned sideways through the grille. "I'm not sure that I even believe."

"It's easy," the priest said, "to worry too much about that. Especially here. The penance I would give to a lot of people if I could is six months' leave. The climate gets you down. It's easy to mistake tiredness for—well, disbelief."

"I don't want to keep you, father. There are other people waiting. I know these are just fancies. But I feel—empty. Empty."

"That's sometimes the moment God chooses," the priest said. "Now go along with you and say a decade of your rosary."

"I haven't a rosary. At least . . ."

"Well, five Our Fathers and five Hail Marys then." He began to speak the words of absolution, but the trouble is, Scobie thought, there's nothing to absolve. The words brought no sense of relief because there was nothing to relieve. They were a formula: the Latin words hustled together—a hocus-pocus. He went out of the box and knelt down again, and this too was part of a routine. It seemed to him for a moment that God was too accessible. There was no difficulty in approaching Him. Like a popular demagogue He was open to the least of His followers at any hour. Looking up at the cross he thought, He even suffers in public.

[3]

i

"I've brought you some stamps," Scobie said. "I've been collecting them for a week—from everybody. Even Mrs. Carter has contributed a magnificent parakeet—look at it—from somewhere in South America. And here's a complete set of Liberians surcharged for the American occupation. I got those from the Naval Observer."

They were completely at ease: it seemed to both of them for that very reason they were safe.

"Why do you collect stamps?" he asked. "It's an odd thing to do—after sixteen."

"I don't know," Helen Rolt said. "I don't really collect. I carry them round. I suppose it's habit." She opened the album and said, "No, it's not just habit. I do love the things. Do you see this green George V halfpenny stamp? It's the first I ever collected. I was eight. I steamed it off an envelope and stuck it in a notebook. That's why my father gave me an album. My mother had died, so he gave me a stamp-album."

She tried to explain more exactly. "They are like snap-shots. They are so portable. People who collect china—they can't carry it around with them. Or books. But you don't have to tear the pages out like you do with snap-shots."

"You've never told me about your husband," Scobie said.

"No."

"It's not really much good tearing out a page because you can see the place where it's been torn?"

"Yes."

"It's easier to get over a thing," Scobie said, "if you talk about it."

"That's not the trouble," she said. "The trouble is—it's so terribly easy to get over." She took him by surprise; he hadn't believed she was old enough to have reached that stage in her lessons, that particular turn of the screw. She said, "He's been dead—how long—is it eight weeks yet? and he's so dead, so completely dead. What a little bitch I must be."

Scobie said, "You needn't feel that. It's the same with everybody, I think. When we say to someone, 'I can't live without you,' what we really mean is, 'I can't live feeling you may be in pain, unhappy, in want.' That's all it is. When they are dead our responsibility ends. There's nothing more we can do about it. We can rest in peace."

"I didn't know I was so tough," Helen said. "Horribly tough."

"I had a child," Scobie said, "who died. I was out here.

My wife sent me two cables from Bexhill, one at five in the evening and one at six, but they mixed up the order. You see she meant to break the thing gently. I got one cable just after breakfast. It was eight o'clock in the morning—a dead time of day for any news." He had never mentioned this before to anyone, not even to Louise. Now he brought out the exact words of each cable, carefully. "The cable said, *Catherine died this afternoon no pain God bless you.* The second cable came at lunch-time. It said, *Catherine seriously ill. Doctor has hope my diving.* That was the one sent off at five. 'Diving' was a mutilation—I suppose for 'darling.' You see there was nothing more hopeless she could have put to break the news than 'doctor has hope.' "

"How terrible for you," Helen said.

"No, the terrible thing was that when I got the second telegram, I was so muddled in my head, I thought, there's been a mistake. She must be still alive. For a moment until I realized what had happened, I was—disappointed. That was the terrible thing. I thought 'now the anxiety begins, and the pain,' but when I realized what had happened, then it was all right, she was dead, I could begin to forget her."

"Have you forgotten her?"

"I don't remember her often. You see, I escaped seeing her die. My wife had that."

It was astonishing to him how easily and quickly they had become friends. They came together over two deaths without reserve. She said, "I don't know what I'd have done without you."

"Everybody would have looked after you."

"I think they are scared of me," she said.

He laughed.

"They are. Flight-Lieutenant Bagster took me to the beach this afternoon, but he was scared. Because I'm not happy and because of my husband. Everybody on the beach was pretending to be happy about something, and I sat there grinning and it didn't work. Do you remember when you went to your first party and coming up the stairs you heard all the voices and you didn't know how to talk to people? That's how I felt, so I sat and grinned in Mrs. Carter's bathing-dress, and Bagster stroked my leg, and I wanted to go home."

"You'll be going home soon."

"I don't mean *that* home. I mean here, where I can shut the door and not answer when they knock. I don't want to go away yet."

"But surely you aren't happy here?"

"I'm so afraid of the sea," she said.

"Do you dream about it?"

"No. I dream of John sometimes—that's worse. Because I've always had bad dreams of him, and I still have bad dreams of him. I mean we were always quarrelling in the dreams and we still go on quarrelling."

"Did you quarrel?"

"No. He was sweet to me. We were only married a month, you know. It would be easy being sweet as long as that, wouldn't it? When this happened I hadn't really had time to know my way around." It seemed to Scobie that she had never known her way around—at least not since she had left her netball team; was it a year ago? Sometimes he saw her lying back in the boat on that oily featureless sea, day after day, with the other child near death and the sailor going mad, and Miss Malcott, and the chief engineer who felt his responsibility to the owners, and sometimes he saw her carried past him on a stretcher grasping her stamp-album, and now he saw her in the borrowed unbecoming bathing-dress grinning at Bagster as he stroked her legs, listening to the laughter and the splashes, not knowing the adult etiquette. . . . Sadly like an evening tide he felt responsibility bearing him up the shore.

"You've written to your father?"

"Oh yes, of course. He cabled that he's pulling strings about the passage. I don't know what strings he can pull from Bury, poor dear. He doesn't know anybody at all. He cabled too about John, of course." She lifted a cushion off the chair and pulled the cable out. "Read it. He's very sweet, but of course he doesn't know a thing about me."

Scobie read, *Terribly grieved for you, dear child, but remember his happiness, Your loving father.* The date stamp with the Bury mark made him aware of the enormous distance between father and child. He said, "How do you mean, he doesn't know a thing?"

"You see, he believes in God and heaven, all that sort of thing."

"You don't?"

"I gave up all that when I left school. John used to pull his leg about it, quite gently you know. Father didn't mind. But he never knew I felt the way John did. If you are a clergyman's daughter there are a lot of things you have to pretend about. He would have hated knowing that John and I went together, oh, a fortnight before we married."

Again he had that vision of someone who didn't know her way around: no wonder Bagster was scared of her. Bagster was not a man to accept responsibility, and how could anyone lay the responsibility for any action, he thought, on this stupid bewildered child? He turned over the little pile of stamps he had accumulated for her and said, "I wonder what you'll do when you get home?"

"I suppose," she said, "they'll conscript me."

He thought: If my child had lived, she too would have been conscriptable, flung into some grim dormitory, to find her own way. After the Atlantic, the A.T.S. or the W.A.A.F., the blustering sergeant with the big bust, the cook-house and the potato peelings, the lesbian officer with the thin lips and the tidy gold hair, and the men waiting on the Common outside the camp, among the gorse bushes . . . compared to that surely even the Atlantic was more a home. He said, "Haven't you got any shorthand? any languages?" Only the clever and the astute and the influential escaped in war.

"No," she said, "I'm not really any good at anything."

It was impossible to think of her being saved from the sea

and then flung back like a fish that wasn't worth catching.

He said, "Can you type?"

"I can get along quite fast with one finger."

"You could get a job here, I think. We are very short of secretaries. All the wives, you know, are working in the secretariat, and we still haven't enough. But it's a bad climate for a woman."

"I'd like to stay. Let's have a drink on it." She called, "Boy, boy."

"You are learning," Scobie said. "A week ago you were so frightened of him . . ." The boy came in with a tray set out with glasses, limes, water, a new gin bottle.

"This isn't the boy I talked to," Scobie said.

"No, that one went. You talked to him too fiercely."

"And this one came?"

"Yes."

"What's your name, boy?"

"Vande, sah."

"I've seen you before, haven't I?"

"No, sah."

"Who am I?"

"You big policeman, sah."

"Don't frighten this one away," Helen said.

"Who were you with?"

"I was with D.C. Pemberton up bush, sah. I was small boy."

"Is that where I saw you?" Scobie said. "I suppose I did. You look after this missus well now, and when she goes home, I get you big job. Remember that."

"Yes, sah."

"You haven't looked at the stamps," Scobie said.

"No, I haven't, have I?" A spot of gin fell upon one of the stamps and stained it. He watched her pick it out of the pile, taking in the straight hair falling in rats' tails over the nape as though the Atlantic had taken the strength out of it for ever, the hollowed face. It seemed to him that he had not felt so much at ease with another human being for years—

not since Louise was young. But this case was different, he told himself: they were safe with each other. He was more than thirty years the older; his body in this climate had lost the sense of lust; he watched her with sadness and affection and enormous pity because a time would come when he couldn't show her around in a world where she was at sea. When she turned and the light fell on her face she looked ugly, with the temporary ugliness of a child. The ugliness was like handcuffs on his wrists.

He said, "That stamp's spoilt. I'll get you another."

"Oh no," she said, "it goes in as it is. I'm not a real collector."

He had no sense of responsibility towards the beautiful and the graceful and the intelligent. They could find their own way. It was the face for which nobody would go out of his way, the face that would never catch the covert look, the face which would soon be used to rebuffs and indifference that demanded his allegiance. The word "pity" is used as loosely as the word "love": the terrible promiscuous passion which so few experience.

She said, "You see, whenever I see that stain I'll see this room. . . ."

"Then it's like a snap-shot."

"You can pull a stamp out," she said with a terrible youthful clarity, "and you don't know that it's ever been there." She turned suddenly to him and said, "It's so good to talk to you. I can say anything I like. I'm not afraid of hurting you. You don't want anything out of me. I'm safe."

"We're both safe." The rain surrounded them, falling regularly on the iron roof.

She said, "I have a feeling that you'd never let me down." The words came to him like a command he would have to obey however difficult. Her hands were full of the absurd scraps of paper he had brought her. She said, "I'll keep these always. I'll never have to pull these out."

Somebody knocked on the door and a voice said, "Freddie Bagster. It's only me. Freddie Bagster," cheerily.

"Don't answer," she whispered, "don't answer." She put her arm in his and watched the door with her mouth a little open as though she were out of breath. He had the sense of an animal which had been chased to its hole.

"Let Freddie in," the voice wheedled. "Be a sport, Helen. Only Freddie Bagster." The man was a little drunk.

She stood pressed against him with her hand on his side. When the sound of Bagster's feet receded, she raised her mouth and they kissed. What they had both thought was safety proved to have been the camouflage of an enemy who works in terms of friendship, trust and pity.

ii

The rain poured steadily down, turning the little patch of reclaimed ground on which his house stood back into swamp again. The window of his room blew to and fro. At some time during the night the catch had been broken by a squall of wind. Now the rain had blown in, his dressing-table was soaking wet, and there was a pool of water on the floor. His alarm clock pointed to 4:25. He felt as though he had returned to a house that had been abandoned years ago. It would not have surprised him to find cobwebs over the mirror, the mosquito-net hanging in shreds and the dirt of mice upon the floor.

He sat down on a chair and the water drained off his trousers and made a second pool around his mosquito-boots. He had left his umbrella behind, setting out on his walk home with an odd jubilation, as though he had rediscovered something he had lost, something which belonged to his youth. In the wet and noisy darkness he had even lifted his voice and tried out a line from Fraser's song, but his voice was tuneless. Now somewhere between the Nissen hut and home he had mislaid his joy.

At four in the morning he had woken. Her head lay in his side and he could feel her hair against his breast. Putting his hand outside the net he found the light. She lay in the odd cramped attitude of someone who has been shot in escaping.

It seemed to him for a moment even then, before his tenderness and pleasure awoke, that he was looking at a bundle of cannon fodder. The first words she said when the light had roused her were, "Bagster can go to hell."

"Were you dreaming?"

She said, "I dreamed I was lost in a marsh and Bagster found me."

He said, "I've got to go. If we sleep now, we shan't wake again till it's light." He began to think for both of them, carefully. Like a criminal he began to fashion in his own mind the undetectable crime: he planned the moves ahead: he embarked for the first time in his life on the long legalistic arguments of deceit. If so-and-so . . . then that follows. He said, "What time does your boy turn up?"

"About six I think. I don't know. He calls me at seven."

"Ali starts boiling my water about a quarter to six. I'd better go." He looked carefully everywhere for signs of his presence: he straightened a mat and hesitated over an ashtray. Then at the end of it all he had left his umbrella standing against the wall. It seemed to him the typical action of a criminal. When the rain reminded him of it, it was too late to go back. He would have to hammer on her door, and already in one hut a light had gone on. Standing in his own room with a mosquito-boot in his hand, he thought wearily and drearily, In future I must do better than that.

In the future—that was where the sadness lay. Was it the butterfly that died in the act of love? But human beings were condemned to consequences. The responsibility as well as the guilt was his—he was not a Bagster: he knew what he was about. He had sworn to preserve Louise's happiness, and now he had accepted another and contradictory responsibility. He felt tired by all the lies he would some time have to tell; he felt the wounds of those victims who had not yet bled. Lying back on the pillow he stared sleeplessly out towards the grey early morning tide. Somewhere on the face of those obscure waters moved the sense of yet another wrong and another victim, not Louise, nor Helen.

Part II

[1]

i

"There. What do you think of it?" Harris asked with ill-concealed pride. He stood in the doorway of the hut while Wilson moved cautiously forward between the brown sticks of Government furniture like a setter through stubble.

"Better than the hotel," Wilson said cautiously, pointing his muzzle towards a Government easy-chair.

"I thought I'd give you a surprise when you got back from Lagos." Harris had curtained the Nissen hut into three: a bedroom for each of them and a common sitting-room. "There's only one point that worries me. I'm not sure whether there are any cockroaches."

"Well, we only played the game to get rid of them."

"I know, but it seems almost a pity, doesn't it?"

"Who are our neighbours?"

"There's Mrs. Rolt who was submarined, and there are two chaps in the Department of Works, and somebody called Clive from the Agricultural Department, Boling, who's in charge of Sewage—they all seem a nice friendly lot. And Scobie, of course, is just down the road."

"Yes."

Wilson moved restlessly around the hut and came to a stop in front of a photograph which Harris had propped against a Government inkstand. It showed three long rows of boys on a lawn: the first row sitting cross-legged on the grass: the second on chairs, wearing high stiff collars, with an elderly man and two women (one had a squint) in the centre: the third row standing. Wilson said, "That woman with a squint—I could swear I'd seen her somewhere before."

"Does the name Snakey convey anything to you?"

"Why, yes, of course." He looked closer. "So you were at that hole too?"

"I saw the *Downhamian* in your room and I fished this out to surprise you. I was in Jagger's house. Where were you?"

"I was a Prog," Wilson said.

"Oh well," Harris admitted in a tone of disappointment, "there were some good chaps among the Progs." He laid the photograph flat down again as though it were something that hadn't quite come off. "I was thinking we might have an old Downhamian dinner."

"Whatever for?" Wilson asked. "There are only two of us."

"We could invite a guest each."

"I don't see the point."

Harris said bitterly, "Well, you are the real Downhamian, not me. I never joined the association. You get the magazine. I thought perhaps you had an interest in the place."

"My father made me a life member and he always forwards the bloody paper," Wilson said abruptly.

"It was lying beside your bed. I thought you'd been reading it."

"I may have glanced at it."

"There was a bit about me in it. They wanted my address."

"Oh, but you know why that is?" Wilson said. "They are sending out appeals to any old Downhamian they can rake up. The panelling in the Founders' Hall is in need of repair. I'd keep your address quiet if I were you." He was one of those, it seemed to Harris, who always knew what was on, who gave advance information on extra halves, who knew why old So-and-So had not turned up to school, and what the row brewing at the Head's special meeting was about. A few weeks ago he had been a new boy whom Harris had been delighted to befriend, to show around. He remembered the evening when Wilson would have put on evening dress for a Syrian's dinner-party if he hadn't been warned. But Harris from his first year at school had been fated to see how quickly new boys grew up: one term he was their kindly mentor—the next he was discarded. He could never progress as quickly as the newest unlicked boy. He remembered how even in the cockroach game—that *he* had invented—his rules had been challenged on the first evening. He said sadly, "I expect you are right. Perhaps I won't send a letter after all." He added humbly, "I took the bed on this side, but I don't mind a bit which I have. . . ."

"Oh, that's all right," Wilson said.

"I've only engaged one steward. I thought we could save a bit by sharing."

"The less boys we have knocking about here the better," Wilson said.

That night was the first night of their new comradeship. They sat reading on their twin Government chairs behind the black-out curtains. On the table was a bottle of whisky for Wilson and a bottle of barley-water flavoured with lime for Harris. A sense of extraordinary peace came to Harris while the rain tingled steadily on the roof and Wilson read a Wallace. Occasionally a few drunks from the R.A.F. mess passed by, shouting or revving their cars, but this only enhanced the sense of peace inside the hut. Sometimes his eyes strayed to the walls seeking a cockroach, but you couldn't have everything.

"Have you got the *Downhamian* handy, old man? I wouldn't mind another glance at it. This book's so dull."

"There's a new one unopened on the dressing-table."

"You don't mind my opening it?"

"Why the hell should I?"

Harris turned first to the old Downhamian notes and read again how the whereabouts of H. R. Harris (1917–1921) was still wanted. He wondered whether it was possible that Wilson was wrong: there was no word here about the panelling in Hall. Perhaps after all he would send that letter and he pictured the reply he might receive from the Secretary. *My dear Harris,* it would go something like that, *we were all delighted to receive your letter from those romantic parts. Why not send us a full length contribution to the mag. and while I'm writing to you, what about membership of the Old Downhamian Association? I notice you've never joined. I'm speaking for all Old Downhamians when I say that we'll be glad to welcome you.* He tried out "proud to welcome you" on his tongue, but rejected that. He was a realist.

The Downhamians had had a fairly successful Christmas term. They had beaten Harpenden by one goal, Merchant Taylors by two, and had drawn with Lancing. Ducker and Tierney were coming on well as forwards, but the scrum was still slow in getting the ball out. He turned a page and read how the Opera Society had given an excellent rendering of *Patience* in the Founders' Hall. F.J.K., who was obviously the English master, wrote: *Lane as Bunthorne displayed a degree of æstheticism which surprised all his companions of Vb. We would not hitherto have described his hand as mediæval or associated him with lilies, but he persuaded us that we had misjudged him. A great performance, Lane.*

Harris skimmed through the account of fives matches, a fantasy called "The Tick of the Clock" beginning *There was once a little old lady whose most beloved possession. . . .* The walls of Downham—the red brick laced with yellow, the extraordinary crockets, the mid-Victorian gargoyles—rose around him: boots beat on stone stairs and a cracked dinner-bell rang to rouse him to another miserable day. He felt the loyalty we feel to unhappiness—the sense that that is where we really belong. His eyes filled with tears, he took a sip of his barley-water and thought, "I'll post that letter whatever Wilson says." Somebody outside shouted, "Bagster. Where are you, Bagster, you sod?" and stumbled in a ditch. He might have been back at Downham, except of course that they wouldn't have used *that* word.

Harris turned a page or two and the title of a poem caught his eye. It was called "West Coast" and it was dedicated to "L.S." He wasn't very keen on poetry, but it struck him as interesting that somewhere on this enormous coastline of sand and smells there existed a third old Downhamian.

> *Another Tristram on this distant coast,* he read
> *Raises the poisoned chalice to his lips,*
> *Another Mark upon the palm-fringed shore*
>   *watches his love's eclipse.*

It seemed to Harris obscure: his eye passed rapidly over the intervening verses to the initials at the foot: E.W. He nearly exclaimed aloud, but he restrained himself in time. In such close quarters as they now shared it was necessary to be circumspect. There wasn't space to quarrel in. Who is L.S., he wondered, and thought, surely it can't be . . . the very idea crinkled his lips in a cruel smile. He said, "There's not much in the mag. We beat Harpenden. There's a poem called 'West Coast.' Another poor devil out here, I suppose."

"Oh."

"Lovelorn," Harris said. "But I don't read poetry."

"Nor do I," Wilson lied behind the barrier of the Wallace.

ii

It had been a very narrow squeak. Wilson lay on his back in bed and listened to the rain on the roof and the heavy breathing of the old Downhamian beyond the curtain. It was as if the hideous years had extended through the intervening mist to surround him again. What madness had induced him to send that poem to the *Downhamian*? But it wasn't madness: he had long since become incapable of anything so honest as madness: he was one of those condemned in childhood to complexity. He knew what he had intended to do: to cut the poem out with no indication of its source and to send it to Louise. It wasn't quite her sort of poem, he knew, but surely, he had argued, she would be impressed to some extent by the mere fact that the poem was in print. If she asked him where it had appeared, it would be easy to invent some convincing coterie name. The *Downhamian* luckily was well printed and on good paper. It was true, of course, that he would have to paste the cutting on opaque paper to disguise what was printed on the other side, but it would be easy to think up an explanation of that. It was as if his profession were slowly absorbing his whole life, just as school had done. His profession was to lie, to have the quick story ready, never to give himself away, and his private life was taking the same pattern. He lay on his back in a nausea of self-disgust.

The rain had momentarily stopped. It was one of those cool intervals that were the consolation of the sleepless. In Harris's heavy dreams the rain went on. Wilson got softly out and mixed himself a bromide; the grains fizzed in the bottom of the glass and Harris spoke hoarsely and turned over behind the curtain. Wilson flashed his torch on his watch and read 2:25. Tiptoeing to the door so as not to waken Harris, he felt the little sting of a jigger under his toenail. In the morning he must get his boy to scoop it out. He stood on the small cement pavement above the marshy ground and let the cool air play on him with his pyjama jacket flapping open. All the huts were in darkness, and the moon was patched with the rain-clouds coming up. He was going to turn away when he heard someone stumble a few yards away and he flashed his torch. It lit on a man's bowed back moving between the huts towards the road. "Scobie," Wilson exclaimed and the man turned.

"Hullo, Wilson," Scobie said. "I didn't know you lived up here."

"I'm sharing with Harris," Wilson said, watching the man who had watched his tears.

"I've been taking a walk," Scobie said unconvincingly. "I couldn't sleep." It seemed to Wilson that Scobie was still a novice in the world of deceit: he hadn't lived in it since childhood, and he felt an odd elderly envy for Scobie, much as an old lag might envy the young crook serving his first sentence, to whom all this was new.

iii

Wilson sat in his little stuffy room in the U.A.C. office. Several of the firm's journals and day-books bound in quarter pigskin formed a barrier between him and the door. Surreptitiously, like a schoolboy using a crib, Wilson behind the barrier worked at his code-books, translating a cable. A commercial calendar showed a week-old date—June 20—and a motto: *The best investments are honesty and enterprise. William P. Cornforth.* A clerk knocked and said, "There's a nigger for you, Wilson, with a note."

"Who from?"

"He says Brown."

"Keep him a couple of minutes, there's a good chap, and then boot him in." However diligently Wilson practised, the slang phrase sounded unnaturally on his lips. He folded up the cable and stuck it in the code-book to keep his place: then he put the cable and the code-book in the safe and pulled the door to. Pouring himself out a glass of water he looked out on the street; the mammies, their heads tied up in bright cotton cloths, passed under their coloured umbrellas. Their shapeless cotton gowns fell to the ankle: one with a design of match-boxes: another with kerosene lamps: the third—the latest from Manchester—covered with mauve cigarette-lighters on a yellow ground. Naked to the waist a young girl passed gleaming through the rain and Wilson watched her out of sight with melancholy lust. He swallowed and turned as the door opened.

"Shut the door."

The boy obeyed. He had apparently put on his best clothes for this morning call: a white cotton shirt fell outside his white shorts. His gym shoes were immaculate in spite of the rain, except that his toes protruded.

"You small boy at Yusef's?"

"Yes, sah."

"You got a message," Wilson said, "from my boy. He tell you what I want, eh? He's your young brother, isn't he?"

"Yes, sah."

"Same father?"

"Yes, sah."

"He says you good boy, honest. You want to be a steward, eh?"

"Yes, sah."

"Can you read?"

"No, sah."

"Write?"

"No, sah."

"You got eyes in your head? Good ears? You see everything? You hear everything?" The boy grinned—a gash of white in the smooth grey elephant hide of his face: he had a look of sleek intelligence. Intelligence, to Wilson, was more valuable than honesty. Honesty was a double-edged weapon, but intelligence looked after number one. Intelligence realized that a Syrian might one day go home to his own land, but the English stayed. Intelligence knew that it was a good thing to work for Government, whatever the Government. "How much you get as small boy?"

"Ten shillings."

"I pay you five shillings more. If Yusef sack you I pay you ten shillings. If you stay with Yusef one year and give me good information—true information—no lies, I give you job as steward with white man. Understand?"

"Yes, sah."

"If you give me lies, then you go to prison. Maybe they shoot you. I don't know. I don't care. Understand?"

"Yes, sah."

"Every day you see your brother at meat market. You tell him who comes to Yusef's house. Tell him where Yusef goes. You tell him any strange boys who come to Yusef's house. You no tell lies, you tell truth. No humbug. If no one comes to Yusef's house you say no one. You no make big lie. If you tell lie, I know it and you go to prison straight away." The wearisome recital went on. He was never quite sure how much was understood. The sweat ran off Wilson's forehead and the cool contained grey face of the boy aggravated him like an accusation he couldn't answer. "You go to prison and you stay in prison plenty long time." He could hear his own voice cracking with the desire to impress; he could hear himself, like the parody of a white man on the halls. He said, "Scobie? Do you know Major Scobie?"

"Yes, sah. He very good man, sah." They were the first words apart from yes and no the boy had uttered.

"You see him at your master's?"

"Yes, sah."

"How often?"

"Once, twice, sah."

"He and your master—they are friends?"

"My master he think Major Scobie very good man, sah." The reiteration of the phrase angered Wilson. He broke furiously out, "I don't want to hear whether he's good or not. I want to know where he meets Yusef, see? What do they talk about? You bring them in drinks some time when steward's busy? What do you hear?"

"Last time they have big palaver," the boy brought ingratiatingly out, as if he were showing a corner of his wares.

"I bet they did. I want to know all about their palaver."

"When Major Scobie go away one time, my master he put pillow right on his face."

"What on earth do you mean by that?"

The boy folded his arms over his eyes in a gesture of great dignity and said, "His eyes make pillow wet."

"Good God," Wilson said, "what an extraordinary thing."

"Then he drink plenty whisky and go to sleep—ten, twelve hours. Then he go to his store in Bond Street and make plenty hell."

"Why?"

"He say they humbug him."

"What's that got to do with Major Scobie?"

The boy shrugged. As so many times before Wilson had the sense of a door closed in his face; he was always on the outside of the door.

When the boy had gone he opened his safe again, moving the knob of the combination first left to 32—his age, secondly right to 10, the year of his birth, left again to 65, the number of his home in Western Avenue, Pinner, and took out the code-books. 32946 78523 97042. Row after row of groups swam before his eyes. The telegram was headed Important, or he would have postponed the decoding till the evening. He knew how little important it really was—the usual ship had left Lobito carrying the usual suspects—diamonds, diamonds, diamonds. When he had decoded the telegram he would hand it to the long-suffering Commissioner, who had already probably received the same information or contradictory information from S.O.E. or one of the other secret organizations which took root on the coast like mangroves. *Leave alone but do not repeat not pinpoint P. Ferreira passenger 1st class repeat P. Ferreira passenger 1st class.* Ferreira was presumably an agent his organization had recruited on board. It was quite possible that the Commissioner would receive simultaneously a message from Colonel Wright that P. Ferreira was suspected of carrying diamonds and should be rigorously searched. 72391 87052 63847 92034. How did one simultaneously leave alone, not repeat not pinpoint, and rigorously search Mr. Ferreira? That luckily was not his worry. Perhaps it was Scobie who would suffer any headache there was.

Again he went to the window for a glass of water and again he saw the same girl pass. Or maybe it was not the same girl. He watched the water trickling down between the two thin wing-like shoulder-blades. He remembered there was a time when he had not noticed a black skin. He felt as though he had passed years and not months on this coast, all the years between puberty and manhood.

iv

"Going out?" Harris asked with surprise. "Where to?"

"Just into town," Wilson said, loosening the knot round his mosquito-boots.

"What on earth can you find to do in town at this hour?"

"Business," Wilson said.

Well, he thought, it was business of a kind, the kind of joyless business one did alone, without friends. He had bought a second-hand car a few weeks ago, the first he had ever owned, and he was not yet a very reliable driver. No gadget survived the climate long and every few hundred yards he had to wipe the windscreen with his handkerchief. In Kru Town the hut doors were open and families sat around the kerosene lamps waiting till it was cool enough to sleep. A dead pye-dog lay in the gutter with the rain running over its white swollen belly. He drove in second gear at little more than a walking pace, for civilian headlamps had to be blacked out to the size of a visiting-card and he couldn't see more than fifteen paces ahead. It took him ten minutes to reach the great cotton tree near the police station. There were no lights on in any of the officers' rooms and he left his car outside the main entrance. If anyone saw it there they would assume he was inside. For a moment he sat with the door open hesitating. The image of the girl passing in the rain conflicted with the sight of Harris on his shoulder-blades reading a book with a glass of squash at his elbow. He thought sadly, as lust won the day, what a lot of trouble it was; the sadness of the after-taste fell upon his spirits beforehand.

He had forgotten to bring his umbrella and he was wet through before he had walked a dozen yards down the hill. It was the passion of curiosity more than of lust that impelled him now. Some time or another if one lived in a place one must try the local product. It was like having a box of chocolates shut in a bedroom drawer. Until the box was empty it occupied the mind too much. He thought: when this is over I shall be able to write another poem to Louise.

The brothel was a tin-roofed bungalow half-way down the hill on the right-hand side. In the dry season the girls sat outside in the gutter like sparrows; they chatted with the policeman on duty at the top of the hill. The road was never made up, so that nobody drove by the brothel on the way to the wharf or the Cathedral: it could be ignored. Now it turned a shuttered silent front to the muddy street, except where a door, propped open with a rock out of the roadway, opened on a passage. Wilson looked quickly this way and that and stepped inside.

Years ago the passage had been whitewashed and plastered, but rats had torn holes in the plaster and human beings had mutilated the whitewash with scrawls and pencilled names. The walls were tattooed like a sailor's arm, with initials, dates, there were even a pair of hearts interlocked. At first it seemed to Wilson that the place was entirely deserted; on either side of the passage there were little cells nine feet by four with curtains instead of doorways and beds made out of old packing-cases spread with a native cloth. He walked rapidly to the end of the passage; then, he told himself, he would turn and go back to the quiet and somnolent security of the room where the old Downhamian dozed over his book.

He felt an awful disappointment, as though he had *not* found what he was looking for, when he reached the end and discovered that the left-hand cell was occupied; in the light of an oil lamp burning on the floor he saw a girl in a dirty shift spread out on the packing-cases like a fish on a counter; her bare pink soles dangled over the words "Tate's Sugar." She lay there on duty, waiting for a customer. She grinned at Wilson, not bothering to sit up and said, "Want jig jig, darling. Ten bob." He had a vision of a girl with a rain-wet back moving forever out of his sight.

"No," he said, "no," shaking his head and thinking, What a fool I was, what a fool, to drive all the way for only this. The girl giggled as if she understood his stupidity and he heard the slop slop of bare feet coming up the passage from the road; the way was blocked by an old mammy carrying a striped umbrella. She said something to the girl in her native tongue and received a grinning explanation. He had the sense that all this was only strange to *him*, that it was one of the stock situations the old woman was accustomed to meet in the dark regions which she ruled. He said weakly, "I'll just go and get a drink first."

"She get drink," the mammy said. She commanded the girl sharply in the language he couldn't understand and the girl swung her legs off the sugar cases. "You stay here," the mammy said to Wilson, and mechanically like a hostess whose mind is elsewhere but who must make conversation with however uninteresting a guest, she said, "Pretty girl, jig jig, one pound." Market values here were reversed: the price rose steadily with his reluctance.

"I'm sorry. I can't wait," Wilson said. "Here's ten bob," and he made the preliminary motions of departure, but the old woman paid him no attention at all, blocking the way, smiling steadily like a dentist who knows what's good for you. Here a man's colour had no value: he couldn't bluster as a white man could elsewhere; by entering this narrow plaster passage, he had shed every racial, social and individual trait, he had reduced himself to human nature. If he had wanted to hide, here was the perfect hiding-place; if he had wanted to be anonymous, here he was simply a man. Even his reluctance, disgust and fear were not personal characteristics; they were so common to those who came here for the first time that the old woman knew exactly what each move would be. First the suggestion of a drink, then the offer of money, after that . . .

Wilson said weakly, "Let me by," but he knew that she wouldn't move; she stood watching him, as though he were a tethered animal on whom she was keeping an eye for its owner. She wasn't interested in him, but occasionally she repeated calmly, "Pretty girl jig jig by-an-by." He held out a pound to her and she pocketed it and went on blocking the way. When he tried to push by, she thrust him backwards with a casual pink palm, saying, "By-an-by. Jig jig." It had all happened so many hundreds of times before.

Down the passage the girl came carrying a vinegar bottle filled with palm wine, and with a sigh of reluctance Wilson surrendered. The heat between the walls of rain, the musty smell of his companion, the dim and wayward light of the kerosene lamp reminded him of a vault newly opened for another body to be let down upon its floor. A grievance stirred in him, a hatred of those who had brought him here. In their presence he felt as though his dead veins would bleed again.

Part III

[1]

i

Helen said, "I saw you on the beach this afternoon." Scobie looked up from the glass of whisky he was measuring. Something in her voice reminded him oddly of Louise. He said, "I had to find Rees—the Naval Intelligence man."

"You didn't even speak to me."

"I was in a hurry."

"You are so careful, always," she said, and now he realized what was happening and why he had thought of Louise. He wondered sadly whether love always inevitably took the same road. It was not only the act of love itself that was the same . . . How often in the last two years he had tried to turn away at the critical moment from just such a scene—to save himself but also to save the other victim. He laughed with half a heart and said, "For once I wasn't thinking of you. I had other things in mind."

"What other things?"

"Oh, diamonds. . . ."

"Your work is much more important to you than I am," Helen said, and the banality of the phrase, read in how many bad novels, wrung his heart.

"Yes," he said gravely, "but I'd sacrifice it for you."

"Why?"

"I suppose because you are a human being. Somebody may love a dog more than any other possession, but he wouldn't run down even a strange child to save it."

"Oh," she said, "why do you always tell me the truth? I don't want the truth all the time."

He put the whisky glass in her hand and said, "Dear, you are unlucky. You are tied up with a middle-aged man. We can't be bothered to lie all the time like the young."

"If you knew," she said, "how tired I get of all your caution. You come here after dark and you go after dark. It's so —so ignoble."

"Yes."

"We always make love—here. Among the junior official's furniture. I don't believe we'd know how to do it anywhere else."

"Poor you," he said.

She said furiously, "I don't want your pity." But it was not a question of whether she wanted it—she had it. Pity smouldered like decay at his heart. He would never rid himself of it. He knew from experience how passion died away and how love went, but pity always stayed. Nothing ever diminished pity. The conditions of life nurtured it. There was only a single person in the world who was unpitiable, oneself.

"Can't you ever risk anything?" she asked. "You never even write a line to me. You go away on trek for days, but you won't leave anything behind. I can't even have a photograph to make this place human."

"But I haven't got a photograph."

"I suppose you think I'd use your letters against you." He thought, if I shut my eyes it might almost be Louise speaking—the voice was younger, that was all, and perhaps less capable of giving pain. Standing with the whisky glass in his hand he remembered another night—a hundred yards away—the glass had then contained gin. He said gently, "You talk such nonsense."

"You think I'm a child. You tiptoe in—bringing me stamps."

"I'm trying to protect you."

"I don't care a bloody damn if people talk." He recognized the hard swearing of the netball team.

He said, "If they talked enough, this would come to an end."

"You are not protecting *me*. You are protecting your wife."

"It comes to the same thing."

"Oh," she said, "to couple me with—that woman." He couldn't prevent the wince. He had underrated her power of giving pain. He could see how she had spotted her success: he had delivered himself into her hands. Now she would always know how to inflict the sharpest stab. She was like a child with a pair of dividers who knows her power to injure. You could never trust a child not to use her advantage.

"Dear," he said, "it's too soon to quarrel."

"That woman," she repeated, watching his eyes. "You'd never leave her, would you?"

"We are married," he said.

"If she knew of this, you'd go back like a whipped dog." He thought with tenderness, she hasn't read the best books, like Louise.

"I don't know."

"You'll never marry me."

"I can't. You know that."

"It's a wonderful excuse being a Catholic," she said. "It doesn't stop you sleeping with me—it only stops you marrying me."

"Yes," he said. He thought: how much older she is than she was a month ago. She hadn't been capable of a scene then, but she had been educated by love and secrecy: he was beginning to form her. He wondered whether if this went on long enough, she would be indistinguishable from Louise. In my school, he thought, they learn bitterness and frustration and how to grow old.

"Go on," Helen said, "justify yourself."

"It would take too long," he said. "One would have to begin with the arguments for a God."

"What a twister you are."

He felt disappointed. He had looked forward to the evening. All day in the office dealing with a rent case and a case of juvenile delinquency he had looked forward to the Nissen hut, the bare room, the junior official's furniture like his own youth, everything that she had abused. He said, "I meant well."

"What do you mean?"

"I meant to be your friend. To look after you. To make you happier than you were."

"Wasn't I happy?" she asked as though she were speaking of years ago.

He said, "You were shocked, lonely . . ."

"I couldn't have been as lonely as I am now," she said. "I go out to the beach with Mrs. Carter when the rain stops. Bagster makes a pass, they think I'm frigid. I come back here before the rain starts and wait for you . . . we drink a glass of whisky . . . you give me some stamps as though I were your small girl . . ."

"I'm sorry," Scobie said. He put out his hand and covered hers: the knuckles lay under his palm like a small backbone that had been broken. He went slowly and cautiously on, choosing his words carefully, as though he were pursuing a path through an evacuated country sown with booby-traps: every step he took he expected the explosion. "I'd do anything—almost anything—to make you happy. I'd stop coming here. I'd go right away—retire . . ."

"You'd be so glad to get rid of me," she said.

"It would be like the end of life."

"Go away if you want to."

"I don't want to go. I want to do what you want."

"You can go if you want to—or you can stay," she said with contempt. "I can't move, can I?"

"If you want it, I'll get you on the next boat somehow."

"Oh, how pleased you'd be if this were over," she said and began to weep. When he put out a hand to touch her she screamed at him, "Go to hell. Go to hell. Clear out."

"I'll go," he said.

"Yes, go and don't come back."

Outside the door, with the rain cooling his face, running down his hands, it occurred to him how much easier life might be if he took her at her word. He would go into his house and close the door and be alone again; he would write a letter to Louise without a sense of deceit and sleep as he hadn't slept for weeks, dreamlessly. Next day the office, the quiet going home, the evening meal, the locked door. . . . But down the hill, past the transport park, where the lorries crouched under the dripping tarpaulins, the rain fell like tears. He thought of her alone in the hut, wondering whether the irrevocable words had been spoken, if all the to-morrows would consist of Mrs. Carter and Bagster until the boat came and she went home with nothing to remember but misery. Inexorably another's point of view rose on the path like a murdered innocent.

As he opened his door a rat that had been nosing at the food-safe retreated without haste up the stairs. This was what Louise had hated and feared; he had at least made her happy, and now ponderously, with planned and careful recklessness, he set about trying to make things right for Helen. He sat down at his table and taking a sheet of type-writing paper—official paper stamped with the Government watermark—he began to compose a letter.

He wrote: *My darling*—he wanted to put himself entirely in her hands, but to leave her anonymous. He looked at his watch and added in the right-hand corner, as though he were making a police report, *12:35 a.m. Burnside, September 5.* He went carefully on, *I love you more than myself, more than my wife. I am trying very hard to tell the truth. I want more than anything in the world to make you happy.* . . . The banality of the phrases saddened him; they seemed to have no truth personal to herself: they had been used too often. If I were young, he thought, I would be able to find the right words, the new words, but all this has happened to me before. He wrote again, *I love you. Forgive me,* signed and folded the paper.

He put on his mackintosh and went out again in the rain. Wounds festered in the damp, they never healed. Scratch your finger and in a few hours there would be a little coating of green skin. He carried a sense of corruption up the hill. A soldier shouted something in his sleep in the transport park —a single word like a hieroglyphic on a wall which Scobie could not interpret—the men were Nigerians. The sky wept endlessly around him; he had the sense of wounds that never healed. He whispered, "O God, I have deserted you. Do not you desert me." When he came to her door he thrust the letter under it; he heard the rustle of the paper on the cement floor but nothing else. Remembering the childish figure carried past him on the stretcher, he was saddened to think how much had happened, how uselessly, to make him now say to himself with resentment: she will never again be able to accuse me of caution.

ii

"I was just passing by," Father Rank said, "so I thought I'd look in." The evening rain fell in grey ecclesiastical folds, and a lorry howled its way towards the hills.

"Come in," Scobie said. "I'm out of whisky. But there's beer—or gin."

"I saw you up at the Nissens, so I thought I'd follow you down. You are not busy?"

"I'm having dinner with the Commissioner, but not for another hour."

Father Rank moved restlessly around the room, while Scobie took the beer out of the ice-box. "Would you have heard from Louise lately?" he asked.

"Not for a fortnight," Scobie said, "but there've been more sinkings in the south."

Father Rank let himself down in the Government arm-chair with his glass between his knees. There was no sound

but the rain scraping on the roof. Scobie cleared his throat
and then the silence came back. He had the odd sense that
Father Rank, like one of his own junior officers, was waiting
there for orders.

"The rains will soon be over," Scobie said.

"It must be six months now since your wife went."

"Seven."

"Will you be taking your leave in South Africa?" Father
Rank asked, looking away and taking a draught of his beer.

"I've postponed my leave. The young men need it more."

"Everybody needs leave."

"*You've* been here twelve years without it, father."

"Ah, but that's different," Father Rank said. He got up
again and moved restlessly down one wall and along another. He turned an expression of undefined appeal toward
Scobie. "Sometimes," he said, "I feel as though I weren't a
working man at all." He stopped and stared and half raised
his hands, and Scobie remembered Father Clay dodging an
unseen figure in his restless walk. He felt as though an appeal were being made to which he couldn't find an answer.
He said weakly, "There's no one works harder than you, father."

Father Rank returned draggingly to his chair. He said,
"It'll be good when the rains are over."

"How's the mammy out by Congo Creek? I heard she was
dying."

"She'll be gone this week. She's a good woman." He took
another draught of beer and doubled up in the chair with
his hand on his stomach. "The wind," he said. "I get the
wind badly."

"You shouldn't drink bottled beer, father."

"The dying," Father Rank said, "that's what I'm here for.
They send for me when they are dying." He raised eyes
bleary with too much quinine and said harshly and hopelessly, "I've never been any good to the living, Scobie."

"You are talking nonsense, father."

"When I was a novice, I thought that people talked to

their priests, and I thought God somehow gave the right words. Don't mind me, Scobie, don't listen to me. It's the rains—they always get me down about this time. God doesn't give the right words, Scobie. I had a parish once in Northampton. They make boots there. They used to ask me out to tea, and I'd sit and watch their hands pouring out, and we'd talk of the Children of Mary and repairs to the church roof. They were very generous in Northampton. I only had to ask and they'd give. I wasn't of any use to a single living soul, Scobie. I thought, in Africa things will be different. You see I'm not a reading man, Scobie. I never had much talent for loving God as some people do. I wanted to be of use, that's all. Don't listen to me. It's the rains. I haven't talked like this for five years. Except to the mirror. If people are in trouble they'd go to you, Scobie, not to me. They ask me to dinner to hear the gossip. And if you were in trouble where would you go?" And Scobie was again aware of those bleary and appealing eyes, waiting through the dry seasons and the rains, for something that never happened. Could I shift my burden there, he wondered: could I tell him that I love two women: that I don't know what to do? What would be the use? I know the answers as well as he does. One should look after one's own soul at whatever cost to another, and that's what I can't do, what I shall never be able to do. It wasn't he who required the magic word, it was the priest, and he couldn't give it.

"I'm not the kind of man to get into trouble, father. I'm dull and middle-aged," and looking away, unwilling to see distress, he heard Father Rank's clapper miserably sounding, "Ho! ho ho!"

iii

On his way to the Commissioner's bungalow, Scobie looked in at his office. A message was written in pencil on his pad. *I looked in to see you. Nothing important. Wilson.* It struck him as odd: he had not seen Wilson for some weeks, and if his visit had no importance why had he so carefully recorded it? He opened the drawer of his desk to find a packet of cigarettes and noticed at once that something was out of order: he considered the contents carefully: his indelible pencil was missing. Obviously Wilson had looked for a pencil with which to write his message and had forgotten to put it back. But why the message?

In the charge-room the sergeant said, "Mr. Wilson come to see you, sah."

"Yes, he left a message."

So that was it, he thought: I would have known anyway, so he considered it best to let me know himself. He returned to his office and looked again at his desk. It seemed to him that a file had been shifted, but he couldn't be sure. He opened his drawer, but there was nothing there which would interest a soul. Only the broken rosary caught his eye—something which should have been mended a long while ago. He took it out and put it in his pocket.

"Whisky?" the Commissioner asked.

"Thank you," Scobie said, holding the glass up between himself and the Commissioner. "Do *you* trust me?"

"Yes."

"Am I the only one who doesn't know about Wilson?"

The Commissioner smiled, lying back at ease, unembarrassed. "Nobody knows officially—except myself and the manager of the U.A.C.—that was essential of course. The Governor too and whoever deals with the cables marked 'Most Secret.' I'm glad you've tumbled to it."

"I wanted you to know that—up to date of course—I've been trustworthy."

"You don't need to tell me, Scobie."

"In the case of Tallit's cousin we couldn't have done anything different."

"Of course not."

Scobie said, "There is one thing you don't know though. I borrowed two hundred pounds from Yusef so that I could send Louise to South Africa. I pay him four per cent interest. The arrangement is purely commercial, but if you want my head for it . . ."

"I'm glad you told me," the Commissioner said. "You see Wilson got the idea that you were being blackmailed. He must have dug up those payments somehow."

"Yusef wouldn't blackmail for money."

"I told him that."

"Do you want my head?"

"I need your head, Scobie. You're the only officer I really trust."

Scobie stretched out a hand with an empty glass in it: it was like a handclasp.

"Say when."

"When."

Men can become twins with age. The past was their common womb; the six months of rain and the six months of sun was the period of their common gestation. They needed only a few words and a few gestures to convey their meaning. They had graduated through the same fevers, they were moved by the same love and contempt.

"Derry reports there've been some big thefts from the mines."

"Commercial?"

"Gem stones. Is it Yusef—or Tallit?"

"It might be Yusef," Scobie said. "I don't think he deals in industrial diamonds. He calls them gravel. But of course one can't be sure."

"The *Esperança* will be in in a few days. We've got to be careful."

"What does Wilson say?"

"He swears by Tallit. Yusef is the villain of his piece—and you, Scobie."

"I haven't seen Yusef for a long while."

"I know."

"I begin to know what these Syrians feel—watched and reported on."

"Wilson reports on all of us, Scobie. Fraser, Tod, Thimblerigg, myself. He thinks I'm too easy-going. It doesn't matter though. Wright tears up his reports, and of course Wilson reports on him."

"I suppose so."

He walked up, at midnight, to the Nissen huts. In the black-out he felt momentarily safe, unwatched, unreported on; in the soggy ground his footsteps made the smallest sounds, but as he passed Wilson's hut he was aware again of the deep necessity for caution. An awful weariness touched him, and he thought: I will go home: I won't creep by to her tonight: her last words had been "don't come back." Couldn't one, for once, take somebody at their word? He stood twenty yards from Wilson's hut, watching the crack of light between the curtains. A drunken voice shouted somewhere up the hill and the first spatter of the returning rain licked his face. He thought: I'll go back and go to bed. In the morning I'll write to Louise and in the evening go to confession: the day after that God will return to me in a priest's hands: life will be simple again. Virtue, the good life, tempted him in the dark like a sin. The rain blurred his eyes, the ground sucked at his feet as they trod reluctantly towards the Nissen hut.

He knocked twice and the door immediately opened. He had prayed between the two knocks that anger might still be there behind the door, that he wouldn't be wanted. He couldn't shut his eyes or his ears to any human need of him; he was not the centurion, but a man in the ranks who had to do the bidding of a hundred centurions, and when the door opened, he could tell the command was going to be given again—the command to stay, to love, to accept responsibility, to lie.

"Oh darling," she said, "I thought you were never coming. I bitched you so."

"I'll always come if you want me."

"Will you?"

"Always. If I'm alive." God can wait, he thought: how can one love God at the expense of one of his creatures?

Would a woman accept the love for which a child had to be sacrificed?

Carefully they drew the curtains close before turning up the lamps.

She said, "I've been afraid all day that you wouldn't come."

"Of course I came."

"I told you to go away. Never pay any attention to me when I tell you to go away. Promise."

"I promise," he said.

"If you hadn't come back . . ." she said, and became lost in thought between the lamps. He could see her searching for herself, frowning in the effort to see where she would have been . . . "I don't know. Perhaps I'd have slutted with Bagster, or killed myself, or both. I think both."

He said anxiously, "You mustn't think like that. I'll always be here if you need me, as long as I'm alive."

"Why do you keep on saying as long as I'm alive?"

"There are thirty years between us."

For the first time that night they kissed. She said, "I can't feel the years."

"Why did you think I wouldn't come?" Scobie said. "You got my letter."

"Your letter?"

"The one I pushed under your door last night."

She said with fear, "I never saw a letter. What did you say?"

He touched her face and smiled. "Everything. I didn't want to be cautious any longer. I put down everything."

"Even your name?"

"I think so. Anyway it's signed with my handwriting."

"There's a mat by the door. It must be under the mat." But they both knew it wouldn't be there. It was as if all along they had foreseen how disaster would come in by that particular door.

"Who would have taken it?"

He tried to soothe her nerves. "Probably your boy threw it

away, thought it was waste paper. It wasn't in an envelope.
Nobody could know whom I was writing to."

"As if that mattered. Darling," she said, "I feel sick. Really sick. Somebody's getting something on you. I wish I'd
died in that boat."

"You're imagining things. Probably I didn't push the note
far enough. When your boy opened the door in the morning
it blew away or got trampled in the mud." He spoke with all
the conviction he could summon: it was just possible.

"Don't let me ever do you any harm," she implored, and
every phrase she used fastened the fetters more firmly round
his wrists. He put out his hands to her and lied firmly,
"You'll never do me harm. Don't worry about a lost letter. I
exaggerated. It said nothing really—nothing that a stranger
would understand. Don't worry."

"Listen, darling. Don't stay tonight. I'm nervous. I feel—
watched. Say good night now and go away. But come back.
Oh my dear, come back."

The light was still on in Wilson's hut as he passed. Opening the door of his own dark house he saw a piece of paper
on the floor. It gave him an odd shock as though the missing
letter had returned, like a cat, to its old home. But when he
picked it up, it wasn't his letter, though this too was a message of love. It was a telegram addressed to him at police
headquarters and the signature written in full for the sake of
censorship, Louise Scobie, was like a blow struck by a boxer
with a longer reach than he possessed. *Have written am on my
way home have been a fool stop love*—and then that name as formal as a seal.

He sat down. His head swam with nausea. He thought: if
I had never written that other letter, if I had taken Helen at
her word and gone away, how easily then life could have
been arranged again. But he remembered his words in the
last ten minutes, "I'll always be here if you need me, as long
as I'm alive"—that constituted an oath as ineffaceable as
the vow by the Ealing altar. The wind was coming up from
the sea—the rains ended as they began with typhoons. The

curtains blew in and he ran to the windows and pulled them shut. Upstairs the bedroom windows clattered to and fro, tearing at hinges. Turning from closing them he looked at the bare dressing-table where soon the photographs and the pots would be back again—one photograph in particular. The happy Scobie, he thought, my one success. A child in hospital said, "Father," as the shadow of a rabbit shifted on the pillow: a girl went by on a stretcher clutching a stamp-album—why me, he thought, why do they need me, a dull middle-aged police officer who had failed for promotion? I've got nothing to give them that they can't get elsewhere: why can't they leave me in peace? Elsewhere there was a younger and better love, more security. It sometimes seemed to him that all he could share with them was his despair.

Leaning back against the dressing-table, he tried to pray. The Lord's Prayer lay as dead on his tongue as a legal document: it wasn't his daily bread that he wanted but so much more. He wanted happiness for others and solitude and peace for himself. "I don't want to plan any more," he said suddenly aloud. "They wouldn't need me if I were dead. No one needs the dead. The dead can be forgotten. O God, give me death before I give them unhappiness." But the words sounded melodramatically in his own ears. He told himself that he mustn't get hysterical: there was far too much planning to do for an hysterical man, and going downstairs again he thought three aspirins or perhaps four were what he required in this situation—this banal situation. He took a bottle of filtered water out of the ice-box and dissolved the aspirin. He wondered how it would feel to drain death as simply as these aspirins which now stuck sourly in his throat. The priests told one it was the unforgivable sin, the final expression of an unrepentant despair, and of course one accepted the Church's teaching. But they taught also that God had sometimes broken his own laws, and was it less possible for him to put out a hand of forgiveness into the suicidal darkness than to have woken himself in the tomb, behind the stone? Christ had not been murdered—you couldn't murder God. Christ had killed himself: he had hung himself on the Cross as surely as Pemberton from the picture-rail.

He put his glass down and thought again, I must not get hysterical. Two people's happiness was in his hands and he must learn to juggle with strong nerves. Calmness was everything. He took out his diary and began to write against the date, Wednesday, September 6. *Dinner with the Commissioner. Satisfactory talk about W. Called on Helen for a few minutes. Telegram from Louise that she is on the way home.*

He hesitated for a moment and then wrote: *Father Rank called in for drink before dinner. A little overwrought. He needs leave.* He read this over and scored out the last two sentences. It was seldom in this record that he allowed himself an expression of opinion.

[2]

i

The telegram lay on his mind all day: ordinary life—the two hours in court on a perjury case—had the unreality of a country one is leaving for ever. One thinks, at this hour, in that village, these people I once knew are sitting down at table just as they did a year ago when I was there, but one is not convinced that any life goes on the same as ever outside the consciousness. All Scobie's consciousness was on the telegram, on that nameless boat edging its way now up the African coastline from the south. God forgive me, he thought, when his mind lit for a moment on the possibility that it might never arrive. In our hearts there is a ruthless dictator, ready to contemplate the misery of a thousand strangers if it will ensure the happiness of the few we love.

At the end of the perjury case Fellowes, the sanitary inspector, caught him at the door. "Come to chop tonight, Scobie. We've got a bit of real Argentine beef." It was too much of an effort in this dream world to refuse an invitation. "Wilson's coming," Fellowes said. "To tell you the truth, he helped us with the beef. You like him, don't you?"

"Yes. I thought it was you who didn't."

"Oh, the club's got to move with the times, and all sorts of people go into trade nowadays. I admit I was hasty. Bit boozed up, I wouldn't be surprised. He was at Downham: we used to play them when I was at Lancing."

Driving out to the familiar house he had once occupied himself on the hills, Scobie thought listlessly, I must speak to Helen soon. She mustn't learn this from someone else. Life always repeated the same pattern; there was always, sooner or later, bad news that had to be broken, comforting lies to be uttered, pink gins to be consumed to keep misery away.

He came to the long bungalow living-room and there at the end of it was Helen. With a sense of shock he realized that never before had he seen her like a stranger in another man's house, never before dressed for an evening's party. "You know Mrs. Rolt, don't you?" Fellowes asked. There was no irony in his voice. Scobie thought with a tremor of self-disgust, how clever we've been: how successfully we've deceived the gossipers of a small colony. It oughtn't to be possible for lovers to deceive so well. Wasn't love supposed to be spontaneous, reckless . . . ?

"Yes," he said, "I'm an old friend of Mrs. Rolt. I was at Pende when she was brought across." He stood by the table a dozen feet away while Fellowes mixed the drinks and watched her while she talked to Mrs. Fellowes, talked easily, naturally. Would I, he wondered, if I had come in tonight and seen her for the first time ever have felt any love at all?

"Now which was yours, Mrs. Rolt?"

"A pink gin."

"I wish I could get my wife to drink them. I can't bear her gin and orange."

Scobie said, "If I'd known you were going to be here, I'd have called for you."

"I wish you had," Helen said. "You never come and see me." She turned to Fellowes and said with an ease that horrified him, "He was so kind to me in hospital at Pende, but I think he only likes the sick."

Fellowes stroked his little ginger moustache, poured himself out some more gin and said, "He's scared of you, Mrs. Rolt. All we married men are."

She said with false blandness, "Do you think I could have one more without getting tight?"

"Ah, here's Wilson," Fellowes said, and there he was with his pink, innocent, self-distrustful face and his badly tied cummerbund. "You know everybody, don't you? You and Mrs. Rolt are neighbours."

"We haven't met though," Wilson said, and began automatically to blush.

"I don't know what's come over the men in this place," said Fellowes. "You and Scobie both neighbours and neither of you see anything of Mrs. Rolt," and Scobie was immediately aware of Wilson's gaze speculatively turned upon him. "*I* wouldn't be so bashful," Fellowes said, pouring out the pink gins.

"Dr. Sykes late as usual," Mrs. Fellowes commented from the end of the room, but at that moment treading heavily up the outside stairs, sensible in a dark dress and mosquito-boots, came Dr. Sykes. "Just in time for a drink, Jessie," Fellowes said. "What's it to be?"

"Double Scotch," Dr. Sykes said. She glared around through her thick glasses and added, "Evening all."

As they went in to dinner, Scobie said, "I've got to see you," but catching Wilson's eye he added, "about your furniture."

"My furniture?"

"I think I could get you some extra chairs." As conspirators they were much too young; they had not yet absorbed a whole code-book into their memory and he was uncertain whether she had understood the mutilated phrase. All through dinner he sat silent, dreading the time when he would be alone with her, afraid to lose the least opportunity; when he put his hand in his pocket for a handkerchief the telegram crumpled in his fingers . . . *have been a fool stop love.*

"Of course you know more about it than we do, Major Scobie," Dr. Sykes said.

"I'm sorry. I missed . . ."

"We were talking about the Pemberton case." So already in a few months it had become a case. When something became a case it no longer seemed to concern a human being: there was no shame or suffering in a case. The boy on the bed was cleaned and tidied, laid out for the textbook of psychology.

"I was saying," Wilson said, "that Pemberton chose an odd way to kill himself. I would have chosen a sleeping-draught."

"It wouldn't be easy to get a sleeping-draught in Bamba," Dr. Sykes said. "It was probably a sudden decision."

"I wouldn't have caused all that fuss," said Fellowes. "A chap's got the right to take his own life, of course, but there's no need for fuss. An overdose of sleeping-draught—I agree with Wilson—that's the way."

"You still have to get your prescription," Dr. Sykes said.

Scobie with his fingers on the telegram remembered the letter signed "Dicky," the immature handwriting, the marks of cigarettes on the chairs, the novels of Wallace, the stigmata of loneliness. Through two thousand years, he thought, we have discussed Christ's agony in just this disinterested way.

"Pemberton was always a bit of a fool," Fellowes said.

"A sleeping-draught is invariably tricky," Dr. Sykes said. Her big lenses reflected the electric globe as she turned them like a lighthouse in Scobie's direction. "*Your* experience will tell you how tricky. Insurance companies never like sleeping-draughts, and no coroner could lend himself to a deliberate fraud."

"How can they tell?" Wilson asked.

"Take luminol, for instance. Nobody could really take enough luminol by accident. . . ." Scobie looked across the table at Helen. She ate slowly, without appetite, her eyes on her plate. Their silences seemed to isolate them: this was a subject the unhappy could never discuss impersonally. Again he was aware of Wilson looking from one to another of them, and Scobie drew desperately at his mind for any phrase that would end their dangerous solitude. They could not even be silent together with safety.

He said, "What's the way out you'd recommend, Dr. Sykes?"

"Well, there are bathing accidents—but even they need a good deal of explanation. If a man's brave enough to step in front of a car, but it's too uncertain . . ."

"And involves somebody else," Scobie said.

"Personally," Dr. Sykes said, grinning under her glasses, "I should have no difficulties. In my position, I should classify myself as an angina case and then get one of my colleagues to prescribe . . ."

Helen said with sudden violence, "What a beastly talk this is. You've got no business to tell . . ."

"My dear," Dr. Sykes said, revolving her malevolent beams, "when you've been a doctor as long as I have been you know your company. I don't think any of us are likely . . ."

Mrs. Fellowes said, "Have another helping of fruit salad, Mrs. Rolt."

"Are you a Catholic, Mrs. Rolt?" Fellowes asked. "Of course they take very strong views."

"No, I'm not a Catholic."

"But they do, don't they, Scobie?"

"We are taught," Scobie said, "that it's the unforgivable sin."

"But do you really, seriously, Major Scobie," Dr. Sykes asked, "believe in hell?"

"Oh yes, I do."

"In flames and torment?"

"Perhaps not quite that. They tell us it may be a permanent sense of loss."

"That sort of hell wouldn't worry *me*," Fellowes said.

"Perhaps you've never lost anything of any importance," Scobie said.

The real object of the dinner-party had been the Argentine beef. With that consumed there was nothing to keep them together (Mrs. Fellowes didn't play cards). Fellowes busied himself about the beer, and Wilson was wedged between the sour silence of Mrs. Fellowes and Dr. Sykes' garrulity.

"Let's get a breath of air," Scobie suggested.

"Wise?"

"It would look odd if we didn't," Scobie said.

"Going to look at the stars?" Fellowes called, pouring out the beer. "Making up for lost time, Scobie? Take your glasses with you."

They balanced their glasses on the rail of the verandah. Helen said, "I haven't found your letter."

"Forget it."

"Wasn't that what you wanted to see me about?"

"No."

He could see the outline of her face against the sky doomed to go out as the rain clouds advanced. He said, "I've got bad news."

"Somebody knows?"

"Oh no, nobody knows." He said, "Last night I had a telegram from my wife. She's on the way home." One of the glasses fell from the rail and smashed in the yard.

The lips repeated bitterly the word "home" as if that were the only word she had grasped. He said quickly, moving his hand along the rail and failing to reach her, "*Her* home. It will never be my home again."

"Oh yes, it will. Now it will be."

He swore carefully, "I shall never again want any home without you." The rain clouds had reached the moon and her face went out like a candle in a sudden draught of wind. He had the sense that he was embarking now on a longer journey than he had ever intended. A light suddenly shone on both of them as a door opened. He said sharply, "Mind the black-out," and thought: at least we were not standing together, but how, how did our faces look? Wilson's voice said, "We thought a fight was going on. We heard a glass break."

"Mrs. Rolt lost all her beer."

"For God's sake call me Helen," she said drearily, "everybody else does, Major Scobie."

"Am I interrupting something?"

"A scene of unbridled passion," Helen said. "It's left me shaken. I want to go home."

"I'll drive you down," Scobie said. "It's getting late."

"I wouldn't trust you, and anyway Dr. Sykes is dying to talk to you about suicide. I won't break up the party. Haven't you got a car, Mr. Wilson?"

"Of course. I'd be delighted."

"You could always drive down and come straight back."

"I'm an early bird myself," Wilson said.

"I'll just go in then and say good night."

When he saw her face again in the light, he thought: do I worry too much? Couldn't this for her be just the end of an episode? He heard her saying to Mrs. Fellowes, "The Argentine beef certainly was lovely."

"We've got Mr. Wilson to thank for it."

The phrases went to and fro like shuttlecocks. Somebody laughed (it was Fellowes or Wilson) and said, "You're right there," and Dr. Sykes' spectacles made a dot dash dot on the ceiling. He couldn't watch the car move off without disturbing the black-out; he listened to the starter retching and retching, the racing of the engine, and then the slow decline to silence.

Dr. Sykes said, "They should have kept Mrs. Rolt in hospital a while longer."

"Why?"

"Nerves. I could feel it when she shook hands."

He waited another half an hour and then he drove home. As usual Ali was waiting for him, dozing uneasily on the kitchen step. He lit Scobie to the door with his torch. "Missus leave letter," he said, and took an envelope out of his shirt.

"Why didn't you leave it on my table?"

"Massa in there."

"What massa?" but by that time the door was open, and he saw Yusef stretched in a chair, asleep, breathing so gently that the hair lay motionless on his chest.

"I tell him go away," Ali said with contempt, "but he stay."

"That's all right. Go to bed."

He had a sense that life was closing in on him. Yusef had never been here since the night he came to inquire after Louise and to lay his trap for Tallit. Quietly, so as not to disturb the sleeping man and bring *that* problem on his heels, he opened the note from Helen. She must have written it immediately she got home. He read, *My darling, this is serius. I can't say this to you, so I'm putting it on paper. Only I'll give it to Ali. You trust Ali. When I heard your wife was coming back . . .*

Yusef opened his eyes and said, "Excuse me, Major Scobie, for intruding."

"Do you want a drink? Beer. Gin. My whisky's finished."

"May I send you a case?" Yusef began automatically and then laughed. "I always forget. I must not send you things."

Scobie sat down at the table and laid the note open in front of him. Nothing could be so important as those next sentences. He said, "What do you want, Yusef?" and read on, *When I heard your wife was coming back, I was angry and bitter. It was stupid of me. Nothing is your fault.*

"Finish your reading, Major Scobie, I can wait."

"It isn't really important," Scobie said, dragging his eyes from the large immature letters, the mistake in spelling. "Tell me what you want, Yusef," and back his eyes went to the letter. *That's why I'm writing. Because last night you made promises about not leaving me and I don't want you ever to be bound to me with promises. My dear, all your promises . . .*

"Major Scobie, when I lent you money, I swear, it was for friendship, just friendship. I never wanted to ask anything of you, anything at all, not even the four per cent. I wouldn't even have asked for *your* friendship . . . I was *your* friend . . . this is very confusing, words are very complicated, Major Scobie."

"You've kept the bargain, Yusef. I don't complain about Tallit's cousin." He read on: *belong to your wife. Nothing you say to me is a promise. Please, please remember that. If you never want to see me again, don't write, don't speak. And, dear, if you just want to see me sometimes, see me sometimes. I'll tell any lies you like.*

"Do finish what you are reading, Major Scobie. Because what I have to speak about is very, very important."

My dear, my dear, leave me if you want to or have me as your hore if you want to. He thought: she's only heard the word, never seen it spelt: they cut it out of the school Shakespeare. *Goodnight. Don't worry, my darling.* He said savagely, "All right, Yusef. What is it that's so important?"

"Major Scobie, I have got after all to ask you a favour. It has nothing to do with the money I lent you. If you can do this for me it will be friendship, just friendship."

"It's late, Yusef, tell me what it is."

"The *Esperança* will be in the day after tomorrow. I want a small packet taken on board for me and left with the captain."

"What's in the packet?"

"Major Scobie, don't ask. I am your friend. I would rather have this be a secret. It will harm no one at all."

"Of course, Yusef, I can't do it. You know that."

"I assure you, Major Scobie, on my word——" he leant forward in the chair and laid his hand on the black fur of his chest—"on my word as a friend the package contains nothing, nothing for the Germans. No industrial diamonds, Major Scobie."

"Gem stones?"

"Nothing for the Germans. Nothing that will hurt your country."

"Yusef, you can't really believe that I'd agree?"

The light drill trousers squeezed to the edge of the chair: for one moment Scobie thought that Yusef was going on his knees to him. He said, "Major Scobie, I implore you. . . . It is important for you as well as for me." His voice broke with genuine emotion, "I want to be a friend."

Scobie said, "I'd better warn you before you say any more, Yusef, that the Commissioner *does* know about our arrangement."

"I daresay, I daresay, but this is so much worse. Major Scobie, on my word of honour, this will do no harm to anyone. Just do this one act of friendship, and I'll never ask another. Do it of your own free will, Major Scobie. There is no bribe. I offer no bribe."

His eye went back to the letter: *My darling, this is serius.* Serius—his eye this time read it as *servus*—a slave: a servant of the servants of God. It was like an unwise command which he had none the less to obey. He felt as though he were turning his back on peace for ever. With his eyes open, knowing the consequences, he entered the territory of lies without a passport for return.

"What were you saying, Yusef? I didn't catch . . ."

"Just once more I ask you . . ."

"No, Yusef."

"Major Scobie," Yusef said, sitting bolt upright in his chair, speaking with a sudden odd formality, as though a stranger had joined them and they were no longer alone, "you remember Pemberton?"

"Of course."

"His boy came into my employ."

"Pemberton's boy?" *Nothing you say to me is a promise.*

"Pemberton's boy is Mrs. Rolt's boy."

Scobie's eyes remained on the letter, but he no longer read what he saw.

"Her boy brought me a letter. You see I asked him to keep his eyes—bare—is that the right word?"

"You have a very good knowledge of English, Yusef. Who read it to you?"

"That does not matter."

The formal voice suddenly stopped and the old Yusef implored again, "Oh, Major Scobie, what made you write such a letter? It was asking for trouble."

"One can't be wise all the time, Yusef. One would die of disgust."

"You see it has put you in my hands."

"I wouldn't mind that so much. But to put three people in your hands . . ."

"If only you would have done an act of friendship . . ."

"Go on, Yusef. You must complete your blackmail. You can't get away with half a threat."

"I wish I could dig a hole and put the package in it. But the war's going badly, Major Scobie. I am doing this not for myself, but for my father and mother, my half-brother, my three sisters—and there are cousins too."

"Quite a family."

"You see if the English are beaten all my stores have no value at all."

"What do you propose to do with the letter, Yusef?"

"I hear from a clerk in the cable company that your wife is on her way back. I will have the letter handed to her as soon as she lands."

He remembered the telegram signed Louise Scobie: *have been a fool stop love*. It would be a cold welcome, he thought.

"And if I give your package to the captain of the *Esperança*?"

"My boy will be waiting on the wharf. In return for the captain's receipt he will give you an envelope with your letter inside."

"You trust your boy?"

"Just as you trust Ali."

"Suppose I demand the letter first and gave you my word . . ."

"It is the penalty of the blackmailer, Major Scobie, that he has no debts of honour. You would be quite right to cheat me."

"Suppose you cheat me?"

"That wouldn't be right. And formerly I was your friend."

"You very nearly were," Scobie reluctantly admitted.

"I am the base Indian."

"The base Indian?"

"Who threw away a pearl," Yusef sadly said. "That was in the play by Shakespeare the Ordnance Corps gave in the Memorial Hall. I have always remembered it."

ii

"Well," Druce said, "I'm afraid we'll have to get to work now."

"One more glass," the captain of the *Esperança* said.

"Not if we are going to release you before the boom closes. See you later, Scobie."

When the door of the cabin closed the captain said breathlessly, "I am still here."

"So I see. I told you there are often mistakes—minutes go to the wrong place, files are lost."

"I believe none of that," the captain said. "I believe you helped me." He dripped gently with sweat in the stuffy cabin. He added, "I pray for you at Mass, and I have brought you this. It was all that I could find for you in Lobito. She is a very obscure saint," and he slid across the table between them a holy medal the size of a nickel piece. "Santa—I don't remember her name. She had something to do with Angola I think," the captain explained.

"Thank you," Scobie said. The package in his pocket seemed to him to weigh as heavily as a gun against his thigh.

He let the last drops of port settle in the well of his glass and then drained them. He said, "This time I have something for *you*." A terrible reluctance cramped his fingers.

"For me?"

"Yes."

How light the little package actually was now that it was on the table between them. What had weighed like a gun in the pocket might now have contained little more than fifty cigarettes. He said, "Someone who comes on board with the pilot at Lisbon will ask you if you have any American cigarettes. You will give him this package."

"Is this Government business?"

"No. The Government would never pay as well as this." He laid a packet of notes upon the table.

"This surprises me," the captain said with an odd note of disappointment. "You have put yourself in my hands."

"You were in mine," Scobie said.

"I don't forget. Nor will my daughter. She is married outside the Church, but she has faith. She prays for you too."

"The prayers we pray then don't count, surely?"

"No, but when the moment of Grace returns they rise," the captain raised his fat arms in an absurd and touching gesture, "all at once together like a flock of birds."

"I shall be glad of them," Scobie said.

"You can trust me, of course."

"Of course. Now I must search your cabin."

"You do not trust me very far."

"That package," Scobie said, "has nothing to do with the war."

"Are you sure?"

"I am nearly sure."

He began his search. Once, pausing by a mirror, he saw poised over his own shoulder a stranger's face, a fat, sweating, unreliable face. Momentarily he wondered: who can that be? before he realized that it was only this new unfamiliar look of pity which made it strange to him. He thought: am I really one of those whom people pity?

BOOK THREE

Part I

[1]

i

The rains were over and the earth steamed. Flies everywhere settled in clouds, and the hospital was full of malaria patients. Farther up the coast they were dying of blackwater, and yet for a while there was a sense of relief. It was as if the world had become quiet again, now that the drumming on the iron roofs was over. In the town the deep scent of flowers modified the zoo smell in the corridors of the police station. An hour after the boom was opened the liner moved in from the south unescorted.

Scobie went out in the police boat as soon as the liner anchored. His mouth felt stiff with welcome; he practised on his tongue phrases which would seem warm and unaffected, and he thought: what a long way I have travelled to make me rehearse a welcome. He hoped he would find Louise in one of the public rooms; it would be easier to greet her in front of strangers, but there was no sign of her anywhere. He had to ask at the purser's office for her cabin number.

Even then, of course, there was the hope that it would be shared. No cabin nowadays held less than six passengers.

But when he knocked and the door was opened, nobody was there but Louise. He felt like a caller at a strange house with something to sell. There was a question-mark at the end of his voice when he said, "Louise?"

"Henry." She added, "Come inside." When once he was within the cabin there was nothing to do but kiss. He avoided her mouth—the mouth reveals so much, but she wouldn't be content until she had pulled his face round and left the seal of her return on his lips. "Oh my dear, here I am."

"Here you are," he said, seeking desperately for the phrases he had rehearsed.

"They've all been so sweet," she explained. "They are keeping away, so that I can see you alone."

"You've had a good trip?"

"I think we were chased once."

"I was very anxious," he said and thought: that is the first lie. I may as well take the plunge now. He said, "I've missed you so much."

"I was a fool to go away, darling." Through the port-hole the houses sparkled like mica in the haze of heat. The cabin smelt closely of women, of powder, nail-varnish, and night-dresses. He said, 'Let's get ashore.'

But she detained him a little while yet. "Darling," she said, "I've made a lot of resolutions while I've been away. Everything now is going to be different. I'm not going to rattle you any more." She repeated, "Everything will be different," and he thought sadly that that at any rate was the truth, the bleak truth.

Standing at the window of his house while Ali and the small boy carried in the trunks he looked up the hill towards the Nissen huts. It was as if a landslide had suddenly put an immeasurable distance between him and them. They were so distant that at first there was no pain, any more than for an episode of youth remembered with the faintest melancholy. Did my lies really start, he wondered, when I wrote that letter? Can I really love her more than Louise? Do I, in my heart of hearts, love either of them, or is it only that this automatic pity goes out to any human need—and makes it worse? Any victim demands allegiance. Upstairs silence and solitude were being hammered away, tin-tacks were being driven in, weights fell on the floor and shook the ceiling. Louise's voice was raised in cheerful peremptory commands.

There was a rattle of objects on the dressing-table. He went upstairs and from the doorway saw the face in the white communion veil staring back at him again: the dead too had returned. Life was not the same without the dead. The mosquito-net hung, a grey ectoplasm, over the double bed.

"Well, Ali," he said, with the phantom of a smile which was all he could raise at this séance, "Missus back. We're all together again." Her rosary lay on the dressing-table, and he thought of the broken one in his pocket. He had always meant to get it mended: now it hardly seemed worth the trouble.

"Darling," Louise said, "I've finished up here. Ali can do the rest. There are so many things I want to speak to you about. . . ." She followed him downstairs and said at once, "I must get the curtains washed."

"They don't show the dirt."

"Poor dear, you wouldn't notice, but I've been away." She said, "I really want a bigger bookcase now. I've brought a lot of books back with me."

"You haven't told me yet what made you . . ."

"Darling, you'd laugh at me. It was so silly. But suddenly I saw what a fool I'd been to worry like that about the Commissionership. I'll tell you one day when I don't mind your laughing." She put her hand out and tentatively touched his arm. "You're really glad . . . ?"

"So glad," he said.

"Do you know one of the things that worried me? I was afraid you wouldn't be much of a Catholic without me around, keeping you up to things, poor dear."

"I don't suppose I have been."

"Have you missed Mass often?"

He said with forced jocularity, "I've hardly been at all."

"Oh, Ticki." She pulled herself quickly up and said, "Henry, darling, you'll think I'm very sentimental, but to-morrow's Sunday and I want us to go to communion together. A sign that we've started again—in the right way."

It was extraordinary the points in a situation one missed—
this he had not considered. He said, "Of course," but his
brain momentarily refused to work.

"You'll have to go to confession this afternoon."

"I haven't done anything very terrible."

"Missing Mass on Sunday's a mortal sin, just as much as
adultery."

"Adultery's more fun," he said with attempted lightness.

"It's time I came back."

"I'll go along this afternoon—after lunch. I can't confess
on an empty stomach," he said.

"Darling, you *have* changed, you know."

"I was only joking."

"I don't mind you joking. I like it. You didn't do it much
though before."

"You don't come back every day, darling." The strained
good humour, the jest with dry lips, went on and on: at
lunch he laid down his fork for yet another "crack." "Dear
Henry," she said, "I've never known you so cheerful." The
ground had given way beneath his feet, and all through the
meal he had the sensation of falling, the relaxed stomach,
the breathlessness, the despair—because you couldn't fall so
far as this and survive. His hilarity was like a scream from a
crevasse.

When lunch was over (he couldn't have told what it was
he'd eaten) he said, "I must be off."

"Father Rank?"

"First I've got to look in on Wilson. He's living in one of
the Nissens now. A neighbour."

"Won't he be in town?"

"I think he comes back for lunch."

He thought as he went up the hill, what a lot of times in
future I shall have to call on Wilson. But no—that wasn't a
safe alibi. It would only do this once, because he knew that
Wilson lunched in town. None the less, to make sure, he
knocked and was taken aback momentarily when Harris
opened to him. "I didn't expect to see you."

"I had a touch of fever," Harris said.

"I wondered whether Wilson was in."

"He always lunches in town," Harris said.

"I just wanted to tell him he'd be welcome to look in. My wife's back, you know."

"I thought I saw the activity through the window."

"You must call on us too."

"I'm not much of a calling man," Harris said, drooping in the doorway. "To tell you the truth women scare me."

"You don't see enough of them, Harris."

"I'm not a squire of dames," Harris said with a poor attempt at pride, and Scobie was aware of how Harris watched him as he picked his way reluctantly towards a woman's hut, watched with the ugly asceticism of the unwanted man. He knocked and felt that disapproving gaze boring into his back. He thought: there goes my alibi: he will tell Wilson and Wilson . . . He thought: I will say that as I was up here, I called . . . and he felt his whole personality crumble with the slow disintegration of lies.

"Why did you knock?" Helen asked. She lay on her bed in the dusk of drawn curtains.

"Harris was watching me."

"I didn't think you'd come today."

"How did you know?"

"Everybody here knows everything—except one thing. How clever you are about that. I suppose it's because you are a police officer."

"Yes." He sat down on the bed and put his hand on her arm; immediately the sweat began to run between them. He said, "What are you doing here? You are not ill?"

"Just a headache."

He said mechanically, without even hearing his own words, "Take care of yourself."

"Something's worrying you," she said. "Have things gone —wrong?"

"Nothing of that kind."

"Do you remember the first night you stayed here? We

didn't worry about anything. You even left your umbrella behind. We were happy. Doesn't it seem odd?—we were happy."

"Yes."

"Why do we go on like this—being unhappy?"

"It's a mistake to mix up the ideas of happiness and love," Scobie said with desperate pedantry, as though, if he could turn the whole situation into a textbook case, as they had turned Pemberton, peace might return to both of them, a kind of resignation.

"Sometimes you are so damnably old," Helen said, but immediately she expressed with a motion of her hand towards him that she wasn't serious. Today, he thought, she can't afford to quarrel—or so she believes. "Darling," she added, "a penny for your thoughts."

One ought not to lie to two people if it could be avoided— that way lay complete chaos, but he was tempted terribly to lie as he watched her face on the pillow. She seemed to him like one of those plants in nature films which you watch age under your eye. Already she had the look of the Coast about her. She shared it with Louise. He said, "It's just a worry I have to think out for myself. Something I hadn't considered."

"Tell me, darling. Two brains . . ." She closed her eyes and he could see her mouth steady for a blow.

He said, "Louise wants me to go to Mass with her, to communion. I'm supposed to be on the way to confession now."

"Oh, is that all?" she asked with immense relief, and irritation at her ignorance moved like hatred unfairly in his brain.

"All?" he said. "All?" Then justice reclaimed him. He said gently, "If I don't go to communion, you see, she'll know there's something wrong—seriously wrong."

"But can't you simply go?"

He said, "To me that means—well, it's the worst thing I can do."

"You don't really believe in hell?"

"That was what Fellowes asked me."

"But I simply don't understand. If you believe in hell, why are you with me now?"

How often, he thought, lack of faith helps one to see more clearly than faith. He said, "You are right, of course: it ought to prevent all this. But the villagers on the slopes of Vesuvius go on. . . . And then, against all the teaching of the Church, one has the conviction that love—any kind of love—does deserve a bit of mercy. One will pay, of course, pay terribly, but I don't believe one will pay for ever. Perhaps one will be given time before one dies. . . ."

"A deathbed repentance," she said with contempt.

"It wouldn't be easy," he said, "to repent of this." He kissed the sweat off her hand. "I can regret the lies, the mess, the unhappiness, but if I were dying now I wouldn't know how to repent the love."

"Well," she said with the same undertone of contempt that seemed to pull her apart from him, into the safety of the shore, "can't you go and confess everything now? After all it doesn't mean you won't do it again."

"It's not much good confessing if I don't intend to try. . . ."

"Well then," she said triumphantly, "be hung for a sheep. You are in—what do you call it?—mortal sin?—now. What difference does it make?"

He thought: pious people, I suppose, would call this the devil speaking, but he knew that evil never spoke in these crude answerable terms: this was innocence. He said, "There *is* a difference—a big difference. It's not easy to explain. *Now* I'm just putting our love above—well, my safety. But the other—the other's really evil. It's like the Black Mass, the man who steals the sacrament to desecrate it. It's striking God when he's down—in my power."

She turned her head wearily away and said, "I don't understand a thing you are saying. It's all hooey to me."

"I wish it were to me. But I believe it."

She said sharply, "I *suppose* you do. Or is it just a trick? I didn't hear so much about God when we began, did I? You aren't turning pious on me to give you an excuse. . . ?"

"My dear," Scobie said, "I'm not leaving you ever. I've got to think, that's all."

ii

At a quarter past six next morning Ali called them. Scobie woke at once, but Louise remained sleeping—she had had a long day. Scobie watched her—this was the face he had loved: this was the face he loved. She was terrified of death by sea and yet she had come back, to make him comfortable. She had borne a child by him in one agony, and in another agony had watched the child die. It seemed to him that he had escaped everything. If only, he thought, I could so manage that she never suffers again, but he knew that he had set himself an impossible task. He could delay the suffering, that was all, but he carried it about with him, an infection which sooner or later she must contract. Perhaps she was contracting it now, for she turned and whimpered in her sleep. He put his hand against her cheek to soothe her. He thought: if only she will go on sleeping, then I will sleep on too, I will oversleep, we shall miss Mass, another problem will be postponed. But as if his thoughts had been an alarm clock she awoke.

"What time is it, darling?"

"Nearly half past six."

"We'll have to hurry." He felt as though he were being urged by a kindly and remorseless gaoler to dress for execution. Yet he still put off the saving lie: there was always the possibility of a miracle. Louise gave a final dab of powder (but the powder caked as it touched the skin) and said, "We'll be off now." Was there the faintest note of triumph in her voice? Years and years ago, in the other life of childhood, someone with his name, Henry Scobie, had acted in the school play, had acted Hotspur. He had been chosen for his seniority and his physique, but everyone said it had been a good performance. Now he had to act again—surely it was as easy as the simpler verbal lie?

Scobie suddenly leant back against the wall and put his hand on his chest. He couldn't make his muscles imitate pain, so he simply closed his eyes. Louise looking in her mirror said, "Remind me to tell you about Father Davis in Durban. He was a very good type of priest, much more intellectual than Father Rank." It seemed to Scobie that she was never going to look round and notice him. She said, "Well, we really must be off," and dallied by the mirror. Some sweat-lank hairs were out of place. Through the curtain of his lashes at last he saw her turn and look at him. "Come along, dear," she said, "you look sleepy."

He kept his eyes shut and stayed where he was. She said sharply, "Ticki, what's the matter?"

"A little brandy."

"Are you ill?"

"A little brandy," he repeated sharply, and when she had fetched it for him and he felt the taste on his tongue he had an immeasurable sense of reprieve. He sighed and relaxed. "That's better."

"What was it, Ticki?"

"Just a pain in my chest. It's gone now."

"Have you had it before?"

"Once or twice while you've been away."

"You must see a doctor."

"Oh, it's not worth a fuss. They'll just say overwork."

"I oughtn't to have dragged you up, but I wanted us to have communion together."

"I'm afraid I've ruined that—with the brandy."

"Never mind, Ticki." Carelessly she sentenced him to eternal death. "We can go any day."

He knelt in his seat and watched Louise kneel with the other communicants at the altar rail: he had insisted on coming to the service with her. Father Rank turning from the altar came to them with God in his hands. Scobie thought: God has just escaped me, but will He always escape? *Domine, non sum dignus . . . Domine, non sum dignus . . . Domine, non sum dignus. . . .* His hand formally, as though he were at drill, beat on a particular button of his uniform. It seemed to him for a moment cruelly unfair of God to have exposed himself in this way, a man, a wafer of bread, first in the Palestinian villages and now here in the hot port, there, everywhere, allowing man to have his will of Him. Christ had told the rich young man to sell all and follow Him, but that was an easy rational step compared with this that God had taken, to put Himself at the mercy of men who hardly knew the meaning of the word. How desperately God must love, he thought with shame. The priest had reached Louise in his slow interrupted patrol, and suddenly Scobie was aware of the sense of exile. Over there, where all these people knelt, was a country to which he would never return. The sense of love stirred in him, the love one always feels for what one has lost, whether a child, a woman, or even pain.

[2]

i

Wilson tore the page carefully out of the *Downhamian* and pasted a thick sheet of Colonial Office notepaper on the back of the poem. He held it up to the light: it was impossible to read the sports results on the other side of his verses. Then he folded the page carefully and put it in his pocket; there it would probably stay, but one never knew.

He had seen Scobie drive away towards the town and with beating heart and a sense of breathlessness, much the same as he had felt when stepping into the brothel, even with the same reluctance—for who wanted at any given moment to change the routine of his life?—he made his way downhill towards Scobie's house.

He began to rehearse what he considered another man in his place would do: pick up the threads at once: kiss her quite naturally, upon the mouth if possible, say, "I've missed you," no uncertainty. But his beating heart sent out its message of fear which drowned thought.

"It's Wilson at last," Louise said. "I thought you'd forgotten me," and held out her hand. He took it like a defeat.

"Have a drink."

"I was wondering whether you'd like a walk."

"It's too hot, Wilson."

"I haven't been up there, you know, since. . . ."

"Up where?" He realized that for those who do not love time never stands still.

"Up at the old station."

She said vaguely with a remorseless lack of interest, "Oh yes . . . yes, I haven't been up there myself yet."

"That night when I got back," he could feel the awful immature flush expanding, "I tried to write some verse."

"What, you, Wilson?"

He said furiously, "Yes, me, Wilson. Why not? And it's been published."

"I wasn't laughing. I was just surprised. Who published it?"

"A new paper called *The Circle*. Of course they don't pay much."

"Can I see it?"

Wilson said breathlessly, "I've got it here." He explained, "There was something on the other side I couldn't stand. It was just too modern for me." He watched her with hungry embarrassment.

"It's quite pretty," she said weakly.

"You see the initials?"

"I've never had a poem dedicated to me before."

Wilson felt sick; he wanted to sit down. Why, he wondered, does one ever begin this humiliating process: why does one imagine that one is in love? He had read somewhere that love had been invented in the eleventh century by the troubadours. Why had they not left us with lust? He said with hopeless venom, "I love you." He thought: it's a lie, the word means nothing off the printed page. He waited for her laughter.

"Oh, no, Wilson," she said, "no. You don't. It's just Coast fever."

He plunged blindly, "More than anything in the world."

She said gently, "No one loves like that, Wilson."

He walked restlessly up and down, his shorts flapping, waving the bit of paper from the *Downhamian*. "You ought to believe in love. You're a Catholic. Didn't God love the world?"

"Oh yes," she said, "He's capable of it. But not many of us are."

"You love your husband. You told me so. And it's brought you back."

Louise said sadly, "I suppose I do. All I can. But it's not the kind of love *you* want to imagine you feel. No poisoned chalices, eternal doom, black sails. We don't *die* for love, Wilson—except, of course, in books. And sometimes a boy play-acting. Don't let's play-act, Wilson—it's no fun at our age."

"I'm not play-acting," he said with a fury in which he could hear too easily the histrionic accent. He confronted her bookcase as though it were a witness she had forgotten. "Do *they* play-act?"

"Not much," she said. "That's why I like them better than *your* poets."

"All the same you came back." His face lit up with wicked inspiration. "Or was that just jealousy?"

She said, "Jealousy? What on earth have I got to be jealous about?"

"They've been careful," Wilson said, "but not as careful as all that."

"I don't know what you are talking about."

"Your Ticki and Helen Rolt."

Louise struck at his cheek and missing got his nose, which began to bleed copiously. She said, "That's for calling him Ticki. Nobody's going to do that except me. You know he hates it. Here, take my handkerchief if you haven't got one of your own."

Wilson said, "I bleed awfully easily. Do you mind if I lie on my back?" He stretched himself on the floor between the table and the meat safe, among the ants. First there had been Scobie watching his tears at Pende, and now—this.

"You wouldn't like me to put a key down your back?" Louise asked.

"No. No thank you." The blood had stained the *Down-hamian* page.

"I really *am* sorry. I've got a vile temper. This will cure you, Wilson." But if romance is what one lives by, one must never be cured of it. The world has too many spoilt priests of this faith or that: better surely to pretend a belief than wander in that vicious vacuum of cruelty and despair. He said obstinately, "Nothing will cure me, Louise. I love you. Nothing," bleeding into her handkerchief.

"How strange," she said, "it would be if it were true."

He grunted a query from the ground.

"I mean," she explained, "if you *were* one of those people who really love. I thought Henry was. It would be strange if really it was you all the time." He felt an odd fear that after all he was going to be accepted at his own valuation, rather as a minor staff officer might feel during a rout when he finds that his claim to know the handling of the tanks will be accepted. It is too late to admit that he knows nothing but what he has read in the technical journals—"O lyric love, half angel and half bird." Bleeding into the handkerchief, he formed his lips carefully round a generous phrase, "I expect he loves—in his way."

"Who?" Louise said. "Me? This Helen Rolt you are talking about? Or just himself?"

"I shouldn't have said that."

"Isn't it true? Let's have a bit of truth, Wilson. You don't know how tired I am of comforting lies. Is she beautiful?"

"Oh no, no. Nothing of that sort."

"She's young, of course, and I'm middle-aged. But surely she's a bit worn after what she's been through."

"She's very worn."

"But she's not a Catholic. She's lucky. She's free, Wilson."

Wilson sat up against the leg of the table. He said with genuine passion, "I wish to God you wouldn't call me Wilson."

"Edward. Eddie. Ted. Teddy."

"I'm bleeding again," he said dismally and lay back on the floor.

"What do you know about it all, Teddy?"

"I think I'd rather be Edward, Louise. I've seen him come away from her hut at two in the morning. He was up there yesterday afternoon."

"He was at confession."

"Harris saw him."

"You're certainly watching him."

"It's my belief Yusef is using him."

"That's fantastic. You're going too far."

She stood over him as though he were a corpse: the blood-stained handkerchief lay in his palm. They neither of them heard the car stop or the footsteps up to the threshold. It was strange to both of them, hearing a third voice from an outside world speaking into this room which had become as close and intimate and airless as a vault. "Is anything wrong?" Scobie's voice asked.

"It's just . . ." Louise said and made a gesture of bewilderment—as though she were saying: where does one start explaining? Wilson scrambled to his feet and at once his nose began to bleed.

"Here," Scobie said and taking out his bundle of keys dropped them inside Wilson's shirt collar. "You'll see," he said, "the old-fashioned remedies are always best," and sure enough the bleeding did stop within a few seconds. "You should never lie on your back," Scobie went reasonably on. "Seconds use a sponge of cold water, and you certainly look as though you'd been in a fight, Wilson."

"I always lie on my back," Wilson said. "Blood makes me ill."

"Have a drink?"

"No," Wilson said, "no. I must be off." He retrieved the keys with some difficulty and left the tail of his shirt dangling. He only discovered it when Harris pointed it out to him on his return to the Nissen, and he thought: that is how I looked while I walked away and they watched side by side.

ii

"What did he want?" Scobie said.

"He wanted to make love to me."

"Does he love you?"

"He thinks he does. You can't ask much more than that, can you?"

"You seem to have hit him rather hard," Scobie said, "on the nose?"

"He made me angry. He called you Ticki. Darling, he's spying on you."

"I know that."

"Is he dangerous?"

"He might be—under some circumstances. But then it would be my fault."

"Henry, do you never get furious at anyone? Don't you mind him making love to me?"

He said, "I'd be a hypocrite if I were angry at that. It's the kind of thing that happens to people. You know, quite pleasant normal people do fall in love."

"Have you ever fallen in love?"

"Oh yes, yes." He watched her closely while he excavated his smile. "*You* know I have."

"Henry, did you really feel ill this morning?"

"Yes."

"It wasn't just an excuse?"

"No."

"Then, darling, let's go to communion together tomorrow morning."

"If you want to," he said. It was the moment he had known would come. With bravado, to show that his hand was not shaking, he took down a glass. "Drink?"

"It's too early, dear," Louise said; he knew she was watching him closely like all the others. He put the glass down and said, "I've just got to run back to the station for some papers. When I get back it will be time for drinks."

He drove unsteadily down the road, his eyes blurred with nausea. O God, he thought, the decisions you force on people, suddenly, with no time to consider. I am too tired to think: this ought to be worked out on paper like a problem in mathematics, and the answer arrived at without pain. But the pain made him physically sick, so that he retched over the wheel. The trouble is, he thought, we know the answers—we Catholics are damned by our knowledge. There's no need for me to work anything out—there is only one answer: to kneel down in the confessional and say, "Since my last confession I have committed adultery so many times et cetera, et cetera"; to hear Father Rank telling me to avoid the occasion: never see the woman alone (speaking in those terrible abstract terms: Helen—the woman, the occasion, no longer the bewildered child clutching the stamp-album, listening to Bagster howling outside the door: that moment of peace and darkness and tenderness and pity, "adultery"). And I to make my Act of Contrition, the promise "never more to offend thee," and then tomorrow the communion: taking God in my mouth in what they call the state of grace. That's the right answer—there *is* no other answer: to save my own soul and abandon her to Bagster and despair. One must be reasonable, he told himself, and recognize that despair doesn't last (is that true?), that love doesn't last (but isn't that the very reason that despair does?), that in a few weeks or months she'll be all right again. She has survived forty days in an open boat and the death of her husband and can't she survive the mere death of love? As I can, as I know I can.

He drew up outside the church and sat hopelessly at the wheel. Death never comes when one desires it most. He thought: of course there's the ordinary honest *wrong* answer, to leave Louise, forget that private vow, resign my job. To abandon Helen to Bagster or Louise to what? I am trapped, he told himself, catching sight of an expressionless stranger's face in the driving mirror, trapped. Nevertheless he left the car and went into the church. While he was waiting for Father Rank to go into the confessional he knelt and prayed: the only prayer he could rake up. Even the words of the Our Father and the Hail Mary deserted him. He prayed for a miracle: "O God, convince me, help me, convince me. Make me feel that I am more important than that girl." It was not Helen's face he saw as he prayed but the dying child who called him father: a face in a photograph staring from the dressing-table: the face of a black girl of twelve a sailor had raped and killed glaring blindly up at him in a yellow paraffin light. "Make me put my own soul first. Give me trust in your mercy to the one I abandon." He could hear Father Rank close the door of his box and nausea twisted him again on his knees. "O God," he said, "if instead I should abandon you, punish me but let the others get some happiness." He went into the box. He thought, a miracle may still happen. Even Father Rank may for once find the word, the right word. . . . Kneeling in the space of an upturned coffin he said, "Since my last confession I have committed adultery."

"How many times?"

"I don't know, father, many times."

"Are you married?"

"Yes." He remembered that evening when Father Rank had nearly broken down before him, admitting his failure to help. . . . Was he, even while he was struggling to retain the complete anonymity of the confessional, remembering it too? He wanted to say, "Help me, father. Convince me that I would do right to abandon her to Bagster. Make me believe in the mercy of God," but he knelt silently waiting: he was unaware of the slightest tremor of hope. Father Rank said, "Is it one woman?"

"Yes."

"You must avoid seeing her. Is that possible?"

He shook his head.

"If you must see her, you must never be alone with her. Do you promise to do that, promise God, not me?" He thought: how foolish it was of me to expect the magic word. This is the formula used so many times on so many people. Presumably people promised and went away and came back and confessed again. Did they really believe they were going to try? He thought: I am cheating human beings every day I live, I am not going to try to cheat myself or God. He replied, "It would be no good my promising that, father."

"You must promise. You can't desire the end without desiring the means."

Ah, but one can, he thought, one can: one can desire the peace of victory without desiring the ravaged towns.

Father Rank said, "I don't need to tell you surely that there's nothing automatic in the confessional or in absolution. It depends on your state of mind whether you are forgiven. It's no good coming and kneeling here unprepared. Before you come here you must know the wrong you've done."

"I do know that."

"And you must have a real purpose of amendment. We are told to forgive our brother seventy times seven and we needn't fear God will be any less forgiving than we are, but nobody can begin to forgive the uncontrite. It's better to sin seventy times and repent each time than sin once and never repent." He could see Father Rank's hand go up to wipe the sweat out of his eyes: it was like a gesture of weariness. He thought: what is the good of keeping him in this discomfort? He's right, of course, he's right. I was a fool to imagine that somehow in this airless box I would find a conviction. . . . He said, "I think I was wrong to come, father."

"I don't want to refuse you absolution, but I think if you would just go away and turn things over in your mind, you'd come back in a better frame of mind."

"Yes, father."

"I will pray for you."

When he came out of the box it seemed to Scobie that for the first time his footsteps had taken him out of sight of hope. There was no hope anywhere he turned his eyes: the dead figure of the God upon the cross, the plaster Virgin, the hideous stations representing a series of events that had happened a long time ago. It seemed to him that he had only left for his exploration the territory of despair.

He drove down to the station, collected a file and returned home. "You've been a long time," Louise said. He didn't even know the lie he was going to tell before it was on his lips. "That pain came back," he said, "so I waited for a while."

"Do you think you ought to have a drink?"

"Yes, until anybody tells me not to."

"And you'll see a doctor?"

"Of course."

That night he dreamed that he was in a boat drifting down just such an underground river as his boyhood hero Allan Quatermain had taken towards the lost city of Milosis. But Quatermain had companions while he was alone, for you couldn't count the dead body on the stretcher as a companion. He felt a sense of urgency, for he told himself that bodies in this climate kept for a very short time and the smell of decay was already in his nostrils. Then, sitting there guiding the boat down the mid-stream, he realized that it was not the dead body that smelt but his own living one. He felt as though his blood had ceased to run: when he tried to lift his arm it dangled uselessly from his shoulder. He woke and it was Louise who had lifted his arm. She said, "Darling, it's time to be off."

"Off?" he asked.

"We're going to Mass," and again he was aware of how

closely she was watching him. What was the good of yet another delaying lie? He wondered what Wilson had said to her. Could he go on lying week after week, finding some reason of work, of health, of forgetfulness for avoiding the issue at the altar rail? He thought hopelessly: I am damned already—I may as well go the whole length of my chain. "Yes," he said, "of course. I'll get up," and was suddenly surprised by her putting the excuse into his mouth, giving him his chance. "Darling," she said, "if you aren't well, stay where you are. I don't want to drag you to Mass."

But the excuse it seemed to him was also a trap. He could see where the turf had been replaced over the hidden stakes. If he took the excuse she offered he would have all but confessed his guilt. Once and for all now at whatever eternal cost, he was determined that he would clear himself in her eyes and give her the reassurance she needed. He said, "No, no. I will come with you." When he walked beside her into the church it was as if he had entered this building for the first time—a stranger. An immeasurable distance already separated him from these people who knelt and prayed and would presently receive God in peace. He knelt and pretended to pray.

The words of the Mass were like an indictment. "I will go in unto the altar of God: to God who giveth joy to my youth." But there was no joy anywhere. He looked up from between his hands and the plaster images of the Virgin and the saints seemed to be holding out hands to everyone, on either side, beyond him. He was the unknown guest at a party who is introduced to no one. The gentle painted smiles were unbearably directed elsewhere. When the Kyrie Eleison was reached he again tried to pray. "Lord have mercy . . . Christ have mercy . . . Lord have mercy," but the fear and the shame of the act he was going to commit chilled his brain. Those ruined priests who presided at a Black Mass, consecrating the Host over the naked body of a woman, consuming God in an absurd and horrifying ritual, were at least performing the act of damnation with an emotion larger than human love: they were doing it from hate of God or some odd perverse devotion to God's enemy. But he had no love of evil or hate of God. How was he to hate this God who of His own accord was surrendering Himself into his power? He was desecrating God because he loved a woman—was it even love, or was it just a feeling of pity and responsibility? He tried again to excuse himself: "You can look after yourself. You survive the cross every day. You can only suffer. You can never be lost. Admit that you must come second to these others." And myself, he thought, watching the priest pour the wine and water into the chalice, his own damnation being prepared like a meal at the altar, I must come last: I am the Deputy Commissioner of Police: a hundred men serve under me: I am the responsible man. It is my job to look after the others. I am conditioned to serve.

Sanctus. Sanctus. Sanctus. The Canon of the Mass had started: Father Rank's whisper at the altar hurried remorselessly towards the consecration. "To order our days in thy peace . . . that we be preserved from eternal damnation. . . ." *Pax, pacis, pacem:* all the declinations of the word "peace" drummed on his ears through the Mass. He thought: I have left even the hope of peace for ever. I am the responsible man. I shall soon have gone too far in my design of deception ever to go back. *Hoc est enim Corpus:* the bell rang, and Father Rank raised God in his fingers—this God as light now as a wafer whose coming lay on Scobie's heart as heavily as lead. *Hic est enim calix sanguinis* and the second bell.

Louise touched his hand. "Dear, are you well?" He thought: here is the second chance. The return of my pain. I can go out. But if he went out of church now, he knew that there would be only one thing left to do—to follow Father Rank's advice, to settle his affairs, to desert, to come back in a few days' time and take God with a clear conscience and a knowledge that he had pushed innocence back where it properly belonged—under the Atlantic surge. Innocence must die young if it isn't to kill the souls of men.

"Peace I leave with you, my peace I give unto you."

"I'm all right," he said, the old longing pricking at the eyeballs, and looking up towards the cross on the altar he thought savagely: take your sponge of gall. You made me what I am. Take the spear thrust. He didn't need to open his Missal to know how this prayer ended. "May the receiving of Thy Body, O Lord Jesus Christ, which I unworthy presume to take, turn not to my judgment and condemnation." He shut his eyes and let the darkness in. Mass rushed towards its end: *Domine, non sum dignus . . . Domine, non sum dignus . . . Domine, non sum dignus. . . .* At the foot of the scaffold he opened his eyes and saw the old black women shuffling up towards the altar rail, a few soldiers, an aircraft mechanic, one of his own policemen, a clerk from the bank: they moved sedately towards peace, and Scobie felt an envy of their simplicity, their goodness. Yes, now at this moment of time they were good.

"Aren't you coming, dear?" Louise asked, and again the hand touched him: the kindly firm detective hand. He rose and followed her and knelt by her side like a spy in a foreign land who has been taught the customs and to speak the language like a native. Only a miracle can save me now, Scobie told himself, watching Father Rank at the altar opening the tabernacle, but God would never work a miracle to save Himself. I am the cross, he thought, He will never speak the word to save Himself from the cross, but if only wood were made so that it didn't feel, if only the nails were senseless as people believed.

Father Rank came down the steps from the altar bearing the Host. The saliva had dried in Scobie's mouth: it was as though his veins had dried. He couldn't look up; he saw only the priest's skirt like the skirt of the mediaeval warhorse bearing down upon him: the flapping of feet: the charge of God. If only the archers would let fly from ambush, and for a moment he dreamed that the priest's steps had indeed faltered: perhaps after all something may yet happen before he reaches me: some incredible interposition.

. . . But with open mouth (the time had come) he made one last attempt at prayer: "O God, I offer up my damnation to you. Take it. Use it for them," and was aware of the pale papery taste of an eternal sentence on the tongue.

[3]

i

The bank manager took a sip of iced water and exclaimed with more than professional warmth, "How glad you must be to have Mrs. Scobie back well in time for Christmas."

"Christmas is a long way off still," Scobie said.

"Time flies when the rains are over," the bank manager went on with his novel cheerfulness. Scobie had never before heard in his voice this note of optimism. He remembered the stork-like figure pacing to and fro, pausing at the medical books, so many hundred times a day.

"I came along . . ." Scobie began.

"About your life insurance—or an overdraft, would it be?"

"Well, it wasn't either this time."

"You know I'll always be glad to help you, Scobie, whatever it is." How quietly Robinson sat at his desk. Scobie said with wonder, "Have you given up your daily exercise?"

"Ah, that was all stuff and nonsense," the manager said. "I had read too many books."

"I wanted to look in your medical encyclopaedia," Scobie explained.

"You'd do much better to see a doctor," Robinson surprisingly advised him. "It's a doctor who's put me right, not the books. The time I would have wasted. . . . I tell you, Scobie, the new young fellow they've got at the Argyll Hospital's the best man they've sent to this colony since they discovered it."

"And he's put you right?"

"Go and see him. His name's Travis. Tell him I sent you."

"All the same, if I could just have a look . . ."

"You'll find it on the shelf. I keep 'em there still because they look important. A bank manager has to be a reading man. People expect him to have solid books around."

"I'm glad your stomach's cured."

The manager took another sip of water. He said, "I'm not bothering about it any more. The truth of the matter is, Scobie, I'm . . ."

Scobie looked through the encyclopaedia for the word Angina and now he read on: CHARACTER OF THE PAIN. *This is usually described as being "gripping," "as though the chest were in a vice." The pain is situated in the middle of the chest and under the sternum. It may run down either arm, perhaps more commonly the left, or up into the neck or down into the abdomen. It lasts a few seconds, or at the most a minute or so.* THE BEHAVIOUR OF THE PATIENT. *This is characteristic. He holds himself absolutely still in whatever circumstances he may find himself.* . . . Scobie's eye passed rapidly down the cross-headings: CAUSE OF THE PAIN. TREATMENT. TERMINATION OF THE DISEASE. Then he put the book back on the shelf. "Well," he said, "perhaps I'll drop in on your Dr. Travis. I'd rather see him than Dr. Sykes. I hope he cheers me up as he's done you."

"Well, my case," the manager said evasively, "had peculiar features."

"Mine looks straightforward enough."

"You seem pretty well."

"Oh, I'm all right—bar a bit of pain now and then and sleeping badly."

"Your responsibilities do that for you."

"Perhaps."

It seemed to Scobie that he had sowed enough—against what harvest? He couldn't himself have told. He said goodbye and went out into the dazzling street. He carried his helmet and let the sun strike vertically down upon his thin greying hair. He offered himself for punishment all the way to the police station and was rejected. It had seemed to him these last three weeks that the damned must be in a special category; like the young men destined for some unhealthy foreign post in a trading company, they were reserved from their humdrum fellows, protected from the daily task, preserved carefully at special desks, so that the worst might happen later. Nothing now ever seemed to go wrong. The sun would not strike, the Colonial Secretary asked him to dinner. . . . He felt rejected by misfortune.

The Commissioner said, "Come in, Scobie. I've got good news for you," and Scobie prepared himself for yet another rejection.

"Baker is not coming here. They need him in Palestine. They've decided after all to let the right man succeed me." Scobie sat down on the window-ledge and watched his hand tremble on his knee. He thought: so all this need not have happened. If Louise had stayed I should never have loved Helen, I would never have been blackmailed by Yusef, never have committed that act of despair. I would have been myself still—the same self that lay stacked in fifteen years of diaries, not this broken cast. But, of course, he told himself, it's only because I have done these things that success comes. I am of the devil's party. He looks after his own in this world. I shall go now from damned success to damned success, he thought with disgust.

"I think Colonel Wright's word was the deciding factor. You impressed him, Scobie."

"It's come too late, sir."

"Why too late?"

"I'm too old for the job. It needs a younger man."

"Nonsense. You're only just fifty."

"My health's not good."

"It's the first I've heard of it."

"I was telling Robinson at the bank today. I've been getting pains, and I'm sleeping badly." He talked rapidly, beating time on his knee. "Robinson swears by Travis. He seems to have worked wonders with him."

"Poor Robinson."

"Why?"

"He's been given two years to live. That's in confidence, Scobie."

Human beings never cease to surprise: so it was the death sentence that had cured Robinson of his imaginary ailments, his medical books, his daily walk from wall to wall. I suppose, Scobie thought, that is what comes of knowing the worst—one is left alone with the worst and it's like peace. He imagined Robinson talking across the desk to his solitary companion. "I hope we all die as calmly," he said. "Is he going home?"

"I don't think so. I suppose presently he'll have to go to the Argyll."

Scobie thought: I wish I had known what I had been looking at. Robinson was exhibiting the most enviable possession a man can own—a happy death. This tour would bear a high proportion of deaths—or perhaps not so high when you counted them and remembered Europe. First Pemberton, then the child at Pende, now Robinson . . . no, it wasn't many, but of course he hadn't counted the blackwater cases in the military hospital.

"So that's how matters stand," the Commissioner said. "Next tour you will be Commissioner. Your wife will be pleased."

I must endure her pleasure, Scobie thought, without anger. I am the guilty man, and I have no right to criticize, to show vexation ever again. He said, "I'll be getting home."

Ali stood by his car, talking to another boy who slipped quietly away when he saw Scobie approach. "Who was that, Ali?"

"My small brother, sah," Ali said.

"I don't know him, do I? Same mother?"

"No, sah, same father."

"What does he do?" Ali worked at the starting handle, his face dripping with sweat, saying nothing.

"Who does he work for, Ali?"

"Sah?"

"I said who does he work for?"

"For Mr. Wilson, sah."

The engine started and Ali climbed into the back seat. "Has he ever made you a proposition, Ali? I mean has he asked you to report on me—for money?" He could see Ali's face in the driving mirror, set, obstinate, closed and rocky like a cave mouth. "No, sah."

"Lots of people are interested in me and pay good money for reports. They think me bad man, Ali."

Ali said, "I'm your boy," staring back through the medium of the mirror. It seemed to Scobie one of the qualities of deceit that you lost the sense of trust. If I can lie and betray, so can others. Wouldn't many people gamble on my honesty and lose their stake? Why should I lose my stake on Ali? I have not been caught and he has not been caught, that's all. An awful depression weighed his head towards the wheel. He thought: I know that Ali is honest: I have known that for fifteen years; I am just trying to find a companion in this region of lies. Is the next stage the stage of corrupting others?

Louise was not in when they arrived. Presumably someone had called and taken her out—perhaps to the beach. She hadn't expected him back before sundown. He wrote a note for her, *Taking some furniture up to Helen. Will be back early with good news for you,* and then he drove up alone to the Nissen huts through the bleak empty middle day. Only the vultures were about—gathering round a dead chicken at the edge of the road, stooping their old men's necks over the carrion, their wings like broken umbrellas sticking out this way and that.

"I've brought you another table and a couple of chairs. Is your boy about?"

"No, he's at market."

They kissed as formally now when they met as a brother and sister. When the damage was done adultery became as unimportant as friendship. The flame had licked them and gone on across the clearing: it had left nothing standing except a sense of responsibility and a sense of loneliness. Only if you trod barefooted did you notice the heat in the grass. Scobie said, "I'm interrupting your lunch."

"Oh no. I've about finished. Have some fruit salad."

"It's time you had a new table. This one wobbles." He said, "They are making me Commissioner after all."

"It will please your wife," Helen said.

"It doesn't mean a thing to me."

"Oh, of course it does," she said briskly. This was another convention of hers—that only she suffered. He would for a long time resist, like Coriolanus, the exhibition of *his* wounds, but sooner or later he would give way: he would dramatize his pain in words until even to himself it seemed unreal. Perhaps, he would think, she is right after all: perhaps I don't suffer. She said, "Of course the Commissioner must be above suspicion, mustn't he, like Caesar." (Her sayings, as well as her spelling, lacked accuracy.) "This is the end of us, I suppose."

"You know there is no end to us."

"Oh, but the Commissioner can't have a mistress hidden away in a Nissen hut." The sting, of course, was in the "hidden away," but how could he allow himself to feel the least irritation, remembering the letter she had written to him, offering herself as a sacrifice any way he liked, to keep or to throw away? Human beings couldn't be heroic all the time: those who surrendered everything—for God or love—must be allowed sometimes in thought to take back their surrender. So many had never committed the heroic act, however rashly. It was the act that counted. He said, "If the Commissioner can't keep you, then I shan't be the Commissioner."

"Don't be silly. After all," she said with fake reasonableness, and he recognized this as one of her bad days, "what do we get out of it?"

"I get a lot," he said, and wondered: is that a lie for the sake of comfort? There were so many lies nowadays he couldn't keep track of the small, the unimportant ones.

"An hour or two every other day perhaps when you can slip away. Never so much as a night."

He said hopelessly, "Oh, I have plans."

"What plans?"

He said, "They are too vague still."

She said with all the acid she could squeeze out, "Well, let me know in time. To fall in with your wishes, I mean."

"My dear, I haven't come here to quarrel."

"I sometimes wonder what you do come here for."

"Well, today I brought some furniture."

"Oh yes, the furniture."

"I've got the car here. Let me take you to the beach."

"Oh, we can't be seen there together."

"That's nonsense. Louise is there now, I think."

"For God's sake," Helen said, "keep that smug woman out of my sight."

"All right then. I'll take you for a run in the car."

"That would be safer, wouldn't it?"

Scobie took her by the shoulders and said, "I'm not always thinking of safety."

"I thought you were."

Suddenly he felt his resistance give way and he shouted at her, "The sacrifice isn't all on your side." With despair he could see from a distance the scene coming up on both of them: like the tornado before the rains, that wheeling column of blackness which would soon cover the whole sky.

"Of course work must suffer," she said with childish sarcasm. "All these snatched half-hours."

"I've given up hope," he said.

"What do you mean?"

"I've given up the future. I've damned myself."

"Don't be so melodramatic," she said. "I don't know what you are talking about. Anyway, you've just told me about the future—the Commissionership."

"I mean the real future—the future that goes on."

She said, "If there's one thing I hate it's your Catholicism. I suppose it comes of having a pious wife. It's so bogus. If you really believed you wouldn't be here."

"But I do believe and I am here." He said with bewilderment, "I can't explain it, but there it is. My eyes are open. I know what I'm doing. When Father Rank came down to the rail carrying the sacrament . . ."

Helen exclaimed with scorn and impatience, "You've told me all that before. You are trying to impress me. You don't believe in hell any more than I do."

He took her wrists and held them furiously. He said, "You can't get out of it that way. I believe, I tell you. I believe that I'm damned for all eternity—unless a miracle happens. I'm a policeman. I know what I'm saying. What I've done is far worse than murder—that's an act, a blow, a stab, a shot: it's over and done, but I'm carrying my corruption around with me. It's the coating of my stomach." He threw her wrists aside like seeds towards the stony floor. "Never pretend I haven't shown my love."

"Love for your wife, you mean. You were afraid she'd find out."

Anger drained out of him. He said, "Love for both of you. If it were just for her there'd be an easy straight way." He put his hands over his eyes, feeling hysteria beginning to mount again. He said, "I can't bear to see suffering, and I cause it all the time. I want to get out, get out."

"Where to?"

Hysteria and honesty receded: cunning came back across the threshold like a mongrel dog. He said, "Oh, I just mean take a holiday." He added, "I'm not sleeping well. And I've been getting an odd pain."

"Darling, are you ill?" The pillar had wheeled on its course: the storm was involving others now: it had passed beyond them. Helen said, "Darling, I'm a bitch. I get tired and fed up with things—but it doesn't mean anything. Have you seen a doctor?"

"I'll see Travis at the Argyll some time soon."

"Everybody says Dr. Sykes is better."

"No, I don't want to see Dr. Sykes." Now that the anger and hysteria had passed he could see her exactly as she was that first evening when the sirens blew. He thought, O God, I can't leave her. Or Louise. You don't need me as they need me. You have your good people, your saints, all the company of the blessed. You can do without me. He said, "I'll take you for a spin now in the car. It will do us both good."

In the dusk of the garage he took her hands again and kissed her. He said, "There are no eyes here. . . . Wilson can't see us. Harris isn't watching. Yusef's boys . . ."

"Dear, I'd leave you tomorrow if it would help."

"It wouldn't help." He said, "You remember when I wrote you a letter—which got lost. I tried to put down everything there, plainly, in black and white. So as not to be cautious any more. I wrote that I loved you more than my wife. . . ." As he spoke he heard another's breath behind his shoulder, beside the car. He said, sharply, "Who's that?"

"What, dear?"

"Somebody's here." He came round to the other side of the car and said sharply, "Who's there? Come out."

"It's Ali," Helen said.

"What are you doing here, Ali?"

"Missus sent me," Ali said. "I wait here for Massa tell him Missus back." He was hardly visible in the shadow.

"Why were you waiting here?"

"My head humbug me," Ali said. "I go for sleep, small small sleep."

"Don't frighten him," Helen said. "He's telling the truth."

"Go along home, Ali," Scobie told him, "and tell Missus I come straight down." He watched him pad out into the hard sunlight between the Nissen huts. He never looked back.

"Don't worry about him," Helen said. "He didn't understand a thing."

"I've had Ali for fifteen years," Scobie said. It was the first time he had been ashamed before him in all those years. He remembered Ali the night after Pemberton's death, cup of tea in hand, holding him up against the shaking lorry, and then he remembered Wilson's boy slinking off along the wall by the police station.

"You can trust him anyway."

"I don't know how," Scobie said. "I've lost the trick of trust."

ii

Louise was asleep upstairs, and Scobie sat at the table with his diary open. He had written down against the date October 31: *Commissioner told me this morning I am to succeed him. Took some furniture to H.R. Told Louise news, which pleased her.* The other life—bare and undisturbed and built of facts—lay like Roman foundations under his hand. This was the life he was supposed to lead; no one reading this record would visualize the obscure shameful scene in the garage, the interview with the Portuguese captain, Louise striking out blindly with the painful truth, Helen accusing him of hypocrisy. . . . He thought: this is how it ought to be. I am too old for emotion. I am too old to be a cheat. Lies are for the young. They have a lifetime of truth to recover in. He looked at his watch, 11:45, and wrote: *Temperature at 2 p.m. 92°.* The lizard pounced upon the wall, the tiny jaws clamping on a moth. Something scratched outside the door—a pye-dog? He laid his pen down again and loneliness sat across the table opposite him. No man surely was less alone with his wife upstairs and his mistress little more than five hundred yards away up the hill, and yet it was loneliness that seated itself like a companion who doesn't need to speak. It seemed to him that he had never been so alone before.

There was nobody now to whom he could speak the truth. There were things the Commissioner must not know, Louise must not know, there were even limits to what he could tell Helen, for what was the use, when he had sacrificed so much in order to avoid pain, of inflicting it needlessly? As for God he could speak to Him only as one speaks to an enemy— there was bitterness between them. He moved his hand on the table, and it was as though his loneliness moved too and touched the tips of his fingers. "You and I," his loneliness said, "you and I." It occurred to him that the outside world if they knew the facts might envy him: Bagster would envy him Helen, and Wilson Louise. What a hell of a quiet dog, Fraser would exclaim with a lick of the lips. They would imagine, he thought with amazement, that I get something out of it, but it seemed to him that no man had ever got less. Even self-pity was denied him because he knew so exactly the extent of his guilt. He felt as though he had exiled himself so deeply in the desert that his skin had taken on the colour of the sand.

The door creaked gently open behind him. Scobie did not move. The spies, he thought, are creeping in. Is this Wilson, Harris, Pemberton's boy, Ali . . . ? "Massa," a voice whispered, and a bare foot slapped the concrete floor.

"Who are you?" Scobie asked, not turning round. A pink palm dropped a small ball of paper on the table and went out of sight again. The voice said, "Yusef say come very quiet nobody see."

"What does Yusef want now?"

"He send you dash—small small dash." Then the door closed again and silence was back. Loneliness said, "Let us open this together, you and I."

Scobie picked up the ball of paper: it was light, but it had a small hard centre. At first he didn't realize what it was: he thought it was a pebble put in to keep the paper steady and he looked for writing which, of course, was not there, for whom would Yusef trust to write for him? Then he realized what it was—a diamond, a gem stone. He knew nothing about diamonds, but it seemed to him that it was probably worth at least as much as his debt to Yusef. Presumably Yusef had information that the stones he had sent by the *Esperança* had reached their destination safely. This was a mark of gratitude—not a bribe, Yusef would explain, the fat hand upon his sincere and shallow heart.

The door burst open and there was Ali. He had a boy by the arm who whimpered. Ali said, "This stinking Mende boy he go all round the house. He try doors."

"Who are you?" Scobie said.

The boy broke out in a mixture of fear and rage, "I Yusef's boy. I bring Massa letter," and he pointed at the table where the pebble lay in the screw of paper. Ali's eyes followed the gesture. Scobie said to his loneliness, "You and I have to think quickly." He turned on the boy and said, "Why you not come here properly and knock on the door? Why you come like a thief?"

He had the thin body and the melancholy soft eyes of all Mendes. He said, "I not a thief," with so slight an emphasis on the first word that it was just possible he was not impertinent. He went on, "Massa tell me to come very quiet."

Scobie said, "Take this back to Yusef and tell him I want to know where he gets a stone like that. I think he steals stones and I find out by-and-by. Go on. Take it. Now, Ali, throw him out." Ali pushed the boy ahead of him through the door, and Scobie could hear the rustle of their feet on the path. Were they whispering together? He went to the door and called out after them, "Tell Yusef I call on him one night soon and make hell of a palaver." He slammed the door again and thought, what a lot Ali knows, and he felt distrust of his boy moving again like fever with the bloodstream. He could ruin me, he thought: he could ruin *them*.

He poured himself out a glass of whisky and took a bottle of soda out of his ice-box. Louise called from upstairs, "Henry."

"Yes, dear?"

"Is it twelve yet?"

"Close on, I think."

"You won't drink anything after twelve, will you? You remember tomorrow?" and of course he did remember, draining his glass: it was November the First—All Saints' Day, and this All Souls' Night. What ghost would pass over the whisky's surface? "You are coming to communion, aren't you, dear?" and he thought wearily: there is no end to this: why should I draw the line now? One may as well go on damning oneself until the end. His loneliness was the only ghost his whisky could invoke, nodding across the table at him, taking a drink out of his glass. "The next occasion," loneliness told him, "will be Christmas—the Midnight Mass—you won't be able to avoid that you know, and no excuse will serve you on that night, and after that"—the long chain of feast days, of early Masses in spring and summer, unrolled themselves like a perpetual calendar. He had a sudden picture before his eyes of a bleeding face, of eyes closed by the continuous shower of blows: the punch-drunk head of God reeling sideways.

"You *are* coming, Ticki?" Louise called with what seemed to him a sudden anxiety, as though perhaps suspicion had momentarily breathed on her again—and he thought again, can Ali really be trusted? and all the stale Coast wisdom of the traders and the remittance men told him, "Never trust a black. They'll let you down in the end. Had my boy fifteen years. . . ." The ghosts of distrust came out on All Souls' Night and gathered around his glass.

"Oh yes, my dear, I'm coming."

"You have only to say the word," he addressed God, "and legions of angels . . ." and he struck with his ringed hand under the eye and saw the bruised skin break. He thought, "And again at Christmas," thrusting the child's face into the filth of the stable. He cried up the stairs, "What's that you said, dear?"

"Oh, only that we've got so much to celebrate tomorrow. Being together and the Commissionership. Life is so happy, Ticki." And that, he told his loneliness with defiance, is my reward, splashing the whisky across the table, defying the ghosts to do their worst, watching God bleed.

[4]

i

He could tell that Yusef was working late in his office on the quay. The little white two-storeyed building stood beside the wooden jetty on the edge of Africa, just beyond the army dumps of petrol, and a line of light showed under the curtains of the landward window. A policeman saluted Scobie as he picked his way between the crates. "All quiet, corporal?"

"All quiet, sah."

"Have you patrolled at the Kru Town end?"

"Oh yes, sah. All quiet, sah." He could tell from the promptitude of the reply how untrue it was.

"The wharf rats out?"

"Oh no, sah. All very quiet like the grave." The stale literary phrase showed that the man had been educated at a mission school.

"Well, good night."

"Good night, sah."

Scobie went on. It was many weeks now since he had seen Yusef—not since the night of the blackmail, and now he felt an odd yearning towards his tormentor. The little white building magnetized him, as though concealed there was his only companionship, the only man he could trust. At least his blackmailer knew him as no one else did: he could sit opposite that fat absurd figure and tell the whole truth. In this new world of lies his blackmailer was at home: he knew the paths: he could advise: even help. . . . Round the corner of a crate came Wilson. Scobie's torch lit his face like a map.

"Why, Wilson," Scobie said, "you are out late."

"Yes," Wilson said, and Scobie thought uneasily, how he hates me.

"You've got a pass for the quay?"

"Yes."

"Keep away from the Kru Town end. It's not safe there alone. No more nose bleeding?"

"No," Wilson said. He made no attempt to move; it seemed always his way—to stand blocking a path: a man one had to walk round.

"Well, I'll be saying good night, Wilson. Look in any time. Louise . . ."

Wilson said, "I love her, Scobie."

"I thought you did," Scobie said. "She likes you, Wilson."

"I love her," Wilson repeated. He plucked at the tarpaulin over the crate and said, "You wouldn't know what that means."

"What means?"

"Love. You don't love anybody except yourself, your dirty self."

"You are overwrought, Wilson. It's the climate. Go and lie down."

"You wouldn't act as you do if you loved her." Over the black tide, from an invisible ship, came the sound of a gramophone playing some popular heart-rending tune. A sentry by the Field Security post challenged and somebody replied with a password. Scobie lowered his torch till it lit only Wilson's mosquito-boots. He said, "Love isn't as simple as you think it is, Wilson. You read too much poetry."

"What would you do if I told her everything—about Mrs. Rolt?"

"But you have told her, Wilson. What you believe. But she prefers my story."

"One day I'll ruin you, Scobie."

"Would that help Louise?"

"I could make her happy," Wilson claimed ingenuously, with a breaking voice that took Scobie back over fifteen years—to a much younger man than this soiled specimen who listened to Wilson at the sea's edge, hearing under the words the low sucking of water against wood. He said gently, "You'd try. I know you'd try. Perhaps . . ." but he had no idea himself how that sentence was supposed to finish, what vague comfort for Wilson had brushed his mind and gone again. Instead an irritation took him against the gangling romantic figure by the crate who was so ignorant and yet knew so much. He said, "I wish meanwhile you'd stop spying on me."

"It's my job," Wilson admitted, and his boots moved in the torchlight.

"The things you find out are so unimportant." He left Wilson beside the petrol dump and walked on. As he climbed the steps to Yusef's office he could see, looking back, an obscure thickening of the darkness where Wilson stood and watched and hated. He would go home and draft a report. "At 11:25 I observed Major Scobie going obviously by appointment . . ."

Scobie knocked and walked right in where Yusef half lay behind his desk, his legs upon it, dictating to a black clerk. Without breaking his sentence—"five hundred rolls matchbox design, seven hundred and fifty bucket and sand, six hundred poker dot artificial silk"—he looked up at Scobie with hope and apprehension. Then he said sharply to the clerk, "Get out. But come back. Tell my boy that I see no one." He took his legs from the desk, rose and held out a flabby hand, "Welcome, Major Scobie," then let it fall like an unwanted piece of material. "This is the first time you have ever honoured my office, Major Scobie."

"I don't know why I've come here now, Yusef."

"It is a long time since we have seen each other." Yusef sat down and rested his great head wearily on a palm like a dish. "Time goes so differently for two people—fast or slow. According to their friendship."

"There's probably a Syrian poem about that."

"There is, Major Scobie," he said eagerly.

"You should be friends with Wilson, not me, Yusef. He reads poetry. I have a prose mind."

"A whisky, Major Scobie?"

"I wouldn't say no." He sat down on the other side of the desk and the inevitable blue syphon stood between them.

"And how is Mrs. Scobie?"

"Why did you send me that diamond, Yusef?"

"I was in your debt, Major Scobie."

"Oh no, you weren't. You paid me off in full with a bit of paper."

"I try so hard to forget that that was the way. I tell myself it was really friendship—at bottom it was friendship."

"It's never any good lying to oneself, Yusef. One sees through the lie too easily."

"Major Scobie, if I saw more of you, I should become a better man." The soda hissed in the glasses and Yusef drank greedily. He said, "I can feel in my heart, Major Scobie, that you are anxious, depressed. . . . I have always wished that you would come to me in trouble."

Scobie said, "I used to laugh at the idea—that I should ever come to you."

"In Syria we have a story of a lion and a mouse . . ."

"We have the same story, Yusef. But I've never thought of you as a mouse, and I'm no lion. No lion."

"It is about Mrs. Rolt you are troubled. And your wife, Major Scobie?"

"Yes."

"You do not need to be ashamed with me, Major Scobie. I have had much woman trouble in my life. Now it is better because I have learned the way. The way is not to care a damn, Major Scobie. You say to each of them, 'I do not care a damn. I sleep with whom I please. You take me or leave me. I do not care a damn.' They always take you, Major Scobie." He sighed into his whisky. "Sometimes I have wished they would not take me."

"I've gone to great lengths, Yusef, to keep things from my wife."

"I know the lengths you have gone, Major Scobie."

"Not the whole length. The business with the diamonds was very small compared . . ."

"Yes?"

"You wouldn't understand. Anyway somebody else knows now—Ali."

"But you trust Ali?"

"I think I trust him. But he knows about you too. He came in last night and saw the diamond there. Your boy was very indiscreet."

The big broad hand shifted on the table. "I will deal with my boy presently."

"Ali's half-brother is Wilson's boy. They see each other."

"That is certainly bad," Yusef said.

He had told all his worries now—all except the worst. He had the odd sense of having for the first time in his life shifted a burden elsewhere. And Yusef carried it—he obviously carried it. He raised himself from his chair and now moved his great haunches to the window, staring at the green black-out curtain as though it were a landscape. A hand went up to his mouth and he began to bite his nails—snip, snip, snip, his teeth closed on each nail in turn. Then he began on the other hand. "I don't suppose it's anything to worry about really," Scobie said. He was touched by uneasiness, as though he had accidentally set in motion a powerful machine he couldn't control.

"It is a bad thing not to trust," Yusef said. "One must always have boys one trusts. You must always know more about them than they do about you." That, apparently, was his conception of trust. Scobie said, "I used to trust him."

Yusef looked at his trimmed nails and took another bite. He said, "Do not worry. I will not have you worry. Leave everything to me, Major Scobie. I will find out for you whether you can trust him." He made the startling claim, "I will look after you."

"How can you do that?" I feel no resentment, he thought with weary surprise. I am being looked after, and a kind of nursery peace descended.

"You mustn't ask me questions, Major Scobie. You must leave everything to me just this once. I understand the way." Moving from the window Yusef turned on Scobie eyes like closed telescopes, blank and brassy. He said with a soothing nurse's gesture of the broad wet palm, "You will just write a little note to your boy, Major Scobie, asking him to come here. I will talk to him. My boy will take it to him."

"But Ali can't read."

"Better still then. You will send some token with my boy to show that he comes from you. Your signet ring."

"What are you going to do, Yusef?"

"I am going to help you, Major Scobie. That is all."
Slowly, reluctantly, Scobie drew at his ring. He said, "He's
been with me fifteen years. I always have trusted him until
now."

"You will see," Yusef said. "Everything will be all right."
He spread out his palm to receive the ring and their hands
touched: it was like a pledge between conspirators. "Just a
few words."

"The ring won't come off," Scobie said. He felt an odd
unwillingness. "It's not necessary, anyway. He'll come if
your boy tells him that I want him."

"I do not think so. They do not like to come to the wharf
at night."

"He will be all right. He won't be alone. Your boy will be
with him."

"Oh yes, yes, of course. But I still think—if you would just
send something to show—well, that it is not a trap. Yusef's
boy is no more trusted, you see, than Yusef."

"Let him come tomorrow, then."

"Tonight is better," Yusef said.

Scobie felt in his pockets: the broken rosary grated on his
nails. He said, "Let him take this, but it's not necessary . . ." and fell silent, staring back at those blank eyes.

"Thank you," Yusef said. "This is most suitable." At the
door he said, "Make yourself at home, Major Scobie. Pour
yourself another drink. I must give my boy instructions. . . ."

He was away a very long time. Scobie poured himself a
third whisky and then, because the little office was so airless,
he drew the seaward curtains after turning out the light and
let what wind there was trickle in from the bay. The moon
was rising and the naval depot ship glittered like grey ice.
Restlessly he made his way to the other window that looked
up the quay towards the sheds and lumber of the native
town. He saw Yusef's clerk coming back from there, and he
thought how Yusef must have the wharf rats well under control if his clerk could pass alone through *their* quarters. I

came for help, he told himself, and I am being looked after
—how, and at whose cost? This was the day of All Saints
and he remembered how mechanically, almost without fear
or shame, he had knelt at the rail this second time and
watched the priest come. Even that act of damnation could
become as unimportant as a habit. He thought: my heart
has hardened, and he pictured the fossilized shells one picks
up on a beach: the stony convolutions like arteries. One can
strike God once too often. After that does one care what
happens? It seemed to him that he had rotted so far that it
was useless to make any effort. God was lodged in his body
and his body was corrupting outwards from that seed.

"It was too hot?" Yusef's voice said. "Let us leave the
room dark. With a friend the darkness is kind."

"You have been a very long time."

Yusef said with what must have been deliberate vague-
ness, "There was much to see to." It seemed to Scobie that
now or never he must ask what was Yusef's plan, but the
weariness of his corruption halted his tongue. "Yes, it's hot,"
he said; "let's try and get a cross-draught," and he opened
the side window on to the quay. "I wonder if Wilson has
gone home."

"Wilson?"

"He watched me come here."

"You must not worry, Major Scobie. I think your boy can
be made quite trustworthy."

He said with relief and hope, "You mean you have a hold
on him?"

"Don't ask questions. You will see." The hope and the relief both wilted. He said, "Yusef, I *must* know . . ." but
Yusef said, "I have always dreamed of an evening just like
this with two glasses by our side and darkness and time to
talk about important things, Major Scobie. God. The family. Poetry. I have great appreciation of Shakespeare. The
Royal Ordnance Corps have very fine actors and they have
made me appreciate the gems of English literature. I am
crazy about Shakespeare. Sometimes because of Shake-

speare I would like to be able to read, but I am too old to learn. And I think perhaps I would lose my memory. That would be bad for business, and though I do not live for business I must do business to live. There are so many subjects I would like to talk to you about. I should like to hear the philosophy of your life."

"I have none."

"The piece of cotton you hold in your hand in the forest."

"I've lost my way."

"Not a man like you, Major Scobie. I have such an admiration for your character. You are a just man."

"I never was, Yusef. I didn't know myself, that's all. There's a proverb, you know, about in the end is the beginning. When I was born I was sitting here with you drinking whisky, knowing . . ."

"Knowing what, Major Scobie?"

Scobie emptied his glass. He said, "Surely your boy must have got to my house now."

"He has a bicycle."

"Then they should be on their way back."

"We must not be impatient. We may have to sit a long time, Major Scobie. You know what boys are."

"I thought I did." He found his left hand was trembling on the desk and he put it between his knees to hold it still. He remembered the long trek beside the border: innumerable lunches in the forest shade, with Ali cooking in an old sardine-tin, and again that last drive to Bamba came to mind—the long wait at the ferry, the fever coming down on him, and Ali always at hand. He wiped the sweat off his forehead and he thought for a moment: this is just a sickness, a fever, I shall wake soon. The record of the last six months—the first night in the Nissen hut, the letter which said too much, the smuggled diamonds, the lies, the sacrament taken to put a woman's mind at ease—seemed as insubstantial as shadows over a bed cast by a hurricane-lamp. He said to himself: I am waking up, and heard the sirens blowing the alert just as on that night, that night. . . . He shook his head and came awake to Yusef sitting in the dark on the other side of the desk, to the taste of the whisky, and the knowledge that everything was the same. He said wearily, "They ought to be here by now."

Yusef said, "You know what boys are. They get scared by the siren and they take shelter. We must sit here and talk to each other, Major Scobie. It is a great opportunity for me. I do not want the morning ever to come."

"The morning? I am not going to wait till morning for Ali."

"Perhaps he will be frightened. He will know you have found him out and he will run away. Sometimes boys go back to bush. . . ."

"You are talking nonsense, Yusef."

"Another whisky, Major Scobie?"

"All right. All right." He thought: am I taking to drink too? It seemed to him that he had no shape left, nothing you could touch and say: this is Scobie.

"Major Scobie, there are rumours that after all justice is to be done and that you are to be Commissioner."

He said with care, "I don't think it will ever come to that."

"I just wanted to say, Major Scobie, that you need not worry about me. I want your good, nothing so much as that. I will slip out of your life, Major Scobie. I will not be a millstone. It is enough for me to have had tonight—this long talk in the dark on all sorts of subjects. I will remember tonight always. You will not have to worry. I will see to that." Through the window behind Yusef's head, from somewhere among the jumble of huts and warehouses, a cry came: pain and fear: it swam up like a drowning animal for air, and fell again into the darkness of the room, into the whisky, under the desk, into the basket of wastepaper, a discarded finished cry.

Yusef said too quickly, "A drunk man." He yelped apprehensively, "Where are you going, Major Scobie? It's not safe—alone." That was the last Scobie ever saw of Yusef, a silhouette stuck stiffly and crookedly on the wall, with the moonlight shining on the syphon and the two drained glasses. At the bottom of the stairs the clerk stood, staring down the wharf. The moonlight caught his eyes: like road studs they showed the way to turn.

There was no movement in the empty warehouses on either side or among the sacks and crates as he moved his torch: if the wharf rats had been out, that cry had driven them back to their holes. His footsteps echoed between the sheds, and somewhere a pye-dog wailed. It would have been quite possible to have searched in vain in this wilderness of litter until morning: what was it that brought him so quickly and unhesitatingly to the body, as though he had himself chosen the scene of the crime? Turning this way and that down the avenues of tarpaulin and wood, he was aware of a nerve in his forehead that beat out the whereabouts of Ali.

The body lay coiled and unimportant like a broken watchspring under a pile of empty petrol drums: it looked as though it had been shovelled there to wait for morning and the scavenger birds. Scobie had a moment of hope before he turned the shoulder over, for after all two boys had been together on the road. The seal-grey neck had been slashed and slashed again. Yes, he thought, I can trust him now. The yellow eyeballs stared up at him like a stranger's, flecked with red. It was as if this body had cast him off, disowned him—"I know you not." He swore aloud, hysterically. "By God, I'll get the man who did this," but under that anonymous stare insincerity withered. He thought: I am the man. Didn't I know all the time in Yusef's room that something was planned? Couldn't I have pressed for an answer? A voice said, "Sah?"

"Who's that?"

"Corporal Laminah, sah."

"Can you see a broken rosary anywhere around? Look carefully."

"I can see nothing, sah."

Scobie thought: if only I could weep, if only I could feel pain; have I really become so evil? Unwillingly he looked down at the body. The fumes of petrol lay all around in the heavy night and for a moment he saw the body as something very small and dark and a long way away—like a broken piece of the rosary he looked for: a couple of black beads and the image of God coiled at the end of it. Oh God, he thought, I've killed you: you've served me all these years and I've killed you at the end of them. God lay there under the petrol drums and Scobie felt the tears in his mouth, salt in the cracks of his lips. You served me and I did this to you. You were faithful to me, and I wouldn't trust you.

"What is it, sah?" the corporal whispered, kneeling by the body.

"I loved him," Scobie said.

Part II

[1]

i

As soon as he had handed over his work to Fraser and closed his office for the day, Scobie started out for the Nissen. He drove with his eyes half-closed, looking straight ahead: he told himself, now, today, I am going to clean up, whatever the cost. Life is going to start again: this nightmare of love is finished. It seemed to him that it had died for ever the previous night under the petrol drums. The sun blazed down on his hands, which were stuck to the wheel by sweat.

His mind was so concentrated on what had to come—the opening of a door, a few words, and closing a door again for ever—that he nearly passed Helen on the road. She was walking down the hill towards him, hatless. She didn't even see the car. He had to run after her and catch her up. When she turned it was the face he had seen at Pende carried past him—defeated, broken, as ageless as a smashed glass.

"What are you doing here? In the sun, without a hat."

She said vaguely, "I was looking for you," standing there, dithering on the laterite.

"Come back to the car. You'll get sunstroke." A look of cunning came into her eyes. "Is it as easy as all that?" she asked, but she obeyed him.

They sat side by side in the car. There seemed to be no object in driving farther: one could say good-bye here as easily as there. She said, "I heard this morning about Ali. Did you do it?"

"I didn't cut his throat myself," he said. "But he died because I existed."

"Do you know who did?"

"I don't know who held the knife. A wharf rat, I suppose. Yusef's boy who was with him has disappeared. Perhaps he did it or perhaps he's dead too. We will never prove anything. I doubt if Yusef intended it."

"You know," she said, "this is the end for us. I can't go on ruining you any more. Don't speak. Let me speak. I never thought it would be like this. Other people seem to have love affairs which start and end and are happy, but with us it doesn't work. It seems to be all or nothing. So it's got to be nothing. Please don't speak. I've been thinking about this for weeks. I'm going to go away—right right away."

"Where to?"

"I told you not to speak. Don't ask questions." He could see in the windscreen a pale reflection of her desperation. It seemed to him as though he were being torn apart. "Darling," she said, "don't think it's easy. I've never done anything so hard. It would be so much easier to die. You come into everything. I can never again see a Nissen hut—or a Morris car. Or taste a pink gin. See a black face. Even a bed . . . one has to sleep in a bed. I don't know where I'll get away from you. It's no use saying in a year it will be all right. It's a year I've got to get through. All the time knowing you are somewhere. I could send a telegram or a letter and you'd have to read it, even if you didn't reply." He thought: how much easier it would be for her if I were dead. "But I mustn't write," she said. She wasn't crying: her eyes when he took a quick glance were dry and red, as he remembered them in hospital, exhausted. "Waking up will be the worst. There's always a moment when one forgets that everything's different."

He said, "I came up here to say good-bye too. But there are things I can't do."

"Don't talk, darling. I'm being good. Can't you see I'm being good? You don't have to go away from me—I'm going away from you. You won't ever know where to. I hope I won't be too much of a slut."

"No," he said, "no."

"Be quiet, darling. You are going to be all right. You'll see. You'll be able to clean up. You'll be a Catholic again—that's what you really want, isn't it, not a pack of women?"

"I want to stop giving pain," he said.

"You want peace, dear. You'll have peace. You'll see. Everything will be all right." She put her hand on his knee and began at last to weep in this effort to comfort him. He thought: where did she pick up this heart-breaking tenderness? Where do they learn to be so old so quickly?

"Look, dear. Don't come up to the hut. Open the car door for me. It's stiff. We'll say good-bye here, and you'll just drive home—or to the office if you'd rather. That's so much easier. Don't worry about me. I'll be all right." He thought, I missed that one death and now I'm having them all. He leant over her and wrenched at the car door: her tears touched his cheek. He could feel the mark like a burn. "There's no objection to a farewell kiss. We haven't quarrelled. There hasn't been a scene. There's no bitterness." As they kissed he was aware of pain under his mouth like the beating of a bird's heart. They sat still, silent, and the door of the car lay open. A few black labourers passing down the hill looked curiously in.

She said, "I can't believe that this is the last time: that I'll get out and you'll drive away, and we won't see each other again ever. I won't go outside more than I can help till I get right away. I'll be up here and you'll be down there. Oh, God, I wish I hadn't got the furniture you brought me."

"It's just official furniture."

"The cane is broken in one of the chairs where you sat down too quickly."

"Dear, dear, this isn't the way."

"Don't speak, darling. I'm really being quite good, but I can't say these things to another living soul. In books there's always a confidant. But I haven't got a confidant. I must say them all once." He thought again: if I were dead, she would be free of me. One forgets the dead quite quickly; one doesn't wonder about the dead—what is he doing now, who is he with? This for her is the hard way.

"Now, darling, I'm going to do it. Shut your eyes. Count three hundred slowly, and I won't be in sight. Turn the car quickly and drive like hell. I don't want to see you go. And I'll stop my ears. I don't want to hear you change gear at the bottom of the hill. Cars do that a hundred times a day. I don't want to hear you change gear."

O God, he prayed, his hands dripping over the wheel, kill me now, now. My God, you'll never have more complete contrition. What a mess I am. I carry suffering with me like a body smell. Kill me. Put an end to me. Vermin don't have to exterminate themselves. Kill me. Now. Now. Now.

"Shut your eyes, darling. This is the end. Really the end." She said hopelessly, "It seems so silly though."

He said, "I won't shut my eyes. I won't leave you. I promised that."

"You aren't leaving me. I'm leaving you."

"It won't work. We love each other. It won't work. I'd be up this evening to see how you were. I couldn't sleep . . ."

"You can always sleep. I've never known such a sleeper. Oh, my dear, look. I'm beginning to laugh at you again just as though we weren't saying good-bye."

"We aren't. Not yet."

"But I'm only ruining you. I can't give you any happiness."

"Happiness isn't the point."

"I'd made up my mind."

"So had I."

"But, darling, what do we *do?*" She surrendered completely. "I don't mind going on as we are. I don't mind the lies. Anything."

"Just leave it to me. I've got to think." He leant over her and closed the door of the car. Before the lock had clicked he had made his decision.

ii

Scobie watched the small boy as he cleared away the evening meal, watched him come in and go out, watched the bare feet flap the floor. Louise said, "I know it's a terrible thing, dear, but you've got to put it behind you. You can't help Ali now." A new parcel of books had come from England and he watched her cutting the leaves of a volume of verse. There was more grey in her hair than when she had left for South Africa, but she looked, it seemed to him, years younger because she was paying more attention to make-up: her dressing-table was littered with the pots and bottles and tubes she had brought back from the south. Ali's death meant little to her: why should it? It was the sense of guilt that made it so important. Otherwise one didn't grieve for a death. When he was young, he had thought love had something to do with understanding, but with age he knew that no human being understood another. Love was the wish to understand, and presently with constant failure the wish died, and love died too perhaps or changed into this painful affection, loyalty, pity. . . . She sat there, reading poetry, and she was a thousand miles away from the torment that shook his hand and dried his mouth. She would understand, he thought, if I were in a book, but would I understand her if she were just a character? I don't read that sort of book.

"Haven't you anything to read, dear?"

"I'm sorry. I don't feel much like reading."

She closed her book, and it occurred to him that after all she had her own effort to make: she tried to help. Sometimes he wondered with horror whether perhaps she knew everything, whether that complacent face which she had worn since her return masked misery. She said, "Let's talk about Christmas."

"It's still a long way off," he said quickly.

"Before you know it will be on us. I was wondering whether we could give a party. We've always been out to dinner: it would be fun to have people here. Perhaps on Christmas Eve."

"Just what you like."

"We could all go on then to Midnight Mass. Of course you and I would have to remember to drink nothing after ten—but the others could do as they pleased."

He looked up at her with momentary hatred as she sat so cheerfully there, so smugly, it seemed to him, arranging his further damnation. He was going to be Commissioner. She had what she wanted—her sort of success, everything was all right with her now. He thought: it was the hysterical woman who felt the world laughing behind her back that I loved. I love failure: I can't love success. And how successful she looks, sitting there, one of the saved, and he saw laid across that wide face like a news-screen the body of Ali under the black drums, the exhausted eyes of Helen, and all the faces of the lost, his companions in exile, the unrepentant thief, the soldier with the sponge. Thinking of what he had done and was going to do, he thought, even God is a failure.

"What is it, Ticki? Are you still worrying . . . ?"

But he couldn't tell her the entreaty that was on his lips: let me pity you again, be disappointed, unattractive, be a failure so that I can love you once more without this bitter gap between us. Time is short. I want to love you too at the end. He said slowly, "It's the pain. It's over now. When it comes—" he remembered the phrase of the textbook—"it's like a vice."

"You must see the doctor, Ticki."

"I'll see him tomorrow. I was going to anyway because of my sleeplessness."

"Your sleeplessness? But, Ticki, you sleep like a log."

"Not the last week."

"You're imagining it."

"No. I wake up about two and can't sleep again—till just before we are called. Don't worry. I'll get some tablets."

"I hate drugs."

"I won't go on long enough to form a habit."

"We must get you right for Christmas, Ticki."

"I'll be all right by Christmas." He came stiffly across the room to her, imitating the bearing of a man who fears that pain may return again, and put his hand against her breast. "Don't worry." Hatred went out of him at the touch—she wasn't as successful as all that: she would never be married to the Commissioner of Police.

After she had gone to bed he took out his diary. In this record at least he had never lied. At the worst he had omitted. He had checked his temperatures as carefully as a sea captain making up his log. He had never exaggerated or minimized, and he had never indulged in speculation. All he had written here was fact. *November 1. Early Mass with Louise. Spent morning on larceny case at Mrs. Onoko's. Temperature 91° at 2 p.m. Saw Y. at his office. Ali found murdered.* The statement was as plain and simple as that other time when he had written: *C. died.*

"November 2." He sat a long while with that date in front of him, so long that presently Louise called down to him. He replied carefully, "Go to sleep, dear. If I sit up late, I may be able to sleep properly." But already, exhausted by the day and by all the plans that had to be laid, he was near to nodding at the table. He went to his ice-box and wrapping a piece of ice in his handkerchief rested it against his forehead until sleep receded. *November 2.* Again he picked up his pen: this was his death-warrant he was signing. He wrote: *Saw Helen for a few minutes.* (It was always safer to leave no facts for anyone else to unearth.) *Temperature at 2 p.m. 92°. In the evening return of pain. Fear angina.* He looked up the pages of the entries for a week back and added an occasional note. *Slept very badly. Bad night. Sleeplessness continues.* He read the entries over carefully: they would be read later by the coroner, by the insurance inspectors. They seemed to him to be in his usual manner. Then he put the ice back on his forehead to drive sleep away. It was still only half after midnight: it would be better not to go to bed before two.

[2]

i

"It grips me," Scobie said, "like a vice."

"And what do you do then?"

"Why nothing. I stay as still as I can until the pain goes."

"How long does it last?"

"It's difficult to tell, but I don't think more than a minute."

The stethoscope followed like a ritual. Indeed there was something clerical in all that Dr. Travis did: an earnestness, almost a reverence. Perhaps because he was young he treated the body with great respect; when he rapped the chest he did it slowly, carefully, with his ear bowed close as though he really expected somebody or something to rap back. Latin words came softly on to his tongue as though in the Mass—*sternum* instead of *pacem.*

"And then," Scobie said, "there's the sleeplessness."

The young man sat back behind his desk and tapped with an indelible pencil; there was a mauve smear at the corner of his mouth which seemed to indicate that sometimes—offguard—he sucked it. "That's probably nerves," Dr. Travis said, "apprehension of pain. Unimportant."

"It's important to me. Can't you give me something to

take? I'm all right when once I get to sleep, but I lie awake for hours, waiting. . . . Sometimes I'm hardly fit for work. And a policeman, you know, needs his wits."

"Of course," Dr. Travis said. "I'll soon settle you. Evipan's the stuff for you." It was as easy as all that. "Now for the pain——" he began his tap, tap, tap, with the pencil. He said, "It's impossible to be certain, of course. . . . I want you to note carefully the circumstances of every attack . . . what seems to bring it on. Then it will be quite possible to regulate it, avoid it almost entirely."

"But what's wrong?"

Dr. Travis said, "There are some words that always shock the layman. I wish we could call cancer by a symbol like H_2O. People wouldn't be nearly so disturbed. It's the same with the word angina."

"You think it's angina?"

"It has all the characteristics. But men live for years with angina—even work in reason. We have to see exactly how much you can do."

"Should I tell my wife?"

"There's no point in not telling her. I'm afraid this might mean—retirement."

"Is that all?"

"You may die of a lot of things before angina gets you—given care."

"On the other hand I suppose it could happen any day?"

"I can't guarantee anything, Major Scobie. I'm not even absolutely satisfied that this is angina."

"I'll speak to the Commissioner then on the quiet. I don't want to alarm my wife until we are certain."

"If I were you, I'd tell her what I've said. It will prepare her. But tell her you may live for years with care."

"And the sleeplessness?"

"This will make you sleep."

Sitting in the car with the little package on the seat beside him, he thought, I have only now to choose the date. He didn't start his car for quite a while; he was touched by a feeling of awe as if he had in fact been given his death sentence by the doctor. His eyes dwelt on the neat blob of sealing-wax like a dried wound. He thought, I have still got to be careful, so careful. If possible no one must even suspect. It was not only the question of his life insurance: the happiness of others had to be protected. It was not so easy to forget a suicide as a middle-aged man's death from angina.

He unsealed the package and studied the directions. He had no knowledge of what a fatal dose might be, but surely if he took ten times the correct amount he would be safe. That meant every night for nine nights removing a dose and keeping it secretly for use on the tenth night. More evidence must be invented in his diary which had to be written right up to the end—November 12. He must make engagements for the following week. In his behaviour there must be no hint of farewells. This was the worst crime a Catholic could commit—it must be a perfect one.

First the Commissioner. . . . He drove down towards the police station and stopped his car outside the church. The solemnity of the crime lay over his mind almost like happiness: it was action at last—he had fumbled and muddled too long. He put the package for safekeeping into his pocket and went in, carrying his death. An old mammy was lighting a candle before the Virgin's statue; another sat with her market basket beside her and her hands folded staring up at the altar. Otherwise the church was empty. Scobie sat down at the back: he had no inclination to pray—what was the good? If one was a Catholic, one had all the answers: no prayer was effective in a state of mortal sin, but he watched the other two with sad envy. They were still inhabitants of the country he had left. This was what human love had done to him—it had robbed him of love for eternity. It was no use pretending as a young man might that the price was worth while.

If he couldn't pray he could at least talk, sitting there at the back, as far as he could get from Golgotha. He said, O God, I am the only guilty one because I've known the answers all the time. I've preferred to give you pain rather than give pain to Helen or my wife because I can't observe your suffering. I can only imagine it. But there are limits to what I can do to you—or them. I can't desert either of them while I'm alive, but I can die and remove myself from their blood stream. They are ill with me and I can cure them. And you too, God—you are ill with me. I can't go on, month after month, insulting you. I can't face coming up to the altar at Christmas—your birthday feast—and taking your body and blood for the sake of a lie. I can't do that. You'll be better off if you lose me once and for all. I know what I'm doing. I'm not pleading for mercy. I am going to damn myself, whatever that means. I've longed for peace and I'm never going to know peace again. But you'll be at peace when I am out of your reach. It will be no use then sweeping the floor to find me or searching for me over the mountains. You'll be able to forget me, God, for eternity. One hand clasped the package in his pocket like a promise.

No one can speak a monologue for long alone—another voice will always make itself heard; every monologue sooner or later becomes a discussion. So now he couldn't keep the other voice silent; it spoke from the cave of his body: it was as if the sacrament which had lodged there for his damnation gave tongue. You say you love me, and yet you'll do this to me—rob me of you for ever. I made you with love. I've wept your tears. I've saved you from more than you will ever know; I planted in you this longing for peace only so that one day I could satisfy your longing and watch your happiness. And now you push me away, you put me out of your reach. There are no capital letters to separate us when we talk together. I am not Thou but simply you, when you speak to me; I am humble as any other beggar. Can't you trust me as you'd trust a faithful dog? I have been faithful to you for two thousand years. All you have to do now is ring a bell, go into a box, confess . . . the repentance is already there, straining at your heart. It's not repentance you lack, just a few simple actions: to go up to the Nissen hut and say good-bye. Or if you must, continue rejecting me but without lies any more. Go to your house and say good-bye to your wife and live with your mistress. If you live you will come back to me sooner or later. One of them will suffer, but can't you trust me to see that the suffering isn't too great?

The voice was silent in the cave and his own voice replied hopelessly: No. I don't trust you. I've never trusted you. If you made me, you made this feeling of responsibility that I've always carried about like a sack of bricks. I'm not a policeman for nothing—responsible for order, for seeing justice is done. There was no other profession for a man of my kind. I can't shift my responsibility to you. If I could, I would be someone else. I can't make one of them suffer so as to save myself. I'm responsible and I'll see it through the only way I can. A sick man's death means to them only a short suffering—everybody has to die. We are all of us resigned to death: it's life we aren't resigned to.

So long as you live, the voice said, I have hope. There's no human hopelessness like the hopelessness of God. Can't you just go on, as you are doing now? the voice pleaded, lowering the terms every time it spoke like a dealer in a market. It explained: there are worse acts. But no, he said, no. That's impossible. I won't go on insulting you at your own altar. You see it's an *impasse*, God, an *impasse*, he said, clutching the package in his pocket. He got up and turned his back on the altar and went out. Only when he saw his face in the driving mirror did he realize that his eyes were bruised with suppressed tears. He drove on towards the police station and the Commissioner.

[3]

i

November 3. Yesterday I told the Commissioner that angina had been diagnosed and that I should have to retire as soon as a successor could be found. Temperature at 2 p.m. 91°. Much better night as the result of Evipan.

November 4. Went with Louise to 7:30 Mass but as pain threatened to return did not wait for communion. In the evening told Louise that I should have to retire before end of tour. Did not mention angina but spoke of strained heart. Another good night as a result of Evipan. Temperature at 2 p.m. 89°

November 5. Lamp thefts in Wellington Street. Spent long morning at Azikawe's store checking story of fire in storeroom. Temperature at 2 p.m. 90°. Drove Louise to Club for library night.

November 6–10. First time I've failed to keep up daily entries. Pain has become more frequent and unwilling to take on any extra exertion. Like a vice. Lasts about a minute. Liable to come on if I walk more than half a mile. Last night or two have slept badly in spite of Evipan, I think from the apprehension of pain.

November 11. Saw Travis again. There seems to be no doubt now that it is angina. Told Louise tonight, but also that with care I may live for years. Discussed with Commissioner on early passage home. In any case can't go for another month as too many cases I want to see through the courts in the next week or two. Agreed to dine with Fellowes on 13th. Commissioner on 14th. Temperature at 2 p.m. 88°.

ii

Scobie laid down his pen and wiped his wrist on the blotting-paper. It was just six o'clock on November 12 and Louise was out at the beach. His brain was clear, but the nerves tingled from his shoulder to his wrist. He thought: I have come to the end. What years had passed since he walked up through the rain to the Nissen hut, while the sirens wailed: the moment of happiness. It was time to die after so many years.

But there were still deceptions to be practised, just as though he were going to live through the night, good-byes to be said with only himself knowing that they were good-byes. He walked very slowly up the hill in case he was observed—wasn't he a sick man?—and turned off by the Nissens. He couldn't just die without some word—what word? O God, he prayed, let it be the right word, but when he knocked there was no reply, no words at all. Perhaps she was at the beach with Bagster.

The door was not locked and he went in. Years had passed in his brain, but here time had stood still. It might have been the same bottle of gin from which the boy had stolen—how long ago? The junior official's chairs stood stiffly around, as though on a film set: he couldn't believe they had ever moved, any more than the pouf presented by —was it Mrs. Carter? On the bed the pillow had not been shaken after the siesta, and he laid his hand on the warm mould of a skull. O God, he prayed, I'm going away from all of you for ever: let her come back in time: let me see her once more, but the hot day cooled around him and nobody came. At 6:30 Louise would be back from the beach. He couldn't wait any longer.

I must leave some kind of a message, he thought, and perhaps before I have written it she will have come. He felt a constriction in his breast worse than any pain he had ever invented to Travis. I shall never touch her again. I shall leave her mouth to others for the next twenty years. Most lovers deceived themselves with the idea of an eternal union beyond the grave, but he knew all the answers: he went to an eternity of deprivation. He looked for paper and couldn't find so much as a torn envelope; he thought he saw a writing-case, but it was the stamp-album that he unearthed, and opening it at random for no reason, he felt fate throw another shaft, for he remembered that particular stamp and how it came to be stained with gin. She will have to tear it out, he thought, but that won't matter: she had told him that you can't see where a stamp has been torn out. There was no scrap of paper even in his pockets, and in a sudden rush of jealousy he lifted up the little green image of George VI and wrote in ink beneath it: *I love you.* She can't take that out, he thought with cruelty and disappointment, that's indelible. For a moment he felt as though he had laid a mine for an enemy, but this was no enemy. Wasn't he clearing

himself out of her path like a piece of dangerous wreckage?
He shut the door behind him and walked slowly down the
hill—she might yet come. Everything he did now was for the
last time—an odd sensation. He would never come this way
again, and five minutes later taking a new bottle of gin from
his cupboard, he thought: I shall never open another bottle.
The actions which could be repeated became fewer and
fewer. Presently there would be only one unrepeatable action left, the act of swallowing. He stood with the gin bottle
poised and thought: then hell will begin, and they'll be safe
from me, Helen, Louise, and You.

At dinner he talked deliberately of the week to come; he
blamed himself for accepting Fellowes's invitation and explained that dinner with the Commissioner the next day was
unavoidable—there was much to discuss.

"Is there no hope, Ticki, that after a rest, a long
rest . . . ?"

"It wouldn't be fair to carry on—to them or you. I might
break down at any moment."

"It's really retirement?"

"Yes."

She began to discuss where they were to live. He felt tired
to death, and it needed all his will to show interest in this
fictitious village or that, in the kind of house he knew they
would never inhabit. "I don't want a suburb," Louise said.
"What I'd really like would be a weatherboard house in
Kent, so that one can get up to town quite easily."

He said, "Of course it will depend on what we can afford.
My pension won't be very large."

"I shall work," Louise said. "It will be easy in wartime."

"I hope we shall be able to manage without that."

"I wouldn't mind."

Bed-time came, and he felt a terrible unwillingness to let
her go. There was nothing to do when she had once gone
but die. He didn't know how to keep her—they had talked
about all the subjects they had in common. He said, "I shall
sit here a while. Perhaps I shall feel sleepy if I stay up half

an hour longer. I don't want to take the Evipan if I can help
it."

"I'm very tired after the beach. I'll be off."

When she's gone, he thought, I shall be alone for ever. His
heart beat and he was held in the nausea of an awful unreality. I can't believe that I'm going to do this. Presently I
shall get up and go to bed, and life will begin again. Nothing, nobody, can force me to die. Though the voice was no
longer speaking from the cave of his belly, it was as though
fingers touched him, signalled their mute message of distress,
tried to hold him. . . .

"What is it, Ticki? You look ill. Come to bed too."

"I wouldn't sleep," he said obstinately.

"Is there nothing I can do?" Louise asked. "Dear, I'd do
anything. . . ." Her love was like a death sentence.

"There's nothing, dear," he said. "I mustn't keep you
up." But so soon as she turned towards the stairs he spoke
again. "Read me something," he said; "you got a new book
today. Read me something."

"You wouldn't like it, Ticki. It's poetry."

"Never mind. It may send me to sleep." He hardly listened while she read. People said you couldn't love two
women, but what was this emotion if it were not love? This
hungry absorption of what he was never going to see again?
The greying hair, the line of nerves upon the face, the thickening body held him as her beauty never had. She hadn't
put on her mosquito-boots, and her slippers were badly in
need of mending. It isn't beauty that we love, he thought,
it's failure—the failure to stay young for ever, the failure of
nerves, the failure of the body. Beauty is like success: we
can't love it for long. He felt a terrible desire to protect—but
that's what I'm going to do, I am going to protect her from
myself for ever. Some words she was reading momentarily
caught his attention:

> "We are all falling. This hand's falling too—
> all have this falling sickness none withstands.

And yet there's always One whose gentle hands
this universal falling can't fall through."

They sounded like truth, but he rejected them—comfort can
come too easily. He thought, those hands will never hold my
fall: I slip between the fingers, I'm greased with falsehood,
treachery. Trust was a dead language of which he had forgotten the grammar.

"Dear, you are half asleep."

"For a moment."

"I'll go up now. Don't stay long. Perhaps you won't need
your Evipan tonight."

He watched her go. The lizard lay still upon the wall. Before she had reached the stairs he called her back. "Say good
night, Louise, before you go. You may be asleep."

She kissed him perfunctorily on the forehead and he gave
her hand a casual caress. There must be nothing strange on
this last night, and nothing she would remember with regret.
"Good night, Louise. You know I love you," he said with
careful lightness.

"Of course and I love you."

"Yes. Good night, Louise."

"Good night, Ticki." It was the best he could do with
safety.

As soon as he heard the door close, he took out the cigarette carton in which he kept the ten doses of Evipan. He
added two more doses for greater certainty—to have ex-
ceeded by two doses in ten days could not, surely, be regarded as suspicious. After that he took a long drink of
whisky and sat still and waited for courage with the tablets
in the palm of his hand. Now, he thought, I am absolutely
alone: this was freezing-point.

But he was wrong. Solitude itself has a voice. It said to
him, Throw away those tablets. You'll never be able to collect enough again. You'll be saved. Give up play-acting.
Mount the stairs to bed and have a good night's sleep. In the

morning you'll be woken by your boy, and you'll drive down to the police station for a day's ordinary work. The voice dwelt on the word "ordinary" as it might have dwelt on the word "happy" or "peaceful."

"No," Scobie said aloud, "no." He pushed the tablets in his mouth six at a time, and drank them down in two draughts. Then he opened his diary and wrote against November 12, *Called on H.R., out; temperature at 2 p.m.* and broke abruptly off as though at that moment he had been gripped by the final pain. Afterwards he sat bolt upright and waited what seemed a long while for any indication at all of approaching death; he had no idea how it would come to him. He tried to pray, but the Hail Mary evaded his memory, and he was aware of his heart-beats like a clock striking the hour. He tried out an Act of Contrition but when he reached, "I am sorry and beg pardon," a cloud formed over the door and drifted down over the whole room and he couldn't remember what it was that he had to be sorry for. He had to hold himself upright with both hands, but he had forgotten the reason why he so held himself. Somewhere far away he thought he heard the sounds of pain. "A storm," he said aloud, "there's going to be a storm," as the clouds grew, and he tried to get up to close the windows. "Ali," he called, "Ali." It seemed to him as though someone outside the room were seeking him, calling him, and he made a last effort to indicate that he was here. He got to his feet and heard the hammer of his heart beating out a reply. He had a message to convey, but the darkness and the storm drove it back within the case of his breast, and all the time outside the house, outside the world that drummed like hammer blows within his ear, someone wandered, seeking to get in, someone appealing for help, someone in need of him. And automatically at the call of need, at the cry of a victim, Scobie strung himself to act. He dredged his consciousness up from an infinite distance in order to make some reply. He said aloud, "Dear God, I love . . ." but the effort was too great and he did not feel his body when it struck the floor or hear the small tinkle of the medal as it span like a coin under the ice-box—the saint whose name nobody could remember.

Part III

[I]

i

Wilson said, "I have kept away as long as I could, but I thought perhaps I could be of some help."

"Everybody," Louise said, "has been very kind."

"I had no idea that he was so ill."

"Your spying didn't help you there, did it?"

"That was my job," Wilson said, "and I love you."

"How glibly you use that word, Wilson."

"You don't believe me?"

"I don't believe in anybody who says love, love, love. It means self, self, self."

"You won't marry me then?"

"It doesn't seem likely, does it, but I might, in time. I don't know what loneliness may do. But don't let's talk about love any more. It was his favourite lie."

"To both of you."

"How has she taken it, Wilson?"

"I saw her on the beach this afternoon with Bagster. And I hear she was a bit pickled last night at the club."

"She hasn't any dignity."

"I never knew what he saw in her. I'd never betray you, Louise."

"You know he even went up to see her the day he died."

"How do you know?"

"It's all written there. In his diary. He never lied in his diary. He never said things he didn't mean—like love."

Three days had passed since Scobie had been hastily buried. Dr. Travis had signed the death certificate—*angina pectoris.* In that climate a post-mortem was difficult, and in any case unnecessary, though Dr. Travis had taken the precaution of checking up on the Evipan.

"Do you know," Wilson said, "when my boy told me he had died suddenly in the night, I thought it was suicide?"

"It's odd how easily I can talk about him," Louise said, "now that he's gone. Yet I did love him, Wilson. I did love him, but he seems so very very gone."

It was as if he had left nothing behind him in the house but a few suits of clothes and a Mende grammar: at the police station a drawer full of odds and ends and a pair of rusting handcuffs. And yet the house was no different: the shelves were as full of books; it seemed to Wilson that it must always have been *her* house, not his. Was it just imagination then that made their voices ring a little hollowly, as though the house were empty?

"Did you know all the time—about her?" Wilson asked.

"It's why I came home. Mrs. Carter wrote to me. She said everybody was talking. Of course he never realized that. He thought he'd been so clever. And he nearly convinced me—that it was finished. Going to communion the way he did."

"How did he square that with his conscience?"

"Some Catholics do, I suppose. Go to confession and start over again. I thought he was more honest though. When a man's dead one begins to find out."

"He took money from Yusef."

"I can believe it now."

Wilson put his hand on Louise's shoulder and said, "You can trust me, Louise. I love you."

"I really believe you do." They didn't kiss; it was too soon for that, but they sat in the hollow room, holding hands, listening to the vultures clambering on the iron roof.

"So that's his diary," Wilson said.

"He was writing in it when he died—oh nothing interesting, just the temperatures. He always kept the temperatures.

He wasn't romantic. God knows what she saw in him to make it worth while."

"Would you mind if I looked at it?"

"If you want to," she said, "poor Ticki, he hasn't any secrets left."

"His secrets were never very secret." He turned a page and read and turned a page. He said, "Had he suffered from sleeplessness very long?"

"I always thought that he slept like a log whatever happened."

Wilson said, "Have you noticed that he's written in pieces about sleeplessness—afterwards?"

"How do you know?"

"You've only to compare the colour of the ink. And all these records of taking his Evipan—it's very studied, very careful. But above all the colour of the ink." He said, "It makes one think."

She interrupted him with horror, "Oh no, he couldn't have done that. After all, in spite of everything, he *was* a Catholic."

ii

"Just let me come in for one little drink," Bagster pleaded.

"We had four at the beach."

"Just one little one more."

"All right," Helen said. There seemed to be no reason so far as she could see to deny anyone anything any more for ever.

Bagster said, "You know it's the first time you've let me come in. Charming little place you've made of it. Who'd have thought a Nissen hut could be so homey?" Flushed and smelling of pink gin, both of us, we are a pair, she thought. Bagster kissed her wetly on her upper lip and looked around again. "Ha ha," he said, "the good old bottle." When they had drunk one more gin he took off his uniform jacket and hung it carefully on a chair. He said, "Let's take our back hair down and talk of love."

"Need we?" Helen said. "Yet?"

"Lighting-up time," Bagster said. "The dusk. So we'll let George take over the controls. . . ."

"Who's George?"

"The automatic pilot, of course. You've got a lot to learn."

"For God's sake, teach me some other time."

"There's no time like the present for a prang," Bagster said, moving her firmly towards the bed. Why not? she thought, why not . . . if he wants it? Bagster is as good as anyone else. There's nobody in the world I love, and out of it doesn't count, so why not let them have their prangs (it was Bagster's phrase) if they want them enough. She lay back mutely on the bed and shut her eyes and was aware in the darkness of nothing at all. I'm alone, she thought without self-pity, stating it as a fact, as an explorer might after his companions have died from exposure.

"By God, you aren't enthusiastic," Bagster said. "Don't you love me a bit, Helen?" and his ginny breath fanned through her darkness.

"No," she said, "I don't love anyone."

He said furiously, "You loved Scobie," and added quickly, "Sorry. Rotten thing to say."

"I don't love anyone," she repeated. "You can't love the dead, can you? They don't exist, do they? It would be like loving the dodo, wouldn't it?" questioning him as if she expected an answer, even from Bagster. She kept her eyes shut because in the dark she felt nearer to death, the death which had absorbed him. The bed trembled a little as Bagster shuffled his weight from off it, and the chair creaked as he took away his jacket. He said, "I'm not all that of a bastard, Helen. You aren't in the mood. See you tomorrow?"

"I expect so." There was no reason to deny anyone anything, but she felt an immense relief because nothing after all had been required.

"Good night, old girl," Bagster said; "I'll be seeing you."

She opened her eyes and saw a stranger in dusty blue pottering round the door. One can say anything to a stranger—they pass on and forget like beings from another world. She asked, "Do you believe in a God?"

"Oh well, I suppose so," Bagster said, feeling at his moustache.

"I wish I did," she said; "I wish I did."

"Oh well, you know," Bagster said, "a lot of people do. Must be off now. Good night."

She was alone again in the darkness behind her lids, and the wish struggled in her body like a child: her lips moved, but all she could think of to say was, "For ever and ever, Amen. . . ." The rest she had forgotten. She put her hand out beside her and touched the other pillow, as though perhaps after all there was one chance in a thousand that she was not alone, and if she were not alone now she would never be alone again.

iii

"*I* should never have noticed it, Mrs. Scobie," Father Rank said.

"Wilson did."

"Somehow I can't like a man who's quite so observant."

"It's his job."

Father Rank took a quick look at her. "As an accountant?"

She said drearily, "Father, haven't you any comfort to give me?" Oh, the conversations, he thought, that go on in a house after a death, the turnings over, the discussions, the questions, the demands—so much noise round the edge of silence.

"You've been given an awful lot of comfort in your life, Mrs. Scobie. If what Wilson thinks is true, it's he who needs our comfort."

"Do you know all that I know about him?"

"Of course I don't, Mrs. Scobie. You've been his wife, haven't you, for fifteen years. A priest only knows the unimportant things."

"Unimportant?"

"Oh, I mean the sins," he said impatiently. "A man doesn't come to us and confess his virtues."

"I expect you know about Mrs. Rolt. Most people did."

"Poor woman."

"I don't see why."

"I'm sorry for anyone happy and ignorant who gets mixed up in that way with one of us."

"He was a bad Catholic."

"That's the silliest phrase in common use," Father Rank said.

"And at the end this—horror. He must have known that he was damning himself."

"Yes, he knew that all right. He never had any trust in mercy—except for other people."

"It's no good even praying. . . ."

Father Rank clapped the cover of the diary to and said furiously, "For goodness' sake, Mrs. Scobie, don't imagine you—or I—know a thing about God's mercy."

"The Church says . . ."

"I know the Church says. The Church knows all the rules. But it doesn't know what goes on in a single human heart."

"You think there's some hope then?" she wearily asked.

"Are you so bitter against him?"

"I haven't any bitterness left."

"And do you think God's likely to be more bitter than a woman?" he said with harsh insistence, but she winced away from the arguments of hope.

"Oh, why, why, did he have to make such a mess of things?"

Father Rank said, "It may seem an odd thing to say—when a man's as wrong as he was—but I think, from what I saw of him, that he really loved God."

She had denied just now that she felt any bitterness, but a little more of it drained out now like tears from exhausted ducts. "He certainly loved no one else," she said.

"And you may be in the right of it there too," Father Rank replied.

The Third Man

EDITOR'S NOTE

*Many readers will be more familiar with the film version of
The Third Man, directed by Sir Carol Reed and starring
Orson Welles, than with the version that follows. Greene
himself calls the film, which he worked on closely
throughout its making, "the finished state of the story."*

*But it began in conventional fictional form. "To me it is
almost impossible to write a film play without first writing a
story," Greene confesses. "Even a film depends on more
than plot, on a certain measure of characterization, on
mood and atmosphere; and these seem to me almost
impossible to capture for the first time in the dull shorthand
of a script. One can reproduce an effect caught in another
medium, but one cannot make the first act of creation in
script form. One must have the sense of more material than
one needs to draw on. The Third Man, therefore, though
never intended for publication, had to start as a story before
those apparently interminable transformations from one
treatment to another."*

*For those who wish to follow the film treatment, the
shooting script has been published by Lorrimer (London).
The original story is presented here as a classic example of
one of Greene's "entertainments."*

*To Carol Reed
in admiration and affection
and in memory of so many early morning
Vienna hours at Maxim's, the Casanova, the Oriental*

[1]

One never knows when the blow may fall. When I saw Rollo Martins first I made this note on him for my security police files: "In normal circumstances a cheerful fool. Drinks too much and may cause a little trouble. Whenever a woman passes raises his eyes and makes some comment, but I get the impression that really he'd rather not be bothered. Has never really grown up and perhaps that accounts for the way he worshipped Lime." I wrote there that phrase "in normal circumstances" because I met him first at Harry Lime's funeral. It was February, and the grave-diggers had been forced to use electric drills to open the frozen ground in Vienna's Central Cemetery. It was as if even nature were doing its best to reject Lime, but we got him in at last and laid the earth back on him like bricks. He was vaulted in, and Rollo Martins walked quickly away as though his long gangly legs wanted to break into a run, and the tears of a boy ran down his thirty-five-year-old face. Rollo Martins believed in friendship, and that was why what happened later was a worse shock to him than it would have been to you or me (you because you would have put it down to an illusion and me because at once a rational explanation—however wrongly—would have come to my mind). If only he had come to tell me then, what a lot of trouble would have been saved.

If you are to understand this strange, rather sad story you must have an impression at least of the background—the smashed dreary city of Vienna divided up in zones among the four powers; the Russian, the British, the American, the French zones, regions marked only by notice-boards, and in the centre of the city, surrounded by the Ring with its heavy public buildings and its prancing statuary, the Inner Stadt under the control of all four powers. In this once fashionable Inner Stadt each power in turn, for a month at a time, takes, as we call it, "the chair," and becomes responsible for security; at night, if you were fool enough to waste your Austrian schillings on a night club, you would be fairly certain to see the International Patrol at work—four military police, one from each power, communicating with each other, if they communicated at all, in the common language of their enemy. I never knew Vienna between the wars, and I am too young to remember the old Vienna with its Strauss music and its bogus easy charm; to me it is simply a city of undignified ruins which turned that February into great glaciers of snow and ice. The Danube was a grey flat muddy river a long way off across the second bezirk, the Russian zone where the Prater lay smashed and desolate and full of weeds, only the Great Wheel revolving slowly over the foundations of merry-go-rounds like abandoned millstones, the rusting iron of smashed tanks which nobody had cleared away, the frost-nipped weeds where the snow was thin. I haven't enough imagination to picture it as it had once been, any more than I can picture Sacher's Hotel as other than a transit hotel for English officers or see the Kärtnerstrasse as a fashionable shopping street instead of a street which exists, most of it, only at eye level, repaired up to the first storey. A Russian soldier in a fur cap goes by with a rifle over his shoulder, a few tarts cluster round the American Information Office and men in overcoats sip ersatz coffee in the windows of the Old Vienna. At night it is just as well to stick to the Inner Stadt or the zones of three of the powers, though even there the kidnappings occur—such senseless kidnappings they sometimes seemed to us—a Ukrainian girl without a passport, an old man beyond the age of usefulness, sometimes of course the technician or the traitor. This was roughly the Vienna to which Rollo Martins came on February seventh last year. I have reconstructed the affair as best I can from my own files and from what Martins told me. It is as accurate as I can make it—I haven't invented a line of dialogue, though I can't vouch for Martins' memory; an ugly story if you leave out the girl: grim and sad and unrelieved if it were not for that absurd episode of the British Council lecturer.

[2]

A British subject can still travel if he is content to take with him only five English pounds which he is forbidden to spend abroad, but if Rollo Martins had not received an invitation from Lime of the International Refugee Office he would not have been allowed to enter Austria, which counts still as occupied territory. Lime had suggested that Martins might write up the business of looking after the international refugees, and although it wasn't Martins' usual line, he had consented. It would give him a holiday, and he badly needed a holiday after the incident in Dublin and the other incident in Amsterdam; he always tried to dismiss women as "incidents," things that simply happened to him without any will of his own, acts of God in the eyes of insurance agents. He had a haggard look when he arrived in Vienna and a habit of looking over his shoulder that for a time made me suspicious of him until I realized that he went in fear that one of, say, six people might turn up unexpectedly. He told me vaguely that he had been mixing his drinks—that was another way of putting it.

Rollo Martins' usual line was the writing of cheap paper-covered Westerns under the name of Buck Dexter. His public was large but unremunerative. He couldn't have afforded Vienna if Lime had not offered to pay his expenses when he got there out of some vaguely described propaganda fund. Lime could also, he said, keep him supplied with paper bafs —the only currency in use from a penny upwards in British hotels and clubs. So it was with exactly five unusable pound notes that Martins arrived in Vienna.

An odd incident had occurred at Frankfurt, where the plane from London grounded for an hour. Martins was eating a hamburger in the American canteen (a kindly airline supplied the passengers with a voucher for sixty-five cents' worth of food) when a man he could recognize from twenty feet away as a journalist approached his table.

"You Mr. Dexter?" he asked.

"Yes," Martins said, taken off his guard.

"You look younger than your photographs," the man said. "Like to make a statement? I represent the local forces paper here. We'd like to know what you think of Frankfurt."

"I only touched down ten minutes ago."

"Fair enough," the man said. "What about views on the American novel?"

"I don't read them," Martins said.

"The well-known acid humour," the journalist said. He pointed at a small grey-haired man with two protruding teeth, nibbling a bit of bread. "Happen to know if that's Carey?"

"No. What Carey?"

"J. G. Carey of course."

"I've never heard of him."

"You novelists live out of the world. He's my real assignment," and Martins watched him make across the room for the great Carey, who greeted him with a false headline smile, laying down his crust. Dexter wasn't the man's assignment, but Martins couldn't help feeling a certain pride—nobody had ever before referred to him as a novelist; and that sense of pride and importance carried him over the disappointment when Lime was not there to meet him at the airport. We never get accustomed to being less important to other people than they are to us—Martins felt the little jab of dispensability, standing by the bus door, watching the snow come sifting down, so thinly and softly that the great drifts among the ruined buildings had an air of permanence, as though they were not the result of this meagre fall, but lay, for ever, above the line of perpetual snow.

There was no Lime to meet him at the Hotel Astoria, where the bus landed him, and no message—only a cryptic one for Mr. Dexter from someone he had never heard of called Crabbin. "We expected you on tomorrow's plane. Please stay where you are. On the way round. Hotel room booked." But Rollo Martins wasn't the kind of man who stayed around. If you stayed around in a hotel lounge, sooner or later incidents occurred; one mixed one's drinks. I can hear Rollo Martins saying to me, "I've done with incidents. No more incidents," before he plunged headfirst into the most serious incident of all. There was always a conflict in Rollo Martins—between the absurd Christian name and the sturdy Dutch (four generations back) surname. Rollo looked at every woman that passed, and Martins renounced them for ever. I don't know which of them wrote the Westerns.

Martins had been given Lime's address and he felt no curiosity about the man called Crabbin; it was too obvious that a mistake had been made, though he didn't yet connect it with the conversation at Frankfurt. Lime had written that he could put Martins up in his own flat, a large apartment on the edge of Vienna that had been requisitioned from a Nazi owner. Lime could pay for the taxi when he arrived, so Martins drove straight away to the building lying in the third (British) zone. He kept the taxi waiting while he mounted to the third floor.

How quickly one becomes aware of silence even in so silent a city as Vienna with the snow steadily settling. Martins hadn't reached the second floor before he was convinced that he would not find Lime there, but the silence was deeper than just absence—it was as if he would not find Harry Lime anywhere in Vienna, and, as he reached the third floor and saw the big black bow over the door handle, anywhere in the world at all. Of course it might have been a cook who had died, a housekeeper, anybody but Harry Lime, but he knew—he felt he had known twenty stairs down—that Lime, the Lime he had hero-worshipped now for twenty years, since the first meeting in a grim school corridor with a cracked bell ringing for prayers, was gone. Martins wasn't wrong, not entirely wrong. After he had rung the bell half a dozen times a small man with a sullen expression put his head out from another flat and told him in a tone of vexation, "It's no use. There's nobody there. He's dead."

"Herr Lime?"

"Herr Lime of course."

Martins said to me later, "At first it didn't mean a thing. It was just a bit of information, like those paragraphs in *The Times* they call 'News in Brief.' I said to him, 'When did it happen? How?' "

"He was run over by a car," the man said. "Last Thursday." He added sullenly, as if really this were none of his business, "They're burying him this afternoon. You've only just missed them."

"Them?"

"Oh, a couple of friends and the coffin."

"Wasn't he in hospital?"

"There was no sense in taking him to hospital. He was killed here on his own doorstep—instantaneously. The right-hand mudguard struck him on his shoulder and bowled him over like a rabbit."

It was only then, Martins told me, when the man used the word "rabbit," that the dead Harry Lime came alive, became the boy with the gun which he had shown Martins the means of "borrowing"; a boy starting up among the long sandy burrows of Brickworth Common saying, "Shoot, you fool, shoot! There," and the rabbit limped to cover, wounded by Martins' shot.

"Where are they burying him?" he asked the stranger on the landing.

"In the Central Cemetery. They'll have a hard time of it in this frost."

He had no idea how to pay for his taxi, or indeed where in Vienna he could find a room in which he could live for five English pounds, but that problem had to be postponed until he had seen the last of Harry Lime. He drove straight out of town into the suburb (British zone) where the Central Cemetery lay. One passed through the Russian zone to reach it, and took a short cut through the American zone, which you couldn't mistake because of the ice-cream parlours in every street. The trams ran along the high wall of the Central Cemetery, and for a mile on the other side of the rails stretched the monumental masons and the market gardeners—an apparently endless chain of gravestones waiting for owners and wreaths waiting for mourners.

Martins had not realized the size of this huge snowbound park where he was making his last rendezvous with Lime. It was as if Harry had left a message to him, "Meet me in Hyde Park," without specifying a spot between the Achilles statue and Lancaster Gate; the avenues of graves, each avenue numbered and lettered, stretched out like the spokes of an enormous wheel; they drove for a half-mile towards the west, and then turned and drove a half-mile north, turned south. . . . The snow gave the great pompous family headstones an air of grotesque comedy; a toupee of snow slipped sideways over an angelic face, a saint wore a heavy white moustache, and a shako of snow tipped at a drunken angle over the bust of a superior civil servant called Wolfgang Gottman. Even this cemetery was zoned between the powers: the Russian zone was marked by huge tasteless statues of armed men, the French by rows of anonymous wooden crosses and a torn tired tricolour flag. Then Martins remembered that Lime was a Catholic and was unlikely to be buried in the British zone for which they had been vainly searching. So back they drove through the heart of a forest where the graves lay like wolves under the trees, winking white eyes under the gloom of the evergreens. Once from under the trees emerged a group of three men in strange eighteenth-century black and silver uniforms with three-cornered hats, pushing a kind of barrow: they crossed a ride in the forest of graves and disappeared again.

It was just chance that they found the funeral in time—one patch in the enormous park where the snow had been shovelled aside and a tiny group was gathered, apparently bent on some very private business. A priest had finished speaking, his words coming secretively through the thin patient snow, and a coffin was on the point of being lowered into the ground. Two men in lounge suits stood at the graveside; one carried a wreath that he obviously had forgotten to drop on to the coffin, for his companion nudged his elbow so that he came to with a start and dropped the flowers. A girl stood a little way away with her hands over her face, and I stood twenty yards away by another grave, watching with relief the last of Lime and noticing carefully who was there—just a man in a mackintosh I was to Martins. He came up to me and said, "Could you tell me who they are burying?"

"A fellow called Lime," I said, and was astonished to see the tears start to this stranger's eyes: he didn't look like a man who wept, nor was Lime the kind of man whom I thought likely to have mourners—genuine mourners with genuine tears. There was the girl of course, but one excepts women from all such generalizations.

Martins stood there, till the end, close beside me. He said to me later that as an old friend he didn't want to intrude on these newer ones—Lime's death belonged to them, let them have it. He was under the sentimental illusion that Lime's life—twenty years of it anyway—belonged to him. As soon as the affair was over—I am not a religious man and always feel a little impatient with the fuss that surrounds death—Martins strode away on his long legs that always seemed likely to get entangled together, back to his taxi. He made no attempt to speak to anyone, and the tears now were really running, at any rate the few meagre drops that any of us can squeeze out at our age.

One's file, you know, is never quite complete; a case is never really closed, even after a century, when all the participants are dead. So I followed Martins: I knew the other three: I wanted to know the stranger. I caught him up by his taxi and said, "I haven't any transport. Would you give me a lift into town?"

"Of course," he said. I knew the driver of my jeep would spot me as we came out and follow us unobtrusively. As we drove away I noticed he never looked behind—it's nearly always the fake mourners and the fake lovers who take that last look, who wait waving on platforms, instead of clearing quickly out, not looking back. Is it perhaps that they love themselves so much and want to keep themselves in the sight of others, even of the dead?

I said, "My name's Calloway."

"Martins," he said.

"You were a friend of Lime?"

"Yes." Most people in the last week would have hesitated before they admitted quite so much.

"Been here long?"

"I only came this afternoon from England. Harry had asked me to stay with him. I hadn't heard."

"Bit of a shock?"

"Look here," he said, "I badly want a drink, but I haven't any cash—except five pounds sterling. I'd be awfully grateful if you'd stand me one."

It was my turn to say "Of course." I thought for a moment and told the driver the name of a small bar in the Kärntnerstrasse. I didn't think he'd want to be seen for a while in a busy British bar full of transit officers and their wives. This bar—perhaps because it was exorbitant in its prices—seldom had more than one self-occupied couple in it at a time. The trouble was too that it really only had one drink—a sweet chocolate liqueur that the waiter improved at a price with cognac—but I got the impression that Martins had no objection to any drink so long as it cast a veil over the present, and the past. On the door was the usual notice saying the bar opened from six till ten, but one just pushed the door and walked through the front rooms. We had a whole small room to ourselves; the only couple were next door, and the waiter, who knew me, left us alone with some caviar sandwiches. It was lucky that we both knew I had an expense account.

Martins said over his second quick drink, "I'm sorry, but he was the best friend I ever had."

I couldn't resist saying, knowing what I knew, and because I was anxious to vex him—one learns a lot that way— "That sounds like a cheap novelette."

He said quickly, "I write cheap novelettes."

I had learned something anyway. Until he had had a third drink I was under the impression that he wasn't an easy talker, but I felt fairly certain that he was one of those who turn unpleasant after their fourth glass.

I said, "Tell me about yourself—and Lime."

"Look here," he said, "I badly need another drink, but I can't keep on scrounging on a stranger. Could you change me a pound or two into Austrian money?"

"Don't bother about that," I said and called the waiter. "You can treat me when I come to London on leave. You were going to tell me how you met Lime?"

The glass of chocolate liqueur might have been a crystal, the way he looked at it and turned it this way and that. He said, "It was a long time ago. I don't suppose anyone knows Harry the way I do," and I thought of the thick file of agents' reports in my office, each claiming the same thing. I believe in my agents; I've sifted them all very thoroughly.

"How long?"

"Twenty years—or a bit more. I met him my first term at school. I can see the place. I can see the notice-board and what was on it. I can hear the bell ringing. He was a year older and knew the ropes. He put me wise to a lot of things." He took a quick dab at his drink and then turned the crystal again as if to see more clearly what there was to see. He said, "It's funny. I can't remember meeting any woman quite as well."

"Was he clever at school?"

"Not the way they wanted him to be. But what things he did think up! He was a wonderful planner. I was far better at subjects like History and English than Harry, but I was a hopeless mug when it came to carrying out his plans." He laughed: he was already beginning, with the help of drink and talk, to throw off the shock of the death. He said, "I was always the one who got caught."

"That was convenient for Lime."

"What the hell do you mean?" he asked. Alcoholic irritation was setting in.

"Well, wasn't it?"

"That was my fault, not his. He could have found someone cleverer if he'd chosen, but he liked me. He was endlessly patient with me." Certainly, I thought, the child is father to the man, for I too had found Lime patient.

"When did you see him last?"

"Oh, he was over in London six months ago for a medical congress. You know he qualified as a doctor, though he never practised. That was typical of Harry. He just wanted to see if he could do a thing and then he lost interest. But he used to say that it often came in handy." And that too was true. It was odd how like the Lime he knew was to the Lime I knew: it was only that he looked at Lime's image from a different angle or in a different light. He said, "One of the things I liked about Harry was his humour." He gave a grin which took five years off his age. "I'm a buffoon. I like playing the silly fool, but Harry had real wit. You know, he could have been a first-class light composer if he had worked at it."

He whistled a tune—it was oddly familiar to me. "I always remember that. I saw Harry write it. Just in a couple of minutes on the back of an envelope. That was what he always whistled when he had something on his mind. It was his signature tune." He whistled the tune a second time, and I knew then who had written it—of course it wasn't Harry. I nearly told him so, but what was the point? The tune wavered and went out. He stared down into his glass, drained what was left, and said, "It's a damned shame to think of him dying the way he did."

"It was the best thing that ever happened to him," I said.

He didn't take in my meaning at once: he was a little hazy with the drinks. "The best thing?"

"Yes."

"You mean there wasn't any pain?"

"He was lucky in that way, too."

It was my tone of voice and not my words that caught Martins' attention. He asked gently and dangerously—I could see his right hand tighten—"Are you hinting at something?"

There is no point at all in showing physical courage in all situations: I eased my chair far enough back to be out of reach of his fist. I said, "I mean that I had his case completed at police headquarters. He would have served a long spell—a very long spell—if it hadn't been for the accident."

"What for?"

"He was about the worst racketeer who ever made a dirty living in this city."

I could see him measuring the distance between us and deciding that he couldn't reach me from where he sat. Rollo wanted to hit out, but Martins was steady, careful. Martins, I began to realize, was dangerous. I wondered whether after all I had made a complete mistake: I couldn't see Martins being quite the mug that Rollo had made out. "You're a policeman?" he asked.

"Yes."

"I've always hated policemen. They are always either crooked or stupid."

"Is that the kind of books you write?"

I could see him edging his chair round to block my way out. I caught the waiter's eye and he knew what I meant—there's an advantage in always using the same bar for interviews.

Martins brought out a surface smile and said gently, "I have to call them sheriffs."

"Been in America?" It was a silly conversation.

"No. Is this an interrogation?"

"Just interest."

"Because if Harry was that kind of racketeer, I must be one too. We always worked together."

"I daresay he meant to cut you in—somewhere in the organization. I wouldn't be surprised if he had meant to give you the baby to hold. That was his method at school—you told me, didn't you? And, you see, the headmaster was getting to know a thing or two."

"You are running true to form, aren't you? I suppose there was some petty racket going on with petrol and you couldn't pin it on anyone, so you've picked a dead man. That's just like a policeman. You're a real policeman, I suppose?"

"Yes, Scotland Yard, but they've put me into a colonel's uniform when I'm on duty."

He was between me and the door now. I couldn't get away from the table without coming into range. I'm no fighter, and he had six inches of advantage anyway. I said, "It wasn't petrol."

"Tyres, saccharin—why don't you policemen catch a few murderers for a change?"

"Well, you could say that murder was part of his racket."

He pushed the table over with one hand and made a dive at me with the other; the drink confused his calculations. Before he could try again my driver had his arms round him. I said, "Don't treat him rough. He's only a writer with too much drink in him."

"Be quiet, can't you, sir," my driver said. He had an exaggerated sense of officer-class. He would probably have called Lime "sir."

"Listen, Callaghan, or whatever your bloody name is . . ."

"Calloway. I'm English, not Irish."

"I'm going to make you look the biggest bloody fool in Vienna. There's one dead man you aren't going to pin your unsolved crimes on."

"I see. You're going to find me the real criminal? It sounds like one of your stories."

"You can let me go, Callaghan. I'd rather make you look the fool you are than black your bloody eye. You'd only have to go to bed for a few days with a black eye. But when I've finished with you, you'll leave Vienna."

I took out a couple of pounds' worth of bafs and stuck them in his breast pocket. "These will see you through to-night," I said, "and I'll make sure they keep a seat for you on tomorrow's London plane."

"You can't turn me out. My papers are in order."

"Yes, but this is like other cities: you need money here. If you change sterling on the black market I'll catch up on you inside twenty-four hours. Let him go."

Rollo Martins dusted himself down. He said, "Thanks for the drinks."

"That's all right."

"I'm glad I don't have to feel grateful. I suppose they were on expenses?"

"Yes."

"I'll be seeing you again in a week or two when I've got the dope." I knew he was angry. I didn't believe then that he was serious. I thought he was putting over an act to cheer up his self-esteem.

"I might come and see you off tomorrow."

"I shouldn't waste your time. I won't be there."

"Paine here will show you the way to Sacher's. You can get a bed and dinner there. I'll see to that."

He stepped to one side as though to make way for the waiter and slashed out at me. I just avoided him, but stumbled against the table. Before he could try again Paine had landed him on the mouth. He went bang over in the alley-way between the tables and came up bleeding from a cut lip. I said, "I thought you promised not to fight."

He wiped some of the blood away with his sleeve and said, "Oh, no, I said I'd rather make you a bloody fool. I didn't say I wouldn't give you a black eye as well."

I had had a long day and I was tired of Rollo Martins. I said to Paine, "See him safely into Sacher's. Don't hit him again if he behaves," and turning away from both of them towards the inner bar (I deserved one more drink), I heard Paine say respectfully to the man he had just knocked down, "This way, sir. It's only just around the corner."

[3]

What happened next I didn't hear from Paine but from Martins a long time afterwards, as I reconstructed the chain of events which did indeed—though not quite in the way he had expected—prove me to be a fool. Paine simply saw him to the head porter's desk and explained there, "This gentleman came in on the plane from London. Colonel Calloway says he's to have a room." Having made that clear, he said, "Good evening, sir," and left. He was probably a bit embarrassed by Martins' bleeding lip.

"Had you already got a reservation, sir?" the porter asked.

"No. No, I don't think so," Martins said in a muffled voice, holding his handkerchief to his mouth.

"I thought perhaps you might be Mr. Dexter. We had a room reserved for a week for Mr. Dexter."

Martins said, "Oh, I am Mr. Dexter." He told me later that it occurred to him that Lime might have engaged a room for him in that name because perhaps it was Buck Dexter and not Rollo Martins who was to be used for propaganda purposes. A voice said at his elbow, "I'm so sorry you were not met at the plane, Mr. Dexter. My name's Crabbin."

The speaker was a stout middle-aged young man with a natural tonsure and one of the thickest pairs of horn-rimmed glasses that Martins had ever seen. He went apologetically on, "One of our chaps happened to ring up Frankfurt and heard you were on the plane. HQ made one of their usual foolish mistakes and wired you were not coming. Something about Sweden, but the cable was badly mutilated. Directly I heard from Frankfurt I tried to meet the plane, but I just missed you. You got my note?"

Martins held his handkerchief to his mouth and said obscurely, "Yes. Yes?"

"May I say at once, Mr. Dexter, how excited I am to meet you?"

"Good of you."

"Ever since I was a boy, I've thought you the greatest novelist of our century."

Martins winced. It was painful opening his mouth to protest. He took an angry look instead at Mr. Crabbin, but it was impossible to suspect that young man of a practical joke.

"You have a big Austrian public, Mr. Dexter, both for your originals and your translations. Especially for *The Curved Prow*, that's my own favourite."

Martins was thinking hard. "Did you say—room for a week?"

"Yes."

"Very kind of you."

"Mr. Schmidt here will give you tickets every day, to cover all meals. But I expect you'll need a little pocket money. We'll fix that. Tomorrow we thought you'd like a quiet day—to look about."

"Yes."

"Of course any of us are at your service if you need a guide. Then the day after tomorrow in the evening there's a little quiet discussion at the Institute—on the contemporary novel. We thought perhaps you'd say a few words just to set the ball rolling, and then answer questions."

Martins at that moment was prepared to agree to anything, to get rid of Mr. Crabbin and also to secure a week's free board and lodging; and Rollo, of course, as I was to discover later, had always been prepared to accept any suggestion—for a drink, for a girl, for a joke, for a new excitement. He said now, "Of course, of course," into his handkerchief.

"Excuse me, Mr. Dexter, have you got toothache? I know a very good dentist."

"No. Somebody hit me, that's all."

"Good God! Were they trying to rob you?"

"No, it was a soldier. I was trying to punch his bloody colonel in the eye." He removed the handkerchief and gave Crabbin a view of his cut mouth. He told me that Crabbin

was at a complete loss for words. Martins couldn't understand why because he had never read the work of his great
contemporary, Benjamin Dexter: he hadn't even heard of
him. I am a great admirer of Dexter, so that I could understand Crabbin's bewilderment. Dexter has been ranked as a
stylist with Henry James, but he has a wider feminine streak
than his master—indeed his enemies have sometimes described his subtle, complex, wavering style as old-maidish.
For a man still just on the right side of fifty his passionate interest in embroidery and his habit of calming a not very tu-
multuous mind with tatting—a trait beloved by his disci-
ples—certainly to others seems a little affected.

"Have you ever read a book called *The Lone Rider of Santa
Fé*?"

"No, I don't think so."

Martins said, "This lone rider had his best friend shot by
the sheriff of a town called Lost Claim Gulch. The story is
how he hunted that sheriff down—quite legally—until his
revenge was completed."

"I never imagined you reading Westerns, Mr. Dexter,"
Crabbin said, and it needed all Martins' resolution to stop
Rollo saying, "But I write them."

"Well, I'm gunning just the same way for Colonel Callaghan."

"Never heard of him."

"Heard of Harry Lime?"

"Yes," Crabbin said cautiously, "but I didn't really know
him."

"I did. He was my best friend."

"I shouldn't have thought he was a very—literary character."

"None of my friends are."

Crabbin blinked nervously behind the horn-rims. He said
with an air of appeasement, "He was interested in the theatre though. A friend of his—an actress, you know—is learning English at the Institute. He called once or twice to fetch
her."

"Young or old?"

"Oh, young, very young. Not a good actress in my opinion."

Martins remembered the girl by the grave with her hands over her face. He said, "I'd like to meet any friend of Harry's."

"She'll probably be at your lecture."

"Austrian?"

"She claims to be Austrian, but I suspect she's Hungarian. She works at the Josefstadt."

"Why claims to be Austrian?"

"The Russians sometimes get interested in the Hungarians. I wouldn't be surprised if Lime had helped her with her papers. She calls herself Schmidt. Anna Schmidt. You can't imagine a young English actress calling herself Smith, can you? And a pretty one, too. It always struck me as a bit too anonymous to be true."

Martins felt he had got all he could from Crabbin, so he pleaded tiredness, a long day, promised to ring up in the morning, accepted ten pounds' worth of bafs for immediate expenses, and went to his room. It seemed to him that he was earning money rapidly—twelve pounds in less than an hour.

He *was* tired: he realized that when he stretched himself out on his bed in his boots. Within a minute he had left Vienna far behind him and was walking through a dense wood, ankle-deep in snow. An owl hooted, and he felt suddenly lonely and scared. He had an appointment to meet Harry under a particular tree, but in a wood so dense as this how could he recognize any one tree from the rest? Then he saw a figure and ran towards it: it whistled a familiar tune and his heart lifted with the relief and joy at not after all being alone. Then the figure turned and it was not Harry at all—just a stranger who grinned at him in a little circle of wet slushy melted snow, while the owl hooted again and again. He woke suddenly to hear the telephone ringing by his bed.

A voice with a trace of foreign accent—only a trace—said, "Is that Mr. Rollo Martins?"

"Yes." It was a change to be himself and not Dexter.

"You wouldn't know me," the voice said unnecessarily, "but I was a friend of Harry Lime."

It was a change too to hear anyone claim to be a friend of Harry's. Martins' heart warmed towards the stranger. He said, "I'd be glad to meet you."

"I'm just round the corner at the Old Vienna."

"Wouldn't you make it tomorrow? I've had a pretty awful day with one thing and another."

"Harry asked me to see that you were all right. I was with him when he died."

"I thought——" Rollo Martins said and stopped. He had been going to say, "I thought he died instantaneously," but something suggested caution. He said instead, "You haven't told me your name."

"Kurtz," the voice said. "I'd offer to come round to you, only, you know, Austrians aren't allowed in Sacher's."

"Perhaps we could meet at the Old Vienna in the morning."

"Certainly," the voice said, "if you are *quite* sure that you are all right till then?"

"How do you mean?"

"Harry had it on his mind that you'd be penniless." Rollo Martins lay back on his bed with the receiver to his ear and thought: come to Vienna to make money. This was the third stranger to stake him in less than five hours. He said cautiously, "Oh, I can carry on till I see you." There seemed no point in turning down a good offer till he knew what the offer was.

"Shall we say eleven, then, at the Old Vienna in the Kärtnerstrasse? I'll be in a brown suit and I'll carry one of your books."

"That's fine. How did you get hold of one?"

"Harry gave it to me." The voice had enormous charm and reasonableness, but when Martins had said good night and rung off, he couldn't help wondering how it was that if Harry had been so conscious before he died he had not had a cable sent to stop him. Hadn't Callaghan too said that Lime had died instantaneously—or without pain, was it?—or had he himself put the words into Callaghan's mouth? It was then that the idea first lodged firmly in Martins' mind that there was something wrong about Lime's death, something the police had been too stupid to discover. He tried to discover it himself with the help of two cigarettes, but he fell asleep without his dinner and with the mystery still unsolved. It had been a long day, but not quite long enough for that.

[4]

"What I disliked about him at first sight," Martins told me, "was his toupee. It was one of those obvious toupees—flat and yellow, with the hair cut straight at the back and not fitting close. There *must* be something phoney about a man who won't accept baldness gracefully. He had one of those faces too where the lines have been put in carefully, like a make-up, in the right places—to express charm, whimsicality, lines at the corners of the eyes. He was made up to appeal to romantic schoolgirls."

This conversation took place some days later—he brought out his whole story when the trail was nearly cold. We were sitting in the Old Vienna at the table he had occupied that first morning with Kurtz, and when he made that remark about the romantic schoolgirls I saw his rather hunted eyes focus suddenly. It was a girl—just like any other girl, I thought, hurrying by outside in the driving snow.

"Something pretty?"

He brought his gaze back and said, "I'm off that for ever. You know, Calloway, a time comes in a man's life when he gives up all that sort of thing . . ."

"I see. I thought you were looking at a girl."

"I was. But only because she reminded me for a moment of Anna—Anna Schmidt."

"Who's she? Isn't she a girl?"

"Oh, yes, in a way."

"What do you mean, in a way?"

"She was Harry's girl."

"Are you taking her over?"

"She's not that kind, Calloway. Didn't you see her at his funeral? I'm not mixing my drinks any more. I've got a hangover to last me a lifetime."

"You were telling me about Kurtz," I said.

It appeared that Kurtz was sitting there, making a great show of reading *The Lone Rider of Santa Fé.* When Martins sat down at his table he said with indescribably false enthusiasm, "It's wonderful how you keep the tension."

"Tension?"

"Suspense. You're a master at it. At the end of every chapter one's left guessing. . . ."

"So you were a friend of Harry's," Martins said.

"I think his best," but Kurtz added with the smallest pause, in which his brain must have registered the error, "except you, of course."

"Tell me how he died."

"I was with him. We came out together from the door of his flat and Harry saw a friend he knew across the road—an American called Cooler. He waved to Cooler and started across the road to him when a jeep came tearing round the corner and bowled him over. It was Harry's fault really—not the driver's."

"Somebody told me he died instantaneously."

"I wish he had. He died before the ambulance could reach us though."

"He could speak, then?"

"Yes. Even in his pain he worried about you."

"What did he say?"

"I can't remember the exact words, Rollo—I may call you Rollo, mayn't I? he always called you that to us. He was anxious that I should look after you when you arrived. See that you were looked after. Get your return ticket for you."

In telling me, Martins said, "You see I was collecting return tickets as well as cash."

"But why didn't you cable to stop me?"

"We did, but the cable must have missed you. What with censorship and the zones, cables can take anything up to five days."

"There was an inquest?"

"Of course."

"Did you know that the police have a crazy notion that Harry was mixed up in some racket?"

"No. But everyone in Vienna is. We all sell cigarettes and exchange schillings for bafs and that kind of thing. You won't find a single member of the Control Commission who hasn't broken the rules."

"The police meant something worse than that."

"They get rather absurd ideas sometimes," the man with the toupee said cautiously.

"I'm going to stay here till I prove them wrong."

Kurtz turned his head sharply and the toupee shifted very very slightly. He said, "What's the good? Nothing can bring Harry back."

"I'm going to have that police officer run out of Vienna."

"I don't see what you can do."

"I'm going to start working back from his death. You were there and this man Cooler and the chauffeur. You can give me their addresses."

"I don't know the chauffeur's."

"I can get it from the coroner's records. And then there's Harry's girl. . . ."

Kurtz said, "It will be painful for her."

"I'm not concerned about her. I'm concerned about Harry."

"Do you know what it is that the police suspect?"

"No. I lost my temper too soon."

"Has it occurred to you," Kurtz said gently, "that you might dig up something—well, discreditable to Harry?"

"I'll risk that."

"It will take a bit of time—and money."

"I've got time and you were going to lend me some money, weren't you?"

"I'm not a rich man," Kurtz said. "I promised Harry to see you were all right and that you got your plane back. . . ."

"You needn't worry about the money—or the plane," Martins said. "But I'll make a bet with you—in pounds sterling—five pounds against two hundred schillings—that there's something queer about Harry's death."

It was a shot in the dark, but already he had this firm instinctive sense that there was something wrong, though he hadn't yet attached the word "murder" to the instinct. Kurtz had a cup of coffee half-way to his lips and Martins watched him. The shot apparently went wide; an unaffected hand held the cup to the mouth and Kurtz drank, a little noisily, in long sips. Then he put down the cup and said, "How do you mean—queer?"

"It was convenient for the police to have a corpse, but wouldn't it have been equally convenient, perhaps, for the real racketeers?" When he had spoken he realized that after all Kurtz had not been unaffected by his wild statement: hadn't he been frozen into caution and calm? The hands of the guilty don't necessarily tremble; only in stories does a dropped glass betray agitation. Tension is more often shown in the studied action. Kurtz had drunk his coffee as though nothing had been said.

"Well—" he took another sip—"of course I wish you luck, though I don't believe there's anything to find. Just ask me for any help you want."

"I want Cooler's address."

"Certainly. I'll write it down for you. Here it is. In the American zone."

"And yours?"

"I've already put it—underneath. I'm unlucky enough to be in the Russian zone—so don't visit me very late. Things sometimes happen round our way." He was giving one of his

studied Viennese smiles, the charm carefully painted in with
a fine brush in the little lines about the mouth and eyes.
"Keep in touch," he said, "and if you need any help . . .
but I still think you are very unwise." He picked up *The Lone
Rider.* "I'm so proud to have met you. A master of suspense,"
and one hand smoothed the toupee, while another, passing
softly over the mouth, brushed out the smile as though it
had never been.

[5]

Martins sat on a hard chair just inside the stage door of the
Josefstadt Theatre. He had sent up his card to Anna
Schmidt after the matinée, marking it "a friend of Harry's."
An arcade of little windows, with lace curtains and the lights
going out one after another, showed where the artists were
packing up for home, for the cup of coffee without sugar, the
roll without butter to sustain them for the evening performance. It was like a little street built indoors for a film set,
but even indoors it was cold, even cold to a man in a heavy
overcoat, so that Martins rose and walked up and down, underneath the little windows. He felt, he said, rather like a
Romeo who wasn't sure of Juliet's balcony.

He had had time to think: he was calm now, Martins not
Rollo was in the ascendant. When a light went out in one of
the windows and an actress descended into the passage
where he walked, he didn't even turn to take a look. He was
done with all that. He thought, Kurtz is right. They are all
right. I'm behaving like a romantic fool. I'll just have a word
with Anna Schmidt, a word of commiseration, and then I'll
pack and go. He had quite forgotten, he told me, the com-
plication of Mr. Crabbin.

A voice over his head called "Mr. Martins," and he
looked up at the face that watched him from between the
curtains a few feet above his head. It wasn't a beautiful face,
he firmly explained to me, when I accused him of once
again mixing his drinks. Just an honest face; dark hair and

eyes which in that light looked brown; a wide forehead, a large mouth which didn't try to charm. No danger any-where, it seemed to Rollo Martins, of that sudden reckless moment when the scent of hair or a hand against the side al-ters life. She said, "Will you come up, please? The second door on the right."

There are some people, he explained to me carefully, whom one recognizes instantaneously as friends. You can be at ease with them because you know that never, never will you be in danger. "That was Anna," he said, and I wasn't sure whether the past tense was deliberate or not.

Unlike most actresses' rooms this one was almost bare; no wardrobe packed with clothes, no clutter of cosmetics and grease paints; a dressing-gown on the door, one sweater he recognized from Act II on the only easy chair, a tin of half-used paints and grease. A kettle hummed softly on a gas ring. She said, "Would you like a cup of tea? Someone sent me a packet last week—sometimes the Americans do, in-stead of flowers, you know, on the first night."

"I'd like a cup," he said, but if there was one thing he hated it was tea. He watched her while she made it, of course, all wrong: the water not on the boil, the teapot un-heated, too few leaves. She said, "I never quite understand why English people like tea."

He drank his cupful quickly like a medicine and watched her gingerly and delicately sip at hers. He said, "I wanted very much to see you. About Harry."

It was the dreadful moment; he could see her mouth stiffen to meet it.

"Yes?"

"I had known him twenty years. I was his friend. We were at school together, you know, and after that—there weren't many months running when we didn't meet. . . ."

She said, "When I got your card, I couldn't say no. But there's nothing really for us to talk about, is there?—noth-ing."

"I wanted to hear——"

"He's dead. That's the end. Everything's over, finished. What's the good of talking?"

"We both loved him."

"I don't know. You can't know a thing like that—afterwards. I don't know anything any more except——"

"Except?"

"That I want to be dead too."

Martins told me, "Then I nearly went away. What was the good of tormenting her because of this wild idea of mine? But instead I asked her one question. 'Do you know a man called Cooler?' "

"An American?" she asked. "I think that was the man who brought me some money when Harry died. I didn't want to take it, but he said Harry had been anxious—at the last moment."

"So he didn't die instantaneously?"

"Oh, no."

Martins said to me, "I began to wonder why I had got that idea so firmly into my head, and then I thought it was only the man in the flat who told me so—no one else. I said to her, 'He must have been very clear in his head at the end —because he remembered about me too. That seems to show that there wasn't really any pain.' "

"That's what I tell myself all the time."

"Did you see the doctor?"

"Once. Harry sent me to him. He was Harry's own doctor. He lived near by, you see."

Martins suddenly saw in that odd chamber of the mind that constructs such pictures, instantaneously, irrationally, a desert place, a body on the ground, a group of birds gathered. Perhaps it was a scene from one of his own books, not yet written, forming at the gate of consciousness. Immediately it faded, he thought how odd that they were all there, just at that moment, all Harry's friends—Kurtz, the doctor, this man Cooler; only the two people who loved him seemed to have been missing. He said, "And the driver? Did you hear his evidence?"

"He was upset, scared. But Cooler's evidence exonerated him, and Kurtz's. No, it wasn't his fault, poor man. I've often heard Harry say what a careful driver he was."

"He knew Harry too?" Another bird flapped down and joined the others round the silent figure on the sand who lay face down. Now he could tell that it was Harry, by the clothes, by the attitude like that of a boy asleep in the grass at a playing field's edge, on a hot summer afternoon.

Somebody called outside the window, "Fräulein Schmidt."

She said, "They don't like one to stay too long. It uses up *their* electricity."

He had given up the idea of sparing her anything. He told her, "The police say they were going to arrest Harry. They'd pinned some racket on him."

She took the news in much the same way as Kurtz. "Everybody's in a racket."

"I don't believe he was in anything serious."

"No."

"But he may have been framed. Do you know a man named Kurtz?"

"I don't think so."

"He wears a toupee."

"Oh." He could tell that that struck home. He said, "Don't you think it was odd they were all there—at the death? Everybody knew Harry. Even the driver, the doctor. . . ."

She said with hopeless calm, "I've wondered that too, though I didn't know about Kurtz. I wondered whether they'd murdered him, but what's the use of wondering?"

"I'm going to get those bastards," Rollo Martins said.

"It won't do any good. Perhaps the police are right. Perhaps poor Harry got mixed up——"

"Fräulein Schmidt," the voice called again.

"I must go."

"I'll walk with you a bit of the way."

The dark was almost down; the snow had ceased for a while to fall, and the great statues of the Ring, the prancing horses, the chariots and the eagles, were gun-shot grey with the end of evening light. "It's better to give up and forget," Anna said. The moony snow lay ankle-deep on the unswept pavements.

"Will you give me the doctor's address?"

They stood in the shelter of a wall while she wrote it down for him.

"And yours too?"

"Why do you want that?"

"I might have news for you."

"There isn't any news that would do any good now." He watched her from a distance board her tram, bowing her head against the wind, a dark question mark on the snow.

[6]

An amateur detective has this advantage over the professional, that he doesn't work set hours. Rollo Martins was not confined to the eight-hour day: his investigations didn't have to pause for meals. In his one day he covered as much ground as one of my men would have covered in two, and he had this initial advantage over us, that he was Harry's friend. He was, as it were, working from inside, while we pecked at the perimeter.

Dr. Winkler was at home. Perhaps he would not have been home to a police officer. Again Martins had marked his card with the sesame phrase: "A friend of Harry Lime's."

Dr. Winkler's waiting-room reminded Martins of an antique shop—an antique shop that specializes in religious objets d'art. There were more crucifixes than he could count, none of later date probably than the seventeenth century. There were statues in wood and ivory. There were a number of reliquaries: little bits of bone marked with saints' names and set in oval frames on a background of tinfoil. If they were genuine, what an odd fate it was, Martins thought, for a portion of Saint Susanna's knuckle to come to rest in Dr. Winkler's waiting room. Even the high-backed hideous chairs looked as if they had once been sat in by cardinals. The room was stuffy, and one expected the smell of incense. In a small gold casket was a splinter of the True Cross. A sneeze disturbed him.

Dr. Winkler was the cleanest doctor Martins had ever seen. He was very small and neat, in a black tail-coat and a high stiff collar; his little black moustache was like an evening tie. He sneezed again: perhaps he was cold because he was so clean. He said, "Mr. Martins?"

An irresistible desire to sully Dr. Winkler assailed Rollo Martins. He said, "Dr. Winkle?"

"Dr. Winkler."

"You've got an interesting collection here."

"Yes."

"These saints' bones . . ."

"The bones of chickens and rabbits." Dr. Winkler took a large white handkerchief out of his sleeve rather as though he were a conjurer producing his country's flag, and blew his nose neatly and thoroughly twice, closing each nostril in turn. You expected him to throw away the handkerchief after one use. "Would you mind, Mr. Martins, telling me the purpose of your visit? I have a patient waiting."

"We were both friends of Harry Lime."

"I was his medical adviser," Dr. Winkler corrected him and waited obstinately between the crucifixes.

"I arrived too late for the inquest. Harry had invited me out here to help him in something. I don't quite know what. I didn't hear of his death till I arrived."

"Very sad," Dr. Winkler said.

"Naturally, under the circumstances, I want to hear all I can."

"There is nothing I can tell you that you don't know. He was knocked over by a car. He was dead when I arrived."

"Would he have been conscious at all?"

"I understand he was for a short time, while they carried him into the house."

"In great pain?"

"Not necessarily."

"You are quite certain that it was an accident?"

Dr. Winkler put out a hand and straightened a crucifix. "I was not there. My opinion is limited to the cause of death. Have you any reason to be dissatisfied?"

The amateur has another advantage over the professional: he can be reckless. He can tell unnecessary truths and propound wild theories. Martins said, "The police have implicated Harry in a very serious racket. It seemed to me that he might have been murdered—or even killed himself."

"I am not competent to pass an opinion," Dr. Winkler said.

"Do you know a man called Cooler?"

"I don't think so."

"He was there when Harry was killed."

"Then of course I have met him. He wears a toupee."

"That was Kurtz."

Dr. Winkler was not only the cleanest, he was also the most cautious doctor that Martins had ever met. His statements were so limited that you could not for a moment doubt their veracity. He said, "There was a second man there." If he had to diagnose a case of scarlet fever he would, you felt, have confined himself to a statement that a rash was visible, that the temperature was so and so. He would never find himself in error at an inquest.

"Had you been Harry's doctor for long?" He seemed an odd man for Harry to choose—Harry who liked men with a certain recklessness, men capable of making mistakes.

"For about a year."

"Well, it's good of you to have seen me." Dr. Winkler bowed. When he bowed there was a very slight creak as though his shirt were made of celluloid. "I mustn't keep you from your patients any longer." Turning away from Dr.

Winkler, he confronted yet another crucifix, the figure hanging with arms above the head: a face of elongated El Greco agony. "That's a strange crucifix," he said.

"Jansenist," Dr. Winkler commented and closed his mouth sharply as though he had been guilty of giving away too much information.

"Never heard the word. Why are the arms above the head?"

Dr. Winkler said reluctantly, "Because He died, in their view, only for the elect."

[7]

As I see it, turning over my files, the notes of conversations, the statements of various characters, it would have been still possible, at this moment, for Rollo Martins to have left Vienna safely. He had shown an unhealthy curiosity, but the disease had been checked at every point. Nobody had given anything away. The smooth wall of deception had as yet shown no real crack to his roaming fingers. When Rollo Martins left Dr. Winkler's he was in no danger. He could have gone home to bed at Sacher's and slept with a quiet mind. He could even have visited Cooler at this stage without trouble. No one was seriously disturbed. Unfortunately for him—and there would always be periods of his life when he bitterly regretted it—he chose to go back to Harry's flat. He wanted to talk to the little vexed man who said he had seen the accident—or had he really not said so much? There was a moment in the dark frozen street when he was inclined to go straight to Cooler, to complete his picture of those sinister birds who sat around Harry's body, but Rollo, being Rollo, decided to toss a coin and the coin fell for the other action, and the deaths of two men.

Perhaps the little man—who bore the name of Koch—had drunk a glass too much of wine, perhaps he had simply spent a good day at the office, but this time, when Rollo Martins rang his bell, he was friendly and quite ready to talk. He had just finished dinner and had crumbs on his moustache. "Ah, I remember you. You are Herr Lime's friend."

He welcomed Martins in with great cordiality and introduced him to a mountainous wife whom he obviously kept under very strict control. "Ah, in the old days I would have offered you a cup of coffee, but now——"

Martins passed round his cigarette case and the atmosphere of cordiality deepened. "When you rang yesterday I was a little abrupt," Herr Koch said, "but I had a touch of migraine and my wife was out, so I had to answer the door myself."

"Did you tell me that you had actually seen the accident?"

Herr Koch exchanged glances with his wife. "The inquest is over, Ilse. There is no harm. You can trust my judgment. The gentleman is a friend. Yes, I saw the accident, but you are the only one who knows. When I say that I saw it, perhaps I should say that I heard it. I heard the brakes put on and the sound of the skid, and I got to the window in time to see them carry the body to the house."

"But didn't you give evidence?"

"It is better not to be mixed up in such things. My office cannot spare me. We are short of staff, and of course I did not actually *see*——"

"But you told me yesterday how it happened."

"That was how they described it in the papers."

"Was he in great pain?"

"He was dead. I looked right down from my window here and I saw his face. I know when a man is dead. You see, it is, in a way, my business. I am the head clerk at the mortuary."

"But the others say that he did not die at once."

"Perhaps they don't know death as well as I do."

"He was dead, of course, when the doctor arrived. He told me that."

"He was dead at once. You can take the word of a man who knows."

"I think, Herr Koch, that you should have given evidence."

"One must look after oneself, Herr Martins. I was not the only one who should have been there."

"How do you mean?"

"There were three people who helped to carry your friend to the house."

"I know—two men and the driver."

"The driver stayed where he was. He was very much shaken, poor man."

"Three men . . ." It was as though suddenly, fingering that bare wall, his fingers had encountered, not so much a crack perhaps, but at least a roughness that had not been smoothed away by the careful builders.

"Can you describe the men?"

But Herr Koch was not trained to observe the living: only the man with the toupee had attracted his eyes—the other two were just men, neither tall nor short, thick nor thin. He had seen them from far above, foreshortened, bent over their burden; they had not looked up, and he had quickly looked away and closed the window, realizing at once the wisdom of not being seen himself.

"There was no evidence I could really give, Herr Martins."

No evidence, Martins thought, no evidence! He no longer doubted that murder had been done. Why else had they lied about the moment of death? They wanted to quieten with their gifts of money and their plane ticket the only two friends Harry had in Vienna. And the third man? Who was he?

He said, "Did you see Herr Lime go out?"

"No."

"Did you hear a scream?"

"Only the brakes, Herr Martins."

It occurred to Martins that there was nothing—except the word of Kurtz and Cooler and the driver—to prove that in fact Harry had been killed at that precise moment. There was the medical evidence, but that could not prove more than that he had died, say, within a half-hour, and in any case the medical evidence was only as strong as Dr. Wink-ler's word: that clean, controlled man creaking among his crucifixes.

"Herr Martins, it just occurs to me—you are staying in Vienna?"

"Yes."

"If you need accommodation and spoke to the authorities quickly, you might secure Herr Lime's flat. It is a requisi-tioned property."

"Who has the keys?"

"I have them."

"Could I see the flat?"

"Ilse, the keys."

Herr Koch led the way into the flat that had been Har-ry's. In the little dark hall there was still the smell of ciga-rette smoke—the Turkish cigarettes that Harry always smoked. It seemed odd that a man's smell should cling in the folds of curtains so long after the man himself had be-come dead matter, a gas, a decay. One light, in a heavily beaded shade, left them in semi-darkness, fumbling for door handles.

The living-room was completely bare—it seemed to Mar-tins too bare. The chairs had been pushed up against the walls; the desk at which Harry must have written was free from dust or any papers. The parquet reflected the light like a mirror. Herr Koch opened a door and showed the bed-room: the bed neatly made with clean sheets. In the bath-room not even a used razor blade indicated that a few days ago a living man had occupied it. Only the dark hall and the cigarette smell gave a sense of occupation.

"You see," Herr Koch said, "it is quite ready for a new-comer. Ilse has cleaned up."

That she certainly had done. After a death there should have been more litter left than this. A man can't go sud-denly and unexpectedly on his longest journey without forgetting this or that, without leaving a bill unpaid, an official form unanswered, the photograph of a girl. "Were there no papers, Herr Koch?"

"Herr Lime was always a very tidy man. His waste-paper basket was full and his brief-case, but his friend fetched that away."

"His friend?"

"The gentleman with the toupee."

It was possible, of course, that Lime had not taken the journey so unexpectedly, and it occurred to Martins that Lime had perhaps hoped he would arrive in time to help. He said to Herr Koch, "I believe my friend was murdered."

"Murdered?" Herr Koch's cordiality was snuffed out by the word. He said, "I would not have asked you in here if I had thought you would talk such nonsense."

"Why should it be nonsense?"

"We do not have murders in this zone."

"All the same your evidence may be very valuable."

"I have no evidence. I saw nothing. I am not concerned. You must leave here at once please. You have been very inconsiderate." He hustled Martins back through the hall; already the smell of the smoke was fading a little more. Herr Koch's last word before he slammed his own door was, "It's no concern of mine." Poor Herr Koch! We do not choose our concerns. Later, when I was questioning Martins closely, I said to him, "Did you see anybody at all on the stairs, or in the street outside?"

"Nobody." He had everything to gain by remembering some chance passer-by, and I believed him. He said, "I noticed myself how quiet and dead the whole street looked. Part of it had been bombed, you know, and the moon was shining on the snow slopes. It was so very silent. I could hear my own feet creaking in the snow."

"Of course it proves nothing. There is a basement where anybody who had followed you could have hidden."

"Yes."

"Or your whole story may be phoney."

"Yes."

"The trouble is I can see no motive for you to have done it. It's true you are already guilty of getting money on false pretences. You came out here to join Lime, perhaps to help him . . ."

Martins said to me, "What was this precious racket you keep on hinting at?"

"I'd have told you all the facts when I first saw you if you hadn't lost your temper so damned quickly. Now I don't think I shall be acting wisely to tell you. It would be disclosing official information, and your contacts, you know, don't inspire confidence. A girl with phoney papers supplied by Lime, this man Kurtz . . ."

"Dr. Winkler . . ."

"I've got nothing against Dr. Winkler. No, if you are phoney, you don't need the information, but it might help you to learn exactly what we know. You see, our facts are not complete."

"I bet they aren't. I could invent a better detective than you in my bath."

"Your literary style does not do your namesake justice." Whenever he was reminded of Mr. Crabbin, that poor harassed representative of the British Council, Rollo Martins turned pink, with annoyance, embarrassment, shame. That too inclined me to trust him.

He had certainly given Crabbin some uncomfortable hours. On returning to Sacher's Hotel after his interview with Herr Koch he had found a desperate note waiting for him from the representative.

"I have been trying to locate you all day," Crabbin wrote. "It is essential that we should get together and work out a proper programme for you. This morning by telephone I have arranged lectures at Innsbruck and Salzburg for next week, but I must have your consent to the subjects, so that proper programmes can be printed. I would suggest two lectures: 'The Crisis of Faith in the Western World' (you are very respected here as a Christian writer, but this lecture should be quite unpolitical and no references should be made to Russia or communism) and 'The Technique of the Contemporary Novel.' The same lectures would be given in Vienna. Apart from this, there are a great many people here who would like to meet you, and I want to arrange a cocktail party for early next week. But for all this I must have a few words with you." The letter ended on a note of acute anxiety. "You will be at the discussion tomorrow night, won't you? We all expect you at eight-thirty and, needless to say, look forward to your coming. I will send transport to the hotel at eight-fifteen sharp."

Rollo Martins read the letter and, without bothering any further about Mr. Crabbin, went to bed.

[8]

After two drinks Rollo Martins' mind would always turn towards women—in a vague, sentimental, romantic way, as a Sex, in general. After three drinks, like a pilot who dives to find direction, he would begin to focus on one available girl. If he had not been offered a third drink by Cooler, he would probably not have gone quite so soon to Anna Schmidt's house, and if—but there are too many "ifs" in my style of writing, for it is my profession to balance possibilities, human possibilities, and the drive of destiny can never find a place in my files.

Martins had spent his lunch-time reading up the reports of the inquest, thus again demonstrating the superiority of the amateur to the professional, and making him more vulnerable to Cooler's liquor (which the professional in duty bound would have refused). It was nearly five o'clock when he reached Cooler's flat, which was over an ice-cream parlour in the American zone: the bar below was full of G.I.s with their girls, and the clatter of the long spoons and the curious free unformed laughter followed him up the stairs.

The Englishman who objects to Americans in general usually carries in his mind's eye just such an exception as Cooler: a man with tousled grey hair and a worried kindly face and long-sighted eyes, the kind of humanitarian who turns up in a typhus epidemic or a world war or a Chinese famine long before his countrymen have discovered the place in an atlas. Again the card marked "Harry's friend" was like an entrance ticket. Cooler was in officer's uniform, with mysterious letters on his flash, and no badges of rank, although his maid referred to him as Colonel Cooler. His warm frank handclasp was the most friendly act that Martins had encountered in Vienna.

"Any friend of Harry is all right with me," Cooler said. "I've heard of you, of course."

"From Harry?"

"I'm a great reader of Westerns," Cooler said, and Martins believed him as he did not believe Kurtz.

"I wondered—you were there, weren't you?—if you'd tell me about Harry's death."

"It was a terrible thing," Cooler said. "I was just crossing the road to go to Harry. He and Mr. Kurtz were on the sidewalk. Maybe if I hadn't started across the road, he'd have stayed where he was. But he saw me and stepped straight off to meet me and this jeep—it was terrible, terrible. The driver braked, but he didn't stand a chance. Have a Scotch, Mr. Martins. It's silly of me, but I get shaken up when I think of it." He said as he splashed in the soda, "In spite of this uniform, I'd never seen a man killed before."

"Was the other man in the car?"

Cooler took a long pull and then measured what was left with his tired kindly eyes. "What man would you be referring to, Mr. Martins?"

"I was told there was another man there."

"I don't know how you got that idea. You'll find all about it in the inquest reports." He poured out two more generous drinks. "There were just the three of us—me and Mr. Kurtz and the driver. The doctor, of course. I expect you were thinking of the doctor."

"This man I was talking to happened to look out of a window—he has the next flat to Harry's—and he said he saw three men and the driver. That's before the doctor arrived."

"He didn't say that in court."

"He didn't want to get involved."

"You'll never teach these Europeans to be good citizens. It was his duty." Cooler brooded sadly over his glass. "It's an odd thing, Mr. Martins, with accidents. You'll never get two reports that coincide. Why, even Mr. Kurtz and I disagreed about details. The thing happens so suddenly, you aren't concerned to notice things, until bang crash, and then you have to reconstruct, remember. I expect he got too tangled up trying to sort out what happened before and what after, to distinguish the four of us."

"The four?"

"I was counting Harry. What else did he see, Mr. Martins?"

"Nothing of interest—except he says Harry was dead when he was carried to the house."

"Well, he was dying—not much difference there. Have another drink, Mr. Martins?"

"No, I don't think I will."

"Well, I'd like another spot. I was very fond of your friend, Mr. Martins, and I don't like talking about it."

"Perhaps one more—to keep you company. Do you know Anna Schmidt?" Martins asked, while the whisky tingled on his tongue.

"Harry's girl? I met her once, that's all. As a matter of fact, I helped Harry fix her papers. Not the sort of thing I should confess to a stranger, I suppose, but you have to break the rules sometimes. Humanity's a duty too."

"What was wrong?"

"She was Hungarian and her father had been a Nazi, so they said. She was scared the Russians would pick her up."

"Why should they want to?"

"We can't always figure out why they do these things. Perhaps just to show that it's not healthy being friends with an Englishman."

"But she lives in the British zone."

"That wouldn't stop them. It's only five minutes ride in a jeep from the Commandatura. The streets aren't well lighted, and you haven't many police around."

"You took her some money from Harry, didn't you?"

"Yes, but I wouldn't have mentioned that. Did she tell you?"

The telephone rang, and Cooler drained his glass. "Hullo," he said. "Why, yes. This is Colonel Cooler." Then he sat with the receiver at his ear and an expression of sad patience, while some voice a long way off drained into the room. "Yes," he said once. "Yes." His eyes dwelt on Martins' face, but they seemed to be looking a long way beyond him: flat and tired and kind, they might have been gazing out across the sea. He said, "You did quite right," in a tone of commendation, and then, with a touch of asperity, "Of course they will be delivered. I gave my word. Good-bye."

He put the receiver down and passed a hand across his forehead wearily. It was as though he were trying to remember something he had to do. Martins said, "Had you heard anything of this racket the police talk about?"

"I'm sorry. What's that?"

"They say Harry was mixed up in some racket."

"Oh, no," Cooler said. "No. That's quite impossible. He had a great sense of duty."

"Kurtz seemed to think it was possible."

"Kurtz doesn't understand how an Anglo-Saxon feels," Cooler replied.

[9]

It was nearly dark when Martins made his way along the banks of the canal: across the water lay the half-destroyed Diana baths and in the distance the great black circle of the Prater Wheel, stationary above the ruined houses. Over there across the grey water was the second bezirk, in Russian ownership. St. Stefanskirche shot its enormous wounded spire into the sky above the Inner City, and, coming up the Kärtnerstrasse, Martins passed the lit door of the Military

Police station. The four men of the International Patrol were climbing into their jeep; the Russian M.P. sat beside the driver (for the Russians had that day taken over the chair for the next four weeks) and the Englishman, the Frenchman, and the American mounted behind. The third stiff whisky fumed into Martins' brain, and he remembered the girl in Amsterdam, the girl in Paris; loneliness moved along the crowded pavement at his side. He passed the corner of the street where Sacher's lay and went on. Rollo was in control and moved towards the only girl he knew in Vienna.

I asked him how he knew where she lived. Oh, he said, he'd looked up the address she had given him the night before, in bed, studying a map. He wanted to know his way about, and he was good with maps. He could memorize turnings and street names easily because he always went one way on foot.

"One way?"

"I mean when I'm calling on a girl—or someone."

He hadn't, of course, known that she would be in, that her play was not on that night in the Josefstadt, or perhaps he had memorized that too from the posters. In at any rate she was, if you could really call it being in, sitting alone in an unheated room, with the bed disguised as a divan, and a typewritten script lying open at the first page on the inadequate too-fancy topply table—because her thoughts were so far from being "in." He said awkwardly (and nobody could have said, not even Rollo, how much his awkwardness was part of his technique), "I thought I'd just look in and look you up. You see, I was passing . . ."

"Passing? Where to?" It had been a good half an hour's walk from the Inner City to the rim of the English zone, but he always had a reply. "I had too much whisky with Colonel Cooler. I needed a walk and I just happened to find myself this way."

"I can't give you a drink here. Except tea. There's some of that packet left."

"No, no thank you." He said, "You are busy," looking at the script.

"I didn't get beyond the first line."

He picked it up and read: "*Enter Louise.* LOUISE: I heard a child crying."

"Can I stay a little?" he asked with a gentleness that was more Martins than Rollo.

"I wish you would." He slumped down on the divan, and he told me a long time later (for lovers talk and reconstruct the smallest details if they can find a listener) that there it was he took his second real look at her. She stood there as awkward as himself in a pair of old flannel trousers which had been patched badly in the seat; she stood with her legs firmly straddled as though she were opposing someone and was determined to hold her ground—a small rather stocky figure with any grace she had folded and put away for use professionally.

"One of those bad days?" he asked.

"It's always bad about this time." She explained, "He used to look in, and when I heard you ring, just for a moment, I thought . . ." She sat down on a hard chair opposite him and said, "Please talk. You knew him. Just tell me anything."

And so he talked. The sky blackened outside the window while he talked. He noticed after a while that their hands had met. He said to me, "I never meant to fall in love, not with Harry's girl."

"When did it happen?" I asked him.

"It was very cold and I got up to close the window curtains. I only noticed my hand was on hers when I took it away. As I stood up I looked down at her face and she was looking up. It wasn't a beautiful face—that was the trouble. It was a face to live with, day in, day out. A face for wear. I felt as though I'd come into a new country where I couldn't speak the language. I had always thought it was beauty one loved in a woman. I stood there at the curtains, waiting to pull them, looking out. I couldn't see anything but my own face, looking back into the room, looking for her. She said, 'And what did Harry do that time?' and I wanted to say, 'Damn Harry. He's dead. We both loved him, but he's dead. The dead are made to be forgotten.' Instead, of course, all I said was, 'What do you think? He just whistled his old tune as if nothing was the matter,' and I whistled it to her as well as I could. I heard her catch her breath, and I looked round and before I could think: is this the right way, the right card, the right gambit?—I'd already said, 'He's dead. You can't go on remembering him for ever.' "

She said, "I know, but perhaps something will happen first."

"What do you mean—something happen?"

"Oh, I mean, perhaps there'll be another war, or I'll die, or the Russians will take me."

"You'll forget him in time. You'll fall in love again."

"I know, but I don't want to. Don't you see I don't want to?"

So Rollo Martins came back from the window and sat down on the divan again. When he had risen half a minute before he had been the friend of Harry, comforting Harry's girl; now he was a man in love with Anna Schmidt who had been in love with a man they had both once known called Harry Lime. He didn't speak again that evening about the past. Instead he began to tell her of the people he had seen. "I can believe anything of Winkler," he told her, "but Cooler—I liked Cooler. He was the only one of his friends who stood up for Harry. The trouble is, if Cooler's right, then Koch is wrong, and I really thought I had something there."

"Who's Koch?"

He explained how he had returned to Harry's flat and he described his interview with Koch, the story of the third man.

"If it's true," she said, "it's very important."

"It doesn't prove anything. After all, Koch backed out of the inquest; so might this stranger."

"That's not the point," she said. "It means that *they* lied: Kurtz and Cooler."

"They might have lied so as not to inconvenience this fellow—if he was a friend."

"Yet another friend—on the spot. And where's your Cooler's honesty then?"

"What do we do? Koch clamped down like an oyster and turned me out of his flat."

"He won't turn me out," she said, "or his Ilse won't."

They walked up the long road to the flat together; the snow clogged on their shoes and made them move slowly like convicts weighed down by irons. Anna Schmidt said, "Is it far?"

"Not very far now. Do you see that knot of people up the road? It's somewhere about there." The group was like a splash of ink on the whiteness, a splash that flowed, changed shape, spread out. When they came a little nearer Martins said, "I think that's his block. What do you suppose this is, a political demonstration?"

Anna Schmidt stopped. She said, "Who else have you told about Koch?"

"Only you and Colonel Cooler. Why?"

"I'm frightened. It reminds me . . ." She had her eyes fixed on the crowd and he never knew what memory out of her confused past had risen to warn her. "Let's go away," she implored him.

"You're crazy. We're on to something here, something big . . ."

"I'll wait for you."

"But you're going to talk to him."

"Find out first what all those people . . ." She said strangely for one who worked behind the footlights, "I hate crowds."

He walked slowly on alone, the snow caking on his heels. It wasn't a political meeting, for no one was making a speech. He had the impression of heads turning to watch him come, as though he were somebody who was expected.

When he reached the fringe of the little crowd, he knew for certain that it was the house. A man looked hard at him and said, "Are you another of them?"

"What do you mean?"

"The police."

"No. What are they doing?"

"They've been in and out all day."

"What's everybody waiting for?"

"They want to see him brought out."

"Who?"

"Herr Koch." It occurred vaguely to Martins that somebody besides himself had discovered Herr Koch's failure to give evidence, though that was hardly a police matter. He said, "What's he done?"

"Nobody knows that yet. They can't make their minds up in there—it might be suicide, you see, and it might be murder."

"Herr Koch?"

"Of course."

A small child came up to his informant and pulled at his hand. "Papa, Papa." He wore a wool cap on his head, like a gnome; his face was pinched and blue with cold.

"Yes, my dear, what is it?"

"I heard them talking through the grating, Papa."

"Oh, you cunning little one. Tell us what you heard, Hansel."

"I heard Frau Koch crying, Papa."

"Was that all, Hansel?"

"No. I heard the big man talking, Papa."

"Ah, you cunning little Hansel. Tell Papa what he said."

"He said, 'Can you tell me, Frau Koch, what the foreigner looked like?'"

"Ha, ha, you see, they think it's murder. And who's to say they are wrong? Why should Herr Koch cut his own throat in the basement?"

"Papa, Papa."

"Yes, little Hansel?"

"When I looked through the grating, I could see some blood on the coke."

"What a child you are. How could you tell it was blood? The snow leaks everywhere." The man turned to Martins and said, "The child has such an imagination. Maybe he will be a writer when he grows up."

The pinched face stared solemnly up at Martins. The child said, "Papa."

"Yes, Hansel?"

"He's a foreigner too."

The man gave a big laugh that caused a dozen heads to turn. "Listen to him, sir, listen," he said proudly. "He thinks you did it just because you are a foreigner. As though there weren't more foreigners here these days than Viennese."

"Papa, Papa."

"Yes, Hansel?"

"They are coming out."

A knot of police surrounded the covered stretcher which they lowered carefully down the steps for fear of sliding on the trodden snow. The man said, "They can't get an ambulance into this street because of the ruins. They have to carry it round the corner." Frau Koch came out at the tail of the procession; she had a shawl over her head and an old sackcloth coat. Her thick shape looked like a snowman as she sank in a drift at the pavement's edge. Someone gave her a hand and she looked round with a lost hopeless gaze at this crowd of strangers. If there were friends there she did not recognize them, looking from face to face. Martins bent as she passed, fumbling at his shoelace, but looking up from the ground he saw at his own eyes' level the scrutinizing cold-blooded gnome gaze of little Hansel.

Walking back down the street towards Anna, he looked back once. The child was pulling at his father's hand and he could see the lips forming round those syllables like the refrain of a grim ballad, "Papa, Papa."

He said to Anna, "Koch has been murdered. Come away from here." He walked as rapidly as the snow would let him, turning this corner and that. The child's suspicion and alertness seemed to spread like a cloud over the city—they could not walk fast enough to evade its shadow. He paid no attention when Anna said to him, "Then what Koch said was true. There *was* a third man," nor a little later when she said, "It must have been murder. You don't kill a man to hide anything less."

The tramcars flashed like icicles at the end of the street: they were back at the Ring. Martins said, "You had better go home alone. I'll keep away from you awhile till things have sorted out."

"But nobody can suspect you."

"They are asking about the foreigner who called on Koch yesterday. There may be some unpleasantness for a while."

"Why don't you go to the police?"

"They are so stupid. I don't trust them. See what they've pinned on Harry. And then I tried to hit this man Callaghan. They'll have it in for me. The least they'll do is send me away from Vienna. But if I stay quiet—there's only one person who can give me away. Cooler."

"And he won't want to."

"Not if he's guilty. But then I can't believe he's guilty."

Before she left him, she said, "Be careful. Koch knew so very little and they murdered him. You know as much as Koch."

The warning stayed in his brain all the way to Sacher's: after nine o'clock the streets are very empty, and he would turn his head at every padding step coming up the street behind him, as though that third man whom they had protected so ruthlessly were following him like an executioner. The Russian sentry outside the Grand Hotel looked rigid with the cold, but he was human, he had a face, an honest peasant face with Mongol eyes. The third man had no face: only the top of a head seen from a window. At Sacher's Mr. Schmidt said, "Colonel Calloway has been in, asking for you, sir. I think you'll find him in the bar."

"Back in a moment," Martins said and walked straight

out of the hotel again: he wanted time to think. But immediately he stepped outside a man came forward, touched his cap, and said firmly, "Please, sir." He flung open the door of a khaki-painted truck with a Union Jack on the windscreen and firmly urged Martins within. He surrendered without protest; sooner or later, he felt sure, inquiries would be made; he had only pretended optimism to Anna Schmidt.

The driver drove too fast for safety on the frozen road, and Martins protested. All he got in reply was a sullen grunt and a muttered sentence containing the word "orders." "Have you orders to kill me?" Martins said and got no reply at all. He caught sight of the Titans on the Hofburg balancing great globes of snow above their heads, and then they plunged into ill-lit streets beyond, where he lost all sense of direction.

"Is it far?" But the driver paid no attention at all. At least, Martins thought, I am not under arrest: they have not sent a guard; I am being invited—wasn't that the word they used?—to visit the station to make a statement.

The car drew up and the driver led the way up two flights of stairs; he rang the bell of a great double door, and Martins was aware of many voices beyond it. He turned sharply to the driver and said, "Where the hell . . . ?" but the driver was already half-way down the stairs, and already the door was opening. His eyes were dazzled from the darkness by the lights inside; he heard but he could hardly see the advance of Crabbin. "Oh, Mr. Dexter, we have been so anxious, but better late than never. Let me introduce you to Miss Wilbraham and the Gräfin von Meyersdorf."

A buffet laden with coffee cups; an urn steamed; a woman's face shiny with exertion; two young men with the happy intelligent faces of sixth-formers; and, huddled in the background, like faces in a family album, a multitude of the old-fashioned, the dingy, the earnest and cheery features of constant readers. Martins looked behind him, but the door had closed.

He said desperately to Mr. Crabbin, "I'm sorry, but——"

"Don't think any more about it," Mr. Crabbin said. "One cup of coffee and then let's go on to the discussion. We have a very good gathering tonight. They'll put you on your mettle, Mr. Dexter." One of the young men placed a cup in his hand, the other shovelled in sugar before he could say he preferred his coffee unsweetened. The youngest man breathed into his ear, "Afterwards would you mind signing one of your books, Mr. Dexter?" A large woman in black silk bore down upon him and said, "I don't mind if the Gräfin does hear me, Mr. Dexter, but I don't like your books, I don't approve of them. I think a novel should tell a good story."

"So do I," Martins said hopelessly.

"Now, Mrs. Bannock, wait for question time."

"I know I'm downright, but I'm sure Mr. Dexter values *honest* criticism."

An old lady, who he supposed was the Gräfin, said, "I do not read many English books, Mr. Dexter, but I am told that yours . . ."

"Do you mind drinking up?" Crabbin said and hustled him through into an inner room where a number of elderly people were sitting on a semicircle of chairs with an air of sad patience.

Martins was not able to tell me very much about the meeting; his mind was still dazed with the death; when he looked up he expected to see at any moment the child Hansel and hear that persistent informative refrain, "Papa, Papa." Apparently Crabbin opened the proceedings, and, knowing Crabbin, I am sure that it was a very lucid, very fair and unbiased picture of the contemporary English novel. I have heard him give that talk so often, varied only by the emphasis given to the work of the particular English visitor. He would have touched lightly on various problems of technique—the point of view, the passage of time—and then he would have declared the meeting open for questions and discussion.

Martins missed the first question altogether, but luckily

Crabbin filled the gap and answered it satisfactorily. A woman wearing a brown hat and a piece of fur round her throat said with passionate interest, "May I ask Mr. Dexter if he is engaged on a new work?"

"Oh, yes—yes."

"May I ask the title?"

" 'The Third Man,' " Martins said and gained a spurious confidence as the result of taking that hurdle.

"Mr. Dexter, could you tell us what author has chiefly influenced you?"

Martins, without thinking, said, "Grey." He meant of course the author of *Riders of the Purple Sage*, and he was pleased to find his reply gave general satisfaction—to all save an elderly Austrian who asked, "Grey. What Grey? I do not know the name."

Martins felt he was safe now and said, "Zane Grey—I don't know any other," and was mystified at the low subservient laughter from the English colony.

Crabbin interposed quickly for the sake of the Austrians, "That is a little joke of Mr. Dexter's. He meant the poet Gray—a gentle, mild, subtle genius—one can see the affinity."

"And he is called Zane Grey?"

"That was Mr. Dexter's joke. Zane Grey wrote what we call Westerns—cheap popular novelettes about bandits and cowboys."

"He is not a great writer?"

"No, no. Far from it," Mr. Crabbin said. "In the strict sense I would not call him a writer at all." Martins told me that he felt the first stirrings of revolt at that statement. He had never regarded himself before as a writer, but Crabbin's self-confidence irritated him—even the way the light flashed back from Crabbin's spectacles seemed an added cause of vexation. Crabbin said, "He was just a popular entertainer."

"Why the hell not?" Martins said fiercely.

"Oh, well, I merely meant——"

"What was Shakespeare?"

Somebody with great daring said, "A poet."

"Have you ever read Zane Grey?"

"No, I can't say——"

"Then you don't know what you are talking about."

One of the young men tried to come to Crabbin's rescue. "And James Joyce, where would you put James Joyce, Mr. Dexter?"

"What do you mean put? I don't want to put anybody anywhere," Martins said. It had been a very full day: he had drunk too much with Colonel Cooler; he had fallen in love; a man had been murdered—and now he had the quite unjust feeling that he was being got at. Zane Grey was one of his heroes: he was damned if he was going to stand any nonsense.

"I mean would you put him among the really great?"

"If you want to know, I've never heard of him. What did he write?"

He didn't realize it, but he was making an enormous impression. Only a great writer could have taken so arrogant, so original a line. Several people wrote Zane Grey's name on the backs of envelopes and the Gräfin whispered hoarsely to Crabbin, "How do you spell Zane?"

"To tell you the truth, I'm not quite sure."

A number of names were simultaneously flung at Martins—little sharp pointed names like Stein, round pebbles like Woolf. A young Austrian with an intellectual black forelock called out, "Daphne du Maurier," and Mr. Crabbin winced and looked sideways at Martins. He said in an undertone, "Be gentle with them."

A kind-faced woman in a hand-knitted jumper said wistfully, "Don't you agree, Mr. Dexter, that no one, no one has written about *feelings* so poetically as Virginia Woolf? In prose, I mean."

Crabbin whispered, "You might say something about the stream of consciousness."

"Stream of what?"

A note of despair came into Crabbin's voice. "Please, Mr.

Dexter, these people are your genuine admirers. They want to hear your views. If you knew how they have *besieged* the Council."

An elderly Austrian said, "Is there any writer in England today of the stature of the late John Galsworthy?"

There was an outburst of angry twittering in which the names of du Maurier, Priestley, and somebody called Layman were flung to and fro. Martins sat gloomily back and saw again the snow, the stretcher, the desperate face of Frau Koch. He thought: if I had never returned, if I had never asked questions, would that little man still be alive? How had he benefited Harry by supplying another victim—a victim to assuage the fear of whom?—Herr Kurtz, Colonel Cooler (he could not believe that), Dr. Winkler? Not one of them seemed adequate to the drab gruesome crime in the basement; he could hear the child saying, "I saw the blood on the coke," and somebody turned towards him a blank face without features, a grey plasticine egg, the third man.

Martins could not have said how he got through the rest of the discussion: perhaps Crabbin took the brunt; perhaps he was helped by some of the audience who got into an animated discussion about the film version of a popular American novel. He remembered very little more before Crabbin was making a final speech in his honour. Then one of the young men led him to a table stacked with books and asked him to sign them. "We have only allowed each member one book."

"What have I got to do?"

"Just a signature. That's all they expect. This is my copy of *The Curved Prow*. I would be so grateful if you'd just write a little something . . ."

Martins took his pen and wrote: "From B. Dexter, author of *The Lone Rider of Santa Fé*," and the young man read the sentence and blotted it with a puzzled expression. As Martins sat down and started signing Benjamin Dexter's title pages, he could see in a mirror the young man showing the inscription to Crabbin. Crabbin smiled weakly and stroked his chin, up and down, up and down. "B. Dexter, B. Dexter, B. Dexter," Martins wrote rapidly—it was not, after all, a lie. One by one the books were collected by their owners; little half-sentences of delight and compliment were dropped like curtsies—was this what it was to be a writer? Martins began to feel distinct irritation towards Benjamin Dexter. The complacent, tiring, pompous ass, he thought, signing the twenty-seventh copy of *The Curved Prow.* Every time he looked up and took another book he saw Crabbin's worried speculative gaze. The members of the Institute were beginning to go home with their spoils: the room was emptying. Suddenly in the mirror Martins saw a military policeman. He seemed to be having an argument with one of Crabbin's young henchmen. Martins thought he caught the sound of his own name. It was then he lost his nerve and with it any relic of common sense. There was only one book left to sign; he dashed off a last "B. Dexter" and made for the door. The young man, Crabbin, and the policeman stood together at the entrance.

"And this gentleman?" the policeman asked.

"It's Mr. Benjamin Dexter," the young man said.

"Lavatory. Is there a lavatory?" Martins said.

"I understood a Mr. Rollo Martins came here in one of your cars."

"A mistake. An obvious mistake."

"Second door on the left," the young man said.

Martins grabbed his coat from the cloakroom as he went and made down the stairs. On the first-floor landing he heard someone mounting the stairs and, looking over, saw Paine, whom I had sent to identify him. He opened a door at random and shut it behind him. He could hear Paine going by. The room where he stood was in darkness; a curious moaning sound made him turn and face whatever room it was.

He could see nothing and the sound had stopped. He made a tiny movement and once more it started, like an impeded breath. He remained still and the sound died away.

Outside somebody called, "Mr. Dexter, Mr. Dexter." Then a new sound started. It was like somebody whispering—a long continuous monologue in the darkness. Martins said, "Is anybody there?" and the sound stopped again. He could stand no more of it. He took out his lighter. Footsteps went by and down the stairs. He scraped and scraped at the little wheel and no light came. Somebody shifted in the dark, and something rattled in mid-air like a chain. He asked once more with the anger of fear, "Is anybody there?" and only the click-click of metal answered him.

Martins felt desperately for a light switch, first to his right hand and then to his left. He did not dare go farther because he could no longer locate his fellow occupant; the whisper, the moaning, the click had all stopped. Then he was afraid that he had lost the door and felt wildly for the knob. He was far less afraid of the police than he was of the darkness, and he had no idea of the noise he was making.

Paine heard it from the bottom of the stairs and came back. He switched on the landing light, and the glow under the door gave Martins his direction. He opened the door and, smiling weakly at Paine, turned back to take a second look at the room. The eyes of a parrot chained to a perch stared beadily back at him. Paine said respectfully, "We were looking for you, sir. Colonel Calloway wants a word with you."

"I lost my way," Martins said.

"Yes, sir. We thought that was what had happened."

[1 0]

I had kept a very careful record of Martins' movements from the moment I knew that he had not caught the plane home. He had been seen with Kurtz, and at the Josefstadt Theatre; I knew about his visit to Dr. Winkler and to Colonel Cooler, his first return to the block where Harry had lived. For some reason my man lost him between Cooler's and Anna Schmidt's flats; he reported that Martins had wandered widely, and the impression we both got was that he had deliberately thrown off his shadower. I tried to pick him up at the hotel and just missed him.

Events had taken a disquieting turn, and it seemed to me that the time had come for another interview. He had a lot to explain.

I put a good wide desk between us and gave him a cigarette. I found him sullen but ready to talk, within strict limits. I asked him about Kurtz and he seemed to me to answer satisfactorily. I then asked him about Anna Schmidt and I gathered from his reply that he must have been with her after visiting Colonel Cooler; that filled in one of the missing points. I tried him with Dr. Winkler, and he answered readily enough. "You've been getting around," I said, "quite a bit. And have you found out anything about your friend?"

"Oh, yes," he said. "It was under your nose but you didn't see it."

"What?"

"That he was murdered." That took me by surprise: I had at one time played with the idea of suicide, but I had ruled even that out.

"Go on," I said. He tried to eliminate from his story all mention of Koch, talking about an informant who had seen the accident. This made his story rather confusing, and I couldn't grasp at first why he attached so much importance to the third man.

"He didn't turn up at the inquest, and the others lied to keep him out."

"Nor did your man turn up—I don't see much importance in that. If it was a genuine accident, all the evidence needed was there. Why get the other chap in trouble? Perhaps his wife thought he was out of town; perhaps he was an official absent without leave—people sometimes take unauthorized trips to Vienna from places like Klagenfurt. The delights of the great city, for what they are worth."

"There was more to it than that. The little chap who told me about it—they've murdered him. You see, they obviously didn't know what else he had seen."

"Now we have it," I said. "You mean Koch."

"Yes."

"As far as we know, you were the last person to see him alive." I questioned him then, as I've written, to find out if he had been followed to Koch's by somebody who was sharper than my man and had kept out of sight. I said, "The Austrian police are anxious to pin this on you. Frau Koch told them how disturbed her husband was by your visit. Who else knew about it?"

"I told Cooler." He said excitedly, "Suppose immediately I left he telephoned the story to someone—to the third man. They had to stop Koch's mouth."

"When you told Colonel Cooler about Koch, the man was already dead. That night he got out of bed, hearing some-one, and went downstairs——"

"Well, that rules me out. I was in Sacher's."

"But he went to bed very early. Your visit brought back the migraine. It was soon after nine when he got up. You returned to Sacher's at nine-thirty. Where were you before that?"

He said gloomily, "Wandering round and trying to sort things out."

"Any evidence of your movements?"

"No."

I wanted to frighten him, so there was no point in telling him that he had been followed all the time. I knew that he hadn't cut Koch's throat, but I wasn't sure that he was quite so innocent as he made out. The man who owns the knife is not always the real murderer.

"Can I have a cigarette?"

"Yes."

He said, "How did you know that I went to Koch's? That was why you pulled me here, wasn't it?"

"The Austrian police——"

"They hadn't identified me."

"Immediately you left Colonel Cooler's, he telephoned to me."

"Then that lets him out. If he had been concerned, he wouldn't have wanted me to tell you my story—to tell Koch's story, I mean."

"He might assume that you were a sensible man and would come to me with your story as soon as you learned of Koch's death. By the way, how did you learn of it?"

He told me promptly and I believed him. It was then I began to believe him altogether. He said, "I still can't believe Cooler's concerned. I'd stake anything on his honesty. He's one of those Americans with a real sense of duty."

"Yes," I said, "he told me about that when he phoned. He apologized for it. He said it was the worst of having been brought up to believe in citizenship. He said it made him feel a prig. To tell you the truth, Cooler irritates me. Of course he doesn't know that I know about his tyre deals."

"Is he in a racket, too, then?"

"Not a very serious one. I daresay he's salted away twenty-five thousand dollars. But I'm not a good citizen. Let the Americans look after their own people."

"I'm damned." He said thoughtfully, "Is that the kind of thing Harry was up to?"

"No. It was not so harmless."

He said, "You know this business—Koch's death—has shaken me. Perhaps Harry did get mixed up in something pretty bad. Perhaps he was trying to clear out again, and that's why they murdered him."

"Or perhaps," I said, "they wanted a bigger cut off the spoils. Thieves fall out."

He took it this time without any anger at all. He said, "We won't agree about motives, but I think you check your facts pretty well. I'm sorry about the other day."

"That's all right." There are times when one has to make a flash decision—this was one of them. I owed him something in return for the information he had given me. I said, "I'll show you enough of the facts in Lime's case for you to understand. But don't fly off the handle. It's going to be a shock."

It couldn't help being a shock. The war and the peace (if you can call it peace) let loose a great number of rackets, but none more vile than this one. The black marketeers in food did at least supply food, and the same applied to all the other racketeers who provided articles in short supply at extravagant prices. But the penicillin racket was a different affair altogether. Penicillin in Austria was supplied only to the military hospitals: no civilian doctor, not even a civilian hospital, could obtain it by legal means. As the racket started, it was relatively harmless. Penicillin would be stolen by military orderlies and sold to Austrian doctors for very high sums—a phial would fetch anything up to seventy pounds. You might say that this was a form of distribution— unfair distribution because it benefited only the rich patient, but the original distribution could hardly have a claim to greater fairness.

This racket went on quite happily for a while. Occasionally an orderly was caught and punished, but the danger simply raised the price of penicillin. Then the racket began to get organized: the big men saw big money in it, and while the original thief got less for his spoils, he received instead a certain security. If anything happened to him he would be looked after. Human nature too has curious twisted reasons that the heart certainly knows nothing of. It eased the conscience of many small men to feel that they were working for an employer: they were almost as respectable in their own eyes as wage-earners; they were one of a group, and if there was guilt, the leaders bore the guilt. A racket works very like a totalitarian party.

This I have sometimes called stage two. Stage three was when the organizers decided that the profits were not large enough. Penicillin would not always be impossible to obtain legitimately; they wanted more money and quicker money while the going was good. They began to dilute the penicillin with coloured water, and, in the case of penicillin dust, with sand. I keep a small museum in one drawer in my desk, and I showed Martins examples. He wasn't enjoying the talk, but he hadn't yet grasped the point. He said, "I suppose that makes the stuff useless."

I said, "We wouldn't worry so much if that was all, but just consider. You can be immunized from the effects of penicillin. At the best you can say that the use of this stuff makes a penicillin treatment for the particular patient ineffective in the future. That isn't so funny, of course, if you are suffering from V.D. Then the use of sand on a wound that requires penicillin—well, it's not healthy. Men have lost their legs and arms that way—and their lives. But perhaps what horrified me most was visiting the children's hospital here. They had bought some of this penicillin for use against meningitis. A number of children simply died, and a number went off their heads. You can see them now in the mental ward."

He sat on the other side of the desk, scowling into his hands. I said, "It doesn't bear thinking about very closely, does it?"

"You haven't showed me any evidence yet that Harry——"

"We are coming to that now," I said. "Just sit still and listen." I opened Lime's file and began to read. At the beginning the evidence was purely circumstantial, and Martins fidgeted. So much consisted of coincidence—reports from agents that Lime had been at a certain place at a certain time; the accumulation of opportunities; his acquaintance with certain people. He protested once, "But the same evidence would apply against me—now."

"Just wait," I said. For some reason Harry Lime had grown careless: he may have realized that we suspected him and got rattled. He held a quite distinguished position in the Relief Organization, and a man like that is the more easily rattled. We put one of our agents as an orderly in the British Military Hospital: we knew by this time the name of our go-between, but we had never succeeded in getting the line right back to the source. Anyway, I am not going to bother the reader now, as I bothered Martins then, with all the

stages—the long tussle to win the confidence of the go-between, a man called Harbin. At last we had the screws on
Harbin, and we twisted them until he squealed. This kind of
police work is very similar to secret service work: you look
for a double agent whom you can really control, and Harbin
was the man for us. But even he only led us as far as Kurtz.

"Kurtz!" Martins exclaimed. "But why haven't you
pulled him in?"

"Zero hour is almost here," I said.

Kurtz was a great step forward, for Kurtz was in direct
communication with Lime—he had a small outside job in
connection with international relief. With Kurtz, Lime
sometimes put things on paper—if he was pressed. I showed
Martins the photostat of a note. "Can you identify that?"

"It's Harry's hand." He read it through. "I don't see anything wrong."

"No, but now read this note from Harbin to Kurtz—
which we dictated. Look at the date. This is the result."

He read them both through twice.

"You see what I mean?" If one watched a world come to
an end, a plane dive from its course, I don't suppose one
would chatter, and a world for Martins had certainly come
to an end, a world of easy friendship, hero-worship, confidence that had begun twenty years before—in a school corridor. Every memory—afternoons in the long grass, the ille-
gitimate shoots on Brickworth Common, the dreams, the
walks, every shared experience was simultaneously tainted,
like the soil of an atomized town. One could not walk there
with safety for a long while. While he sat there, looking at
his hands and saying nothing, I fetched a precious bottle of
whisky out of a cupboard and poured out two large doubles.
"Go on," I said, "drink that," and he obeyed me as though I
were his doctor. I poured him out another.

He said slowly, "Are you certain that he was the real
boss?"

"It's as far back as we have got so far."

"You see, he was always apt to jump before he looked."

I didn't contradict him, though that wasn't the impression he had before given of Lime. He was searching round for some comfort.

"Suppose," he said, "someone had got a line on him, forced him into this racket, as you forced Harbin to double-cross . . ."

"It's possible."

"And they murdered him in case he talked when he was arrested."

"It's not impossible."

"I'm glad they did," he said. "I wouldn't have liked to hear Harry squeal." He made a curious little dusting movement with his hand on his knee as much as to say, "That's that." He said, "I'll be getting back to England."

"I'd rather you didn't just yet. The Austrian police would make an issue if you tried to leave Vienna at the moment. You see, Cooler's sense of duty made him call them up too."

"I see," he said hopelessly.

"When we've found the third man . . ." I said.

"I'd like to hear *him* squeal," he said. "The bastard. The bloody bastard."

[1 1]

After he left me, Martins went straight off to drink himself silly. He chose the Oriental to do it in, the dreary smoky little night club that stood behind a sham Eastern façade. The same semi-nude photographs on the stairs, the same half-drunk Americans at the bar, the same bad wine and extra-ordinary gins—he might have been in any third-rate night haunt in any other shabby capital of a shabby Europe. At one point of the hopeless early hours the International Patrol took a look at the scene, and a Russian soldier made a bolt for the stairs at the sight of them, moving with bent averted head like a small harvest animal. The Americans never stirred and nobody interfered with them. Martins had drink after drink; he would probably have had a woman too, but the cabaret performers had all gone home, and there were practically no women left in the place, except for one beautiful shrewd-looking French journalist who made one remark to her companion and fell contemptuously asleep.

Martins moved on: at Maxim's a few couples were dancing rather gloomily, and at a place called Chez Victor the heating had failed and people sat in overcoats drinking cocktails. By this time the spots were swimming in front of Martins' eyes, and he was oppressed by a sense of loneliness. His mind reverted to the girl in Dublin, and the one in Amsterdam. That was one thing that didn't fool you—the straight drink, the simple physical act: one didn't expect fidelity from a woman. His mind revolved in circles—from sentiment to lust and back again from belief to cynicism.

The trams had stopped, and he set out obstinately on foot to find Harry's girl. He wanted to make love to her—just like that: no nonsense, no sentiment. He was in the mood for violence, and the snowy road heaved like a lake and set his mind on a new course towards sorrow, eternal love, renunciation. In the corner of a sheltering wall he was sick in the snow.

It must have been about three in the morning when he climbed the stairs to Anna's room. He was nearly sober by that time and had only one idea in his head, that she must know about Harry too. He felt that somehow this knowledge would pay the mortmain that memory levies on human beings, and he would stand a chance with Harry's girl. If you are in love yourself, it never occurs to you that the girl doesn't know: you believe you have told it plainly in a tone of voice, the touch of a hand. When Anna opened the door to him, with astonishment at the sight of him tousled on the threshold, he never imagined that she was opening the door to a stranger.

He said, "Anna, I've found out everything."

"Come in," she said, "you don't want to wake the house." She was in a dressing-gown; the divan had become a bed, the kind of tumbled bed that showed how sleepless the occupant had been.

"Now," she said, while he stood there, fumbling for words, "what is it? I thought you were going to keep away. Are the police after you?"

"No."

"You didn't really kill that man, did you?"

"Of course not."

"You're drunk, aren't you?"

"I am a bit," he said sulkily. The meeting seemed to be going on the wrong lines. He said angrily, "I'm sorry."

"Why? I would like a drink myself."

He said, "I've been with the British police. They are satisfied I didn't do it. But I've learned everything from them. Harry was in a racket—a bad racket." He said hopelessly, "He was no good at all. We were both wrong."

"You'd better tell me," Anna said. She sat down on the bed and he told her, swaying slightly beside the table where her typescript part still lay open at the first page. I imagine he told it to her pretty confusedly, dwelling chiefly on what had stuck most in his mind, the children dead with meningitis and the children in the mental ward. He stopped and they were silent. She said, "Is that all?"

"Yes."

"You were sober when they told you? They really proved it?"

"Yes." He added drearily, "So that, you see, was Harry."

"I'm glad he's dead now," she said. "I wouldn't have wanted him to rot for years in prison."

"But can you understand how Harry—your Harry, my Harry—could have got mixed up . . . ?" He said hopelessly, "I feel as though he had never really existed, that we'd dreamed him. Was he laughing at fools like us all the time?"

"He may have been. What does it matter?" she said. "Sit down. Don't worry." He had pictured himself comforting *her*—not this other way about. She said, "If he was alive now, he might be able to explain, but we've got to remember him as he was to us. There are always so many things one doesn't know about a person, even a person one loves—good things, bad things. We have to leave plenty of room for them."

"Those children———"

She said angrily, "For God's sake stop making people in *your* image. Harry was real. He wasn't just your hero and my lover. He was Harry. He was in a racket. He did bad things. What about it? He was the man we knew."

He said, "Don't talk such bloody wisdom. Don't you see that I love you?"

She looked at him in astonishment. "You?"

"Yes, me. I don't kill people with fake drugs. I'm not a hypocrite who persuades people that I'm the greatest—I'm just a bad writer who drinks too much and falls in love with girls . . ."

She said, "But I don't even know what colour your eyes are. If you'd rung me up just now and asked me whether you were dark or fair or wore a moustache, I wouldn't have known."

"Can't you get him out of your mind?"

"No."

He said, "As soon as they've cleared up this Koch murder, I'm leaving Vienna. I can't feel interested any longer in whether Kurtz killed Harry—or the third man. Whoever killed him it was a kind of justice. Maybe I'd kill him myself under these circumstances. But you still love him. You love a cheat, a murderer."

"I loved a man," she said. "I told you—a man doesn't alter because you find out more about him. He's still the same man."

"I hate the way you talk. I've got a splitting headache, and you talk and talk . . ."

"I didn't ask you to come."

"You make me cross."

Suddenly she laughed. She said, "You are so comic. You come here at three in the morning—a stranger—and say you love me. Then you get angry and pick a quarrel. What do you expect me to do—or say?"

"I haven't seen you laugh before. Do it again. I like it."

"There isn't enough for two laughs," she said.

He took her by the shoulders and shook her gently. He said, "I'd make comic faces all day long. I'd stand on my head and grin at you between my legs. I'd learn a lot of jokes from the books on after-dinner speaking."

"Come away from the window. There are no curtains."

"There's nobody to see." But automatically checking his statement, he wasn't quite so sure: a long shadow that had moved, perhaps with the movement of clouds over the moon, was motionless again. He said, "You still love Harry, don't you?"

"Yes."

"Perhaps I do. I don't know." He dropped his hands and said, "I'll be pushing off."

He walked rapidly away. He didn't bother to see whether he was being followed, to check up on the shadow. But, passing by the end of the street, he happened to turn, and there just around the corner, pressed against a wall to escape notice, was a thick stocky figure. Martins stopped and stared. There was something familiar about that figure. Perhaps, he thought, I have grown unconsciously used to him during these last twenty-four hours; perhaps he is one of those who have so assiduously checked my movements. Martins stood there, twenty yards away, staring at the silent motionless figure in the dark side street who stared back at him. A police spy, perhaps, or an agent of those other men, those men who had corrupted Harry first and then killed him—even possibly the third man?

It was not the face that was familiar, for he could not make out so much as the angle of the jaw; nor a movement, for the body was so still that he began to believe that the whole thing was an illusion caused by shadow. He called sharply, "Do you want anything?" and there was no reply. He called again with the irascibility of drink, "Answer, can't you," and an answer came, for a window curtain was drawn petulantly back by some sleeper he had awakened, and the light fell straight across the narrow street and lit up the features of Harry Lime.

[1 2]

"Do you believe in ghosts?" Martins said to me.

"Do you?"

"I do now."

"I also believe that drunk men see things—sometimes rats, sometimes worse."

He hadn't come to me at once with his story—only the danger to Anna Schmidt tossed him back into my office, like something the sea had washed up, tousled, unshaven, haunted by an experience he couldn't understand. He said, "If it had been just the face, I wouldn't have worried. I'd been thinking about Harry, and I might easily have mistaken a stranger. The light was turned off again at once, you see. I only got one glimpse, and the man made off down the street—if he was a man. There was no turning for a long way, but I was so startled I gave him another thirty yards' start. He came to one of those newspaper kiosks and for a moment moved out of sight. I ran after him. It only took me ten seconds to reach the kiosk, and he must have heard me running, but the strange thing was he never appeared again. I reached the kiosk. There wasn't anybody there. The street was empty. He couldn't have reached a doorway without my seeing him. He'd simply vanished."

"A natural thing for ghosts—or illusions."

"But I can't believe I was as drunk as all that!"

"What did you do then?"

"I had to have another drink. My nerves were all in pieces."

"Didn't that bring him back?"

"No, but it sent me back to Anna's."

I think he would have been ashamed to come to me with his absurd story if it had not been for the attempt on Anna Schmidt. My theory, when he did tell me his story, was that there had been a watcher—though it was drink and hysteria that had pasted on the man's face the features of Harry Lime. The watcher had noted his visit to Anna, and the member of the ring—the penicillin ring—had been warned by telephone. Events that night moved fast. You remember that Kurtz lived in the Russian zone—in the second bezirk to be exact, in a wide, empty, desolate street that runs down to the Prater Platz. A man like that had probably obtained his influential contacts. It was ruin for a Russian to be observed on very friendly terms with an American or an Englishman, but the Austrian was a potential ally—and in any case one doesn't fear the influence of the ruined and defeated.

You must understand that at this period co-operation between the Western Allies and the Russians had practically, though not yet completely, broken down.

The original police agreement in Vienna between the Allies confined the military police (who had to deal with crimes involving Allied personnel) to their particular zones, unless permission was given to them to enter the zone of another power. This agreement worked well enough between the three Western powers. I only had to get on the phone to my opposite number in the American or French zones before I sent in my men to make an arrest or pursue an investigation. During the first six months of the occupation it had worked reasonably well with the Russians: perhaps forty-eight hours would pass before I received permission, and in practice there are few occasions when it is necessary to work quicker than that. Even at home it is not always possible to obtain a search warrant or permission from one's superiors to detain a suspect with any greater speed. Then the forty-eight hours turned into a week or a fortnight, and I remember my American colleague suddenly taking a look at his records and discovering that there were forty cases dating back more than three months where not even an acknowledgment of his requests had been received. Then the trouble started. We began to turn down, or not to answer, the Russian requests, and sometimes without permission they would send in police, and there were clashes. . . . At the date of this story the Western powers had more or less ceased to put in applications or reply to the Russian ones. This meant that if I wanted to pick up Kurtz it would be as well to catch him outside the Russian zone, though of course it was always possible his activities would offend the Russians and his punishment be more sudden and severe than any we should inflict. Well, the Anna Schmidt case was one of the clashes: when Rollo Martins went drunkenly back at four o'clock in the morning to tell Anna that he had seen the ghost of Harry, he was told by a frightened porter who had not yet gone back to sleep that she had been taken away by the International Patrol.

What happened was this. Russia, you remember, was in the chair as far as the Inner Stadt was concerned, and when Russia was in the chair, you expected certain irregularities. On this occasion, half-way through the patrol the Russian policeman pulled a fast one on his colleagues and directed the car to the street where Anna Schmidt lived. The British military policeman that night was new to his job: he didn't realize, till his colleagues told him, that they had entered a British zone. He spoke a little German and no French, and the Frenchman, a cynical hard-bitten Parisian, gave up the attempt to explain to him. The American took on the job. "It's all right by me," he said, "but is it all right by you?" The British M.P. tapped the Russian's shoulder, who turned his Mongol face and launched a flood of incomprehensible Slav at him. The car drove on.

Outside Anna Schmidt's block the American took a hand in the game and demanded in German what it was all about. The Frenchman leaned against the bonnet and lit a stinking Caporal. France wasn't concerned, and anything that didn't concern France had no genuine importance to him. The Russian dug out a few words of German and flourished some papers. As far as they could tell, a Russian national wanted by the Russian police was living there without proper papers. They went upstairs and the Russian tried Anna's door. It was firmly bolted, but he put his shoulder to it and tore out the bolt without giving the occupant an opportunity of letting him in. Anna was in bed, though I don't suppose, after Martins' visit, that she was asleep.

There is a lot of comedy in these situations if you are not directly concerned. You need a background of central European terror, of a father who belonged to a losing side, of house searches and disappearances, before the fear outweighs the comedy. The Russian, you see, refused to leave the room while Anna dressed: the Englishman refused to remain in the room: the American wouldn't leave a girl unprotected with a Russian soldier, and the Frenchman—well, I think the Frenchman must have thought it was fun. Can't you imagine the scene? The Russian was just doing his duty and watched the girl all the time, without a flicker of sexual interest; the American stood with his back chivalrously turned, but aware, I am sure, of every movement; the Frenchman smoked his cigarette and watched with detached amusement the reflection of the girl dressing in the mirror of the wardrobe; and the Englishman stood in the passage wondering what to do next.

I don't want you to think the English policeman came too badly out of the affair. In the passage, undistracted by chivalry, he had time to think, and his thoughts led him to the telephone in the next flat. He got straight through to me at my flat and woke me out of that deepest middle sleep. That was why when Martins rang up an hour later I already knew what was exciting him; it gave him an undeserved but very useful belief in my efficiency. I never heard another crack from him about policemen or sheriffs after that night.

I must explain another point of police procedure. If the International Patrol made an arrest, they had to lodge their prisoner for twenty-four hours at the International Headquarters. During that period it would be determined which power could justifiably claim the prisoner. It was this rule that the Russians were most ready to break. Because so few of us can speak Russian and the Russian is almost debarred from explaining his point of view (try and explain your own point of view on any subject in a language you don't know well—it's not as easy as ordering a meal), we are apt to regard any breach of an agreement by the Russians as deliberate and malign. I think it quite possible that they understood this agreement as referring only to prisoners about whom there was a dispute. It's true that there was a dispute about nearly every prisoner they took, but there was no dispute in their own minds, and no one has a greater sense of self-righteousness than a Russian. Even in his confessions a Russian is self-righteous—he pours out his revelations, but he doesn't excuse himself, he needs no excuse. All this had to form the background of one's decision. I gave my instructions to Corporal Starling.

When he went back to Anna's room a dispute was raging. Anna had told the American that she had Austrian papers (which was true) and that they were quite in order (which was rather stretching the truth). The American told the Russian in bad German that they had no right to arrest an Austrian citizen. He asked Anna for her papers and when she produced them, the Russian snatched them from her hand.

"Hungarian," he said, pointing at Anna. "Hungarian," and then, flourishing the papers, "bad, bad."

The American, whose name was O'Brien, said, "Give the goil back her papers," which the Russian naturally didn't understand. The American put his hand on his gun, and Corporal Starling said gently, "Let it go, Pat."

"If those papers ain't in order we got a right to look."

"Just let it go. We'll see the papers at HQ."

"If we get to HQ. You can't trust these Russian drivers. As like as not he'll drive straight through to the second bezirk."

"We'll see," Starling said.

"The trouble about you British is you never know when to make a stand."

"Oh, well," Starling said; he had been at Dunkirk, but he knew when to be quiet.

They got back into the car with Anna, who sat in the front between the two Russians dumb with fear. After they had gone a little way the American touched the Russian on the shoulder. "Wrong way," he said. "HQ that way." The Russian chattered back in his own tongue making a conciliatory gesture, while they drove on. "It's what I said," O'Brien told Starling. "They are taking her to the Russian zone." Anna stared out with terror through the windscreen. "Don't worry, little goil," O'Brien said, "I'll fix them all right." His hand was fidgeting round his gun again. Starling said, "Look here, Pat, this is a British case. You don't have to get involved."

"You are new to this game. You don't know these bastards."

"It's not worth making an incident about."

"For Christ's sake," O'Brien said, "not worth . . . that little goil's got to have protection." American chivalry is always, it seems to me, carefully canalized—one still awaits the American saint who will kiss a leper's sores.

The driver put on his brakes suddenly: there was a road block. You see, I knew they would have to pass this military post if they did not make their way to the International HQ in the Inner City. I put my head in at the window and said to the Russian haltingly, in his own tongue, "What are you doing in the British zone?"

He grumbled that it was "orders."

"Whose orders? Let me see them." I noted the signature —it was useful information. I said, "This tells you to pick up a certain Hungarian national and war criminal who is living with faulty papers in the British zone. Let me see the papers."

He started on a long explanation, but I saw the papers

sticking in his pocket and I pulled them out. He made a grab at his gun, and I punched his face—I felt really mean at doing so, but it's the conduct they expect from an angry officer and it brought him to reason—that and seeing three British soldiers approaching his headlights. I said, "These papers look to me quite in order, but I'll investigate them and send a report of the result to your colonel. He can, of course, ask for the extradition of this lady at any time. All we want is proof of her criminal activities. I'm afraid we don't regard Hungarian in itself as Russian nationality." He giggled at me (my Russian was probably half incomprehensible) and I said to Anna, "Get out of the car." She couldn't get by the Russian, so I had to pull him out first. Then I put a packet of cigarettes in his hand, said, "Have a good smoke," waved my hand to the others, gave a sigh of relief, and that incident was closed.

[1 3]

While Martins told me how he went back to Anna's and found her gone, I did some hard thinking. I wasn't satisfied with the ghost story or the idea that the man with Harry Lime's features had been a drunken illusion. I took out two maps of Vienna and compared them. I rang up my assistant and, keeping Martins silent with a glass of whisky, asked him if he had located Harbin yet. He said no; he understood he'd left Klagenfurt a week ago to visit his family in the adjoining zone. One always wants to do everything oneself; one has to guard against blaming one's juniors. I am convinced that I would never have let Harbin out of our clutches, but then I would probably have made all kinds of mistakes that my junior would have avoided. "All right," I said. "Go on trying to get hold of him."

"I'm sorry, sir."

"Forget it. It's just one of those things."

His young enthusiastic voice—if only one could still feel that enthusiasm for a routine job; how many opportunities, flashes of insight one misses simply because a job has become just a job—tingled up the wire. "You know, sir, I can't help feeling that we ruled out the possibility of murder too easily. There are one or two points——"

"Put them on paper, Carter."

"Yes, sir. I think, sir, if you don't mind my saying so" (Carter is a very young man), "we ought to have him dug up. There's no real evidence that he died just when the others said."

"I agree, Carter. Get on to the authorities."

Martins was right. I had made a complete fool of myself, but remember that police work in an occupied city is not like police work at home. Everything is unfamiliar: the methods of one's foreign colleagues, the rules of evidence, even the procedure at inquests. I suppose I had got into the state of mind when one trusts too much to one's personal judgment. I had been immensely relieved by Lime's death. I was satisfied with the accident.

I said to Martins, "Did you look inside the newspaper kiosk or was it locked?"

"Oh, it wasn't exactly a newspaper kiosk," he said. "It was one of those solid iron kiosks you see everywhere plastered with posters."

"You'd better show me the place."

"But is Anna all right?"

"The police are watching the flat. They won't try anything else yet."

I didn't want to make a fuss in the neighbourhood with a police car, so we took trams—several trams—changing here and there, and came into the district on foot. I didn't wear my uniform, and I doubted anyway, after the failure of the attempt on Anna, whether they would risk a watcher. "This is the turning," Martins said and led me down a side street. We stopped at the kiosk. "You see, he passed behind here and simply vanished—into the ground."

"That was exactly where he did vanish to," I said.

"How do you mean?"

An ordinary passer-by would never have noticed that the

kiosk had a door, and of course it had been dark when the man disappeared. I pulled the door open and showed Martins the little curling iron staircase that disappeared into the ground. He said, "Good God, then I didn't imagine him!"

"It's one of the entrances to the main sewer."

"And anyone can go down?"

"Anyone. For some reason the Russians object to these being locked."

"How far can one go?"

"Right across Vienna. People used them in air raids; some of our prisoners hid for two years down there. Deserters have used them—and burglars. If you know your way about you can emerge again almost anywhere in the city through a manhole or a kiosk like this one. The Austrians have to have special police for patrolling these sewers." I closed the door of the kiosk again. I said, "So that's how your friend Harry disappeared."

"You really believe it was Harry?"

"The evidence points that way."

"Then whom did they bury?"

"I don't know yet, but we soon shall, because we are digging him up again. I've got a shrewd idea, though, that Koch wasn't the only inconvenient man they murdered."

Martins said, "It's a bit of a shock."

"Yes."

"What are you going to do about it?"

"I don't know. It's no good applying to the Russians, and you can bet he's hiding out now in the Russian zone. We have no line now on Kurtz, for Harbin's blown—he must have been blown or they wouldn't have staged that mock death and funeral."

"But it's odd, isn't it, that Koch didn't recognize the dead man's face from the window?"

"The window was a long way up and I expect the face had been damaged before they took the body out of the car."

He said thoughtfully, "I wish I could speak to him. You see, there's so much I simply can't believe."

"Perhaps you are the only one who could speak to him. It's risky enough, because you know too much."

"I still can't believe—I only saw the face for a moment." He said, "What shall I do?"

"He won't leave the Russian zone now. Perhaps that's why he tried to have the girl taken over—because he loves her? because he doesn't feel secure? I don't know. I do know that the only person who could persuade him to come over would be you—or her, if he still believes you are his friend. But first you've got to speak to him. I can't see the line."

"I could go and see Kurtz. I have the address."

I said, "Remember. Lime may not want you to leave the Russian zone when once you are there, and I can't protect you there."

"I want to clear the whole damned thing up," Martins said, "but I'm not going to act as a decoy. I'll talk to him. That's all."

[1 4]

Sunday had laid its false peace over Vienna; the wind had dropped and no snow had fallen for twenty-four hours. All the morning trams had been full, going out to Grinzing where the young wine was drunk and to the slopes of snow on the hills outside. Walking over the canal by the makeshift military bridge, Martins was aware of the emptiness of the afternoon: the young were out with their toboggans and their skis, and all around him was the after-dinner sleep of age. A notice-board told him that he was entering the Russian zone, but there were no signs of occupation. You saw more Russian soldiers in the Inner City than here.

Deliberately he had given Kurtz no warning of his visit. Better to find him out than a reception prepared for him. He was careful to carry with him all his papers, including the laissez-passer of the four powers that on the face of it allowed him to move freely through all the zones of Vienna. It was extraordinarily quiet over here on the other side of the canal, and a melodramatic journalist had painted a picture of silent terror; but the truth was simply the wider streets, the greater shell damage, the fewer people—and Sunday afternoon. There was nothing to fear, but all the same, in this huge empty street where all the time you heard your own feet moving, it was difficult not to look behind.

He had no difficulty in finding Kurtz's block, and when he rang the bell the door was opened quickly, as though Kurtz expected a visitor, by Kurtz himself.

"Oh," Kurtz said, "it's you, Mr. Martins," and made a perplexed motion with his hand to the back of his head. Martins had been wondering why he looked so different, and now he knew. Kurtz was not wearing the toupee, and yet his head was not bald. He had a perfectly normal head of hair cut close. He said, "It would have been better to have telephoned to me. You nearly missed me; I was going out."

"May I come in a moment?"

"Of course."

In the hall a cupboard door stood open, and Martins saw Kurtz's overcoat, his raincoat, a couple of soft hats, and, hanging sedately on a peg like a wrap, Kurtz's toupee. He said, "I'm glad to see your hair has grown," and was astonished to see, in the mirror on the cupboard door, the hatred flame and blush on Kurtz's face. When he turned Kurtz smiled at him like a conspirator and said vaguely, "It keeps the head warm."

"Whose head?" Martins asked, for it had suddenly occurred to him how useful that toupee might have been on the day of the accident. "Never mind," he went quickly on, for his errand was not with Kurtz. "I'm here to see Harry."

"Harry?"

"I want to talk to him."

"Are you mad?"

"I'm in a hurry, so let's assume that I am. Just make a

note of my madness. If you should see Harry—or his ghost— let him know that I want to talk to him. A ghost isn't afraid of a man, is it? Surely it's the other way round. I'll be waiting in the Prater by the Big Wheel for the next two hours— if you can get in touch with the dead, hurry." He added, "Remember, I was Harry's friend."

Kurtz said nothing, but somewhere, in a room off the hall, somebody cleared his throat. Martins threw open a door: he had half expected to see the dead rise yet again, but it was only Dr. Winkler who rose from a kitchen chair, in front of the kitchen stove, and bowed very stiffly and correctly with the same celluloid squeak.

"Dr. Winkle," Martins said. Dr. Winkler looked extraordinarily out of place in a kitchen. The debris of a snack lunch littered the kitchen table, and the unwashed dishes consorted very ill with Dr. Winkler's cleanness.

"Winkler," the doctor corrected him with stony patience.

Martins said to Kurtz, "Tell the doctor about my madness. He might be able to make a diagnosis. And remember the place—by the Great Wheel. Or do ghosts only rise by night?" He left the flat.

For an hour he waited, walking up and down to keep warm, inside the enclosure of the Great Wheel; the smashed Prater with its bones sticking crudely through the snow was nearly empty. One stall sold thin flat cakes like cartwheels, and the children queued with their coupons. A few courting couples would be packed together in a single car of the Wheel and revolve slowly above the city, surrounded by empty cars. As the car reached the highest point of the Wheel, the revolutions would stop for a couple of minutes and far overhead the tiny faces would press against the glass. Martins wondered who would come for him. Was there enough friendship left in Harry for him to come alone, or would a squad of police arrive? It was obvious from the raid on Anna Schmidt's flat that he had a certain pull. And then as his watch hand passed the hour, he wondered: was it all an invention of my mind? are they digging up Harry's body now in the Central Cemetery?

Somewhere behind the cake stall a man was whistling, and Martins knew the tune. He turned and waited. Was it fear or excitement that made his heart beat—or just the memories that tune ushered in, for life had always quickened when Harry came, came just as he came now, as though nothing much had happened, nobody had been lowered into a grave or found with cut throat in a basement, came with his amused deprecating take-it-or-leave-it manner—and of course one always took it.

"Harry."

"Hullo, Rollo."

Don't picture Harry Lime as a smooth scoundrel. He wasn't that. The picture I have of him in my files is an excellent one: he is caught by a street photographer with his stocky legs apart, big shoulders a little hunched, a belly that has known too much good food for too long, on his face a look of cheerful rascality, a geniality, a recognition that *his* happiness will make the world's day. Now he didn't make the mistake of putting out a hand that might have been rejected, but instead just patted Martins on the elbow and said, "How are things?"

"We've got to talk, Harry."

"Of course."

"Alone."

"We couldn't be more alone than here."

He had always known the ropes, and even in the smashed pleasure park he knew them, tipping the woman in charge of the Wheel, so that they might have a car to themselves. He said, "Lovers used to do this in the old days, but they haven't the money to spare, poor devils, now," and he looked out of the window of the swaying, rising car at the figures diminishing below with what looked like genuine commiseration.

Very slowly on one side of them the city sank; very slowly on the other the great cross-girders of the Wheel rose into sight. As the horizon slid away the Danube became visible, and the piers of the Kaiser Friedrich Brücke lifted above the houses. "Well," Harry said, "it's good to see you, Rollo."

"I was at your funeral."

"That was pretty smart of me, wasn't it?"

"Not so smart for your girl. She was there too—in tears."

"She's a good little thing," Harry said. "I'm very fond of her."

"I didn't believe the police when they told me about you."

Harry said, "I wouldn't have asked you to come if I'd known what was going to happen, but I didn't think the police were on to me."

"Were you going to cut me in on the spoils?"

"I've never kept you out of anything, old man, yet." He stood with his back to the door as the car swung upwards, and smiled back at Rollo Martins, who could remember him in just such an attitude in a secluded corner of the school quad, saying, "I've learned a way to get out at night. It's absolutely safe. You are the only one I'm letting in on it." For the first time Rollo Martins looked back through the years without admiration, as he thought: he's never grown up. Marlowe's devils wore squibs attached to their tails: evil was like Peter Pan—it carried with it the horrifying and horrible gift of eternal youth.

Martins said, "Have you ever visited the children's hospital? Have you seen any of your victims?"

Harry took a look at the toy landscape below and came away from the door. "I never feel quite safe in these things," he said. He felt the back of the door with his hand, as though he were afraid that it might fly open and launch him into that iron-ribbed space. "Victims?" he asked. "Don't be melodramatic, Rollo. Look down there," he went on, pointing through the window at the people moving like black flies at the base of the Wheel. "Would you really feel any pity if one of those dots stopped moving—for ever? If I said you can have twenty thousand pounds for every dot that stops, would you really, old man, tell me to keep my money—without hesitation? Or would you calculate how many dots you could afford to spare? Free of income tax, old man. Free of income tax." He gave his boyish conspiratorial smile. "It's the only way to save nowadays."

"Couldn't you have stuck to tyres?"

"Like Cooler? No, I've always been ambitious."

"You are finished now. The police know everything."

"But they can't catch me, Rollo, you'll see. I'll pop up again. You can't keep a good man down." The car swung to a standstill at the highest point of the curve and Harry turned his back and gazed out of the window. Martins thought: One good shove and I could break the glass, and he pictured the body falling, falling, through the iron struts, a piece of carrion dropping among the flies. He said, "You know the police are planning to dig up your body. What will they find?"

"Harbin," Harry replied with simplicity. He turned away from the window and said, "Look at the sky."

The car had reached the top of the Wheel and hung there motionless, while the stain of the sunset ran in streaks over the wrinkled papery sky beyond the black girders.

"Why did the Russians try to take Anna Schmidt?"

"She had false papers, old man."

"Who told them?"

"The price of living in this zone, Rollo, is service. I have to give them a little information now and then."

"I thought perhaps you were just trying to get her here— because she was your girl? Because you wanted her?"

Harry smiled. "I haven't all that influence."

"What would have happened to her?"

"Nothing very serious. She'd have been sent back to Hungary. There's nothing against her really. A year in a labour camp perhaps. She'd be infinitely better off in her own country than being pushed around by the British police."

"She hasn't told them anything about you."

"She's a good little thing," Harry repeated with satisfaction and pride.

"She loves you."

"Well, I gave her a good time while it lasted."

"And I love her."

"That's fine, old man. Be kind to her. She's worth it. I'm glad." He gave the impression of having arranged everything to everybody's satisfaction. "And you can help to keep her mouth shut. Not that she knows anything that matters."

"I'd like to knock you through the window."

"But you won't, old man. Our quarrels never last long. You remember that fearful one in the Monaco, when we swore we were through. I'd trust you anywhere, Rollo. Kurtz tried to persuade me not to come, but I know you. Then he tried to persuade me to, well, arrange an accident. He told me it would be quite easy in this car."

"Except that I'm the stronger man."

"But I've got the gun. You don't think a bullet wound would show when you hit *that* ground?" Again the car began to move, sailing slowly down, until the flies were midgets, were recognizable human beings. "What fools we are, Rollo, talking like this, as if I'd do that to you—or you to me." He turned his back and leaned his face against the glass. One thrust. . . . "How much do you earn a year with your Westerns, old man?"

"A thousand."

"Taxed. I earn thirty thousand free. It's the fashion. In these days, old man, nobody thinks in terms of human beings. Governments don't, so why should we? They talk of the people and the proletariat, and I talk of the mugs. It's the same thing. They have their five-year plans and so have I."

"You used to be a Catholic."

"Oh, I still *believe*, old man. In God and mercy and all that. I'm not hurting anybody's soul by what I do. The dead are happier dead. They don't miss much here, poor devils," he added with that odd touch of genuine pity, as the car reached the platform and the faces of the doomed-to-be-victims, the tired pleasure-hoping Sunday faces, peered in at them. "I could cut you in, you know. It would be useful. I have no one left in the Inner City."

"Except Cooler? And Winkler?"

"You really mustn't turn policeman, old man." They passed out of the car and he put his hand again on Martins' elbow. "That was a joke, I know you won't. Have you heard anything of old Bracer recently?"

"I had a card at Christmas."

"Those were the days, old man. Those were the days. I've got to leave you here. We'll see each other sometime. If you are in a jam, you can always get me at Kurtz's." He moved away and, turning, waved the hand he had had the tact not to offer: it was like the whole past moving off under a cloud. Martins suddenly called after him, "Don't trust me, Harry," but there was too great a distance now between them for the words to carry.

[1 5]

"Anna was at the theatre," Martins told me, "for the Sunday matinée. I had to see the whole dreary comedy through a second time. About a middle-aged composer and an infatuated girl and an understanding—a terribly understanding —wife. Anna acted very badly—she wasn't much of an actress at the best of times. I saw her afterwards in her dressing-room, but she was badly fussed. I think she thought I was going to make a serious pass at her all the time, and she didn't want a pass. I told her Harry was alive—I thought she'd be glad and that I would hate to see how glad she was, but she sat in front of her make-up mirror and let the tears streak the grease-paint and I wished afterwards that she had been glad. She looked awful and I loved her. Then I told her about my interview with Harry, but she wasn't really paying much attention because when I'd finished she said, 'I wish he was dead.'

" 'He deserves to be,' I said.

" 'I mean he would be safe then—from everybody.' "

I asked Martins, "Did you show her the photographs I gave you—of the children?"

"Yes. I thought, it's got to be kill or cure this time. She's got to get Harry out of her system. I propped the pictures up among the pots of grease. She couldn't avoid seeing them. I said, 'The police can't arrest Harry unless they get him into this zone, and we've got to help.'

"She said, 'I thought he was your friend.' I said, 'He *was* my friend.' She said, 'I'll never help you to get Harry. I don't want to see him again, I don't want to hear his voice. I don't want to be touched by him, but I won't do a thing to harm him.'

"I felt bitter—I don't know why, because after all I had done nothing for her. Even Harry had done more for her than I had. I said, 'You want him still,' as though I were accusing her of a crime. She said, 'I don't want him, but he's in me. That's a fact—not like friendship. Why, when I have a sex dream, he's always the man.' "

I prodded Martins on when he hesitated. "Yes?"

"Oh, I just got up and left her then. Now it's your turn to work on me. What do you want me to do?"

"I want to act quickly. You see, it was Harbin's body in the coffin, so we can pick up Winkler and Cooler right away. Kurtz is out of our reach for the time being, and so is the driver. We'll put in a formal request to the Russians for permission to arrest Kurtz and Lime: it makes our files tidy. If we are going to use you as our decoy, your message must go to Lime straight away—not after you've hung around in this zone for twenty-four hours. As I see it, you were brought here for a grilling almost as soon as you got back into the Inner City; you heard then from me about Harbin; you put two and two together and you go and warn Cooler. We'll let Cooler slip for the sake of the bigger game—we have no evidence he was in on the penicillin racket. He'll escape into the second bezirk to Kurtz, and Lime will know you've played the game. Three hours later you send a message that the police are after you: you are in hiding and must see him."

"He won't come."

"I'm not so sure. We'll choose our hiding place carefully —where he'll think there's a minimum of risk. It's worth trying. It would appeal to his pride and his sense of humour if he could scoop you out. And it would stop your mouth."

Martins said, "He never used to scoop me out—at school." It was obvious that he had been reviewing the past with care and coming to conclusions.

"That wasn't such serious trouble and there was no danger of your squealing."

He said, "I told Harry not to trust me, but he didn't hear."

"Do you agree?"

He had given me back the photographs of the children and they lay on my desk. I could see him take a long look at them. "Yes," he said, "I agree."

[1 6]

All the first arrangements went according to plan. We delayed arresting Winkler, who had returned from the second bezirk, until after Cooler had been warned. Martins enjoyed his short interview with Cooler. Cooler greeted him without embarrassment and with considerable patronage. "Why, Mr. Martins, it's good to see you. Sit down. I'm glad everything went off all right between you and Colonel Calloway. A very straight chap, Calloway."

"It didn't," Martins said.

"You don't bear any ill-will, I'm sure, about my letting him know about you seeing Koch. The way I figured it was this—if you were innocent you'd clear yourself right away, and if you were guilty, well, the fact that I liked you oughtn't to stand in the way. A citizen has his duties."

"Like giving false evidence at an inquest."

Cooler said, "Oh, that old story. I'm afraid you are riled

at me, Mr. Martins. Look at it this way—you as a citizen, owing allegiance——"

"The police have dug up the body. They'll be after you and Winkler. I want you to warn Harry. . . ."

"I don't understand."

"Oh, yes, you do." And it was obvious that he did. Martins left him abruptly. He wanted no more of that kindly tired humanitarian face.

It only remained then to bait the trap. After studying the map of the sewer system I came to the conclusion that a café anywhere near the main entrance of the great sewer, which was placed in what Martins had mistakenly called a newspaper kiosk, would be the most likely spot to tempt Lime. He had only to rise once again through the ground, walk fifty yards, bring Martins back with him, and sink again into the obscurity of the sewers. He had no idea that this method of evasion was known to us: he probably knew that one patrol of the sewer police ended before midnight, and the next did not start till two, and so at midnight Martins sat in the little cold café in sight of the kiosk, drinking coffee after coffee. I had lent him a revolver; I had men posted as close to the kiosk as I could, and the sewer police were ready when zero hour struck to close the manholes and start sweeping the sewers inwards from the edge of the city. But I intended, if I could, to catch him before he went underground again. It would save trouble—and risk to Martins. So there, as I say, in the café Martins sat.

The wind had risen again, but it had brought no snow; it came icily off the Danube and in the little grassy square by the café it whipped up the snow like the surf on top of a wave. There was no heating in the café, and Martins sat warming each hand in turn on a cup of ersatz coffee—innumerable cups. There was usually one of my men in the café with him, but I changed them every twenty minutes or so irregularly. More than an hour passed. Martins had long given up hope and so had I, where I waited at the end of a phone several streets away, with a party of the sewer police ready to go down if it became necessary. We were luckier than Martins because we were warm in our great boots up to the thighs and our reefer jackets. One man had a small searchlight about half as big again as a car headlight strapped to his breast, and another man carried a brace of Roman candles. The telephone rang. It was Martins. He said, "I'm perishing with cold. It's a quarter past one. Is there any point in going on with this?"

"You shouldn't telephone. You must stay in sight."

"I've drunk seven cups of this filthy coffee. My stomach won't stand much more."

"He can't delay much longer if he's coming. He won't want to run into the two o'clock patrol. Stick it another quarter of an hour, but keep away from the telephone."

Martins' voice said suddenly, "Christ, he's here! He's——" and then the telephone went dead. I said to my assistant, "Give the signal to guard all manholes," and to my sewer police, "We are going down."

What had happened was this. Martins was still on the telephone to me when Harry Lime came into the café. I don't know what he heard, if he heard anything. The mere sight of a man wanted by the police and without friends in Vienna speaking on the telephone would have been enough to warn him. He was out of the café again before Martins had put down the receiver. It was one of those rare moments when none of my men was in the café. One had just left and another was on the pavement about to come in. Harry Lime brushed by him and made for the kiosk. Martins came out of the café and saw my men. If he had called out then it would have been an easy shot, but it was not, I suppose, Lime the penicillin racketeer who was escaping down the street; it was Harry. He hesitated just long enough for Lime to put the kiosk between them; then he called out "That's him," but Lime had already gone to ground.

What a strange world unknown to most of us lies under our feet: we live above a cavernous land of waterfalls and rushing rivers, where tides ebb and flow as in the world above. If you have ever read the adventures of Allan Quatermain and the account of his voyage along the underground river to the city of Milosis, you will be able to picture the scene of Lime's last stand. The main sewer, half as wide as the Thames, rushes by under a huge arch, fed by tributary streams: these streams have fallen in waterfalls from higher levels and have been purified in their fall, so that only in these side channels is the air foul. The main stream smells sweet and fresh with a faint tang of ozone, and everywhere in the darkness is the sound of falling and rushing water. It was just past high tide when Martins and the policeman reached the river: first the curving iron staircase, then a short passage so low they had to stoop, and then the shallow edge of the water lapped at their feet. My man shone his torch along the edge of the current and said, "He's gone that way," for just as a deep stream when it shallows at the rim leaves an accumulation of debris, so the sewer left in the quiet water against the wall a scum of orange peel, old cigarette cartons, and the like, and in this scum Lime had left his trail as unmistakably as if he had walked in mud. My policeman shone his torch ahead with his left hand, and carried his gun in his right. He said to Martins, "Keep behind me, sir, the bastard may shoot."

"Then why the hell should you be in front?"

"It's my job, sir." The water came half-way up their legs as they walked; the policeman kept his torch pointing down and ahead at the disturbed trail at the sewer's edge. He said, "The silly thing is the bastard doesn't stand a chance. The manholes are all guarded and we've cordoned off the way into the Russian zone. All our chaps have to do now is to sweep inwards down the side passages from the manholes." He took a whistle out of his pocket and blew, and very far away, here and again there, came the notes of a reply. He said, "They are all down here now. The sewer police, I mean. They know this place just as I know the Tottenham Court Road. I wish my old woman could see me now," he said, lifting his torch for a moment to shine it ahead, and at that moment the shot came. The torch flew out of his hand and fell in the stream. He said, "God blast the bastard!"

"Are you hurt?"

"Scraped my hand, that's all. A week off work. Here, take this other torch, sir, while I tie my hand up. Don't shine it. He's in one of the side passages." For a long time the sound of the shot went on reverberating: when the last echo died a whistle blew ahead of them, and Martins' companion blew an answer.

Martins said, "It's an odd thing—I don't even know your name."

"Bates, sir." He gave a low laugh in the darkness. "This isn't my usual beat. Do you know the Horseshoe, sir?"

"Yes."

"And the Duke of Grafton?"

"Yes."

"Well, it takes a lot to make a world."

Martins said, "Let me come in front. I don't think he'll shoot at me, and I want to talk to him."

"I had orders to look after you, sir. Careful."

"That's all right." He edged round Bates, plunging a foot deeper in the stream as he went. When he was in front he called out, "Harry," and the name sent up an echo, "Harry, Harry, Harry!" that travelled down the stream and woke a whole chorus of whistles in the darkness. He called again, "Harry. Come out. It's no use."

A voice startlingly close made them hug the wall. "Is that you, old man?" it called. "What do you want me to do?"

"Come out. And put your hands above your head."

"I haven't a torch, old man. I can't see a thing."

"Be careful, sir," Bates said.

"Get flat against the wall. He won't shoot at me," Martins said. He called, "Harry, I'm going to shine the torch. Play fair and come out. You haven't got a chance." He flashed the torch on, and twenty feet away, at the edge of the light and the water, Harry stepped into view. "Hands above the head, Harry." Harry raised his hand and fired.

The shot ricocheted against the wall a foot from Martins' head, and he heard Bates cry out. At the same moment a searchlight from fifty yards away lit the whole channel, caught Harry in its beams, Martins, the staring eyes of Bates slumped at the water's edge with the sewage washing to his waist. An empty cigarette carton wedged into his armpit and stayed. My party had reached the scene.

Martins stood dithering there above Bates' body, with Harry Lime half-way between us. We couldn't shoot for fear of hitting Martins, and the light of the searchlight dazzled Lime. We moved slowly on, our revolvers trained for a chance, and Lime turned this way and that way like a rabbit dazzled by headlights; then suddenly he took a flying jump into the deep central rushing stream. When we turned the searchlight after him he was submerged, and the current of the sewer carried him rapidly on, past the body of Bates, out of the range of the searchlight into the dark. What makes a man, without hope, cling to a few more minutes of existence? Is it a good quality or a bad one? I have no idea.

Martins stood at the outer edge of the searchlight beam, staring downstream. He had his gun in his hand now, and he was the only one of us who could fire with safety. I thought I saw a movement and called out to him, "There. There. Shoot." He lifted his gun and fired, just as he had fired at the same command all those years ago on Brinkworth Common, fired, as he did then, inaccurately. A cry of pain came tearing back like calico down the cavern: a reproach, an entreaty. "Well done," I called and halted by Bates' body. He was dead. His eyes remained blankly open as we turned the searchlight on him; somebody stooped and dislodged the carton and threw it in the river, which whirled it on—a scrap of yellow Gold Flake: he was certainly a long way from the Tottenham Court Road.

I looked up and Martins was out of sight in the darkness. I called his name and it was lost in a confusion of echoes, in the rush and the roar of the underground river. Then I heard a third shot.

Martins told me later, "I walked downstream to find Harry, but I must have missed him in the dark. I was afraid to lift the torch: I didn't want to tempt him to shoot again. He must have been struck by my bullet just at the entrance of a side passage. Then I suppose he crawled up the passage to the foot of the iron stairs. Thirty feet above his head was the manhole, but he wouldn't have had the strength to lift it, and even if he had succeeded the police were waiting above. He must have known all that, but he was in great pain, and just as an animal creeps into the dark to die, so I suppose a man makes for the light. He wants to die at home, and the darkness is never home to *us*. He began to pull himself up the stairs, but then the pain took him and he couldn't go on. What made him whistle that absurd scrap of a tune I'd been fool enough to believe he had written himself? Was he trying to attract attention, did he want a friend with him, even the friend who had trapped him, or was he delirious and had he no purpose at all? Anyway I heard his whistle and came back along the edge of the stream, and felt the wall end and found my way up the passage where he lay. I said, 'Harry,' and the whistling stopped, just above my head. I put my hand on an iron handrail and climbed. I was still afraid he might shoot. Then, only three steps up, my foot stamped down on his hand, and he was there. I shone my torch on him: he hadn't got a gun; he must have dropped it when my bullet hit him. For a moment I thought he was dead, but then he whimpered with pain. I said, 'Harry,' and he swivelled his eyes with a great effort to my face. He was trying to speak, and I bent down to listen. 'Bloody fool,' he said—that was all. I don't know whether he meant that for himself— some sort of act of contrition, however inadequate (he was a Catholic)—or was it for me—with my thousand a year taxed and my imaginary cattle rustlers who couldn't even shoot a rabbit clean? Then he began to whimper again. I couldn't bear it any more and I put a bullet through him."

"We'll forget that bit," I said.

Martins said, "I never shall."

[1 7]

A thaw set in that night, and all over Vienna the snow melted, and the ugly ruins came to light again; steel rods hanging like stalactites, and rusty girders thrusting like bones through the grey slush. Burials were much simpler than they had been a week before when electric drills had been needed to break the frozen ground. It was almost as warm as a spring day when Harry Lime had his second funeral. I was glad to get him under earth again, but it had taken two men's deaths. The group by the grave was smaller now: Kurtz wasn't there, nor Winkler—only the girl and Rollo Martins and myself. And there weren't any tears.

After it was over the girl walked away without a word to either of us down the long avenue of trees that led to the main entrance and the tram stop, splashing through the melted snow. I said to Martins, "I've got transport. Can I give you a lift?"

"No," he said, "I'll take a tram back."

"You win, you've proved me a bloody fool."

"I haven't won," he said. "I've lost." I watched him striding off on his overgrown legs after the girl. He caught her up and they walked side by side. I don't think he said a word to her: it was like the end of a story except that before they turned out of my sight her hand was through his arm—which is how a story usually begins. He was a very bad shot and a very bad judge of character, but he had a way with Westerns (a trick of tension) and with girls (I wouldn't know what). And Crabbin? Oh, Crabbin is still arguing with the British Council about Dexter's expenses. They say they can't pass simultaneous payments in Stockholm and Vienna. Poor Crabbin. Poor all of us, when you come to think of it.

The Destructors

[1]

It was on the eve of August Bank Holiday that the latest recruit became the leader of the Wormsley Common gang. No one was surprised except Mike, but Mike at the age of nine was surprised by everything. "If you don't shut your mouth," somebody once said to him, "you'll get a frog down it." After that Mike had kept his teeth tightly clamped except when the surprise was too great.

The new recruit had been with the gang since the beginning of the summer holidays, and there were possibilities about his brooding silence that all recognized. He never wasted a word even to tell his name until that was required of him by the rules. When he said "Trevor" it was a statement of fact, not as it would have been with the others a statement of shame or defiance. Nor did anyone laugh except Mike, who finding himself without support and meeting the dark gaze of the new-comer opened his mouth and was quiet again. There was every reason why T., as he was afterwards referred to, should have been an object of mockery—there was his name (and they substituted the initial because otherwise they had no excuse not to laugh at it), the fact that his father, a former architect and present clerk, had "come down in the world" and that his mother considered herself better than the neighbours. What but an odd quality of danger, of the unpredictable, established him in the gang without any ignoble ceremony of initiation?

The gang met every morning in an impromptu car-park, the site of the last bomb of the first blitz. The leader, who was known as Blackie, claimed to have heard it fall, and no one was precise enough in his dates to point out that he would have been one year old and fast asleep on the down platform of Wormsley Common Underground Station. On one side of the car-park leant the first occupied house, number 3, of the shattered Northwood Terrace—literally leant, for it had suffered from the blast of the bomb and the side walls were supported on wooden struts. A smaller bomb and some incendiaries had fallen beyond, so that the house stuck up like a jagged tooth and carried on the further wall relics of its neighbour, a dado, the remains of a fireplace. T., whose words were almost confined to voting "Yes" or "No" to the plan of operations proposed each day by Blackie, once startled the whole gang by saying broodingly, "Wren built that house, father says."

"Who's Wren?"

"The man who built St. Paul's."

"Who cares?" Blackie said. "It's only Old Misery's."

Old Misery—whose real name was Thomas—had once been a builder and decorator. He lived alone in the crippled house, doing for himself: once a week you could see him coming back across the common with bread and vegetables, and once as the boys played in the car-park he put his head over the smashed wall of his garden and looked at them.

"Been to the loo," one of the boys said, for it was common knowledge that since the bombs fell something had gone wrong with the pipes of the house and Old Misery was too mean to spend money on the property. He could do the redecorating himself at cost price, but he had never learnt plumbing. The loo was a wooden shed at the bottom of the narrow garden with a star-shaped hole in the door: it had escaped the blast which had smashed the house next door and sucked out the window-frames of number 3.

The next time the gang became aware of Mr. Thomas was more surprising. Blackie, Mike, and a thin yellow boy, who for some reason was called by his surname Summers, met him on the common coming back from the market. Mr. Thomas stopped them. He said glumly, "You belong to the lot that play in the car-park?"

Mike was about to answer when Blackie stopped him. As the leader he had responsibilities. "Suppose we are?" he said ambiguously.

"I got some chocolates," Mr. Thomas said. "Don't like 'em myself. Here you are. Not enough to go round, I don't suppose. There never is," he added with sombre conviction. He handed over three packets of Smarties.

The gang were puzzled and perturbed by this action and tried to explain it away. "Bet someone dropped them and he picked 'em up," somebody suggested.

"Pinched 'em and then got in a bleeding funk," another thought aloud.

"It's a bribe," Summers said. "He wants us to stop bouncing balls on his wall."

"We'll show him we don't take bribes," Blackie said, and they sacrificed the whole morning to the game of bouncing that only Mike was young enough to enjoy. There was no sign from Mr. Thomas.

Next day T. astonished them all. He was late at the rendezvous, and the voting for that day's exploit took place without him. At Blackie's suggestion the gang was to disperse in pairs, take buses at random, and see how many free rides could be snatched from unwary conductors (the operation was to be carried out in pairs to avoid cheating). They were drawing lots for their companions when T. arrived.

"Where you been, T.?" Blackie asked. "You can't vote now. You know the rules."

"I've been *there*," T. said. He looked at the ground, as though he had thoughts to hide.

"Where?"

"At Old Misery's." Mike's mouth opened and then hurriedly closed again with a click. He had remembered the frog.

"At Old Misery's?" Blackie said. There was nothing in the rules against it, but he had a sensation that T. was treading on dangerous ground. He asked hopefully, "Did you break in?"

"No. I rang the bell."

"And what did you say?"

"I said I wanted to see his house."

"What did he do?"

"He showed it me."

"Pinch anything?"

"No."

"What did you do it for then?"

The gang had gathered round: it was as though an impromptu court were about to form and to try some case of deviation. T. said, "It's a beautiful house," and still watching the ground, meeting no one's eyes, he licked his lips first one way, then the other.

"What do you mean, a beautiful house?" Blackie asked with scorn.

"It's got a staircase two hundred years old like a corkscrew. Nothing holds it up."

"What do you mean, nothing holds it up. Does it float?"

"It's to do with opposite forces, Old Misery said."

"What else?"

"There's panelling."

"Like in the Blue Boar?"

"Two hundred years old."

"Is Old Misery two hundred years old?"

Mike laughed suddenly and then was quiet again. The meeting was in a serious mood. For the first time since T. had strolled into the car-park on the first day of the holidays his position was in danger. It only needed a single use of his real name and the gang would be at his heels.

"What did you do it for?" Blackie asked. He was just, he had no jealousy, he was anxious to retain T. in the gang if he could. It was the word "beautiful" that worried him—that belonged to a class world that you could still see parodied at the Wormsley Common Empire by a man wearing a top hat and a monocle, with a haw-haw accent. He was tempted to say, "My dear Trevor, old chap," and unleash his hell hounds. "If you'd broken in," he said sadly—that indeed would have been an exploit worthy of the gang.

"This was better," T. said. "I found out things." He continued to stare at his feet, not meeting anybody's eye, as though he were absorbed in some dream he was unwilling— or ashamed—to share.

"What things?"

"Old Misery's going to be away all tomorrow and Bank Holiday."

Blackie said with relief, "You mean we could break in?"

"And pinch things?" somebody asked.

Blackie said, "Nobody's going to pinch things. Breaking in—that's good enough, isn't it? We don't want any court stuff."

"I don't want to pinch anything," T. said. "I've got a better idea."

"What is it?"

T. raised eyes, as grey and disturbed as the drab August day. "We'll pull it down," he said. "We'll destroy it."

Blackie gave a single hoot of laughter and then, like Mike, fell quiet, daunted by the serious implacable gaze. "What'd the police be doing all the time?" he said.

"They'd never know. We'd do it from inside. I've found a way in." He said with a sort of intensity, "We'd be like worms, don't you see, in an apple. When we came out again there'd be nothing there, no staircase, no panels, nothing but just walls, and then we'd make the walls fall down— somehow."

"We'd go to jug," Blackie said.

"Who's to prove? And anyway we wouldn't have pinched anything." He added without the smallest flicker of glee, "There wouldn't be anything to pinch after we'd finished."

"I've never heard of going to prison for breaking things," Summers said.

"There wouldn't be time," Blackie said. "I've seen housebreakers at work."

"There are twelve of us," T. said. "We'd organize."

"None of us know how—"

"I know," T. said. He looked across at Blackie. "Have you got a better plan?"

"Today," Mike said tactlessly, "we're pinching free rides—"

"Free rides," T. said. "You can stand down, Blackie, if you'd rather. . . ."

"The gang's got to vote."

"Put it up then."

Blackie said uneasily, "It's proposed that tomorrow and Monday we destroy Old Misery's house."

"Here, here," said a fat boy called Joe.

"Who's in favour?"

T. said, "It's carried."

"How do we start?" Summers asked.

"He'll tell you," Blackie said. It was the end of his leadership. He went away to the back of the car-park and began to kick a stone, dribbling it this way and that. There was only one old Morris in the park, for few cars were left there except lorries: without an attendant there was no safety. He took a flying kick at the car and scraped a little paint off the rear mudguard. Beyond, paying no more attention to him than to a stranger, the gang had gathered round T.; Blackie was dimly aware of the fickleness of favour. He thought of going home, of never returning, of letting them all discover the hollowness of T.'s leadership, but suppose after all what T. proposed was possible—nothing like it had ever been done before. The fame of the Wormsley Common car-park gang would surely reach around London. There would be headlines in the papers. Even the grown-up gangs who ran the betting at the all-in wrestling and the barrow-boys would hear with respect of how Old Misery's house had been destroyed. Driven by the pure, simple, and altruistic ambition of fame for the gang, Blackie came back to where T. stood in the shadow of Misery's wall.

T. was giving his orders with decision: it was as though this plan had been with him all his life, pondered through the seasons, now in his fifteenth year crystallized with the pain of puberty. "You," he said to Mike, "bring some big nails, the biggest you can find, and a hammer. Anyone else who can better bring a hammer and a screwdriver. We'll need plenty of them. Chisels too. We can't have too many chisels. Can anybody bring a saw?"

"I can," Mike said.

"Not a child's saw," T. said. "A real saw."

Blackie realized he had raised his hand like any ordinary member of the gang.

"Right, you bring one, Blackie. But now there's a difficulty. We want a hacksaw."

"What's a hacksaw?" someone asked.

"You can get 'em at Woolworth's," Summers said.

The fat boy called Joe said gloomily, "I knew it would end in a collection."

"I'll get one myself," T. said. "I don't want your money. But I can't buy a sledge-hammer."

Blackie said, "They are working on number fifteen. I know where they'll leave their stuff for Bank Holiday."

"Then that's all," T. said. "We meet here at nine sharp."

"I've got to go to church," Mike said.

"Come over the wall and whistle. We'll let you in."

[2]

On Sunday morning all were punctual except Blackie, even Mike. Mike had had a stroke of luck. His mother felt ill, his father was tired after Saturday night, and he was told to go to church alone with many warnings of what would happen if he strayed. Blackie had had difficulty in smuggling out the saw, and then in finding the sledge-hammer at the back of number 15. He approached the house from a lane at the rear of the garden, for fear of the policeman's beat along the main road. The tired evergreens kept off a stormy sun: another wet Bank Holiday was being prepared over the Atlantic, beginning in swirls of dust under the trees. Blackie climbed the wall into Misery's garden.

There was no sign of anybody anywhere. The loo stood like a tomb in a neglected graveyard. The curtains were drawn. The house slept. Blackie lumbered nearer with the saw and the sledge-hammer. Perhaps after all nobody had turned up: the plan had been a wild invention: they had woken wiser. But when he came close to the back door he could hear a confusion of sound, hardly louder than a hive in swarm: a clickety-clack, a bang bang bang, a scraping, a creaking, a sudden painful crack. He thought, It's true, and whistled.

They opened the back door to him and he came in. He had at once the impression of organization, very different from the old happy-go-lucky ways under his leadership. For a while he wandered up and down stairs looking for T. Nobody addressed him: he had a sense of great urgency, and already he could begin to see the plan. The interior of the house was being carefully demolished without touching the outer walls. Summers with hammer and chisel was ripping out the skirting-boards in the ground floor dining-room: he had already smashed the panels of the door. In the same room Joe was heaving up the parquet blocks, exposing the soft wood floor-boards over the cellar. Coils of wire came out of the damaged skirting and Mike sat happily on the floor, clipping the wires.

On the curved stairs two of the gang were working hard with an inadequate child's saw on the banisters—when they saw Blackie's big saw they signalled for it wordlessly. When he next saw them a quarter of the banisters had been dropped into the hall. He found T. at last in the bathroom —he sat moodily in the least cared-for room in the house, listening to the sounds coming up from below.

"You've really done it," Blackie said with awe. "What's going to happen?"

"We've only just begun," T. said. He looked at the sledge-hammer and gave his instructions. "You stay here and break the bath and the wash-basin. Don't bother about the pipes. They come later."

Mike appeared at the door. "I've finished the wire, T.," he said.

"Good. You've just got to go wandering round now. The

kitchen's in the basement. Smash all the china and glass and bottles you can lay hold of. Don't turn on the taps—we don't want a flood—yet. Then go into all the rooms and turn out drawers. If they are locked get one of the others to break them open. Tear up any papers you find and smash all the ornaments. Better take a carving-knife with you from the kitchen. The bedroom's opposite here. Open the pillows and tear up the sheets. That's enough for the moment. And you, Blackie, when you've finished in here crack the plaster in the passage up with your sledge-hammer."

"What are you going to do?" Blackie asked.

"I'm looking for something special," T. said.

It was nearly lunch-time before Blackie had finished and went in search of T. Chaos had advanced. The kitchen was a shambles of broken glass and china. The dining-room was stripped of parquet, the skirting was up, the door had been taken off its hinges, and the destroyers had moved up a floor. Streaks of light came in through the closed shutters where they worked with the seriousness of creators—and destruction after all is a form of creation. A kind of imagination had seen this house as it had now become.

Mike said, "I've got to go home for dinner."

"Who else?" T. asked, but all the others on one excuse or another had brought provisions with them.

They squatted in the ruins of the room and swapped unwanted sandwiches. Half an hour for lunch and they were at work again. By the time Mike returned, they were on the top floor, and by six the superficial damage was completed. The doors were all off, all the skirtings raised, the furniture pillaged and ripped and smashed—no one could have slept in the house except on a bed of broken plaster. T. gave his orders—eight o'clock next morning—and to escape notice they climbed singly over the garden wall, into the car-park. Only Blackie and T. were left; the light had nearly gone, and when they touched a switch, nothing worked—Mike had done his job thoroughly.

"Did you find anything special?" Blackie asked.

T. nodded. "Come over here," he said, "and look." Out of both pockets he drew bundles of pound notes. "Old Misery's savings," he said. "Mike ripped out the mattress, but he missed them."

"What are you going to do? Share them?"

"We aren't thieves," T. said. "Nobody's going to steal anything from this house. I kept these for you and me—a celebration." He knelt down on the floor and counted them out—there were seventy in all. "We'll burn them," he said, "one by one," and taking it in turns they held a note upwards and lit the top corner, so that the flame burnt slowly towards their fingers. The grey ash floated above them and fell on their heads like age. "I'd like to see Old Misery's face when we are through," T. said.

"You hate him a lot?" Blackie asked.

"Of course I don't hate him," T. said. "There'd be no fun if I hated him." The last burning note illuminated his brooding face. "All this hate and love," he said, "it's soft, it's hooey. There's only things, Blackie," and he looked round the room crowded with the unfamiliar shadows of half things, broken things, former things. "I'll race you home, Blackie," he said.

[3]

Next morning the serious destruction started. Two were missing—Mike and another boy, whose parents were off to Southend and Brighton in spite of the slow warm drops that had begun to fall and the rumble of thunder in the estuary like the first guns of the old blitz. "We've got to hurry," T. said.

Summers was restive. "Haven't we done enough?" he said. "I've been given a bob for slot machines. This is like work."

"We've hardly started," T. said. "Why, there's all the floors left, and the stairs. We haven't taken out a single window. You voted like the others. We are going to *destroy* this house. There won't be anything left when we've finished."

They began again on the first floor picking up the top floor-boards next the outer wall, leaving the joists exposed. Then they sawed through the joists and retreated into the hall, as what was left of the floor heeled and sank. They had learnt with practice, and the second floor collapsed more easily. By the evening an odd exhilaration seized them as they looked down the great hollow of the house. They ran risks and made mistakes: when they thought of the windows it was too late to reach them. "Cor," Joe said, and dropped a penny down into the dry rubble-filled well. It cracked and span among the broken glass.

"Why did we start this?" Summers asked with astonishment; T. was already on the ground, digging at the rubble, clearing a space along the outer wall. "Turn on the taps," he said. "It's too dark for anyone to see now, and in the morning it won't matter." The water overtook them on the stairs and fell through the floorless rooms.

It was then they heard Mike's whistle at the back. "Something's wrong," Blackie said. They could hear his urgent breathing as they unlocked the door.

"The bogies?" Summers asked.

"Old Misery," Mike said. "He's on his way." He put his head between his knees and retched. "Ran all the way," he said with pride.

"But why?" T. said. "He told me. . . ." He protested with the fury of the child he had never been, "It isn't fair."

"He was down at Southend," Mike said, "and he was on the train coming back. Said it was too cold and wet." He paused and gazed at the water. "My, you've had a storm here. Is the roof leaking?"

"How long will he be?"

"Five minutes. I gave Ma the slip and ran."

"We better clear," Summers said. "We've done enough, anyway."

"Oh, no, we haven't. Anybody could do this—" "This" was the shattered hollowed house with nothing left but the walls. Yet walls could be preserved. Façades were valuable.

They could build inside again more beautifully than before. This could again be a home. He said angrily, "We've got to finish. Don't move. Let me think."

"There's no time," a boy said.

"There's got to be a way," T. said. "We couldn't have got thus far . . ."

"We've done a lot," Blackie said.

"No. No, we haven't. Somebody watch the front."

"We can't do any more."

"He may come in at the back."

"Watch the back too." T. began to plead. "Just give me a minute and I'll fix it. I swear I'll fix it." But his authority had gone with his ambiguity. He was only one of the gang. "Please," he said.

"Please," Summers mimicked him, and then suddenly struck home with the fatal name. "Run along home, Trevor."

T. stood with his back to the rubble like a boxer knocked groggy against the ropes. He had no words as his dreams shook and slid. Then Blackie acted before the gang had time to laugh, pushing Summers backward. "I'll watch the front, T.," he said, and cautiously he opened the shutters of the hall. The grey wet common stretched ahead, and the lamps gleamed in the puddles. "Someone's coming, T. No, it's not him. What's your plan, T.?"

"Tell Mike to go out to the loo and hide close beside it. When he hears me whistle he's got to count ten and start to shout."

"Shout what?"

"Oh, 'Help,' anything."

"You hear, Mike," Blackie said. He was the leader again. He took a quick look between the shutters. "He's coming, T."

"Quick, Mike. The loo. Stay here, Blackie, all of you till I yell."

"Where are you going, T.?"

"Don't worry. I'll see to this. I said I would, didn't I?"

Old Misery came limping off the common. He had mud on his shoes and he stopped to scrape them on the pavement's edge. He didn't want to soil his house, which stood jagged and dark between the bomb-sites, saved so narrowly, as he believed, from destruction. Even the fan-light had been left unbroken by the bomb's blast. Somewhere somebody whistled. Old Misery looked sharply round. He didn't trust whistles. A child was shouting: it seemed to come from his own garden. Then a boy ran into the road from the car-park. "Mr. Thomas," he called, "Mr. Thomas."

"What is it?"

"I'm terribly sorry, Mr. Thomas. One of us got taken short, and we thought you wouldn't mind, and now he can't get out."

"What do you mean, boy?"

"He's got stuck in your loo."

"He'd no business— Haven't I seen you before?"

"You showed me your house."

"So I did. So I did. That doesn't give you the right to—"

"Do hurry, Mr. Thomas. He'll suffocate."

"Nonsense. He can't suffocate. Wait till I put my bag in."

"I'll carry your bag."

"Oh, no, you don't. I carry my own."

"This way, Mr. Thomas."

"I can't get in the garden that way. I've got to go through the house.

"But you *can* get in the garden this way, Mr. Thomas. We often do."

"You often do?" He followed the boy with a scandalized fascination. "When? What right . . ."

"Do you see . . . ? The wall's low."

"I'm not going to climb walls into my own garden. It's absurd."

"This is how we do it. One foot here, one foot there, and over." The boy's face peered down, an arm shot out, and Mr. Thomas found his bag taken and deposited on the other side of the wall.

"Give me back my bag," Mr. Thomas said. From the loo a boy yelled and yelled. "I'll call the police."

"Your bag's all right, Mr. Thomas. Look. One foot there. On your right. Now just above. To your left." Mr. Thomas climbed over his own garden wall. "Here's your bag, Mr. Thomas."

"I'll have the wall built up," Mr. Thomas said. "I'll not have you boys coming over here, using my loo." He stumbled on the path, but the boy caught his elbow and supported him. "Thank you, thank you, my boy," he murmured automatically. Somebody shouted again through the dark. "I'm coming, I'm coming," Mr. Thomas called. He said to the boy beside him, "I'm not unreasonable. Been a boy myself. As long as things are done regular. I don't mind you playing round the place Saturday mornings. Sometimes I like company. Only it's got to be regular. One of you asks leave and I say Yes. Sometimes I'll say No. Won't feel like it. And you come in at the front door and out at the back. No garden walls."

"Do get him out, Mr. Thomas."

"He won't come to any harm in my loo," Mr. Thomas said, stumbling slowly down the garden. "Oh, my rheumatics," he said. "Always get 'em on Bank Holiday. I've got to go careful. There's loose stones here. Give me your hand. Do you know what my horoscope said yesterday? 'Abstain from any dealings in first half of week. Danger of serious crash.' That might be on this path," Mr. Thomas said. "They speak in parables and double meanings." He paused at the door of the loo. "What's the matter in there?" he called. There was no reply.

"Perhaps he's fainted," the boy said.

"Not in my loo. Here, you, come out," Mr. Thomas said, and giving a great jerk at the door he nearly fell on his back when it swung easily open. A hand first supported him and then pushed him hard. His head hit the opposite wall and he sat heavily down. His bag hit his feet. A hand whipped the key out of the lock and the door slammed. "Let me out," he called, and heard the key turn in the lock. "A serious crash," he thought, and felt dithery and confused and old.

A voice spoke to him softly through the star-shaped hole in the door. "Don't worry, Mr. Thomas," it said, "we won't hurt you, not if you stay quiet."

Mr. Thomas put his head between his hands and pondered. He had noticed that there was only one lorry in the car-park, and he felt certain that the driver would not come for it before the morning. Nobody could hear him from the road in front, and the lane at the back was seldom used. Anyone who passed there would be hurrying home and would not pause for what they would certainly take to be drunken cries. And if he did call "Help," who, on a lonely Bank Holiday evening, would have the courage to investigate? Mr. Thomas sat on the loo and pondered with the wisdom of age.

After a while it seemed to him that there were sounds in the silence—they were faint and came from the direction of his house. He stood up and peered through the ventilation-hole—between the cracks in one of the shutters he saw a light, not the light of a lamp, but the wavering light that a candle might give. Then he thought he heard the sound of hammering and scraping and chipping. He thought of burglars—perhaps they had employed the boy as a scout, but why should burglars engage in what sounded more and more like a stealthy form of carpentry? Mr. Thomas let out an experimental yell, but nobody answered. The noise could not even have reached his enemies.

[4]

Mike had gone home to bed, but the rest stayed. The question of leadership no longer concerned the gang. With nails, chisels, screwdrivers, anything that was sharp and penetrating they moved around the inner walls worrying at the mortar between the bricks. They started too high, and it was Blackie who hit on the damp course and realized the work could be halved if they weakened the joints immediately above. It was a long, tiring, unamusing job, but at last it was finished. The gutted house stood there balanced on a few inches of mortar between the damp course and the bricks.

There remained the most dangerous task of all, out in the open at the edge of the bomb-site. Summers was sent to watch the road for passers-by, and Mr. Thomas, sitting on the loo, heard clearly now the sound of sawing. It no longer came from his house, and that a little reassured him. He felt less concerned. Perhaps the other noises too had no significance.

A voice spoke to him through the hole. "Mr. Thomas."

"Let me out," Mr. Thomas said sternly.

"Here's a blanket," the voice said, and a long grey sausage was worked through the hole and fell in swathes over Mr. Thomas's head.

"There's nothing personal," the voice said. "We want you to be comfortable tonight."

"Tonight," Mr. Thomas repeated incredulously.

"Catch," the voice said. "Penny buns—we've buttered them, and sausage-rolls. We don't want you to starve, Mr. Thomas."

Mr. Thomas pleaded desperately. "A joke's a joke, boy. Let me out and I won't say a thing. I've got rheumatics. I got to sleep comfortable."

"You wouldn't be comfortable, not in your house, you wouldn't. Not now."

"What do you mean, boy?" but the footsteps receded. There was only the silence of night: no sound of sawing. Mr. Thomas tried one more yell, but he was daunted and rebuked by the silence—a long way off an owl hooted and made away again on its muffled flight through the soundless world.

At seven next morning the driver came to fetch his lorry. He climbed into the seat and tried to start the engine. He was vaguely aware of a voice shouting, but it didn't concern him. At last the engine responded and he backed the lorry until it touched the great wooden shore that supported Mr. Thomas's house. That way he could drive right out and down the street without reversing. The lorry moved forward, was momentarily checked as though something were pulling it from behind, and then went on to the sound of a long rumbling crash. The driver was astonished to see bricks bouncing ahead of him, while stones hit the roof of his cab. He put on his brakes. When he climbed out the whole landscape had suddenly altered. There was no house beside the car-park, only a hill of rubble. He went round and examined the back of his car for damage, and found a rope tied there that was still twisted at the other end round part of a wooden strut.

The driver again became aware of somebody shouting. It came from the wooden erection which was the nearest thing to a house in that desolation of broken brick. The driver climbed the smashed wall and unlocked the door. Mr. Thomas came out of the loo. He was wearing a grey blanket to which flakes of pastry adhered. He gave a sobbing cry. "My house," he said. "Where's my house?"

"Search me," the driver said. His eye lit on the remains of a bath and what had once been a dresser and he began to laugh. There wasn't anything left anywhere.

"How dare you laugh," Mr. Thomas said. "It was my house. My house."

"I'm sorry," the driver said, making heroic efforts, but when he remembered the sudden check to his lorry, the crash of bricks falling, he became convulsed again. One moment the house had stood there with such dignity between the bomb-sites like a man in a top hat, and then, bang, crash, there wasn't anything left—not anything. He said, "I'm sorry. I can't help it, Mr. Thomas. There's nothing personal, but you got to admit it's funny."

A Small Affair

EDITOR'S NOTE
In his preface to Brighton Rock *in the Collected Edition,
Greene writes: "Some critics have referred to a strange
violent 'seedy' region of the mind . . . which they call
Greeneland, and I have sometimes wondered whether they
go around the world blinkered. 'This is Indo-China,' I want
to exclaim, 'this is Mexico, this is Sierra Leone carefully
and accurately described. I have been a newspaper
correspondent as well as a novelist. I assure you the dead
child lay in the ditch in just that attitude. In the canal of
Phat Diem the bodies stuck out of the water. . . .' But I
know the argument is useless. They won't believe the world
they haven't noticed is like that."*

The following passage from The Quiet American *may be
taken, then, as an extract from that novel or as a sample of
Greene's journalism. It was, in fact, printed separately in*
The Listener *as a news report on the defense of Phat Diem
two years before the novel was published.*

I had to push my way through the crowd to get out, past the
lake and the white statue with its sugary outspread arms,
into the long street. I could see for nearly three-quarters of a
mile each way, and there were only two living beings in all
that length beside myself—two soldiers with camouflaged
helmets going slowly away up the edge of the street, their
sten guns at the ready. I say living because one body lay in a
doorway with its head in the road. The buzz of flies collecting there and the squelch of the soldiers' boots growing
fainter and fainter were the only sounds. I walked quickly
past the body, turning my head the other way. A few minutes later, when I looked back, I was quite alone with my
shadow and there were no sounds except the sounds I made.

I felt as though I were a mark on a firing range. It occurred to me that if something happened to me in this street it might be many hours before I was picked up: time for the flies to collect.

When I had crossed two canals, I took a turning that led to a church. A dozen men sat on the ground in the camouflage of parachutists, while two officers examined a map. Nobody paid me any attention when I joined them. One man who wore the long antennae of a walkie-talkie said, "We can move now," and everybody stood up.

I asked them in my bad French whether I could accompany them. An advantage of this war was that a European face was in itself a passport on the field: a European could not be suspected of being an enemy agent.

"Who are you?" the lieutenant asked.

"I am writing about the war," I said.

"American?"

"No, English."

He said, "It is a very small affair, but if you wish to come with us . . ." He began to take off his steel helmet.

"No, no," I said, "that is for combatants."

"As you wish."

We went out behind the church in single file, the lieutenant leading, and halted for a moment on a canal bank for the soldier with the walkie-talkie to get contact with the patrols on either flank. The mortar shells tore over us and burst out of sight. We had picked up more men behind the church and were now about thirty strong. The lieutenant explained to me in a low voice, stabbing a finger at his map, "Three hundred have been reported in this village here. Perhaps massing for tonight. We don't know. No one has found them yet."

"How far?"

"Three hundred yards."

Words came over the wireless, and we went on in silence, to the right the straight canal, to the left low scrub and fields and scrub again. "All clear," the lieutenant whispered with a reassuring wave as we started. Forty yards on, another canal, with what was left of a bridge, a single plank without rails, ran across our front. The lieutenant motioned to us to deploy, and we squatted down, facing the unknown territory ahead, thirty feet off, across the plank. The men looked at the water and then, as though by a word of command, all together, they looked away. For a moment I didn't see what they had seen, but, when I saw, my mind went back, I don't know why, to the Chalet and the female impersonators and the young soldiers whistling and Pyle saying, "This isn't a bit suitable."

The canal was full of bodies; I am reminded now of an Irish stew containing too much meat. The bodies overlapped; one head, seal-grey, and anonymous as a convict with a shaven scalp, stuck up out of the water like a buoy. There was no blood; I suppose it had flowed away a long time ago. I have no idea how many there were; they must have been caught in a cross-fire, trying to get back, and I suppose every man of us along the bank was thinking, Two can play at that game. I too took my eyes away; we didn't want to be reminded of how little we counted, how quickly, simply, and anonymously death came. Even though my reason wanted the state of death, I was afraid like a virgin of the act. I would have liked death to come with due warning, so that I could prepare myself. For what? I didn't know, nor how, except by taking a look around at the little I would be leaving.

The lieutenant sat beside the man with the walkie-talkie and stared at the ground between his feet. The instrument began to crackle instructions, and with a sigh as though he had been roused from sleep he got up. There was an odd comradeliness about all their movements, as though they were equals engaged on a task they had performed together times out of mind. Nobody waited to be told what to do. Two men made for the plank and tried to cross it, but they were unbalanced by the weight of their arms and had to sit astride and work their way across a few inches at a time. Another man had found a punt hidden in some bushes down the canal, and he worked it to where the lieutenant stood.

Six of us got in, and he began to pole it towards the other bank, but we ran on a shoal of bodies and stuck. He pushed away with his pole, sinking it into this human clay, and one body was released and floated up all its length beside the boat, like a bather lying in the sun. Then we were free again, and once on the other side we scrambled out, with no backward look. No shots had been fired; we were alive; death had withdrawn perhaps as far as the next canal. I heard somebody just behind me say with great seriousness, "Gott sei Dank." Except for the lieutenant they were most of them Germans.

Beyond was a group of farm buildings. The lieutenant went in first, hugging the wall, and we followed at six-foot intervals, in single file. Then the men, again without an order, scattered through the farm. Life had deserted it—not so much as a hen had been left behind, though hanging on the walls of what had been the living room were two hideous oleographs of the Sacred Heart and the Mother and Child which gave the whole ramshackle group of buildings a European air. One knew what these people believed even if one didn't share their belief; they were human beings, not just grey drained cadavers.

So much of war is sitting around and doing nothing, waiting for somebody else. With no guarantee of the amount of time you have left, it doesn't seem worth starting even a train of thought. Doing what they had done so often before, the sentries moved out. Anything that stirred ahead of us now was enemy. The lieutenant marked his map and reported our position over the radio. A noonday hush fell; even the mortars were quiet, and the air was empty of planes. One man doodled with a twig in the dirt of the farmyard. After a while it was as if we had been forgotten by war. I hoped that Phuong had sent my suits to the cleaners. A cold wind ruffled the straw of the yard, and a man went modestly behind a barn to relieve himself. I tried to remember whether I had paid the British consul in Hanoi for the bottle of whisky he had allowed me.

Two shots were fired to our front, and I thought, This is it. Now it comes. It was all the warning I wanted. I awaited, with a sense of exhilaration, the permanent thing.

But nothing happened. Once again I had "overprepared the event." Only long minutes afterwards one of the sentries entered and reported something to the lieutenant. I caught the phrase—"Deux civils."

The lieutenant said to me, "We will go and see," and following the sentry, we picked our way along a muddy overgrown path between two fields. Twenty yards beyond the farm buildings, in a narrow ditch, we came on what we sought: a woman and a small boy. They were very clearly dead—a small neat clot of blood on the woman's forehead, and the child might have been sleeping. He was about six years old, and he lay like an embryo in the womb with his little bony knees drawn up. "Malchance," the lieutenant said. He bent down and turned the child over. He was wearing a holy medal round his neck, and I said to myself, The juju doesn't work. There was a gnawed piece of loaf under his body. I thought, I hate war.

The lieutenant said, "Have you seen enough?" speaking savagely, almost as though I had been responsible for these deaths; perhaps to the soldier the civilian is the man who employs him to kill, who includes the guilt of murder in the pay envelope and escapes responsibility. We walked back to the farm and sat down again in silence on the straw, out of the wind, which, like an animal, seemed to know that dark was coming. The man who had doodled was relieving himself, and the man who had relieved himself was doodling. I thought how in those moments of quiet, after the sentries had been posted, they must have believed it safe to move from the ditch. I wondered whether they had lain there long—the bread had been very dry. This farm was probably their home.

The radio was working again. The lieutenant said wearily, "They are going to bomb the village. Patrols are called in for the night." We rose and began our journey back, punting again around the shoal of bodies, filing past the church. We hadn't gone very far, and yet it seemed a long enough journey to have made with the killing of those two as the only result. The planes had gone up, and behind us the bombing began.

1955   from *The Quiet American*

A Shocking Accident

[1]

Jerome was called into his housemaster's room in the break between the second and the third class on a Thursday morning. He had no fear of trouble, for he was a warden—the name that the proprietor and headmaster of a rather expensive preparatory school had chosen to give to approved, reliable boys in the lower forms (from a warden one became a guardian and finally before leaving, it was hoped for Marlborough or Rugby, a crusader). The housemaster, Mr. Wordsworth, sat behind his desk with an appearance of perplexity and apprehension. Jerome had the odd impression when he entered that he was a cause of fear.

"Sit down, Jerome," Mr. Wordsworth said. "All going well with the trigonometry?"

"Yes, sir."

"I've had a telephone call, Jerome. From your aunt. I'm afraid I have bad news for you."

"Yes, sir?"

"Your father has had an accident."

"Oh."

Mr. Wordsworth looked at him with some surprise. "A serious accident."

"Yes, sir?"

Jerome worshipped his father: the verb is exact. As man re-creates God, so Jerome re-created his father—from a restless widowed author into a mysterious adventurer who travelled in far places—Nice, Beirut, Majorca, even the Canaries. The time had arrived about his eighth birthday when Jerome believed that his father either "ran guns" or was a member of the British Secret Service. Now it occurred to him that his father might have been wounded in "a hail of machine-gun bullets."

Mr. Wordsworth played with the ruler on his desk. He seemed at a loss how to continue. He said, "You knew your father was in Naples?"

"Yes, sir."

"Your aunt heard from the hospital today."

"Oh."

Mr. Wordsworth said with desperation, "It was a street accident."

"Yes, sir?" It seemed quite likely to Jerome that they would call it a street accident. The police, of course, had fired first; his father would not take human life except as a last resort.

"I'm afraid your father was very seriously hurt indeed."

"Oh."

"In fact, Jerome, he died yesterday. Quite without pain."

"Did they shoot him through the heart?"

"I beg your pardon. What did you say, Jerome?"

"Did they shoot him through the heart?"

"Nobody shot him, Jerome. A pig fell on him." An inexplicable convulsion took place in the nerves of Mr. Wordsworth's face; it really looked for a moment as though he were going to laugh. He closed his eyes, composed his features, and said rapidly, as though it were necessary to expel the story as rapidly as possible, "Your father was walking along a street in Naples when a pig fell on him. A shocking accident. Apparently in the poorer quarters of Naples they keep pigs on their balconies. This one was on the fifth floor. It had grown too fat. The balcony broke. The pig fell on your father."

Mr. Wordsworth left his desk rapidly and went to the window, turning his back on Jerome. He shook a little with emotion.

Jerome said, "What happened to the pig?"

[2]

This was not callousness on the part of Jerome as it was interpreted by Mr. Wordsworth to his colleagues (he even discussed with them whether, perhaps, Jerome was not yet fitted to be a warden). Jerome was only attempting to visualize the strange scene and to get the details right. Nor was Jerome a boy who cried; he was a boy who brooded, and it never occurred to him at his preparatory school that the circumstances of his father's death were comic—they were still part of the mystery of life. It was later in his first term at his public school, when he told the story to his best friend, that he began to realize how it affected others. Naturally, after that disclosure he was known, rather unreasonably, as Pig.

Unfortunately his aunt had no sense of humour. There was an enlarged snap-shot of his father on the piano: a large sad man in an unsuitable dark suit posed in Capri with an umbrella (to guard him against sunstroke), the Faraglioni rocks forming the background. By the age of sixteen Jerome was well aware that the portrait looked more like the author of *Sunshine and Shade* and *Rambles in the Balearics* than an agent of the Secret Service. All the same, he loved the memory of his father: he still possessed an album filled with picture-postcards (the stamps had been soaked off long ago for his other collection), and it pained him when his aunt embarked with strangers on the story of his father's death.

"A shocking accident," she would begin, and the stranger would compose his or her features into the correct shape for interest and commiseration. Both reactions, of course, were false, but it was terrible for Jerome to see how suddenly, midway in her rambling discourse, the interest would become genuine. "I can't think how such things can be allowed in a civilized country," his aunt would say. "I suppose one has to regard Italy as civilized. One is prepared for all kinds of things abroad, of course, and my brother was a great traveller. He always carried a water-filter with him. It was far less expensive, you know, than buying all those bottles of mineral water. My brother always said that his filter paid for his dinner wine. You can see from that what a careful man he was, but who could possibly have expected when he was walking along the Via Dottore Manuele Panucci on his way to the Hydrographic Museum that a pig would fall on him?" That was the moment when the interest became genuine.

Jerome's father had not been a very distinguished writer, but the time always seems to come, after an author's death, when somebody thinks it worth his while to write a letter to *The Times Literary Supplement* announcing the preparation of a biography and asking to see any letters or documents or receive any anecdotes from friends of the dead man. Most of the biographies, of course, never appear—one wonders whether the whole thing may not be an obscure form of blackmail and whether many a potential writer of a biography or thesis finds the means in this way to finish his education at Kansas or Nottingham. Jerome, however, as a chartered accountant, lived far from the literary world. He did not realize how small the menace really was, nor that the danger period for someone of his father's obscurity had long passed. Sometimes he rehearsed the method of recounting his father's death so as to reduce the comic element to its smallest dimensions—it would be of no use to refuse information, for in that case the biographer would undoubtedly visit his aunt, who was living to a great old age with no sign of flagging.

It seemed to Jerome that there were two possible methods—the first led gently up to the accident, so well prepared that the death came really as an anticlimax. The chief danger of laughter in such a story was always surprise. When he rehearsed this method Jerome began boringly enough.

"You know Naples and those high tenement buildings? Somebody once told me that the Neapolitan always feels at home in New York just as the man from Turin feels at home in London because the river runs in much the same way in both cities. Where was I? Oh, yes, Naples, of course. You'd be surprised in the poorer quarters what things they keep on the balconies of those skyscraping tenements—not washing, you know, or bedding, but things like livestock, chickens or even pigs. Of course the pigs get no exercise whatever and fatten all the quicker." He could imagine how his hearer's eyes would have glazed by this time. "I've no idea, have you, how heavy a pig can be, but those old buildings are all badly in need of repair. A balcony on the fifth floor gave way under one of those pigs. It struck the third-floor balcony on its way down and sort of ricocheted into the street. My father was on the way to the Hydrographic Museum when the pig hit him. Coming from that height and that angle it broke his neck." This was really a masterly attempt to make an intrinsically interesting subject boring.

The other method Jerome rehearsed had the virtue of brevity.

"My father was killed by a pig."

"Really? In India?"

"No, in Italy."

"How interesting. I never realized there was pig-sticking in Italy. Was your father keen on polo?"

In course of time, neither too early nor too late, rather as though, in his capacity as a chartered accountant, Jerome had studied the statistics and taken the average, he became engaged to be married: to a pleasant fresh-faced girl of twenty-five whose father was a doctor in Pinner. Her name was Sally, her favourite author was still Hugh Walpole, and she had adored babies ever since she had been given a doll at the age of five which moved its eyes and made water. Their relationship was contented rather than exciting, as became the love affair of a chartered accountant; it would never have done if it had interfered with the figures.

One thought worried Jerome, however. Now that within a year he might himself become a father, his love for the dead man increased; he realized what affection had gone into the picture-postcards. He felt a longing to protect his memory, and uncertain whether this quiet love of his would survive if Sally were so insensitive as to laugh when she heard the story of his father's death. Inevitably she would hear it when Jerome brought her to dinner with his aunt. Several times he tried to tell her himself, as she was naturally anxious to know all she could that concerned him.

"You were very small when your father died?"

"Just nine."

"Poor little boy," she said.

"I was at school. They broke the news to me."

"Did you take it very hard?"

"I can't remember."

"You never told me how it happened."

"It was very sudden. A street accident."

"You'll never drive fast, will you, Jemmy?" (She had begun to call him "Jemmy.") It was too late then to try the second method—the one he thought of as the pig-sticking one.

They were going to marry quietly at a registry-office and have their honeymoon at Torquay. He avoided taking her to see his aunt until a week before the wedding, but then the night came, and he could not have told himself whether his apprehension was more for his father's memory or the security of his own love.

The moment came all too soon. "Is that Jemmy's father?" Sally asked, picking up the portrait of the man with the umbrella.

"Yes, dear. How did you guess?"

"He has Jemmy's eyes and brow, hasn't he?"

"Has Jerome lent you his books?"

"No."

"I will give you a set for your wedding. He wrote so tenderly about his travels. My own favourite is *Nooks and Crannies*. He would have had a great future. It made that shocking accident all the worse."

"Yes?"

How Jerome longed to leave the room and not see that loved face crinkle with irresistible amusement.

"I had so many letters from his readers after the pig fell on him." She had never been so abrupt before.

And then the miracle happened. Sally did not laugh. Sally sat with open eyes of horror while his aunt told her the story, and at the end, "How horrible," Sally said. "It makes you think, doesn't it? Happening like that. Out of a clear sky."

Jerome's heart sang with joy. It was as though she had appeased his fear forever. In the taxi going home he kissed her with more passion than he had ever shown, and she returned it. There were babies in her pale blue pupils, babies that rolled their eyes and made water.

"A week today," Jerome said, and she squeezed his hand. "Penny for your thoughts, my darling."

"I was wondering," Sally said, "what happened to the poor pig?"

"They almost certainly had it for dinner," Jerome said happily and kissed the dear child again.

1957   *May We Borrow Your Husband?*

The Signing-Up of 59200/5

EDITOR'S NOTE

Wormold, the sad clown hero of Our Man in Havana, *fails as a vacuum-cleaner salesman turned spy because he cannot take seriously the melodramatic directives he receives from*

*59200, chief Caribbean agent Hawthorne. But he has a good
fling for his money before he accepts defeat (and an O.B.E.),
and his warm whimsical character saves the novel from
being just a sparkling situation comedy.*

*The situation in question involves Hawthorne's elaborate
overtures to Wormold which eventually separate him from
his old friend Hasselbacher and entangle him in the M.I.6
web.*

For some reason that morning he had no wish to meet Dr.
Hasselbacher for his morning daiquiri. There were times
when Dr. Hasselbacher was a little too carefree, so he looked
in at Sloppy Joe's instead of at the Wonder Bar. No Havana
resident ever went to Sloppy Joe's, because it was the rendezvous of tourists, but tourists were sadly reduced nowadays in number, for the President's regime was creaking
dangerously towards its end. There had always been unpleasant doings out of sight, in the inner rooms of the Je-
fatura, which had not disturbed the tourists in the Nacional
and the Seville-Biltmore, but one tourist had recently been
killed by a stray bullet while he was taking a photograph of
a picturesque beggar under a balcony near the palace, and
the death had sounded the knell of the all-in tour "including
a trip to Varadero beach and the night-life of Havana." The
victim's Leica had been smashed as well, and that had impressed his companions more than anything with the destructive power of a bullet. Wormold had heard them talking afterwards in the bar of the Nacional. "Ripped right
through the camera," one of them said. "Five hundred dollars gone just like that."

"Was he killed at once?"

"Sure. And the lens—you could pick up bits for fifty yards
around. Look. I'm taking a piece home to show Mr. Hum-
pelnicker."

The long bar that morning was empty except for the elegant stranger at one end and a stout member of the tourist
police who was smoking a cigar at the other. The Eng-

lishman was absorbed in the sight of so many bottles and it was quite a while before he spotted Wormold. "Well I never," he said, "Mr. Wormold, isn't it?" Wormold wondered how he knew his name, for he had forgotten to give him a trade-card. "Eighteen different kinds of Scotch," the stranger said, "including Black Label. And I haven't counted the bourbons. It's a wonderful sight. Wonderful," he repeated, lowering his voice with respect. "Have you ever seen so many whiskies?"

"As a matter of fact I have. I collect miniatures and I have ninety-nine at home."

"Interesting. And what's your choice today? A Dimpled Haig?"

"Thanks, I've just ordered a daiquiri."

"Can't take those things. They relax me."

"Have you decided on a cleaner yet?" Wormold asked for the sake of conversation.

"Cleaner?"

"Vacuum cleaner. The things I sell."

"Oh, cleaner. Ha-ha. Throw away that stuff and have a Scotch."

"I never drink Scotch before the evening."

"You Southerners!"

"I don't see the connection."

"Makes the blood thin. Sun, I mean. You were born in Nice, weren't you?"

"How do you know that?"

"Oh well, one picks things up. Here and there. Talking to this chap and that. I've been meaning to have a word with you as a matter of fact."

"Well, here I am."

"I'd like it more on the quiet, you know. Chaps keep on coming in and out."

No description could have been less accurate. No one even passed the door in the hard straight sunlight outside. The officer of the tourist police had fallen contentedly asleep after propping his cigar over an ash-tray; there were no tourists at this hour to protect or to supervise. Wormold said, "If it's about a cleaner, come down to the shop."

"I'd rather not, you know. Don't want to be seen hanging about there. Bar's not a bad place after all. You run into a fellow countryman, have a get-together, what more natural?"

"I don't understand."

"Well, you know how it is."

"I don't."

"Well, wouldn't you say it was natural enough?"

Wormold gave up. He left eighty cents on the counter and said, "I must be getting back to the shop."

"Why?"

"I don't like to leave Lopez for long."

"Ah, Lopez. I want to talk to you about Lopez." Again the explanation that seemed most probable to Wormold was that the stranger was an eccentric inspector from headquarters, but surely he had reached the limit of eccentricity when he added in a low voice, "You go to the Gents and I'll follow you."

"The Gents? Why should I?"

"Because I don't know the way."

In a mad world it always seems simpler to obey. Wormold led the stranger through a door at the back, down a short passage, and indicated the toilet. "It's in there."

"After you, old man."

"But I don't need it."

"Don't be difficult," the stranger said. He put a hand on Wormold's shoulder and pushed him through the door. Inside there were two washbasins, a chair with a broken back, and the usual cabinets and pissoirs. "Take a pew, old man," the stranger said, "while I turn on a tap." But when the water ran he made no attempt to wash. "Looks more natural," he explained (the word "natural" seemed a favourite adjective of his), "if someone barges in. And of course it confuses a mike."

"A mike?"

"You're quite right to question that. Quite right. There probably wouldn't be a mike in a place like this, but it's the drill, you know, that counts. You'll find it always pays in the end to follow the drill. It's lucky they don't run to waste-plugs in Havana. We can just keep the water running."

"Please will you explain . . . ?"

"Can't be too careful even in a Gents, when I come to think of it. A chap of ours in Denmark in 1940 saw from his own window the German fleet coming down the Kattegat."

"What gut?"

"Kattegat. Of course he knew then the balloon had gone up. Started burning his papers. Put the ashes down the lav and pulled the chain. Trouble was—late frost. Pipes frozen. All the ashes floated up into the bath down below. Flat belonged to an old maiden lady—Baronin someone or other. She was just going to have a bath. Most embarrassing for our chap."

"It sounds like the Secret Service."

"It *is* the Secret Service, old man, or so the novelists call it. That's why I wanted to talk to you about your chap Lopez. Is he reliable or ought you to fire him?"

"Are you in the Secret Service?"

"If you like to put it that way."

"Why on earth should I fire Lopez? He's been with me ten years."

"We could find you a chap who knew all about vacuum cleaners. But of course—naturally—we'll leave that decision to you."

"But I'm not in your Service."

"We'll come to that in a moment, old man. Anyway we've traced Lopez—he seems clear. But your friend Hasselbacher, I'd be a bit careful of him."

"How do you know about Hasselbacher?"

"I've been around a day or two, picking things up. One has to on these occasions."

"What occasions?"

"Where was Hasselbacher born?"

"Berlin, I think."

"Sympathies East or West?"

"We never talk politics."

"Not that it matters—East or West they play the German game. Remember the Ribbentrop Pact. We won't be caught that way again."

"Hasselbacher's not a politician. He's an old doctor and he's lived here for thirty years."

"All the same, you'd be surprised. . . . But I agree with you, it would be conspicuous if you dropped him. Just play him carefully, that's all. He might even be useful if you handle him right."

"I've no intention of handling him."

"You'll find it necessary for the job."

"I don't want any job. Why do you pick on me?"

"Patriotic Englishman. Been here for years. Respected member of the European Traders' Association. We must have our man in Havana, you know. Submarines need fuel. Dictators drift together. Big ones draw in the little ones."

"Atomic submarines don't need fuel."

"Quite right, old man, quite right. But wars always start a little behind the times. Have to be prepared for conventional weapons too. Then there's economic intelligence—sugar, coffee, tobacco."

"You can find all that in the Government yearbooks."

"We don't trust them, old man. Then political intelligence. With your cleaners you've got the entrée everywhere."

"Do you expect me to analyse the fluff?"

"It may seem a joke to you, old man, but the main source of the French intelligence at the time of Dreyfus was a charwoman who collected the scraps out of the wastepaper baskets at the German Embassy."

"I don't even know your name."

"Hawthorne."

"But who are you?"

"Well, you might say I'm setting up the Caribbean network. One moment. Someone's coming. I'll wash. You slip into a closet. Mustn't be seen together."

"We *have* been seen together."

"Passing encounter. Fellow countrymen." He thrust Wormold into the compartment as he had thrust him into the lavatory—"It's the drill, you know"—and then there was silence except for the running tap. Wormold sat down. There was nothing else to do. When he was seated his legs still showed under the half door. A handle turned. Feet crossed the tiled floor towards the pissoir. Water went on running. Wormold felt an enormous bewilderment. He wondered why he had not stopped all this nonsense at the beginning. No wonder Mary had left him. He remembered one of their quarrels. "Why don't you do something, act some way, any way at all? You just stand there. . . ." At least, he thought, this time I'm not standing, I'm sitting. But in any case what could he have said? He hadn't been given time to get a word in. Minutes passed. What enormous bladders Cubans had, and how clean Hawthorne's hands must be getting by this time. The water stopped running. Presumably he was drying his hands, but Wormold remembered there were no towels. That was another problem for Hawthorne, but he would be up to it. All part of the drill. At last the feet passed towards the door. The door closed.

"Can I come out?" Wormold asked. It was like a surrender. He was under orders now.

He heard Hawthorne tiptoeing near. "Give me a few minutes to get away, old man. Do you know who that was? The policeman. A bit suspicious, eh?"

"He may have recognized my legs under the door. Do you think we ought to change trousers?"

"Wouldn't look natural," Hawthorne said, "but you are getting the idea. I'm leaving the key of my room in the basin. Fifth floor Seville-Biltmore. Just walk up. Ten tonight. Things to discuss. Money and so on. Sordid issues. Don't ask for me at the desk."

"Don't you need your key?"

"Got a pass key. I'll be seeing you."

Wormold stood up in time to see the door close behind the elegant figure and the appalling slang. The key was there in the wash basin—room 510. . . .

§

Wormold said, "Well, I'll be saying good night, Hassel-bacher. I'm late."

"The least I can do, Mr. Wormold, is to accompany you and explain how I came to delay you. I'm sure when I tell your friend of my good fortune he will understand."

"It's not necessary. It's really not necessary," Wormold said. Hawthorne, he knew, would jump to conclusions. A reasonable Hawthorne, if such existed, was bad enough, but a suspicious Hawthorne . . . his mind boggled at the thought.

He made towards the lift with Dr. Hasselbacher trailing behind. Ignoring a red signal light and a warning *Mind the Step,* Dr. Hasselbacher stumbled. "Oh dear," he said, "my ankle."

"Go home, Hasselbacher," Wormold said with despera-tion. He stepped into the lift, but Dr. Hasselbacher, putting on a turn of speed, entered too. He said, "There's no pain that money won't cure. It's a long time since I've had such a good evening."

"Sixth floor," Wormold said. "I want to be alone, Hassel-bacher."

"Why? Excuse me. I have the hiccups."

"This is a private meeting."

"A lovely woman, Mr. Wormold? You shall have some of my winnings to help you stoop to folly."

"Of course it isn't a woman. It's business, that's all."

"Private business?"

"I told you so."

"What can be so private about a vacuum cleaner, Mr. Wormold?"

"A new agency," Wormold said, and the liftman announced, "Sixth floor."

Wormold was a length ahead and his brain was clearer than Hasselbacher's. The rooms were built like prison cells round a rectangular balcony; on the ground floor two bald heads gleamed upwards like traffic globes. He limped to the corner of the balcony where the stairs were, and Dr. Hasselbacher limped after him, but Wormold was practised in limping. "Mr. Wormold," Dr. Hasselbacher called, "Mr. Wormold, I'd be happy to invest a hundred thousand of my dollars. . . ."

Wormold got to the bottom of the stairs while Dr. Hasselbacher was still manoeuvring the first step; 501 was close by. He unlocked the door. A small table lamp showed him an empty sitting-room. He closed the door very softly—Dr. Hasselbacher had not yet reached the bottom of the stairs. He stood listening and heard Dr. Hasselbacher's hop, skip, and hiccup pass the door and recede. Wormold thought, I feel like a spy, I behave like a spy. This is absurd. What am I going to say to Hasselbacher in the morning?

The bedroom door was closed and he began to move towards it. Then he stopped. Let sleeping dogs lie. If Hawthorne wanted him, let Hawthorne find him without his stir, but a curiosity about Hawthorne induced him to make a parting examination of the room.

On the writing desk were two books—identical copies of Lamb's *Tales from Shakespeare*. A memo pad—on which perhaps Hawthorne had made notes for their meeting—read, "1. Salary. 2. Expenses. 3. Transmission. 4. Charles Lamb. 5. Ink." He was just about to open the Lamb when a voice said, "Put up your hands. *Arriba los manos.*"

"*Las manos,*" Wormold corrected him. He was relieved to see that it was Hawthorne.

"Oh, it's only you," Hawthorne said.

"I'm a bit late. I'm sorry. I was out with Hasselbacher."

Hawthorne was wearing mauve silk pyjamas with a monogram *H.R.H.* on the pocket. This gave him a royal air.

He said, "I fell asleep and then I heard you moving around." It was as though he had been caught without his slang; he hadn't yet had time to put it on with his clothes. He said, "You've moved the Lamb," accusingly, as though he were in charge of a Salvation Army chapel.

"I'm sorry. I was just looking round."

"Never mind. It shows you have the right instinct."

"You seem fond of that particular book."

"One copy is for you."

"But I've read it," Wormold said, "years ago, and I don't like Lamb."

"It's not meant for reading. Have you never heard of a book code?"

"As a matter of fact—no."

"In a minute I'll show you how to work it. I keep one copy. All you have to do when you communicate with me is to indicate the page and line where you begin the coding. Of course it's not so hard to break as a machine code, but it's hard enough for the mere Hasselbachers."

"I wish you'd get Dr. Hasselbacher out of your head."

"When we have your office here properly organized, with sufficient security—a combination safe, radio, trained staff, all the gimmicks—then of course we can abandon a primitive code like this, but except for an expert cryptologist it's damned hard to break without knowing the name and edition of the book."

"Why did you choose Lamb?"

"It was the only book I could find in duplicate except *Uncle Tom's Cabin*. I was in a hurry and had to get something at the C.T.S. bookshop in Kingston before I left. Oh, there was something too called *The Lit Lamp: A Manual of Evening Devotion*, but I thought somehow it might look conspicuous on your shelves if you weren't a religious man."

"I'm not."

"I brought you some ink as well. Have you got an electric kettle?"

"Yes. Why?"

"For opening letters. We like our men to be equipped against an emergency."

"What's the ink for? I've got plenty of ink at home."

"Secret ink of course. In case you have to send anything by the ordinary mail. Your daughter has a knitting needle, I suppose?"

"She doesn't knit."

"Then you'll have to buy one. Plastic is best. Steel sometimes leaves a mark."

"Mark where?"

"On the envelopes you open."

"Why on earth should I want to open envelopes?"

"It might be necessary for you to examine Dr. Hasselbacher's mail. Of course, you'll have to find a sub-agent in the post office."

"I absolutely refuse . . ."

"Don't be difficult. I'm having traces of him sent out from London. We'll decide about his mail after we've read them. A good tip—if you run short of ink use bird shit, or am I going too fast?"

"I haven't even said I was willing . . ."

"London agrees to a hundred and fifty dollars a month, with another hundred and fifty as expenses—you'll have to justify those, of course. Payment of sub-agents, et cetera. Anything above that will have to be specially authorized."

"You are going much too fast."

"Free of income tax, you know," Hawthorne said and winked slyly. The wink somehow didn't go with the royal monogram.

"You must give me time. . . ."

"Your code number is 59200 stroke 5." He added with pride, "Of course *I* am 59200. You'll number your sub-agents 59200 stroke 5 stroke 1 and so on. Got the idea?"

"I don't see how I can possibly be of use to you."

"You are English, aren't you?" Hawthorne said briskly.

"Of course I'm English."

"And you refuse to serve your country?"

"I didn't say that. But the vacuum cleaners take up a great deal of time."

"They are an excellent cover," Hawthorne said. "Very well thought out. Your profession has quite a natural air."

"But it *is* natural."

"Now if you don't mind," Hawthorne said firmly, "we must get down to our Lamb."

1958   from *Our Man in Havana*

The Blessing

The Archbishop was a quarter of an hour late, and Weld, who was uncomfortably pressed into the crowd on the dock, below a heavy glaring sky, resented the delay. It seemed to him absurd that he was there at all. The ceremony could not possibly rate more than a couple of sticks in tomorrow's paper, insufficient to justify even his train-fare from the capital. He suspected that for some obscure reason Smiley, his chief, had wanted him out of the office for the day. Perhaps someone of importance was arriving from London. . . . Smiley had not been too pleased when Weld's story of a small pacifist demonstration had been raised to the head of a column on the principal news-page. He had made a slighting reference to the chief sub-editor of the foreign room— "He never had a sense of values."

"You never know," Smiley had said to him that morning with the sour expression which belied his name, "some of your beloved pacifists may make a protest."

"It's very improbable. Even if they do . . ."

"Try to make a story out of the ceremony itself. You have a pretty sense of irony. Or so Crowe thinks" (Crowe was the chief sub-editor). "There are no Catholics on the board—as far as I know."

But were there? Perhaps that was the point of sending him south. Perhaps Smiley was trying to blacken his reputation in London by encouraging him to take a false step.

When he arrived at the port Weld went straight to the taverna in the upper town where he could expect to find his colleagues, if anyone beside himself had troubled to come so far for so little. But he had been over-pessimistic. At least the agencies were represented by their junior men—Hughes of the AP, Collins of the United Press, Tumbril of Reuters, and of course all the natives. He saw no sign of the *Telegraph*, the *Express* or the *Mail*.

One of the natives was drinking a horrible aperitif made out of artichokes and he was in the course of being interrogated by Tumbril when Weld arrived. Tumbril was a very serious young man, but under these circumstances he had the support of Hughes, who was obviously just as unhappy at being there as Weld.

"You haven't answered Tumbril's question," Hughes said.

"Oh, heretics like you cannot be expected to understand." He uttered the word "heretics" with a smile as an Englishman might have said "bastards."

"You told me yourself," Tumbril persisted, "that you thought this was an unjust war." They spoke in English in a hazy hope that the barman might not understand.

"Well . . . perhaps . . ."

"How can you bless the weapons which are to be used in an unjust war?"

"I do not suppose it will make them more efficacious, if that is what you fear."

"Are you going to bless the canisters of poison gas?"

"There is a difference. The canisters contain only gas—not human beings."

"What earthly good . . . ?"

"No earthly good. I assure you, no earthly good."

"You are escaping with a quibble," Hughes said.

"What is a quibble?"

Collins said to Weld, "What's yours?"

"A Negroni."

"What are you here for?"

"What are *you* here for?"

"Caper thought there might possibly be a demonstration."

"Against an Archbishop? Here? Not a chance."

"That's what I said. I was going down to the sea with Martha. You know Martha?"

"Oh, yes. Yes." Martha was the plump and prehensile wife of a German correspondent who was suspected of strong Nazi sympathies. She was said to look after men's needs with a simple and indiscriminate fervour, and most men felt a strong moral duty to betray her husband.

"Why didn't you bring her with you?"

"I did. She's waiting for me at"—and he named a resort popular with pederasts, lesbians and English tourists.

"You won't have much time. These ceremonies are always late—and prayers drag on so.

"I was hoping, old man, that you'd do me a favour. Tumbril won't and Hughes—for reasons of his own which I can only surmise—can't. I thought perhaps you'd telephone to me when it's all over at the Grand Hotel—I mean only if something unexpected occurs. I've seen so many of these affairs. I've got this one all written up—I just need an insurance, that's all."

"Very well. I'll ring you between five and six. It's going to be bloody hot."

"They'll have rigged up something over the tribune."

"I'm not going on any tribune. The only chance of a story will be in the crowd."

"What an optimist you are, Weld."

"I said the only chance. What's yours?"

"Campari soda. Cigarette?"

"Thanks." Weld took the cigarette, the tenth of the day, handling it like an enemy. He knew that later in the afternoon his smoker's cough would inevitably begin, rasping the dry throat, keeping him awake all the short night before the sun struck through the shutters at five. He had promised himself not to smoke till the ceremony was over, but the Negroni had weakened his resistance.

"What about the men they are going to kill? Will the blessing help *them?*" Hughes returned to the attack.

"The 'unarmed savages' you are always writing about?"

"Not me, old man. If you work for an agency you can't afford fancy words. What's good for the *Express* is poison for the *Mail*. We give them the so-called facts and leave the irony and the indignation to men like Weld here."

Two hours later Weld stood on the dock in a crowd that smelt of garlic and sweat-soaked cloth. He was a tall man and he could see easily, in spite of the police who were ranked shoulder to shoulder in front of them. There was no tribune, and, when the moment came, very little ceremony. In the space between the troopship and the crowd, tanks were lined up. Sullied with camouflage, they looked secondhand, like old cars on a city parking-lot waiting for a buyer or the scrap-heap. The crews lounged a little apart as though disowning them. A child screamed persistently close to Weld and was finally given the breast. Only the flags on the troopship, the strident posters on the walls of the customs indicated that at least someone had an enthusiasm for the war blundering on beyond the sun-polished horizon. The crowd had none. It seemed to Weld that they had come here like himself in case something happened. There was a general tone of black because of the number of women, so that he had the sense of forming part of a nation in mourning rather than of a nation under arms.

He was looking the other way at the houses beyond the railway, where the bright bed-covers hung from the windows in place of flags, when someone gave an order, and, as he turned, the crews snapped to attention beside their machines, and a little old man in a black cassock with a crimson silk edging shuffled slowly down their ranks. He wore a stole over his shoulders and violet stockings, and he picked his way in silver-buckled shoes. The lace on his cotta looked old like himself. A young priest towered over him from be-

hind carrying a purple biretta. There was a small flurry of
priests, and in the dazzling day they seemed to scatter like
feathers; Weld had the impression of a pigeon being
plucked, a small plump pigeon. The crowd was cheering
now—so it wasn't, after all, a funeral. As the Archbishop
came to each tank he paused, and a priest thrust a great
prayer-book in front of him from which he read, bending
very close to the page as though his old eyes could see no
more than an inch or two ahead. Then another priest put a
censer into his hand and he swung it to and fro, and whatever breeze there was from the sea sent the blue smoke back
towards the crowd, so that for a moment the sweet smell dis-
persed the sweat and the garlic.

"Ah mother of God, sweet mother of God," said the man
who stood by Weld, and Weld saw that he was weeping. It
shocked him. He had never been quite so close before to superstition. The man's face was wrinkled like a windfall
apple which has lain too long upon the ground. "The good
old man, the good old man," he kept on repeating. "Ah, the
saint of God." He spoke in the accent of the country, not of
the port. Weld was irritated by the man's piety, by his simplicity, or perhaps by the great heat of the day.

"So this is a holy war," he said scornfully.

The old man looked at him with surprise. "It is a cursed
war," he said. "Two men in my village will never come
home. Why should we fight over there? The devil makes
wars, not God."

"Then why not let the devil bless the tanks?"

"The devil does not bless. He does not know how to
bless."

"You are against the war," Weld said, "and yet you see
nothing wrong in an archbishop blessing tanks?"

"Why should he not bless the tanks?" the old man asked.
The Archbishop passed on, and the old man clapped and
yelled, "A saint. A saint," gleefully now as though he and
the Archbishop were sharing a joke together. Some children
were flinging crackers over the heads of the police, the cere-

mony was nearly over, and there had been no demonstration. The holy mutter passed out of hearing, while the smell of incense faded.

Weld said to the old man, speaking very simply because his command of the language was weak, "I do not understand. You say this is a cursed war. Those tanks are going to kill men with spears and old rifles who are defending their country. How can your holy Archbishop bless these instruments of evil?"

"I don't like them myself," the old man said, "ugly dangerous things—but then, if you have the desire to bless, you bless."

"I do not understand."

"I do a lot of blessing myself," the old man said. "It's when you want to love and you can't manage it. You stretch out your hands and you say God forgive me that I can't love but bless this thing anyway. I had a spade, the handle was always coming loose, and I cut my foot with it, so I blessed it—I had to bless it or break it—and I couldn't afford to break it. A woman comes to me every week complaining of my dog. She wants it gelded, poor woman. I can't do that, it's against nature, she calls me all kinds of names, I hold out my hand—the next thing you know I'm blessing her, poor thing, because I can't love her."

Weld could not follow. It was as though he had found himself in a very simple landscape, yet one where every path led into a maze from which there was no visible exit.

"But the Archbishop," he said, "dressed up like that, the incense, the prayers. . . ." He said, "All the world knows you have been using mustard gas. . . ." He broke off; it was an absurd accusation to bring against one peasant. "And these tanks . . ."

"Ugly dangerous things," the old man repeated. "They don't even shine like a new plough does. They look as though they had spotted fever. Perhaps the Archbishop hates them—I wouldn't be surprised. We have to bless what we hate. I remember hating once—it was a great grey rat and it killed my pullets. I had it cornered at last, so I put out my hands, and I blessed it. It died after that, run over by the priest's car. Maybe these tanks will die too and the poor souls in them. I've never known a blessing save a life. But then, if you want to bless, you bless. It would be better to love, but that's not always possible."

It was after five before Weld got back to the taverna in the upper town. He telephoned to Collins at the Grand Hotel. Collins replied petulantly—perhaps the afternoon had not gone as well as he had hoped, perhaps Weld had interrupted something, he thought he heard a woman's laugh. Collins said, "I only asked you to telephone if something interesting happened."

"Nothing happened."

"Well, all right, good-bye then," and he rang off without a word of thanks.

Hughes and Tumbril came into the bar while Weld was telephoning, and so the ritual of paying for rounds of whisky began. Weld found that he had lost his packet of cigarettes. It had probably been stolen from him in the crowd. "A packet of Players," he said to the barman. The grime of the long hot afternoon had dried his throat. A cigarette would not help, it would only start his cough again, and he hesitated a moment with his hand raised before he took the packet; perhaps he could wait a little longer—say, until the third round.

"Look at Weld," Hughes said to Tumbril. "He's blessing the cigarettes."

"I bless the whisky," Tumbril said, passing his hand over the glass. "Sweet product of the fields. Sweet golden grain. I love you as dearly as the Archbishop loves his dear old tanks."

"You don't bless what you love," Weld said.

"What about your cigarettes then?"

"They are my enemy. They'll kill me in the end." He couldn't wait any longer. He lit one and almost immediately he began to cough. "I've never known a blessing save a life," he said. The sentence sounded like a familiar quotation.

Cheap in August

[1]

It was cheap in August: the essential sun, the coral reefs, the bamboo bar and the calypsos—they were all of them at cut prices, like the slightly soiled slips in a bargain sale. Groups arrived periodically from Philadelphia in the manner of school-treats and departed with less *bruit,* after an exact exhausting week, when the picnic was over. Perhaps for twenty-four hours the swimming-pool and the bar were almost deserted, and then another school-treat would arrive, this time from St. Louis. Everyone knew everyone else; they had bussed together to an airport, they had flown together, together they had faced an alien customs; they would separate during the day and greet each other noisily and happily after dark, exchanging impressions of "shooting the rapids," the botanic gardens, the Spanish fort. "We are doing that tomorrow."

Mary Watson wrote to her husband in Europe, "I had to get away for a bit and it's so cheap in August." They had been married ten years and they had only been separated three times. He wrote to her every day and the letters arrived twice a week in little bundles. She arranged them like newspapers by the date and read them in the correct order. They were tender and precise; what with his research, with preparing lectures and writing letters he had little time to *see* Europe—he insisted on calling it "your Europe" as though to assure her that he had not forgotten the sacrifice which she must have made by marrying an American professor from New England, but sometimes little criticisms of "her Europe" escaped him—the food was too rich, cigarettes too expensive, wine too often served, and milk very difficult to obtain at lunch-time—which might indicate that, after all, she ought not to exaggerate her sacrifice. Perhaps it would have been a good thing if James Thomson, who was his special study at the moment, had written *The Seasons* in America—an American autumn, she had to admit, was more beautiful than an English one.

Mary Watson wrote to him every other day, but sometimes a postcard only, and she was apt to forget if she had repeated the postcard. She wrote in the shade of the bamboo bar, where she could see everyone who passed on the way to the swimming-pool. She wrote truthfully, "It's so cheap in August; the hotel is not half full, and the heat and the humidity are very tiring. But, of course, it's a change." She had no wish to appear extravagant; the salary, which to her European eyes had seemed astronomically large for a professor of literature, had long dwindled to its proper proportions, relative to the price of steaks and salads—she must justify with a little enthusiasm the money she was spending in his absence. So she wrote also about the flowers in the botanic gardens—she had ventured that far on one occasion—and with less truth of the beneficial changes wrought by the sun and the lazy life on her friend Margaret who from "her England" had written and demanded her company: a Margaret, she admitted frankly to herself, who was not visible to any eye but the eye of faith. But then Charlie had complete faith. Even good qualities become with the erosion of time a reproach. After ten years of being happily married, she thought, one undervalues security and tranquillity.

She read Charlie's letters with great attention. She longed to find in them one ambiguity, one evasion, one time-gap which he had ill explained. Even an unusually strong expression of love would have pleased her, for its strength might have been there to counterweigh a sense of guilt. But she couldn't deceive herself that there was any sense of guilt in Charlie's facile flowing informative script. She calculated that if he had been one of the poets he was now so closely studying, he would have completed already a standard-sized epic during his first two months in "her Europe," and the letters, after all, were only a spare-time occupation. They filled up the vacant hours, and certainly they could have left no room for any other occupation. "It is ten o'clock at night, it is raining outside and the temperature is rather cool for August, not above fifty-six degrees. When I have said good night to you, dear one, I shall go happily to bed with the thought of you. I have a long day tomorrow at the museum and dinner in the evening with the Henry Wilkinsons who are passing through on their way from Athens—you remember the Henry Wilkinsons, don't you?" (Didn't she just?) She had wondered whether, when Charlie returned, she might perhaps detect some small unfamiliar note in his love-making which would indicate that a stranger had passed that way. Now she disbelieved in the possibility, and anyway the evidence would arrive too late—it was no good to her now that she might be justified later. She wanted her justification immediately, a justification not—alas!—for any act that she had committed but only for an intention, for the intention of betraying Charlie, of having, like so many of her friends, a holiday affair (the idea had come to her immediately the dean's wife had said, "It's so cheap in Jamaica in August").

The trouble was that, after three weeks of calypsos in the humid evening, the rum punches (for which she could no longer disguise from herself a repugnance), the warm martinis, the interminable red snappers, and tomatoes with everything, there had been no affair, not even the hint of one. She had discovered with disappointment the essential morality of a holiday resort in the cheap season; there were no opportunities for infidelity, only for writing postcards—with great brilliant blue skies and seas—to Charlie. Once a woman from St. Louis had taken too-obvious pity on her, when she sat alone in the bar writing postcards, and invited her to join their party, which was about to visit the botanic gardens— "We are an awfully jolly bunch," she had said with a big turnip smile. Mary exaggerated her English accent to repel her better and said that she didn't much care for flowers. It had shocked the woman as deeply as if she had said she did not care for television. From the motion of the heads at the other end of the bar, the agitated clinking of the Coca-Cola glasses, she could tell that her words were being repeated from one to another. Afterwards, until the jolly bunch had taken the airport limousine on the way back to St. Louis, she was aware of averted heads. She was English, she had taken a superior attitude to flowers, and as she preferred even warm martinis to Coca-Cola, she was probably in their eyes an alcoholic.

It was a feature common to most of these jolly bunches that they contained no male attachment, and perhaps that was why the attempt to look attractive was completely abandoned. Huge buttocks were exposed in their full horror in tight large-patterned Bermuda shorts. Heads were bound in scarves to cover rollers which were not removed even by lunch-time—they stuck out like small mole-hills. Daily she watched the bums lurch by like hippos on the way to the water. Only in the evening would the women change from the monstrous shorts into monstrous cotton frocks, covered with mauve or scarlet flowers, in order to take dinner on the terrace, where formality was demanded in the book of rules, and the few men who appeared were forced to wear jackets and ties though the thermometer stood at close on eighty degrees after sunset. The market in femininity being such, how could one hope to see any male foragers? Only old and broken husbands were sometimes to be seen towed towards an Issa store advertising free-port prices.

She had been encouraged during the first week by the sight of three young men with crew-cuts who went past the bar towards the swimming-pool wearing male bikinis. They were far too young for her, but in her present mood she would have welcomed altruistically the sight of another's romance. Romance is said to be contagious, and if in the candle-lit evenings the "informal" coffee tavern had contained a few young amorous couples, who could say what men of maturer years might not eventually arrive to catch the infection? But her hopes dwindled. The young men came and went without a glance at the Bermuda shorts or the pinned hair. Why should they stay? They were certainly more beautiful than any girl there and they knew it.

By nine o'clock most evenings Mary Watson was on her way to bed. A few evenings of calypsos, of quaint false impromptus, and the hideous jangle of rattles had been enough. Outside the closed windows of the hotel-annexe the boxes of the air-conditioners made a continuous rumble in the starry palmy night like over-fed hotel guests. Her room was full of dried air which bore no more resemblance to fresh air than the dried figs to the newly picked fruit. When she looked in the glass to brush her hair she often regretted her lack of charity to the jolly bunch from St. Louis. It was true she did not wear Bermuda shorts nor coil her hair in rollers, but her hair was streaky none the less with heat and the mirror reflected more plainly than it seemed to do at home her thirty-nine years. If she had not paid an advance for a four-weeks *pension* on her individual round-trip tour, with tickets exchangeable for a variety of excursions, she would have turned tail and returned to the campus. Next year, she thought, when I am forty, I must feel grateful that I have preserved the love of a good man.

She was a woman given to self-analysis, and perhaps because it is a great deal easier to direct questions to a particular face rather than to a void (one has the right to expect some kind of a response even from eyes one sees many times a day in a compact), she posed the questions to herself with a belligerent direct stare into the looking-glass. She was an honest woman, and for that reason the questions were all the cruder. She would say to herself: I have slept with no one other than Charlie (she wouldn't admit as sexual experiences the small exciting halfway points that she reached before marriage); why am I now seeking to find a strange body, which will probably give me less pleasure than the body I already know? It had been more than a month before Charlie brought her real pleasure. Pleasure, she learnt, grew with habit, so that if it were not really pleasure that she looked for, what was it? The answer could be only the unfamiliar. She had friends, even on the respectable campus, who had admitted to her, in the frank admirable American way, their adventures. These had usually been in Europe—a momentary marital absence had given the opportunity for a momentary excitement, and then with what a sigh of relief they had found themselves safely at home. All the same they felt afterwards that they had enlarged their experience; they understood something that their husbands did not really understand—the real character of a Frenchman, an Italian, even—there were such cases—of an Englishman.

Mary Watson was painfully aware, as an Englishwoman, that her experience was confined to one American. They all, on the campus, believed her to be European, but all she knew was confined to one man and he was a citizen of Boston who had no curiosity for the great Western regions. In a sense she was more American by choice than he was by birth. Perhaps she was less European even than the wife of the Professor of Romance Languages, who had confided to her that once—overwhelmingly—in Antibes . . . it had happened only once because the sabbatical year was over . . . her husband was up in Paris checking manuscripts before they flew home. . . .

Had she herself, Mary Watson sometimes wondered, been just such a European adventure which Charlie mistakenly had domesticated? (She couldn't pretend to be a tigress in a cage, but they kept smaller creatures in cages, white mice, love-birds). And to be fair Charlie too was her adventure, her American adventure, the kind of man whom at twenty-seven she had not before encountered in frowsy London. Henry James had described the type, and at that moment in her history she had been reading a great deal of Henry James: "A man of intellect whose body was not much to him and its senses and appetites not importunate." All the same, for a while she had made the appetites importunate.

That was her private conquest of the American continent,

and when the Professor's wife had spoken of the dancer of Antibes (no, that was a Roman inscription—the man had been a *marchand de vin*) she had thought: the lover I know and admire is American and I am proud of it. But afterwards came the thought: American or New England? Yet to know a country must one know every region sexually?

It was absurd at thirty-nine not to be content. She had her man. The book on James Thomson would be published by the University Press, and Charlie had the intention afterwards of making a revolutionary break from the romantic poetry of the eighteenth century into a study of the American image in European literature—it was to be called *The Double Reflection*; the effect of Fenimore Cooper on the European scene: the image of America presented by Mrs. Trollope—the details were not yet worked out. The study might possibly end with the first arrival of Dylan Thomas on the shores of America—at the Cunard quay or at Idlewild? That was a point for later research. She examined herself again closely in the glass—the new decade of the forties stared frankly back at her—an Englander who had become a New Englander. After all, she hadn't travelled very far— Kent to Connecticut. This was not just the physical restlessness of middle age, she argued; it was the universal desire to see a little bit further, before one surrendered to old age and the blank certitude of death.

[2]

Next day she picked up her courage and went as far as the swimming-pool. A strong wind blew and whipped up the waves in the almost land-girt harbour—the hurricane season would soon be here. All the world creaked around her: the wooden struts of the shabby harbour, the jalousies of the small hopeless houses which looked as though they had been knocked together from a make-it-yourself kit, the branches of the palms—a long, weary, worn-out creaking. Even the water of the swimming-pool imitated in miniature the waves of the harbour.

She was glad that she was alone in the swimming-pool, at least for all practical purposes alone, for the old man splashing water over himself, like an elephant, in the shallow end hardly counted. He was a solitary elephant and not one of the hippo band. They would have called her with merry cries to join them—and it's difficult to be stand-offish in a swimming-pool, which is common to all as a table is not. They might even in their resentment have ducked her—pretending like school children that it was all a merry game; there was nothing she put beyond those thick thighs, whether they were encased in bikinis or Bermuda shorts. As she floated in the pool her ears were alert for their approach. At the first sound she would get well away from the water, but today they were probably making an excursion to Tower Isle on the other side of the island, or had they done that yesterday? Only the old man watched her, pouring water over his head to keep away sun-stroke. She was safely alone, which was the next best thing to the adventure she had come here to find. All the same, as she sat on the rim of the pool and let the sun and wind dry her, she realized the extent of her solitude. She had spoken to no one but black waiters and Syrian receptionists for more than two weeks. Soon, she thought, I shall even begin to miss Charlie—it would be an ignoble finish to what she had intended to be an adventure.

A voice from the water said to her, "My name's Hickslaughter—Henry Hickslaughter." She couldn't have sworn to the name in court, but that was how it had sounded at the time, and he never repeated it. She looked down at a polished mahogany crown surrounded by white hair; perhaps he resembled Neptune more than an elephant. Neptune was always outsize, and, as he had pulled himself a little out of the water to speak, she could see the rolls of fat folding over the blue bathing-slip, with tough hair lying like weeds along the ditches. She replied with amusement, "My name is Watson. Mary Watson."

"You're English?"

"My husband's American," she said in extenuation.

"I haven't seen him around, have I?"

"He's in England," she said with a small sigh, for the geographical and national situation seemed too complicated for casual explanation.

"You like it here?" he asked and lifting a hand-cup of water he distributed it over his bald head.

"So-so."

"Got the time on you?"

She looked in her bag and told him, "Eleven-fifteen."

"I've had my half-hour," he said and trod heavily away towards the ladder at the shallow end.

An hour later, staring at her lukewarm martini with its great green unappetizing olive, she saw him looming down at her from the other end of the bamboo bar. He wore an ordinary shirt open at the neck and a brown leather belt; his type of shoes in her childhood had been known as co-respondent, but one seldom saw them today. She wondered what Charlie would think of her pick-up; unquestionably she had landed him, rather as an angler struggling with a heavy catch finds that he has hooked nothing better than an old boot. She was no angler; she didn't know whether a boot would put an ordinary hook out of action altogether, but she knew that *her* hook could be irremediably damaged. No one would approach her if she were in his company. She drained the martini in one gulp and even attacked the olive so as to have no excuse to linger in the bar.

"Would you do me the honour," Mr. Hickslaughter asked, "of having a drink with me?" His manner was completely changed; on dry land he seemed unsure of himself and spoke with an old-fashioned propriety.

"I'm afraid I've only just finished one. I have to be off." Inside the gross form she thought she saw a tousled child with disappointed eyes. "I'm having lunch early today." She got up and added rather stupidly, for the bar was quite empty, "You can have my table."

"I don't need a drink that much," he said solemnly. "I was just after company." She knew that he was watching her as she moved to the adjoining coffee tavern, and she thought with guilt, At least I've got the old boot off the hook. She refused the shrimp cocktail with tomato ketchup and fell back as was usual with her on a grapefruit, with grilled trout to follow. "Please no tomato with the trout," she implored, but the black waiter obviously didn't understand her. While she waited she began with amusement to picture a scene between Charlie and Mr. Hickslaughter, who happened for the purpose of her story to be crossing the campus. "This is Henry Hickslaughter, Charlie. We used to go bathing together when I was in Jamaica." Charlie, who always wore English clothes, was very tall, very thin, very concave. It was a satisfaction to know that he would never lose his figure—his nerves would see to that, and his extreme sensibility. He hated anything gross; there was no grossness in *The Seasons*, not even in the lines on spring.

She heard slow footsteps coming up behind her and nearly panicked. "May I share your table?" Mr. Hickslaughter asked. He had recovered his terrestrial politeness, but only so far as speech was concerned, for he sat firmly down without waiting for her reply. The chair was too small for him; his thighs overlapped like a double mattress on a single bed. He began to study the menu.

"They copy American food; it's worse than the reality," Mary Watson said.

"You don't like American food?"

"Tomatoes even with the trout!"

"Tomatoes? Oh, you mean tomatoes," he said, correcting her accent. "I'm fond of tomatoes myself."

"And fresh pineapple in the salad."

"There's a lot of vitamins in fresh pineapple." Almost as if he wished to emphasize their disagreement, he ordered shrimp cocktail, grilled trout, and a sweet salad. Of course, when her trout arrived, the tomatoes were there. "You can have mine if you want to," she said, and he accepted with pleasure. "You are very kind. You are really very kind." He held out his plate like Oliver Twist.

She began to feel oddly at ease with the old man. She would have been less at ease, she was certain, with a possible adventure: she would have been wondering about her effect on him, while now she could be sure that she gave him pleasure—with the tomatoes. He was perhaps less the old anonymous boot than an old shoe comfortable to wear. And curiously enough, in spite of his first approach and in spite of his correcting her over the pronunciation of tomatoes, it was not really an old American shoe of which she was reminded. Charlie wore English clothes over his English figure, he studied English eighteenth-century literature, his book would be published in England by the Cambridge University Press, who would buy sheets, but she had the impression that he was far more fashioned as an American shoe than Hickslaughter. Even Charlie, whose manners were perfect, if they had met for the first time today at the swimming-pool, would have interrogated her more closely. Interrogation had always seemed to her a principal part of American social life—an inheritance perhaps from the Indian smoke-fires. "Where are you from? Do you know the So-and-so's? Have you been to the botanic gardens?" It came over her that Mr. Hickslaughter, if that were really his name, was perhaps an American reject—not necessarily more flawed than the pottery rejects of famous firms you find in bargain-basements.

She found herself questioning *him*, with circumlocutions, while he savoured the tomatoes. "I was born in London. I couldn't have been born more than four hundred miles from there without drowning, could I? But you belong to a continent thousands of miles wide and long. Where were you born?" (She remembered a character in a Western movie directed by John Ford who asked, "Where do you hail from, stranger?" The question was more frankly put than hers.)

He said, "St. Louis."

"Oh, then there are lots of your people here—you are not alone." She felt a slight disappointment that he might belong to the jolly bunch.

"I'm alone," he said. "Room sixty-three." It was in her own corridor on the third floor of the annexe. He spoke firmly, as though he were imparting information for future use. "Five doors down from you."

"Oh."

"I saw you come out your first day."

"I never noticed you."

"I keep to myself unless I see someone I like."

"Didn't you see anyone you liked from St. Louis?"

"I'm not all that fond of St. Louis, and St. Louis can do without me. I'm not a favourite son."

"Do you come here often?"

"In August. It's cheap in August." He kept on surprising her. First there was his lack of local patriotism, and now his frankness about money or rather about the lack of it, a frankness that could almost be classed as an un-American activity.

"Yes."

"I have to go where it's reasonable," he said, as though he were exposing his bad hand to a partner at gin.

"You've retired?"

"Well—I've been retired." He added, "You ought to take salad. . . . It's good for you."

"I feel quite well without it."

"You could do with more weight." He added appraisingly, "A couple of pounds." She was tempted to tell him that he could do with less. They had both seen each other exposed.

"Were you in business?" She was being driven to interrogate. He hadn't asked her a personal question since his first at the pool.

"In a way," he said. She had a sense that he was supremely uninterested in his own doings; she was certainly discovering an America which she had not known existed.

She said, "Well, if you'll excuse me . . ."

"Aren't you taking any dessert?"

"No, I'm a light luncher."

"It's all included in the price. You ought to eat some fruit." He was looking at her under his white eyebrows with an air of disappointment which touched her.

"I don't care much for fruit and I want a nap. I always have a nap in the afternoon."

Perhaps, after all, she thought, as she moved away through the formal dining-room, he is disappointed only because I'm not taking full advantage of the cheap rate.

She passed his room going to her own: the door was open and a big white-haired mammy was making the bed. The room was exactly like her own—the same pair of double beds, the same wardrobe, the same dressing-table in the same position, the same heavy breathing of the air-conditioner. In her own room she looked in vain for the Thermos of iced water; then she rang the bell and waited for several minutes. You couldn't expect good service in August. She went down the passage; Mr. Hickslaughter's door was still open, and she went in to find the maid. The door of the bathroom was open too, and a wet cloth lay on the tiles.

How bare the bedroom was. At least she had taken the trouble to add a few flowers, a photograph, and half a dozen books on a bedside table, which gave her room a lived-in air. Beside his bed there was only a digest magazine lying open and face down; she turned it over to see what he was reading—as she might have expected, it was something to do with calories and proteins. He had begun writing a letter at his dressing-table and with the simple unscrupulousness of an intellectual she began to read it with her ears cocked for any sound in the passage.

"Dear Joe," she read, "The draft was two weeks late last month and I was in real difficulties. I had to borrow from a Syrian who runs a tourist junk-shop in Curaçao and pay him interest. You owe me a hundred dollars for the interest. It's your own fault. Mom never gave us lessons on how to live on an empty stomach. Please add it to the next draft and be sure to do that, you wouldn't want me coming back to collect. I'll be here till the end of August. It's cheap in August, and a man gets tired of nothing but Dutch, Dutch, Dutch. Give my love to Sis."

The letter broke off unfinished. Anyway, she would have had no opportunity to read more because someone was approaching down the passage. She went to the door in time to see Mr. Hickslaughter on the threshold. He said, "You looking for me?"

"I was looking for the maid. She was in here a minute ago."

"Come in and sit down."

He looked through the bathroom door and then at the room in general. Perhaps it was only an uneasy conscience which made her think that his eyes strayed a moment to the unfinished letter.

"She's forgotten my iced water."

"You can have mine if it's filled." He shook his Thermos and handed it to her.

"Thanks a lot."

"When you've had your sleep——" he began and looked away from her. Was he looking at the letter?

"Yes?"

"We might have a drink."

She was, in a sense, trapped. She said, "Yes."

"Give me a ring when you wake up."

"Yes." She said nervously, "have a good sleep yourself."

"Oh, I don't sleep." He didn't wait for her to leave the room before turning away, swinging that great elephantine backside of his towards her. She had walked into a trap baited with a flask of iced water, and in her room she drank the water gingerly as though it might have a flavour different from hers.

[3]

She found it difficult to sleep: the old fat man had become an individual now that she had read his letter. She couldn't help comparing his style with Charlie's. "When I have said good night to you, my dear one, I shall go happily to bed with the thought of you." In Mr. Hickslaughter's there was an ambiguity, a hint of menace. Was it possible that the old man could be dangerous?

At half past five she rang up room 63. It was not the kind of adventure she had planned, but it was an adventure none the less. "I'm awake," she said.

"You coming for a drink?" he asked.

"I'll meet you in the bar."

"Not the bar," he said. "Not at the prices they charge for bourbon. I've got all we need here."

She felt as though she were being brought back to the scene of a crime, and she needed a little courage to knock on the door.

He had everything prepared: a bottle of Old Walker, a bucket of ice, two bottles of soda. Like books, drinks can make a room inhabited. She saw him as a man fighting in his own fashion against the sense of solitude.

"Siddown," he said, "make yourself comfortable," like a character in a movie. He began to pour out two highballs.

She said, "I've got an awful sense of guilt. I did come in here for iced water, but I was curious too. I read your letter."

"I knew someone had touched it," he said.

"I'm sorry."

"Who cares? It was only to my brother."

"I had no business . . ."

"Look," he said, "if I came into your room and found a letter open I'd read it, wouldn't I? Only your letter would be more interesting."

"Why?"

"I don't write love letters. Never did and I'm too old

now." He sat down on a bed—she had the only easy chair. His belly hung in heavy folds under his sports shirt, and his fly was a little open. Why was it always fat men who left them unbuttoned? He said, "This is good bourbon," taking a drain of it. "What does your husband do?" he asked—it was his first personal question since the pool, and it took her by surprise.

"He writes about literature. Eighteenth-century poetry," she added, rather inanely under the circumstances.

"Oh."

"What did you do? I mean when you worked."

"This and that."

"And now?"

"I watch what goes on. Sometimes I talk to someone like you. Well, no, I don't suppose I've ever talked to anyone like you before." It might have seemed a compliment if he had not added, "A professor's wife."

"And you read the *Digest*?"

"Ye-eh. They make books too long—I haven't the patience. Eighteenth-century poetry. So they wrote poetry back in those days, did they?"

She said, "Yes," not sure whether or not he was mocking her.

"There was a poem I liked at school. The only one that ever stuck in my head. By Longfellow, I think. You ever read Longfellow?"

"Not really. They don't read him much in school any longer."

"Something about Spanish sailors with bearded lips and the something and mystery of the ships and the something of the sea. It hasn't stuck all that well, after all, but I suppose I learned that sixty years ago and even more. Those were the days."

"The nineteen-hundreds?"

"No, no. I meant pirates—Kidd and Bluebeard and those fellows. This was their stamping ground, wasn't it? The Caribbean. It makes you kind of sick to see those women going around in their shorts here." His tongue had been tingled into activity by the bourbon.

It occurred to her that she had never really been curious about another human being; she had been in love with Charlie, but he hadn't aroused her curiosity except sexually, and she had satisfied that only too quickly. She asked him, "Do you love your sister?"

"Yes, of course, why? How do you know I've got a sister?"

"And Joe?"

"You certainly read my letter. Oh, he's O.K."

"O.K.?"

"Well you know how it is with brothers. I'm the oldest in my family. There was one that died. My sister's twenty years younger than I am. Joe's got the means. He looks after her."

"You haven't got the means?"

"I had the means. I wasn't good at managing them, though. We aren't here to talk about myself."

"I'm curious. That's why I read your letter."

"You? Curious about me?"

"It could be, couldn't it?"

She had confused him, and now that she had the upper hand, she felt that she was out of the trap; she was free, she could come and go as she pleased, and if she chose to stay a little longer, it was her own choice.

"Have another bourbon?" he said. "But you're English. Maybe you'd prefer Scotch?"

"Better not mix."

"No." He poured her another glass. He said, "I was wondering—sometimes I want to get away from this joint for a little. What about having dinner down the road?"

"It would be stupid," she said. "We've both paid our *pension* here, haven't we? And it would be the same dinner in the end. Red snapper. Tomatoes."

"I don't know what you have against tomatoes," but he did not deny the good sense of her economic reasoning: he was the first unsuccessful American she had ever had a drink with. One must have seen them in the street. . . . But

even the young men who came to the house were not yet unsuccessful. The Professor of Romance Languages had perhaps hoped to be head of a university—success is relative,
but it remains success.

He poured out another glass. She said, "I'm drinking all
your bourbon."

"It's in a good cause."

She was a little drunk by now and things—which only
seemed relevant—came to her mind. She said, "That thing of
Longfellow's. It went on—something about 'the thoughts of
youth are long, long thoughts.' I must have read it somewhere. That was the refrain, wasn't it?"

"Maybe. I don't remember."

"Did you want to be a pirate when you were a boy?"

He gave an almost happy grin. He said, "I succeeded.
That's what Joe called me once—'pirate.'"

"But you haven't any buried treasure?"

He said, "He knows me well enough not to send me a
hundred dollars. But if he feels scared enough that I'll come
back—he might send fifty. And the interest was only
twenty-five. He's not mean, but he's stupid."

"How?"

"He ought to know I wouldn't go back. I wouldn't do one
thing to hurt Sis."

"Would it be any good if I asked you to have dinner with
me?"

"No. It wouldn't be right." In some ways he was obviously
very conservative. "It's as you said—you don't want to go
throwing money about." When the bottle of Old Walker
was half empty, he said, "You'd better have some food even
if it is red snapper and tomatoes."

"Is your name really Hickslaughter?"

"Something like that."

They went downstairs, following rather carefully in each
other's footsteps like ducks. In the formal restaurant open to
all the heat of the evening, the men sat and sweated in their
jackets and ties. They passed, the two of them, through the

bamboo bar into the coffee tavern, which was lit by candles that increased the heat. Two young men with crew-cuts sat at the next table—they weren't the same young men she had seen before, but they came out of the same series. One of them said, "I'm not denying that he has a certain style, but even if you *adore* Tennessee Williams . . ."

"Why did he call you a pirate?"

"It was just one of those things."

When it came to the decision there seemed nothing to choose except red snapper and tomatoes, and again she offered him her tomatoes; perhaps he had grown to expect it, and already she was chained by custom. He was an old man, he had made no pass which she could reasonably reject—how could a man of his age make a pass to a woman of hers?—and yet all the same she had a sense that she had landed on a conveyor belt. . . . The future was not in her hands, and she was a little scared. She would have been more frightened if it had not been for her unusual consumption of bourbon.

"It was good bourbon," she commented for something to say, and immediately regretted it. It gave him an opening.

"We'll take another glass before bed."

"I think I've drunk enough."

"A good bourbon won't hurt you. You'll sleep well."

"I always sleep well." It was a lie—the kind of unimportant lie one tells a husband or a lover in order to keep some privacy. The young man who had been talking about Tennessee Williams rose from his table. He was very tall and thin and he wore a skin-tight black sweater; his small elegant buttocks were outlined in skin-tight trousers. It was easy to imagine him a degree more naked. Would he have looked at her, she wondered, with any interest if she had not been sitting there in the company of a fat old man so horribly clothed? It was unlikely; his body was not designed for a woman's caress.

"I don't."

"You don't what?"

"I don't sleep well." The unexpected self-disclosure after all his reticences came as a shock. It was as though he had put out one of his square brick-like hands and pulled her to him. He had been aloof, he had evaded her personal questions, he had lured her into a sense of security, but now every time she opened her mouth she seemed doomed to commit an error, to invite him nearer. Even her harmless remark about the bourbon. . . . She said stupidly, "Perhaps it's the change of climate."

"What change of climate?"

"Between here and . . . and . . ."

"Curaçao? I guess there's no great difference. I don't sleep there either."

"I've got some very good pills . . ." she said rashly.

"I thought you said you slept well."

"Oh, there are always times. It's sometimes just a question of digestion."

"Yes, digestion. You're right there. A bourbon will be good for that. If you've finished dinner . . ."

She looked across the coffee tavern to the bamboo bar, where the young man stood *déhanché,* holding a glass of crème de menthe between his face and his companion's like an exotically coloured monocle.

Mr. Hickslaughter said in a shocked voice, "You don't care for that type, do you?"

"They're often good conversationalists."

"Oh, conversation . . . If that's what you want." It was as though she had expressed an un-American liking for snails or frogs' legs.

"Shall we have our bourbon in the bar? It's a little cooler tonight."

"And listen to their chatter? No, we'll go upstairs."

He swung back again in the direction of old-fashioned courtesy and came behind her to pull her chair—even Charlie was not so polite, but was it politeness or the determination to block her way of escape to the bar?

They entered the lift together. The black attendant had a

radio turned on, and from the small brown box came the voice of a preacher talking about the Blood of the Lamb. Perhaps it was a Sunday, and that would explain the temporary void around them—between one jolly bunch and another. They stepped out into the empty corridor like undesirables marooned. The boy followed them out and sat down upon a chair beside the elevator to wait for another signal, while the voice continued to talk about the Blood of the Lamb. What was she afraid of? Mr. Hickslaughter began to unlock his door. He was much older than her father would have been if he had been still alive; he could be her grandfather—the excuse, "What will the boy think?" was inadmissible—it was even shocking, for his manner had never ceased to be correct. He might be old, but what right had she to think of him as "dirty"?

"Damn the hotel key," he said. "It won't open."

She turned the handle for him. "The door wasn't locked."

"I can sure do with a bourbon after those nancies. . . ."

But now she had her excuse ready on the lips. "I've had one too many already, I'm afraid. I've got to sleep it off." She put her hand on his arm. "Thank you so much. . . . It was a lovely evening." She was aware how insulting her English accent sounded as she walked quickly down the corridor leaving it behind her like a mocking presence, mocking all the things she liked best in him: his ambiguous character, his memory of Longfellow, his having to make ends meet.

She looked back when she reached her room: he was standing in the passage as though he couldn't make up his mind to go in. She was reminded of an old man whom she had passed one day on the campus leaning on his broom among the unswept autumn leaves.

[4]

In her room she picked up a book and tried to read. It was Thomson's *Seasons*. She had carried it with her, so that she could understand any references to his work that Charlie might make in a letter. This was the first time she had opened it, and she was not held:

And now the mounting Sun dispels the Fog:
The rigid Hoar-Frost melts before his Beam;
And hung on every Spray, on every Blade
Of Grass, the myriad Dew-Drops twinkle round.

If she could be so cowardly, she thought, with a harmless old man like that, how could she have faced the real decisiveness of an adventure? One was not, at her age, "swept off the feet." Charlie had been proved just as sadly right to trust her as she was right to trust Charlie. Now with the difference in time he would be leaving the Museum, or rather, if this were a Sunday as the Blood of the Lamb seemed to indicate, he would probably have just quit writing in his hotel room. After a successful day's work he always resembled an advertisement for a new shaving-cream: a kind of glow. . . . She found it irritating, like living with a halo. Even his voice had a different timbre and he would call her "old girl" and pat her bottom patronizingly. She preferred him when he was touchy with failure: only temporary failure, of course, the failure of an idea which hadn't worked out, the touchiness of a child's disappointment at a party which has not come up to his expectations, not the failure of the old man—the rusted framework of a ship transfixed once and for all upon the rock where it had struck.

She felt ignoble. What earthly risk could the old man represent to justify refusing him half an hour's companionship? He could no more assault her than the boat could detach itself from the rock and steam out to sea for the Fortunate Islands. She pictured him sitting alone with his half-empty bottle of bourbon seeking unconsciousness. Or was he perhaps finishing the crude blackmailing letter to his brother? What a story she would make of it one day, she thought with self-disgust as she took off her dress, her evening with a blackmailer and "pirate."

There was one thing she could do for him: she could give him her bottle of pills. She put on her dressing-gown and re-trod the corridor, room by room, until she arrived at 63. His voice told her to come in. She opened the door and in the light of the bedside lamp saw him sitting on the edge of the bed wearing a crumpled pair of cotton pyjamas with broad mauve stripes. She began, "I've brought you . . ." and then she saw to her amazement that he had been crying. His eyes were red and the evening darkness of his cheeks sparkled with points like dew. She had only once before seen a man cry—Charlie, when the University Press had decided against his first volume of literary essays.

"I thought you were the maid," he said. "I rang for her."

"What did you want?"

"I thought she might take a glass of bourbon," he said.

"Did you want so much . . . I'll take a glass." The bottle was still on the dressing-table, where they had left it and the two glasses—she identified hers by the smear of lipstick. "Here you are," she said, "drink it up. It will make you sleep."

He said, "I'm not an alcoholic."

"Of course you aren't."

She sat on the bed beside him and took his left hand in hers. It was cracked and dry, and she wanted to clean back the cuticle until she remembered that was something she did for Charlie.

"I wanted company," he said.

"I'm here."

"You better turn off the bell-light or the maid will come."

"She'll never know what she missed in the way of Old Walker."

When she returned from the door he was lying back against the pillows in an odd twisted position, and she thought again of the ship broken-backed upon the rocks. She tried to pick up his feet to lay them on the bed, but they were like heavy stones at the bottom of a quarry.

"Lie down," she said. "You'll never be sleepy that way. What do you do for company in Curaçao?"

"I manage," he said.

"You've finished the bourbon. Let me put out the lights."

"It's no good pretending to you," he said.

"Pretending?"

"I'm afraid of the dark."

She thought, I'll smile later when I think of who it was I feared. She said, "Do the old pirates you fought come back to haunt you?"

"I've done some bad things," he said, "in my time."

"Haven't we all?"

"Nothing extraditable," he explained as though that were an extenuation.

"If you take one of my pills . . ."

"You won't go—not yet?"

"No, no. I'll stay till you're sleepy."

"I've been wanting to talk to you for days."

"I'm glad you did."

"Would you believe it—I didn't have the nerve." If she had shut her eyes it might have been a very young man speaking. "I don't know your sort."

"Don't you have my sort in Curaçao?"

"No."

"You haven't taken the pill yet."

"I'm afraid of not waking up."

"Have you so much to do tomorrow?"

"I mean ever." He put out his hand and touched her knee, searchingly, without sensuality, as if he needed support from the bone. "I'll tell you what's wrong. You're a stranger, so I can tell you. I'm afraid of dying, with nobody around, in the dark."

"Are you ill?"

"I wouldn't know. I don't see doctors. I don't like doctors."

"But why should you think . . . ?"

"I'm over seventy. The Bible age. It could happen any day now."

"You'll live to a hundred," she said with an odd conviction.

"Then I'll have to live with fear a hell of a long time."

"Was that why you were crying?"

"No. I thought you were going to stay awhile, and then suddenly you went. I guess I was disappointed."

"Are you never alone in Curaçao?"

"I pay not to be alone."

"As you'd have paid the maid?"

"Ye-eh. Sort of."

It was as though she were discovering for the first time the interior of the enormous continent on which she had elected to live. America had been Charlie, it had been New England; through books and movies she had been aware of the wonders of nature like some great Cinerama film with Lowell Thomas cheapening the Painted Desert and the Grand Canyon with his clichés. There had been no mystery anywhere from Miami to Niagara Falls, from Cape Cod to the Pacific Palisades; tomatoes were served on every plate and Coca-Cola in every glass. Nobody anywhere admitted failure or fear; they were like "sins hushed up"—worse perhaps than sins, for sins have glamour—they were bad taste. But here stretched on the bed, dressed in striped pyjamas which Brooks Brothers would have disowned, failure and fear talked to her without shame, and in an American accent. It was as though she were living in the remote future, after God knew what catastrophe.

She said, "I wasn't for sale? There was only the Old Walker to tempt *me*."

He raised his antique Neptune head a little way from the pillow and said, "I'm not afraid of death. Not sudden death. Believe me, I've looked for it here and there. It's this certain-sure business, closing in on you, like tax-inspectors. . . ."

She said, "Sleep now."

"I can't."

"Yes, you can."

"If you'd stay with me awhile . . ."

"I'll stay with you. Relax." She lay down on the bed beside him on the outside of the sheet. In a few minutes he was deeply asleep and she turned off the light. He grunted several times and spoke only once, when he said, "You've got me wrong," and after that he became for a little while like a dead man in his immobility and his silence, so that during that period she fell asleep. When she woke she was aware from his breathing that he was awake too. He was lying away from her so that their bodies wouldn't touch. She put out her hand and felt no repulsion at all at his excitement. It was as though she had spent many nights beside him in the one bed, and when he made love to her, silently and abruptly in the darkness, she gave a sigh of satisfaction. There was no guilt; she would be going back in a few days, resigned and tender, to Charlie and Charlie's loving skill, and she wept a little, but not seriously, at the temporary nature of this meeting.

"What's wrong?" he asked.

"Nothing. Nothing. I wish I could stay."

"Stay a little longer. Stay till it's light." That would not be very long. Already they could distinguish the grey masses of the furniture standing around them like Caribbean tombs.

"Oh, yes, I'll stay till it's light. That wasn't what I meant." His body began to slip out of her, and it was as though he were carrying away her unknown child, away in the direction of Curaçao, and she tried to hold him back, the fat old frightened man whom she almost loved.

He said, "I never had this in mind."

"I know. Don't say it. I understand."

"I guess after all we've got a lot in common," he said, and she agreed in order to quieten him. He was fast asleep by the time the light came back, so she got off the bed without waking him and went to her room. She locked the door and began with resolution to pack her bag: it was time for her to leave, it was time for term to start again. She wondered afterwards, when she thought of him, what it was they could have had in common, except the fact, of course, that for both of them Jamaica was cheap in August.

1967   *May We Borrow Your Husband?*

Travel Tips from Aunt Augusta

EDITOR'S NOTE

What better way to represent raffish indomitable Aunt Augusta, mainspring of Greene's latest novel, than to record some of the quips and tips she so liberally distributes in her seductive conversations with her elderly nephew, the retired bank manager Henry Pulling? For, hard as it is to pin down this seventy-five-year-old globetrotter geographically, she remains steadily true to character. Catch her in Paris, Paraguay, Istanbul, Heathrow, Rome, Boulogne, or Brighton, she is still the same girlish, surprising, irreverent person. She is by a long shot Greene's most engaging female character.

The selection begins with Henry's appreciation of her baroque rhetorical style.

I wish I could reproduce more clearly the tones of her voice. She enjoyed talking, she enjoyed telling a story. She formed her sentences carefully like a slow writer who foresees ahead of him the next sentence and guides his pen towards it. Not for her the broken phrase, the lapse of continuity. There was something classically precise, or perhaps it would be more accurate to say, old-world in her diction. The bizarre phrase, and occasionally, it must be agreed, a shocking one, gleamed all the more brightly from the old setting. As I grew to know her better, I began to regard her as bronze rather than brazen, a bronze which has been smoothed and polished by touch, like the horse's knee in the lounge of the Hôtel de Paris in Monte Carlo, which she once described to me, caressed by generations of gamblers.

"I only take a plane when there is no alternative means of travel. . . . It is a matter of choice, not nerves. I knew Wilbur Wright very well indeed at one time. He took me for several trips. I always felt quite secure in his contraptions. But I cannot bear being spoken to all the time by irrelevant loud-speakers. One is not badgered at a railway station. An airport always reminds me of a Butlin's Camp."

"The Pullings have all been great travellers. I think I must have caught the infection through your father. . . . He travelled from one woman to another, Henry, all through his life. That comes to much the same thing. New landscapes, new customs. The accumulation of memories. A long life is not a question of years. A man without memories might reach the age of a hundred and feel that his life had been a very brief one."

"I have always liked fat men. They have given up all unnecessary effort, for they have the sense to realize that women do not, as men do, fall in love with physical beauty. . . . It's easier to feel at home with a fat man. Perhaps travelling with me you will put on a little weight yourself."

"They have now taken to spot-checks on passengers leaving the country. They whittle away our liberties one by one. When I was a girl you could travel anywhere on the continent except Russia without a passport and you took what you liked in the way of money. Until recently they only *asked* what money you had, or at the very worst they wanted to see your wallet. If there's one thing I hate in any human being it is mistrust."

"The difference between first and tourist fares is nearly wiped out by the caviar and the smoked salmon, and surely between us we can probably put away half a bottle of vodka. Not to speak of the champagne and cognac. . . . A friend of mine calculated once that on a long flight to Tahiti—it took in those days more than sixty-four hours—he recuperated nearly twenty pounds, but of course he was a hard drinker."

"Luck doesn't enter into my calculations. Only a fool would trust to luck. . . . The official mind is remarkably innocent. . . . I've always been interested in human nature. Especially the more imaginative sides of it."

"I have an impression that you are really a little shocked by trivial illegalities. When you reach my age you will be more tolerant. Years ago Paris was regarded as the vice-centre of the world, as Buenos Aires was before that, but Madame de Gaulle altered things there. Rome, Milan, Venice and Naples survived a decade longer, but then the only cities left were Macao and Havana. Macao has been cleaned up by the Chinese Chamber of Commerce and Havana by Fidel Castro. For the moment Heathrow is the Havana of the West. It won't last very long, of course, but one must admit that at the present time London Airport has a glamour that certainly puts Britain first."

"A little honest thieving hurts no one, especially when it's a question of gold. Gold needs free circulation. The Spanish Empire would have decayed far more quickly if Sir Francis Drake had not kept a proportion of the Spanish gold in circulation."

"You mustn't think me strait-laced. I am all for a little professional sex. . . . It seems to me that the old professional brothel system was far healthier than these exaggerated amateur distractions. But then an amateur always goes too far. An amateur is never in proper control of his art. There was a discipline in the old-time brothels. The madame in many ways played a role similar to that of the headmistress of Roedean. A brothel after all is a kind of school, and not least a school of manners. I have known several madames of real distinction who would have been just as at home in Roedean and have lent distinction to any school."

"The young do not particularly care for luxury. They have other interests than spending and can make love satisfactorily on a Coca-Cola, a drink which is nauseating in age. They have little idea of real pleasure: even their love-making is apt to be hurried and incomplete. Luckily in middle age pleasure begins, pleasure in love, in wine, in food. Only the taste for poetry flags a little, but I would have always gladly lost my taste for the sonnets of Wordsworth . . . if I could have bettered my palate for wine. Love-making too provides as a rule a more prolonged and varied pleasure after forty-five. Aretino is not a writer for the young."

"You must surrender yourself first to extravagance. Poverty is apt to strike suddenly like influenza, it is well to have a few memories of extravagance in store for bad times."

"Switzerland is only bearable covered with snow, like some people are only bearable under a sheet."

" 'All the world's a stage,' of course, but a metaphor as general as that loses all its meaning. Only a second-rate actor could have written such a line out of pride in his second-rate calling. There were occasions when Shakespeare was a very bad writer indeed. You can see how often in books of quotations. People who like quotations love meaningless generalizations."

"Politics in Turkey are taken more seriously than they are at home. It was only quite recently that they executed a Prime Minister. We dream of it, but they act."

"Am I really a Roman Catholic? Yes, my dear, only I just don't believe in all the things they believe in."

"I like men who are untouchable. I've never wanted a man who needed me. . . . A need is a claim."

"You are not untouchable, Aunt Augusta."

"That's why I need a man who is. Two touchables together, what a terrible life they always make of it, two people suffering, afraid to speak, afraid to act, afraid of hurting. Life can be bearable when it's only one who suffers. It's easy to put up with your own suffering, but not someone else's. I'm not afraid of making Mr. Visconti suffer. I wouldn't know how. I have a wonderful feeling of freedom. I can say what I like, and it will never get under that thick dago skin of his."

"Paraguay is very peaceful, only an occasional gun-shot after dark."

"Do you know what you'll think about when you can't sleep in your double bed? Not of women. . . . You will think how every day you are getting a little closer to death. It will stand there as close as the bedroom wall. And you'll become more and more afraid of the wall because nothing can prevent you from coming nearer and nearer to it every night. . . ."

"You may be right, Aunt Augusta, but isn't it the same everywhere at our age?"

"Not here it isn't. Tomorrow you may be shot in the street by a policeman because you haven't understood Guarani, or a man may knife you in a cantina because you can't speak Spanish and he thinks you are acting in a superior way. Next week, when we have our Dakota, perhaps it will crash with you over Argentina. . . . My dear Henry, if you live with us, you won't be edging day by day across to any last wall. The wall will find you of its own accord without your help, and every day you live will seem to you a kind of victory. 'I was too sharp for it that time,' you will say when night comes, and afterwards you'll sleep well. . . ."

1969   from *Travels with My Aunt*

III. CRITICISM

. . . interest in the technicalities of his art
can alone prevent the mind dulling, the
imagination losing power.
　　　—"Fiction," *The Spectator*, November 3, 1933

EDITOR'S PREFACE

Greene is surely one of the most literary of contemporary novelists. His books are full of allusions to other writers, past and present, the famous and the long forgotten. The habit of wide reading began early in the well-stocked library of Berkhamsted School. It continued at Oxford, where Greene read history and edited an undergraduate literary magazine. Later, during the lean apprentice years in the thirties, to eke out a decent living he reviewed books and cinema regularly for *The Spectator* and other London journals. He has published a brilliant volume of *Collected Essays* which illustrates the range, perceptiveness, and wit of his criticism, but these eighty pieces are just the tip of the iceberg. By my count, from 1932 through 1960 he wrote five hundred review articles covering more than a thousand books, films, and plays.

I have chosen nine of these which represent the writers who most influenced Greene, and some of his main areas of interest—Catholic eccentrics, African explorers, and sixteenth-century recusants.

There are half a dozen essays on James in *Collected Essays*; I have resurrected one more—Greene's review of James's prefaces—to stand as a capsule tribute to the Master. The piece on Ford Madox Ford is slightly different from the one in *Collected Essays*; it comes from the introduction to the Bodley Head *Ford Madox Ford*, which Greene edited. The essays on Evelyn Waugh's *The Loved One* and on John Gerard's *Autobiography of an Elizabethan* are uncollected. Greene says that he would have included them if he had remembered their existence when preparing *Collected Essays*.

The Lesson of the Master

No writer has been the victim of more misleading criticism than Henry James, from the cruel caricature by Mr. Wells to the rather snappy sentimentalities of Mr. Van Wyck Brooks. Mr. MacCarthy, too, has contributed to the common idea of James as a man who withdrew shrinkingly from "real life" into an ivory tower where he contented himself with beautifully portraying the surface of civilized society. A great deal of superficiality and intellectual dishonesty has gone to this misrepresentation: one remembers Mr. MacCarthy's astounding statement that the religious sense is almost entirely absent from James's work, and innumerable examples come to mind from Mr. Brooks's bright modish criticism of deviations from the truth. It is quite forgotten that the novel which lends its title, *The Ivory Tower*, to so many grudging appraisals has a subject as "real," even gross, as it is religious: "the black and merciless things that are behind great possessions."

James needed to express his sense of the cruelties and deceptions beneath civilized relationships. He was a puritan with a nose for the Pit, as religious as Bunyan and as violent as Shakespeare. Life is violent and art has to reflect that violence: you can't avoid Hyacinth Harvey's suicide, Milly Theale's betrayal, the swindling of Gray. Those who complain that James's men and women never reach the point of a proposal forget that they often reach the point of suicide, adultery, even murder. Their complaint is the best evidence that James's method, described in his prefaces to the collected edition, was successful. The novel by its nature is dramatic, but it need not be melodramatic, and James's problem was to admit violence without becoming violent. He mustn't let violence lend the tone (that is melodrama): violence must draw its tone from all the rest of life; it must be subdued, and it must not, above all, be sudden and inexplicable. The violence he worked with was not accidental; it was corrupt; it came from the Pit, and therefore it had to be fully understood. Otherwise, the moral background would be lost. This, too, helped to determine his method, for fully to understand, unless the author indulged in tiresome explanation, in the "platitude of statement," you had to be yourself inside the story, within a consciousness of unusual intelligence.

The prefaces represent the means to his end: and it is absurd to make out that the means ever became more important to him than the end. He never hesitated to break his own rules, but he broke them with a full consciousness of his responsibility, shivering a little with the temerity of his "exquisite treacheries"; and it remains true today that no novelist can begin to write until he has taken those rules into consideration; you cannot be a protestant before you have studied the dogmas of the old faith. James's argument, as Mr. Blackmur has written, was "that in art what is merely stated is not presented, what is not presented is not vivid, what is not vivid is not represented, and what is not represented is not art." That is a dogma which no one will dispute. The long care which James gave to the technique of his art was all a gain for vividness, and the kind of ivory tower that he inhabited admitted life more truthfully than a hatter's castle. His rules were not cramping; they had as their object the liberation of his genius, and the extent of the liberation is best seen when we compare him to his great contemporary Thomas Hardy. Hardy wrote as he pleased, just as any popular novelist does, quite unaware of the particular problems of his art, and yet it is Hardy who gives the impression of being cramped, of being forced into melodramatic laocoön attitudes, so that we begin to appreciate his novels only for the passages where the poet subdues the novelist. In James the poet and the novelist were inseparable.

This is the chief importance of James's prefaces: that they have made future novelists conscious: that the planned effect has been substituted for the lucky stroke (and Hardy shows how seldom even genius can depend on the lucky stroke). But to the common reader they should have an almost equal value, for our enjoyment of a novel is increased when we can follow the method of the writer (if they are sometimes difficult reading it is only because James had to invent his terms; he was the first critic of the novel). There is an uneducated pleasure to be obtained from pictures and music; but few will dispute that a subtler pleasure is enjoyed by the educated. The numinous pleasure is not lost if we know a little of the way in which it has been transmitted; a fine stroke by a novelist should be at least as exciting as a fine stroke by a batsman. And there is no reason for sentimentalists to be afraid. We have watched James choose his point of view, work out his ironic antitheses, arrange his scenes, but the peculiar aptitude remains; even given the directions no one has equalled him.

1935   *The Lost Childhood*

From Feathers to Iron

Stevenson's reputation has suffered perhaps more from his early death than from any other cause. He was only forty-four when he died, and he left behind him what mainly amounts to a mass of juvenilia. Gay, bright, and perennially attractive though much of his work may be, it has a spurious maturity which hides the fact that, like other men, he was developing. Indeed it was only in the last six years of his life —the Samoan years—that his fine dandified talent began to shed its disguising graces, the granite to show through. And how rich those last years were: *The Wrong Box*, *The Master of Ballantrae*, *The Island Nights' Entertainments*, *The Ebb Tide*, and *Weir of Hermiston*. Could he have kept it up? Henry James wondered of the last unfinished book and added with gracious pessimism, "the reason for which he didn't reads itself back into his text as a kind of beautiful rash divination in him that he mightn't have to. Among prose fragments it stands quite alone, with the particular grace and sanctity of mutilation worn by the marble morsels of masterwork in another art."*

Unfortunately Stevenson's reputation was not left in the hands of so cautious and subtle a critic. The early affected books of travel by canoe and donkey, the too personal letters full of "rot about a fellow's behaviour," with a slang that rings falsely on the page like an obscenity in a parson's mouth, the immature musings on his craft ("Fiction is to the grown man what play is to the child"), the early ethical essays of *Virginibus Puerisque*, all these were thrust into the foreground by the appearance of collected edition after collected edition: his youthful thoughts still sprinkle the commercial calendars with quotations. His comparatively uneventful life (adventurous only to the sedate Civil Service minds of Colvin and Gosse) was magnified into a saga: early indiscretions were carefully obliterated from the record, until at last his friends had their reward—that pale hollow stuffed figure in a velvet jacket with a Lang moustache, kneeling by a chair of native wood, with the pokerwork mottoes just behind the head—"to travel hopefully is a better thing than to arrive," etc., etc. Did it never occur to these industrious champions that as an adventurer, as a man of religion, as a traveller, as a friend of the "coloured races" he must wither into insignificance beside that other Scotsman, with the name rather like his own but the letters reshuffled into a stronger pattern, Livingstone? If he is to survive for us today, it will not be as Tusitala or the rather absurd lover collapsing at Monterrey or the dandy of Davos, but as the tired disheartened writer of the last eight years, pegging desperately away at what he failed to recognize as his masterworks.

Miss Cooper in her short biography* has followed conventionally the well-worn tracks which James noticed had been laid carefully by the hero himself. "Stevenson never

* *Robert Louis Stevenson*, by Lettice Cooper.

covered his tracks," James wrote. "We follow them here, from year to year and from stage to stage, with the same charmed sense with which he has made us follow some hunted hero in the heather." As an interpreter of his work she is incomparably less sensitive than Miss Janet Adam Smith, who has already written to my mind the best possible book on Stevenson of this length. One cannot really dismiss *The Wrong Box* as "a *tour de force* sometimes enlivened by a faintly ghoulish humour, but with no breath of reality in the characters," and criticism such as this (Miss Cooper is dealing with *The Master of Ballantrae*) has too much of the common touch even for a popular series: "The reader feels Henry's unhappiness, even when he finds it difficult to care very much about Henry, who is, it must be confessed, a dull dog." Of *The Ebb Tide* the ignorant reader will learn only that it is "a grim study of shady characters in the South Seas."

However, here for those who want it (though insufficiently charted with dates) is the obvious rail: we can watch Stevenson scatter his scraps of paper across the clearings for his pursuers to spy. His immense correspondence was mainly written with an eye on his pursuers—he encouraged Colvin to arrange it for publication. Miss Emily Dickinson wrote with some lack of wisdom in one of her poems, "I like a look of agony because I know it's true," but we are never, before the last years, quite sure of the agony. Compare his Davos letters—"Here a sheer hulk lies poor Tom Bowling and aspires, yes, C.B., with tears after the past" or doing his courageous act, "I am better. I begin to hope that I may, if not outlive this wolverine on my shoulder, at least carry him bravely"—with the letters of his last year (for suffering like literature has its juvenilia: men mature and graduate in suffering):

> The truth is I am nearly useless at literature, and I will ask you to spare *St Ives* when it goes to you. . . . No toil has been spared over the ungrateful canvas: and it *will not* come together, and I must live, and my family. Were it not for my health, which made it impossible, I could not

find it in my heart to forgive myself that I did not stick to an honest commonplace trade when I was young, which might have now supported me during these ill years. . . . It was a very little dose of inspiration, and a pretty little trick of style, long lost, improved by the most heroic industry. So far I have managed to please the journalists. But I am a fictitious article and have long known it.

A month before this he had written to his friend Baxter, admitting his life-long attempt to turn "Bald Conduct" into an emotional religion and comparing with the dreariness of his own creed the new spirit of the anarchists in Europe, men who "commit dastardly murders very basely, die like saints, and leave beautiful letters behind 'em . . . people whose conduct is inexplicable to me, and yet their spiritual life higher than that of most." *"Si vieillesse pouvait,"* he quoted, while Colvin supplied the asterisks. He was on the eve of *Weir*: the old trim surface was cracking up: the granite was coming painfully through. It is at that point, where the spade strikes the edge of the stone, that the biographer should begin to dig.

1948   *Collected Essays*

Rider Haggard's Secret

How seldom in the literary life do we pause to pay a debt of gratitude except to the great or the fashionable, who are like those friends that we feel do us credit. Conrad, Dostoevsky, James, yes, but we are too ready to forget such figures as A. E. W. Mason, Stanley Weyman, and Rider Haggard, perhaps the greatest of all who enchanted us when we were young. Enchantment is just what this writer exercised; he fixed pictures in our minds that thirty years have been unable to wear away: the witch Gagool screaming as the rock-door closed and crushed her; Eric Brighteyes fighting his doomed battle; the death of the tyrant Chaka; Umslopagaas holding the queen's stairway in Milosis. It is odd how many violent images remain like a prophecy of the future; the love passages were quickly read and discarded from the mind, though now they seem oddly moving (as when Queen Nylepta declares her love to Sir Henry Curtis in the midnight hall), a little awkward and stilted perhaps, but free from ambiguities and doubts, and with the worn rhetoric of honesty.

I am glad that his daughter's vivid and well-written biography* leaves Rider Haggard where he was in the imagination: the tall bearded figure with the presence of Sir Henry Curtis and the straightforwardness of Quatermain. This life does not belong to the unhappy world of letters; there are no rivalries, jealousies, nerve storms, no toiling miserably against the grain, no ignoble ambivalent vision which finds a kind of copy even in personal grief. The loss of his only son in childhood nearly broke Haggard in middle life, but yet his grief had the common direct quality: he was not compelled to watch himself turn it into words. "Jock was dead, so he mustn't be mentioned," Sir Godfrey Haggard writes.

> To come on a book or a toy that once belonged to my young cousin (whom I never knew) was to strike a hush over the room such as might almost have been observed towards a relative who had been hanged for murder. There was a guilty silence. Jock haunted the house far more obtrusively because everyone there pretended they could not see him, and the poor schoolboy wraith seemed to be begging piteously for some notice, so that at last he might be laid to rest.

A few words from Allan Quatermain on how the joy of life had left him with his son's death—"I have just buried my boy, my poor handsome boy of whom I was so proud, and my heart is broken. It is very hard having only one son to lose him thus; but God's will be done. Who am I that I

* *The Cloak That I Left*, by Lilias Rider Haggard.

should complain?" This is all Haggard allowed himself. He was a public author and the private life remained the private life in so far as he could control it.

The poetic element in Haggard's work breaks out where the control fails. Because the hidden man was so imprisoned, when he does emerge through the tomb it is against enormous pressure, and the effect is often one of horror, a risen Lazarus—next time he must be buried deeper. Perhaps that is why some of his early readers found his work obscene (it seems incredible to us). An anonymous letter-writer wrote to him:

> As regards *She*, it is a tissue of the most sickening trash that was ever printed, the only parts worth reading are borrowed—I could quote the books if I liked. None but a foul-minded liar could invent such sickening details. I trace a good deal of the diabolical murders that have been lately committed to the ideas promulgated by your foul trash. Of course, it *pays* and you don't care a damn, nevertheless the opinion of the decent public is that you are a skunk and a very foul one.

Even of *King Solomon's Mines* another anonymous correspondent wrote: "We approached this book with feelings of curiosity—we left with those of loathing and disgust."

It is simple to trace the influence of the public life on his work, the public life of the boy as well as of the man. There is, for example, a neighbouring farmer, "a long lank man in a smocked frock, called Quatermain." In Zululand, where he went whilst still a boy on the staff of the Governor of Natal, he met Gagool in the body (we suspect he had met her in the spirit long before). Pagéte's warriors are performing a war dance. "Suddenly there stood before us a creature, a woman—tiny, withered, and bent nearly double by age, but in her activity passing comprehension. Clad in a strange jumble of snake skins, feathers, furs and bones, a forked wand in her outstretched hand, she rushed to and fro before the little group of white men, crying:

> *"Ou, Ou, Ai, Ai, Ai,*
> *Oh! ye warriors that shall dance before the*
>   *great ones of the earth, come!*
> *Oh! ye dyers of spears, ye plumed suckers of*
>   *blood, come!*
>
> *I, the witch finder;*
> *I, the wise woman;*
> *I, the seer of strange sights;*
> *I, the reader of dark thoughts; call ye!"*

Umslopagaas with the great hole in his head above the left temple, carrying his spiked axe Imkosi-kaas, came down one day from Swaziland and became Haggard's friend. All through his life we can find superficial material for his books, even for the dull adult books like *Mr. Meeson's Will.* His life provides Zulu impis, war, flight, shipwreck, a treasure hunt in Mexico, even the City of London, but what we do not so easily detect is the very thing that makes these books live today with undiminished vitality—the emergence of the buried man.

There are some revealing passages in his friendship with Rudyard Kipling. Fishing together for trout at Bateman's, these two elderly men—in some ways the most successful writers of their time, linked together to their honour even by their enemies ("the prose that knows no reason, and the unmelodious verse," "When the Rudyards cease from Kipling, and the Haggards ride no more"), suddenly let out the secret. "I happened to remark," Haggard wrote, "that I thought this world was one of the hells. He replied he did not think—he was certain of it. He went on to show that it had every attribute of hell; doubt, fear, pain, struggle, bereavement, almost irresistible temptations springing from the nature with which we are clothed, physical and mental suffering, etc., ending in the worst fate man can devise for man, Execution!"

Haggard's comment starts shockingly from the page in its

very casualness, and then we begin to remember the passages we skated so lightly over in the adventure stories when
we were young and the world held promise: there was, for
example, Allan Quatermain dying and resigned:

> Well, it is not a good world—nobody can say that it is,
> save those who wilfully blind themselves to the facts. How
> can a world be good in which Money is the moving
> power, and Self-Interest the guiding star? The wonder is
> not that it is so bad but that there should be any good left
> in it.

Quatermain remembers the good things of life, how he
"watched the wild game trek down to the water in the
moonlight. But I should not wish to live again." And we remember too the Brethren and the quite casual comment,
not unlike Haggard's to Kipling, "So they went, talking earnestly of all things, but, save in God, finding no hope at all."

They seemed so straightforward to us once, those books
we first encountered behind the steel grille of the school library, casting a glow over the dull neighbouring H's: Henty
already abandoned and Hope not yet enjoyed: *The Wan-
derer's Necklace* (with the hero blinded by the queen to whom
he remains faithful to the last), *Montezuma's Daughter* (and
her suicide beside her lover), *Ayesha* (with the mad Khan's
hunting), *Nada the Lily* (and the death of the beloved). We
did not notice the melancholy end of every adventure or
know that the battle scenes took their tension from the fear
of death which so haunted Haggard from one night in his
childhood when he woke in the moonlight:

> He put out his hand . . . how odd it looked in the
> moonlight, dead—dead. Then it happened. He realized
> that one day that hand would be limp also, that he could
> not lift it any more—it would be dead—he would be
> dead. The awful, inescapable certainty hung over him
> like a pall of misery. He felt it would be better if he died
> at once—he wished he were dead, rather than have to live
> with that in front of him.

Haggard's own melancholy end, with falling royalties and the alienation of the Norfolk lands he loved, departing from the doomed house with a flower in his button-hole to the operation he guessed would be final, comes closer to adult literature perhaps than any of his books. It is not the sound of Umslopagaas's axe that we hear, cracking the marble monument in the moment of his death, so much as the sound of trees falling, the strokes of the axe far away in the cherry orchard. We think again of how much we loved him when we were young—the gleam of Captain Good's monocle, the last stand of the Greys, de Garcia tracked through the snows—and of how little we knew. "Occasionally one sees the Light, one touches the pierced feet, one thinks that the peace which passes understanding is gained—then all is gone again." Could we ever have believed that our hero wrote that, or have been interested if we had known?

François Mauriac

After the death of Henry James a disaster overtook the English novel; indeed long before his death one can picture that quiet, impressive, rather complacent figure, like the last survivor on a raft, gazing out over a sea scattered with wreckage. He even recorded his impressions in an article in *The Times Literary Supplement*, recorded his hope—but was it really hope or only a form of his unconquerable oriental politeness?—in such young novelists as Mr. Compton Mackenzie and Mr. David Herbert Lawrence, and we who have lived after the disaster can realize the futility of those hopes.

For with the death of James the religious sense was lost to the English novel, and with the religious sense went the sense of the importance of the human act. It was as if the world of fiction had lost a dimension: the characters of such distinguished writers as Mrs. Virginia Woolf and Mr. E. M. Forster wandered like cardboard symbols through a world that was paper-thin. Even in one of the most materialistic of our great novelists—in Trollope—we are aware of another world against which the actions of the characters are thrown into relief. The ungainly clergyman picking his black-booted way through the mud, handling so awkwardly his umbrella, speaking of his miserable income and stumbling through a proposal of marriage, exists in a way that Mrs. Woolf's Mr. Ramsay never does, because we are aware that he exists not only to the woman he is addressing but also in a God's eye. His unimportance in the world of the senses is only matched by his enormous importance in another world.

The novelist, perhaps unconsciously aware of his predicament, took refuge in the subjective novel. It was as if he thought that by mining into layers of personality hitherto untouched he could unearth the secret of "importance," but in these mining operations he lost yet another dimension. The visible world for him ceased to exist as completely as the spiritual. Mrs. Dalloway walking down Regent Street was aware of the glitter of shop-windows, the smooth passage of cars, the conversation of shoppers, but it was only a Regent Street seen by Mrs. Dalloway that was conveyed to the reader: a charming whimsical rather sentimental prose poem was what Regent Street had become: a current of air, a touch of scent, a sparkle of glass. But, we protest, Regent Street too has a right to exist; it is more real than Mrs. Dalloway, and we look back with nostalgia towards the chop houses, the mean courts, the still Sunday streets of Dickens. Dickens's characters were of immortal importance, and the houses in which they loved, the mews in which they damned themselves were lent importance by their presence. They were given the right to exist as they were, distorted, if at all, only by their observer's eye—not further distorted at a second remove by an imagined character.

M. Mauriac's first importance to an English reader, therefore, is that he belongs to the company of the great traditional novelists: he is a writer for whom the visible world has not ceased to exist, whose characters have the solidity and importance of men with souls to save or lose, and a writer who claims the traditional and essential right of a novelist, to comment, to express his views. For how tired we have become of the dogmatically "pure" novel, the tradition founded by Flaubert and reaching its magnificent tortuous climax in England in the works of Henry James. One is reminded of those puzzles in children's papers which take the form of a maze. The child is encouraged to trace with his pencil a path to the centre of the maze. But in the pure novel the reader begins at the centre and has to find his way to the gate. He runs his pencil down avenues which must surely go straight to the circumference, the world outside the maze, where moral judgments and acts of supernatural importance can be found (even the writing of a novel indeed can be regarded as a more important action, expressing an intention of more vital importance, than the adultery of the main character or the murder in chapter three), but the printed channels slip and twist and slide, landing him back where he began, and he finds on close examination that the designer of the maze has in fact overprinted the only exit.

I am not denying the greatness of either Flaubert or James. The novel was ceasing to be an aesthetic form and they recalled it to the artistic conscience. It was the later writers who by accepting the technical dogma blindly made the novel the dull devitalized form (form it retained) that it has become. The exclusion of the author can go too far. Even the author, poor devil, has a right to exist, and M. Mauriac reaffirms that right. It is true that the Flaubertian form is not so completely abandoned in this novel* as in *Le Baiser au lépreux*; the "I" of the story plays a part in the action; any commentary there is can be attributed by purists to this fictional "I," but the pretence is thin—"I" is dominated by I. Let me quote two passages:

* *La Pharisienne.*

— Et puis, tellement beau, tu ne trouves pas?

Non, je ne le trouvais pas beau. Qu'est-ce que la beauté pour un enfant? Sans doute, est-il surtout sensible à la force, à la puissance. Mais cette question dut me frapper puisque je me souviens encore, après toute une vie, de cet endroit de l'allée où Michèle m'interrogea ainsi, à propos de Jean. Saurais-je mieux définir aujourd'hui, ce que j'appelle beauté? saurais-je dire à quel signe je la reconnais, qu'il s'agisse d'un visage de chair, d'un horizon, d'un ciel, d'une couleur, d'une parole, d'un chant? A ce tressaillement charnel et qui, pourtant, intéresse l'âme, à cette joie désespérée, à cette contemplation sans issue et que ne récompense aucune étreinte. . . .

Ce jour-là, j'ai vu pour la première fois à visage découvert, ma vieille ennemie la solitude, avec qui je fais bon ménage aujourd'hui. Nous nous connaissons: elle m'a asséné tous les coups imaginables, et il n'y a plus de place où frapper. Je ne crois avoir évité aucun de ses pièges. Maintenant elle a fini de me torturer. Nous tisonnons face à face, durant ces soirs d'hiver où la chute d'une "pigne", un sanglot de nocturne ont autant d'intérêt pour mon cœur qu'une voix humaine.

In such passages one is aware, as in Shakespeare's plays, of a sudden tensing, a hush seems to fall on the spirit—this is something more important than the king, Lear, or the general, Othello, something which is unconfined and unconditioned by plot. "I" has ceased to speak, I is speaking.

One is never tempted to consider in detail M. Mauriac's plots. Who can describe six months afterwards the order of events, say in *Ce qui était perdu*? One remembers the simple outlines of *Le Baiser au lépreux*, but the less simple the events of the novel the more they disappear from the mind, leaving in our memory only the characters, whom we have known so intimately that the events at the one period of their lives chosen by the novelist can be forgotten without forgetting them. (The first lines of *La Pharisienne* create completely the horrible Comte de Mirbel: " 'Approche ici, garçon!' Je me retournai, croyant qu'il s'adressait à un de mes camarades. Mais non, c'était bien moi qu'appelait l'ancien zouave pontifical, souriant. La cicatrice de sa lèvre supérieure rendait le sourire hideux.") M. Mauriac's characters exist with extraordinary physical completeness (he has affinities here we feel to Dickens), but their particular acts are less important than the force, whether God or Devil, that compels them, and though M. Mauriac rises to dramatic heights in his great "scenes," as when Jean de Mirbel, the boy whose soul is in such danger (a kind of unhappy tortured Grand Meaulnes), is the silent witness outside the country hotel of his beloved mother's vulgar adultery, the "joins" of his plot, the events which should make a plausible progression from one scene to another, are often oddly lacking. Described as plots his novels would sometimes seem to flicker like an early film. But who would attempt to describe them as plots? Wipe out the whole progression of events and we would be left still with the characters in a way I can compare with no other novelist. Take away Mrs. Dalloway's capability of self-expression and there is not merely no novel but no Mrs. Dalloway: take away the plot from Dickens and the characters who have lived so vividly from event to event would dissolve. But if the Comtesse de Mirbel had not committed adultery, if Jean's guardian, the evil Papal Zouave, had never lifted a hand against him, if the clumsy well-meaning saintly priest, the Abbé Calou, had never been put in charge of the boy, the characters, we feel, would have continued to exist in identically the same way. We are saved or damned by our thoughts, not by our actions.

The events of M. Mauriac's novels are used not to change characters (how little in truth are we changed by events: how romantic and false in comparison is a book such as Conrad's *Lord Jim*) but to reveal characters—reveal them gradually with an incomparable subtlety. His moral and religious insight is the reverse of the obvious: you will seldom find the easy false assumption, the stock figure in M. Mauriac. Take for example the poor pious usher M. Puybaraud. He is what we call in England a creeping Jesus, but M. Mauriac shows how in truth the creeping Jesus may creep towards Jesus. La Pharisienne herself under her layer of destructive egotism and false pity is disclosed sympathetically to the religious core. She learns through hypocrisy. The hypocrite cannot live insulated for ever against the beliefs she professes. There is irony but no satire in M. Mauriac's work.

I am conscious of having scattered too many names and comparisons in this short and superficial essay, but one name—the greatest—cannot be left out of any consideration of M. Mauriac's work, Pascal. This modern novelist, who allows himself the freedom to comment, comments, whether through his characters or in his own "I," again in the very accents of Pascal.

> Les êtres ne changent pas, c'est là une vérité dont on ne doute plus à mon âge; mais ils retournent souvent à l'inclination que durant une vie ils se sont épuisés à combattre. Ce qui ne signifie point qu'ils finissent toujours par céder au pire d'eux-mêmes: Dieu est la bonne tentation à laquelle beaucoup d'hommes succombent à la fin.

> Il y a des êtres qui tendent leurs toiles et peuvent jeûner longtemps avant qu'aucune proie s'y laisse prendre: la patience du vice est infinie.

> Il ne faut pas essayer d'entrer dans la vie des êtres malgré eux: retiens cette leçon, mon petit. Il ne faut pas pousser la porte de cette seconde ni de cette troisième vie que Dieu seul connaît. Il ne faut jamais tourner la tête vers la ville secrète, vers la cité maudite des autres, si on ne veut pas être changé en statue de sel.

> Notre-Seigneur exige que nous aimions nos ennemis; c'est plus facile souvent que de ne pas haïr ceux que nous aimons.

If Pascal had been a novelist, we feel, this is the method and the tone he would have used.

1945   *Collected Essays*

The Redemption of Mr. Joyboy[*]

"We are made a spectacle unto God, unto His angels and unto men," so Campion quoted on the scaffold, and if one were to choose a single motto to represent the spirit of Mr. Waugh's work, from *Decline and Fall* to Campion's life, to *Brideshead Revisited* and now to *The Loved One*, could a better be found? The emphasis in the early books was on "a spectacle to men": from a distance, far enough, though below the angels' viewpoint, Mr. Waugh regarded the absurd and pathetic antics of his characters—"the sound of the English country families baying for broken glass" in the quad of Scone College; poor Grimes trapped into marriage with the headmaster's daughter, "Oh why did nobody warn me? I should have been told. They should have told me in so many words. They should have warned me about Flossie, not about the fires of hell." In these books there was an innocence in the spectator, typified by Paul Pennyfeather, a good humour, a natural charity, which sometimes we find ourselves missing now. The spectator is no longer innocent, Dennis Barlow of *The Loved One* is conspicuously astute and cold-blooded, and the reader can no longer idly smile and lay the book down without his thoughts wandering through wider spaces, the regions of good and evil. If Captain Grimes emerged again from his Dartmoor grave, we should no longer laugh so readily: we should be aware of a different standard of criticism. The huge ceiling of eternity has closed

[*] This originally appeared as a review of *The Loved One* in *The Month*, January 1949.

over Mr. Waugh's work: the delightful minor novelist has
developed into one of the major writers of his day, and if we
have lost some pleasures in the process, we have gained a
world. "I thought of the joyful youth with the teddy-bear
under the flowering chestnuts. 'It's not what I would have
foretold,' I said."

It is not that Mr. Waugh now takes a God-like view of the
world; far from it. God may forgive the things we do, it is his
métier, but not Mr. Waugh. In the savagery of his approach
to the strange burial customs of the Californians—in this
horrible and exquisitely funny story (as we call an agony exquisite) of the great human cemetery of Whispering Glades
and the animal cemetery of the Happy Hunting Ground, of
the loves of the morticians—he may have thought himself to
be returning towards the pure comedy of *Decline and Fall* (it
is certainly his funniest since that wonderful young book),
but we cannot help recognizing the genuine note of hate, the
hate of a man who loves, of one aware that it was for this
grotesque world a God died, who is bitterly ashamed of what
we have made of ourselves. There was a dignity about those
who mocked in the presence of Christ absent from this world
of Bel Air and Beverly Hills, of Sunset Boulevard and the
floodlit motels, where dogs are buried with religious rites
and the mourners receive their cards of remembrance
("Your little Arthur is thinking of you in Heaven today and
wagging his tail"), where the Mortuary Hostesses discuss the
choice of inhumement, entombment, innurement, immure-
ment, or insarcophagusment to the strains of the Hindu
Love Song, and the non-sectarian clergyman advertises
"Confessions heard in strict confidence."

    . . . "Tell me, how does one become a non-sectarian
clergyman?"
    "One has the Call."
    "Yes, of course; but after the Call, what is the process? I
mean, is there a non-sectarian bishop who ordains you?"
    "Certainly not. Anyone who has received the Call has
no need for human intervention."

"You just say one day 'I am a non-sectarian clergyman' and set up shop?"

"There is considerable outlay. You need buildings. But the banks are usually ready to help. . . ."

Mr. Waugh gives us two warnings. First, that "This is a purely fanciful tale, a little nightmare," much as Henry James disowned that profound study of evil, *The Turn of the Screw*, calling it a little story suitable for Christmas, but we need pay no attention to this warning. It is only a few months ago that a famous film star was buried at Forest Lawn and the pall bearers were stopped for autographs and interviews, and Mr. Pat O'Brien, a film actor, told the Press, "This is the hardest matinée that Carole and I have ever played together," and the Bishop who preached the funeral oration (I suspect he may have been non-sectarian) referred to a famous comparison: As Shakespeare put it "some are stars, and some only bit players." No, Mr. Waugh's world is as near to ours as the country of the Yahoos.

Mr. Waugh's second warning is to the squeamish, and this may be taken more seriously. With what admirable diligence he must have studied the necrophilous details of Whispering Glades, the secrets of embalming, of preparing a corpse for the casket, before he sat down to write his little tragic tale of Anglo-American misunderstanding, of the dubious love of the English poet, Dennis Barlow, employed at the Happy Hunting Ground, for Miss Thanatogenos, the naïve, bewildered young cosmetician of Whispering Glades ("My memory's very bad for live faces"), torn between the poet and Mr. Joyboy, the chief embalmer who wooed her by the tender plastic smiles on the features of his corpses. If it were not so funny, how revolting it would be. The grotesque details are pressed firmly, relentlessly, home by Mr. Waugh's thumb like sand in a child's pail. Sometimes his diligence seems to go too far, and I found myself questioning the cruel ending—the illicit disposal in the veterinary incinerator of Miss Thanatogenos after her suicide—much as I questioned the cannibalism at the end of *Black Mischief*, for after all this is a redeemed world and a God died for Mr. Joyboy too. But this is a small criticism, for the sand has been very firmly set and this castle is likely to endure as long as any against the sea of time.

1949Uncollected

Ford Madox Ford

Ford had once described himself, before the great disaster of 1914: "I may humbly write myself down a man in his early forties a little mad about good letters." By the very nature of his birth and early years he was condemned to the life of an artist. Son of Hueffer, the distinguished musical critic of *The Times* and grandson of Ford Madox Brown, the famous Victorian painter, brought up in the strange mansion in Fitzroy Square immortalized by Thackeray in *The Newcomes*, with small Rossetti cousins tumbling downstairs at his feet and Swinburne, as like as not, lying drunk in the bath on the top floor, he had little choice: one might have prophesied almost anything for him from a staggered laudanum death to membership of the Royal Academy.

One would have been wrong about the details, but not about the fact that, in the age of Kipling, Haggard, and Wells, an age of increasing carelessness among good writers, he was an artist. No one in our century except James has been more attentive to the craft of letters. He was not only a designer; he was a carpenter: you feel in his work the love of the tools and the love of the material. He may sometimes have been over-elaborate, an accusation which after he had spent more than forty years in writing fiction can be brought against his last novels. But who else, except James, has shown such a capacity for growth, even misguided growth, over so long a span of years? Ford's first novel was published in 1892 and his last in 1937. Even so, when he died, he had not reached the limit of his technical experiments.

How seldom a novelist chooses the material nearest to his hand; it is almost as if he were driven to earn experience the hard way. Ford, whom we might have expected to become a novelist of artistic bohemia, a kind of English Murger, did indeed employ the material of Fitzroy Square incomparably well in his volumes of reminiscence—and some people might regard those as his finest novels, for he brought to his dramatizations of people he had known—James, Conrad, Crane, Hudson, Hardy—the same astonishing knack he showed with his historical figures. Most writers dealing with real people find their invention confined, but that was not so with Ford. "When it has seemed expedient to me I have altered episodes that I have witnessed, but I have been careful never to distort the character of the episode. *The accuracies I deal in are the accuracies of my impressions.* If you want factual accuracies you must go to . . . but no, no, don't go to anyone, stay with me." (The italics are mine: it is a phrase worth bearing in mind in reading all his works.)

In fact as a novelist Ford began to move further and further from bohemia for his material. His first period as an historical novelist, which he began by collaborating with Conrad in that underrated novel *Romance*, virtually closed with his Tudor trilogy. There were to be two or three more historical novels, until in *Ladies Whose Bright Eyes* . . . he came half out into the contemporary world and began to find his true subject. It could even be argued that in *The Fifth Queen* he was nearest as a novelist to Fitzroy Square. There is the sense of saturation: something is always happening on the stairs, in the passages the servants come and go on half-explained errands, and the great King may at any moment erupt upon the scene, half kindly, half malevolent, rather as we feel the presence of Madox Brown in the gas-lit interstices of number 37.

Most historical novelists use real characters only for purposes of local colour—Lord Nelson passes up a Portsmouth street or Doctor Johnson enters ponderously to close a chapter, but in *The Fifth Queen* we have virtually no fictional characters—the King, Thomas Cromwell, Katharine Howard, they are the principals; we are nearer to the historical plays of Shakespeare than to the fictions of such historical writers as Miss Irwin or Miss Heyer.

"The accuracies I deal in are the accuracies of my impressions." In *The Fifth Queen* Ford tries out the impressionist method which he was later to employ with triumphant ease in the great confused Armistice Day scene of *A Man Could Stand Up.* The whole story of the struggle between Katharine and Cromwell for the King seems told in shadows—shadows which flicker with the flames of a log-fire, diminish suddenly as a torch recedes, stand calm awhile in the candlelight of a chapel: a cresset flares and all the shadows leap together. Has a novel ever before been lit as carefully as a stage production? Nicolas Udal's lies, which play so important a part in the first volume, take their substance from the lighting: they are monstrously elongated or suddenly shrivel: one can believe anything by torchlight. (The power of a lie—that too was a subject he was to pursue through all his later books: the lies of Sylvia Tietjens which ruined her husband's army career and the monstrous lie of "poor Florence" in *The Good Soldier* which brought death to three people and madness to a fourth.)

If *The Fifth Queen* is a magnificent bravura piece—and you could say that it was a better painting than ever came out of Fitzroy Square with all the mingled talents there of Madox Brown and Morris, Rossetti and Burne-Jones—in *The Good Soldier* Ford triumphantly found his true subject and oddly enough, for a child of the Pre-Raphaelites, his subject was the English "gentleman," the "black and merciless things" which lie behind that façade.

Edward Ashburnham was the cleanest looking sort of chap;—an excellent magistrate, a first rate soldier, one of the best landlords, so they said, in Hampshire, England. To the poor and to hopeless drunkards, as I myself have witnessed, he was like a painstaking guardian. And he never told a story that couldn't have gone into the columns of the *Field* more than once or twice in all the nine years of my knowing him. He didn't even like hearing them; he would fidget and get up and go out to buy a cigar or something of that sort. You would have said that he was just exactly the sort of chap that you could have trusted your wife with. And I trusted mine and it was madness.

The Good Soldier, which Ford had wished to call *The Saddest Story*, concerns the ravages wrought by a passionate man who had all the virtues but continence. The narrator is the betrayed husband, and it is through his eyes alone that we watch the complications and involvements left by Ashburnham's blind urge towards satisfaction. Technically the story is undoubtedly Ford's masterpiece: the book is simultaneously a study of the way memory works. The time-shifts are valuable not merely for purposes of suspense—they lend veracity to the appalling events. This is just how memory does work, and we become involved with the narrator's memory as though it were our own. Ford's apprenticeship with Conrad had borne its fruit, but he improved on the Master.

I have, I am aware, told this story in a very rambling way so that it may be difficult for anyone to find their path through what may be a sort of maze. I cannot help it. I have stuck to my idea of being in a country cottage with a silent listener, hearing between the gusts of the wind and amidst the noises of the distant sea, the story as it comes. And when one discusses an affair—a long, sad affair—one goes back, one goes forward. One remembers points that one has forgotten and one explains them all the more minutely since one recognizes that one has forgotten to mention them in their proper places and that one may have given, by omitting them, a false impression. I console myself with thinking that this is a real story and that, after all, real stories are probably told best in the way a person telling a story would tell them. They will then seem most real.

A short enough book it is to contain two suicides, two ruined lives, a death, and a girl driven insane: it may seem odd to find the keynote of the book is restraint, a restraint which is given it by the gentle character of the narrator ("I am only an ageing American with very little knowledge of life") who never loses his love and compassion for the characters concerned. "Here were two noble people—for I am convinced that both Edward and Leonora had noble natures—here, then, were two noble natures, drifting down life, like fireships afloat on a lagoon and causing miseries, heartaches, agony of the mind and death. And they themselves steadily deteriorated. And why? For what purpose? To point what lesson? It is all a darkness." He condemns no one; in extremity he doesn't even condemn human nature, and I find one of the most moving understatements in literature his summing up of Leonora's attitude to her husband's temporary infatuation for the immature young woman, Maisie Maidan: "I think she would really have welcomed it if he could have come across the love of his life. It would have given her a rest."

I don't know how many times in nearly forty years I have come back to this novel of Ford's, every time to discover a new aspect to admire, but I think the impression which will be left most strongly on the reader is the sense of Ford's involvement. A novelist is not a vegetable absorbing nourishment mechanically from soil and air: material is not easily or painlessly gained, and one cannot help wondering what agonies of frustration and error lay behind *The Saddest Story*.

1962

Frederick Rolfe:
Edwardian Inferno

The obscurity and what we curiously believe to be the cru-
dity and violence of the distant past make a suitable background to the Soul. Temptation, one feels, is seldom today so
heroically resisted or so devastatingly succumbed to as in the
days of Dante or of Milton; Satan, as well as sanctity, demands an apron stage. It is, therefore, with a shock of startled incredulity that we become aware on occasion even
today of eternal issues, of the struggle between good and evil,
between vice that really demands to be called satanic and
virtue of a kind which can only be called heavenly.

How much less are we prepared for it in the Edwardian
age, in the age of bicycles and German bands and gold
chamber ware, of Norfolk jackets and deerstalker caps. How
distressingly bizarre seems the whole angelic conflict which
centred around Frederick Rolfe, self-styled Baron Corvo, the
spoilt priest, who was expelled from the Scots College at
Rome, the waster who lived on a multitude of generous
friends, the writer of genius, author of *Hadrian the Seventh* and
Don Tarquinio and *Chronicles of the House of Borgia*. When
Rolfe's fictional self prayed in his Hampstead lodging:

> "God, if ever You loved me, hear me, hear me. *De Pro-
> fundis ad Te, ad Te clamavi.* Don't I want to be good and
> clean and happy? What desire have I cherished since my
> boyhood save to serve in the number of Your mystics?
> What but that have I asked of You Who made me? Not a
> chance do You give me—ever—ever—"

it is disquieting to remember how in the outside world Mr.
Wells was writing *Love on Wheels*, the Empire builders after
tiffin at the club were reading "The Song of the Banjo," and
up the crowded stairway of Grosvenor House Henry James
was bearing his massive brow; disquieting too to believe that

Miss Marie Corelli was only palely limping after truth when she brought the devil to London. For if ever there was a case of demonic possession it was Rolfe's: the hopeless piety, the screams of malevolence, the sense of despair which to a man of his faith was the sin against the Holy Ghost. "All men are too vile for words to tell."

The greatest saints have been men with more than a normal capacity for evil, and the most vicious men have sometimes narrowly evaded sanctity. Frederick Rolfe in his novel *Hadrian the Seventh* expressed a sincere, if sinister, devotion to the Church that had very wisely rejected him; all the good of which he was capable went into that book, as all the evil went into the strange series of letters which Mr. Symons has described for the first time,* written at the end of his life, when he was starving in Venice, to a rich acquaintance.

> He had become a habitual corrupter of youth, a seducer of innocence, and he asked his wealthy accomplice for money, first that he might use it as a temptation, to buy bait for the boys whom he misled, and secondly, so that he might efficiently act as pander when his friend revisited Venice. Neither scruple nor remorse was expressed or implied in these long accounts of his sexual exploits or enjoyments, which were so definite in their descriptions that he was forced, in sending them by post, so to fold them that only blank paper showed through the thin foreign envelopes.

These were the astonishing bounds of Corvo: the starving pander on the Lido and the man of whom Mr. Vincent O'Sullivan wrote to his biographer: "He was born for the Church: that was his main interest." Between these bounds, between the Paradise and the Inferno, lay the weary purgatorial years through which Mr. Symons has been the first to track him with any closeness. Mr. Symons's method, unchronological, following the story as he discovered it from witness to witness, lends Rolfe's vacillating footprints a pain-

* *The Quest for Corvo*, by A. J. A. Symons.

ful drama. Continually, with the stamp of an obstinate courage, they turn back towards Paradise: from the rim of the Inferno they turn and go back: but on the threshold of Paradise they turn again because of the devilish pride which would not accept even Heaven, except on his own terms; this way and that, like the steps of a man pacing a room in agony of mind. It is odd to realize that all the time common-or-garden life is going on within hailing distance, publishers are making harsh bargains, readers are reporting adversely on his work, friends are forming hopeless plans of literary collaboration. Mr. Grant Richards and Monsignor Benson and Mr. Pirie-Gordon and the partners of Chatto and Windus beckon and speak like figures on the other side of a distorting glass pane. They have quite a different reality, much thinner reality, they are not concerned with eternal damnation. And their memories of Rolfe are puzzled, a little amused, a little exasperated, as if they cannot understand the eccentricity of a man who chooses to go about sheathed in flame in the heyday of the Entente Cordiale, of Sir Ernest Cassel, and Lily Langtry.

Mr. O'Sullivan wrote of Rolfe to Mr. Symons as a man "who had only the vaguest sense of realities," but the phrase seems a little inaccurate. His realities were less material than spiritual. It would be easy to emphasize his shady financial transactions, his pose as the Kaiser's godson, his complete inability to earn a living. It is terrible to think what a figure of cruel fun a less imaginative writer than Mr. Symons might have made of Rolfe, turned out of an Aberdeen boarding house in his pyjamas, painting pictures with the help of magic-lantern slides, forced to find employment as a gondolier, begging from strangers, addressing to the Pope a long indictment of living Catholics. But against this material reality Mr. Symons with admirable justice sets another: the reality of *Hadrian the Seventh*, a novel of genius, which stands in relation to the other novels of its day much as *The Hound of Heaven* stands in relation to the verse. Rolfe's vice was spiritual more than it was carnal: it might be said that he was a pander and a swindler because he cared for nothing but his faith. He would be a priest or nothing, so nothing it had to be and he was not ashamed to live on his friends; if he could not have Heaven, he would have Hell, and the last footprints seem to point unmistakably towards the Inferno.

1934   *Collected Essays*

"Sore Bones; Much Headache"

It is a sad thing about small nationalities that like a possessive woman they trap their great men: Walter Scott, Stevenson, Burns, Livingstone—all have to some extent been made over by their countrymen, they have not been allowed to grow or to diminish with time. How can they even shift in the grave under the weight of their national memorials? A whole industry of trinkets and souvenirs and statuettes depends on the conformity of the dead. A Civil Service of curators, secretaries, and guides takes charge of the memory. (Sixty-five thousand people pass annually through the turnstiles of the Livingstone Memorial House at Blantyre with its coloured statuary and its Ancestry Room, Youth Room, Adventure Room.) An explorer can suffer from his legend as much as a writer—the explorer, too, has a passion to create, and just as a body carried to its grave at the summit of a Samoan hill obscures the writer struggling with the character of Hermiston, so the last trek of Livingstone's faithful carriers to the coast, with the obvious drama and the missionary moral, has intruded between us and the patience, the monotony, and the weariness incurred in adding a new line to a map, surveying an uncharted range, correcting an erroneous reading; above all it has obscured Livingstone's failure—you will not find photographs of the Lari massacre at Blantyre. (Dr. Macnair does not help us to escape the legend by writing always in capital letters of the Explorer, the Traveller, the Missionary. I prefer the admirably clear and sensible geographical notes by Dr. Ronald Miller.*)

The virtue of this selection from Livingstone's travel books and journals is its dullness—the reader must dig himself for the vivid fact or the revealing sentence. Livingstone was not primarily concerned with the beauty of the scenery or the drama of his journeys: he was concerned, at the beginning, with the location of healthy mission stations, later with discovering trade routes (which he considered might help towards the extinction of slavery)—the discoveries of Lake Shira and Lake Nyasa had no drama for him: they were incidental.

> We discovered Lake Nyasa a little before noon on September 16, 1859. Its southern end is 14° 25′ South lat., 35° 30′ E. long. At this point the valley is about 12 miles wide. There are hills on both sides of the lake.

The plot of the novel catches the attention, but the subject lies deeper. "The Nile sources are valuable only to me as a means of opening my mouth with power."

Literary expression was not Livingstone's object—a compass reading was more important for his mission. ("It seems a pity that the important facts about two healthy ridges should not be known to Christendom.") But in the early years when he wrote for publication, *Missionary Travels and Researches*, *The Zambesi and Its Tributaries*, he thought it necessary to take as his model the work of other Victorian travel books.

> We proceeded rapidly up-river. The magnificent stream is often more than a mile broad and is adorned by many islands from three to five miles in length. The beauty of the scenery on some of these islands is greatly increased by the date-palm with its gracefully curved fronds and refreshing light-green colour, while the lofty palmyra towers above and casts its feathery foliage

* *Livingstone's Travels*, edited by Dr. James I. Macnair.

against a cloudless sky. The banks of the river are equally covered by forest and most of the trees on the brink of the water send down roots from their branches, like the banian. The adjacent country is rocky and undulating, abounding in elephants and all other large game, except leches and nakongs, which seem generally to avoid stony ground.

The airs and graces were to be shed when he was no longer concerned in advancing the sales of his books at home and increasing his opportunities for work. In the final journals we get the hard truthful writing of which he was capable. Written for no one but himself during that terrible seven-year journey, they present a picture quite different to those bas-reliefs of a missionary in a peaked consular cap, Bible in hand, surrounded by his native followers. Tired out, disillusioned (for now he was dependent upon the very slave traders whom he wished to put out of business for ever), uncertain of everything (even of the Zambesi whose navigability had been his obstinate dream) except of his simple evangelical faith, so free from the complex dogmas of a theologian—just God the Father, God the Son and God the Holy Ghost. (The Apostles' Creed was nearer to him than the Athanasian.)

How little experience is needed in a reader to make him realize the appalling nature of the seven-year journey. This writer has experienced only four weeks of African travel on foot, one strike of carriers, one bad chief, a single night of high fever, only a few days when provisions grew short—but multiplying that small experience nearly a hundred times in days and how many hundred times in privation, it seems almost incredible that Livingstone could have gone on for so long without returning to civilization. Dr. Miller admirably describes the condition of all African travel—the spider-web of tracks that may lead somewhere or nowhere:

> One of the amazing features of Africa is the close network of footpaths that exists everywhere—and leads ev-

erywhere—highly convenient for movement within a limited neighbourhood, but most confusing for the stranger wishing to make a long cross-country traverse; and placing him at the mercy of guides who may mislead him, deliberately or accidentally, or simply immobilise him by withdrawing their services. . . . Thus we find Livingstone, like many other African travellers, subjected to expensive and infuriating delays by the refusal of chiefs to supply guides. He navigated and fixed the framework of his maps by means of sextant observations, of course, but these could not tell him which fork of the path led merely to an outfield, and which to the next village on his route; which to a swamp and which to the ford on the river."

Here are a few jottings of his journey:

Christmas Day 1866. "A little indigestible porridge, of hardly any taste, is now my fare and it makes me dream of better."

January 1867 (the great journey was not yet a year old). Deserting carriers stole: "all the dishes, a large box of powder, the flour we had purchased dearly to help us as far as the Chambesi, the tools, two guns and a cartridge pouch; but the medicine chest was the sorest loss of all. I felt as if I had received a sentence of death, like poor Bishop Mackenzie."

October 1867. "Sore bones; much headache; no appetite; much thirst."

December 1867. "I am so tired of exploration. . . ."

July 1868. "Here we cooked a little porridge, and then I lay down on one side, and the canoe men and my attendants at the fire in the middle. I was soon asleep and dreamt I had apartments in Mivart's hotel."

July 5, 1872 (Stanley by this time had come and gone). "Weary! Weary!"—but there were still ten months to go.

All the last months of the seven years' trek were spent in a flat prairie waste of water; the earth, what there was of it, was like adhesive plaster. In one night six inches of rain fell. Canoes sank and stuck; tents became rotten, clothes were never dry. There are moments when the reader feels as though Livingstone had forgotten his true purpose, which was not to explore the limit of human endurance but to reach the Lualaba river and sail down it in the hope that it might lead him to the Nile and its sources (even that was only a means to the great white trade routes, the blessings as he believed of commerce, the end of slavery). He was in Childe Roland's territory now—"a lion wandered into this world of water and ant-hills and roared night and morning." What a long way he had come from the gracefully curved fronds, the magnificent streams, the lofty palmyra towers. Like Stevenson struggling with *Weir* he had reached rock at the moment of death.

The comparison between these two Scotsmen is oddly close. Under the literary polish of the Vailima Prayers was a simplicity of faith very similar to Livingstone's. Does it come from a Scottish upbringing—this ability to feel regret without remorse, to pardon oneself and accept one's weakness, the ability to leave oneself to God? "For our sins forgiven or prevented, for our shame unpublished, we bless and thank Thee, O God." Thus Stevenson, and thus Livingstone:

> We now end 1866. It has not been so fruitful or useful as I intended. Will try to do better in 1867, and be better —more gentle and loving. And may the Almighty, to whom I commit my way, bring my desires to pass, and prosper me. Let all the sins of '66 be blotted out for Jesus' sake.

At the end they shared the same sense of failure. Who suffered more? Stevenson two months before his death writing, "I am a fictitious article and have long known it. I am read by journalists, by my fellow novelists, and by boys," or Livingstone finding himself embroiled in the slave trade he hated: "I am heart sore and sick of human blood. . . . I doubt whether the divine favour and will is on my side."

For the end their wish was the same. It is impossible not to recall the grave on Mount Vaea and the over-familiar verses, "Here he lies where he longed to be," when we read in Livingstone's journal on June 25, 1868:

> We came to a grave in the forest. It was a little rounded mound, as if the occupant sat in it. It was strewn over with flour, and a number of large beads had been put on it. A little path showed that it had visitors. That is the sort of grave I should prefer. To lie in the still, still forest, with no hand ever to disturb my bones. Graves at home seem to me miserable and without elbow room, especially those in cold, damp clay.

Stevenson's wishes were the more respected, for Livingstone's embalmed body was brought home to the damp clay and the lack of elbow room in the nave of Westminster Abbey.

Less than a hundred years has gone by since Livingstone's death and we can see the measure of his failure in East Africa today. The trade routes have been opened up, the slave trade abolished, but the true lesson of Livingstone's life was completely forgotten. "In attempting their moral elevation," Livingstone wrote of the Africans, "it is always more conductive to the end desired that the teacher should come unaccompanied by any power to cause either jealousy or fear." In the same book he wrote, "Good manners are as necessary among barbarians as among the civilized," but during those weeks in Stanley's company he had failed to influence his companion except superficially. It was to Stanley and his Maxim guns and rawhide whips that the future in East Africa belonged, and it was Stanley's methods that left a legacy of hatred and distrust throughout Africa.

1954   *Collected Essays*

John Gerard*

"This last era of a declining and gasping world"—so Gerard describes in his modest preface the setting of his *Autobiography*. How strange that phrase would have sounded to a Victorian ear, to the ear of Archdeacon Grantly or Mr. Micawber—a phrase, it would have seemed to them, as outlandish as the details of Gerard's adventure (it would be more accurate, when we remember his narrow escapes, his disappointments and betrayals, the long terrible scene of his torture, to call it his Passion). This history would have been as remote from them as an historical novel, and as an historical novel they would have preferred *Esmond*, with its remote romanticism, the dandyism of snuff-box and cane. They would have been a little disturbed even by Gerard's love story, for this, when you come to think of it, is a love story, the story of a man who loved his fellows to the worst point of pain.

Outlandish, yes; but for a quarter of a century now we have been travelling slowly back towards those outlands of danger through which Gerard moved in his disguise of fashion, with his talk of the hunt and of cards. We can read the *Autobiography* like a contemporary document or perhaps as something still a little ahead of our time, as though in a dream we had been allowed to read an account of life in 1960: life as it is going to be lived.

This is what gives the book, in its excellent translation from the Latin, such a sense of excitement, of immediacy. Listen to the narrative of Gerard's arrival in his native country: the danger in the familiar lane, death lying in wait in all the peaceful countryside.

> After crossing the sea we sailed up the English coast. On the third day my companion and I saw what seemed a

* This originally appeared as an Introduction in John Gerard, *The Autobiography of a Hunted Priest*, translated by Philip Caraman, published by Farrar, Straus & Giroux, Inc.

good place to put ashore in the ship's boat. As we thought it would be dangerous for all of us to land together, we asked God's guidance in prayer. Then we consulted our companions and ordered the ship to cast anchor off the point till nightfall. At the first watch of the night we were taken ashore in the boat and dropped there. The ship spread its canvas and sailed on.

For a few moments we prayed and commended ourselves to the keeping of God, then we looked about for a path to take us as far inland as possible and put a good distance between us and the sea before dawn broke. But the night was dark and overcast, and we could not pick the path we wanted and get away into the open fields. Every track we took led up to a house—as we knew at once when the dogs started to bark. This happened two or three times. Afraid we might wake the people inside and be set on for attempting to burgle them, we decided to go off into a nearby wood and rest there till the morning. It was about the end of October, raining and wet, and we passed a sleepless night. Nor did we dare to talk for the wood was close to a house. However, in little more than a whisper we held a conference. Would it be better to make for London together or separate so that if one of us was caught the other might get away safely? We discussed both courses thoroughly. In the end we decided to part company and each to go his own way.

That homecoming has been enacted in many countries during our half-century since Father Pro landed at Vera Cruz in his bright cardigan and his striped tie and his brown shoes, but here, in Gerard's narrative, it is happening in our own Norfolk, to us.

Father Gerard's prose is plain, accurate, vivid. The act of writing is very like the act of sculpture: one is presented with a rude block of facts, out of which one has to cut the only details that matter. "As exciting as a novel"—how often we have read that misleading phrase in a publisher's advertisement, and how seldom, in fact, is the novel exciting. How seldom do we find the novelist properly detaching his subject matter, his characters, his mood, his scene, from the preliminary stone as Gerard does.

We have seen in his account of his landing how quietly and almost modestly Gerard sets his scene, the mood of suspense and pursuit conveyed in the simplest terms—an overcast night, a strange house, the barking of dogs. One could have quoted more dramatic scenes—Father Southwell's Mass interrupted by the priest hunters, Gerard's own arrest and torture, his escape from the Tower. For his ability to draw character, quickly, in the running course of his narrative, there are many examples. Father Southwell, who will be known to many readers only as the poet who wrote "The Burning Babe," as much a lay figure as his fellow poets of the time of whom we know so little, comes alive in Gerard's narrative as he worries over the correct technical terms to maintain his superficial disguise as a country gentleman.

When I got the opportunity I spoke about hunting and falconry, a thing no one could do in correct technical language unless he was familiar with the sports. It is an easy thing to trip up in one's terms, as Father Southwell used to complain. Frequently, as he was travelling about with me later, he would ask me to tell him the correct terms and worried because he couldn't remember and use them when the need arose: for instance, when he fell in with Protestant gentlemen who had practically no other conversation except, perhaps, obscene subjects, or rant against the saints and the Catholic faith. On occasions like this there is often a chance of bringing the conversation round to some other topic simply by throwing out a remark about horses or hounds or the like.

Was it some such experience as this that brought the metaphors of the hunt even into the poems of the Blessed Henry Walpole, whose cell in the Tower Gerard was later to occupy?

> The falkener seeks to see a flight
> the hunter beates to see his gamme

Longe thou my soule to see that sight
    and labour to enjoy the same.

Southwell is a major character in Gerard's story, but how
easily he touches in even his anonymous figures, the warder
who wept over his torture, or this convert, identified by Father Caraman as Sir Oliver Manners, sketched so vividly in
the margin of the narrative that we seem to see him full
length, the very cut of his doublet, the shape of his leg, the
spread of the long Elizabethan fingers on his book, though
Gerard has used not one phrase of physical description.

> You might see him in the court or in the Presence
> Chamber, as it is called, when it was crowded with cour-
> tiers and famous ladies, turning aside to a window and
> reading a chapter of Thomas à Kempis's *Imitation of Christ*.
> He knew the book from cover to cover. And after reading
> a little he would turn to the company, but his mind was
> elsewhere. He stood absorbed in his thoughts. People
> imagined that he was admiring some beautiful lady, or
> wondering how to climb to a higher position.

Compared with these Topcliffe might be thought an easy
character to draw, but the priest hunter has been the bogey
man of so many stories that we feel a certain surprise at
finding him start up here as evil in fact as in fiction, wearing
a court dress with a sword hanging at his side "old and
hoary and a veteran in evil." (It is rather as though Mr.
Hyde had stepped out of Stevenson's pages into the authen-
tic Edinburgh streets.)

> "I will see that you are brought to me and placed in my
> power. I will hang you up in the air and will have no pity
> on you; and then I shall watch and see whether God will
> snatch you from my grasp."

There is one portrait in this gallery one sadly misses. On
April 14, 1597, five men reported on their examination of
Gerard in the Tower: only two of them were known to Ge-
rard, but one, we learn from Father Caraman, was Francis

Bacon. For a moment one would like to imagine oneself a follower of the Baconian heresy and to believe that it was William Shakespeare who faced Gerard across the board, for isn't there one whole area of the Elizabethan scene that we miss even in Shakespeare's huge world of comedy and despair? The kings speak, the adventurers speak (so that we can imagine in Faulconbridge's rough tones the very language of Francis Drake), the madmen and the lovers, the soldiers and the poets, but the martyrs are quite silent—one might say that the Christians are silent except for the diplomatic tones of a Wolsey or Pandulpho or the sudden flash of conscience in Hamlet's uncle at prayers. What Franciscan ever resembled Friar Lawrence with his little moral apothegms, his tags of Latin and his herbs? One might have guessed from Shakespeare's plays that there was a vast vacuum where the Faith had been—the noise and bustle of pilgrimages have been stilled: we come out of the brisk world of Chaucer into the silence of Hamlet's court after the Prince's departure, out of the colours of Canterbury into the grey world of Lear's blasted heath. An old Rome has taken the place of the Christian Rome—the pagan philosophers and the pagan gods seem to have returned. Characters speak with the accent of stoics, they pay lip service to Venus and Bacchus. How far removed they are from the routine of the torture chamber.

> When the Lieutenant saw that I could speak he said: "Don't you see how much better for you it would be if you submitted to the Queen instead of dying like this?"
>
> God helped me and I was able to put more spirit into my answer than I had felt up to now.
>
> "No, no I don't!" I said. "I would prefer to die a thousand times rather than do as they suggest."
>
> "So you won't confess, then?"
>
> "No, I won't," I said. "And I won't as long as there is breath left in my body."
>
> "Very well, then, we must hang you up again now, and a second time after dinner."

He spoke as though he were sorry to have to carry out his orders.

"Eamus in nomine Domini," I said. "I have only one life, but if I had several I would sacrifice them all for the same cause."

I struggled to my feet and tried to walk over to the pillar but I had to be helped. I was very weak now and if I had any spirit left in me it was given by God and given to me, although most unworthy, because I shared the fellowship of the Society.

I was hung up again. The pain was intense now, but I felt a great consolation of soul, which seemed to me to come from a desire of death. Whether it arose from a true love of suffering for Christ, or from a selfish longing to be with Christ, God knows best. But I thought then that I was going to die. And my heart filled with great gladness as I abandoned myself to His will and keeping and contemned the will of men.

If Shakespeare had sat where Bacon had sat and given the orders for the torture, one wonders whether into the great plays which present on the inner side, however much on the outer Lear may rave or Antony lust, so smooth and ambiguous a surface, there would have crept a more profound doubt than Hamlet's, a sense of a love deeper than Romeo's.

1951   Uncollected

IV. COMMITMENTS

Be disloyal. It's your duty to the human race.
The human race needs to survive and it's the
loyal man who dies first from anxiety or a
bullet or overwork. If you have to earn a
living . . . and the price they make you pay is
loyalty, be a double agent—and never let
either of the two sides know your real
name. . . .

—"Under the Garden," *A Sense of Reality*

EDITOR'S PREFACE

The title and design of this section are Greene's idea. Instead of the usual "Letters and Essays" he wanted something more pointed, something that would reflect his current concern for repressed and miserable countries and people, and his hatred of injustice and intolerance.

Of course he has always been a committed writer. He began with socialist sympathies. His trip to Mexico led to a period of Catholic commitment. He now considers himself only as a recruit to the Foreign Legion as far as the Church is concerned, but he has become involved politically again, this time on a world scale. If space permitted, here is where some of his journalism should be included. From 1951, with the first of a dozen reports on the French war in Indo-China, he has sent in many personal diagnoses of inflammation points in a troubled world, from Cuba, Haiti, Paraguay, the Congo, Kenya, Berlin, and Poland. In all these articles his political preferences are clearly stated: pro-Castro in Cuba, anti-Duvalier in Haiti, pro-Allende in Chile, pro-Kikuyu in Kenya, anti-Communist in Malaya, anti-American in Vietnam. . . .

But although he has been very outspoken on political issues, he cannot be judged by his allegiances, for they are not determined by belief in any particular ideology but are prompted rather by a writer's concern for individuals. That is why, in his novels, as in the selections that follow, the basic freedom that he recognizes is the freedom to dissent, and the essential virtue, "the virtue of disloyalty." Most of these pieces are uncollected, and two of them appear in English for the first time.

Two Statements on Commitment

A Meditation by Brown

Perhaps there is an advantage in being born in a city like Monte Carlo, without roots, for one accepts more easily what comes. The rootless have experienced, like all the others, the temptation of sharing the security of a religious creed or a political faith, and for some reason we have turned the temptation down. We are the faithless; we admire the dedicated, the Doctor Magiots and the Mr. Smiths, for their courage and their integrity, for their fidelity to a cause, but through timidity, or through lack of sufficient zest, we find ourselves the only ones truly committed—committed to the whole world of evil and of good, to the wise and to the foolish, to the indifferent and to the mistaken. We have chosen nothing except to go on living, "rolled round on Earth's diurnal course, With rocks and stones and trees."

A Letter from Doctor Magiot

Dear friend,
    I write to you because I loved your mother and in these last hours I want to communicate with her son. My hours are limited: I expect any moment that knock upon the door. They can hardly ring the bell, for the electricity as usual is off. The American Ambassador is about to come back and Baron Samedi will surely pay a little tribute in return. It happens like that all over the world. A few Communists can always be found, like Jews and Catholics. Chiang Kai-shek, the heroic defender of Formosa, fed us, you remember, into the boilers of railway-engines. God knows for what medical research Papa Doc may find me useful. I only ask you to remember *ce si gros neg*. Do you remember that evening when Mrs. Smith accused me of being a Marxist? Accused is too strong a word. She is a kind woman who hates injustice. Yet

I have grown to dislike the word "Marxist." It is used so often to describe only a particular economic plan. I believe of course in that economic plan—in certain cases and in certain times, here in Haiti, in Cuba, in Vietnam, in India. But Communism, my friend, is more than Marxism, just as Catholicism—remember I was born a Catholic too—is more than the Roman Curia. There is a *mystique* as well as a *politique*. We are humanists, you and I. You won't admit it perhaps, but you are the son of your mother and you once took that dangerous journey which we all have to take before the end. Catholics and Communists have committed great crimes, but at least they have not stood aside, like an established society, and been indifferent. I would rather have blood on my hands than water like Pilate. I know you and love you well, and I am writing this letter with some care because it may be the last chance I have of communicating with you. It may never reach you, but I am sending it by what I believe to be a safe hand—though there is no guarantee of that in the wild world we live in now (I do not mean my poor insignificant little Haiti). I implore you—a knock on the door may not allow me to finish this sentence, so take it as the last request of a dying man—if you have abandoned one faith, do not abandon all faith. There is always an alternative to the faith we lose. Or is it the same faith under another mask?

1966   from *The Comedians*

Convenience and Morality

To the Editor of *The Times* [London]

July 7, 1969

Sir,

The days of ideals—and ideologies which are their political expression—are certainly over. The invasion of Czecho slovakia by the Soviet Union and her allies was an echo of the invasion of the Dominican Republic by the United States and her allies. Now your paper today prints a photograph of Governor Rockefeller presenting a letter from President Nixon to that murderer and torturer, President Duvalier of Haiti. Of course we cannot tell what the letter contains, but the public presentation will appear as an encouragement of tyranny to all those brave men who have been risking their lives in attempts to overthrow Papa Doc. The convenience of the major powers now is all and morality counts for nothing in international politics.

Let us remember that, when the United States—or the Soviet Union—demand "moral support" for their policies. Of course the two super powers do not need our support—they are allies in all but name.

Yours sincerely,
GRAHAM GREENE

The Last Pope[*]

No doubt because he continues an uninterrupted tradition of Christian state of mind, thought, and style, the French novelist seems to move easily among abstractions: they surround his childhood, and the liturgy is as familiar to him as his nursery rhymes. When a door opens in a novel by Mauriac, even before one leaves the shadows to enter the well-lit room where the characters are assembled, one is aware of forces of Good and Evil that slide along the walls and press their fingers against the window-pane ready to crowd in. This awareness is, in general, banished from the English

[*] The text of an address given at Les Grandes Conférences Catholiques in Brussels in January 1948 on the theme "Is Christian Civilization in Peril?" Translation by Philip Stratford.

novel. Perhaps it is because we live in a northern island where the sun shines so spasmodically and where we can be cut off from the continent for days at a time by fog or storm, an island to which Christianity came like a stranger from across the sea—perhaps because of this we tend to be more materialistic in our reactions and more concrete in imagination than those who live in sunnier lands who can permit themselves the luxury of shadow. The English novelist has become accustomed to bypass eternity. Evil appears in Dickens's novels only as an economic factor, nothing more. Christianity is a woman serving soup to the poor. How vivid are his images of the still Sunday streets, the dark, mean little courts near the river, the prison buildings, but how barren and dim is the life of the spirit! In Dickens, Evil has lost its supernatural quality, it has become something that the power of money, an amendment to the law, or perhaps simply death can abolish, for when a character dies, the evil dies with him. The English novel always makes us live within time.

Is Christian civilization in peril? For each of you these words possess the solidity of statues. You move freely among them like a man making his way past the overpopulated side-chapels of a great cathedral: the Immaculate Conception stretches out its arms of stone to you; the Sacred Heart is there made out of carved and painted wood; the candles burn with a tangible flame. But I feel as though I am surrounded by shadows. Civilization is a thing I learned in books, and Christianity is something that happens somewhere else, beyond my range of vision, perhaps in another country, certainly in another heart. I cannot touch the words unless they are given a human shape. The Apostle Thomas should be the patron saint of people in my country, for we must see the marks of the nails and put our hands in the wounds before we can understand.

So this question, even before I begin to consider it, becomes three questions. First, what is a Christian civilization in terms of human characters, human acts, and the daily commerce of human lives? Second, has this civilization ever existed, and does it exist today in any part of the world? It is only if the reply to this second question is affirmative that it will be necessary to ask whether Christian civilization is in danger.

Naturally, it would be convenient to adopt a rigid and clearly defined attitude, to represent Christian civilization as a corporate arrangement of human life that would permit everyone to follow, without the least hindrance from his fellows, the teaching of the Sermon on the Mount. In that case, without further ado, we could examine our own age, retrace the course of history, and declare that such a civilization has never existed. But in adopting such an attitude—and the enemies of Christianity have often used this kind of argument—we are confusing the city of man and the City of God. The perfect imitation of Christ is impossible here, but our very imperfection is sanctified, for didn't God imitate man, and weren't man's despair and failure expressed by God himself on the cross? So in our definition of a Christian civilization we should not be led astray by the presence of wars, injustice and cruelty, or by the absence of charity. All those things can exist in a Christian state. They are not marks of Christianity, but of man.

But if we give up all thought of achieving or even of pursuing perfection, what clues can we hope to find that will help us distinguish a Christian from a pagan civilization? Perhaps, truthfully, we can count on nothing more than the divided mind, the uneasy conscience, and the sense of personal failure.

Of course this sense of guilt was already present in Greek civilization; it hangs over Greek drama like a heavy cloud. But it is a kind of impersonal guilt that a Christian literature might have produced on the theme of the fall of man if there had been the Revelation without the Incarnation, or if we had experienced personal failure without having had the model. In Greek literature any excess is synonymous with fear—excess of riches, happiness, luck, or power—but this fear is only an abstract fear. The fortunate man believes in justice operating like a pendulum; he follows like all men the swing of the pendulum; he has no sense of an individual failure which differentiates him from other men equally fortunate.

My conviction that the Christian conscience is the only satisfactory sign of a Christian civilization is reinforced by the fact that this trait was completely lacking in the pagan powers that so recently reigned over the world. How the Nazis strutted in their hour of triumph and how they justified themselves in their defeat! How deliberately and explicitly they followed the doctrine which consists in doing evil to achieve good—their own personal good! The totalitarian state contrives, by educating its citizens, to suppress all sense of guilt, all indecision of mind. Let the State assume the responsibility for the crime, I am innocent. My only crime is my loyalty. The parrot voices proclaim with a terrifying pathetic resignation, "My chief gave the order." No soldier makes a cross of sticks to hand his victim.

The years we have just lived through are perhaps not the worst Europe has known. Many times in Christian civilization cities have been sacked and prisoners tortured, but doesn't one always find these tyrants of the past haunted by a sense of guilt? Let me read you a passage from the Anglo-Saxon Chronicles which describes the situation in England in the twelfth century, in the reign of Stephen. It is a contemporary report. It is at least equal in horror to anything we have seen in Europe in the past few years.

. . . They sorely burdened the unhappy people of the country with forced labour on the castles; and when the castles were built, they filled them with devils and wicked men. By night and by day they seized those whom they believed to have any wealth, whether they were men or women; and in order to get their gold and silver, they put them into prison and tortured them with unspeakable tortures, for never were martyrs tortured as they were. They hung them up by the feet and smoked them with foul smoke. They strung them up by the thumbs, or by the head, and hung coats of mail on their feet. They tied knotted cords round their heads and twisted it till it entered the brain. They put them in dungeons wherein were adders and snakes and toads, and so destroyed them. Some they put into a "crucethus"; that is to say, into a short, narrow, shallow chest into which they put sharp stones; and they crushed the man in it until they had broken every bone in his body.

. . . Then was corn dear and flesh and cheese and butter, for there was none in the land. The wretched people perished with hunger; some, who had been great men, were driven to beggary, while others fled from the country. Never did a country endure greater misery, and never did the heathen act more vilely than they did.

. . . If two or three men came riding towards a village, all the villagers fled for fear of them, believing that they were robbers. The bishops and the clergy were for ever cursing them, but that was nothing to them, for they were all excommunicated and forsworn and lost.

Wherever the ground was tilled the earth bore no corn, for the land was ruined by such doings; and men said openly that Christ and His saints slept. Such things and others more than we know how to relate we suffered nineteen years for our sins.

I would not refuse the name of Christian civilization to those sombre years. Don't we, in fact, in reading this chronicle get the distinct impression of a bad conscience, of an acute sense of guilt? There were still some who raised voices in protest, the chronicle tells us so. The saints slept, but they were not disowned. Darkness covered the face of the island, but Christianity continued to move in the shadows. The possibility of an enormous repentance counterbalanced the possibility of enormous crimes. Take an example from English history. Our great king Henry II, in his grief, made a deliberate pact with the enemy of God. When he saw his native city burned in Normandy he made this great oath (so Christian even in its denial of Christ): "O God, since you have seen well to take from me the thing I loved most, the city where I was born and bred, I swear that I, too, will take from you that which you love the most in me." How could one class among the enemies of God this saint in reverse who gave us a true saint, Thomas of Canterbury, and who, after the murder of Saint Thomas, demanded to be whipped publicly by the monks. Contrition was born at the same time as the crime: twin births of sin and punishment.

Our enemies can call to witness many crimes committed in Christ's name. But in the long run what importance do such crimes have? In all our poetry you can hear a common note, the note of what I have called the divided mind—in the words of Sir Thomas Browne: "There's another man within me that's angry with me."

. . . This is the signature of a Christian civilization. Challenged by our enemies we can admit our crimes because throughout history it is possible to point to our repentance.

If you accept my definition of the distinguishing mark of a Christian civilization, we can now easily answer the second question, "Has such a civilization ever existed?" The answer is "Yes." In a large part of the world man's conscience remains sensitive to moral failure. To cite only one recent example, it was not just political opportunism that determined the liberation of India. Half a century ago it would have seemed absurd to suggest that Christian civilization was in any danger. There have been so many wars and revolutions that a few more or less matter very little in the eyes of history. No new weapon can kill the impetus of Christianity. If that were possible, gunpowder would have finished it off. The atom bomb is powerless against conscience. But in the last twenty years we have witnessed an attempt to kill it by means of a new philosophy designed to persuade men that Lazarus is without importance. Dives, in a fancy dress uniform, receives the acclamations of the crowd in the treets of Berlin or from a balcony in Red Square. Perhaps my countrymen are not entirely wrong to mistrust those abstract words which allowed Dives to become a hero, by replacing Lazarus with "the people" or "the proletariat" or "the working class." In countries that were formerly democratic, and nowadays in countries that are still democratic, we have seen abstractions extend their domain in man's thought and leave their rightful place in philosophy and theology to invade history, economics and politics, subjects which, by their very nature, should be treated in concrete terms. Read any article in the popular press, even if the subject is as matter of fact as the extraction of iron ore, or estimates of this year's crop yield—one seeks in vain for a concrete image. Abstractions have been administered to our democracies like a drug. A phrase like "render unto Caesar" is translated by political journalists into "our responsibilities towards the State." Abstract expressions help dictators to power by troubling the clear waters of thought. William Blake said that whoever wishes to do good to his neighbour should do so on small occasions, for the general good is always invoked by scoundrels, hypocrites and flatterers.

We can no longer take lightly the danger that threatens Christian civilization. Between 1933 and 1945 civilization was almost completely destroyed in Germany. That abscess has been lanced, but the totalitarian poison can still spread to countries which escaped the first infection. It is terrifying to think of the distance Russia has travelled in less than a hundred years. Remember in *The Brothers Karamazov* Aliosha stripping himself of everything for the service of God: "I cannot give up two roubles instead of 'all thou hast' or just go to morning mass instead of 'come and follow me.' " And remember Father Zossima and his all-embracing charity: "Hate not atheists, the teachers of evil, materialists, even the most wicked of them, let alone the good ones among them. . . Remember them in your prayers thus: 'Save, O Lord, all who have no one to pray for them, and save those, too, who do not want to pray to thee.' " And then think of the

Moscow Trials and of Prosecutor Vishinsky and of that in accessible grey figure in the Kremlin with his skin-deep bon homie reserved for state banquets and the dark in the depth of his eyes.

And yet it would surely be a sin against faith to exagger ate the danger. We are bound to believe that Christianit cannot die. A hundred years is, after all, a very short time Perhaps it will turn out that it is Mitya Karamazov wh rules in Russia today. You remember his words: "If I am t precipitate myself into the abyss, I shall do so without a mo ment's reflection, head over heels, and indeed I shall be glad to fall in such a degrading attitude and consider it beautifu for a man like me. And it is at this very moment of sham and disgrace that I suddenly begin to intone this hymn.' Perhaps if we were well enough informed we could discern here and there in Russia, too, the signs of an uneasy con science. For we must not forget that in Germany's darkes days the voice of conscience was heard intermittently, neve among the leaders of the state, but among the leaders of th Church—Faulhaber, Galen, Niemöller, and others too ob scure or too unimportant to escape death. I remember one o my friends, von Bernstorff. Before Hitler's rise to power h was First Secretary of the German Embassy in London. H resigned in 1933 and was executed in 1944 in Dachau be cause he belonged to a secret organization that continued t help Jews escape from Germany even during the war. Wha a strange fate that this heavy, superficial man, who loved the good life and a good laugh, with his aristocratic indo lence and his taste for old cognac, should be transformed into a martyr for the cause of charity!

As I have said, we are bound to believe that Faith canno die. It can suffer reverses, large parts of the world can b conquered by its enemies, but there will always exist pocket of Christian resistance. In England during the sinister yea 1940 we used to say, "But just look at the map of the world, meaning that if our island seemed tiny and desperately im perilled in relation to Europe, all the same, hope was rekin dled at the sight of allied territories in Africa, Australia and Canada. Christians, too, should look at the map of the world from time to time. Suppose the whole of Europe should become a totalitarian state; we are not the world.

It is not impossible that we might see the whole world succumb to a totalitarian and atheistic regime. Even so, it would still not be the end. In that case we, the spies of God, would have to draw up large-scale maps of every city and every village. There, in such and such a street, behind the café, at the crossroads in the town of X, in the fifteenth house on the right, there is a cellar, and in this cellar a child, playing, has traced a clumsy cross on the plaster wall. . . .

Permit me to close with a story which I once intended to write—a fantasy in a melodramatic vein, which takes place in the distant future, say two centuries from now, when the whole world is governed by a single party and organized with an efficiency undreamt of today. The curtain rises on a sordid little hotel in London or New York, it doesn't matter which. It is late at night. An old man, tired, down-hearted, nondescript, wearing a shabby raincoat and carrying a battered suitcase, comes up to the reception desk and asks for a room. He signs the register and disappears wearily up the stairs (the hotel is too poor to have an elevator). The house detective looks at the register and says to the clerk:

"Did you see who that was?"

"No."

"It's the Pope."

"The Pope? Who's that?"

Catholicism has been successfully stamped out. Only the Pope survives, elected thirty years before at the last conclave (a secret conclave, its members believed, though in reality monitored by an even more secret police), and doomed to rule over a Church which has virtually ceased to exist. After the conclave the cardinals had met the fate of the rest of the priests: a white wall and a firing squad. But the Pope was authorized to live. He even receives a small pension from the State because he is of use in demonstrating how dead the

Church is, and because there is always the possibility that some survivor will betray himself by trying to get in touch with him. But there are no more survivors. Rome, naturally, has been renamed for over a century.

I was going to describe this little man, this little Pope, drifting miserably here and there, purposelessly, driven on by the vague hope that somewhere, some day, he might encounter a sign to show him that the Faith survived after all and he need no longer be haunted by the fear that what he had professed to be eternal might die with him. I won't bore you with the story of his useless wanderings and his deceptions, each duly recorded and filed at the headquarters of the World Police. In the end the World Dictator got tired of the game. He wanted to put an end to it in his own lifetime, for although he was only fifty while the Pope had long since passed seventy, accidents happen to dictators and he did not wish to surrender his place in history as the man who, with his own finger on the trigger of the revolver, had put an end to the Christian myth.

So at the end of this story which I never wrote, the Pope was brought by the police into the Dictator's secret room with its soundproof, bulletproof walls, and there, in the padded silence, the Dictator, after offering the Pope a cigarette, which he refused, and a glass of wine, which he accepted, told him he was going to die on the spot—the last Christian, the last man in the world who still believed. After dismissing the detectives the Dictator took a revolver out of his desk drawer. He granted the Pope a moment to pray (he had read in a book that this was customary), but he didn't listen to the prayer. Then he shot him in the left side of the chest and leaned forward over the body to give the coup de grâce. At that instant, in the second between the pressure on the trigger and the skull cracking, a thought crossed the Dictator's mind: "Is it just possible that what this man believed is true?" Another Christian had been born.

Colette's Funeral Rites*

An Open Letter to the Cardinal Archbishop of Paris

Your Eminence,

Those of us who loved Colette and her books gathered today to honour her in a ceremony that must have seemed strangely curtailed to Catholics present. We are used to pray for our dead. In our faith the dead are never abandoned. It is the right of every person baptized a Catholic to be accompanied to the tomb by a priest. This right cannot be lost—as one can lose one's citizenship in a temporary country—due to some crime or misdemeanour, because no human being is capable of judging another or of deciding where his faults begin or his merits end.

But today, by your decision, no priest offered public prayers at Colette's funeral. We all know your reasons. But would they have been brought forward if Colette had been less famous? Forget the great writer and think only of an old woman of eighty who, at a time when Your Eminence had not yet been ordained, made an unhappy marriage through no fault of her own (unless innocence is a fault) and later broke the Church's law by a second and then a third civil marriage. Are two civil marriages so unforgivable? The lives of some of our saints provide worse examples. Of course they repented. But to repent means to rethink one's life, and no one can say what passes through a mind trained in habits of lucidity when it is confronted with the imminent fact of death. You have made your condemnation on insufficient evidence, for you were not with her then, nor were any of your ministers.

Your Eminence has unconsciously given the impression

---

* This letter was published in *Le Figaro Littéraire* on August 7, 1954. Translation by Philip Stratford.

that the Church pursues the fault beyond the grave. What was Your Eminence's purpose in making an example of this case? Was it to warn your flock of the danger of taking the marriage laws lightly? It would surely have been more to the point to warn them of the danger of condemning others too easily and to guard them from lack of charity. Religious authorities frequently remind writers of their responsibilities towards simple souls and of the risk of scandal. But there is also another risk, which is to scandalize the enlightened. Has Your Eminence considered that a scandal of this kind might be caused by his decision? It may seem to non-Catholics that the Church itself is lacking in charity; it may seem capable of refusing prayers at the moment of greatest need. How different was the treatment accorded Gide by the Protestant Church when he died! (Your Eminence will pardon the warmth of these remarks when he remembers that a writer whose books we love becomes someone dear to us. This is no abstract case drawn from a text in moral theology designed for the use of seminarians.)

Of course, upon reflection, Catholics may consider that the voice of an Archbishop is not necessarily the voice of the Church, but many Catholics, not only in France but also in England and America where Colette's works are known and loved, will feel personally wounded by the fact that Your Eminence, through such a strict interpretation of the rule, seems to deny the hope of that final intervention of grace upon which surely Your Eminence and each one of us will depend at the last hour.

With my humble respect for the Sacred Purple,

Graham Greene

A Superstition to Live By

A conversation between Querry and Doctor Colin

"The fathers believe they have the Christian truth behind them, and it helps them in a place like this. You and I have no such truth. Is the Christian myth that you talked about enough for you?"

"I want to be on the side of change," the doctor said. "If I had been born an amoeba who could think, I would have dreamed of the day of the primates. I would have wanted anything I did to contribute to that day. Evolution, as far as we can tell, has lodged itself finally in the brains of man. The ant, the fish, even the ape has gone as far as it can go, but in our brain evolution is moving—my God—at what a speed! I forget how many hundreds of millions of years passed between the dinosaurs and the primates, but in our own lifetime we have seen the change from diesel to jet, the splitting of the atom, the cure of leprosy."

"Is change so good?"

"We can't avoid it. We are riding a great ninth evolutionary wave. Even the Christian myth is part of the wave, and perhaps, who knows, it may be the most valuable part. Suppose love were to evolve as rapidly in our brains as technical skill has done. In isolated cases it may have done, in the saints . . . if the man really existed, in Christ."

"You can really comfort yourself with all that?" Querry asked. "It sounds like the old song of progress."

"The nineteenth century wasn't as far wrong as we like to believe. We have become cynical about progress because of the terrible things we have seen men do during the last forty years. All the same through trial and error the amoeba did become the ape. There were blind starts and wrong turnings even then, I suppose. Evolution today can produce Hitlers as well as St. John of the Cross. I have a small hope, that's all, a very small hope, that someone they call Christ was the fertile element, looking for a crack in the wall to plant its seed. I think of Christ as an amoeba who took the right turning. I want to be on the side of the progress which survives. I'm no friend of pterodactyls."

"But if we are incapable of love?"

"I'm not sure such a man exists. Love is planted in man now, even uselessly in some cases, like an appendix. Sometimes of course people call it hate."

"I haven't found any trace of it in myself."

"Perhaps you are looking for something too big and too important. Or too active."

"What you are saying seems to me every bit as superstitious as what the fathers believe."

"Who cares? It's the superstition I live by."

1961   from *A Burnt-Out Case*

Slide into Barbarism

To the Editor of *The Times* [London]

November 6, 1964

Sir,

In the past few weeks photographs have appeared in the British Press showing the tortures inflicted on Viet-Cong prisoners by troops of the Vietnam army.

In the long, frustrating war—now nearly twenty years old—there has, of course, always been a practice of torture —torture by Viet-Minh, torture by Vietnamese, torture by the French—but at least in the old days hypocrisy paid a tribute to virtue by hushing up the torture inflicted by its own soldiers and condemning the torture inflicted by the other side.

The strange new feature about the photographs of torture now appearing in the British and American Press is that they have been taken with the approval of the torturers and are published over captions that contain no hint of condemnation. They might have come out of a book on insect life. "The white ant takes certain measures against the red ant after a successful foray."

But these, after all, are not ants but men. The long, slow slide into barbarism of the western world seems to have quickened. For these photographs are of torturers belonging to an army which could not exist without American aid and counsel.

Does this mean that the American authorities sanction torture as a means of interrogation? The photographs certainly are a mark of honesty, a sign that the authorities do not shut their eyes to what is going on, but I wonder whether this kind of honesty without conscience is really to be preferred to the old hypocrisy.

Yours faithfully,
GRAHAM GREENE

Letter to a West German Friend[*]

What a relief it is sometimes to find oneself on a material frontier, a frontier visible to the eyes, tangible—even when in Berlin it is a wall. For most of us have all our lives in this unhappy century carried an invisible frontier around with us, political, religious, moral. . . . Nearly forty years ago I stepped across such a frontier when I became a Catholic, but the frontier did not cease to exist for me because I had crossed it. Often I have returned and looked over it with nostalgia, like the little groups on either side of the Brandenburg Gate who on holidays stare across at each other trying to recognize a friend.

I was reminded of my invisible frontier when I stayed

* Published in *The New Statesman*, May 31, 1963.

with you in West Berlin. Up at night in the roof-garden of the Hilton Hotel—a garden where vari-coloured bottles take the place of flowers—you pointed out to me the great arc of lights around the west, and the deep space of darkness beyond, broken only by occasional short chains of yellow beads. "You can see," you said, "where the East lies"; yet it is the mark of frontiers—the evil of frontiers perhaps—that things look quite different when you pass them. Four days later, driving into East Berlin from Dresden and Potsdam, I was not particularly aware of darkness—not at any rate a greater darkness than you will find in the industrial quarter of any large city at ten o'clock at night. It was true there was no Kurfürstendam, though that name conveys now none of the gay haggard associations of the twenties. The big new restaurant in the Unter den Linden was still bright with lights; the shop windows too were lit and there was an elegance too in the window-dressing which you do not find in Moscow. Alone of Communist cities Moscow seems to frown on the allure of consumer-goods—she makes the worst of what she has, while in East Berlin and Bucharest and Warsaw they make the most. . . .

There is a wall neurosis: the visitor is more aware of it in the West than in the East because there the wall is geographically inescapable. Take a drive in the evening as we did in the little patch of country still belonging to West Berlin: the road is packed with cars, driven by people seeking the illusion of space and air, until suddenly there the wall is again, not of brick or cement this time, but of wire and water, the water divided by buoys and patrolled by eastern police boats.

Belief, like it or not, is a magnet. Even what seem the extravagant claims of a belief are magnetic. In a commercial world of profit and loss man is hungry often for the irrational. I do not believe that the little knots of people who gather near Checkpoint Charlie are there to demonstrate repugnance, as do the bus loads at the Brandenburg Gate. Part of Berlin has become a foreign land and they are staring into the strangeness, some with enmity, others with apprehension, but all with a certain fascination. Behind them lies the new city, the smart hotels, the laden stores; but capitalism is not a belief, and so it is not a magnet. It is only a way of life to which one has grown accustomed.

To take the few steps beyond Checkpoint Charlie can be compared with the acceptance of the last difficult dogma—say the infallibility of the Pope. There are moments when the possible convert is in a state of rebellion; he can see the wall and nothing but the wall. There are moments when he will gladly stretch his faith to the furthest limits. Perhaps there is always one moment when he shuts his eyes and walks into the wide ruined spaces beyond the checkpoint. He looks back, over his shoulder and the dogma has suddenly changed. What had been a threat can even appear like a protection. . . .

Naturally this was the way the wall was presented to me by the young officer at the Brandenburg Gate in a speech too long, too prepared and too innocently propagandist: a protection from spies, saboteurs and black marketeers. His stories of deaths along the wall almost too carefully duplicated the circumstances of deaths on the western side. Crosses and wreaths are a popular expression, and though they may be as misleading as photographs, they are a great deal more convincing. It was not from this officer that one gained the sense of the wall as protection, nor from the booklet purporting to give the names, addresses and telephone numbers of the C.I.A. staff in West Berlin, beginning with a Mr. Harry Grant of 15 Taylorstrasse and ending with a Miss Jane Rowlay of 17 Stuartstrasse (telephone 76-49-87). There were private tragedies of divided families *before* the wall was built as well as after—families divided by the temptations of the West.

The West is too inclined to attach heroic motives to all those who escape across or through the wall. Courage they certainly have, but how many are "choosing freedom" for romantic motives, love of a girl, of a family, of a way of life, and how many are merely tempted by a standard which includes transistor radio-sets, American blue jeans and leather jackets? As long as living standards differ, there'll always be motives less than noble.

You may think I was conditioned by the friends I made on the other side of the wall, for true it is, when I passed Checkpoint Charlie returning west, I felt as if I were leaving something simple behind me and coming out again into the complex world of Bonn. In a few more minutes I would be talking again with my western friends about the case of *Der Spiegel*, about the wiles of the old Chancellor, about Doenitz's school speech in defence of the Nazis and the headmaster's suicide; I would be asking about the record of General Speidel and the latest Nazi scandal in the government of Bonn.

There have been scandals, of course, on the other side, but they have been ruthlessly cured: the sore does not continue to run there indefinitely. In West Germany one hesitates to probe the past of any man in his fifties or sixties. I felt no such hesitation in the East. Of four friends I made there two were old Communists who had spent the war in a refugee camp in Shanghai; one had served in the British Army, landing with a Scottish regiment in Normandy; one, having fought with the International Brigade in Spain, saw the war out in South America. Perhaps the old Catholic convert has something in common with the old Communist convert which makes it easy for the two to get on terms—he has lived through the period of enthusiasm and now recognizes the differing regions of acceptance and doubt. One Communist, who had been an orthodox Jew, said to me, "I gave up my faith when I was eighteen and joined the party. Now at fifty one realizes that everything is not known." There's a funny story—told in the East. Khrushchev has been asked by the Central Committee to visit the Pope and try to reduce the tension of the Cold War. He reports to the Committee when he returns: "I have reached a compromise with the Pope." (The members express uneasiness at the very idea of compromise.) "I have agreed that the world was made in seven days." (A tumult follows.) "Yes, but listen to what the Pope has agreed—that it was made under the leadership of the Communist Party."

On this side of the wall we are apt to believe that we have a monopoly of laughter and self-mockery. Brigitte Bardot is playing in the East. . . .

The Daniel-Sinyavsky Trial*

March 28, 1968

. . . One of the traces left on the world by Christianity, I think, is a phrase like "There but for the grace of God go I," or in Donne's more literary fashion, "For whom the bell tolls." We can sympathize with a forger, or a blackmailer, or even that man, even that genocide, who drops the bombs on innocent peasants in Vietnam. But in any government there grows up a hideous Establishment of stupid men. What seems to me appallingly absent among these stupid men is a feeling of community. I wrote—if you'll forgive me being personal—to the Union of Writers in Moscow, asking them to hand over my royalties which are banked there to the wives of the imprisoned writers Sinyavsky and Daniel. After about three months I got a cold response that they could not hand over *my* money to anyone but myself. Legal enough, fair enough. But I knew the answer to that, and so I wrote to Mr. Alexander Chakovsky, the editor of the *Literary Gazette*, who is also a member of the Supreme Soviet, and asked him if I took out a deed of attorney at the Russian Embassy in Paris and sent it to him, whether he would draw out my money and hand it to these ladies. I didn't expect a very

* Statement by Graham Greene recorded in the minutes of the International PEN Defence Committee for Soviet and Greek Writers in Prison.

good response, but I didn't expect really such a reply, smooth as ice. Can I read it to you?

> My dear Greene,
> It goes without saying that I remember our encounters quite well, and those are very pleasant memories indeed. There's no need to tell you that I am prepared to comply with any of your requests if it is within my power to do so. I am extremely sorry that in this case I have to start with a refusal. The fact is that we do not see eye to eye with regard to the matter raised in your letter. My attitude towards this matter being what it is, I would not like to be involved in it or get in touch with persons who in one way or another are connected with it. This is the reason why I cannot comply with your request. Please accept my best wishes for the New Year.

One must say that no bell tolls in Mr. Chakovsky's ears: no thought that when we defend others we are defending ourselves. Because, one day, God knows, we shall need to be defended.

Shame of the Catholics, Shame of the English*

To be at the same time a Catholic and an Englishman is today to be ashamed on both counts. As a Catholic one is ashamed that more than a thousand years of Christianity have not abated the brutality of those Catholic women who shaved a young girl's head and poured tar and red lead over her body because she intended to marry an English soldier. As an Englishman the shame is even greater.

* This letter, written from Paris, was published by *The Times* of London on November 26, 1971, and by *The New York Times* on December 2, 1971.

"Deep interrogation"—a bureaucratic phrase which takes the place of the simpler word "torture" and is worthy of Orwell's *1984*—is on a different level of immorality than hysterical sadism or the indiscriminating bomb of urban guerrillas. It is something organized with imagination and a knowledge of psychology, calculated and cold-blooded, and it is only half condemned by the Compton probe.

Mr. Maudling, in his blithe jolly style, reminiscent of that used by defenders of corporal punishment when they remember their school days, suggests that no one has suffered permanent injury from this form of torture, by standing long hours pressed against a wall, hooded in darkness, isolated and deprived of hearing as well as sight by permanent noise, prevented in the intervals of the ordeal from sleep—these were the methods we condemned in the Slansky trial in Czechoslovakia and in the case of Cardinal Mindszenty in Hungary.

Slansky is dead; he cannot be asked by Mr. Maudling how permanent was the injury he suffered, but one would like to know the opinion of the Cardinal on methods which when applied by Communists or Fascists we call "torture" and when applied by the British become down-graded to "ill treatment." If I, as a Catholic, were living in Ulster today I confess I would have one savage and irrational ambition—to see Mr. Maudling pressed against a wall for hours on end, with a hood over his head, hearing nothing but the noise of a wind machine, deprived of sleep when the noise temporarily ceases by the bland voice of a politician telling him that his brain will suffer no irreparable damage.

The effect of these methods extends far beyond the borders of Ulster. How can any Englishman now protest against torture in Vietnam, in Greece, in Brazil, in the psychiatric wards of the U.S.S.R., without being told, "You have a double standard: one for others and another for your own country."

And after all the British tortures and Catholic outrages, what comes next? We all know the end of the story, however long the politicians keep up their parrot cry of "no talk until violence ends." When I was young it was the same cliché they repeated. Collins was "a gunman and a thug." "We will not talk to murderers." No one doubts that it was in our power then to hold Ireland by force. The Black and Tans matched the Republicans in terror. It was the English people who in the end forced the politicians to sit down at a table with "the gunman and the thug."

Now too, when the deaths and the tortures have gone on long enough to blacken us in the eyes of the world and to sicken even a Conservative of the right, there will inevitably be a temporary truce and a round-table conference—Mr. Maudling or his successor will sit down over the coffee and the sandwiches with representatives of Eire and Stormont, of the I.R.A. and the Provisional I.R.A. to discuss with no pre-ordained conditions changes in the constitution and in the borders of Ulster. Why not now rather than later?

The Virtue of Disloyalty*

Surely if there is one supreme poet of conservatism, of what we now call the Establishment, it is Shakespeare. In his great poetic history of England, he began with Henry VI, who was almost as close to his own time as we are to the war of 1870, and then worked backwards, receding from the dangerous present, the England of plots and persecutions, into the safer past. Shakespeare's father was a Roman Catholic, who did not conform, but the only line I can recall of Shakespeare's which reflects critically on the Reformation is a metaphor in the Sonnets which could easily be explained away.

* An address given by Graham Greene, June 6, 1969, upon the award of the Shakespeare Prize by the University of Hamburg.

Bare ruined choirs where once the sweet birds sang.

If there is one word which chimes through Shakespeare's early plays it is the word "peace." In times of political trouble the Establishment always appeals to this ideal of peace.

> God's gentle sleeping peace.

> The troubler of the poor world's peace.

Peace as a nostalgia for a lost past: peace which Shakespeare associated like a retired colonial governor with firm administration.

> Peace it bodes, and love and quiet life,
> An awe-full rule, and right supremacy.

There are moments as he mocks at poor Jack Cade and his peasant rebels when we revolt against this bourgeois poet on his way to the house at Stratford and his coat of arms, and we sometimes tire even of the great tragedies, where the marvellous beauty of the verse takes away the sting and the last lines heal all, with right supremacy re-established by Fortinbras, Malcolm and Octavius Caesar. Then we are inclined to use against him the accusation flung at Antonio in *The Merchant of Venice*.

> You have too much respect upon the world:
> They lose it that do buy it with such care.

Of course he is the greatest of all poets, but we who live in times just as troubled as his, times full of the deaths of tyrants, a time of secret agents, assassinations and plots and torture chambers, sometimes feel ourselves more at home with the sulphurous anger of Dante, the self-disgust of Baudelaire and the blasphemies of Villon, poets who dared to reveal themselves whatever the danger, and the danger was very real. The first earned exile, the second a trial for obscenity, and the third possibly a hangman's cord.

So we think in our own day of Pasternak, Daniel, Sinyavsky, Ginsberg, Solzhenitsyn in Russia: Roa Bastos a fugitive from Paraguay: George Seferis making his brave protest in Greece. On this roll of honour the name of Shakespeare does not appear, and yet, and yet . . . I like to believe that if he had lived a little longer, his name would not have been absent. We grow a little tired of the artificial problem of the Prince of Denmark (a mother's incest and a father's murder is not an experience we can easily share) and a young suicide today is unlikely to brood so deliberately in the Wittenberg manner on the dilemma "To be or not to be." But in his last years Shakespeare did strike the same note of outrage as Dante and Villon in the two characters I prefer to think of as one composite character, Timon-Caliban.

> You taught me language; and my profit on't
> Is, I know how to curse.

If only he had lived a few more years, so that we could have seen the great poet of the Establishment defect to the side of the disloyal, to the side of the poet Southwell disembowelled for so-called treason, to the side of those who by the very nature of their calling will always be "troublers of the poor world's peace"—Zola writing *J'accuse*, Dostoevsky before a firing squad, Victor Hugo following Dante into exile, the Russian writers in their labour camps. One cannot help putting a higher value on what their rulers have regarded as disloyalty than the musical sentiments of loyalty expressed by so unlikely a character as John of Gaunt:

> This happy breed of men, this little world.

We all learnt the lines at school.

> This blessed plot, this earth, this realm, this England.

These complacent lines were published in 1597. Two years before, Shakespeare's fellow poet Southwell had died on the scaffold after three years of torture. If only Shakespeare had shared his disloyalty, we could have loved him better as a man.

It has always been in the interests of the State to poison the psychological wells, to encourage cat-calls, to restrict human sympathy. It makes government easier when the people shout Galilean, Papist, Fascist, Communist. Isn't it the story-teller's task to act as the devil's advocate, to elicit sympathy and a measure of understanding for those who lie outside the boundaries of State approval? The writer is driven by his own vocation to be a protestant in a Catholic society, a catholic in a Protestant one, to see the virtues of the capitalist in a Communist society, of the communist in a Capitalist state. Thomas Paine wrote, "We must guard even our enemies against injustice."

If only writers could maintain that one virtue of disloyalty—so much more important than chastity—unspotted from the world. Honours, even this prize-giving, State patronage, success, the praise of their fellows all tend to sap their disloyalty. The house at Stratford must not be endangered. If they don't become loyal to a Church or a country, they are apt to become loyal to some invented ideology of their own, until they are praised for consistency, although the writer should always be ready to change sides at the drop of a hat. He stands for the victims, and the victims change. Loyalty confines you to accepted opinions: loyalty forbids you to comprehend sympathetically your dissident fellows; but disloyalty encourages you to roam through any human mind: it gives the novelist an extra dimension of understanding.

I am not advocating propaganda in any cause. Propaganda is only concerned to elicit sympathy for one side, what the propagandist regards as the good side: he too poisons the wells. But the novelist's task is to draw his own likeness to any human being, to the guilty as much as to the innocent—There, and may God forgive me, goes myself.

If we enlarge the bounds of sympathy in our readers we succeed in making the work of the State a degree more difficult. That is a genuine duty we owe society, to be a piece of grit in the State machinery. However acceptable for the moment the Soviet State may find the great classic writers, Dostoevsky, Tolstoy, Turgenev, Gogol, Chekhov, they have surely made the regimentation of the Russian spirit an imperceptible degree more difficult or more incomplete. You cannot talk of the Karamazovs in terms of a class, and if you speak with hatred of the kulak doesn't the rich humorous memory of the hero of *Dead Souls* come back to kill your hatred? Sooner or later the strenuous bugle note of loyalty, of social responsibility, of the greatest material good of the greatest number must die in the ear, and then perhaps certain memories will come back, of long purposeless discussions in the moonlight about life and art, the click of a billiard ball, the sunny afternoons of that month in the country.

A great German theologian confronted, in the worst days of our lifetime, this issue of loyalty and disloyalty: "Christians in Germany," he wrote, "will face the terrible alternative of either willing the defeat of their nation in order that Christian civilization may survive, or willing the victory of their nation and thereby destroying our civilization. I know which of those alternatives I must choose."

Dietrich Bonhoeffer chose to be hanged like our English poet Southwell. He is a greater hero for the writer than Shakespeare. Perhaps the deepest tragedy Shakespeare lived was his own: the blind eye exchanged for the coat of arms, the prudent tongue for the friendships at Court and the great house at Stratford.